EX
LIBRIS

Dear Reader,

It's hard for me to believe that Silhouette Intimate Moments has been here for ten years, striving to bring you the most exciting contemporary romance novels we could find, but it's true. In those ten years you've helped make stars of our authors, taken the line to number one on the romance bestseller lists and watched as your favorite authors took home award after award from the Romance Writers of America and other writers' groups and romance publications. In short, your enthusiasm and loyalty have made Intimate Moments the six-book-a-month success story it is today.

Now, on our tenth anniversary, it's our turn to do something for *you*. We've put together a fabulous collection of firsts—the first Intimate Moments novels from three of your favorite authors. And what a collection this is! *New York Times* bestselling author Heather Graham Pozzessere shows off her *Night Moves*. Emilie Richards, a veteran of numerous bestseller lists, introduces us to a *Lady of the Night*. And Kathleen Korbel, who has won three RWA Rita Awards for her Intimate Moments novels, tempts us with *A Stranger's Smile*.

If you read these books when they first appeared, you'll be thrilled to add this collector's edition to your bookshelf. And if you missed one, two or even all three of them, what better way to get acquainted with some of the most memorable characters in romance?

I have only one thing left to say: Enjoy!

Yours,

Leslie Wainger
Senior Editor and Editorial Coordinator

INTIMATE MOMENTS®
10TH
Anniversary

Heather Graham Pozzessere
Emilie Richards
Kathleen Korbel

Silhouette®
INTIMATE MOMENTS®

Published by Silhouette Books New York
America's Publisher of Contemporary Romance

SILHOUETTE BOOKS
300 East 42nd St., New York, N.Y. 10017

SILHOUETTE INTIMATE MOMENTS
Tenth Anniversary Collection
Copyright © 1993 by Silhouette Books

ISBN: 0-373-15233-7

Night Moves
Copyright © 1985 by Heather Graham Pozzessere
Originally published as Silhouette Intimate Moments #118

Lady of the Night
Copyright © 1986 by Emilie McGee
Originally published as Silhouette Intimate Moments #152

A Stranger's Smile
Copyright © 1986 by Eileen Dreyer
Originally published as Silhouette Intimate Moments #163

CONTENTS

NIGHT MOVES

Heather Graham Pozzessere

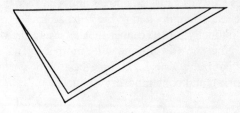

For Sally Schoenweiss,
whose friendship has so enriched my life.

HEATHER GRAHAM POZZESSERE

considers herself lucky to live in Florida, where she can indulge her love of water sports, such as swimming and boating, year-round. Her background includes stints as a model, actress and a bartender. She was once actually tied to the railroad tracks to garner publicity for the dinner theater where she was acting. Now she's a full-time wife, mother of five and, of course, a *New York Times* bestselling writer of historical and contemporary romances.

Books by Heather Graham Pozzessere

Silhouette Intimate Moments

Night Moves #118
The di Medici Bride #132
Double Entendre #145
The Game of Love #165
A Matter of Circumstance #174
Bride of the Tiger #192
All in the Family #205
King of the Castle #220
Strangers in Paradise #225
Angel of Mercy #248
This Rough Magic #260
Lucia in Love #265
Borrowed Angel #293
A Perilous Eden #328
Forever My Love #340
Wedding Bell Blues #352
Snowfire #386
Hatfield and McCoy #416
Mistress of Magic #450
Between Roc and a Hard Place #499
The Trouble with Andrew #525

Silhouette Shadows

The Last Cavalier #1

Silhouette Books

Silhouette Christmas Stories 1991
"The Christmas Bride"

Silhouette Shadows Story Collection 1992
"Wilde Imaginings"

Prologue

He was as one with the night.

His tread upon the damp earth was as silent as the soft breeze that cooled the night, and as he moved carefully through the neatly manicured foliage, he was no more than shadow.

A distant heritage had given him these gifts, and that same distant heritage had taught him to move with the grace of the wild deer, to hunt with the acute and cunning stalk of the panther, and to stand firm in his determination with the tenacity of the golden eagle.

Yet that distant heritage had nothing to do with the his secretive stalk of this dark evening. Nor with the clothes he wore, black Levi's jeans and a black turtleneck sweater.

And black Adidas sneakers.

Black, which could be swallowed into the night.

Hunched down and balanced on the balls of his feet, he watched the house patiently for half an hour. Then he began to move, circling around it within the shelter of palms and hibiscus.

No light shone from within. All was silent. Not even the trailing fingers of the pines gave off a rustle.

Puzzled, he relaxed somewhat, then began another stealthy walk to circle the contemporary dwelling once more.

Near the rear of the house he paused, hearing nothing, but sensing movement on the air. And then he did hear it. Footsteps. Padding cautiously, slowly.

A silhouette appeared against the pale glimmer of the moon.

A figure, also clad in black from head to toe.

Black jeans. Loose-fitting, bulky black sweater. And a black ski mask that hid the wearer's features, rendering it sexless, an intruder with one intent: to get into the house.

The slender form paused as if strung upon the air, something like a young doe, seeming to sense danger. But there was no tangible danger, and so the form moved again, scurrying this time, rushing from the cover of the foliage to a double-paned window.

He waited tensely as he watched the figure struggle for several seconds to lift the window. A cloud suddenly slipped over the moon, dimming the meager natural light of the night until it was almost nonexistent. There was nothing but pure shadow, a mist of blindness, and even the shadow was sensed rather than seen.

The figure continued to work at the window. At last it gave, and the form leaped nimbly to the sill, paused again, then disappeared within.

Only then did he move himself, silent as the shadow of the night once more, his steps making no sound. He peered through the window. A small, furtive light gleamed, the beam of a small flashlight. It moved across the room, disappearing past a white framed doorway that momentarily caught its reflection.

Swiftly, smoothly, he hopped to the sill and eased himself over.

He followed in the wake of the flashlight, past several doors, until he came to a large and spacious room. He paused in the darkness of the hallway, watching as the light was played quickly about. A modular sofa, strewn with colorful afghans, was comfortably arranged in one corner; a piano set upon a dais, and bookshelves lined opposing walls. Where there was space, attractive Western prints were hung; there was a rifle rack, and also a display of antique bows, arrows and spears.

Far to the left, past a tiled foyer, was another raised section, separated from the main room by a handsome wrought-iron rail from which hung curling ivy. And within the enclosed section sat a large teakwood desk.

It was here that the figure had stopped.

The flashlight was set on top of a leather framed blotter; busy hands began hurriedly pulling at the drawers and rifling through them. With narrowed eyes he watched the action for a moment, and then, with the stealthy tread of a panther, he began to close in.

A desk drawer slammed. Too loud. The intruder froze for a moment and sent the light flashing nervously around.

He ducked behind a section of the sofa and waited until he heard the sound of riffled papers once again.

Now... now he was ready to strike.

Like a rush of wind he moved across the room, his movement fluid as he plucked an arrow from the wall, sprang over the ivy covered railing and clamped an arm about the stunned intruder's throat.

"Who the hell are you?" he growled, pressing the arrow point threateningly to the intruder's ribs. "And what the hell do you want?"

He felt the cold rush of terror that flooded through the intruder, the rigid, frozen stance.

"I—" The tremulous whisper was choked off almost immediately. He relaxed the pressure of his hold somewhat and dropped the arrow as he realized his enemy's weakness.

"We'll get some light on the situation," he finally muttered dryly, releasing his victim altogether and moving confidently toward the desk.

But he had underestimated his wily opponent. The figure spun about, jumping the rail with a fluid grace and tearing blindly through the shadowed house toward the hallway.

"Hell!" he swore, gripping the rail and hurdling over once again. He raced through the hall. Past closed doors. To the den. Just in time to see the silhouette perched on the windowsill.

"Stop!" he commanded, allowing for no weakness this time. Reflexively he bunched his muscles and hurled himself at the figure. Instead of jumping out, the black-clad wraith jumped inward, eluding him. Almost.

He caught a handfull of soft wool. His grip was so tight that the sweater ripped, a swatch coming free in his hand.

The figure spun from him in wild desperation, realized that it would be impossible to reach the window and pelted toward the door.

He rolled, sprang to his feet and followed in hot pursuit again, aware now of something that the figure wasn't: There was no other way out.

Back into the living room they raced, to the stairwell rising to the balcony and the second floor. He was certain that the fleeing wraith was reasoning no more; just running blindly in desperation.

Running foolishly in panic. Clinging to the hope of escape until the last possible moment.

Their footsteps flew down the length of the wood-railed balcony that overlooked the living room. To the door at the end of the long hallway. The figure managed to throw the door open, then twisted wildly to see him an arm's length away...

The figure turned again, bolted into the room and tried to slam the door shut.

He sprang, his shoulder sending a thudding shudder rippling through the wood of the door, his arms clasping the intruder.

Together they flew through the darkness with the force of his impetus, landing hard upon the queen-sized bed in the center of the room. Arms flailed madly against him; thrashing legs kicked. The wraith writhed beneath him like a pinned cat. He worked silently and grimly to subdue the figure, and started for just a moment when his hands brushed something very lush. Firm, but soft. Full and tempting.

A woman's breast.

"No! Please!" The cry was very feminine. Panicked. No, terrified. He could feel her racing heartbeat, hear the rush of air in her lungs as she fought to breathe. But still she struggled . . .

With a grunt he straddled her and made quick work of securing her wrists.

"All right!" he muttered furiously and repeated, "Who the hell are you, and what the hell are you doing here?"

As suddenly as it had come earlier to create blackness, the cloud that had covered the moon drifted away. A silver glow poured through the glass panes of the French doors that led to the master suite's sky-topped terrace.

He could see her clearly, as she could see him.

He reached for the black ski mask that covered her head and face and ripped it away, exposing a wealth of shiny hair that caught the moonglow and gleamed as richly as a newly minted penny. And exposing her features . . .

Wide, thick-lashed, cat-green eyes stared into his. He quickly studied the woman's face. High, delicate cheekbones. Copper brows. Straight, acquiline nose. Well defined mouth with a lower lip that hinted at an innate sensuality.

She was still beneath him, only the rampant rise and fall of her breasts betraying the depth of her fear.

He sat back, resting his weight on his haunches yet keeping her firmly a prisoner with the pressure of his thighs about her hips. He crossed his arms over his chest and kept staring at her, his eyes narrowing to a dangerous gold-tinted gleam, his lips forming a mocking smile of cynicism.

He knew the luminous, cat-green eyes that stared into his. Just as he knew the lustrous length of deep copper hair.

And he knew why she had been able to leap the downstairs rail with ease, and spin and pivot with the ease of a dancer.

She was one.

He even knew something of the soft and supple form that quivered now beneath his. He had held her once, in the creation of an illusion. Held her, and started up a long, curving staircase.

And when his back had shielded her face from the camera, he had seen the hard glimmer of hostility fill her eyes. Felt in her rigid form dislike for the fact that she had to endure those moments in his arms . . .

He had seen her before the camera, and he had seen her behind the camera.

And he had seen her dance.

"Ah, Miss Keller. How very nice to have you over—yet, how strange this seems! You were reluctant to join me for a glass of wine, yet here we meet—touching hip to hip—upon my bed. Should I be flattered, Miss Keller? Pity, but I think not." He leaned low suddenly, palms on either side of her head, eyes flashing a chilling gold fire and bronzed features warningly tensed.

"Speak to me, Bryn. Why did you break in? What are you looking for? You didn't find it last night—"

"Last night!" she broke in with whispered alarm.

"Oh, cut it, will you?" he spat out harshly. "Yes, last night. Believe me, honey, I know when my place has been searched."

"But it wasn't me—"

"Shhh!"

Suddenly he shifted again, his back straightening, his broad shoulders entirely still.

And then she heard it, too.

Someone moving...prowling about the living room. He started to rise, then paused as they both heard the creak of a footstep on the bottom step.

Abruptly but quietly he moved, crossing his arms and grabbing the bottom of his turtleneck to hurriedly struggle out of it. His chest, broad, tapering to a drum hard abdomen, rippling with taut muscle, gleamed bronze in the moonlight.

"Get your sweater off!" he hissed at her, rolling onto his side and ripping the covers from his half of the bed.

"I will not!"

"You will too—and fast!" he whispered, rolling her indignant form beside his so that he could tug at the other half of the bedding and pull it back up over the two of them. "Damn it, woman!" His voice was as insubstantial as the air, but she heard the angry, warning timbre. "No one will believe we're sleeping soundly after a torrid session of lovemaking if you're in bed with your clothes on! This is your game you've drawn me into, sweetheart, not mine, but now you'll damn well play by my rules!"

She hesitated, but his hands, long-fingered, broad-backed, powerful, were upon her, tugging at what was left of the sweater.

"Stop!" she whispered, and quickly shed the garment herself, then started to ease down under the covers, her heart thumping madly.

"The bra, too!" he snapped. "What's the matter with you? Haven't you ever made love?"

She was shaking with outrage and humiliation, but she sensed that he knew what he was doing. Still, her fingers trembled too badly to release the hook. He touched her back, sending ripples that chilled and then burned all along the length of her spine. The hood gave in to his practiced flick of the thumb, and she clutched at the front of the lacy garment then shoved it beneath the covers before he could.

It didn't help her much. She almost cried out when she felt his arm come around her, his hand comfortably upon her ribs, his fingers splayed so that they teased the curve beneath her breast. He pulled her close until the supple length of her spine was pressed against the heat of his chest, his long legs curled intimately about her. She could hear the whisper of his breath against her neck, against the lobe of her ear...

To an observer, they might easily have just made love. They might have been sleeping, comfortably, intimately, as lovers did...

But she knew he was far from asleep. Far from comfortably at ease. She felt the vitality, the heat, exuding from him. She knew that his ears were keenly attuned to the slightest sound, that his entire being was acutely aware, that he could spring like a panther at a split second's notice. Even as he lay still, she felt the ripple of perfectly toned muscle, the vibrant, primal male power that was his essence...

And she was frightened. Frightened of the danger she had brought; frightened of the footsteps that kept coming, slowly...so slowly and carefully...up the stairway.

And beyond that fear was something else. Something that reached inside of her. Despite it all, she was achingly aware of him. Of the fingers that brushed her bare breasts; of the hot male flesh pressed so tightly to her own. She felt vulnerable, and yet she felt protected. To feel his touch, to let him in, would be to become completely possessed on the most elemental of levels. He was a man who would take a woman body and soul. She would be completely his. And in return he would give her something as old as time, as staunch and firm as the mountains. His shielding strength; his sword against the world...

If he wanted her.

She was afraid of him. Had been from the beginning. Had sensed that if she gave in to the slightest weakness—

The footsteps were coming closer. His arm moved, drawing her even more tightly to him, fingers inadvertently teasing higher over her breast. Sensation rippled through her like lightning, mingling and joining with the rapid-fire gusts of terror...

"Keep your eyes closed!"

How had he known they were open to the darkness?

His were, she was certain. Yet heavy-lidded, so no one would see that piercing gleam of night gold.

The footsteps halted at the open door. She caught her breath, paralyzed with the terror of knowing that she was being watched—and not even able to watch back....

Creak... A telltale floorboard was giving. This intruder, now satisfied with the whereabouts of the house's occupants, turned away again, starting back down the stairs.

The man beside her was up like a flash, tearing toward the door. Ready now to attack, with surprise on his side. He started down the stairs. "What the bloody hell are you doing in my house?"

An explosion of gunfire, ripping through the darkness in an instant of blood red and sun yellow, was his only answer.

He ducked and heard the bullet whiz by his ear, then sink into the wood of the doorframe.

The intruder ran, clattering now, down the stairway.

He tried to follow, ducking again behind the banister when another shot was fired. The bolts were blown out of the door, and the intruder was swallowed into the night.

He followed, but to no avail. The roar of a car engine could already be heard; tires spat out gravel and grass, and the lightless vehicle was gone.

He turned and pelted hurriedly back up the stairway.

She was sitting up in the bed, the covers pulled chastely to her breast. Her hair spilled about her now parchment-white features and shoulders like an aura of sunset. Her eyes, those pools of green that had enchanted and beguiled him, were wide. Tipped slightly at the corners. Adding allure to the beauty of her fragile features and striking coloring.

They still held fear within their depths.

He smiled grimly as he entered the room, closing the door behind him.

She jumped at the sound of the door clicking, and his dangerous smile broadened.

She damned well better be a little bit afraid of him. She had broken into his home, rifled through his belongings and brought another intruder in her wake to riddle his walls with bullets.

"All right, Bryn. Out with it. What's going on?"

She moistened her lips nervously with the tip of her tongue, and her eyes darted to the floor, where her sweater had fallen. She clutched the sheet more tightly to her and leaned over awkwardly to reach for her garment, but a flash of silent movement stopped her.

He was sitting on the bed beside her, still smiling. But his left sneaker was planted firmly over her sweater.

"No more defenses of any kind, Bryn. The only way to reach you is to make you as vulnerable as possible, and if that means half naked, well . . ."

He lifted his hands casually in a resigned manner, then allowed them to fall back to his knees. She sank back against the pillow, biting her lip, and suddenly wishing she had never made him an enemy.

He wanted vulnerable. Oh, God, was she vulnerable!

"Bryn!" His voice was a threat.

"I . . . I . . . can't tell you," she began.

"You'd better. Or else I can give a call to the police."

"No! Oh, please, Lee! Please, don't—"

"Then tell me why my house was broken into last night—and the night before. And why I was shot at by some thug. And what you're doing here now."

"All right, all right! But please, you must swear not to go to the police!" Her lime-green eyes, capable of being brilliant and innocent, sultry and seductive, proud and sometimes haughty, but never, never opaque with naked humility and pleading, were brimming with the glitter of tears. Tears that she held back with the greatest strength of will. Her lips quivered. "Look, Lee, I know I haven't been especially decent to you, but I had some legitimate, personal reasons. I realize I haven't the right now, but I have to ask you to help me. Please, Lee! Promise me that you won't involve the police! The...the people involved with this...they...they have Adam!"

His brows shot up with surprise and grim commitment. "Okay, Bryn," he said quietly. "I'm not going to call the police—not yet, anyway. I promise."

"It's the pictures!" she blurted out.

"The pictures?" he replied with a frown of puzzlement. "The ones you took last Thursday?"

"Yes."

He leaned over and flicked on the bedside light, then stood and walked over to his closet, pulling it open and searching through it absently. Then he tossed a long sleeved pin-striped shirt to her and ordered briefly, "Put that on. Your sweater has about had it. I'm going downstairs to make some coffee. Be in the kitchen in five minutes flat, and be prepared to tell me this whole story—with no holes."

He walked out the door, and Bryn closed her eyes in bleak misery. Why was this all happening, she wondered bleakly. If she had only aimed her lens in a different direction...

Adam would still be at home.

And she wouldn't be forced now to rely upon a man to whom she had shown nothing but hostility and antagonism since they had first met.

A man she had misjudged—and sadly underestimated.

And who scared her silly, even as he drew her to him. Who could play upon her senses with a whispered word, make her shiver with a mere touch...

And yet could easily use her, then toss her over like windswept driftwood upon a white-sand shore of emptiness.

She was lying in his bed now. Had lain beside him in it, had felt his touch almost as a lover might...

She wrenched the sheets from her and leaped to her feet, fingers trembling as she slipped her arms into the shirt-sleeves, then labored quickly with the buttons.

She had come to know him fairly well. He didn't make idle threats, or hand out orders he didn't expect to be obeyed. If she didn't appear in the kitchen in five minutes, he would be back up the stairs, soundlessly, swiftly—determinedly—to drag her down. She might resent the idea, but she wasn't about to take any more chances.

Because if he touched her again tonight, she might break into a thousand tiny pieces and be forever lost.

Bryn breathed a soft sigh of resignation. It was almost a relief to have no choice but to tell all. To Lee. If she had come to him to begin with, things might not have gotten this far.

This frightening...

There might be dangerous men after her, but...

But he had to be the most damned dangerous man she had ever met.

Bryn closed her eyes tightly and breathed deeply for strength. She was going to have to go down and talk to him. Tell him everything, from the beginning.

From the beginning.

Who could have known...?

Chapter 1

"Arggghhh!"

At the sound of the loud and piercing scream, Bryn Keller dropped the trade paper she had been industriously reading onto the comfortably stuffed love seat, sprang to her feet and rushed to the door, flinging it open.

In her year and a half of being a pseudoparent, she still hadn't learned to decipher which screams were of pain, and which were of play.

Luckily, this one seemed to have been play.

Brian, at the grand age of seven, the oldest of her nephews, had been the perpetrator of the sound. He met her eyes curiously as he saw her anxious stare.

"We're playing, Aunt Bryn." He puffed out his chest proudly and waved a plastic sword. "I'm Gringold! God of water and light! And I'm battling the forces of the Dark Hound."

"And I'm Tor the Magnificent!" chimed in Keith. He was six, and second-in-command among the trio. They only owned two plastic swords, and he carried the second.

"Oh?" Bryn raised her eyebrows and suppressed a grin. She didn't have to ask who had the honor of being the Dark Hound. Her eyes traveled to little Adam. At four, he was the youngest and therefore always elected to be the bad guy. The boys were using the tops of garbage cans as shields, but just as there were only two plastic swords, there were only two can tops. Adam carried a giant plastic baseball bat and a ripped-up piece of cardboard.

Adam graced her with a beautiful smile, and she forgot that she had been about to knock all three heads together for the scare they had just given her. She laughed suddenly, narrowed her eyes at Keith and raced over to Adam, stealing his baseball bat. "Tor the Magnificent, eh? Well, I'm the White Witch!" she told them all gravely. "And I'm going to get the lot of you for turning my hair gray way before its time!"

The boys squealed with delight as she chased them about the small yard, catching their little bottoms with light taps of the bat. At last they began to gang up on her, rushing her, hugging her and knocking her to the ground.

"Beg for mercy, White Witch!" Brian demanded.

"Never!" she cried in mock horror. Then she started as she heard the phone ringing in the kitchen.

"Cry for mercy!" Keith echoed Brian.

"Off! Off, you hoodlums! I'll cry for mercy later, I promise, but right now the White Witch has to answer the phone."

"Ahh, Auntie Bryn!"

The boys grumbled but let her up. Bryn threw them a kiss as she rushed back into the house and flew to the phone.

"Bryn?"

"Barbara?"

"Yes, of course, it's Barbara. What were you doing? You didn't take up jogging, I hope? You sound absolutely breathless. I didn't interrupt anything—or did I? I would just love for you to be doing something that I could worry about interrupting!"

Bryn gave the receiver an affectionate grimace. Barbara couldn't understand her friend's withdrawal from male society since her broken engagement. Especially since it had been Bryn who had made the final break.

"No, you didn't interrupt anything except for a wild battle between the forces of good and evil. What's up?"

"I've got something for you."

"Work? Oh, great! I'm just about to wind up those wildlife shots, and Cathy's ankle got better, so she returned to the dinner show last night. I've been worrying about finances already. What have you got, a dance gig or a shoot?"

Barbara's delighted laughter came to her over the phone. "Bryn! What a card you are. And what a lucky card to have me for an agent. How many people can sell you as a photographer, and a dancer?"

"Probably not many," Bryn replied dryly. "I can see the billboard now: 'Jack of all trades—master of none.'"

"Hey, don't undersell yourself, Bryn. You do damn well at both your trades."

Bryn remained silent. She was a good dancer and a good photographer. But she had learned through life that "good" did not mean success. It meant that, if you were lucky, you could keep working.

She laughed suddenly. "Maybe if I had decided earlier whether I wanted to grow up to be either Martha Graham or Matthew Brady, I might have made it as one or the other!"

"Maybe, but it wouldn't have helped you this time, chick. 'Cause I've got two jobs for you. One shooting and one dancing."

"Well, great!" Bryn approved enthusiastically. "Who am I shooting, and who am I dancing for?"

"They're one and the same."

"They are?" Bryn queried curiously. "That's strange. Who is this 'one and the same'?"

"Lee Condor."

"The Indian rock star?"

"Half Indian, and he refers to himself as a musician," Barbara said with cool aplomb. "Remember that, sweets."

"The *half* Indian or the musician?" Bryn asked dryly.

"Both!" Barbara chuckled. "He never denies the Blackfoot blood, but he doesn't make a big deal of it, either. And he spent two years at Julliard, where his mother was a teacher, then two years at the Royal Conservatory. He has a right to call himself a musician."

"I don't know, Barbara. It makes me a little uncomfortable. I don't tend to care for men with purple hair who behave like sexual athletes and jump all over the stage."

"Honey, his hair isn't purple! It's jet black. And he's never acted like a sexual athlete. He was married for five years, and not even the *National Enquirer* could make an attack on the relationship. He's a widower now, and besides, you don't have to fall in love with him, just work for him!" Barbara exclaimed with exasperation. "And what's gotten into you all of sudden? You've worked for dozens of males of all varieties and disparaged the interested like the iceberg did the Titanic. Why are you afraid to work for a man you've never met?"

"I'm not afraid," Bryn replied instantly, but then realized that, inexplicably, she was. At the mention of Condor's name, hot flashes of electricity had started to attack her; now they ran all the way up and down her spine. She knew of him, just as she knew of the Beatles, the Rolling Stones, Duran Duran, and so forth, but there was absolutely no reason to *fear* the man or even to be apprehensive that he might be...weird.

Still...she was definitely afraid. Silly, she told herself. Ridiculous. And then she knew where the feeling came from.

A video that he had already done.

The kids had been watching an old Dickens classic on HBO one night, and when the movie had ended, the video had come on.

Lee Condor's video.

There had been no shots of the group with smoke coming from their guitars, no absurb mechanizations, or anything of the like. There hadn't even been shots of Condor or his group playing their individual instruments. It had been a story video; the popular love song was based on a fantasy affair. The scenes had been as good as many movies: knights on destriers pounding through mist to reach the castle; a great battle; the heroine being rescued too late and dying in her lover's arms.

Bryn had found herself watching the four minutes of tape without moving.

And at the very end, there had been a face shot. Not a full face shot, but a picture of the knight with his visor on, gold-glinted eyes staring dangerously through.

She could still remember those eyes—too easily. And even now, the thought of them disturbed her.

"I'm not afraid, Barbara," Bryn repeated more staunchly, her irritation with herself growing. "I just don't really get this. Why would Lee Condor come to Tahoe to do a video? What's the matter with Hollywood these days?"

"Hey, he went over to Scotland to film his last video. And he doesn't live in Hollywood. He has a home in Ft. Lauderdale, and one here."

"Here?"

"Yeah, he's owned it for years. But he seems to be a very private person, so few people know about it, or much about him."

"You seem to know enough," Bryn teased lightly.

"Ummm. I wish I knew a little more."

"You like that hard-rock type, huh?" Bryn kept up with a chuckle.

To her surprise, Barbara hesitated. "He's a strange man, Bryn. Cordial, and quiet. But you have the feeling that he sees everything around him and that...that he *absorbs* more than most people. He's dynamite to look at, with those gold-tinged eyes and dark hair. Seems like he's long and wiry until you get close to him and see the real breadth of his shoulders..." Barbara sighed. "I admit he does give me goose bumps. I've never come across a man so...so...*male*...before."

Bryn laughed, but she sounded uneasy even to her own ears.

She had known a man like that before. Known him a little too well. Was that what gave her fever-chills of instant hostility? Had just that flash-fast glimpse of elemental fire in those gold eyes warned her that his sensual appetites were as natural to him as breathing, just as they had been with Joe?

There were signs of warning as clear as neon lights about such men...once you learned to read them. Signs that might read: Women, beware! He can take you to the stars, and dash you back upon the gates of hell.

But a woman only got messed up with a man like that once in her life, never a second time.

Bryn shook away her thoughts and the uneasy feeling of fever along her spine. This was business.

"Okay, he's doing a video and hiring dancers. But where does the photography come in?"

"You know those promo shots you took for Vic and Allen when they started playing the Stardust Lounge? He saw them, stared at them for a long time and asked if I knew the photographer. Well, of course, I hopped right in with your name!"

"Thanks," Bryn murmured.

"What's an agent for?" Barbara laughed happily. "But listen, I've got to run. I have another twenty dancers to line up. Boy, oh boy, am I in love with the man! Think of my percentages! And I'm going to put on the old answering machine and dance myself. Oh, Bryn! This has been a heck of a windfall!"

This time when Bryn laughed, it was with honest delight. She and Barbara were a lot alike. Barbara spent her days as an agent and her nights as a showgirl in a popular nightclub that was part of a new casino. Barbara loved to wheel and deal, and she also loved to dance. She could easily have gotten Bryn a job in her own show, but Bryn considered it a little too risque for a woman who was raising children and also for her own comfort. Barbara was an efficient businesswoman and had concluded deals for a number of big names, but even so, this did sound like a nice windfall.

"You're right, the whole thing sounds great, Barb. I'm happy for you."

"Be happy for yourself, honey. You're going to make enough to come close to a real nice down payment for that new house you've been dreaming about."

Bryn bit her lip. Money was, unfortunately, one of the key factors of life. One you couldn't live without.

Before her brother Jeff's death, she had always felt that she had all she needed to survive. She could take the jobs she liked, turn down those she didn't.

If only he were still alive! Not because she resented her nephews—she loved them and would fight hell and high water to keep them—but because...because she had loved her brother, too, and life had seemed so normal once, simple, right and easy. She couldn't wallow in self-pity. She had to accept reality. Jeff was dead.

And he had died without a shred of life insurance. But growing boys had to be fed and clothed, taken to doctors and dentists—and brought to a baby-sitter when Bryn worked nights. Keith and Brian went to school, but Adam's day care was costly. She'd had to sell her two-seater Trans-Am and buy a small Ford van. And her pretty little two bedroom town house had become way too small. The boys had been moved into the darkroom, and the darkroom had been moved to the storage shed.

And the stuff that had been in storage . . .

Well, it was stuck into closets, cabinets and any little nook that would hold anything.

Since she wasn't ready to fall back on being a showgirl, she couldn't afford to get fussy about jobs just because a man's eyes—seen on screen!—made her nervous.

"You still there, Bryn?"

"Yeah, Barb."

"Be at the old Fulton place at ten sharp on Tuesday. He's a real stickler for punctuality."

"The old Fulton place?" The house was on one of the long roads leading to the desert; it had been built around the middle of the nineteenth century, and had been deserted for as long as Bryn could remember. School kids still dared one another to go into it, as it had, of course, acquired a reputation for housing ghosts.

"You won't recognize what's been done with it!" Barbara laughed. "Ten o'clock, with everything you'll need for a full workout."

"I'll be there," Bryn promised. "Oh Barb? How many days' work is it? And when do I take the PR photos?"

"Probably three or four weeks on the video. It's going to run about fifteen minutes, I think. But there will be a day or two off during that time for the photos. I'll let you know when."

"Thanks again, Barb."

"Arggggghhhhhh!"

Another ear-splitting scream sounded from outside.

"Got to go, Barb. The natives are getting restless."

"Give them all a kiss and a hug for me!"

"I will."

Bryn slammed down the receiver and raced outside again, anxiously scanning little faces.

Adam was crying his eyes out. And soon as he saw her, he ran toward her as fast as his chubby little legs would carry him and buried his head in her lap.

"What happened?" Bryn demanded of the older two.

"I think a bug stung him!" Brian answered worriedly, coming over and stroking his little brother's blond curls. "Adam—"

Adam began to wail again. Bryn picked him up. "Come on, Adam, you have to tell me what happened."

He raised a red and swollen pinky to her, the tears still streaming from his huge green eyes just a shade darker than her own.

"Bug!" he pronounced with a shudder. "It was a bad bug! Hurts, Aunt Bryn . . ."

She whirled and hurried into the house, where she plopped Adam onto the counter between the kitchen and the dining room, and filled a small bowl with water and ice cubes. "Put your finger in the water, Adam, and it will feel better, I promise."

Adam, his tears drying as he tremulously took a deep breath, did as he was told. Bryn glanced over the counter to see that Keith and Brian, their eyes frightened as they stared at their brother, had followed her.

She grimaced, then gave them an encouraging smile. "It's not that bad, guys, really. I think it must have been a little honeybee."

Brian compressed his lips for a minute, then lowered his eyes. Bryn frowned as she watched him.

"What's the matter, Brian?"

"He...he..."

"He what, Brian?"

Brian mouthed the words behind Adam's back, his eyes stricken. "He's not going to die, is he, Aunt Bryn?"

"No!" Bryn exclaimed. "Of course not!" She lowered her own lashes and pretended to turn around to survey the contents of the refrigerator.

It was strange that Brian had come up with the question. It seemed as if all three of the boys had adjusted so well in the past year and a half. They accepted her as their figure of authority, and they were touchingly ready to give her their trust and their love.

But maybe it wasn't so strange. Sue had died of a case of pneumonia that had defied medical science when Adam was just a year old; Jeff had followed her in the reckless accident less than two years later. No matter how well-adjusted the boys seemed, it was natural that they should worry.

And natural that they should cling to her, fearing sometimes that she would leave them, too...

She pulled out a pack of hot dogs and turned back to smile at the three; Adam with his pain-puckered and rosy cheeks; Brian and Keith, both pale with uncertainty.

"Hey! Why the long faces? Adam, you just keep your finger in that water—"

"Too cold!"

"Okay, take it out for a minute, but then put it back in. Keith, Brian, go and take your baths. Then we'll have hot dogs and ice cream and I'll play your Muppet tape, and then everybody can go to bed. Tomorrow's a school day." And, she added silently, I'm going to have to finish up those last proofs and run out and buy some new tights. I don't have a pair left without a dozen holes.

Three hours later the boys were all bathed—including Adam—the hot dogs had been long-consumed and *The Great Muppet Caper* was drawing to a close.

Brian was on her left side, Keith on her right. And Adam was perched on her lap.

A painful shaft of memory suddenly ripped through Bryn, and she bit her lip so the boys wouldn't notice the tears that had stung her eyes.

She loved them so very much.

And she felt so fiercely loyal to them. Partially because they were beautiful kids and partially because they had been Jeff's. And no matter what happened, no matter how she had to struggle, no matter what she had to give up, she would never, never, let them down.

Jeff had never let her down.

She had been only sixteen when her mother and father had died in a freak mountain slide on the ski slopes. Sixteen, lost, bewildered, and stricken with grief. The only certainty in her life had been Jeff, and Jeff had battled for her. He fought distant aunts and uncles, and he had fought the courts.

He had taught her to accept their parents' deaths, and he had somehow gone on to school, kept a job and created a home for the two of them, until she had been ready to leave for college. He had never failed her; he had been only three years older, but no girl, no job, no social event, had ever come before her.

Even when he and Sue had married, she had never been made to feel like an outsider. She had waited at the hospital when each one of the boys had been born. And she had been the one to stay with Sue each time she had come home with a new baby.

No, she would never let anyone stop her from loving the kids, or giving them the same loyalty and devotion that their natural parents would have given them.

Not even a man like Joe.

She had always considered herself to be confident and self-assured, but Joe had swept her off her feet. He had come to Tahoe for a vacation when the football season had ended, and from the first moment he had seen her, he had pursued her with a vengeance.

Bryn had been amused at first, accepting the situation with the proverbial grain of salt. She didn't consider herself particularly beautiful, but she was aware that there was something about her trim, wiry form and slightly tilted "cat eyes" that made her appealing to the opposite sex. She wasn't sure if she liked the attraction that she held. It was often uncomfortable to know that the male of the species looked upon her and wondered not what she was like as a person, but what she would be like in bed. For a long time she laughed with good humor when Joe tried every compliment and trick in the book to get her to go out with him.

But somewhere along the line, something had become real. She had convinced herself that even football heroes needed to be loved and to give love in return. And it had seemed that he had loved her.

Things had started going badly with Sue's death. Joe had resented the time she spent with her brother, although he tolerated it. Football season rolled around again, and Joe went back to work. In December he called to tell her that he had one night in which he could fly in.

But she was due at Jeff's that night. He was a pilot, and Bryn had assured him that she would stay with the children.

Joe was livid. She asked him to come to Jeff's house, but he didn't want to play baby-sitter, he wanted to be alone. Bryn entreated him, trying to make him understand...

He hung up on her.

But the next week he was on the phone again, pretending that nothing had happened.

She traveled with him for a while. But then the telegram had come from Tahoe. Jeff had been killed while fooling around with a hang glider.

Joe had been comforting, but also aloof. He hadn't come back with her to bury her brother, nor had he seen the faces of the three little boys who had lost both parents and were now lost and alone and frightened....

Bryn couldn't pay the mortgage on Jeff's big house, so she moved the kids into the town house.

When Joe returned the first time, things went fairly smoothly. She hired a baby-sitter, stayed at Joe's hotel room until 2:00 A.M., then rushed home to be there if the kids woke up with nightmares.

There had been a fight when she wasn't ready to go back out on the road. But again he called her in a few days, behaving as if nothing had happened.

Except that something *had* happened. Bryn had watched his team on TV. And in the shots of the victorious players in the aftermath of their glory, she had seen Joe—and he hadn't been alone. He had been in the company of a very young, very beautiful and very sleek redhead.

Joe had sensed Bryn's withdrawal during their phone conversation, and he had arrived in Tahoe the next Wednesday. Even with the children up and awaiting dinner, he had pursued her for answers. When she had accused him of infidelity, he had thundered in rage, "I'm a normal, vital, healthy male! You know how it is with football players. There are always women hanging around."

Bryn had looked anxiously about the kitchen, but the kids were all in the living room watching TV. She dropped her voice to a low whisper. "Oh, so you didn't sleep with her?"

"If I did, what difference would it make? She meant nothing to me. She was just there—and willing. Which you weren't at the time. You were too busy playing little homemaker. And I warn you, Bryn, no man is going to play a waiting game while you want to be Mother Goose. Not when he has a Sleeping Beauty on his arm."

Somehow she had refrained from throwing a pan of boiling peas in his face. She had emptied them into a serving dish and headed past the counter for the dining-room table. "Dinner's ready, Joe." She could still remember her icy pronunciation of the words. "And call me Mother Goose if you like, but I don't intend to discuss any of this in front of the kids. Understand?"

He had nodded and taken his place at the table while she called the boys. But Brian must have heard part of the argument. He had been silently hostile when Joe had tried to talk to him. And then, when Joe had sworn silently beneath his breath, Brian had dipped his spoon into his peas and sent them flying across the table and into Joe's face.

It had been the last straw, Joe told her later. Sure, she had to be responsible for the kids. But she'd damn well better hire a housekeeper to stay with them. Then she could travel with him, and he wouldn't have to fall for the groupies who awaited the players.

He had proved himself unfaithful, and scarcely charitable. Knowing he had been with another woman had been painful, and then numbing. And it had hurt all over again when she answered him.

"Forget it, Joe. Just forget the whole thing."

"What?"

"I mean it. I don't want to marry you. It would be a disaster from start to finish."

"You're crazy! Do you know what you're giving up?"

"Yes, a man who feels it's his right to cheat if 'his woman' isn't available to fall into bed on his terms, at his times."

There had been more. A lot more. But in the end it had all been more of the same, and the engagement had definitely been over.

"Aunt Bryn? There's nothing but squiggly stuff on the TV."

Bryn started back to the present. "So there is, Brian. And there won't be anything but squiggly stuff in your mind tomorrow if you don't get some sleep! Bedtime, guys!"

They grumbled but obeyed. Bryn checked Adam's finger and saw that the swelling was down, and that only a small red area remained to show where the "boo-boo" was. And Adam was half asleep before he hit the pillow, so she knew he was well on his way to recovery.

With the boys tucked in, Bryn threw on an old leotard, tights and leg warmers, and hurried back downstairs. She could get in some limbering exercises and catch up on the news at the same time.

The trustworthy face of the weatherman came on the screen, announcing that the days would show a warming trend, but the nights would remain cool. Then the anchorman came on and began to talk about a young politician, Dirk Hammarfield, who was beginning his campaign for the U.S. senate in Lake Tahoe.

Between leg stretches, Bryn watched with casual interest. The man had the energetic smile of a young Kennedy. He was of medium stature, with nice sandy hair and blue eyes.

He'd probably get a lot of votes, she thought with a shrug. Maybe even her own.

Bryn lay down on her stomach, but with her legs stretched, she suddenly froze.

The story on the tube had shifted again.

A pretty anchorwoman was talking; at the left-hand corner of the screen was a picture of a man.

Lee Condor.

Bryn didn't hear what was being said; she was mesmerized by the picture. And by the gold-flecked eyes that were so arresting, even in a still shot.

Perhaps, she tried to tell herself analytically, his eyes were so arresting because they were so very dark—except for the crystalline effect of the gold. Or perhaps because his face was so interesting. High, broad forehead. Dark, defined and arching brows. Straight—dead straight—nose. High cheekbones. Firm, ruggedly square jawline. And his mouth...even in a still, it looked mobile. As if he could smile easily, yet compress his lips into a line of determined intent...or anger.

His hair was almost a pure jet black—a little long, but still, he looked more as if he could be a businessman than a rock star. Maybe not a businessman. A steelworker, more likely. There was something about him, even in a picture, that hinted at a lean and powerful physical prowess.

Something, as Barbara had mentioned, that made him appear almost overwhelmingly male, all the more so because it was something of which he didn't seem to be aware himself....

The story suddenly went off the air, and a commercial for sandwich bags came on.

Bryn abruptly relaxed her ridiculous pose and shook the tension out of her muscles. I've never even met him, she reminded herself.

But even when she had finished with her exercises, showered, and fallen into bed for the night, she couldn't stop thinking about him.

And wondering what he would be like.

And whether she would ever be able to control the disturbing fever that raced along her spine when she saw that gold fire in his dark eyes.

It won't matter, she assured herself. He'll probably barely notice me, what with all the others....

On that note, she slept.

But her hope was proved false on Tuesday, when she had been at the Fulton place for barely fifteen minutes.

She had been chatting idly and nervously with Barbara as the two did some warm-up exercises when the friendly dance director pulled Barbara away. Moments later Barbara and the director came bearing down on her and excitedly dragged her away.

"He says he thinks you're perfect—" Barbara began.

"It will mean a hike in your pay scale, of course," the director cut in.

"And very little extra work."

"Lee can explain it to you himself."

She suddenly found herself standing before him, and she hadn't even seen him come in. Barbara was issuing an enthusiastic introduction, and he was vaguely smiling, barely attentive to her words.

His eyes—they were a strange hazel, she realized, mahogany at the rim, yellow-green by the pupil—were on her. They swept over her from head to toe, lingering slowly, coming to rest on her own.

"Bryn Keller? You're the photographer, then, too. It's a pleasure to meet you."

His hand was on hers. Rough—there were heavy calluses on his palms. Large—it enveloped her slender fingers.

And hot...

As if a burning energy poured through his system, making him as combustible as an active volcano, except that his power was deceptively calm, like the snowcapped peak of a mountain beneath a blue sky....

The fire seemed to rip along her spine.

She pulled her hand—jerked it, rather—from his, and stepped back a foot. "Yes, I'm Bryn Keller. If you'll explain what you want, I'll let you know if I'll be capable or not."

Ice... There could have been no better description of her voice. She hadn't really meant to be cold, but...

She had been cold to the point of rudeness.

The gold-tinged eyes narrowed, but barely perceptibly. His voice was a lazy drawl. "Oh, I'm quite sure that you'll be capable, Miss Keller. Quite sure. Tony can explain the concept."

He turned and walked away.

Chapter 2

Lee Condor's first glimpse of the girl was an intriguing one.

When he arrived at the Fulton place, the door was open, and a flurry of activity was already in progress. No one noticed him as he walked in; the dancers—in all shapes and forms of workout clothing—were milling about, stretching and warming up. A gray-haired carpenter was finishing up at the top of the long, curving stairway, and Tony Asp, the dance director, and Gary Wright, the general director, were arguing midway up the stairs.

Lee glanced quickly around the elegant entryway and oversized ballroom. Neither Perry nor Andrew—nor even Mick—seemed to have arrived yet, but it was still only ten to ten, and they had all spent the night at the casino, gotten a little nostalgic about being back in Tahoe, then toasted themselves until the dawn.

Still, he thought with a knowing, inward smile, Perry and Andrew would arrive by ten. They had learned long ago that when they worked they were a team, and as a team, they were courteous to one another without fault. That meant not wasting the other guys' time by not showing up.

Lee ran his eyes casually over the dancers. Ten men, ten women. Most of them very young. Probably kids just out of high school, or maybe college, trying to get a break with a show in Tahoe. Well, if he was giving anyone a break, he was damned glad. Breaks were hard to come by.

It was while he was idly staring about that he noticed her—or at least part of her. His first sight was of long, long legs. The backs of them, to be precise.

The girl was bent over at the waist, first stretching her spine parallel with the ground, then dangling over until the top of her head almost touched the floor. Her tights were pink, and her leg warmers were black, as was her leotard. He really didn't have much of an impression of her face, all he noticed at first sight were those legs, slim, yet sinewy. And he couldn't help but notice her nicely rounded derriere. Not when it topped those long legs and faced him so pointedly...

She straightened, stretched her arms as if reaching for the sky, then slid into a graceful split.

Something about the action mesmerized him, and when he realized that he was watching her with his tongue practically hanging out, he laughed inwardly at himself.

She probably wouldn't appreciate the fact that he would have loved to bark out an order, empty the room and jump her like a madman.

But to him, it was nice to have the feeling. There had been women since Victoria, but none that had made him feel this way at first sight. Victoria's death had changed him, and not for the better.

And, he reminded himself, if he had ever thought of Victoria that way and she had found out, she would definitely have considered him a madman. No, a savage. That had been her favorite term....

He gave himself a little shake. Whatever mistakes he had made, whatever mistakes she had made, they were in the past. Over. Agonizing over all that had happened had never done him any good. It was too late to go back.

"Lee, you're here! I didn't see you come in."

Lee turned as Tony Asp approached him, grinning broadly, his hand stretched out in greeting.

"Hi, Tony," Lee said, shaking the offered hand and returning the grin. "I just walked in." He waved an arm to indicate the entryway, the staircase and the grand ballroom. "The place looks great. What do you think?"

"Day and night," Tony replied with a grimace. "I have to admit, I thought you were crazy to buy the place and renovate it, but you were right. From what I hear, it cost less than renting, and you've got yourself a dynamite house. You gonna move in here after the shoot?"

Lee shook his head. "I like my old house. Or new house, depending on how you look at it."

"Well, for the video, it looks great. I don't think you could find anything that looked more antebellum in the heart of Georgia."

"I hope you're right—" Lee began, but just then a hand clamped down hard on his shoulder and he turned to see Gary Wright, a too-thin bundle of nervous energy, but a brilliant conceptual director, standing behind him.

"Lee! How was the concert tour? Good to be back with you."

"The tour was fine, Gary, but I think it was our last. And it's good to be back with you, too."

The three men shared a good business relationship, although it had been an awkward one when they had first come together a year ago in Scotland to work on the first video. Tony had made his name in classical ballet, and Gary had earned his reputation as a director for PBS. They had been skeptical about working with Lee, but Lee had learned early that there were two things about him that could draw prejudice: he was a Blackfoot, and he was a rock musician.

Growing up, he had learned to be tough. Growing older, he had learned to shrug his shoulders and quietly prove his points.

And he had proved himself to both Tony and Gary.

But never to Victoria...

That's over, he reminded himself. Over...

There had been some compromises made throughout the entire month's work on the first video, but the result had been so gratifying that before the final wrap they had found themselves fast friends. And the video had hit the tube with astounding success, both commercial and critical.

"I only have one disagreement with you, Lee," Gary was saying now. "I like the concept; I have to admit I even like the arrangement of the song. But I think—with your career in mind—that we should have shots of you guys with your instruments. I know you're going to tell me that it's a Civil War ballad, which it is, but think of it this way—"

"Excuse me, Gary," Tony cut in quickly. "I'm going to go and get started with the dancers."

"Sure, Tony," Gary said. "Go ahead. Now, Lee, I'm not talking about a shot of more than a second or two—"

"Sorry, Gary," Lee interrupted this time, his eyes following Tony as he started across the ballroom toward the group of colorfully clad dancers. "I'll be right back."

"But, Lee..."

"Go with it, Gary. Go with whatever you want!" A smile spread across Gary's features, but Lee didn't notice, nor would he have minded. He was anxious to catch up with the dance director.

"Tony!"

The other man stopped quickly and turned around.

"Tony, see the willowy redhead over there?"

"Redhead? I don't see a redhead."

"*Dark* red, Tony. She's in a black leotard, pink tights. About five-foot-six. Tony, are you blind?"

"Oh! Yeah, I see her now. Boy, do I see her now!"

"Quit gawking, Tony. You should be accustomed to nice bodies."

"I am, but, hey…"

"Tony, we're being aesthetic here for a minute, okay? What do you think about using her for our Lorena?"

Tony's "aesthetic" mind went into action. "Perfect! Nice long hair, good height against yours. Thin waist—good for the costume. And nice full breasts—*great* for the costume. She's perfect!"

"If she can dance."

"I guarantee you, Lee, they can all dance. Barbara Vinton doesn't cast people unless they know their business. I'll chat with Barbara for a minute, make sure the girl's one of the best and bring her over to meet you."

"Good. I see Perry and Andrew. I'm going to talk with them for a minute, then take a look at the staircase."

Tony nodded, then hurried over to the group of dancers. Lee walked toward the door to greet his fellow band members, Andrew McCabe, Perry Litton and Mick Skyhawk.

"Damn, Lee, the place looks great!" Andrew said admiringly.

"Super," Mick agreed.

"Glad you like it," Lee laughed. "I just hope you're really seeing it. Even for a red man, you have red eyes, my friend!"

Mick, a full-blooded Blackfoot, flushed, making his naturally bronzed features darken to rust. The others laughed; Mick joined in with them good-naturedly.

"Hey, I'm here, aren't I? And you're the ones who keep telling me I need to settle down. How will I ever settle down if I don't spend an evening now and then with a member of the opposite sex?"

"You spend plenty of evenings with members of the opposite sex," Andrew told him, sighing with feigned exasperation. "It would help if you spent these nights with the *same* member of the opposite sex."

Lee felt his smile fade a little uneasily. Be careful, Mick, he thought fleetingly. Sometimes you're better off when you don't know a woman well, when you both come and go in the dark. Because you may think that you know her, but you never will, and dark secrets can hide in the heart….

"I want to go and take a look at the staircase," Lee murmured, "Mick, they've set your piano up at the rear of the ballroom, if you want to go take a look."

"I'll do that," Mick replied.

The group parted, and Lee headed toward the gracefully curving stairway. He smiled for a minute, pleased and proud that the Fulton place had turned out so well. When he had first seen it, the old marble floors had been covered in inches of dust. The stairway had been charred and broken in places, and the elegant light fixtures—including a couple of priceless chandeliers—had been so tangled in spider-webs as to be unrecognizable. They had all thought he was crazy when he decided to buy the place and renovate it for the video of "Lorena." But now, cleaned up and fixed up, the place was perfect.

Just as music had always been a passion with him, an intregal part of living, film had become an almost-obsession.

"Lee, good morning! I'd like you to meet Bryn Keller. Bryn, Lee Condor."

He had turned instantly at the sound of Barbara's voice, greeting her with a warm smile. Keller...the name was familiar.

He smiled at the woman he had chosen and extended a hand in greeting. As he studied her, he murmured something polite in return to the introduction.

Even before she spoke, he felt it: a wave of cold antagonism that was startling. So strong he could almost see a sheet of ice in the air between them.

Ice...and fire.

She seemed even more perfect now that she was standing before him. Her hair was a shade that was not quite mahogany, not quite red—something deeper than either, making him think of the hottest, most inner flame of a raging blaze. It was caught at her nape, and just a few straying tendrils curled about her forehead. Her eyes were lime-green and tilted slightly, like those of a sleek and mysterious cat. And like her hair, despite the aura of coldness about her, they hinted of fire. Deepest, hidden fire.

When she did speak, her words were soft, well-modulated, but they sent another gust of cool wind into the air between them, and no matter how softly spoken her words were, they were blunt and blatantly rude.

Her attitude made him want to slap her.

He smiled. And replied quietly. He wasn't sure what he had said, or even what she had said. It didn't matter. She still made a perfect Lorena. She was welcome to dislike him as much as she chose as long as she didn't let it interfere with her work.

But as he turned away, he was more bothered than he wanted to admit. Did she dislike him because he was a rock performer? Or because she had a hang-up about heritage? Maybe she was Custer's great-great-granddaughter or something, he thought with impatience. Well, he wasn't going to let it get to him. He would just leave her alone.

Lee smiled suddenly as he climbed the staircase. He could hear Tony explaining the entire concept of the video to her. It was obvious that she was going to stick—he was paying nicely.

A streak of mischief deepened his smile.

She was in it strictly for money. Well, she would get a chance to earn her money.

* * *

The traffic was bad getting back into town, and with each bumper-to-bumper snarl she came upon, Bryn cursed Lee Condor and his endless filming anew.

Tony Asp had explained it all to her; the song "Lorena" was a ballad written and made popular during the Civil War. Scenes had already been filmed in which the blue met the gray. In her scenes, the Fulton place would be the site of a ball to which the soldier returned to find that his Lorena had met and married another.

A dream sequence followed in a field of mist, the soldier imagining what he would like to do: take Lorena and force her to remember her vows of love.

In reality, he would walk away, understanding that circumstances had changed everything for them both.

The main scene with Lorena would take place on the stairway. She would try to flee his wrath, but he would whirl her back and into his arms and carry her into the mist.

"It won't be more than a minute and a half of film time," Tony had told her, "but there can't be a misstep in it. And if it isn't entirely graceful, the full effect will be lost. You'll be in authentic period costume, so you need to get the moves down pat. And the main responsibility will be on you. Lee is something of a gymnast, but he's not a dancer. You'll be part of the group doing the Virginia reel first, so go ahead and get back with the others now, and we'll start rehearsal with the group. During their break, we'll work on your stuff."

And so there had been the rehearsal with the group, four hours of getting down the moves. And going over and over them until they began to synchronize . . .

"You look tired, Miss Keller," Tony had called her when they had broken. "Take five minutes."

Five minutes had meant five minutes—to the second. And then she had begun with Tony on the staircase. Four steps, whirl, fall. No, try it a little higher. Oh, don't worry about Lee. He'll definitely catch you. . . .

Then it had been back to the group and another three hours of back-breaking rehearsal. . . .

She had perspired so much that now she felt like a salt lick for a whole herd of cattle.

And to make it worse, *he* had been there the entire time. Watching. Quietly making suggestions to Tony. He had stood out of the way, arms crossed over his chest, or hands stuffed into his pockets. He had worn blue jeans and a blue, button down work shirt. But if he had just tied a bandana around his forehead, she could easily have imagined him on a flashy pinto, shrieking out a war cry and bearing down on the town to burn it out. . . .

Brian and Keith's school bused them to Adam's day-care center when she was late, so at least she only had one stop to make. But all three boys were bickering.

"Keith stepped on my toe!" Adam wailed loudly.

"He hit me!" Keith protested.

"Did not! It was an ax-see-dent!"

"That was no accident."

"I saw you!" Brian butted in. "And it was no accident!"

"Stop it!" Bryn snapped. "Stop it, all three of you. Get in the van!"

It might have ended there, but something about the heat and her state of irritated exhaustion had gotten to her through and through, and she snapped at Keith again as he got into the van.

"Keith! Damn it, get in and get your seat belt on. You've been dawdling for five minutes now."

Keith hurried into his place in the back seat, snapped on his seat belt and stared at her with hurt eyes. Although the boys had been fighting like cats and dogs, now they joined together against a common enemy: her. Three pairs of green eyes stared at her with silent reproach; all three sets of little lips were compressed in hostile silence.

Bryn didn't say anything then, but as she walked around to climb into the driver's seat, guilt overwhelmed her. As soon as she turned the key in the ignition, she twisted around to face Keith with a grimace.

"Sorry, Keith. I've had a bad day." That was no excuse, she reminded herself. Especially for the "damn." If she said it, the kids said it.

He gave her a half smile, and she sighed. "How did swimming go today, Adam?"

"Don't like it!" Adam, at her side, replied, scrunching up his little nose. "Mr. Beacon tried to drown me!"

"He isn't trying to drown you, he's trying to make you learn. Keith, what did you get on your spelling test?"

Keith started to answer her, and she listened to him ramble on for a while, not hearing him. Suddenly she did hear something: the dead silence in the van.

At the next red light she stared around at their faces. They were all looking at her reproachfully again.

"What's the matter with you, Aunt Bryn?" Brian, the spokesman for the group, asked.

"Nothing, nothing," she replied quickly. Someone was beeping at her; she was ignoring the turn light. "Damn!" she muttered, but this time the oath was beneath her breath.

"Aunt Bryn..." Brian persisted.

"Really, guys, nothing is wrong. Nothing at all. Just that stupid red-skinned tom-tom player."

"Red-skinned tom-tom player?"

"Oh, God!" Bryn groaned. What had she said? And in front of the kids... "No one, honey. Please, pretend I never said that." They were all looking at her; she sensed it. "Really—please, I was being horrible, and I didn't mean what I said. I was just angry and frustrated, so I was searching for anything to say to be mean. Do you understand?"

"Of course," Brian said. "Daddy always said not to say anything at all if you couldn't say something nice. Is that it?"

"Sort of," Bryn murmured uneasily. "But it's a little deeper than that. You don't need to...to..." She paused, wishing she had thought before she had spoken. "You don't ever need to attack someone for what he is just because he's made you angry."

"I see," Brian agreed sagely, nodding. "You shouldn't have said that a man was a stupid red-skinned tom-tom player because you were mad."

"Right," Bryn said.

"What's a red-skinned tom-tom player?" Keith asked.

"The American Indians were called 'redskins' by the early settlers," Brian educated him. "Don't you ever watch 'Rin Tin Tin' on TV?" he asked with impatience.

Bryn wanted to crawl under her seat. What would Jeff—with his absolute impatience for intolerence of any kind—think of her, or the way she was raising his children now?

"Brian!" she said sharply, ashamed of herself, yet hoping to make a point. "You're watching too much television. Keith—"

"Is it wrong to be an Indian tom-tom player?" Keith interrupted innocently.

"No!" Bryn gasped out. "Oh, please! Let's forget this. Stick with the 'if you can't say anything nice, don't say anything at all.' I was wrong, very wrong, and I didn't mean what I said." Quickly she continued. "I...uh...I'm working on a videotape—"

"Oh, wow!" Keith said. "You mean like on MTV?"

"Yeah, like on MT—"

"Wow!" Brian leaned up as far as he could.

"For who, Aunt Bryn?"

"Lee Condor."

"Wow!" Even Adam echoed their excitement.

Brian turned to Keith. "Mrs. Lowe told us to watch his last video if we wanted to see the Middle Ages recreated perfectly!"

"Perfectly," Adam imitated his older brother.

"Perfect," Bryn muttered. "Everything's just perfect!"

It was almost seven o'clock before she made it home, and almost nine before she had the kids fed, bathed and in bed.

Then she had to spend another hour in the darkroom. She had done a wildlife layout for a Tahoe tour folder, and only after having chosen five shots from the proofs had they decided on a different set of animals. But the folder could lead to more work in the future, so she didn't want to take a chance on quibbling with the nervous exec from the ad company.

At least, when she finally got to bed, she wasn't haunted by dreams, or by visions of strange dark and golden eyes. She fell into an exhausted slumber the minute her head touched her pillow.

Wednesday was, if possible, worse than Tuesday.

She arrived at 9:00 A.M., as Tony Asp had asked her to before she left the night before.

She thought that the place was empty when she first walked in, and it felt strange to be there. It was almost as if she had stepped back in time. The huge chandelier glowed in the ballroom, illuminating the striking marble floor and the beautifully carved strips of wall trim that contrasted with the lightly patterned wallpaper. The staircase rose into misty darkness, and for a minute she felt as if she had actually stepped back to intrude upon another lifetime.

A sudden blast of music almost sent her rocketing up to the ceiling; her heart slowed its wild pounding as she realized a tape had been turned on. A tape of Lee Condor and his group doing "Lorena."

It began with a drum beat that had a rock sound about it, but more than that, it projected the image of men marching off to war. A fiddle joined in. Then, softly, the sound of a keyboard.

And then Condor's voice.

It was a unique sound. His voice was a tenor, but a husky one, and it seemed as if it could reach inside the soul with its slightly raspy edge.

Bryn's nerves felt more on edge than ever. She felt as if his voice, like his eyes, could discover her secrets. As if it were an instrument that could strip one bare, expose the heart and the mind and leave them naked and vulnerable.

The song was beautiful. When other voices joined his in perfect harmony for the refrain, she felt an absurb rush of tears sting her eyes. You could feel it all, the love found, the love lost, the wisdom and sadness of resignation.

"Bryn, you're here. Great!"

Tony Asp was coming down the stairway, a tape recorder in his hand.

"Can't you just imagine when it's all done?" he asked jovially. "It's going to be wonderful. Just wonderful."

Bryn dredged up a weak smile. "I'm sure it will be."

"Set your bag down, honey, and take a minute to warm up. I'll be ready at the foot of the stairs."

Bryn obediently did as she was told, wryly thinking she didn't need much of a warm-up. They had "warmed her up" so much yesterday that she should be stretched and limber for years to come.

Still, she knew the importance of keeping her muscles and tendons from being strained, so she set into a quick routine of exercises. Pliés and stretches and, on the floor, more stretches. She rose, absently dusted her hands on her tights and walked the few feet to the stairway.

"All set, Tony," she told the dance director.

"Good. We're going to start back at the beginning, nice and slow," he told her with a smile. "You'll start working with Lee today instead of me."

"Lee?" She couldn't prevent dismay from sounding in her voice.

"Yes, Miss Keller. Me."

She hadn't seen him; she hadn't had the slightest idea that he was anywhere about.

But he was. Walking down the stairway. And his movements were so quiet that it made perfect sense that she hadn't heard him, but still she felt like screaming at him.

It was obvious that he had been there all along. Watching her. Not covertly, openly. She just hadn't known....

Hadn't sensed his presence.

And now it was suddenly overwhelming.

She stared at him blankly as he continued down to meet her. He was in a short-sleeved knit Izod, kelly-green. The color seemed to bring out the glitter of gold in his eyes. His arms were bare, and his biceps bespoke wiry, muscled strength. The shirt hugged his torso, the trim, flat expanse of his waist, the triangular breadth of his chest and shoulders. Barbara had been right again: he appeared slim at a distance, but the closer he came, the more you became aware of the power of his frame.

She was still looking up when he reached the bottom step. He stood a full head taller than she. And when he was there, right there before her, she sensed him again, as well as saw him. His after-shave was very light, and it made her think of cool, misty woods. It was pleasant, seductive....

And as frightening as that hot, leashed sense of energy about him.

"Good morning, Miss Keller."

The sound of his voice razored through her blood stream. Chills, then fever, assailed her again.

"Good morning."

"Tony has been through this with me already, so we might as well give it a quick spin and see where the problems will be. I like the idea of the five steps—if you can handle the distance. I assure you, I'll catch you when you fall."

"Fine," Bryn said crisply.

"Tony?"

"I'm ready. Walk it through from the foot of the stairs. Then we'll try it with the music."

It had been so easy the day before. Today, as soon as Lee put his hands on her upper arms, she wanted to wrench away from him and run. She glanced uneasily at the fingers that locked over her gently. They were bronze from the sun, long, the nails blunt and clean. A spattering of jet hair feathered the backs of his hands. She found herself thinking that they were definitely a man's hands....

"When you're ready, Miss Keller."

She stared into his eyes. She saw the gold again, a deep burning fire, plunging into her soul. He was amused by her. She saw it as his lips twisted slightly into a sardonic smile.

The spin! she reminded herself. She could wrench away from him....

She spun into a pirouette, paused, turning right, and then left, then flew up the stairs. One, two, three, four, five...

She felt his hand on her arm, gripping her, stopping her, spinning her around again. She executed the kick without thinking, then prayed that he would be there to catch her....

He was. His right arm locked around her waist as she fell against the rock hardness of his torso; his left arm slipped beneath her, bending her knees, and she was floating as he began to carry her up the stairs. Floating...and staring into his eyes again. Feeling their heat...and that of his powerful arms about her...

"Great!" Tony approved from the foot of the stairs. "Rough, but great. Bryn, the kick was a little slow. Lee, look angrier, less tense. You're not going to drop her. Now let's try it with the music."

The first try might have been "great," but the second was a disaster. Bryn tripped on the second step. And, to her horror, she repeated the fumble once, and then again.

It was Condor, she thought with defensive and heated anger. It was all his fault for that half smile of vast amusement he gave her each time he saw the resentment in her eyes....

"Miss Keller, just what is the problem?" he inquired politely, but she could still see the laughter. "Have you had coffee yet? Tony, how could you let this young lady go to work without coffee?"

She wanted to protest; she wanted to tell him that all she wanted was to get the rehearsal over. But before she could say anything, she found herself being ushered into a drawing room opposite the ballroom and staircase.

And she was completely alone with him.

Bryn stood silently as he poured a cup of coffee from a drip brewer.

"Sugar?"

"Black, please."

He handed her the cup and poured one for himself. He sipped from it, staring at her so pointedly that she wished she could disappear into the floorboards.

"Have I ever met you before, Miss Keller?"

"No."

"I was quite sure I hadn't. I can't imagine forgetting you. But if we've never met, I certainly can't see how I might have offended you in any way. Why do you dislike me?"

"I...I don't," Bryn protested.

"But you do. Why?"

Inadvertently she moistened her lips. It would be futile to lie. He wasn't asking her *if* she disliked him, he was asking her *why* she did. And in the secluded drawing room, he suddenly seemed ridiculously dangerous to her. Taut, trim and powerful. Able to move soundlessly with the grace of a great cat. She surreptitiously scanned his hard features. The jet hair, short and feathered in front, longer in back, dead straight. She imagined him with a bandanna across his forehead again. His shirt off, a loincloth in place of jeans. Moving stealthily through the dark, attacking with a bloodcurdling war cry keening from his full lips...

He wouldn't need the costume. In jeans and knit shirt, the fluid agility of his body was still evident. His dry, mocking smiles added to her certainty that he was more than healthy—he was exceptionally virile, a sexual and sensual man. Dangerous? Yes, very. He was being cordial now, testing her. Perhaps giving her a chance. But she knew as he stared at her with that look that was as hard as flint that things were done his way. He wouldn't tolerate dissention in the ranks of his employees. She would dance to his tune—or not at all.

Anger made an abrupt appearance, welling up from deep inside her. He wanted things on the line. Well, so did she.

"To be quite truthful, Mr. Condor, I don't quite know why I dislike you myself. But I won't let it interfere with my work—here, or when we do your promo shots."

He laughed, easily, and his features didn't seem so hard as a grin, which displayed a nice set of even white teeth, softened them.

"Fine, Miss Keller, I'll trust in your professionalism. Just as I'll trust my own."

"What does that mean?" Bryn queried quickly.

"It means, Miss Keller, that I may know you better than you know yourself. I believe you think that I mentally undress you each time I look at you."

"Perhaps," Bryn replied coolly, hoping that her cheeks weren't turning a telltale crimson.

"Ummm. And perhaps you're worried that I chose you from a crowd because I'd like to see more of you. Or drag you into bed."

"I don't presume—"

He chuckled softly again, and she heard the sound like a hot whisper that swept through the blood, caressing her heart.

"Miss Keller, presume all you like. I chose you for Lorena because you're talented, and you fit my image of the woman perfectly. As to the other... I'm afraid you're right. I would like to see more of you — and I would definitely like to seduce you into bed. But don't worry, I won't let it interfere with work. Here, or when we do the promo shots."

She should have slapped him. She should have done something. But she was too stunned. She just stared at him as he set his cup on the fold-up table and sauntered out of the room. Silently.

With a panther-light tread that was dangerously deceptive, totally contrary to all that the man was proving himself to be.

He was professional, and competent — but he was *there*.

And no matter how she fought the ridiculousness of it, he frightened the hell out of her.

Chapter 3

Bryn knew soon after she sat down at the large booth that the Chinese restaurant had been a mistake. Noodles were sliding across the slick veneer tabletop in seconds as the hungry kids grabbed at them; a water glass was tipped over almost immediately, and Adam slid off the plastic seat cover, bumped his head and broke into tears.

Why couldn't I have picked McDonald's, she asked herself as she alternately soothed Adam and tried to sound like the wrath of God to Brian and Keith in a quiet tone so that they would settle down.

Yes, it had definitely been a mistake.

When Friday night had at last rolled around after the grueling and nerve-racking week, she had been ecstatic. She had promised herself that she was going to forget it all, go home cool and calm, and be entirely decent and loving to the kids.

And for the first half hour everything had gone fine, just fine. But she had carried her Mother Goose act a little too far. And while she had been helping Brian to read Burrough's "Tarzan," Adam had looked up from his coloring book to inform her, "Something stinks!"

"Yeah," Keith had volunteered helpfully. "And it's burning, too!"

"Oh—" Don't say it! Don't say it! "Oh—sugar!" she groaned, flying up from the bottom bunk, bashing her head, and racing down to the kitchen. The meatloaf was irretrievably burned; her spinach was green glue inside the saucepan.

The kids loved Chinese food, and they even ate Chinese vegetables. Wong's was a great restaurant where they had a high tolerance for children. And she had already copped out with burgers and fries, and with pizza. They needed something healthy to eat.

So here she was at Wong's, wishing that she wasn't.

"I want the sweet and sour chicken..." Keith began.

"Can I have the cashew chicken? We always have to order what Keith wants."

"Uggh! I don't like cashew chicken. I don't like cashews."

"Stop!" Bryn hissed as quietly as it was possible to do while still putting menace in her voice. She kissed Adam on the top of his blond head, sopped up the spilled water and did her best to collect the straying noodles. Then she gave the two older boys her most threatening scowl, until Keith lowered his red head, and Brian bowed his darker one in silent submission.

"You three *will* act decent in a restaurant!" she warned, but then she leaned back more comfortably in the booth, resting her head against its back for a minute. It wasn't their fault that it was so late and that they were half starving. Nor was it their fault that her week had been so miserable.

It wasn't anyone's fault but her own. And Lee Condor's.

He had barely spoken to her since they had talked in the drawing room. He had been professional and competent to a fault, polite—and strictly proper. It was almost as if he had actually asked her for a date and she had said a clear "No," leaving him to agree with a simple "Fine."

And then again, it was if he was waiting...watching her. As if he knew that she had come to a point where she could sense his presence even when he silently appeared several feet away, sense the subtle, woodsy, masculine aroma of his after-shave.

It was as if he knew that currents, alternately ice and fire, plagued her, rippling along her spine, playing havoc with her blood, each time he touched her.

And he always looked at her as he walked up that stairway with her in his arms. The gold flame seemed to ignite something within her, and as soon as she could, she would close her eyes and hear his husky laughter....

She couldn't help but wonder about him. She knew that he had made a whole host of new fans in Tahoe; everyone working on the video was crazy about him. He knew when to work, and when to laugh. When to demand discipline, when to let loose. And just as she sensed that dangerous fire within his eyes, she sensed a deep wisdom within their depths, one that had come from living...and from hurting? It was hard to imagine that he might have known trauma or pain. But Barbara had told her that he was widower. Was it possible that such a man could have loved one woman, and loved her so completely that her death had brought him a never-ending pain?

"Aunt Bryn?" Brian asked quietly. "Can I get cashew chicken?"

They usually had to share a meal. There were no children's portions here, and the tab could get high. But tonight...

She waved a hand in the air with helpless resignation. "Get whatever you want." She closed her eyes again for a minute. When she opened them, a pretty Oriental girl was waiting to take her order. "A large glass of wine first, please," Bryn murmured. "And we'll have the cashew chicken, the sweet and sour chicken—and Adam, what would you like?"

"A hot dog!" Adam said.

"They don't have hot dogs, Adam. This is a Chinese restaurant."

"Ummm...chicken."

Bryn shrugged at the waitress. "I'd better take a side order of egg rolls and ribs. And the special fried rice with the shrimp, please."

The waitress was a doll. She returned quickly with Bryn's wine, and with sodas for the boys with little umbrellas sticking out of the straws.

That will be good for at least two minutes' entertainment, Bryn thought gratefully.

The food arrived while they were still engrossed with the umbrellas, giving Bryn a chance to dole out portions to the three boys, and to dissect Adam's eggroll. He didn't like the "dark green things" in it.

Well, if nothing else, she reminded herself as she spooned out the fried rice, the wildlife shots were all completed. And Barbara was taking a few weeks off from her show and had promised to baby-sit a couple nights next week so that Bryn could go out and have dinner and drinks with a few of the other dancers. That would be nice. A night of utter relaxation...

"Aunt Bryn."

It was Brian's voice. Low, excited.

"There's a man coming this way. I think he's coming to see you."

Her eyes flew open, and she stared across the restaurant in dismay. There *was* a man coming toward them, and he was definitely coming to see her.

It was Lee Condor.

What was he doing here, she wondered bleakly. The restaurant was nice, but not ritzy. He should have been at some sleek night spot, dining on steak Diane, dancing, and throwing some of his overabundance of money away at the crap tables.

"Hello, Miss Keller." His eyes moved quickly around the table; Brian and Keith were surveying him with open mouths, and Adam was showing overt hostility, with his mouth set in a pout.

"Hello," Bryn murmured. She was surprised that he had come to see her when she had three small children at her table. Most men would have run in the other direction.

But there were nice smile lines that crinkled about his eyes, and he looked both interested and amused as he turned his gaze to her once more. "Is this your family? Foolish question, they must be. They all bear a resemblance."

"She's not our mother!" Brian supplied quickly. "She's our aunt."

"Oh, is she?" Lee queried. "Not yours, huh?" he asked Bryn.

"Not mine—but, yes, mine."

Keith liked to think of himself as old and mature; but his lip trembled a little when he hopped into the conversation. "My mother and father are...they live with Jesus now. And we live with Aunt Bryn."

"Well, that sounds like a good arrangement," Lee said amiably. "And you're—"

"Keith Keller. That's Adam."

"Well, Keith Keller, would you mind scooting over for a minute? I'd like to join you for a few seconds, if you don't mind."

Keith agreeably scooted over. And to Bryn's horror Lee Condor sat down and smiled at her.

She tried to smile back, but the effort was a dismal failure. At least, she thought, he wouldn't want to hop into bed with her after tonight. She had showered, but that had been it. Her hair was still damp; it felt as if it was plastered to her shoulders. She hadn't bothered with new makeup, and she had thrown on an old tube top and a faded calico wraparound skirt.

And now she was wearing half of the Chinese noodles that had been on the table.

Bryn picked up her glass of wine and nervously downed three-quarters of it, then tried a polite smile once again. "What are you doing here?" she asked him.

"I like Chinese food," he replied with a shrug.

"No date?" Bryn queried, instantly wishing she hadn't.

He chuckled. "Not unless you want to consider Mick and Perry dates. They're over there." He waved toward the rear of the room. She had met Mick and Perry earlier in the week. They had both impressed her as being down to earth pleasant men, the opposite of what she had expected. Sandy-haired Perry with his sexy lopsided smile waved to her; Mick, with his sparkling dark eyes, grinned broadly and waved, too.

Bryn waved back, then found her eyes returning of their own accord to meet Lee Condor's.

"Would you...ah...like some cashew chicken? Fried rice, an egg roll, a rib...?"

"Thank you, no. I've eaten, and I'm all done."

So am I, Bryn thought, looking down at her plate and knowing she wouldn't be able to consume another mouthful.

"I'm...surprised to see you here," she heard herself say lamely.

"I've had a home in Tahoe for the last ten years," he explained. "I know all the spots where the food is really good and the service amiable."

"Oh," Bryn murmured. "They do serve delicious food. And they're very nice. They're always great with the . . . children."

"She means she's not embarrassed to bring us here," Brian volunteered.

"Brian!"

"Oh, I don't think your aunt is embarrassed to bring you places. It's just that some places are very accustomed to adults, but they don't understand how to feed children—or deal with them. But you know something, Brian? Most people who care about children tend to be nice people. So knowing that they're nice to you here makes me like the restaurant even better."

"Do you have any children?" Brian asked, wide-eyed.

Did Bryn imagine it, or did a flicker of the pain that she had sensed pass quickly through his eyes?

"No, I don't have any children. But I would like to one day."

"A boy?"

"Sure, but I'd take a daughter, too."

"Are you really a red-skinned tom-tom player?"

"Oh, God!" Bryn breathed, frozen in absolute terror as she waited for an explosion of righteous fury.

There was no explosion. His eyes returned to hers, heavily laced with humor. "A red-skinned tom-tom player?"

"Are you?" Brian persisted.

"Brian!" Bryn snapped. "I swear to God, I'm going to skin you alive. . . ."

Lee turned his attention back to the boy and repeated the description one more time. "A red-skinned tom-tom player. Hmmm. Yes, well, I guess in a way I am."

"You're Lee Condor, aren't you?" Keith asked excitedly.

"Yes." He glanced at Bryn with amused reproach. "I guess your aunt forgot her manners, but aunts do that sometimes."

"Then you really are an Indian?" Brian asked.

"Real live," he laughed. "Or at least half."

Brian looked confused. "Which half?"

Bryn wanted to sink under the table and die; Lee laughed again and motioned to the waitress. "I think I'm going to order your aunt another drink, and then I'll explain." He glanced at Bryn. "Chablis, isn't it?"

She could only nod. She would gladly have downed the entire bottle if they would have brought it.

Lee ordered another wine for her, glanced at her with an upraised brow and ordered a Scotch for himself.

The drinks arrived quickly, and he sipped his while replying to Brian. "My dad is a full-blooded Blackfoot. But my mom is German. That makes me half Blackfoot and half German. And all American."

"Oh, wow!" Keith approved. "Does your dad live in a teepee? Does he have horses and bows and arrows and all those neat things?"

"Sorry. My dad lives in an apartment in New York City. He's a lawyer. They live there because my mom teaches at a music school."

"Oh," Keith said, and his disappointment was evident.

"But," Lee continued, "my grandfather lives in a teepee during the summer. And he wears buckskins and hunts deer and lives by all the old ways."

"I wish I could meet him!" Keith sighed enviously.

"Well, he lives in the Dakota Black Hills, and that's pretty far away. But I have a nice collection of old bows and arrows and Indian art, if your aunt would like to bring you by to see them some time."

"Oh, Aunt Bryn, could we?" Brian begged instantly.

"I . . . uh . . ."

"Oh, I forgot. I have tom-toms, too."

By now she was halfway through her second glass of wine, but it hadn't eased the desire to be swallowed into the floor one bit. She was certain that she was as red as the lobster being served at the next table, and she was completely lost for a reply. But it didn't matter, not anymore. Because Adam, who had an innate resentment against any man who claimed his aunt's attention, and who had been ignored throughout the preceding conversation, chose that minute to strike.

A large spoonful of pork fried rice went flying across the table.

"Oh, Adam!" Bryn gasped in horror. She didn't think to reprimand him further; she was too busy staring across the table as Lee picked the pieces of food off himself and wondering if she might still possibly have a job.

"Lee, I'm sorry. Truly sorry. Really." She stood up nervously and began to help dust the rice off the sleeve of his navy shirt. It was linen, she thought, feeling ill. Expensive, and hard to clean.

And then she couldn't help but remember the last time food had flown across a table; it had been the last straw. This was different, but . . .

Tears suddenly stung her eyes. She was inadequate. She couldn't handle disciplining the boys, and she couldn't give them all that they needed. She was suddenly on the defensive as she kept dusting his already dusted arm.

"He's not a bad child, he really isn't. He's just four years old, and he's lost so much . . . ."

"Bryn."

His voice was quiet and soft, but commanding. His hand, bronze and broad and powerful, enveloped hers, stopping its futile motion.

His eyes rose to hers, and she saw a gentle empathy in the soft flicker of gold and deeper brown. "It's all right. It's no big thing. Would you please sit back down?"

She did so, biting her lower lip miserably as she continued to stare at him. He smiled at her, inclining his head slightly as if to tell her to go ahead—but to what she wasn't sure—and turned his attention to Adam. "Adam, I'm sorry that we weren't including you in the conversation. That was very rude of us. But throwing your food across the table is a very bad thing to do. Do it again, and your aunt or I will take you outside and give you a good talking to there. Understand?"

Adam shifted closer to Bryn and pressed as far into the vinyl seat as he could. He didn't reply, but he didn't throw anything again, either.

Bryn wondered briefly if she should have resented Lee taking over the initiative on discipline. But she didn't feel any resentment; all she felt was a pounding headache coming on.

"Guys," she murmured, and her voice held a husky tremor, "please finish your dinners; we have to get home."

Get it together, Bryn Keller, she warned herself. It had been nice to see the empathy in Lee Condor's extraordinary eyes, but she didn't want empathy to become pity. She could control her situation; only rarely did she fall prey to frustration.

"Want some coffee?" Lee asked her after Brian and Keith had looked from her to Lee to her again, then begun busily eating. Adam didn't budge, but his plate was almost empty anyway. She decided to let it go.

Bryn lowered her lashes suddenly. Lee even seemed to know that gulping two glasses of wine was too much for her. Yes, she did want coffee. There was Chinese tea on the table, but it wouldn't perk her up enough to drive.

"Yes, I would," she murmured.

Lee signaled to the waitress, and she wondered for a moment if the American Indian and the Chinese shared a special sign language, because two cups of coffee were instantly brought.

"How did you do that?" Bryn inquired curiously.

He laughed. "No great talent. I mouthed the word 'coffee.'"

"Oh." She flushed uneasily, lowering her lashes once again, and scalded her lip on the hot coffee.

"Hi, Bryn."

She glanced up to see that Perry and Mick had wandered over to their booth.

"Hi," she returned, wishing her voice didn't sound so shy. She was accustomed to being assured; why did she worry about what these particular men thought of her?

Because they're Lee's co-workers, an inner voice that she didn't want to hear told her. And, more important, they're his friends.

"Nice looking family," Mick said with a grin that proved he meant it.

"Thanks," she replied, then added swiftly, "Guys, meet Mr. Sky-hawk and Mr. Litton. They work with Mr. Condor."

Perry chuckled. "You make us sound like the Mafia, Bryn. Guys, I'm Perry, and this is Mick. And who are you?"

"That's Brian, and that's Keith, and this is— Oh!" She glanced down at Adam to see that he had fallen asleep against her side. His left thumb was securely in his mouth—he had broken the habit during the day, but not at night—and he had bunched a fistful of her skirt into his hand like a security blanket. Bryn glanced back up at Mick and Perry and shrugged. "Rip Van Winkle here is Adam."

"Hi, Brian, hi, Keith," Mick said.

Bryn knew before they opened their mouths that she was in trouble again, but there wasn't a damn thing she could do to prevent it, short of grabbing the tablecloth and throwing it over both their heads.

"You're an Indian, too!" they exclaimed in unison.

Lee laughed along with Perry and Mick, and Perry purposely egged the boys on. "Me? An Indian? No, I'm not. I'm a perfect American Heinz 57! A little Scotch, a little Irish. Some English, some French. Oh! I forgot about the Lithuanian!"

"Not you!" Mick exclaimed in mock horror. "They mean me. Hey, you can't fool kids these days. They know a real Indian when they see one."

Brian and Keith stared at each other in confusion, then broke up giggling. Bryn wasn't sure whether she wanted to kiss the lot of them, or still crawl beneath the table.

"Indians are fun!" Keith told Brian gravely.

"And green-eyed dancers can turn lovely shades of red, can't they?" Lee said, grinning up wickedly at his friends.

"Sure can," Mick agreed. He smiled at Bryn, then turned his attention to Lee. "We were about to head on out. I think they needed our table. But we can wait around outside if you want."

Lee looked across the table at Bryn. "If Miss Keller won't mind the assistance, I'll give her a hand getting her brood home."

"Oh, no, really. I can handle them fine. I don't want to hold you up!" Bryn protested. Don't help me, she pleaded silently. It's too easy to accept help. Too easy to lean on strength. And too easy to find your support gone, and you falling deeper....

"Go on, Perry, Mick," Lee said comfortably. He was looking at Bryn again. "We're just fooling around with some new tunes tonight. Andrew had a date and won't make it until eleven, eleven-thirty. I'll carry our little rice-throwing Rip Van Winkle over there so you don't have to wake him up. Then I'll give Mick and Perry a call, and one of them can come back to get me."

"Oh, no, really . . ."

"You already said that." Mick grinned. "No problem, Bryn. Just make sure he gives us the right address when he calls."

She didn't get a chance to protest again; they were already waving and leaving the restaurant.

"Are you ready?" Lee asked.

"I just have to get the check."

"I already paid it."

"What? How? When?"

"How indignant you can get! I asked them to add your tab to mine when I saw you in here."

"But you had no right—"

"Bryn, it's a lousy dinner check."

"Mr. Condor, I earn my salary, and I pay my own bills."

"Ah . . . I just became 'Mr. Condor' again. I liked it when you used my given name. Okay, let's set the record straight. You *do* earn your salary. You more than earn it. But I wanted to pick up your check. No strings, no, 'You owe me something.' Just dinner. It's been worth it to have a meal with kids. Now, do you want to get out of here before Rip awakens and starts to bawl in the middle of the restaurant?"

"All right, all right!" Bryn snapped. "Let's go. I'll carry Adam until we get to my van."

"The blue Ford?"

"Yes."

She almost forgot about Keith and Brian as she struggled to stand with Adam scooped into her arms. It was Lee who turned back to them. "Brian, Keith? You guys all set?"

They came with him as meekly as lambs.

Outside the restaurant, Lee turned around and smoothly plucked Adam from Bryn's arms. She didn't say anything; Adam was a good forty pounds, and she had already been puffing. Lee carried him as easily as a football.

She didn't speak at all during the short drive home, but it didn't really seem to matter. Lee talked to the boys. And she had to admit that he had a nice way about him. It wasn't so much that he spoke to them as if they were adults; he spoke to them as if they were *people*—a talent which many grown-ups were sadly lacking. She vaguely heard a conversation that began dealing with different Indian tribes in the United States and went on to history in general.

"My teacher said your medieval video was great!"

"Well, thank your teacher for me, Brian. There was a time when I thought I might be a history teacher myself."

"What happened?"

"I found out that I liked being a drummer better."

"I thought you played the tom-toms?"

"Well, they're a lot alike."

A few moments later Bryn pulled into the driveway. She began to hope that she hadn't left laundry scattered anywhere, and that she had remembered to dust sometime within the past month.

After parking, she turned around to look at Lee, who still held Adam.

"I've got him," Lee assured her. "Just lead the way."

Brian and Keith bounded out of the van; Bryn followed them at a more reserved pace. She didn't fumble with the key, but she did have difficulty finding the light switch.

"Upstairs," she told Lee, trying to hide the trace of nervousness in her voice. "Brian, Keith, please don't trip Mr. Condor."

She followed him up the stairs, along with their boisterous escort of two. "Adam is the bottom bunk!" Brian informed Lee in a low whisper. "I'm the top, and Keith has the bed over there."

"Okay!" Lee whispered, ducking low to deposit Adam on the bunk.

"And Aunt Bryn sleeps in her own bed down the hall. She has her own room, you know."

Bryn gritted her teeth and clenched her fists at her sides, shooting her eldest nephew a murderous glare. If I did what I wanted to do to you right now, Brian Keller, she thought, I would definitely be arrested for child abuse.

"You two go brush your teeth and get ready for bed!" Sometimes she could swear that they were sixteen and seventeen instead of six and seven.

"I guess you want to slip his jeans off or something," Lee told her with a smile. "Mind if I wait for you downstairs?"

"No, that'd be fine, thanks," Bryn replied.

Lee disappeared. Bryn could hear water splashing in the upstairs bath as she tugged off Adam's jeans. He'd be all right in his T-shirt, she decided. A tender smile tugged at her lips as she maneuvered the child about. He looked so sweet and vulnerable in his sleep.

"But you have to stop throwing food, young man!" she whispered, bending to kiss his forehead. "You're bad for my image. You're wreaking havoc with my aura of self-control!"

Still smiling, she tucked the covers about him and tiptoed out of the room. Brian and Keith had apparently given their teeth a lick and a promise. They were already downstairs, chatting away to Lee. He had made himself comfortable on the love seat, with his left ankle crossed over his knee, his arms stretched behind him.

"Brian, Keith—to bed. Now," she told them.

"Ahhhh..."

"No 'Ahhhs.' To bed."

Thank God they chose to obey her! Rising, they gave her the usual kisses and hugs, then started for the stairs.

"Would you like to tell Mr. Condor good-night and thank him for the meal?"

"Sure!" Brian readily agreed. "Night, Lee. Thanks for dinner."

"Night, thanks!" Keith echoed.

As soon as they started up the stairs, Bryn started to wonder why she hadn't let them stay up. Now she was alone with Lee Condor.

"Can I get you anything?" she asked him, surreptitiously glancing around the living room. Things looked pretty much in order. There were fingerprint smudges on the glass-topped coffee table, but the magazines on it were neatly stacked, and the long fingers of a philodendron hid a multitude of sins.

"Not a thing," he replied, watching her, a slight smile playing upon his lips, and that glint of golden amusement sparkling from his eyes. "Why don't you sit down for a minute?"

His eyes indicated the small space remaining on the love seat. Bryn lowered her lashes for a minute, then raised her eyes to his.

"Because I don't trust you," she answered honestly.

He chuckled, and she noticed again how nice his features looked with the ease of laughter.

"What's not to trust? I lay everything on the line."

"Hmm. Quite on the line."

"Do you still dislike me?"

"No. Yes. No. Lee, it's not a matter of like or dislike. You've been very frank about wanting to hop into bed, and I don't feel like being used that way. You were nice with the kids tonight, and I appreciate that, just like I appreciate working. But—"

"Hey, wait a minute." He had been sitting comfortably, but he was suddenly standing, gripping her arms and staring deeply into her eyes. Amusement was gone; his golden gaze was as hard as the tension about his features.

"They don't coincide, Miss Keller, not in the least. I didn't buy you dinner, or be nice to the kids, in hopes of any kind of trade. I enjoy children, and frankly, a dinner check is no big deal. Yes, I still want to go to bed with you. It's a rather natural urge when a man meets a truly beautiful woman. But that doesn't mean that I want to *use* you. Any more than you would be using me. I'm talking about something that should be thoroughly enjoyed by both parties—that gives to each."

Why did she have to swallow so much when he stared at her, Bryn wondered, nervously moistening her lips. Because he was right? She had felt the attraction before she had known him. And now...she could feel his heat and energy, and the soft texture of his shirt. His grip was firm, but not painful, and she could think of nothing but the touch of his hands on her arms. She had to tilt her head to meet his eyes, and his thumb moved to her chin, caressing it with a touch of rough magic.

"Lee, you can probably have any number of women...."

He emitted an impatient oath. "Bryn, you keep trying to label me with archaic attitudes. Do you think that all a man wants is a sound body attached to a nice face? I do not run around having indiscriminate affairs. There was something about you that fascinated me from the moment I saw you."

"It's a nice line," Bryn heard herself say harshly.

"Line? Damn it—"

"Yes, line, damn it! Or are you swearing eternal devotion?"

"Is that what you want—eternal devotion? I can't believe that. We've just met. I'm trying to get to know you better, but you're making it damned hard. Maybe there is eternal devotion in it. But how can any of us know where any path leads unless we take the first steps and then follow it?"

"I don't want to get involved!" Bryn flared. "I don't want to get—"

Hurt. That was the word. But she didn't want to say it. It had a very vulnerable sound about it.

"I don't want to get involved," she repeated coldly. Panic was setting in. The longer he stood there, the more she wanted to throw herself against him. The more excitement she felt. How exhilarating it would be to lie down beside him, to explore the taut, muscular length of his body. How nice to be with a man whose very presence spoke of strength and character, power and tenderness. To wake up beside him, feel his arms securely about her...

"Bryn..."

Suddenly his arm was about her, pressing her close until she felt scorched by his body heat, touched by the thunder of his heart. The bronze fingers on her chin held her firm as his lips lowered to hers, firm like his hands, commanding, but persuasive. A touch like lightning. Like the warmth of the sun. So sensual that she felt dizzy, as if her body were spinning along with the earth. His tongue rimmed her lips with a subtle expertise, parted them, delved beyond them. Deeper, deeper, sweetly, firmly exploring, filling her with a current of swiftly burning desire. Somehow hinting of another fulfillment with the crush of his hips against hers, a touch so close that it blatantly spoke to her body of the force of his need...

"No!"

He didn't stop her as she jerked away from him. If he had attempted to, he would easily have succeeded. She was well aware of his strength.

"Please!" she murmured, meeting the disappointed narrowing of his eyes. Panic swelled again. He knew her. Too well. Frighteningly, threateningly. Knew that she didn't dislike him, that she did want him. She had to say something that would dissuade him before she set herself up for the biggest fall of her life.

"Damn it!" she spat. "Are you incapable of believing that someone seriously might not want your...attentions? Listen to me! I—do—not—want—to—get—involved. I do not like rock stars—or any form of 'star,' for that matter. I don't like your type of man. *Please!* I—You're making me very nervous. I'm asking you to leave my house."

She expected anger; she even flinched involuntarily. But his contemptuous stare was worse than anything she could have anticipated. "Relax, Miss Keller. I'm not sure what my 'type' of man is, but I don't run around raping women, or striking them. I'm just sorry that you feel compelled to be such a liar. And to shield yourself in a glass house. Good night."

Bryn bit her lip, feeling the tears well into her eyes. What was she doing? He had every right to fire her, and she would much prefer that he did strike her than fire her! God, what was she doing?

Watching the breadth of his shoulders and his proud carriage as he moved to the door, she felt shamed by the extent of his quiet dignity.

"Lee..." she gulped out quickly. "The phone...uh...you need to call Mick or Perry."

"Thanks—I'll find a pay phone. I can use a nice brisk walk in the evening air."

"Lee, you don't understand. I—"

He stopped at the door and turned back to her with a grim smile. "There are wonderful benefits to being a 'tom-tom' player, Bryn. You can go and beat the hell out of the drums and control all your savage tendencies with that outlet. You can close your mouth, Bryn. And don't look so terrified. I would never fire an employee over a personal problem. You still have a job. In fact, Barbara should be calling you over the weekend. We're doing the pictures on Monday. Rehearsal at the Fulton place is still at 9:00 A.M.; but have your equipment with you, because we'll be going directly to the Timberlane Country Club right after to do some shots with the group."

Bryn stared at him, feeling her face flame crimson. Words! The power of words! She had carelessly issued a few in front of the children—words she had spoken only in frustration and anger—and now it seemed she was to pay for them forever.

I'm sorry....

The thought welled in her throat; she wanted to tell him that she had never meant anything cruel. She even wanted to explain that she could be hurt too easily by any involvement, that she couldn't trust a man to care for a woman—and three young children.

She had wanted so badly to get rid of him. And now, right now in this moment, she wanted nothing more than to explain. But she had

shouted and she had been cruel, and now it was too late. Words—
words that she desperately needed now—refused to come to her aid.

The door opened quietly.

And it closed just as quietly behind him.

Chapter 4

He hadn't dreamed in a long time. And during swatches of semi-consciousness, when he realized that his restless sleep was being pierced by dreams, he mentally assured himself that it was probably a normal occurence. Bryn Keller's words would combine with Victoria's face and the sense of helplessness that had assailed him at the time would come back with a painful force.

Sometimes, when he closed his eyes, the dreamworld took him back. Far back. It had all been fairly simple in South Dakota. Half the people in his small town had Indian blood. He had loved being a Blackfoot then. Loved the days with grandfather. Peaceful days, perfect days. Days in which he had eagerly learned to stalk deer, to watch the flight of the hawk and move through the night as one with it.

But then had come the move to New York. And the taunts from the kids in the streets. And the fights.

And his mother's soft voice.

"You must learn to smile at the taunts, my love, for they are only testing you. And courage is not always in violence, Lee, but in the dignity to stand against it. You needn't call people names in return. You are part Blackfoot. And part German American. Be very proud of them both. You are young, Lee. But you know that your father and your grandfather are two of the finest men living...."

He had started playing the drums then. And started gymnastics. The two had settled his restless soul, and he had found the peace—and price—that he had sought.

There had been attacks of a different variety when the band had formed. Professors who ranted against the new music and said that Lee was wasting a God-given talent with "noise."

The service and military action in the Middle East had put hold on things, but when he had come back, it had been his father who set his mind at ease.

"Each man follows his own path—his own destiny, if you will. And only he is responsible for the choice. You know where your heart longs to fly; give it wings."

And so the group had formed. Each year they knew one another better; the music grew. Their lyrics grew. The crawl to the top was slow, but steady. Their talents had blossomed along with them.

But then there had been Victoria....

Violet eyed, golden-haired. Fragile and beautiful. He had met her on tour in Boston and fallen violently in love.

"She is very, very, delicate, like thin crystal," his father had warned. Lee hadn't cared; he had been madly in love. Victoria was everything that he was not. So fair, so ethereal, so lovely...

Too fair; too fragile. The first years were good ones; he still liked to think so. But then he had taken her to the Black Hills, and he had had to bring her to the hospital in the middle of the night because a bear had brought on a case of severe hysteria....

Was it that night that she had turned from him? Or the night of the break-in at their Ft. Lauderdale home? He had crept up on the robber and wrestled him to the ground. Victoria had screamed and screamed. What should he have done, he demanded. Let the guy rob the place and perhaps attack them in their sleep? No argument did any good; he had become a "savage." And no matter how softly he spoke, or how gently he touched her, she claimed that he was rough...and savage. He left her alone, baffled and hurt. And he had taken her to doctor after doctor, because he had never stopped loving her.

Then had come the shock of learning that she was pregnant, when he hadn't touched her in countless months. Strange, but he hadn't been furious, just horribly confused. And hurt to the depths of his soul. He talked to her, he promised her that things would be okay, that they would raise the child together and learn to trust each other again....

Where had he failed?

In his sleep he covered his head with his hands and began rocking as the pain threatened to rip apart his insides again. He would never, never forget the doctor calling.

Victoria was dead. She had tried to abort the baby herself....

Somehow none of it had gotten into the papers. He had returned to the Black Hills and slowly nursed the deep and bitter wound with his grandfather's wisdom.

"Along our chosen paths, we all meet up with demons. We must meet them, and battle them, even when they are nothing but mist in the night. Your wife could not meet her demons, and you could not battle them for her with all your strength, for such demons lurk in the soul. But now you must battle those that plague your own soul."

Lee shot up in the bed, suddenly wide awake. His skin was covered with perspiration, despite the coolness of the night.

He slid his legs over the side of the bed and padded silently out to the terrace, naked. The fresh breeze cooled his damp flesh, and the last vestiges of his dreams were swept away.

There was a full moon rising, he noted. Shadowed to silver by drifting clouds. It would rain tomorrow he thought. There might even be some snow in the mountains.

Damn her!

The thought flashed thought his mind even as he tried not to allow it. Damn Bryn Keller.

Damn her to a thousand hells....

No, he thought with a soft sigh. It wasn't her fault that he had felt more than fascination. Each time he saw her, he saw something new. Her beauty was in her movement, in the determined straightness of her spine, in her eyes when she pleaded that Adam was not a bad child, just lost and lonely and groping....

"We're all groping, Miss Keller," he said softly to the night breeze. "But if you would just let me touch you... You hold so desperately to your independence and pride. I wouldn't take those from you. I would just be there...a hand, a heart, to reach across and lift you when you stumble...."

He stared at the moon, and at the beautiful velvet stretch of the stars across the heavens. And then he laughed out loud at himself. "Talking to the night, eh, Condor? Standing naked on a balcony—and talking to the moon. Even the Blackfoot would call you crazy!"

He walked back into his bedroom, leaving the French doors to the terrace open. He liked the night air. And nature's sounds of the night. The night could embrace a man as no woman could; and yet, there was a similarity there, too. Loving a woman was like loving the night. It was knowing the dangers and respecting them; knowing all the secret fears and frailties and tenderly protecting them. Learning what was needed, and giving it.

He had failed once. And he had never thought to allow himself to care again. But this woman...

Bryn was strong in her own right. He could make her stronger.

A scowl tightened his ruggedly handsome features.

Savage, he reminded himself.

He started to crawl into bed to go back to sleep. Instead he glanced at his bedside clock.

Six A.M. It was already Monday morning. He might as well get dressed.

Dawn was just breaking when he reached the old Fulton place. They had picked up his drums and set them up on the second-floor landing yesterday afternoon, because they wanted to see the effect of certain camera angles before they started actually shooting everyone in full costume.

He was glad to see his drums. He could feel the rhythm flow through his blood when he climbed up the stairs and approached them.

As the sun blazed a streak in the sky, he picked up his drumsticks and heralded the morning with a wild and chaotic rhythm.

He was still pounding the drums when Bryn Keller walked in two hours later.

She felt the thunder of the beat long before she slipped in the front door.

The weekend had given her a certain courage and strength; she had done the right thing. It was hard now to pull away from him but it would be far more difficult if she allowed herself to be swayed. Loneliness was easier when you became accustomed to it, and since she had cried herself sick after the breakup with Joe, she had become accustomed to managing on her own.

But when she heard the drumbeat, she knew it was going to be a long day.

Bryn closed the door softly behind her, but it wouldn't have mattered if she had slammed it. The sound wouldn't have been heard.

Tony Asp and Gary Wright were already there, standing in the rear of the ballroom and somehow managing to discuss the work for the day. Mick Skyhawk was sitting backward on the piano bench, his long legs stretched out before him. Perry and Andrew McCabe—the last of the group—were lounging on either side of him.

Mick saw Bryn enter and waved at her. She smiled a little nervously in return and walked over to join him and the others. But her eyes strayed up the staircase as she walked through the entryway, and shivers rippled along her spine.

Lee was shirtless as he belted out the rhythm. A fine sheen of perspiration made his bronze torso gleam and clearly delineated the muscles in his arms and chest. His features were intense; his eyes were narrowed in concentration. He might have been alone in the world, alone with his drums and a primeval beat. It was somehow an awesome sight. Primitive, but beautiful. The sheer power of it, the male perfection and the thunder that touched the heart, were beautiful.

"Want some coffee, Bryn?"

She started when she realized she had backed into the ballroom until she was almost on Mick's lap.

"Yes, thanks," she murmured.

She was pretty sure that it was Andrew who set the cup in her hand, and she mumbled "Thanks" again.

"It's going to be a long day!" Perry sighed.

Bryn smiled at him. "Why do you guys show up so early? You don't really have to be here through the tedium of all the rehearsals, do you? Especially this early."

"Ouch!" Perry chuckled.

"We do have to be here, love," Andrew told her, the soft flicker of his native Cork accent not at all affected—just weary. "You see, we're like a miniature democracy. We vote on all decisions: musical, business and aesthetic. Our names and faces are out on the album so it's in our own best interest."

"Oh," Bryn murmured.

The drums were struck in another tempestuous burst of sound.

"It's going to be a long day." Mick reiterated Perry's words bleakly.

"A long day," Andrew agreed.

The pounding rose to a shattering crescendo, and then the silence became overwhelming.

A second later Lee came briskly down the stairway, wiping his face with a towel, then throwing it around his shoulders.

"Ah, good morning, Miss Keller! Let's get right to work, shall we? Hey, Mick, mind playing the piece for this? That recording is awful." His eyes, full of nothing but intense energy, turned to Bryn. "The sound will be mixed in the studio for the real thing, of course, but we're going to have to do better even to take it here for the cameras. Some decent speakers or something. Are you ready?"

"Yes, of course."

Bryn gulped down her coffee and accepted the hand that gripped hers to lead her across the room.

Somewhere during the next hour she became convinced that he was a sadist, and that his drumming was a ritual to summon the devil, who rewarded him with superhuman energy and endurance.

They rehearsed on the staircase for an hour; then the other dancers arrived, and they rehearsed for another hour. She was able to breathe for ten minutes when he donned an infantry uniform so that they could take the shots of him playing on the stairway in the thick mist rising from a large block of dry ice.

Then they were dancing again. Shots were taken of Mick at the piano, Andrew with an old acoustic guitar and Perry with a fiddle. Bryn loved the fiddle music, but she only heard it for a few minutes, because then Tony led her away because he wanted to see what would happen if they tried working six steps up the stairway instead of five.

It felt awfully high for her to trust someone enough to be able to fall back blindly into his arms.

Too high. Bryn looked up the staircase and swallowed, trying to allay her fear. Why did the idea of heights make her so shaky and breathless? She couldn't fall in front of Lee; she just couldn't.

"Is it too high? I promise you that I can catch you, but if it makes you uneasy, say so."

"No..." she murmured. It was obviously a lie.

"Bryn—" He was touching her, she realized. His hands were on her shoulders, and he was looking into her eyes, not unkindly at all. "A phobia about heights isn't anything to worry about. We can go back down a step."

For a moment she was caught by the tawny gold of his eyes, feeling horribly ashamed of herself. After last night, after the things she had said and the way she had acted, he was showing her both sensitivity and kindness. *I could care for him,* she thought. *I could really care for him....*

She gave herself a little shake. "No, the six steps will be fine." She hesitated, slipping from his hold and looking up the stairway again. "I'll be all right. But...thank you."

At least she had seen his arms in action. She knew they were strong.

The gentling she had felt toward him faded as the morning slipped by and his energy continued to be boundless. He didn't ask of others what he wasn't willing to do himself, but in a matter of hours her feet, legs—and everything else—were hurting.

Bryn rehearsed with Lee, then with the other dancers. It seemed to be never-ending.

Somewhere in midst of all the action she had a chance to whisper to Barbara. "I think he's trying for the perfect crime: mass asphyxiation of twenty dancers!"

Barbara laughed, but then Barbara hadn't been required to give up her break time to work on the stairway. "He is a perfectionist, isn't he?"

Perfectionist, hmmmf! Bryn thought.

It was only noon.

But her time was coming soon. Very soon.

By one o'clock the dancers and cameramen had been released. Bryn stood on the lawn beside the golf course of the Timberlane Country Club and stared across the velvety green expanse to the whitecapped mountains beyond.

Bryn had loaded her Canon with a roll of 1000 ASA film, and now she checked the view she had just approved through the lens. The setting was good. All the band's equipment was being moved onto the green, and there would be nothing but sky and grass and the mountains and—

And the flaring neon light for the Sweet Dreams hotel, a rather tawdry spot that embarrassed the country club by having the audacity simply to sit on the opposite side of the road.

"Damn!" Bryn muttered. She moved the camera, then moved herself. No matter what she did, the building and the parking lot would show when she took long shots, but she could probably avoid the neon lights. And the hotel would be so far in the background that everything about it would be minuscule.

Bryn sighed. She would have to warn Lee. Then it would be on his shoulders....

"How's it look, kid?"

Bryn spun around to smile as Barbara approached her. Barbara never looked ruffled. With her short blond hair, near regal height and perpetual calm, she could come from a laborious dance workout and look as if she had been sitting around drinking mint juleps.

"Pretty good, Barb, but look. Follow that slope down and you'll see the—"

"Ah, yes! The ol' Sweet Dreams hotel. Den of water beds, mirrored ceilings and smutty cable!" Barbara laughed. "Is it really going to be a problem?"

"I don't think so. As long as I don't catch the lights. It will be pretty far in the background, but I thought I ought to warn Lee, and see if he wants to choose a new spo—"

"Oh, no! Bryn, don't do that! The maitre d' is already going crazy because he has that politician who's running for the senate coming in for one of those big money luncheons."

"Barb, you're the one who told me Lee Condor is a perfectionist."

"He is, he is. But you just said the hotel would be completely in the background. Look how far away it is!"

"Barb..."

"Oh, shush! Bryn, please!" Barbara lowered her voice. "Honey, everything has gone perfectly for Lee so far, everything that I've been in charge of. This is real important to me, honey: you know that. He's friends with all the top stars in the music world, and if he recommends me to others we could both live off the results for years!" Barbara looked anxiously over Bryn's shoulder. "It won't matter, Bryn. I'm sure of it. He's coming now...."

Barbara shot a dazzling smile past Bryn, but Bryn didn't need to see the smile to be forewarned that Lee was near. She had acquired something like radar since she had met him. The same fever that quickly became chills whipped along her spine whenever he approached.

"I think we're ready here, Lee!" Barbara called out cheerfully.

Bryn spun around. Lee, hands on his hips, still exuding tension and energy, was staring at her with a golden glare that was totally enigmatic. No anger, no passion. They might have just met.

"Bryn, are you pleased with the location?"

"Yes, yes it's fine," she heard herself reply. Except now, she could see golfers in the distance. She hesitated, then added. "Close-ups will be perfect. When we do group shots, there might be a little interference in the background. See, there are a couple of men over there playing the fifteenth hole."

Lee waved a hand impatiently. "That's no problem. These don't need to look like we live alone in the world. Let's go, shall we? I have things to do later."

Bryn felt the coolness of his words like a slap in the face. She smiled sweetly. Things to do? His life couldn't compare with hers. And if he could be a semisadist with his dancers, she could damn well be the same with her "artistic subjects."

"Ready when you are, Mr. Condor. Let's start on the lawn with the four of you grouped behind your instruments."

Perry, Andrew and Mick had come up behind Lee, and they cheerily nodded their assent. Sorry guys, Bryn thought with a tinge of guilt, but you're going to have to suffer a little along with your almighty leader....

But the group was positioned before she had even moved. Bryn bent to grab her camera bag and chased after them. Then she paused, turning to face Barbara.

"Hey, Barb. Come along and keep close tabs on the light meter for me, huh?"

"Sure," Barbara agreed. "Just tell me what I'm keeping tabs on."

Bryn smiled sweetly. It was going to be one thing to attempt a little return torture, but in the process she wanted to make damn sure she took good shots.

"Great, guys! Great!" She applauded as she checked out their positions through her lens. "Perry, chin down a bit. Lee, head up. Andrew, move just a shade to the right. Oh, no, now, wait a minute. Perry, your collar is up in the back."

Bryn kept the others waiting as she meticulously fixed Perry's collar. They all looked nice—really nice—in red tailored shirts and black dress jeans. More than nice. Sexy. Especially Lee with his magnetic eyes and broad-shouldered, athletic build. And jet dark hair.

And thoroughly irate expression.

"Great," Bryn said cheerfully again. She clicked five quick pictures. "All right, Lee, behind the drums. Let's try Perry to the left, Mick in front stooped on one knee. And Andrew to the right. Mick, dangle your hand as if you're relaxed. A little bit of a smile, not too much. A little more teeth, Perry. I need a smile, please, Lee. Not a scowl. Oh, no, wait a minute. This isn't going to do. Andrew will be better in front, because Perry and Mick are the same height...."

She moved them and moved them, and adjusted them and adjusted them. She kept them in place when she disappeared to change her film—and leisurely enjoyed a cup of coffee. She took close-up shots, and another entire roll of long shots. In the background she caught the golf course, the street beyond, and the beauty of the snow-laden mountains. Then she shot the entire roll again, telling them that there had been just too many golfers in the background.

And it wasn't a lie. At first there had been only one man, fooling around in some distant sand pit. He had probably been obscured by the drums. But he had barely been there a minute or two before a group of people had followed him, appearing at the top of the slope behind him like a horde of Mongols.

She was about to start on a fourth roll when Lee at last broke his impatient silence. "Might I suggest you hurry up here, Miss Keller? It's going to rain."

Bryn looked up at the sky. It didn't look like rain. She smiled at Lee. "I just have one more roll to do out here, Mr. Condor. I want to make sure I missed that neon sign for the Sweet Dreams motel over there. Unless, of course, you want it in the pictures...."

"I don't give a damn if it's in the pictures or not, Miss Keller," Lee replied softly. "I'm sure you value your camera and equipment—just as we value our instruments. And it's going to rain."

"Oh, come now! Don't be impatient, Mr. Condor. I'm trying to assure you a choice of really good proofs. It doesn't look at all like rain!"

"Well, I'll tell you one thing," Andrew groaned. "I've got to take a cigarette break."

"Bryn!" Barbara said, nudging her shoulder. "You know this little meter you told me to watch? Well, it just took a big dip."

The meter *had* dipped. The light had changed drastically. Damn it, Bryn thought, but it was going to rain!

And just as she made the sad realization, the first drops started to fall.

"Let's move 'em!" Lee called out, and each member of the group went into efficient motion, carrying the musical instruments quickly beneath the candy-striped awning of the terrace. Barbara helped Bryn grab her tripod and bag and raced after them.

It took two trips to save the drum set, and if Bryn had now accepted that the sky forecast a storm, Lee's features did so doubly. Inadvertently she felt herself backing against the wall.

"Well, Miss Keller, do you think we're quite done?"

"Except for the inside shots," she said quickly, hoping to brazen this out.

He threw up his hands in disgust. "And those will take another four hours, I assume?"

"You are a known perfectionist, Mr. Condor."

He didn't reply, just turned around to the others. "Think we should take a meal break? This could go till next Sunday."

"Yeah, I'm starving. Let's troop on in," Mick suggested.

Bryn felt her elbow being firmly gripped, and she glanced nervously up at Lee's eyes. They seemed as dark as night, except for that wicked gold glitter.

"Come on, Miss Keller. Let's go."

But it was almost impossible to move inside the country club.

"Oh, dear, dear!" the effusive maitre d' sighed. "We've been crowded with members all day, Mr. Condor. Hoping to get a sight of you and your group. And now we have a political rally going on, too, and oh, what a mess! Besides yourselves and the politician, we also have a PGA tournament going on! One of the big money classics. I warned them that we had overbooked but no one listened. I can do nothing about the dining room. If I'd only known that you required a meal..."

"Think you could set us up on the terrace?" Lee asked him.

"Yes, yes, of course. And we'll bring out a special vintage wine for you while you wait—on the house, of course, sir!"

"Come on, Bryn, back to the terrace. I've got a few words to say to you before the others join us."

"I...uh...later, Lee. I have to find the ladies' room."

"Bryn!"

"I'm sorry!"

She fled before he could stop her and decided that she had better really head for the ladies' room—whether she needed to or not. But she had barely woven her way through the crowd when she found herself walking right into the politician who had just turned away from the reporters.

Startled, Bryn just stood there staring at the man. It was Dirk Hammarfield, the man she had watched on the news last week. And as his features crinkled into a friendly smile, she decided that he definitely did have a lot of charisma. His eyes were cornflower blue; he was a nice trim six feet, and his hair was light and tousled. What an all-American candidate, she thought.

"I'm so sorry!" he apologized.

"My fault, I'm afraid, Mr. Hammarfield."

"Ah, so you know me!" He beamed.

Bryn suddenly looked beyond his shoulder. Even through the crowd her eyes were riveted on another man.

Lee. He had followed her. And he now was watching her. Quietly, leaning nonchalantly against the wall, his hands in his pockets, his eyes narrowed and hard.

Bryn gave the young politician a magnificent smile. "Of course I know you, Mr. Hammarfield. I've been following your campaign closely! I'm sure you'll be Nevada's next senator!"

She noticed dimly that Lee had disappeared. Suddenly none of it seemed to matter. Dirk Hammarfield kept beaming, and he started to chatter about something, but all she wanted to do was get away.

"Who is the young lady with the camera, Dirk?"

Bryn jumped as a new voice cut in on the conversation. She glanced quickly at the man who had joined Dirk Hammarfield.

"Miss...?" Dirk queried hurriedly.

"Keller. Bryn Keller."

"Miss Bryn Keller, meet my aide-de-camp, Pete Lars."

"How do you do?" Bryn stretched out her hand, feeling uneasy. Aide-de-camp? The man was short, and not fat, but squat, and as solid as a rock. He was in a dark, nondescript suit. And his features, she thought quizzically, were just the same: totally nondescript. He looked more like a hit man from an old gangster movie than an aide-de-camp.

"What were you taking pictures of, Miss Keller?" Pete Lars asked politely.

"Lee Condor and his group," she returned. She was equally cordial, but she wished she could just get by them both.

"How nice. He's quite famous, isn't he?"

"Yes, I believe so. Well, it's been a pleasure to meet you both. Good luck with the campaign."

She managed to brush past both the clean-cut politician and his gruesome gorilla friend, and then she sped into the ladies' room.

She was shaking, and she didn't know why.

Maybe she was afraid she had pushed too far, and that this time Lee Condor would fire her. Or maybe she was afraid that he was somehow beginning to overwhelm her every time he was near, and that she would be the one to break, and go running to him, begging that he hold her close for just a moment and allow her to believe that there could be a forever-after for her....

She ran a brush through her hair and decided that she was going to have to face the music. When she emerged she saw that Lee had come inside again and been pinned down by a number of autograph seekers.

She slipped past him and started for the terrace, only to find herself hemmed in at the front doors again. Another group of autograph seekers had surrounded a man she was certain she had never seen before. Trying to be polite, she wedged her way through the sea of people, only to find herself pressed against the man receiving all the attention, and she didn't even know who he was!

A quick glance at his sport shirt and trim figure told her that he was a golfer. He was about thirty-five, wore his brown hair short and radiated health. Friendly brown eyes fell to hers.

"Uh...great game," Bryn murmured. "Wonderful game..."

"Thanks. For a minute there I didn't think I'd take the championship!"

"Oh, but you did! Congratulations, Mr...."

He laughed pleasantly. "Mike Winfeld."

Winfeld. Winfeld. Yes, he was young, but despite her complete disinterest in sports, she had heard the name. They had said that he would make it to the top, and apparently he had.

He chuckled softly. "Your blush is gorgeous, but don't be embarrassed. You weren't here for the game, were you? You're with Lee Condor."

With Condor? No, not the way he meant it!

"I'm a photographer. I'm doing publicity shots for him."

"You were taking pictures? Here? Today?"

"Yes, on the other side of the terrace."

"How nice. Hey, if Condor hired you, you must be damned good. Have you got a card?"

"I...uh...yes, I do."

Bryn rummaged around in her purse for her business card. She stuffed it into the golfer's hand, then grimaced as she was jostled into him. "Thanks for asking. Give me a call anytime. I'm going to slip by before your fans decide to hang me!"

"Bryn Keller," he murmured, smiling and waving as she moved through the crowd. "You'll be hearing from me!"

She waved in return.

Maybe some real good would come from this, she thought as she hurried out to join the others on the terrace.

Barbara looked up from her fan-back wicker chair beside the wrought-iron table. "Bryn, that's your glass of wine there. I went ahead and ordered you a crab cocktail and the spinach salad." Barbara lifted her hands with a shrug. "You were gone so long..."

"Sounds great, Barbara," Bryn murmured nervously, taking the empty seat beside Barbara. The only other empty seat had been the next one. No matter which she had chosen, she would still have been forced to sit beside Lee. She picked up her wineglass and began to sip. It was good. Dry, but smooth.

Perry was telling Barbara about the castle where they had filmed in Scotland. His story was bright and amusing, but Bryn found her mind wandering. Glancing through the French doors to the main room of the club, she saw that Lee had now been halted by the politician. The two men spoke for a few minutes; then they were joined by the championship golfer. A meeting of the fabulously famous and rich, Bryn thought somewhat bitterly. Then she pretended to busy herself with her wineglass, because Lee was at last coming through the doors and heading for the table. She sensed his growing irritation as his chair scraped against the concrete when he pulled it out to take his seat.

She felt his eyes openly on her and was compelled to turn in his direction as he took a sip of wine, watching her over the rim of the glass.

"What?" she demanded in an impatient murmur. The others were still talking, not noticing them—she hoped.

"Nothing, Miss Keller, nothing at all."

"Then would you quit looking at me like that?" she whispered.

"Like what?"

"Like..."

"Like you're playing stupid games? Dirk Hammarfield is married, you know. And I know that even a 'perfectionist' doesn't need to take that many rolls of film to come up with a good shot."

"First of all," Bryn replied in a heated whisper, glad that he hadn't seen her with the personable golfer, as well, "if Dirk Hammarfield is married, that's just wonderful. Secondly, all I was trying to do was make sure that you would be pleased—"

"Like hell!" he interrupted impatiently.

"I—"

"You're a coward, Bryn. The worst sort. You're afraid of me, and instead of facing the real reasons, you feel compelled to attack. Don't bother. And don't feel that you have to make a fool of yourself with another man because of me. We'll keep this strictly business. You don't even have to develop the damn prints. Just get me the proof sheets and the negatives and I'll handle the rest. And don't worry about your paycheck. It won't suffer any."

"I wasn't—"

"Worried about your paycheck? Oh, yes, you were. But that's all right. I understand."

"No you don't, you insufferable bastard!"

Why, oh, *why*, did she let him goad her? Was it because she saw the fury flashing in his eyes even as he kept his voice discreetly soft? Or because she couldn't help watching his throat, handsomely bronze, where his pulse beat so strongly?

He stood up, ignoring the food that had been placed before him, his only reply a curt nod. "I think Bryn has decided to call it quits for the day, guys. She can always take some individual close-ups at the house. I've got some things to do. Excuse me, will you? I'll see you all at the house tonight for practice."

He started to walk away. The others called out cheerfully, "See you later!" and waved him on.

Bryn swallowed nervously, then stood to follow him. "Lee!"

He paused, turning back to her.

"I'm sorry."

"So am I." It wasn't an apology; it was a statement of fact. And again he seemed impatient.

"Damn you! You don't know what it's like to...to be entirely responsible to others."

"That's where you're wrong, Bryn," he said tiredly. "I've had my share of— Oh, never mind. That's why I really don't pressure you. I can't make you take a chance on living. That has to be entirely your decision—"

Bryn was startled when he suddenly broke off, staring pensively beyond her.

"Lee?" Shivers rippled along her spine as she watched him. He had gone rigidly tense...as if he were waiting, ready to spring....

"Lee?"

Someone was watching them, Lee thought, curiously at first, and then tensely. Someone from the brush beyond the terrace. Imagination, he tried to tell himself. But it wasn't his imagination. He knew when he was being watched....

He placed his hands on Bryn's shoulders to brush past her and find out why he was being covertly stared at. But he never took a step.

Whomever it had been left with a hurried rustle of the brush.

He turned back to Bryn quickly. "Want to come home with me and have a glass of wine?"

"No...I..."

"Fine. You've got a day off tomorrow, but see if you can't get me the proofs by midday. Just get them to Barbara; she can bring them to my house."

He turned and left her. Bryn bit her lip and walked miserably back to the table. She tried to find some enthusiasm for her crab cocktail, but she could only pick at it. Thirty minutes later she excused herself. She would be able to pick up the boys a little early.

Lee hadn't left the club.

Slunk low in the seat of his beige Olds wagon, he waited patiently on a hunch.

He watched Bryn's van pull out of the club parking lot. His eyes narrowed, and his brow creased into a frown as a dark sedan pulled out after her.

He twisted his keys in the ignition and turned the wagon to follow the sedan.

Rush hour traffic had begun, and he was forced to swerve between lanes as he followed the two vehicles. He had fallen behind when Bryn reached the day-care center, but he arrived just in time to see her enter the flow of traffic again.

The dark sedan was still between them.

He knew the streets to Bryn's house, but traffic became worse and worse. A gas truck cut him off at the next corner, and he was swearing softly as he tried to catch up again.

When he reached Bryn's house she was apparently already inside with the boys.

And the dark sedan was burning rubber to make a hasty retreat down the street.

Chapter 5

For some mysterious reason the boys opted to behave like angels that night. Bryn decided that God was real and occasionally showed mercy to the weary.

She had them fed, bathed and in bed by eight o'clock, and as soon as the last little forehead had been kissed, she rushed back down the stairs and called Barbara. The answering machine came on, and Bryn started to swear softly, only to hear Barbara's chuckling after the recorded message had beeped away.

"Temper, temper, honey! What is the problem?"

"I want to run this film out to be developed tonight, Barb. I hate to ask you this, but the kids are all asleep. Do you think you'd mind stopping by and watching them for just a few minutes?"

"Bryn, I wouldn't mind in the least, whether they were awake or asleep. But I've got a show tonight. No vacation till next week."

"Oh!" Bryn moaned with dismay.

"Why are you sending it out? You always develop your own. 'Half the art,' remember?"

"Yeah, but not with these. Condor just wants the proofs and negatives—ASAP. And I'm exhausted. I just don't think that I could stand to do them tonight." She didn't want to do them. She wanted them out of her way; she just wanted to wash her hands of the whole deal.

Barbara hesitated a minute. "Having trouble with him?"

"Lee? We just don't seem to get on well."

"That's foolish, Bryn. The man admires you so much."

"He told me he wants the proofs, Barb. Period."

Barbara sighed. "It's all in your attitude, Bryn. And I don't see what for. He's charming. A bit remote at times, a little stern, but always courteous. A little scary with that kind of silent strength, but I think that just adds to the sexuality—and sensuality!—of the man. And he's really such a wonderful human being."

"Barbara!" Bryn groaned. She thought that if she heard any more praise of the man when she would truly love to break a drum over his head, she would start screaming and go mad. "Please, I work with him all day. Don't make me hear about him all night."

There was silence on the wire, and then she heard Barbara sigh. "Okay, you two are adults. I'll drop it. And listen. I can't sit for you, but how about this? Tell me where you want the film taken and I'll run it by."

"Will you? Bless you Barb! It needs to go to Kelly's Kodak. I'll call Kelly, and he'll be expecting you. Thanks, Barabara. Thanks so much. I'm sure I can get them back tomorrow, give them to you to deliver and be done with the whole thing!"

"Hmm," Barbara replied enigmatically. "I'll be by in ten minutes. I'll beep; just run out to the car, okay?"

"You got it! Bless you!"

Bryn hung up the phone, then hurriedly called Kelly Crane, the owner of a small camera shop who had helped her out a number of times. He groaned when she said she wanted the proofs by the next day, then woefully told her that he had no hot dates that night anyway. She thanked him, carefully bagged all her film and waited for Barbara's beep. Ten minutes on the dot, Barbara drove away while Bryn was still thanking her.

The night had gone so well at first that Bryn could barely believe it was already eleven o'clock when she finished arranging clothes and lunches for the next day. She hopped quickly in and out of the shower, then decided that a glass of wine along with the news might help her sleep.

But the news wasn't conducive to sleep. The local segment dealt with all the excitement at the Timberlane Country Club.

How had she missed all the media people, she wondered.

The first story was on Dirk Hammarfield. He was shown with his wife—a chubby little brunette—smiling that famous smile. He was applauded for being a wonderful family man, a true "American Hero," living the all-American dream. The newscaster announced that there were rumors regarding his associations with a number of the big gambling concerns, but apparently those associations were all above-board. Gambling was legal in Nevada.

Bryn began to gnaw on her lip as the next film turned out to be of Lee Condor busily signing autographs and laughing with real humor as he tousled a small boy's hair as he signed an album cover.

The newscaster gushed over Lee even more than Barbara had. Bryn was tempted to throw something at her televison, but thanks to some dubious sense of maturity, she knew she'd only break her TV.

Mick Jagger, Michael Jackson and the Beach Boys all rolled into one. Traces of Willie Nelson and Paul Anka. He topped the charts along with Duran, Duran, The Police, etc. etc.

Bryn stood up, ready to change the channel; then she paused, because the story switched to Mike Winfeld, the man who had taken the PGA tournament and added two hundred fifty thousand dollars to his winnings.

Not a bad reason for chasing a little white ball all around a green field, Bryn thought dryly.

She started to sit again, but froze instead. The picture of Winfeld had *her* in it, smiling away, flushing and handing him her business card.

With a groan she sank back into the sofa.

If Lee Condor watched the news tonight he would really be on her case. Flirting with a married politician, then with a championship golfer. Oh, God.

"Oh, what difference does it make?" she groaned aloud. Wasn't that what she wanted? To make it clear that she did like people—men in general—not just him?

Bryn flicked off the television, checked the doors and climbed the stairs to her room. With determination she got into her bed and curled into a comfortable position. Sleep, sleep, she had to sleep, she was so tired....

But she couldn't stop thinking about him. About his eyes when they met hers... About his hands... About the size and strength of his naked shoulders and chest as he hammered away at the drums with perfect rhythm and haunting power...

The man appeared at her front door just as she threw it open to usher the kids out to the van.

She stared at him blankly for a moment, frowned and then smiled reflexively as he greeted her with a broad grin and a friendly, "Good morning! Miss Keller, I believe."

"I, uh, yes, I'm Bryn Keller. I'm in a bit of a hurry though. If I can help you...?"

"Well, I'm hoping I can help you."

"Who is it? Who is it?" Brian demanded, trying to push his way past her. Bryn caught the top of his head with the palm of her hand and pushed him back behind her.

"What are you talking about?" she asked, curiously assessing the stranger. He was medium height and of medium build. His hair was neither dark nor light, nor were his eyes any particular color. They were kind of an opaque gray. He might have been thirty or forty or even older. He was dressed in brown slacks and a short-sleeved tan shirt.

"Well, I'd like to buy something you have."

"Buy something? I'm afraid I haven't got anything of value."

He laughed easily. "Value, like beauty, is in the eye of the beholder. I can see you're in a hurry, so I'll get right to the point. I know you took a bunch of pictures of Lee Condor yesterday. I'm one hell of a fan of his! I'm prepared to pay you five thousand dollars, but I want the lot of them. For a private collection, you know."

"Five thousand..." Bryn echoed, frowning with incredulity. If she believed for one moment that this idiot might be serious, she could be well tempted. But he wasn't serious. And besides, she thought uneasily, even if he was, she didn't think she would dare, no matter how tempting his offer. Lee owned those pictures, and all rights to them. It was stated in the contract. And she still thought of him as having the potential to be a dangerous man. A very dangerous man. She wouldn't want to cross him in a business deal.

"I'm sorry, I'm afraid even if you offered me half of Tahoe I'd still have to turn it down. Lee Condor owns those pictures."

The stranger's smile turned to an ugly scowl. "You're being a fool, you know. Just tell him that the film was overexposed or something and you can find yourself quite a bit richer."

"Nice thought," Bryn said wearily, "but sorry. Now, if you'll excuse me..."

The boys had all grouped behind her. Bryn allowed them to push through so that, between the four of them, the annoying stranger was pushed off the porch. She hurried the boys into the van and hopped into the driver's seat, waving to the man who still stood watching them. "I hope I locked the door," she murmured absently.

"You did, Aunt Bryn," Keith assured her. "I saw you."

"Good," she murmured back. "Thanks, Keith."

A few minutes later she forgot the episode. Traffic was at its horrendous best. She was still thinking about the pictures, but she was thinking that she wanted to get to Kelly's as fast as she could, pick up the proofs and dump them into Barbara's hands. One headache out of the way!

Kelly had the proofs ready. He was a lanky young man who looked more like fifteen than twenty-five, but Bryn was always thankful that she had stumbled on him a year ago. When she found herself in a jam, he was great—and more, he was talented.

"These are only proofs, of course, Bryn, but I think you're going to have some great shots. The backgrounds are wonderful. Looks like you managed to avoid any flaws. And Condor, what an interesting subject! I'd love to photograph him. All this commerical stuff, you usually get 'pretty boys.' Condor's face has such character. A painter would go crazy with him."

"Yeah, thanks, Kelly. I hope I did get some good shots. Well, let me pay you."

"Only a few of the backgrounds will give you problems, and those will be so minimal that—"

"Kelly! Please! I can't tell you how much I appreciate this rush job, but I'm still in a hurry!" She wasn't really—she had the day off—but she didn't want to talk about Lee.

"Okay, Bryn, let me just tally you up. And hey...I really don't mind the rush at all. Just remember me when you get rich and famous, okay?"

"It's a promise, Kelly. But I don't think either of us should hold our breath!"

After she had paid Kelly and left the camera shop, Bryn forced herself to stop in a corner restaurant and circle the shots she liked best on the proof sheets while she sipped two cups of coffee and consumed a slightly rubbery grilled-cheese sandwich. By one o'clock she had dropped the large envelope at Barbara's office, and by two o'clock she was home. She did a load of laundry, and while it went through she studiously exercised—not so much because she felt she couldn't afford a day of rest, but because she thought the strenuous activity might erase Condor from her mind.

But an hour's work didn't help, and when she had switched the laundry from the washer to the dryer, she hurried over to the complex pool and tried swimming. That didn't help either.

But the kids did. They were thrilled to see her pick them up early again, and she found herself giving the afternoon over to them. They made a huge batch of chocolate chip cookies and ate them while she read a space story out loud. The cookies left them all too stuffed for a big dinner, so Bryn—bemoaning her lack of expertise as a dietician—decided they would have a huge salad for dinner, with apples for dessert. It went well, and she felt as if she had semi-succeeded in being a decent parent by the time she tucked her three charges into bed.

At nine the phone rang. It was Barbara, calling quickly before starting work. The proofs and negatives had been turned over to Lee; he had said little, but seemed pleased enough.

"See you tomorrow!" Barbara said, ringing off.

Tomorrow—another grueling day with the drum-beating sadist!

Bryn forced herself into bed early. She was pleasantly exhausted and fairly relaxed, or so she thought.

She did fall asleep. She knew she had fallen asleep easily because her dreams awoke her with such a shattering clarity.

She had not just dreamed of his eyes, or his hands, or his shoulders.

She had dreamed of being with him. Lying beside him, naked, feeling him touch her all over...

She awoke shaking, shivering, covered with a fine sheen of perspiration, and feeling as if she were on fire.

"Oh, my God, I need a psychiatrist!" she moaned softly to the night. But she didn't need a psychiatrist, and she knew it. Whether she liked it or not, she was attracted to Lee Condor. And it was very normal. He was an extremely sensual man, and his aura of tension and strength was enhanced by the power of his character. No one who knew him would ever forget him.

Nibbling absently on her lower lip, Bryn hugged her pillow and came to a sad realization. She was capable of independence, but she missed loving, and she missed sharing. When she had been with Joe, she had given him her whole heart. Loyalty hadn't been a virtue for her, it had been her nature. And caring that way, she had been able to give so freely....

Bryn tossed about, burying her head in the pillow. She wanted Condor. More than she had ever wanted Joe. But Joe had loved her, or at least at the time she had believed that he did. Completely. And sex was the strangest thing. She had friends who thought a woman was crazy not to enjoy a lot of experience before settling down. Bare acquaintances went to bed together nightly by the hundreds or thousands, she assumed. But to her it was all so intimate. It meant a bond between two people. Condor probably didn't want bonds, and she didn't want to be bonded to Condor. Not in any way.

So why did she still want him so badly that he haunted her dreams?

"He'll go away," she promised herself. "And I'll forget, and I'll stop dreaming. And maybe someday I will meet a man who loves me, who I can love, who doesn't mind an instant family...."

She lay awake a long time, dismally accepting the ways of the world—and of nature.

She must have slept again, because she awoke to hear the phone insistently ringing away. It rang ten times before she made it to the kitchen; she was certain she would answer it just as the caller hung up.

"Hello!" she gasped out breathlessly.

"Bryn Keller?"

"Yes," she said, a frown creasing her brow as she tried to shake the fog of broken sleep from her mind. The voice sounded like something out of a late-night horror movie. It was a husky whisper—neither masculine nor feminine.

"I want the pictures. Do you hear me?"

"Yes, I hear you." She definitely heard the voice, but she couldn't believe the words. This had to be a joke. There was a menacing quality to the voice; it sent chills of fear running along her flesh.

"The pictures, Miss Keller. All of them. The proofs *and* the negatives. No omissions."

"Now wait a minute—"

"Do you like living, Miss Keller?"

"I'm going to call the police—"

She broke off as an eerie and ruthless chuckle interrupted her. "Sounds like you have a death wish, pretty lady. I would be real sorry to see you...disfigured. But then, there's not just you, is there? You wouldn't want to lose one of those little boys, now would you?"

"No! No!" Bryn shrieked in panic. It wasn't a joke; she was suddenly certain that it was no joke.

"Then drop the pictures—"

"Wait, oh, please, wait! I haven't got the pictures. I've already—"

"What?"

"I haven't got the pictures. I've already turned them—"

"I don't believe you."

"But, I—"

"Shut up and listen to me. I'll check it out. Start praying if you've lied, lady. And pay sharp attention here. Don't call the police. Or whisper a word of this conversation to anyone. I'll know. And you'll be really sorry. *Really* sorry. Understand? Especially don't go to Condor. I'll know. And I'll check out what you've told me."

"I'm telling you—"

"You'll be hearing from me."

"*Wait!*"

A sharp click and a dull buzz told Bryn that the caller was no longer on the line. She stared at the receiver, numb with fear and incredulity.

"Aunt Bryn?"

She started shaking when Brian's voice startled her from her state of numbness.

"Aunt Bryn, what's the matter?"

"Nothing, nothing," she lied. She started dragging bowls and cereal boxes from the cabinets, but her movements were rough and jerky. "Brian, go get your brothers. Your clothes are laid out on the dresser. Help Adam for me, will you? Then hurry on down. We're running late this morning."

As the terror of actually hearing the voice began to fade, Bryn tried to convince herself that it had been a joke after all. The fan who had appeared at her door was trying a scare tactic, that was all. She wasn't really in any danger. And she didn't have the pictures anymore. Lee had them. The caller would find that out, and that would be the end of it.

It had to be...it had to be...it had to be...

Somehow she managed to act normal. She hesitated when it was time to open the front door, but Keith bounded on past her and threw it open. A scream rose to her throat as she saw a man on the step again, but it disappeared unvoiced as she realized that today the male on her porch was only Andrew.

"Andrew! What are you doing here?"

He grimaced, lowering his head, then meeting her eyes sheepishly. "I...uh...had a late date. I'm in a state of...uh...mild intoxication. But I recognized your neighborhood and, well, would you give a hitchhiker a lift?"

Under normal circumstances she would have laughed. Andrew, the handsome, sexy, popular rock idol standing on her steps after a clandestine appointment like a delinquent child.

She didn't laugh. She was too glad to see him. He was flesh and blood and real, and his presence made the nightmare of the whispered voice fade away.

"Of course, Andrew. Hop in!" She pointed to the van.

"Want me to drive?" he queried.

Had he seen her hands shaking? "No, I'm used to the route," she told him. He laughed with the kids as she ushered them all into the vehicle. He began to talk about music, and Bryn slowly felt herself relax.

But something was troubling her. Andrew was in the back, next to Keith. She glanced at him in the mirror.

He didn't look like he had been out on a late date last night. He looked extremely well rested. And fastidiously neat. There wasn't a wrinkle anywhere on his clothing....

Bryn issued a soft sigh. Andrew was always impeccably neat. He probably folded his clothes carefully no matter how intoxicated he was—and she was certain he would shower and shave, even if he had to remove his whiskers with a sharp rock. She sure as hell wasn't going to worry about his appearance, not when...

No! She didn't want to think about the phone call. It was a joke; it was all over.

She discreetly started to tease Andrew about his wild night out, telling him that she was glad he had happened to be near her house, that next time he might not be so lucky.

"Oh, I'm a survivor by nature!" he teased back, but something in his eyes was more serious than his tone implied.

Bryn hadn't been at the Fulton House for more than an hour before she became fully convinced that Lee Condor was a direct descendant of the Marquis de Sade.

Over and over, over and over...

Every muscle in her body ached. Muscles that she hadn't known she had—even as a dancer—ached.

And Lee seemed exceptionally tense. His eyes, when he looked at her, seemed to burn through her; his hands on her were almost rough.

Once again he wanted to try the fall from another step up. She agreed, simply because he seemed so brooding that she hadn't the strength to argue with him.

But she was frightened. She had never liked heights. She hated to fly; she hated tall buildings. It wasn't a neurosis; at least, she didn't think it was. Being high up just scared her. It made her feel uncomfortable.

"If you can't do it, Miss Keller..." he began in exasperation, his hands on his hips.

"I can do it," she replied curtly.

And she did. But her heart thundered a thousand times in the brief seconds as she spun and fell, seconds that seemed like an eternity. But his arms were there. Powerful and secure. Catching her smoothly, except for the sense of...

Tension.

He was always tense. Always radiating energy, always ready to spin and turn and come up behind you with silent agility.

"Ready for a second try?"

"Ready."

She managed the feat a second time. And a third. And she was so frightened each time she took the fall that she forgot to be frightened of the whisper that had threatened her that morning....

They did break for lunch. Bryn was too nervous to do more than pick at her yogurt. Like a stalked animal, she kept an alert eye out for Lee. And each time she looked for him, she found him watching her.

He approached her as she threw away the half-eaten yogurt. "Is that all you ever eat? No wonder you look like a scared rabbit today."

"I'm sorry if I resemble a rabbit," she said briefly.

"What's wrong with you?"

"Nothing is wrong with me!"

"Do you know, Bryn, the truth sometimes suffices where a lie is ridiculous."

"There is nothing wrong with me. I'm just a little tired."

"You should get more sleep."

"Yes, I should. But don't worry, I won't let my work slip."

"I wasn't worried."

She glanced at him sharply, only to discover that he really wasn't worried. He wasn't even looking at her.

He was scanning the room, eyes keenly alert. She had the sudden impression that if she had felt like something hunted, he definitely seemed like a stalking cat. It was all part of that new tension. He was watching, waiting...searching....

For what?

She was being ridiculous.

He was tense because he was always tense. He was always a hard taskmaster. And he seemed like a powerful cat on a stealthy prowl because he was...

Lee Condor.

She was a nervous wreck, and so she was reading ominous signals into everything she saw. She had done it that morning to Andrew, and she was trying to do it now to Lee.

She began to pray for the day to end.

They were all gone, the dancers, the cameramen, the workers—everyone. Only Lee and the group remained behind.

"I think the police should be called in," Mick stated flatly.

Lee lifted his hands in an absent gesture, then crossed them over his chest again. "And what am I going to say, Mick? I think my house has been broken into several nights in a row? There won't be any prints. This guy is good. I never heard anything. I'm going strictly on intuition. Of course it might have been while I was out."

"But if you report it—" Andrew suggested.

"No," Lee interrupted, shaking his head. "If I do that, I'll never know how Bryn is involved. If she *is*. The car might have just been some guy hoping for a date with a beautiful woman."

"But you don't believe that."

"No, I don't Perry, it's your turn to watch her house tonight."

"No problem," Perry agreed.

"Yeah, but don't ask her for a ride in tomorrow morning. I think she was suspicious," Andrew warned.

"That's because you didn't have the sense to mess your clothes up!" Perry teased.

"Hold it!" Lee laughed. "Perry, just disappear into the trees when she gets ready to leave. I'll pick you up. That will solve that problem."

"What about your house, Lee?" Andrew asked. "I really think one of us should be with you."

"Thanks, Andrew, but no. If I'm going to catch a sneak thief, I'm going to have to be a better sneak than he is. That means being alone."

"Take care," Andrew advised gruffly. "I mean, I like being a musician. Without you, we might have to start back at the bottom, and I've gotten quite fond of an adquate income, you know."

Lee chuckled. "Don't worry, Andrew. I'm pretty sure I know what I'm doing—so far, at least."

"I'm aware you're no fool, Lee. And that you know how to take care of yourself. Like I said—just take care."

"I will."

"Well," Andrew murmured lightly, "since it seems I'm off for the night, I'm going to go ahead and try to enjoy myself." He started for the door with the others behind him, then turned back. "I'll be by my phone, Lee, Perry, if you need me."

"So will I," Mick added bluntly.

"Thanks," Lee told them. He shrugged. "Maybe I am crazy."

They all shrugged. Not one of them thought so.

The phone was ringing as she turned the key in the front door.

Bryn felt chills, and her fingers shook. She didn't want to answer it.

"Hurry, Aunt Bwyn!" Adam said, slurring the *r* in her name as he sometimes did. "The phone is ringing!"

"I know," she murmured. The door opened and swung inward. The boys rushed in ahead of her, the older ones tearing toward the phone together.

"Don't answer it!" she snapped sharply, but too late. Brian was already saying "Hello?"

A wave of cold swept over her as she watched her nephew, a feeling that she would fall ... that she would faint ....

"It's Barbara, Aunt Bryn. Something about a picture for the travel agency."

Relief was almost worse than the fear. Her voice crackled when she took the phone from Brian.

"Hi, Barb, what's up?"

"Nothing big, honey. I just need another print of the iguana by the cactus. Can you do me an eight by ten tonight?"

"Sure."

"Great. You can bring it to me tomorrow."

"Sure."

"You okay, Bryn?"

"Yeah, I'm fine. Just tired."

"Umm ... even I have to admit that Condor was a devil today. Oh, well, I'll let you get going."

"Barbara, wait! I know this sounds a little ridiculous, but could you get those pictures back?"

"Of Lee?" Barbara queried, puzzled.

"Yes."

"How could I do that? I told you I already turned them over to him. I haven't got a single proof or a negative. Why?"

"Oh, nothing. Never mind. I had just ... ah ... wanted to take another look at them."

"Well, I'm sorry."

"Don't worry about it."

"Okay, see you tomorrow."

Bryn hung up, glad for once that work and the kids kept her so busy. She told the boys to do their homework while she heated up some chili and mentally thanked Clarence Birdseye for packaging a spinach concotion that all three would eat. She tried not to think about anything but pots and pans and the convenience of boil-in bags.

After dinner she switched on the Disney Channel, supplied the kids with crayons and coloring books and warned them to watch out for Adam. "I'll be in the darkroom, and don't barge in without knocking unless there's an emergency, okay? I have to develop a print."

They all nodded solemnly, then started bickering about the crayons before she unlocked the back door leading to the darkroom. She kept it locked because of the kids. To get in from the back she had to slink around the filing cabinet which almost completely blocked the door.

It took her a moment to squeeze her way in; it would probably have been easier to just go around and unlock the front door but she was accustomed to working in semidarkness, and she wasn't at all worried as she fumbled around to find the string to the overhead light.

No, she wasn't worried. She didn't have the slightest premonition or foreboding.

Which made it all the worse when she found the switch and filled the room with pale, artificial light.

For a moment she was stunned. Too stunned to assimilate all that she saw. And then the cold set in. A wave of icy fear that seemed to begin in the pit of her stomach and spread to paralyze her limbs.

A scream rose in her throat, yet as if in a dream, she found she couldn't release it. The constriction was horrible; she couldn't scream, couldn't breath....

She could only stare at the total destruction within the small room.

Pictures...old pictures, meaningless pictures, new pictures...all joined together in a savage, silent pattern of horror. They were hung from the drying line and spread across the floor. Littered over her desk. All slashed to macabre ribbons.

And her desk! Each drawer had been ripped out, its contents scattered to the far corners. Gallon jugs of developer and chemicals had been emptied and dumped; the destruction was complete.

In a daze, Bryn started to move toward her desk, compelled by a piece of a photo.

She realized that the other pieces of the photo were beside it, purposely set apart in a slashed jigsaw.

She knew the picture, though she hadn't taken it herself. It was blurred and out of focus, but she had loved it. Barbara had taken it of her with the boys when they had shared a Sunday picnic right after Christmas....

But now the photo was clearly a threat. Adam had been cut out and laid separately aside, as had Brian and Keith.

She was left as the center piece, smiling brilliantly. It had been a nice, laughter filled day. But now her smile mocked her. It seemed grotesque. Her cheap little nail-file letter opener had been slammed into it, angled from her mouth to her throat.

"Oh, God!"

Sound at last tore from her, but it wasn't a scream. It was a whisper. She grabbed the desk because she was going to fall. She couldn't hold on to the light; darkness was swamping her....

No joke, no joke, it wasn't a joke.

Something rose to salvage her consciousness right before the darkness could cover her. It was anger. She had been scared half to death; her things had been ravaged. She had been violated on a very personal level....

"Son of..." she began softly, grating her teeth. She wasn't going to scream. She wasn't going to send the boys into a panic. She was going to think, calmly. And then decide what to do.

Just as she came to that determined decision, the phone began to ring.

And ring...

Chapter 6

Bryn stumbled through the refuse as she hurried to wedge her way past the file cabinet and back into the house.

"Brian! Keith!" she yelled, grunting as she hurried. "Don't you dare! Do you hear me? Don't you dare answer that phone!"

Raw emotion must have given an edge of authority to her voice; when she charged back into the house both boys were standing near the phone, but they were staring at her rather than touching it.

She swept past them and grabbed the receiver, practically shouting into it. "Hello?"

There was a slight hesitation at the other end, then a quiet, masculine voice. "Miss Keller?"

"Yes," Bryn said nervously.

"This is Mike Winfeld. We met at the Timberlane Country Club the other day."

"Oh, yes. How are you, Mr. Winfeld?"

She really didn't give a damn. All she wanted was for the man to get off the phone! Don't be a fool, Bryn. Be warm, be polite! she warned herself. He might need publicity photos, and he seems to be a very pleasant person.

"Fine. Fine, thank you. But I've been thinking about you."

"Oh?"

"Yes. I know we only met briefly, but I wonder if you wouldn't consider the possibility of going to dinner with me? I'd like to discuss the possibility of your doing some pictures for me."

Why not? Bryn asked herself. Normally, she wouldn't mind going at all. It might be a come-on, but she could handle that. And if he turned out to be a really nice and aboveboard man...

Normally. How could she do anything normally now? How could she even think about doing anything when terror tactics were invading her household and she was frightened out of her wits by every phone call?

"Oh, Mr. Winfeld—"

"Mike, please. You make me sound old and decrepit, and I'd rather not be that—especially to you."

Bryn managed to laugh. "Okay, Mike. I'd love to have dinner with you sometime, but I'm tied up for...about two, three weeks. Will you give me a call back?"

"I'd rather not have to, but if that's my choice..." He allowed his voice to trail away hopefully, then chuckled again. "Merciless to a poor fellow, aren't you, Miss Keller? But I will call back. Two weeks?"

"Umm. And please call me Bryn."

"With pleasure. You'll be hearing from me, Bryn."

"Great."

"Bye then, for now."

"Bye."

She was breathing easily enough when she replaced the receiver, but her hand was still on the phone when it started ringing again. She jerked it back to her ear.

"Hello?"

"I assume you've seen your darkroom by now, Miss Keller."

"Yes, I've seen it. And what you've done is criminal. How dare you invade my life like that! You will be caught. And you'll rot in a jail cell for a—"

"Miss Keller, your darkroom was only the beginning."

"Don't you understand?" She was shouting. She could see that both Brian and Keith were staring at her with startled alarm, but she couldn't help herself. "*I don't have the damn pictures!*"

"Do stay calm, Miss Keller. I believe that you don't have the pictures. But I also believe you can get them back."

"Condor has the pictures; go plague him!"

There was the slightest hesitation at the other end of the wire. "I think you can get those pictures back, Miss Keller."

"Condor—"

"Condor wouldn't be half so enjoyable to harass."

"Because he'd tell you to go to hell!"

"Possibly. He's a far tougher adversary, though you seem tough enough yourself, Miss Keller. I can well imagine your being brave enough—or stupid enough—to tell me to go to hell. But you won't, will you? Not when you have three little children to think about. I want the pictures. A woman like yourself can surely con a man into doing what she wants. I'll give you a few days. But get them. And remember, I'll be watching. So far, I've only damaged property. Oh—and don't think that you can put anything over on me. I have an acquaintance at the police station. I'll know if you've called them. And as far as Condor goes . . . Well, I just wouldn't let him in on the situation—not unless you've twisted him around your finger real, real good. He's the type who might just insist on calling the cops, and well, I've just explained that all to you. Clearly. You just keep thinking about two things. Those little boys, and the pictures. 'Cause it's going to be one or the other, kind of, if you understand my meaning. . . ."

She was clenching the phone and staring at it stupidly long after she realized it had gone dead.

Meanwhile her mind raced away. It couldn't be a "fan" of Lee's. Fans might squabble and scramble and risk personal injury to get close to a star, but they didn't break into private homes—not for pictures! No, someone wanted these pictures in a very real way. Why? Oh, God! Did it matter when she was the one caught in the situation? She was no detective, and the Riptide guys certainly weren't going to come along and solve her desperate problems in an hour the way they did on TV. She was a woman alone who barely knew the barrel from the butt of a gun, yet three little children were dependent on her. So all right, yes! There was something deeper going on here, deep and wrong and perhaps even terrible, but that couldn't be her concern. She was human and vulnerable and terrified, and she didn't want to solve any mysteries, she just wanted to feel safe, to believe again that the children were safe. . . .

"Aunt Bryn?"

She jerked herself around to stare at Brian and Keith. "Where's Adam?" she demanded.

"Coloring," Keith supplied.

"What was that all about, Aunt Bryn?" Brian asked.

"Nothing. I mean, nothing that I can explain right now. Listen to me guys, and pay attention, please. I'm . . . uh . . . having a few professional problems. Help me out tonight. Please go upstairs and take your baths and help Adam for me, okay? And please! No soap fights, no yelling or screaming. Please?"

They both nodded at her solemnly. She heard Brian calling to Adam, and then the three boys were traipsing upstairs together.

When she heard the bathwater running, she started to cry.

Several minutes passed as she stood there, just allowing the tears to slide down her face. Then she dried her cheeks with her knuckles, made herself a cup of tea and sat down at the kitchen table.

She wanted to call the police, but she couldn't! Not after the warning she had been given. But what if it had been a bluff? Call the police, she told herself firmly. It would be the logical and intelligent thing to do.

No! She couldn't. Because the warning might not have been a bluff.

And whoever the whispering voice belonged to had a definite flair for destruction. Her darkroom was proof of that.

Oh, God! Bryn started to shake; she covered her face with her hands, fighting back a rush of hysteria. The boys had to be protected above all else...and how could she watch them and protect them at all times while she was working to support them? Even if she wasn't working, she could never be with all three of them always.

There was only one answer. She had to get the pictures back.

Yes, she had to.

Bryn took a deep breath; the decision helped to calm her. She couldn't give way to frustration. She couldn't afford to sit there in tears. She had to think of the boys, and remember that they were precious above anything else in her life.

Her fingers were shaking. She stared at them, until she willed them to be still.

Bryn finished her tea and walked upstairs. The boys were just finishing buttoning their pajamas. Adam's were off center by a mile.

"Hey!" she told him, sitting on the bunk to hold him close and start the buttoning process over. "Almost, Adam, but not quite!"

The tears started to well into her eyes, and she crushed him close.

"Smotherin' me, Aunt Bryn!" Adam protested.

"Sorry, sweetheart. Sorry." She kissed his forehead and stood briskly to tuck him in. Then she kissed Brian and Keith, who both watched her solemnly. "Thanks for being real good tonight, guys. I needed the help."

"Aunt Bryn—"

"I'm really okay now. I promise. Aunts just get a little crazy now and then. Good night."

She turned off their light and closed the door most of the way, leaving it open just enough for a little of the bathroom light to stream through.

In the hallway she realized that she wasn't all right at all. She was scared to death. If someone had gotten into her darkroom, wasn't it possible that they could get into the house...?

She hurried downstairs and started to arm herself with a kitchen knife, then decided against it. If an attacker was large, she wouldn't be able to fend him off, and she might just wind up stabbed by her own knife.

She chose the broom for a weapon, then checked every closet and every nook and cranny in the house, holding her breath in panic each time she threw a door open.

At last she convinced herself that if someone wanted her to get the pictures, he—or she—wasn't going to murder her until she had achieved that project, or at least tried to.

But she still wasn't going to be able to sleep easily. She didn't even bother to go up to bed, but spent the night on the couch with the television on to give her some desperately needed company.

She never really heard the television, though. She just lay awake, staring at the ceiling, trying to make plans.

She was going to have to play up to Lee. Be sweet, be charming—be seductive. To a point, at least. Enough so that she could convince him to trust her. To return the pictures on her promise that she could do much, much better now that she...cared for him more. Understood him so much more

... She tossed on the couch, beset with anxiety—and blood spinning heat. She couldn't move in that close on Lee—but she had to. She had to...she had to. And somehow she had to play the role so well that she could also keep a distance that was safe for her heart.

No, no, none of it could matter! She could think only of the boys! Lee had to help her. Surely he would. She would do her act well. He would give her the pictures back, and the nightmare would be over.

But what if...what if he still refused?

Her mind drew a blank. If he still refused, then she'd have to resort to desperate measures. If he refused to give them back, then she was going to have to take them back.

On Friday she was in for a tremendous disappointment; Lee didn't come to rehearsal. Andrew told her that he'd flown to Los Angeles to sign some papers and wouldn't be back until Monday.

Her weekend was sheer hell. She forced herself to restore the darkroom, and she took the boys swimming both days, packing a picnic lunch and staying out of the house as long as she could. Each time the phone rang she almost jumped through the roof. But the whisperer didn't call and nothing happened.

Except that massive shadows formed beneath her eyes from lack of sleep. And her nerves were stretched as tightly as a drum.

She had never been more grateful to see a Monday roll around. Was she still being watched? If so, the watcher would know that she couldn't have gotten to Lee until today....

Lee still seemed tense, distracted, and now, very distant. That made it all the harder for her to approach him, but she had to. It was also difficult to admit that he looked wonderful to her. Hard to accept that no matter how remotely he touched her, it felt good to be touched by him again. The seconds she spent in his arms made her feel inexplicably secure. His scent was pleasant and masculine; the power of his hold warmed her....

But there was a definite chill to his cool and courteous manner.

She had prayed that an opportunity might pop up, that he would single her out for a conversation as he so often had, but he didn't come near her unless he had to. Finally, during the last break of the day, she gathered up her nerve and two cups of coffee and walked over to the piano where he was idly picking out a tune.

"I thought you might like some coffee," she began when his eyes fell upon her. He raised a brow and she blushed. They both knew she had no great tendency to worry about what he might or might not like.

"Thanks," he said briefly. He accepted the cup but set it down on the piano. His fingers continued to run over the keys. They seemed so large, long and bronze as they skimmed over the ivory.

"I didn't realize you played the piano, too," Bryn murmured, leaning against it and hoping her pose was sultry and not ridiculous.

He glanced her way sharply. "Well, I do."

Not, "Yeah, well, I learned at school," or "It's an important instrument for any musician to play"—not anything that was conversational. Just "Well, I do."

He wasn't making it easy for her. But what had she expected after all this pure antagonism?

Plunge in and lie like hell, and do it well, she told herself. She stretched out a hand and touched his arm. He stopped playing, staring at her hand for several curious moments before raising his eyes to hers.

The irony of it was that *she* understood her antagonism, even if he didn't. Now, at this moment, she could see her folly so clearly. She had judged him by another man, and she had based her hostility on the simple fact that he was a man with whom a woman could easily—too easily—fall in love. And rather than take that chance, she had built a wall of ice. She still needed that wall, but she needed his trust more than anything else.

"Lee, I'm sorry," she murmured quickly before she could lose her nerve. "I mean about everything. I've been horrible to you since we met. I...I'd like an opportunity to change that."

At last he sat back, giving her his full, dubious attention. "Oh?" he queried dryly.

God, how she wanted to slap him! He was just staring at her with those golden eyes, his expression as hard as granite. She gritted her teeth and reminded herself that she had more at stake than even she could fathom.

"I..." Her voice started to fail her, but it was a blessing in disguise, for it gave her an idea for a new tactic.

"Oh, never mind!" she cried, allowing a trace of pathos to edge into her tone. Then she spun away.

It worked. She hadn't gone a step before she felt his hand clamp down on her shoulder. She was spun back around, and she allowed herself to fall against the warm breadth of his chest.

"All right, Bryn. What are you saying?" he asked.

"That I'd like to know you better," she said without flinching.

"Seriously?"

"Seriously." How long would she have to rot in Purgatory for a lie like that? She was breathless, which was no lie. But the effect he had on her was what made the description all the more unbearable. Yes! She had judged him wrong. He was a decent man, strong but often decent, often kind—as well as having that powerful...sexual draw that was almost overwhelming. Oh, God, she thought, it was getting worse and worse; if she was honest, she would admit that she cared for him. She couldn't allow herself to be honest—it would be a disastrous mistake. She had to maintain her walls. Adam! she reminded herself. It wouldn't be so hard to be deceitful, cold, hot—or anything. All she had to do was remember his sweet little face and she could do anything!

"I'll pick you up and the kids for a picnic or something on Sunday, if that's okay," Lee said.

Sunday? No, it was days away! She cleared her throat. Her voice was still husky. Very husky. As sensual as...a practiced whore's. "You asked me over for a glass of wine. If that invitation still stands, I'd like to drive over tonight."

His brows rose again; she could sense his skepticism. But then he shrugged. "You're welcome anytime. We're not having a band practice tonight, so I'll be free."

Bryn swallowed and nodded. Now her voice seemed thin, as if someone else were talking. "I have to see if Barb can stay with the kids, but she promised that she would this week. Eight-thirty."

"Whenever you can come."

He released her, then dug in his pockets for a pencil. He turned back to the piano bench and found an old scrap of paper, scratched out an address and handed it to her.

"See you later then," he murmured. Andrew was calling to him. He stepped by her and Bryn realized that she was shaking again.

At eight o'clock that night Lee sat on his living-room sofa with his feet propped up on the coffee table, brooding as he stared at the glass of Scotch in his hand.

His eyes scanned the handsomely appointed room, and he scowled.

He knew someone had been in the house again. He had locked it securely when he had suddenly been called in to sign a contract amendment, but he was certain that someone had been in. He felt it. But there had been no way to get one of the others to house sit for all those hours, not when he wanted them to keep an eye on Bryn. He might still be going on something entirely crazy.

He sighed and glanced at his wristwatch. Eight-fifteen. She was due any minute. Which led to another dilemma. Why the sudden change in Bryn? He had wanted her since he had first seen her; his fascination had soon grown into something much greater. He should be enthusiastic and glad to know that she would shortly be here....

The pity was, he didn't trust her, or the situation, or something. Yet, he thought, smiling slowly, there had been no way for him not to accept the invitation she had given. She might be up to something, but he was enough the male savage to let her have her way until he discovered just what it was....

"Not a savage, just a fool!" he mocked himself aloud, raising his glass to the arrow collection that decked the wall. "A fool who is definitely falling more than a little in love."

The doorbell rang, and he laughed at himself dryly as he rose. She was here. Early. He knew for a fact that she wanted something, but as he had promised himself, he was going to let her try to get it.

He wasn't quite as hardened and prepared as he would have liked to have been when he opened the door. Not when he saw her.

She had dressed the part.

Her hair was loose and flowing, curling and waving over sleek shoulders bared by the halter top of the backless sun dress she wore. It was perfect. Not overly dressy; casual, but completely feminine. The skirt was blue; it swayed about her knees while the tight waistline emphasized the beauty of her dancer's figure.

Her eyes were dazzling as she greeted him with a brilliant smile. "Hi. I...uh...made it."

He stepped back and offered her a deep welcoming bow. "Then step into the wolf's den, Miss Keller." He chuckled softly as he saw her ivory skin blanche. "Just teasing, Bryn. But do come on in."

She stepped inside, and he closed the door behind her. She carried a soft gauze wrap, and he took it from her and hung it in the entry closet. She was gazing about the room when he turned back to her.

"It's a beautiful place," she said softly.

"Thanks. It's home."

She laughed a little nervously. "I think I expected something different. Iron gates and a crowd of servants."

"I don't like a lot of people around," he said briefly. "I have a housekeeper who comes in daily, but that's it. Would you like a tour?"

"Sure."

He smiled. "Over there you will see the piano where I do most of my work in its initial stages. Over there you will see my desk. Over there you will see a small bar. What can I get you?"

"Gin and tonic?"

"With lime?"

"Please."

She was still standing in the exact same spot after he had mixed her drink. He carried it over to her, took her clutch purse and tossed it on the couch, and took her elbow.

"I thought you came willingly," he told her with one brow lifted sardonically high. She flushed, but he still sensed her unease. She took a quick sip of her drink and pointed to the arrows on the wall.

"Can you really shoot those things?"

"Yes, I can really shoot them."

He felt an almost imperceptible shiver charge along her arm and he led her from the living room along the hall. "The kitchen and formal dining room are on the other side," he said conversationally. "Game room and den are down here."

"Nice," Bryn murmured.

"I like it."

They started walking back. He felt he could hear the pounding of her heart more thoroughly than any drumbeat. She glanced up the stairway to the open balcony. "Gives you a good sense of spaciousness," she approved.

"Want to see upstairs?"

"Sure."

She preceded him up the stairway, pausing to stare down below. "This really should be in 'House Beautiful' or something," she said, offering him a soft smile.

"Thanks. The length of this hallway is all bedrooms until you get past mine. There's a sound studio beyond it."

"A studio? In the house?"

"Umm. Come on, I'll show you."

The studio was fascinating. If Bryn hadn't had a million worries on her mind, she would have loved to have explored it thoroughly. It occupied more than half of the upstairs, the half that sat over the kitchen and dining room, she surmised.

From the floor rose about four feet of handsome paneling; from there up, the wall was glass. From outside she could see the drums and an elaborate keyboard system. A number of guitars, zipped away in their cases, lay against the far wall. There were wires and speakers all about; on a back wall was another assortment of instruments: tambourines, wind pipes, several wooden flutes and some things she didn't even recognize. Within the glass-encased room there was another smaller room, housing all sorts of mechanical boards.

"We record some of our things right here," Lee told her. "It's a complete sound studio. And this—" he rapped firmly on the outer glass "—is completely soundproof. We can play our hearts out and not even disturb the plants!"

"It's wonderful," Bryn murmured. "I had no idea you could keep something so complete in your own home."

He was standing right next to her. Close enough so that she could feel him. His energy, his heat...his fascinating masculinity. She felt drawn to him, like metal to a magnet, and yet she wanted to run as far as she could, before she found herself consumed by his fire. She couldn't run. She had to charm him, play the hunter rather than the hunted....

Not yet! Not yet! She was shaking and shivering; chills racked her, followed by that dizzying sense of heat.

Bryn swallowed, clenching her teeth, afraid suddenly that she would burst into tears. It seemed that it would be so easy right now to turn to him, to tell him the situation, to throw herself on his mercy and beg for his help.

No, no! she reminded herself painfully. She had been warned. Don't tell Condor; don't tell the police. She didn't dare tell him; she just couldn't take the chance. Not when the children had been threatened and she could still close her eyes and see the remains of what had been her darkroom. And Lee... If she told him the truth now, he would despise her for the deception she had already played on him. He would be furious; he would never cooperate. He would demand that she call the police.

No, she had to keep trying to seduce him. Well, not seduce him all the way. Just enough so that he would be willing to cater to her whims...

She turned suddenly, smiling at him. "What's behind this next door?" Nervously she opened it, then wished she hadn't.

It was obviously his bedroom.

Neat and sparse, but having a feel of the man. The bed was large, covered with an Indian print spread. Throw rugs picked up the browns and oranges of the pattern, and the room gave her a sense of basic earthiness—as well as something a little raw and primeval. Despite all the rock star trappings that came along with Lee Condor, you could strip him down and still find a man, strong in his own right.

She turned around to face him and saw that he was smiling with cool amusement. She had walked into his bedroom; he hadn't led her there.

"The doors are lovely," she said, wondering if he was aware that she had swallowed quickly before she could manage to speak.

"They lead to another balcony," He walked across the room and threw open the French doors. Turning, he offered his hand to her. She set her drink on the bedside table as he had, then followed him out.

The night was breathtaking. Thousands of stars seemed to glitter in the heavens, diamonds on black velvet. The air was pleasantly cool; she could feel it keenly on her bare shoulders and back.

And the balcony looked over a lushly landscaped pool, complete with a Jacuzzi that sent a waterfall spilling into the larger body of water.

A cry of real delight escaped her; the sight was beautiful. Garden lights in blue and green enhanced the mystical impression of a tropical lagoon; she would have loved to have forgotten everything and lost herself in the surroundings.

Bryn moved to the railing to fully see and appreciate the view. "Did you design that yourself?"

"Yes."

"It's really..."

Her voice trailed away as she felt his hands on her shoulders. The caress was gentle, and yet the roughness of his palms seemed to emphasize the complete maleness of him. She felt that he watched the movement of his hands over her flesh, and that his eyes caressed her. His body was solid and hard behind hers; she could feel his breathing and his being.

And then he was turning her around. One arm slipped around her back; his free hand cupped her chin, tilting her head so that their eyes met.

Slowly he lowered his lips to hers. They touched down gently, persuasively, and yet with full, consuming purpose. Her lips parted to his, and his leisurely exploration continued. His tongue was rough velvet as it delved to find hers and gently duel. She found herself moving closer to him, feeling all of him with that kiss, the male power and security of his embrace, the pressure of his hips, the potency of his manhood. It frightened her; it fascinated her. It made her breathless as the night spun around her. The scent and taste of him, the wonder...

She could so easily be lost. So easily forget pain, forget the future. Forget that it would be easy to fall in love with him, love him deeply if she gave herself half a chance, and then know a heartache as deep as her love, regret as bitter as his touch was sweet. Forget...

Forget...the pictures!

Bryn placed her hands against his chest and at length broke the embrace, lowering her head against his shoulder, then trying to smile enticingly as she met his eyes again. She needed to seduce; not to be seduced. If he had any more of her, he would have the power; he would have control of her senses, and his strength, if she played too far, was far greater than hers. You couldn't tease a man like this one....

"Go slowly, please, Lee?" she whispered shakily, but at least it sounded real. Her lips were moist and trembling; her head was spinning.

He smiled, releasing her, and at last she felt steady—and annoyed to realize that the kiss had played far more havoc with her senses than his.

"As slow as you like," he told her.

She smiled again, moving away a bit.

"Let's go back downstairs," he said. She nodded, collected her drink from him, took his hand and followed him out.

Lee showed her the large, modern kitchen, the handsomely appointed dining room, then led her back to the modular sofa.

"Want your drink freshened?"

"Please."

A moment later he was sitting beside her again. Watching her. A little shiver rippled through her as she gazed back into his eyes. The gold seemed extremely sharp and alert. Did he know that she had come in pursuit of something?

"Tell me about yourself, Lee," she said hurriedly, taking a long sip of her gin and tonic. "Where were you born?"

"In the Black Hills."

"You grew up there?"

"Some. But we spent a lot of time in New York. You?"

"Born and raised in Lake Tahoe." Bryn hesitated, wondering why she was asking the question. "Barbara said that you had been married... for five years. That you're a widower."

"Yes."

Just yes, nothing more. She didn't seem to be wedging her way into his confidence very well.

Lee was surprised when she turned to him slightly and touched his face, gently running her knuckles over the contours of his cheeks. Her eyes followed her movements; her lips were slightly parted, and though she had claimed she wanted to go slowly, she was very seductively poised.

Too seductively. He wasn't sure how far he could trust his control if she moved against him again, sleek, coming to him like an elegant kitten. She closed her eyes and came even closer, seeming to melt into his arms. He could feel the contours of her body, so gracefully sliding against him. And she was a very beautiful woman, especially in the physical sense. The breasts that taunted him were high and provocatively full. His hand moved to her invitingly trim waistline; the flare of her hip was an irresistible temptation...

She kissed him. Lightly. She had meant to move away quickly, he was certain, but he caught her and swept her long legs over his lap, imprisoning her in his embrace. He deepened the kiss and allowed his palm to move leisurely down her cheek to her throat, to cover and caress the swell of her breast....

He took his lips from hers, but kissed her cheek. His fingers tangled in the silk of her hair, and he kissed that ivory length, drawing lazy patterns with the tip of his tongue.

"Lee..."

"Hmmm?"

"We...uh...we still haven't talked much."

He stopped kissing her and stared into her eyes. There was a gentle, amused gleam in them as he cradled her close.

"Talk," he said softly. She didn't detect the note of suspicion and danger in his tone.

"I...uh..."

He tried not to increase his pleasant smile as she stumbled; he was moving his fingers higher and higher up the sleek, nyloned length of her leg. And it was obviously causing her distress. She was rigid, but she didn't stop him.

She cleared her throat. "I've been thinking, Lee. I really don't think I did you justice."

"Oh?" He started to draw lazy circles high on her thigh, moving intimately close.

"Those...pictures I took." She started as the casual graze on her flesh traveled to her inner thigh.

"Yes? The pictures?"

"I want them back, Lee. I owe you so much more. I can take a new set—"

His left hand stayed on her thigh. His right began to caress the base of her throat. "You want the pictures back, is that it, Bryn?"

"Yes. I was being rather obnoxious that day, and I..." He was making it impossible to concentrate. "I think it influenced my work. I think I could do much better...for you."

"It's nice of you...to be concerned."

He lowered his head and kissed her again. She returned the kiss with all the emotion she could, stroking his cheek, edgy, but willing herself not to fight the intimacy of his hands. She explored the sensual line of his lips with the tip of her tongue, then joined him again in a passionate meeting of their mouths that allowed her hunger to soar with his.

They were both breathless as they broke apart, their arms laced around each other.

"Can I...take the pictures back, Lee?" she begged with a sultry look.

His eyes were on her, gleaming a cat gold. He smoothed a straying hair tenderly from her cheek. "How badly do you want them?"

"What?" Bryn whispered.

He chuckled, a husky sound that meant many things. It was teasing...and a little sinister. And even a little exciting. And so dangerously insinuating that she knew she could do nothing but stall for time.

"You heard me, Bryn." He was smiling as if it were all a sexual game, nothing more. But a serious game. She had thought she could seduce him just so far, have her way with a winning smile and sultry kisses. She had never expected to reach this point. But she had, and it seemed as if her body was inwardly torn, shaken with electrical charges. What should she do? What should she say? She had always known that she could want him; she was learning now that she liked him, was fascinated by him.

She lowered her lashes quickly. She had to have the pictures. She would do anything to obtain them. That was real; it was a fact. But wasn't there more that she would also have to admit? That it would be no great noble act, no sacrifice. She would be able to...know him, explore the mystical, fulfill her secret desires—and still, in her heart and mind, fall back on the belief that she'd had no choice.

"Bryn?"

She laughed as he had, so nervous that it was a sultry breath of air, a bantering...a teasing.

"Lee...does it matter?" She touched his chin tenderly with one nail. "Events will take their course, no matter what we say or do. But I would like to have those pictures. Very badly. Will you give them to me? I'll—" For a minute she didn't think she could go through with it. Her turmoil was too great. He was too close to her, touching her; but though the touch was tender, she knew there was an underlying male strength and power that could sweep her away and leave her heart bruised and battered on a distant shore. And would she deserve any more? She was—despite the sensual laughter and banter—selling herself.

Did any of that matter, she screamed in silent impatience. The pictures mattered; her nephews mattered; her peace of mind and possibly her health mattered. The children's health...

"I'll do anything...for the pictures," she said clearly, as sweetly and as sensually as she could.

He picked up her hands. He kissed them both. His eyes met hers, and he smiled.

"Lee...?"

"No," he said bluntly.

"What?" she gasped.

He dropped her hands, setting her free from him with a swift movement, and stood, arms crossed over his chest as he confronted her.

"You heard me—no. I don't believe you're 'concerned' for a second. The charade's over. I don't know what this is all about, and since it seems you're not going to tell me, you're not going to use sex to back out on a business deal." The cat-gold gleam swept over her assessingly. "The prize is tempting, my love, but I'm afraid a bartered bedding is not quite good enough."

She stared at him a second, a myriad of emotions racing through her. Rage won out. She'd made an absolute fool of herself—for nothing!

"You bastard! You egotistical bastard!"

She was on her feet and he thought it only natural that she would try to strike him. He was ready, and caught her flying fist.

"When you want *me*, Bryn, come back."

"Hell will freeze over first!" she promised, wrenching her wrist away. She spun blindly to leave and tripped over the sofa. He tried to help her, but she slapped his hand away.

He chuckled softly. "Maybe hell *will* freeze over," he told her with a mocking tone.

"Never! I hope you rot. I hope you die. I hope your fans tear you into little pieces and feed you to the vultures—"

"I get your drift, Bryn."

He was standing before the rack of arrows, golden eyes narrowed, hands firmly on his hips—the total image of masculine power and danger—when she slammed out the front door, still cursing like crazy.

In the car, she burst into tears as the wheels spun, sending the gravel flying.

Chapter 7

Bryn spent the fifteen minutes it took her to drive home alternating between rage and despair.

What was she going to do now? When the damned whisperer called again, she would have to say that she had tried everything, and if the pictures were so important, Condor was the man that they had to be gotten from. It was that simple.

She should have called the police. At the very beginning. Spared herself the fear and the anguish and the aggravation and the...

Humiliation of this disastrous evening!

He had known from the beginning that she wanted something. From the very beginning. And he had played her along, picked up on her game with the same smooth expertise with which he played the drums. Letting her come to him, back off, come again, knowing all the while that he didn't intend to give her a thing.

Damn him! She had made a fool of herself, made something *worse* of herself with her sexual bargaining. And she didn't even have the pictures!

She screeched the van into the driveway, then sat, shaking, at the wheel, stunned to find herself actually home already. It was a good thing she knew Lake Tahoe like the back of her hand. Instinct had brought her home.

Deep breaths, Bryn, she told herself silently. And calm down. You have to go inside and speak with Barbara calmly, as if nothing in the world is going on.

She had grabbed her bag, but her wrap was still at Condor's. Small loss. She felt like burning the dress she was wearing.

Don't slam the door, Bryn! Don't. The kids are asleep. Come up with a nice wide smile for Barbara; tell her you had a few drinks and a nice evening.

It wasn't until she was actually at the door that a frown began to spread its way across her brow.

The porch light wasn't on. Barbara was a fanatic about the porch light—much more so than Bryn. Anytime she went out, Barbara put the light on. Muggers, Barb was convinced, would be far more prone to attack in the darkness than if a glaring light was burning.

Bryn forgot about Lee as she fumbled to fit her key in the lock. The door swung inward, and she paused, puzzled.

She could hear the television set. The parlor light was on, as was the kitchen light. Everything appeared to be normal. She could even see Barb's feet propped up at the end of the couch.

"Barb?" Bryn called softly.

There was no reply. Tentatively Bryn stepped into the house and tiptoed over to the sofa. Barbara was lying there, apparently comfortable as she stretched out. But she appeared to be a little pale, and she had to be sleeping soundly not to have heard Bryn yet.

"Barb?" Bryn shook her friend's shoulder. Barbara groaned and winced, but her eyes didn't open. Anxiously, Bryn shook her friend with more force. "Barb!"

Barbara groaned again; her eyelids began to flutter, and then they opened. She stared up at Bryn blankly.

"Barb, it's Bryn. What's the matter? Are you all right?"

Recognition registered in Barbara's eyes. She blinked again, as if bewildered. "Bryn..." She started to move, then groaned, clutching her head.

"Barbara! What's wrong?" Bryn demanded again, truly anxious now.

"I...I don't know..." Barbara murmured. "I must have fallen asleep, but oh, God! My head. I feel like I've been hit by a ton of bricks. I...remember sitting here. I was watching that new miniseries. And I...I don't remember anything after!"

"Can you sit up, Barb?"

"Yes...I think so."

Bryn moved quickly to sit beside Barbara. She grasped Barbara's hands, pulling them from her head, and gingerly worked over her friend's scalp. Rivers of ice seemed to congeal her blood as she found a knot the size of a walnut near Barbara's nape.

"Oh, sweet Jesus, Barb! It feels like you *have* been hit with a ton of bricks. I'm going to get an ice pack. Sit tight."

Bryn sped into the kitchen, dropped ice all over the floor in her desperate effort to hurry, then rushed back to Barbara.

"Lie back down on your side, Barb, and let me get the ice on this. Think Barb. Something must have happened."

Barbara sank gratefully back to the couch. "I swear to you, honey, I haven't lost my mind—just bruised it. I was sitting here watching television. I did not get up and trip and forget all about it or anything. I—"

Barbara's eyes flew open, filled with horror. She stared at Bryn; then her eyes nervously scanned the room, and then she stared at Bryn again.

"Bryn!" Her voice was a terrified whisper. "Someone must have been in here! Someone had to hit me from behind!"

Bryn swallowed as the terror washed over her again. Yes, it was obvious. Someone had been in the house. They had struck Barbara on the head. Then they had left—or had they?

"Oh, God!" Bryn whispered.

Barbara started to rise. "We've got to call the police right away."

"No!" Bryn almost screamed the word. As Barbara stared at her as if she had gone crazy, Bryn lowered her voice to a whisper again. "No...wait. Let's...let's check out the house. The boys..."

"I think we should get on the phone right away—"

"No, Barb, please! I just... Wait. Wait and I'll try to explain. Just first..."

She stood up and started for the stairs, walking backward as she kept a pleading eye on Barbara. "The boys...I can't call the police. Oh, God, I know how this sounds. I realize you've just been criminally attacked and that we should call the police, but—"

"Wait up, Bryn! Where are you going?" Barbara asked.

"I have to check on the boys!" Bryn whispered, tears forming in her eyes. If she was lucky, her mysterious caller had knocked Barbara out, then destroyed her room. And another phone call would come. If she wasn't lucky...

"Wait for me, Bryn Keller!" Barbara called softly. "You're not going up there alone!"

"Get the broom!"

"The broom?"

"It's my best weapon."

"A knife—"

"We'd wind up dead!"

Apparently Barbara saw the sense of it. She hurried into the kitchen and brought back the broom and the mop—a lance for each of them.

Their eyes turned simultaneously up the stairway. It was dark; the bathroom light wasn't on. Bryn had never felt greater terror in her life than when she looked up into that realm of shadow that promised nothing but a never-ending nightmare.

"Go!" Barbara whispered.

Bryn took a step. Barbara followed. Another step. Barbara coughed softly, and Bryn almost screamed. Her heart pounded painfully and seemed to lodge in her throat.

She took another step, and another; Barbara was with her, a shadow glued to her back.

"Do you see anything?" Barbara demanded.

"No!"

"Keep moving."

Bryn took another step. They had almost reached the landing when suddenly a figure loomed before them.

Bryn and Barbara screamed together, knocking each other with the broom and the mop as they tried to raise them.

The reply to their scream was a terrified little echo, and then the sound of a child crying.

Bryn stood dead still. "Adam?" she queried softly.

"No, it's Keith. You scared me, Aunt Bryn!" An accusing hiccup and sob followed his words. "The light is out. I have to go, and I can't find the bathroom."

Bryn raced on up the stairs, breathing a sigh of relief. She fumbled her way into the bathroom and turned on the light. The hallway no longer appeared ominous, and if Keith was fine, so were Brian and Adam. "Here, honey. Barb and I won't forget to put it on again."

Barbara—white and shaky, but poised—managed a smile that was only slightly sick. But as soon as the little boy had closed the door behind him, she whispered to Bryn, "I had that light on, Bryn Keller! You know I always leave the bathroom light on for the boys."

"I know, I know!" Bryn wailed. "Just let's finish checking the house, and I'll try to explain."

"This is one you're going to have to explain, Bryn! I still have a lump the size of an egg on my head! And the way I see it, we're going to have to call the police."

"Just wait till you hear everything, please?"

"Let's check out your bedroom."

They both poised with their household lances before her closet door, but when they had glanced at each other and nervously thrown it open, they found nothing but Bryn's clothing.

And nothing had been done to her room. Not a thing was out of place.

"I don't think there's anywhere else anyone could be hiding. We were running all around the kitchen. And the parlor. The bathroom is certainly too small to hide anything but a gremlin."

"I think you're right. Except for the darkroom," Bryn murmured, chewing on her lip.

"We'll go and check."

Bryn nodded. "Just let me tuck Keith back into bed."

Keith was rubbing his eyes and heading for the stairs rather than his bedroom. Bryn caught his shoulders and propelled him in the right direction. "Get back in bed. Good night now, sweetheart."

He kissed her dutifully and crawled into his bed. Unease suddenly pricked Bryn's spine and she spun to stare at the boy's closet. But the door was open, and she could see that the closet wasn't harboring anything more sinister than clothing, Castle Grayskull and an assortment of *Star Wars* figures.

The intruder was not in the house.

Bryn turned back to tuck in Keith's covers. He was already sound asleep again. She walked over to the bunk and adjusted Brian's covers, then bent to do the same for Adam.

Except that there was no Adam in the bottom bunk.

For a moment she didn't believe it; she was sure she just hadn't looked in the right place. But it was the right place, and no matter how she ran her hands over the sheets, she couldn't find a little boy.

Bryn rushed over to the wall and turned on the light. She stared about frantically, then raced to the closet, tearing apart the clothing, throwing toys around haphazardly. She lowered herself to the floor and checked under the beds.

There was no Adam. Anywhere.

"Aunt Bryn! The light hurts!"

It was Brian, starting to stir.

"Brian," Bryn began, desperately trying to sound calm. "Honey, did you hear anything tonight? Did you see anything? Do you know where your brother—"

She didn't finish her sentence, because the phone began to ring. "Go back to sleep, Brian," she said, her tone faint as a feeling of sickness clutched at her abdomen and almost doubled her over. "I'll turn out the light."

She hurried to do so, then gathered her failing strength and rushed back into the hall to race down the stairs.

Barbara was ready to reach for the phone.

"Don't answer it!" Bryn shrilled out.

Barbara paused as she took a look at her friend's panicked face. Bryn swept by her, half sobbing. "Barb, we have to do it my way! They've got Adam!"

She picked up the phone, shaking too badly to speak for a moment. The caller wasn't deterred.

"Miss Keller? Answer me—quickly."

"Yes! Yes, I'm here!" Bryn screamed. "And I want him back! I want Adam back right now. You bring him back, or so help me God I'll call the police! I'll kill you with my bare hands—"

"Shut up, and don't get carried away. Yes, we have Adam. And do you know what? He's just fine right now. He just had a nice fudge sundae and curled up to sleep. We'll continue to take real, real good care of him, Miss Keller. But you don't get him back. Not until I get the pictures. You messed up tonight. I knew you would. You weren't taking me seriously enough. Now you'll take me seriously—and maybe you'll do it right."

"Oh, God! Don't you understand! I can't get the damned pictures! Condor won't—"

"*You are* going to get them back from Condor."

"I tried...."

The whispered voice suddenly turned to a growl. "You didn't try hard enough. You ran away. You see, Miss Keller, I know your type. I know what you did. I even know how you think. I see everything. So don't mess with me, eh? And keep your mouth shut, you understand? I wouldn't want to have to return your little boy in bits and pieces."

"I tried!" Bryn pleaded again. "I would have done anything—"

"Like I said, Miss Keller, try harder. It's rumored that Condor has a real thing for you. And I have faith, Miss Keller. A woman with your obvious assets can get a man where she wants him. Do it. And soon."

"You knocked out my friend," Bryn charged the caller bitterly. "She wants me to call the police—"

"If she's your friend, she won't."

"But—"

"Get the pictures, Miss Keller. Quickly. You're running out of time."

The phone went dead in Bryn's hand. Dead. What a word. Oh, God, what was she going to do?

She felt a hand on her shoulder and she almost jumped through the roof. It was just Barb. Bryn covered her face with her hands and burst into tears.

Barbara put an arm around her and led her to sit at the kitchen table. "Where's the brandy?"

"Under the sink."

Barbara stuck a snifter full of the fiery liquid beneath Bryn's nose. "Drink it all down at once. All of it."

Bryn did as she was told. She choked, and her throat burned, but she managed to stop crying.

"Okay, now. Let me hear this whole story."

In a dull monotone Bryn told Barbara everything, starting with the strange man who had appeared on her porch offering her five thousand dollars for the photos. She told her about the darkroom, and about all the phone calls—and about her catastrophic efforts to win back the proofs that night.

"It's simple," Barbara said. "You've got to tell Lee."

"No!" Bryn wailed. "I can't! That's one of the main things this person keeps telling me! Not to tell Lee."

"Because he's probably afraid of Lee. Honey, when he's got Adam, he has you by the nose. But if you just tell Lee, he'll give you the pictures back. He'd never jeopardize the life of a little boy."

"But he might try! He might be furious about all this and determined to catch these people. Oh, Barbara. I can't take the chance. Not now! They have Adam!"

"Lee's no fool, Bryn. He'd handle things discreetly."

"I just can't risk it, Barbara! Someone managed to break into my darkroom in broad daylight and rip it to shreds. Tonight, he or she broke in here, knocked you out and abducted Adam—all without a sound! Barb, look. The lock was picked. It seems this person can come and go at will. And I think he knows where I am and where I go. I just can't take a chance, Barbara. Oh, please! You've got to help me! We've just got to do this my way!"

Barbara lowered her lashes, then looked at Bryn squarely. "You're taking another risk, you know."

Bryn swallowed. She knew what Barbara meant, but she had to ask. "What are you talking about?"

"If these people are that ruthless, Adam is in danger no matter what you do."

Bryn shook her head. "All they want is the pictures, I can't let myself believe that they would hurt Adam."

"What are you going to tell his brothers?"

"That...that...he went to stay with your sister."

"I don't have a sister."

"You do now."

Barbara sighed. "All right, Bryn. Adam is your nephew; I can't make you do what would terrify you, even if I do think that the police should be called in. But what are you going to do?"

"I've tried charm, now I'm going to try robbery."

"What?"

"I'm going to break into his house tomorrow night."

"Oh, God in heaven! Now you really have gone crazy!"

"No, no, Barbara! I was in the house tonight, remember? There's a little alcove off the living room with his desk and business papers and the like. And a file cabinet. The proofs have to be there somewhere."

"Marvelous. What if he has a burglar alarm?"

"He doesn't...at least, I'm almost certain he doesn't. And I went through the house. There's a den window that was open tonight. I'm sure I can slip through it."

"This is insane."

"I'm desperate, Barbara!"

Barbara shook her head. "I still say it's insane. You're going to wind up in jail, and then what will happen?"

"I won't wind up in jail," Bryn said with far more confidence than she felt.

Barbara sighed. "Pass the brandy, will you please? This is going to be a long night. And somehow we're both going to have to show up for work tomorrow morning."

Bryn poured Barbara a stiff brandy, then poured another one for herself. God bless Barbara! she thought in sudden meditation. She'd been knocked unconscious, dragged into terror and now showed no signs of deserting the ship. At least Bryn now had a sympathetic shoulder to lean on....

"How many brandies to you think it will take us to get to sleep?"

Bryn grimaced. "The bottle."

But ten bottles of brandy wouldn't have allowed her to sleep that night. All she could think about was Adam. If she could only hold him now, she would promise him that he could shoot peas across any restaurant that he wanted for the rest of his life....

Oh, Adam! Please come home. Dear God, please let him come home....

Before Andrew neared the door of the Fulton place, he could hear the drums. A heavy rock beat was being pounded out, and he pictured Lee before he saw him; face set in a grim mask, biceps and pectorals straining and bulging with the muscular force needed to create such driving thunder from the drums.

He was right. But as soon as he opened the door, Lee stopped pounding. He was either angry, brooding or puzzled, Andrew knew, but no matter what his state, he wouldn't abuse a friend.

The cymbals crashed together as Lee rose and came to the balcony railing to wave at him. "Hey, Andrew. You're early."

"I've been trying to call you all morning."

Lee shrugged. "I've been here. Why? Has something happened?"

"I'm not sure."

Lee left the railing and came pelting down the stairs. "Coffee is on. Let's get some, and you tell me what you mean."

A few minutes later, Andrew had already gulped down one cup of coffee and had begun on another, leaning against the table in the den.

"Last night, as you know, was my turn to watch Bryn's house again. I had a few errands to run first, but I didn't worry about time too much because you had told me Bryn would be coming over to your house. I figured the earliest she could get home would be about ten, so I planned to get there about nine-thirty. But she was already home—at least her van was in the drive—when I got there."

"She left early," Lee said dryly. "Please, Andrew, go on. What happened?"

"Well, nothing, really. Nothing happened, I mean. It was just strange. The lights never went off. Barbara didn't leave, and the television stayed on all night."

Lee frowned, and then shrugged. "Maybe they stayed up talking and fell asleep with the TV and the lights on."

"Maybe," Andrew said, but his look was dubious. "I have a feeling, and intuition, that something did happen before I got there."

Lee was silent for a minute; then he said, "Andrew, don't worry about it, there's probably nothing wrong."

"I should have been there earlier."

"Don't worry about it. It sure as hell isn't your fault that Bryn left my place early."

Andrew still appeared unhappy, but he asked, "What about your place last night?"

"No one came in last night; they waited until I left this morning."

"How do you know that?"

"'Cause Maria just called. And she knows my habits like she knows the Psalms. She's been keeping that place for five years now. She wanted to know why there was a file on my desk. She knows I always keep them in the cabinets."

"And you didn't leave a file on your desk?"

"No."

"You know, Lee, maybe we can't handle this thing. Maybe we need to get some security men in or something."

Lee shook his head. "I still don't know for what. The police would laugh me out of their office and tell me I'm a paranoid 'star.' I could hire private detectives, but something tells me not to right now. Nothing has really happened—that I know about. I don't want to just catch some flunky prowling around my house. I want to know what's going on."

Andrew yawned. "Well, I bloody well hope we find out soon. I could use a week of solid sleep. Oh, by the way. How did your date go?"

"It didn't. As you know, she left early."

"Oh, sorry."

"So was I. Sorry enough to wish I had made a bargain."

"What?"

"Never mind. Thanks for helping me keep up the vigil, Andrew."

"No problem—" Andrew began. He broke off as they heard the front door open. From the den they could see that a tall figure was silhouetted in the doorway.

"Condor?"

Lee looked puzzled; then he frowned as he realized who the man was. "What in hell does he want?" he asked Andrew.

"He who?" Andrew demanded softly.

"It's that damned politician. Remember, the guy from the country club. He said he wanted to see what we had done here, and like an idiot, I told him to stop by anytime."

"Public relations," Andrew reminded him dryly.

"Yeah, public relations!"

Lee set down his coffee cup and stepped out of the den. "Mr. Hammarfield. Come on in. This is it."

The politician was, as always, followed by several men. As they came in the foyer, Andrew moved up by Lee and asked discreetly, "What the bloody hell *is* he doing here?"

"Maybe he needs a testimonial to win the youth vote. I don't know."

Dirk Hammarfield approached him with a wide grin and an extended hand. Lee accepted the handshake and introduced Hammarfield to Andrew. "Can we help you with something?" Lee asked.

"No, no, I just wanted to take a look at the old Fulton place now that you've got it all fixed up. I have to get to the city soon, so I just thought I'd stop by. Too early to catch any of the action, huh?"

"I'm afraid so," Lee replied.

"I'll be on my way then. But I'm having a fund-raising dinner next week at the Swan. You—and your boys—are welcome to attend. On me, of course."

"Thanks. We'll let you know."

Hammarfield smiled, then turned to leave with his navy-suited escorts following behind.

"Why don't I trust him?" Andrew asked.

"Because he smiles too much," Lee replied. He walked to the foyer and stared out the triangular door window. He frowned. Bryn and Barbara had arrived, together. And Hammarfield was approaching them, greeting them with enthusiasm. Too much enthusiasm. He was kissing Bryn on the cheek. And it wasn't a brotherly gesture. The politician was still smiling with the innocence of a bright boy, but his eyes sizzled with nothing less than lust.

"What is his game?" Lee hissed softly.

"It's hard to tell," Andrew supplied dryly. "But unless you want to be known as 'I Spy,' I'd come away from the door."

Lee grimaced and did so. When Barbara opened the door, he greeted her with a smile, then tried to hide the frown that followed as he realized that the usually imperturbable blonde looked decidedly nervous and a bit like she'd been through hell.

Bryn looked even worse. She pretended not to see him, which was a feat in itself since he was standing in her way, and continued through to the den and the coffeepot.

On an impulse he followed her. She jumped when he came through the door, scowled and cleaned up the coffee she had spilled. "What do you want?" she asked sharply.

"Just to inquire after your welfare," he replied in a dry drawl.

"Well, I'm just fine. And I'll stay just fine as long as you stay away from me."

He leaned against the doorway and lifted one brow. "Yesterday she purred, today she stretches her claws. Well, I can't very well stay away from you. We work together. Unless you've decided to quit?"

He could tell she was grinding her teeth as she gave her attention to her coffee cup. "No, I haven't decided to quit." She gazed at him again. "Am I fired?"

"No."

He wanted to shake her; he walked away instead. There had been something about her eyes....

More than anger haunted them. She looked scared. No, not just scared. She was nervous, high strung...and terrified.

Each time he touched her during the day, he was tempted to refuse to release her. To hold her ever tighter and demand that she talk to him. To force her to rest and give some of the fear and worry over to him...

But her eyes flashed each time they met his. A cold war had truly begun.

"You really are crazy, Bryn," Barbara said flatly. "And I'm telling you right now, when you call from the county jail, I'm not coming to pick you up. I'm going to pretend that I don't know a thing about it. Bryn, if you would just talk to him, if you were even halfway decent to him, it wouldn't be so bad. But you're hateful! When he catches you..."

Bryn pulled her black sweater over her head. "I tried to be decent to him. I'd kiss his feet if I thought it would work. It wouldn't. And he isn't going to catch me, Barbara. I stumbled into him and Mick right before he left, and Mick was saying something about its being 'his turn,' and Lee said to try and be there by nine at the latest. So they're either going out, or they're going to rehearse. And if they rehearse, they'll be in that soundproof room. I could explode a bomb and no one would hear me."

"Oh, Bryn, I just don't like it. Not one bit," Barbara said wearily. They were up in Bryn's bedroom, and for the tenth time Barbara walked to the window and assured herself that it was bolted. "I did lock the kids' window, didn't I?"

"We both checked it, Barb. No one is getting in here tonight. But then again, I don't believe anyone will try." She sighed nervously. "I'm ready. Come with me and make sure you lock both bolts as soon as I'm out."

Barbara nodded unhappily. They were halfway down the stairs when the doorbell started to ring. Both women froze; then Bryn shook herself. "Whisperers don't ring doorbells," she assured Barbara—and herself. But she gazed out the peephole carefully, then leaned against the door in dismay. "It's that damned golfer!" she told Barbara.

"Golfer?"

"Mike Winfeld. I met him at the country club."

"The pro? He's a doll. You get all the good ones!" Barbara peered through the peephole herself and sighed a little wistfully. "Just like *Rebel Without a Cause*—except that he's got one now."

"What are you talking about?" Bryn demanded impatiently.

"Mike Winfeld," Barbara replied, surprised by the question. "He was a street kid—getting into drugs, petty thefts, tough-kid kinds of things. But in one of his foster homes he met a golfer, and it was success ever after."

"That's just wonderful, Barbara," Bryn muttered, "but I have to get out of here now."

"So open the door and explain that you've an appointment."

"But what if—"

"If he comes in, I'll entertain him for you."

Bryn cast Barbara a sharp scowl, then opened the door with a brilliant smile. "Mike! How nice to see you. What brings you here?"

"The hope of catching just a minute of your time."

Bryn allowed her smile to fade. "Oh, Mike! I'm so sorry. I was just on my way to keep an appointment. But Barbara is here... Barbara, did you get a chance to meet Mike Winfeld?"

"No, I didn't," Barbara had her hand graciously extended. "What a pleasure, Mr. Winfeld."

"I was just on my way out," Bryn apologized.

For a moment she was really sorry; his handsome features were composed in a mask of disappointment, and she was struck again by what a pleasant individual he was. But she had to get going, and he was in her way! She couldn't really think about anything else when she was so horribly worried about Adam. She had barely made it through the day. She could hardly remember anything about the nightmare hours of waiting....

"Well," Mike laughed, "just remember I'm a determined man! Barbara, nice meeting you."

"Thanks," Barbara murmured.

"Can I walk you to your van?" Mike asked.

"Of course," Bryn murmured. "Barb, I'll see you soon."

"I hope so," Barbara remarked in a dire tone.

"What was that all about?" Mike asked with a laugh as he walked to the van with Bryn.

"Oh, she doesn't like to baby-sit late," Bryn said. They reached the van, and she unlocked the door to crawl lithely into the driver's seat. "It was nice of you to come by."

"Not nice . . . just determined."

Bryn grimaced. "I really am horribly busy for the next few weeks."

"I believe you. Have a nice night."

"Thanks, you too."

He smiled and waved with a disconsolate shrug as he backed away from the van. Bryn turned the key in the ignition and pulled out of the drive.

In her rearview mirror she saw him climb into a small dark Porsche. When she reached the highway, his car was behind hers. She waved once more, and then forgot about him as her problems took control of her mind.

Barbara was right. She was crazy. She was about to break into a man's house like a common burglar. Fear raced through her. She was going to crawl around a dark house and try to break in. And then she was going to rifle through a man's belongings and try to get out again with the all-important prize she craved. . . .

Crazy . . . crazy . . . crazy . . . it was crazy. . . .

Before she knew it, before she was ready, she had pulled into the secluded road that led to Lee's estate.

Bryn pulled the van onto the shoulder beneath the shade of some sloping pine trees. She cut the engine, and then the lights.

Darkness surrounded her. She felt as if she could hear the night, and its whisper was ominous.

She forced herself to grab her flashlight and hop quietly out of the car. She closed the door softly, but it sounded as if it had been slammed.

She could see Lee's house through the trees.

It, too, was dark. Deathly dark.

Go, coward, go! It's your only chance. Think of Adam!

She started walking. All around her the night seemed to close in. She heard every rustle of the trees, ever nuance of the wind. Crickets rose in a chorus to mock her; a fly buzzed past her face and she batted at it in panic.

A fly, only a fly, she told herself.

Feeling like an idiot, she pulled a black knit ski mask from her pocket and pulled it over her head, stuffing her hair into it and beneath the collar of her sweater.

Now she really felt like a sneak thief.

But she would almost disappear into the darkness.

The impulse to turn back was so strong that she almost whipped around like a quarter horse to run in the opposite direction.

But she kept walking. And finally she was standing before the dark house. He *had* gone out. Thank God. But why did his home have to be so isolated? It was a good thing it was, she reminded herself. If he had lived in a giant condo, she would never have been able to break in....

Break in. That was why she had come. She had to start thinking like a burglar.

Bryn bit her lip and ducked behind a bush. She moved closer to the house.

Make sure he isn't here, she warned herself silently, and she carefully began to circle the dwelling.

She couldn't see a sign of life. It was now or never, now or never....

Barely breathing, Bryn moved around to the far right side of the house and the window that led to the den.

Tentatively she reached toward it. She had come this far; she was going all the way.

From the moment she crawled into the house, Bryn should have realized that she had entered a realm of nightmares.

Oh, she should have known!

The ski mask itched, and she tried to scratch her cheek as she nervously shone the flashlight about. Had the mask really been necessary? Yes, because if someone showed up there was a good chance she could outrun them. And as long as they didn't see her features, she could keep her identity secret.

Bryn moved swiftly from the den to the hall, then hurried to the living room. She played the flashlight quickly around her. Nothing had changed. It was the same as it had been last night.

No, it wasn't. The house seemed ominous tonight. Shadowed and ominous. The flashlight picked up the rifle case, and she swept it quickly by, only to see the display of bows and arrows. A quiver chilled her backbone. Yes, he had told her he knew how to use them....

Get to the desk! she warned herself. The house was shadowy and frightening because she was an intruder, a thief. And the faster she worked, the quicker she could get out of here.

Bryn hurried up the single step that led to the little alcove. What if he locked his desk? She tugged at a drawer. She was grateful when it glided open to her nervous touch. Gingerly she began to go through the contents. No prints.

They had to be here. Either in the drawers or in the filing cabinet. She tried the second drawer, then the third. Then the center drawer. Nothing! Nothing but bills and letters and scribbled notes! She closed the center drawer and jumped in startled panic as it snapped shut with a sharp click. Her blood seemed to congeal, and then to flow again. She swept the flashlight quickly around the room. Nothing. What had she been expecting? The arrows to jump down from the walls and come flying at her?

Stay calm, Bryn, she cautioned herself. Stay calm. There are three more drawers on the left-hand side....

But she never touched the left-hand side of the desk. Panic—as strong as the stranglehold about her neck and as cold and sharp as the arrow tip against her ribs—rose up to engulf her.

"Who the hell are you and what the hell do you want?"

"I..." She couldn't speak; she couldn't even think. Terror had taken complete possession of her. She realized vaguely that Lee Condor was her captor, but not a Lee Condor that she knew. The whispered demand was laced with a primal, deep-drawn fury. His hold was cruel and ruthless....

But as suddenly as she had been grabbed, she found herself released, and she heard him speak bitingly once more. "We'll get some light on the situation."

Free! Bryn realized. She was free! With no other thought in her mind, she grabbed the wrought-iron railing that enclosed the alcove and pelted over it. The hallway loomed before her; in desperation she ran, fear shooting through her limbs.

"Hell!" he snapped out behind her.

She reached the window and leaped to the sill. "Stop!" he commanded harshly. She looked back to see that he had sprung with the lithe agility of a panther, hurling himself at her. She couldn't go out; she had to come back in to avoid him.

She jumped back a split second before his shoulder slammed against the window. But what now, she wondered in dismay. Run, don't think. *Run!*

She started to run, but not fast enough. A hand grabbed her sweater. Frantically she jerked back, and her sweater tore away in his hand. Without reason or thought, with blind panic guiding her, she charged into the hallway.

Not back to the den! It was a dead end. She raced furiously up the stairway and was on the landing before she realized that this, too, was a dead end. No way out. If he caught her, he would rip her to shreds or call the police. Or rip her to shreds *and* call the police.

He was right behind her. She heard his feet on the stairs; she could almost feel the warmth of his breath against her skin....

Her eyes fell on the door at the end of the hall and she raced toward it. Reached it, and flung herself into the room. He was behind her! Slam it, slam it, slam it—It wouldn't slam!

No, it wouldn't slam because he had braced himself against it. Bryn gasped as the air was suddenly sucked from her lungs when his charge brought his strength crashing against her, his shoulder bearing into her abdomen and sweeping her off her feet.

She had the sensation of flying and then of brutally crashing. Against the bed. And he was on top of her....

"No! Please!" she gasped.

She started to fight, almost insane with terror as she felt him climb on top of her, pinning her down. She struck out at him with all her strength, but it was futile. He caught her flailing arms and pinned them down, too.

Mercilessly he ripped the ski mask from her head and face. The fickle moon suddenly sprinkled the room with a soft glow, and she was meeting his narrowed, gleaming eyes.

"Ah, Miss Keller..."

Caught...she had been caught. He kept talking; she tried to answer. So frightened, so terrified—so very sorry that she had always shown him such hostility.

But even that was not the end of it. No.

The nightmare had only begun.

She was not the only intruder. There was the sound of footsteps, and suddenly she was lying beside him half naked—barely breathing as the intruder approached. Knowing the meaning of fear, yet knowing Lee's touch, feeling him, sensing his strength and determination...

Then he was gone, and again she knew terror as she was left with only the echo of his anger—and the sound of bullets.

Bullets!

But Lee was all right. Thank God! Except that he was quizzing her again, and she was answering, trying to answer, and then he was warning her. "Be in the kitchen in five minutes flat, and be prepared to tell me this whole story—with no holes!"

Her five minutes were up. It was time to get to the kitchen.

Chapter 8

Lee turned on the hall light as he passed it; it seemed senseless to keep the house in darkness now. He glanced at the doorframe where the first bullet had lodged. No real problem there; a little putty would take care of it. But the front door was going to be another story.

A shaft of anger stabbed him. Pictures! For a lousy set of pictures someone tormented Bryn to near lunacy and shot at him, nearly killing him and ripping the hell out of his home.

He paused. At least now...now he could begin to understand Bryn.

He padded down the stairs and looked at the front door. He could wire it closed for the night, but he'd have to replace both it and the lock in the morning. He frowned then, thinking that the police should really be called. But Bryn seemed to be in a real panic. He couldn't blame her, not when the child was involved.

Nor could he be angry anymore about last night. She had come to him because she had been desperate.

So why the hell hadn't she just talked to him, he wondered, pain knifing through him. Did she really dislike and distrust him so thoroughly that she couldn't trust him, even when she was desperate?

They would, he decided grimly, get to the bottom of things, and as soon as he understood it more fully, he was determined that he would see an end to it all.

He would listen to her. But she was going to have to be made to understand that they had to do things his way. Maybe she would be ready to accept his help at last. She needed help. His help. On many levels, and she was afraid to take it on all of them.

His lips compressed as he wedged a chair beneath the doorknob and walked on into the kitchen. He hit the light switch and illuminated the spotlessly clean room. He filled the percolator with water and measured out four scoops of coffee, then added another. Then he set the pot on a burner and leaned against the counter absently as his thoughts continued to roam.

Why would someone want a bunch of publicity shots badly enough to kidnap a little boy and hold him for ransom?

There had to be something else in those pictures. Something so harmful that . . .

"Lee?"

He glanced across the kitchen to see Bryn standing nervously in the doorway. His shirt engulfed her, overlapping her black jeans to the knees. It seemed strange, but she looked all the more bewitchingly feminine in a man's shirt.

A covert glance at his wristwatch told him that exactly five minutes had passed. He would have smiled if the situation had been less tense.

"Sit down." A wave of his arm indicated the wicker stools that surrounded the kitchen's butcher-block table. She lowered her lashes and did so. Lee felt his heart pound achingly within his chest. He wanted to rush over to her and hold her. Touch her and soothe her and convince her that it was going to be all right.

This wasn't the time. Nor would he allow himself to reach for her again—no pressure, no bargains. She would have to come to him, and she would have to do so because she wanted to. Badly enough to cast aside all her doubts and fears.

He turned around and rummaged in the cupboard for mugs. "Start talking," he told her flatly.

"I . . ."

"Don't hedge!" he said sharply. "Talk."

He could almost hear her grind her teeth. But she began. Sporadically, choppily, but bluntly, she told him the story. "The morning after . . . after I took the pictures . . . a man appeared at my door. He offered me five thousand dollars for them. I don't know whether I believed him or not, but I explained that you owned all the rights to them. I kind of forgot about the incident. But then I got a threatening phone call."

"From a man?"

"I'm not sure. The voice is always a whispered hiss."

"Always?"

"Yes, I've had several calls."

Bryn watched Lee as he poured out two cups of coffee, set them on the table and drew out the stool opposite from her. I'll never be able to explain this with him sitting there bare-chested and staring at me, she thought, despising herself for a coward. But she was going to have to explain. The way he was looking at her, jaw firm and eyes relentless, she had no choice.

"Keep going," he told her.

"I might get a little lost—"

"I'll bear with you. Go on."

Bryn tried to sip her coffee and almost scalded her lips. She set the mug back on the table and stared at it. "I'd given my film to a friend who owns a camera shop the night I shot it, and then I turned the proofs right over to Barbara, so I never had them in the house. But when I came home from work, I found all my film, file pictures and some personal photos destroyed. My darkroom was literally ripped apart—chemicals emptied, anything that could be done was done. Another phone call followed that, threatening me again."

As Lee watched her, he saw a flush spread across her cheeks. "That's when you decided to seduce me into giving the pictures back?"

"Yes," Bryn admitted softly, still staring at her coffee.

"You should have just asked me; I would have given them to you." Her startled eyes flew to his and he smiled bitterly.

"I don't like being taken for a fool, Bryn."

She stared quickly back down to her cup again. "They've got Adam. They kidnapped him."

"How? And when?"

She swallowed painfully and moistened her lips. "Last…last night. When I left here, I went home and found Barbara knocked out on the couch. She never knew what hit her. At first we were afraid that someone was still in the house. That's when I discovered that Adam was gone. And—"

"You got another phone call right away?" Lee's words were more like a flat statement than a question.

Bryn nodded. A flush rose to her cheeks again. "The voice…suggested that if I tried harder, I could…seduce you. And that if I didn't get the pictures from you, I wouldn't see Adam again."

"But you decided not to seduce me, but to rob me instead," Lee stated dryly.

"I…" Bryn paused, her words catching in her throat. He certainly wasn't trying to make this any easier for her. "I was desperate, Lee. And I knew…what the whisperer didn't. That…that I'd failed, and that—"

"That what?"

"Another try wasn't going to change anything," Bryn said softly, her eyes on her coffee cup again.

Lee was silent for a minute, not responding to her words. Then he asked, "What did Barbara have to say to all this?"

Bryn shrugged. "That I should call the police. And that...I should tell you what was going on."

"You should have."

She stared at him miserably. "I...couldn't. Lee, I couldn't take any risk whatsoever, not when the kids were threatened and then when...Adam was taken."

"Damn it, Bryn!" he muttered impatiently. "Whatever your personal opinion of me, I can't believe that you would think I would turn you away when a child was at stake!"

Bryn shook her head. Her lashes swept her cheeks, but rose again instantly. "The caller kept warning me not to let you know what was going on. I wasn't afraid that you wouldn't try to help me, but just that you would insist on calling the police or becoming involved. And I can't risk that, Lee. I have to get Adam back!"

He was silent for a moment, and then he leaned across the table. "Do you know anyone with a dark sedan, Bryn?"

Her frown convinced him that she thought he was crazy. "No, why?"

"Because one followed you home the night after you shot the pictures."

She stared at him, stunned.

"Someone has been in my house twice—that I know of. I thought I had caught my sneak tonight when I found you. And I don't know how this person has been managing to break into your home so smoothly. One of the band has been watching your house every night since."

"Then you've known all along that something has been going on?"

"Yes."

Bryn finally managed to take a drink of her coffee. She wanted to phrase her next words carefully. She set the cup down and faced him squarely. She had learned belatedly that honesty was the best policy with Lee Condor.

"Lee, will you give me the proofs and negatives back and forget everything that's happened? Please? I really believe that's the only way I can ensure Adam's safety."

Lee took a sip of his coffee, his eyes on hers over the rim of his mug. "Bryn, haven't you stopped to wonder what's in those pictures that would make someone this determined to get hold of them?"

"No—yes—no! I don't *care,* and I don't *want* to care!" Bryn swore vehemently. "All I want is to get Adam back!"

"Bryn," Lee said quietly, "I understand that. And we'll get Adam back. But don't you see? The threat to you may not end there. Someone is desperate. There has to be something in those pictures that is extremely harmful to someone. And that someone is going to keep wondering if you know what it is."

"But I don't."

"They don't know that."

"But why would they care? We'll just give them the damn pictures—"

"Bryn, it isn't that simple!" Lee stood impatiently. "Who's at your house? Barbara?"

"Yes."

"Call her. Ask her to stay the night."

"Why?" Bryn asked uneasily.

"Because we've got some talking to do. And some playing."

"Lee, I will not—"

"Jeopardize Adam. I know. Neither will I. But neither will I allow you to jeopardize yourself or those other two kids. Never mind; I'll call Barbara. What's your number?"

He moved to the wall phone at the end of the kitchen counter. Bryn stared at him for a minute, tempted to fall at his feet and beg him to give her the pictures and let her go.

But no matter how she humiliated herself, it wouldn't work. She could see the steely determination in the set of his jaw. Whether she liked it or not, he was involved. He was stepping in, and he was going to force her to face all the implications.

She swallowed as a little lightning bolt of electricity seized her. She gazed at the bare bronze of his chest and broad shoulders. At the way his body narrowed at the hips and waist. He was too powerful and too competent for her to fight at this moment.

She wearily rattled off her phone number.

Barbara must have been extremely anxious; in fact, she must have prepared a heart-rending defense for Bryn. Lee had barely identified himself before Bryn heard the faint and garbled voice returning to him over the wires.

"Barbara, Barbara, hold it!" Lee laughed, and Bryn noted the attractive glitter of humor that touched his eyes and softened the ruthless severity of his features. "She's here, she's fine, and there's no problem—other than the major one. But listen, I don't think she should drive home tonight, so I'm going to have her stay here. But don't worry, you're not alone. Andrew is outside. Go to the porch and call him in. He'll explain. If the phone rings, answer it and do your best, but I don't think anyone will call tonight."

Bryn heard the crackle of conversation from the other end again. Lee said, "All right," and then leaned casually against the counter. "She's calling Andrew in," he explained to Bryn. Bryn just nodded. It suddenly seemed logical that Andrew would be standing outside her door.

"Hey there," Lee said, and by the change of tone, Bryn knew he was talking to Andrew, "you don't mind being inside, do you?"

Whatever Andrew replied must have been in the affirmative, because Lee laughed. "Okay. I'll see you there—early."

He hung up, and Bryn watched him nervously as he strode thoughtfully back to the table. "Okay, Bryn. This is it. At sunrise we'll head back to your place and wait for the phone to ring. You'll arrange an exchange for the pictures and Adam. It has to be a public place—near a phone. As soon as they drop Adam, you'll drop the pictures. If you were supposed to seduce me into agreement, this person will expect me to be near you. And they'll know that I'm in on it somehow. I'd have to be after they shot at me, right?"

"I...suppose," Bryn murmured. Then she added hopefully, "And that will be it?"

"No, that will not be it! Who's your friend who did the pictures?"

"His name is Kelly. His shop is Kelly's Kodak."

"Call him."

"Now?"

"Now."

"But—"

"Tell him you'll be bringing the original negatives back and having a set of prints made. That way we can return everything and still have them, but no one will see any activity *in your darkroom* until Adam is returned and they presumably have everything."

Bryn rubbed her temple. He was right, and she knew it. She just didn't want to see it. She stood up. "Lee, I'm afraid. This guy seems to know everything that I do. He specifically demanded the negatives. What if he finds out that I've ordered more prints?"

"He won't. And we need them, Bryn. We have to figure this out."

"Lee! If we bring the photos by—"

"*We* won't, Bryn. *Bryn!* Pay attention to me. I don't want *you* doing the pictures, because someone might very well be watching your house right now. But if Kelly—"

"Lee—"

"Bryn, it's all right. You and I will not go near Kelly's. Mick has the pictures; he'll get them dropped off. Now this whisperer of yours might have a pretty decent spy system going, but he can't possibly watch you and me and the rest of the world, too."

Bryn was silent for several seconds. His thinking was rational and reasonable. He was right, she was sure. She was just so frightened.

"All right," she said at last. "I'd better call Kelly quickly. But what do I say? When will Mick bring the pictures?"

"Tonight."

Bryn nodded bleakly. Mick had the pictures. No matter how efficiently she had burglarized Lee's house, she would never have gotten them that way.

Kelly moaned and groaned when she called him, but she pleaded sweetly and he promised to do his best. Lee called Mick, spoke to him briefly, and then he and Bryn found themselves staring at each other across the table again.

"We're going to have to start thinking and remember everything that happened at that country club," Lee told her.

Bryn lifted her hands and grimaced. "Everything was happening at the country club. Dirk Hammarfield was there, and that PGA tournament was going on. But that's what I don't get. What could I have gotten on film? A lot of sloping hills and velvety grass?"

"That politican is slippery."

"Hammarfield?"

"Ummm. He was nosing around the Fulton place."

"He wasn't nosing around!" Bryn protested. "He says he's a great fan of yours. And I think he'd like you to endorse him."

"Maybe," Lee said with a shrug. "But I think he's slippery."

"He's polite."

"Charming?" Lee mocked dryly.

"More so than some people I know," Bryn snapped too quickly in response to his cynicism.

"I see. And golfers are far more charming than drummers, too?"

There was an edge to his voice. Bryn shivered slightly. Apparently he had seen the news the night that she was shown smiling and chatting away with Mike Winfeld.

"Yes," Bryn said tightly. "The golfers I've met are far more charming than the drummers of my acquaintance."

He didn't reply. He stood up and stretched, picking up his cup to rinse it out in the sink. Bryn bit her lower lip miserably. Why was she still being so hostile? He had bent to her wishes as far as a man like him could possibly do. He might have called in the police....

"I'm going to rig up the front door. This whisperer of yours seems to be a fairly dangerous fellow. He shot the door right off its hinges. Then..." He paused, staring at her, and she couldn't begin to fathom his expression. "Then I'm going to go to bed," he told her curtly. "There are three guest rooms upstairs. Take your pick."

"I don't think I can sleep," Bryn murmured.

"Then go lie down and think," Lee advised. "About the pictures. Think of anything at all that might have been in the backgrounds."

He rummaged beneath the sink and came up with a hammer, nails and a skein of wire. His golden gaze fell on her enigmatically; then he walked out of the kitchen.

Bryn sat at the table for a while, her emotions playing havoc within her. Where was Adam? Was he all right? She had to believe that he was. She had to live on the hope that he would be returned to her tomorrow. She would have the pictures. She would give them back....

Thanks to Lee. She had to be grateful.

She stood up and walked out to the living room. He had one nail stuck in his mouth while he hammered another into the door. He paused as she walked up to him, a brow raised.

"Lee...thank you," she told him.

He slipped the nail to the corner of his mouth. "Go to bed, Bryn."

She nodded and started up the stairs, then paused. "Does it matter which room?" she asked politely.

He didn't glance at her, but he did stop hammering for a minute. "No. They're all set up for company."

Bryn bit her lip as she watched. His back was bowed over his task, his powerful arms rippling and glistening with each firm whack of the hammer. Then she continued up the stairway.

She stepped through the first door she came upon and flicked on the light. As he had said, the room was ready for company. The rose-wood bed set was gleaming; the teal spread and striped sheets had a clean fresh scent. Bryn found a small nightlight on the mirrored dresser, turned it on and the overhead light off. She shed her sneakers and jeans and climbed beneath the sheets.

But as she lay there, she couldn't stop thinking about Lee. About the times she had lain in his arms. Dreamed of him. Wanted him.

He had given her everything. And demanded nothing of her.

She closed her eyes tightly and tried to shut out his image.

It could not be shut out.

She saw his features in the moonlight: the high forehead; dead straight nose; firm, square jaw; full, sensuous mouth. His eyes full of riveting golden power...

Think about the pictures, she told herself. The Timberlane Country Club. The background...

His scent had always seemed to beckon her. Subtle. Clean, and yet very male. She remembered the way the bronze of his shoulders had gleamed beneath the soft light of the moon. She remembered staring at his chest. Tight and broad, devoid of hair, sheer bronze masculine strength. She had wanted to reach out and touch him.

She'd known for a long time that she had been wrong about him. From the beginning he had meant to offer her friendship. He'd been attracted to her, yes, but he would never have pushed her.

He had always cared; he had always shown her sensitivity. He had sensed her fear of heights; he had reassured her. He had known she needed money; he had never—not once, despite everything that she had done—threatened to fire her. And at the restaurant when Adam— Oh, Adam! Where are you?

When Adam had thrown food, Lee hadn't been horrified. He had understood that bad behavior didn't make a bad child, just a little boy who was insecure and needed a lot of love.

Adam! It hurt to think of him and to be so helpless, waiting and waiting, praying.

Adam, she thought, I do love you. I'll get you back again, and I'll do everything to make you forget that you ever were afraid or frightened or alone...

Love... Such a varied and strange emotion. Love for a child. Love for a man. No, she wasn't in love with Lee. She could admit now that she liked him, that she cared for him. But she couldn't risk loving him. He liked children, but that didn't mean that he wanted them. And he cared for Bryn, but how deeply—and for how long?

She groaned aloud. It hurt to be so torn. So worried about Adam. So alone herself. She needed Lee tonight. Even if she couldn't hold on to love, she needed to feel it.

No, she had to be hard and independent. She had to take care of herself, because she herself was her only guarantee....

There were no guarantees.

Bryn covered her face with her hands and swallowed convulsively.

Who was she kidding? Herself? No longer. She had always wanted him. She did need him; but most of all, she wanted him.

And maybe she was just a little bit in love with him. Maybe she had known that she would be, even before she had met him. And she had been afraid—of herself, of being vulnerable. Not really of him.

Bryn realized suddenly that the hammering had stopped. She waited a minute, listening to the night. Then she crawled out of the bed and walked to her door, opening it softly.

The hall light was still on, but the downstairs was dark and silent.

Close the door and go back to bed, she told herself.

But she didn't close the door. She stepped out into the hall.

You know that you want him. Go to him.

Yes, but did he still want her?

She could be hurt again, she warned herself. He could send her away.... He could still be angry.

He might not want her anymore.

She had to risk it. There might be pain in the future, but for tonight...

Her heart thundered painfully in her chest, but her feet started to carry her down the hall. She came to his door and hesitated. It was open. She moved into the doorway, her blood seeming to flame within her veins, and then to freeze with a nervous apprehension....

"Come in, Bryn."

She realized then that he was sitting up in his bed, casually watching her. His back was straight; the moon bathed his shoulders and caught the golden glitter of his eyes.

He had expected her; he had awaited her. He knew all the moves of the night; he sensed them with an ancient and primitive awareness.

Run, she told herself. This is the greatest danger you have faced. You'll wind up losing your soul to him.

Her heart continued to beat like thunder. Her body and soul seemed gripped by fear and pain.

But she took a step into the room. Going to him. From the very beginning, she had been compelled to do so.

Chapter 9

The room was shadowed in the mist of night, and yet he saw color, enhanced by the gentle beams of the moon. He saw the long and luxurious copper waves of her hair, the dark fringed lime of her widened eyes.

The ivory of her flesh. Of her throat, exposed by the open collar of her shirt, of her supple legs, bared beneath its tails.

Color, and provocative silver mist.

Her form was part substance, part mist, as she created a striking silhouette in the doorway. The moonbeams cut through the shadows, and her slender frame was highlighted as the fabric of his shirt was made translucent. He could see the fullness of her curves, and he longed to touch the deeper shadow where the night conspired to shield her in a cloak of enticing innocence.

She seemed to hover uncertainly, and he thought of her then with a touch of wistful fancy. She was a bit like a beautiful nymph, caught by the silver of the moon. A sweet promise of the night, delicate and breathtakingly lovely. But like a glimmering shaft of moon silver, she would be ethereal. He could not do as his heated passions dictated and bolt to the door to imprison her in his arms; like a mist in darkness she could disappear, and he would hold nothing but empty air....

She *was* real. A woman of soft, warm flesh and vibrantly flowing blood. And his heart longed to reach out to her as much as his hands. But his instinct to hold back was also real. He had to allow her to come to him. He didn't understand why she was afraid, only that she was.

And that she had to take the first steps herself if he was ever to truly hold her.

And so after his inital invitation, he sat silently, waiting. Scarcely breathing. His pose was relaxed, but within he trembled, desire and tenderness combining to flow explosively through his system.

She started to walk to him. Slowly. And with each step she became more real. He heard the soft whisper of her breath. The subtle scent of her perfume wafted over him like a tantalizing caress.

At the foot of the bed she stopped, her eyes beseeching him. Her lashes fell, and she bowed her head slightly. Soft tendrils of silken hair fell about her features to cloak them in a copper enigma.

"Lee?" she murmured, and there was pleading in her quiet tone.

He leaned forward, determined that when he reached out, it would not be for an illusion. "Let me see your eyes, Bryn," he told her. She lifted her head once more, tossing back her hair with a gesture of defiant bravado. Her eyes met his.

"I have to know," he told her, and his voice came out far more harshly than he had intended. "Are you here because you're frightened?"

"No," she said softly. "Would it matter?"

He smiled. "No. Not tonight."

And it was true. He had let her slip through his fingers once; tonight, no matter why she had come, he had to have her. But he also had to ask her.

And now he felt that he had forced her to come far enough. He could feel that she stood there, quivering, and that she could come no farther unless he did reach out to her.

He tossed his sheet aside and stood, and she saw that he was naked. Her eyes ran inadvertently over the length of his body and then met his once more. He started walking toward her, as slowly as she had come to him.

He paused, a hair's breadth away, not touching her. His voice was still harsh. "You don't owe me anything, you know," he told her.

"I know," she said simply.

His hands moved out to encircle her neck, his thumbs absently massaging her cheeks. And then they moved, sliding beneath the collar of the shirt to mold her shoulders and collarbone. His further advance was restricted by the buttons, and he withdrew for a moment, staring at her as he opened the first button, then following the movement of his fingers with his eyes until he reached the last.

His hands slipped beneath the collar of the shirt again. This time they followed the slopes of her shoulders, gently parting the shirt and forcing it to whisper from her form to the floor.

He stood back once more, making no aplogy for the long, silent assessment he gave her. Bryn stood still, her chin lifted as she tried not to shiver beneath his golden gaze.

And then she felt his arms about her. Strong and tender. He was still silent as he lifted her, staring into her eyes as he carried her to the bed and laid her upon it. His length slid along hers, and when the warm, callused touch of his palm caressed and held her hip, she at last sighed and slipped her arms around his neck. His lips touched hers, lightly, and then they were gone. He leaned upon an elbow, one hand upon her, a rough-haired leg angled over her softer one.

She saw his eyes, and she saw a million things in them. Tenderness. Caring. Empathy.

And a raw streak of desire. Glittering golden heat and a savage intensity tempered only by the streak of tenderness ...

Bryn felt herself shudder. But she didn't want to look away from him. His hunger seemed to warm her. To reach inside of her. To build a pulsing need deep within her that flowed through her heart and her limbs. Hot, sweet fire, centering low in her belly, spreading, burning with a wild thirst ...

His hand began to move, running lightly, caressingly, along her hip. His palm and fingers were rough, made hard by the force with which he beat his drums, yet his touch was like a brush of soaring wings, evocative and thrilling. Bryn caught her breath as she felt his hand move upon her, exploring her, knowing her with this new sense as he had with his eyes: thoroughly.

He drew soft circles over her belly with the heel of his palm, circles that climbed steadily higher so that she ached with anticipation. But his hand stopped below her breast, and he lowered his head to tease its crest with the tip of his tongue. She swallowed back a little cry. She longed for him so badly.

In answer to her need his hand closed over the swelling mound, and the demand of his mouth grew harder, tugging, nipping, sending currents of ecstasy sweeping through her. Her fingers tensely gripped his back. His body moved against hers like a rhythmic liquid fire, and she whimpered a soft cry of complete surrender to his desire, and to her own.

She nipped gently at his shoulder, bathing the tiny hurt with the tip of her tongue, washing it in a rain of passionate kisses. She moaned and arched to him as his lips moved across the valley of her breasts to render the same exquisite care a second time. And now, as his lips hungrily teased and assaulted the hardened crest and aching mound, his hand ran free again, exploring the angle of her hip, the flatness of her belly, the soft copper sheath of feminine hair, the slight swell of her thigh....

Then suddenly he rose above her. He watched her as he wedged his knee between her thighs, his arms holding his weight from her as he slid his length firmly between her legs. His features were tense and strained with passion; his eyes glittered with a pure golden fire. And yet there was still something controlled within them; he held himself above her, waiting....

He groaned, a harsh, guttural sound, eased his weight against her and caught her head between the rough grasp of his hands, his fingers entwining in her hair as his lips caught hers in a demanding, all consuming kiss.

His ardor was a delicious tempest. For one brief moment she was frightened, as one was frightened facing the swirling winds of a storm, or the soaring fall of a roller coaster. Already he had taken her past reason or thought, swept her into a realm of intensity from which there was no return. One step further and she would be completely his; with such a man it would mean total abandon. The heights of ecstasy would be hers; his passion would be wild and as demanding as it was giving.

The risk of pain would be as great as the thunder of joy.

His mouth moved against hers; his kisses roamed over her cheek and fell to her throat. But then she found that he was looking at her again, and that his golden eyes burned into hers with a ruthless and questing brilliancy.

"Do you trust me?" he whispered huskily.

"I don't know," she told him, her breath mingling with his, their lips almost touching.

"I want you...so much," he said. A shudder raked the length of his body. She knew that he wanted her; the potency of his male desire was hard against her thigh, taunting her, frightening her, thrilling her. The length of his tightly sinewed body thrilled and excited her. She was touching him, yet she wanted to touch more and more of him, to run her fingers, her lips over the clean-muscled bronzeness of him.

"Can I have you?" he asked softly, almost whimsically. And she knew that he, like she, wanted everything that could be given. In the most gentle terms, he asked for what he could easily take: submission to his will in the most primal roles of man and woman.

Bryn couldn't answer him. She locked her arms about his neck and tried to bury her head against his shoulder. He laughed softly and nuzzled his mouth against her ear in a sensuous whisper that sent the fires flaring through her again.

"Have me, Bryn. Touch me, know me, love me...."

His words trailed away as he rubbed his body along hers, sliding lower against it. His hands moved over her, their caress firm now, the power of his desire unleashed. His mouth covered her, his tongue, his kisses laved her, loving her with a wild, erotic passion she had never known. The winds soared as she had known they would; he was the driving tempest of his drums, and she was lost to the sheer force of primal rhythm.

She cried out when his kisses moved to her thighs, and her nails raked over his shoulders; then her fingers dug hard into his hair. The sensuous pleasure was so great that it was almost pain. Yet it did not stop there. His hands slipped beneath her, firmly molding the lush curve of her buttocks, arching her to his whim. His intimate caress was more than she could bear; she began to writhe and moan in an utter and splendid abandon.

Yet still he did not grant her mercy. She felt his triumph, his pleasure in her, and she cried out his name in a broken plea. He came to her then, holding her, caressing her, entangling his hands in her hair and whispering her name over and over. She moaned as she swept her fingers over his back, trailed the tips over his hard buttocks, pressed him from her so that she could hungrily shower his throat and chest with the damp caress of her tongue.

He shifted, wedging her thighs farther apart, and she touched him, her inhibitions swept away as if by the rush of the wind. She gasped with wonder at the heat and strength of him, shuddered as he moved with a swift, driving thrust and took her completely, sending the force of himself, the tension, the vibrancy, the unleashed power, into her, to become a part of her.

She had never known there would be anything like this. It was the excitement, the demand, the thrill—and the wild beat of his thundering drums. It was gentle, it was rough, savage and sweet. It swept through aeons of time, and yet it was over too quickly. The pinnacle was the most pure physical rapture she had ever known. She had twisted and turned and abandoned herself completely; she felt windswept and ravaged....

And absolutely delicious.

And when he had withdrawn from her, she still felt a part of him. As if she would be his for all the days of her life.

He moved away, easing his weight from her. She curled against him, the damp copper tendrils of her hair waving over his chest as she burrowed against it. He was silent for a long time, but she knew that he lay awake, his head propped on the crook of his elbow as he stared into the night.

After a time she felt his fingers idly smoothing her hair. "What happened to you?" he asked her softly.

Bryn felt the first twinge of remorse for her abandon. "What do you mean?" she asked tensely.

He chuckled softly. "Don't go getting rigid on me. I can't remember ever enjoying such pleasure with a woman as I have with you."

"And there have been plenty, I take it?" Bryn snapped acidly, her nails inadvertently digging into his flesh.

He chuckled softly and grabbed her hand. "Ouch! There have been a few, but not the scores you're trying to credit me with. And I was asking the questions, remember."

"I don't know what you mean," Bryn muttered uneasily, glad that her face was shielded from him by the tangle of her hair.

"Yes, you do. You were afraid of me. Before I did more than shake your hand."

Bryn shrugged. "You must know you make women nervous. You have an aura of leashed energy and...sexuality."

"Sexuality shouldn't be frightening."

Bryn bit her lip, then shrugged against him. He would probe at her until she answered him. "I was engaged once."

"Ah...and so all men become the enemy."

"No, not all men, and not the enemy. I just decided that I had to be careful for a while and avoid a certain type."

She could sense his frown. "What type is that? Don't tell me you were engaged to another musician?"

Bryn hesitated. What difference did it make if she told him or not? She rolled away from him, her arms encircling her pillow as she leaned her cheek against it. "No. I was engaged to a man named Joe Lansky. He was—is—a football player."

"Joe Lansky?" Lee whistled softly. "Big stuff with the NFL."

A surge of unease settled over her as he said the name. "Yes. He enjoys his share of fame. You know him?"

"We met briefly once. In L.A., at a benefit dinner. He seemed a decent sort."

"Oh, Joe is decent. He just...doesn't care much for children. Other people's, that is."

"Adam threw rice at him too, huh?"

"No, peas."

Lee laughed and swept her back into his arms despite her indignant protest. He kissed her on the nose. "I'm awfully glad you and Joe broke it off, Bryn," he told her huskily. "But I'm sorry that you compared me with him. Why did you?"

Bryn remained stiff against him. "You're both accustomed to fame and easy adoration."

"He cheated?"

"My fault, according to him. I couldn't be with him, and his groupies could."

"I see," Lee told her, and she felt a tightening of anger in his hold. "You assumed I jump into bed at any invitation?"

"Not exactly," she murmured.

"Then what, *exactly*?"

"Oh, I don't know!" Bryn exclaimed, trying to break the hold that kept her crushed against him, face-to-face. "I'm grounded in reality, and superstars live in a fantasy world."

"That's absurd. You're categorizing people. Just because Lansky broke it off with you—"

"Joe didn't break it off, I did," Bryn said wearily, rather than defensively. "He wanted me to drop everything and be at his beck and call. I couldn't do that. I didn't want to do that. And I think a regular man would have difficulty dealing with the package of commitments that come with me—much less a quote unquote 'idol.'"

She couldn't fathom his dark expression. "Quote unquote 'idols' are made of flesh and blood. The usual stuff. They bleed and hurt and fall in love. But if you and Lansky couldn't deal with your commitments, be glad you discovered it before you married him."

"I am," Bryn murmured uneasily. She still couldn't fathom the dark tension in his features.

As if he sensed her curiosity, he started idly trailing his fingers along her spine and abruptly changed the subject. "You have the sexiest build I've ever seen. I have to admit pure lust welled within me the moment I saw you."

There was something so honest in his statement that, despite its content, she started to smile. Lee returned the grin, but then he frowned as he saw her smile fade and her face go pale.

"What's wrong?"

"I just . . . I just started thinking about Adam. Oh, God, Lee! I've been here . . . like this . . . with you . . . when poor Adam—"

"Bryn!" Lee exclaimed, cradling her. "Hush. Don't worry about Adam. We'll get him back tomorrow, I promise!"

"How can you be sure! You told me we had to keep the pictures because it could be dangerous if we didn't discover what was in them! If these people could be dangerous later—"

"Bryn, why do you think that they took Adam and not Keith or Brian? Adam is a very little boy. He's not going to be able to point out where he's been, or cause any problems. You're a nice, sharp adult. There's a big difference. Bryn, I know that Adam is all right. He's their bargaining chip."

"But he's so little, and he's alone," Bryn murmured.

"Tomorrow, Bryn. If you just go to sleep, it will be time to start getting him back when you wake up."

"God! I want to sleep so badly. I just haven't been able to."

Lee kissed her forehead. "Didn't wear you out enough, did I?"

Bryn blushed. "You wore me out completely."

"Did I? We'll see in a minute or two. But since you're so wide awake and already worried, I want you to think about the country club. Do you remember anything about the background?"

Bryn thought for only a second. "Yes. I remember the Sweet Dreams motel."

"The what? Oh, that place with the glaring neon lights?"

"That's it."

"Well, that will be well worth looking into. What else?"

"Nothing, really. Oh . . . except the golfers. A whole horde of them came over a hill when I was shooting one roll."

"We'll have to look into that, too. We'll just keep blowing up the shots until we come up with something."

"I just can't see how there could be anything!" Bryn exclaimed, her tone frustrated and tired. "Believe it or not, I looked the proofs over very carefully before I gave them to Barbara. There just wasn't anything to be seen. Maybe it *is* just some mad fan determined to have a bunch of private shots of Lee Condor and his group."

"Bryn, you know that's ludicrous."

"But I looked—"

"At proofs. Little tiny pictures. Bryn, someone is obviously certain that there is something in those pictures. I would say that means that obviously there is. And we'll have to find out what."

She sighed softly and he smiled. "You need to get some sleep."

"I just can't seem to turn my mind off."

"Well, I believe that I can oblige in that direction . . ." His voice grew muffled and then trailed away as his lips fell to her shoulders. A tiny bite sent a shudder rippling through her; the rough velvet lick of his tongue turned the shudder into a liquid quiver. Bryn closed her eyes as he rolled her to her back.

He was right. The warm touch of his hands and the practiced strokes of his tongue could all too easily strip her mind of reason and thought. . . .

She became aware of the distant melody before she fully awoke. And as she struggled from a deep web of sleep, she began to realize that she was hearing the soft strains of the downstairs piano.

And Lee.

She frowned for a minute, blinking against the glow of dawn that bathed the room in pink and yellow light. The tune he sang was an old one, "Follow That Dream." And as she lay there, loathe to leave the comfort of bed, she felt a curious smile tugging at her lips, and a tenderness she didn't want to feel rising within her.

She had never heard him sing in person before. On the radio, on TV. Most of his music was rock, although he did a number of softer ballads. Still, she had never heard him like this.

His voice was as gentle and full of crystal clarity as the piano. It was a tenor, husky and deep. And just as he was an expert with the instrument he played, so he was with that that was a part of him. Bryn mused that certain people were definitely naturals, and for a moment she begrudged him the talent that had been a birthright; then she smiled again and allowed the timbre of his voice to sweep through her and touch her. She couldn't deny that she admired him, was attracted to him... and was also at least halfway in love with him.

That thought brought her wide awake.

Don't be a fool, she warned herself. Be with him now, since you cannot deny him. But never forget that this is only a strange interlude in your life....

An interlude that dealt with Adam!

Bryn scrambled out of bed and searched the floor for the shirt he had lent her. By the time she found it, she realized that the music had stopped. The house seemed silent.

It took her another several seconds of scrambling around at the foot of the bed to find her underwear. She didn't bother to run into the other room for her jeans; she was certain they were still alone in the house. She just rushed out of the bedroom and scampered hurriedly down the stairs.

Lee was nowhere in sight in the living room, but she heard a clatter of sound from the kitchen and moved quickly to the swinging doors. She stopped short when she stared at the butcher-block table.

She had been right on one count: Lee was in the kitchen, leaning against the counter as he spoke on the phone.

But she had been wrong to assume that they were alone in the house. Mick was sitting at the table, feet propped on the opposite chair as he sipped a cup of coffee. He didn't seemed surprised to see her, but his dark eyes glistened with amusement as he saw the red flush of embarassment that rushed to her cheeks.

"Morning, Bryn. Ready for coffee?"

She knew she would look rather absurd if she went rushing back through the swinging doors, so she convinced herself that Lee's shirt did cover her decently and walked on over to take a seat at the table.

"Coffee would be lovely, Mick. Thanks."

He smiled and poured her a cup from the pot that sat in the center of the table. There was a packet there, too, and he pushed it toward her. "This is the set of negatives and proofs that gets turned over."

Bryn glanced at him and then at Lee. He was murmuring monosyllables into the phone, but he grimaced dryly at her, and then smiled. It was a nice, natural look of reassurance. She glanced back to Mick, not questioning his understanding of the situation.

"You got them quickly! I never thought Kelly was awake this early, much less open for business."

"That Kelly seems to be a nice kid, and he likes you. We paid him well, but he was willing to do a super rush job even before I offered him a bonus."

"All right," Bryn heard Lee say. "See you tonight. Hopefully everything will go as planned."

He hung up the phone and walked to the table, poured himself a cup of coffee and sat opposite Bryn. He didn't offer her any explanation about his conversation, but slipped a bare foot along her calf instead. "You look rested," he said softly.

"Do I?" she murmured, her lashes falling to her cheeks.

"Ummm. In fact, you look great. A little tousled, maybe, but I always did like a bit of a wild look."

"Thanks," she murmured dryly.

"Hey, you two. I'm here, remember?" Mick queried. "And I'm not really sure I can handle this! My own sex life has been going all to hell for the past week!"

Both Bryn and Lee stared at Mick, startled. Then they laughed, and when their eyes met again, it was with a mute pleasure and amusement that scared Bryn.

It was too, too easy to like way too much about Lee Condor. She sobered quickly and said, "What now, Lee?"

"You get dressed and we go on over to your place. Mick goes on into work and explains that neither of us will be in, and he and Andrew and Perry get to crack the whip for the day. If I'm playing my hunches right, your phone will ring by ten o'clock."

"Do you really think so?" Bryn asked huskily.

"Yes, I really think so."

Mick stood up and stretched, then kissed Bryn quickly on the cheek. "Good luck, gorgeous. I'll be banking on you."

"Thanks," Bryn murmured. Lee was rising to walk Mick out to the battered front door. Bryn followed them both with her cup of coffee in hand. They were discussing the rehearsal, and Lee was advising Mick to get everyone working in costume. Mick said something about the door and offered to pick up a new one with a double dead-bolt.

"Great, that will save me a trip," Lee said; then his eyes fell on Bryn. "Run on up and get dressed," he told her. She had a feeling that he was going to say something to Mick that he didn't want her to hear, but she was too anxious to get back to her town house to disobey his soft command. She hurried back upstairs.

In the guest room she found her bra, jeans and shoes, and quickly donned them. A shower would have to wait, but she longed to wash up, so she walked into the room's ample bath, only to discover that there was no soap or towels. Or toothpaste. And if she couldn't brush her teeth, she could at least smother them with some toothpaste and feel a little better.

She walked back to Lee's room. His bathroom, as she had discovered late last night, was huge. The tiled tub was equipped with a Jacuzzi and was almost the size of her bedroom at the town house. There was a separate, glass-encased shower, double sinks, a linen closet and a wall of glass medicine chests. She opened the linen closet and was thrilled to discover a stack of new toothbrushes, piles of soap and neat stacks of washcloths and towels.

She washed her face and scrubbed her teeth, then realized that she had left the linen closet open. She absently walked back over to close it, then paused.

Along with the customary items—the towels and soap and such—she was surprised to see a stack of music sheets. Curiously she picked one up. The ink that comprised the notes was sightly faded; the paper was faintly yellowed. The sheets were not brittle, not like old, old paper, but she was certain that the music had been written at least a year or two ago.

She couldn't read music, so her eyes automatically fell to the lyrics scripted below.

Time has drifted by, my love, Leaves have blown, and white flakes fall, Still I wonder why, my love, How love could cause it all. "Oh, Victoria ... Death departs, The savage heart.
What did I see in violet eyes, That made me blind, immune to lies? Had I but seen, I might have been, The man to let you touch the skies; Oh, Victoria ... Dust and ashes, Tattered heart.

"What the hell do you think you're doing?"

Bryn started violently. She stared from the paper in her hand to the bathroom doorway to find Lee standing there, hands on his hips, bronzed features tense and dark and twisted into a menacing scowl. She was so stunned to see him there when she had become so engrossed in his lyrics that at first she didn't register the depth of his anger.

"Lee, I've never heard this song. It's so pretty, and sad—"

She broke off with a startled gasp as he took a furious stride toward her and brutally wrenched the paper from her hand, crumpling it into his fist. "Stay the hell out of things that aren't yours and don't concern you!" he ground out, his jaw rigid and his eyes branding her with his wrath. He didn't give her a chance to reply; he spun around and left her. For once she heard his footsteps clearly. She heard the hard slap of his feet against the carpeted bedroom floor—and the sharp slam of the door.

Sudden tears stung her eyes; he had made her feel like a child, a thief and a nosy intruder all in one. What had she done? Nothing but open a closet door for a towel ...

The hurt brought anger, and humiliation. She had spent the night very intimately in bed with him, but let her take a glance at his life, and she might have been a total stranger, or any one of a number of women who had provided entertainment, but never entered into his soul....

"Bastard!" she hissed, clenching her fists and wishing fervently that she had obeyed her instincts for self-preservation and used him, instead of allowing him to use her.

She heard his shout from downstairs despite the fact that she was in the bathroom and he had slammed the bedroom door.

"Bryn! Let's get going!"

At that moment she would rather have jumped out the window than obey any of his commands. But thoughts of Adam rose within her mind and welled within her heart. She clenched her teeth, strode as furiously as he had across the bedroom, slammed the bedroom door in her wake, then managed to sprint down the stairs with a modicum of control.

She didn't look at him as she swept by him and out the front door he had opened for her. When he asked her for her van keys, she didn't argue with him, but dug into her front pocket and produced them. Once inside the car, she stared out the window.

She felt his tension, and she knew that he glanced her way several times as he left his secluded road behind and entered the stream of traffic. She continued to stare at the distant Sierra Nevada.

They were nearing her town house when at last he spoke. "I'm sorry, Bryn."

"Fine," she said curtly.

"I mean it, Bryn. I'm very sorry. I never should have snapped at you like that."

She glanced at him, unable to ease the anguish he had evoked in her heart. "I said fine."

He had pulled the van into her driveway behind Barbara's car. Bryn started to hop out before he had put it into Park. She heard him swearing that she was a little idiot as he pulled the key from the ignition, but she was already halfway to the door, which had opened, as Barbara, expecting them, peeked her head out.

And then Bryn forgot about the petty quarrel that had cast her into an emotional turmoil. Because even as she reached the porch, the phone began to ring.

She met Barbara's panicked eyes, froze for a split second, then rushed into the kitchen. On the fifth ring she breathlessly grabbed the receiver.

"Hello?"

She heard husky, macabre laughter. "Miss Keller?"

"Yes."

"One, two, three, four, five, six, seven; All good children go to heaven!"

"No! No!" she screamed hysterically into the receiver, tears stinging her eyes and spilling over onto her cheeks. She could barely hold the phone. She was going to drop it; she was going to fall, cast into darkness by fear....

No, she wasn't going to fall. She was suddenly supported by strong arms; the phone taken from her hand.

"Listen, joker, whoever you are, you needn't bother with any more threats. This is Lee Condor—yes, I'm in on it. Obviously I'm in on it. What do you expect when my house is all shot up? But your problems are over. Just give the little boy back and the pictures are yours. No tricks. All we want is the boy."

Lee glanced down into her eyes as he listened to the whisperer. Then he laughed harshly. "Don't worry. Bryn will be the one to bring them to you. I'll be completely out of the way. I'll put her on and you can negotiate the details."

He pressed the phone into her hand. She stared at him, and she felt as if some of his strength radiated into her. She brought the receiver to her mouth, and her voice was sure and strong.

"You'll get the pictures. I'll drop them wherever you want. But first I want to talk to Adam. *Now*."

She bit her lip and began to pray.

"Aunt Bwyn?"

Tears filled her eyes again as she heard the pathetic little voice.

"Adam! Oh, Adam! Are you okay, honey? Are you hurt? Adam, talk to me!"

A jagged sob and a sniff came over the wire. "Not hurt. I want to come home, Aunt Bwyn. Want to come home."

"Oh, honey, you're going to come home! You're going to come soon. I promise! Adam? Adam?"

"See, Miss Keller?" The whisperer was back on. "He's just fine. And he'll stay that way as long as you cooperate. And make sure that your boyfriend does, too."

"We will cooperate!" Bryn cried out bitterly. "I've already told you that—"

"Yeah, I heard you. But I don't trust Condor, honey, so you keep him in line."

Bryn glanced nervously at Lee. She knew that he was purposely standing close enough to hear both sides of the conversation.

"Lee isn't going to interfere. He's promised me."

The whisperer chuckled. "I told you that you charm your way into a man's good graces, Miss Keller. You just keep being charming. 'Cause remember, I'm good. One step I don't like, and I can get this little kid again. Or a bigger little kid. You can't watch them every second, Miss Keller. Keep that in mind."

"I want Adam back," Bryn said. "Where and how?"

"You haven't messed with the negatives, have you, Miss Keller?"

Bryn glanced sharply at Lee, but replied with an exasperated sigh, "Of course not! When the hell would I have been able to?"

"Okay, honey, just see that you don't. 'Cause I'll be watching you, and I'll know. Now, when the time is right I want you—and you alone—to meet at the Cutter Pass—"

Bryn's startled scream cut off the whisperer's words as Lee yanked the receiver from her.

"Nothing doing," he told the caller angrily. "Then you'll have the pictures, the kid and Bryn. Think of something else. We don't want the damned pictures, but I sure as hell don't trust you, either."

"Lee!" Bryn gasped, horrified and furious. She'd happily go anywhere to get Adam back. Lee shook his head at her, his expression a dark scowl. She clawed at his hand, and he pulled her to him so that they could both hear.

"You got a suggestion I can trust, Condor?" the voice mocked.

"Yes. Yes, I do. Bryn can sit on that big red couch in the lobby of the Mountain View. There's a pay phone there. I'll get the number. As soon as she learns that the boy is walking up to the porch here, she'll drop the pictures on the couch and leave."

"Uh-uh. Too public."

"She isn't going anywhere that isn't public."

"What kind of guarantees do I have that someone else isn't going to be around? Like you, Condor." The whisperer laughed crudely. "I don't feel like getting scalped by some punk rocker."

Lee ignored the gibe. "I'll be here. On the porch."

"You seem to think there's more than one person in on this, Condor."

"I know there's more than one person in on this."

"All right," the whisperer said. "No tricks. Remember, I can shoot the boy while he's still standing on the porch."

"I hear you."

"And make sure you don't have any cars cruising too close to that town house. I see anything the least suspicious and there won't be any kid. Got it."

"Yeah, I got it."

"Just watch your step, Condor. If something goes wrong, it will be real easy to terrorize a woman with three kids for a long, long time to come. The exchange will be at ten. One hour from now. And like I said—"

"Don't worry. Nothing is going to go wrong. But do you want to know something?"

"What?"

"You watch your step. 'Cause if anything happens to that kid, if he has one little scratch on him, I won't scalp you. I'll send an arrow piercing straight to your heart. Now I think we understand each other."

"Yeah, Condor, you and I understand each other real good. You would try something if you could, Condor. But thanks to your lady friend, I don't think you'll take any chances. Still, just to keep her on edge—and you in line—I think I'll keep the little boy for a while."

"What?" Lee demanded hoarsely. Bryn started pulling on his arm.

"You heard me. The exchange is going to be Sunday. I'll give you a call in the morning and set the time. And remember, I'll be watching you both. I'll be watching her darkroom. And do you know what I want to see, Condor? Nothing, except two people coming and going from work. Got that?"

Bryn had heard. She wrenched the receiver back. Tears had formed in her eyes. And she started shouting hysterically. "*No!* I want Adam today. So help me God, I don't care about your pictures. I want my nephew! Please, please—"

She broke off, strangling on her tears.

"You get him Sunday, Miss Keller. Just so long as you and the rock star behave. Be home; you'll hear from me by nine."

The line went dead. Bryn heard the dull buzz.

"*No!*" she screeched, throwing the receiver so that it fell to the floor. "*No, no, no!*"

"Bryn... Lee began, but she was totally out of control, unable to believe that she was going to have to endure the torture and torment of four more long—unendurably long—days without having Adam back. The grief, the horror and the fear ripped and wrenched through her; she was crying and laughing—and she needed a scapegoat to be able to accept the horror she needed to accept, so she turned on Lee with a vengeance, pounding her fists against his chest with all her strength.

"It's you! He knows you want to pull something, so he's keeping Adam away from me. It's you.... It's all your fault, Lee. Oh, damn you, damn you, *damn you!*"

"Bryn, stop it! Bryn!" He tried to hold her, but she had a strength born of her terror and fury. She was like a wildcat, hysterical, tearing into him. For a moment he allowed her to scream and cry and curse him with knotted fists flying, praying it would help. But she seemed to grow more hysterical by the second. "*Bryn!*" She didn't even hear him. He closed his eyes for a minute, feeling all her pain and aching to relieve it. Then he closed his arms around her, forcing her to the floor and pinning her there.

For a minute she fought him, still wild, flailing and shouting. He held her firmly, hands at her wrists, knees about her hips. "Bryn..." he said more softly, and at last she went still, staring at him with dull and tear-filled eyes.

"I can't do it," she murmured pathetically. "I can't wait. I can't walk around normally when Adam..."

"Bryn..."

A soft, feminine voice had broken in. Barbara's, as she knelt down beside them. "Bryn, you're going to wake Brian and Keith, honey, if you haven't already. You've just got to be strong, for them. You don't want them scared to pieces now, do you?"

Bryn gazed at Barbara. She had forgotten that her friend was there. And beyond Barbara's shoulder, she saw Andrew. Watching her with so much empathy and concern.

And above her... was Lee. Holding her, not hurting her. Tolerating her... no matter what she did to him.

She started to weep quietly. He shifted his weight and pulled her into his arms, soothing her as if she were a child. His fingers tenderly smoothed her hair back, gently caressing her cheek.

"Adam is fine, Bryn. You know that; you talked to him. The waiting is hard. I know how hard, Bryn. But we've got to handle it. We've got to."

"I can't, Lee. I feel as if there's a knife in me—"

"Hush. You can. You're strong, Bryn. You'll do it."

Was it his faith in her? Or was it just that the boys chose to come down the stairs then? Brian and Keith. The older two. Wise in their childish ways, ready to pick up on trouble.

She couldn't let them know this kind of fear and pain.

"What were you shouting about, Aunt Bryn?" Brian demanded.

"Oh, you know your aunt. What a temper!" Lee answered smoothly for her. "She was mad at me, but she's decided to forgive me. Hey, aren't you two supposed to be at school? We'd better get going."

"Are you going to take us to school, Lee?" Keith asked, wide-eyed.

"Wow!" Brian said. He looked at Keith. "The kids will be green! Man, it's too bad Adam has to miss this!"

Somehow Bryn had managed to leave the support of Lee's arms. "Get dressed and get on down here for breakfast, you two. On the double. We're running horribly late."

And somehow, somehow she managed to get through the day. Like a mechanical being. Lee and Andrew took the boys to school. She and Barbara showered and went to work.

Lee came home with her, and they sat through dinner with the children.

And miraculously, she fell to sleep on the couch, emotionally worn and exhausted, her head against his shoulder.

She had survived her first day of waiting.

Chapter 10

When she awoke the next morning the pain was still with her. And the fear, and the horrible anxiety, but she seemed to have it all in check, at a rational level.

She was in her own bed. Apparently Lee had undressed her and put here there. She stared about the room numbly, and at last her eyes came to rest on Lee. He was standing by her dresser, slipping his watch onto his wrist. He caught her eyes in the mirror and turned to her.

"Morning."

She tried to smile, but the effort fell flat. He walked over to her and sat on the bed by her knees.

"You okay?"

She nodded. "Yes."

He picked up one of her hands idly and massaged the palm. "I—I guess I have to get up and get Brian and Keith going..." she said.

"They're already at school. I took them."

"You took them?" Bryn mumbled, a little dazed, a little incredulous. "But..."

"Don't worry. I fed them, and they're neat and presentable."

She nodded, then murmured, "I guess my neighbors will all realize shortly that I'm...sleeping with you."

"Does it matter?"

"I...no, not for me. I was just thinking about the kids."

"Bryn, I hope you know I wouldn't do anything to hurt you, your reputation, the boys, or your life-style here. But I can't leave you alone now, either. Not while...this...is going on."

"I know," Bryn whispered. A shudder rippled through her, but strangely it made her feel a little better. She looked at him and saw in his eyes all the things that made him the powerful and charismatic man that he was. Warmth, strength and sensitivity.

"Lee?"

"Yes?"

"Thank you."

He smiled and brushed her chin with his knuckles. "We've got a ways to go yet. I'm going to go down and put more coffee on. Get dressed. We've got to go to work, remember?"

He left her. Bryn rose, shivered and hurried into the bathroom for a shower. The days would pass, she promised herself, and then she thought about her nudity again.

It seemed strangely natural, even comforting, that Lee had taken on such an intimate task, that of putting her to bed. Not a sexual act, but rather one that spoke of a longtime relationship, as if they had been lovers and friends for aeons.

She was going to get hurt, she warned herself. But it didn't matter. Nothing could really matter much now. Not until she had Adam home again.

She showered and dressed, and she felt a little stronger. Once the day had passed she would be a day closer to Adam.

By the time they had spent the day at the Fulton place, taken Brian and Keith out for pizza and put them to bed, Bryn had calmed herself to a point where she was fairly rational and willing to talk to Lee about the situation.

She made tea and brought it out to the parlor. Lee was on the sofa, head back, eyes momentarily closed. He rubbed them, then opened them as she approached.

He's been so good, Bryn thought for the hundredth time.

"Tea...great," he said as he accepted a mug.

Bryn sat beside him. "Lee, the more I think about it, the more I don't get this. Shouldn't this guy want the pictures back right away? I mean, the longer we have them, the longer we have to look at them."

Lee shrugged and stretched an arm across the back of the sofa to tug lightly at a stray lock of her hair. "I've thought about that. I'm sure he's thought about it, too. He just knows he has you over a barrel with Adam. And I don't think he's really afraid of our looking at a set of proofs—or even a set of normal prints. What's in the picture, or pictures, is small. Something you'd only find by constant enlargement.

Something hard to find. You'd have to work in your darkroom for hours to get to it."

"Then why go to so much trouble to get the pictures back?"

"Because it *is* there—somewhere—and could be found," Lee said simply. He sipped his tea and looked at her. "Bryn, I think we should move to my house."

"Your house! I can't! He's going to call—"

"We'll be here for the call. But I called yesterday to have a security system installed. My place will be safer."

"I don't know. The boys..."

"The boys will love it. It's huge, and it has a pool."

"But..."

"I'm right, Byrn. You know I am. Please don't argue with me."

Bryn fell silent. Lee began to talk again. "I think we should do something else. That Dirk Hammarfield—the politician I find so sleazy—asked the group to a political dinner this Saturday night. I think he wants us to play, and I think we're going to do it. You and Barbara will come, and maybe, just maybe, we'll find something out."

"No! It could be dangerous when Adam is still gone. Lee, you're crazy!"

"No, I'm not, damm it, Bryn. Look, we're not going to fool around with the pictures until Adam is back. We're doing everything that we're supposed to. But eventually we will need to know what's going on. Think, Bryn! Do you want to go through your life like this, constantly worried that this guy could strike again? And if Hammarfield is the culprit, do you want a kidnapper in public office? Besides, it will be something to keep you occupied and sane on Saturday night."

Bryn was still looking for excuses. "What about Brian and Keith? I can't leave them, and if you want Barabara and I both to go..."

"They'll be at my house and I can get my housekeeper to come in and stay. Marie is a doll; they'll love her. And I've known her for years; she's responsible, gentle and totally reliable."

Again Bryn fell silent. Why not? It would probably make sense to go to the dinner. But could she carry it off? Could she see Hammarfield and act as if everything was normal? No, more than that! Lee wanted her to keep her eyes and ears open, to seek out evidence. Could she do it?

Yes...she could. She was learning that she could do what she had to do. She was managing to get through these days....

Bryn gazed covertly at Lee. At his profile, then at the hand that wound around his cup. She thought suddenly about his anger when she had found his song, but then she realized that she didn't want to think. He had helped her so much. He had been there to hold her and give her strength and security, never pressuring her.

She needed him. Wanted him very badly...tonight.

She set her teacup down and his eyes met hers. "I'm—I'm going up to bed," she told him, then hesitated just slightly. "Are you coming?"

He stared into her eyes for a long time, then nodded slowly. He stood and put an arm around her. Together they walked up the stairs.

And that night Bryn made love to him with a fierce and desperate passion.

So this is a political dinner, Bryn thought, looking around as she sat beside Barbara at their assigned table in the grand ballroom of the Mountain View hotel. The chandeliers gleamed like diamonds rather than cut glass, and the footsteps of the uniformed waiters were deadened by the plushness of the maroon carpet. The tableware glimmered and gleamed; women dressed to the nines in jewels and furs clung to the arms of men decked out handsomely in tuxedos.

It could have been interesting to be here. Intriguing. If only she weren't so overcome by nerves. If only Adam were at Lee's house with his brothers...

But this was it, she told herself. Tomorrow, tomorrow, she would have Adam back. After all the waiting, the end at last seemed close. That she had only one more night to endure was a promise of happiness, and despite her nerves she felt a rush of adrenaline something like excitement. Occasionally that excitement dropped and she was beset by nerves again. Something was going to happen—soon. She would find something out tonight...and if she didn't, she had only to awaken in the morning and events would be set in motion for her to get her nephew back....

She stared around again, suddenly very tense. Was Dirk Hammarfield—the ever-smiling politician—a kidnapper? She had looked through the prints today, but at five by seven they were too small to show much in the background. Once Adam was back she would use the negatives to enlarge the backgrounds until...

Her mind began to move in circles...Hammarfield...the Sweet Dreams motel...pictures...politics...Adam!

Barbara jabbed her with a toe beneath the table. "Stop staring, Bryn!" she commanded. "We'll look suspicious."

Bryn looked at her friend, and new thoughts filled her mind. That afternoon she and Lee had returned from his house to her town house so that she could choose something dressy for the night. When Byrn and Lee had left on Friday, Andrew had suggested that he stay there—to keep an eye on things. Bryn hadn't thought much about it. Not until she had gone there today and discovered Barbara's things—as well as Andrew's—all over her bedroom.

She had never realized that anything was going on between the two. Not that she had realized much of *anything* since Adam had been taken. She had been a little shocked. Not shocked, surprised. And then worried. But Barbara and Andrew were both adults, and as much as Bryn cared for Barbara, she had no right to question her friend's affairs.

We're both going to get hurt, though, she thought sadly. Walloped.

"Well, what do you think?" Barbara murmured, nudging her. They were alone at their table, since Lee and Andrew had eaten quickly, then hurried backstage to check on some last-minute wiring details.

"I think that half the national debt could have been paid with the cost of this dinner," Bryn whispered back.

Barbara laughed nervously. "I mean, what do you think of our would-be congressman?"

Bryn shrugged. Dirk Hammarfield had just finished speaking to the assembled group. "I think Lee and Andrew were only pretending to have something to do to escape the 'thank yous.'"

Barbara lowered her voice even further. "I mean, do you think that he's the whisperer?"

The chills that were never fully quenched started to flutter within Bryn. Could he be the whisperer? Could he be the man who was holding Adam this very minute?

He didn't look it. He just didn't look the part.

"I don't know," she told Barbara truthfully. "But for some reason, I just can't believe it. He's too pleasant and too married!"

"The 'too married' men are the ones you have to watch out for!" Barbara warned.

Bryn raised a cryptic brow to her friend, and allowed herself to muse curiously on Barbara's appearance. She had never seen Barb look better. Her dress was simple and sleek, made of beige silk, and her short blond hair swung freely about her features. Bryn decided that the reason Barbara looked so spectacular was the glow about her face and the diamond sparkle of her eyes. "Let's not talk about it," Bryn murmured. "I'm nervous enough already."

"What do you want to talk about?"

Bryn shrugged. Not Hammarfield. Not Adam. "I'd like to know about you—and Andrew."

Barbara smiled without a blush or a pause. "I think he's wonderful. He's sensitive and caring, not afraid to have fun, and irresistibly sexy. And considering his position in life, he's admirably unaffected. I've met a lot of so-called stars. All of *these* guys are unique. They're grounded in reality."

Bryn played with the swizzle stick in her half-consumed gin and tonic. "What I mean is, what do you think will come of it?"

Barbara laughed. "We haven't been seeing each other all that long, you know."

"I know, but if you like someone that well . . ."

"Then you walk the road and see where it leads."

"Aren't you ever afraid?"

"Bryn, you care very much about Lee, don't you?"

"I—I don't know. That's a lie. Yes, I care about him," Bryn admitted softly. "But there's so much about him, about his past. So many things I'm afraid of, so many things that I don't understand."

Barbara was about to reply, but she halted as their attention was drawn to the stage. Hammarfield managed to introduce the band quickly; there was wild applause, and then the curtains parted to reveal Lee and the group. They started playing with a loud crash of the drums; Lee began to sing a rock number from their first album.

Bryn, as always, felt his voice sweep around her and embrace her. Like him, it was rugged and masculine, a burnished, rough velvet. The group had worn tuxedos tonight, with ruffled white shirts.

Bryn had never seen Lee in such formal attire before, and she felt a warm flush rush over her now just as it had when she had first seen him dress that evening. The elegant white shirt enhanced his dark good looks, contrasting sharply with the rugged angles and planes of his features.

I will never be able to stop wanting him, she admitted ruefully to herself. I allowed myself to fall, and now I will never be able to escape....

Barbara turned back to her, touching her shoulder and leaning closer so that she could be heard. "I hate to sound like a philosopher," Barbara said dryly, "but some sayings are true. Nothing good in life comes easy."

"The video will be done soon."

"And you're thinking that he'll be gone as smoothly as he came? I can't tell you that that won't happen, Bryn. I *can* tell you that it's obvious he's entirely taken with you."

Bryn grimaced. "Maybe just because...because he feels responsible for everything that's happened. I mean—" she lowered her voice to a hushed whisper again "—all this started with the pictures that I took of him."

Barbara sniffed. "I don't think you know your man very well, honey. If he felt responsible, he'd be responsible. But if he didn't want to be with you, he wouldn't be. And any fool could see the sexual attraction between the two of you from the beginning."

"Umm," Bryn murmured dryly. She was about to retort to Barbara's bluntness when she felt a tap on her shoulder. She turned around to see Dirk Hammarfield staring down at her with his perpetual smile.

"Enjoying the evening, ladies?"

Bryn felt the chill again. How long had he been there? Was this benignly smiling man the same one who had made a living hell out of her life?

She wanted to shout at him, she wanted to scream, Where is Adam? Where is my nephew now? If I don't get him back tomorrow, if he's been harmed the least little bit I'll . . .

What? What? *She* was the one completely at someone's mercy. What was she doing here? What could she possibly find out?

"It's lovely, thank you," Bryn heard herself say. Then she started babbling. "The roast duck was absolutely delicious. And that salad dressing! Out of this world."

"The artichoke hearts were wonderful," Barbara added. They glanced at each other. Did being nervous instantly turn one into a blithering idiot, incapable of normal speech?

"Glad to hear the food was good," Hammarfield replied. Was his smile really benign? Or did it have a malicious twist? "Seems," Hammarfield continued, indicating the stage, "that Condor has chosen a nice soft ballad just for me. Would you share a dance with me, Miss Keller?"

No! she wanted to scream.

She gave him her hand and a smile as plastic as his own. "I'd love to, Mr. Hammarfield."

Dirk Hammarfield glanced at Barbara. "If you don't mind . . .?"

"Not at all," Barbara said quickly.

Bryn felt uncomfortable as soon as they reached the dance floor. Dirk Hammarfield believed in dancing cheek to cheek and body to body. Bryn tried to move away from him, but without making a scene she wasn't going to achieve much. Damn Lee! She was going to have to tell him to play fast tunes all night.

She managed to pull her face far enough away from Dirk's shoulder to talk. "So, Mr. Hammarfield, how's the campaigning going?"

"Good. Great!" he told her boisterously. His hand slipped to the small of Bryn's back, then to her rear as he made a sudden swing with his body.

Bryn realized that they were right in front of the stage. She gazed up to see that although Lee's voice hadn't faltered, nor had he missed a beat on his drums, he was staring at her. And she knew that particular glimmer in his eyes. Anger. Was he thundering particularly hard on the drums? She wanted to hit him. What did he think? That she liked being pawed by the polician? It had been his idea that she come here.

"How did your pictures come out, Miss Keller?"

Bryn's heart skipped a beat. "I really don't know," she lied. "I gave Lee the film and the proofs right after they were taken."

She felt as if her knees would give way, but she kept her eyes on his, determined to see if he would react at all to the lie.

"What a pity. I would have loved to have seen them." No reaction; his eyes stayed steadily on hers. His hand was slipping lower and lower. He was almost caressing her.

She ground her teeth, grabbed his hand and smiled. She couldn't stand it anymore. He could very well be a kidnapper.... He could be holding Adam right now...and he had the audacity to be touching her like a lover. She would start screaming, or faint or get sick. It would have to end. She wasn't getting anywhere anyway.

"Where is your wife, Mr. Hammarfield?" she asked. "I haven't had the pleasure of meeting her yet."

Hammarfield paled visibly. He opened his mouth, about to reply, but then he turned abruptly. Bryn realized he had been tapped on the shoulder.

"May I cut in on you, sir? I suppose it's a rude thing to do to the man of the hour, but I'm afraid I might never get another chance to dance with the lady."

"Of course, of course!" Hammarfield patted the newcomer on the back, and Bryn grinned broadly. She had been saved from minor-molestation-on-the-dance-floor and possible illness by the young golfer, Mike Winfeld. He was wholesome and attractive with his out-of-doors appeal, and Bryn was definitely grateful to see him.

"May I?" he asked her.

"Of course!" she murmured. It was really a gasp of relief. This whole thing had been a mistake.

He clasped her to him and quickly danced them across the floor. "I didn't think I'd get a chance to see you so soon," he said reproachfully.

"I really have been busy!" Bryn said.

"Photographing the famous?"

"Dancing for Lee's video. I'm a dancer, too," Bryn said.

"You bet you are," he told her approvingly.

"How's your game going?" Bryn asked him.

"Oh, great. Every once in a while you hit a sand trap, but there's usually a way out of it. When can you do my photos?"

"I really don't know yet," Bryn said apologetically. "I'm still working for Lee."

"Oh," he told her sadly, spinning around again. Bryn decided that she was glad that she was a dancer. Only a professional dancer could hope to keep up with his dips and turns.

Then she found herself being clasped as tightly to him as she had been to Hammarfield. And golfers—as well as politicians—had roving hands. The problem with Winfeld was that he was so fast, she couldn't move quickly enough to escape his roaming fingers....

Lee was glad that playing music was like breathing to him. His mind was wandering. No, damn it! It wasn't wandering. It was set on Bryn.

It was miserable to watch her with Hammarfield and with the golfer. She was dressed in a thin-strapped, black silk dress that was belted at the waist. The silk clung gracefully to her curves, and when she danced . . . when she moved . . . she was fluid and lithe and beautiful.

And as enticing as a rose in full bloom.

He shouldn't be watching her, he thought. Drumming was like breathing, but the drums wouldn't play themselves. And although he had sung this song a thousand times, at this rate . . .

He couldn't look away from her. And he couldn't stop his anger from rising and sky rocketing. She was laughing as she talked to the golfer. Laughing . . . and her eyes were sparkling with a beautiful radiance.

You don't own her, he warned himself sharply.

But he felt as if he did, in a way. Because he was completely entranced with her. She was naked magic in his arms at night, sleek and satin passion. To see another man touching her . . . that way. . . .

It made him feel like being savage, all right.

His biceps strained and bulged beneath the white ruffled shirt; he sang the last words of the song, and rolled out a fading beat.

He barely heard the applause. He had been stupid to do the dinner. Nothing was going to be achieved tonight.

What had he expected?

Something . . . something to happen.

But nothing had. Except that his temper had been stretched to the snapping point.

"Hammarfield is interested in the pictures," Bryn said as Lee revved the engine of his car. It was late; only the cleanup crews still remained. And Lee had been distantly silent since she had met him on the stage when the band had been breaking down their equipment.

Lee kept his eyes on the road and replied with a low grunt.

"Are you listening to me, Lee? Hammarfield asked me about the pictures."

"I heard you. What else did he ask you about?"

"What?" Bryn murmured, confused by the hostility that lay beneath the question.

He glanced her way briefly, a quick gaze of yellow fire, before turning his attention to the road once again. "I asked you what else he talked about."

Bryn shrugged, still not understanding the brooding emotion simmering within him, but finding herself on the defensive anyway. "I don't remember."

"I see. It's hard to listen very closely when you're dancing that close."

"Dancing that close! It wasn't my idea!"

"Umm. You never thought about pushing the man away, I assume."

"I did!"

"That's funny. I never found you ineffective at repulsing a man when you chose to do so. And what about that jock golfer?"

"Mike Winfeld?"

"Is that his name?"

Bryn felt her anger rise to meet his. "Look, Lee, I don't know what your problem is tonight, but I'm not going to sit here and take this from you. It was your idea to play for this dinner, and your idea that Barbara and I come along. You insisted that I might get something out of Hammarfield. You—" She bit off her words, determined not to fly into a name-calling fit. But she was furious. The night had been incredibly tense to begin with, and now he was suddenly coming down on her for things that had been his fault. "You bastard!" she grated out against her best intentions. "How do you think I felt? The man might be still holding Adam. I didn't want to be anywhere near him!"

"Hmm. And what about Winfeld?"

"Winfeld? Just drop it, Lee."

"You told me you liked golfers."

She was worn and frazzled—and not at all prepared for the conversation. Tears stung her eyes, and she determined to fight back—hurting him as she was hurt. "All right—I love golfers! It's none of your damn business. Drop it!"

"Bryn," he began, but then he mutterd. "Oh, hell!"

He shifted in the driver's seat, keeping his steely glare upon the highway. They would be turning off in a minute. Bryn thought, arriving at his house. It seemed as if the car were filled with a static electricity. She wasn't terribly sure she wanted to go into the house with him. The rigid strain on his features, the vise grip he held on the steering wheel, the lethal tension that radiated from him, all promised an explosion waiting to happen.

"It wasn't my idea to watch the woman I'm sleeping with being petted publicly on a dance floor," he said suddenly.

"Petted!" Bryn snapped. "Damn it, Lee—"

The car veered sharply into his drive and jerked to a halt before the front door.

He turned to her, a pulse throbbing along his jaw. "Petted. Yes, the word fits, I think. What else would you call it when a man's hands are all over you?"

Bryn stared at him for a minute, wishing she could strike him, hoping she wouldn't burst into ridiculous tears. The attack was unfair. "I didn't want to be where I was!"

"You were smiling away a mile a minute at the golfer. Seems to me you were quite happy where you were."

Bryn hopped out of the front seat, slamming the door behind her. Her van was parked in front of the garage, and she started walking toward it, her heels clicking sharply against the gravel driveway.

"Where the hell do you think you're going?" he called after her, crawling from the driver's seat and staring after her.

"Home," she said briefly, fumbling in her bag for her keys. "I'll get things ready for Adam to come back tomorrow. With or without your help. And I'll be here to get the boys before they wake up."

"No you will not, because you're not leaving."

"Oh? Because I'm 'the woman you're sleeping with'? You don't own me, Lee. You don't even have a lease on me. And since I've already been 'petted' for the night, I think I'd prefer to sleep in my own bed." Her fingers locked around her keys and she pulled them from her small clutch purse.

He started to swear softly, and his shoes crunched loudly as he strode across the gravel. Bryn felt her heart begin to pound viciously in her chest. Had she wanted him to stop her in her anger? Or had she believed that he might deny his own words and say that she was much, much more than just the woman he was sleeping with?

She wasn't sure; she just knew that she was suddenly frightened. She turned to the van, but she knew that she'd never get the door open before he got there.

She didn't. She felt his hand on her shoulder, his grip painful as he spun her around.

He spoke softly, enunciating each word carefully. "Bryn—even if I hated, loathed and despised you, and if your feelings for me were exactly the same, I wouldn't let you get into that van and drive away. Not tonight. Now act reasonably and turn around and *get in the house!*"

"Reasonably?" Bryn shrieked. It was a foolish thing to do. His lips compressed and his eyes seemed to sizzle in the moonlight with white fire.

"Have it your way," he told her.

He ducked with a fluid movement, catching her about the midriff and flinging her over his shoulder. She swore at him violently as he headed for the door and carefully punched out the code for the new security lock. As soon as they were inside, he flicked on the hall light and set her down.

Shaken and feeling as if her own temper possessed her entire body in a reckless grip, Bryn clenched her hands into fists at her sides and tossed back the tangled waves of her hair to meet his gaze with a fiery one of her own.

"I'll walk out of this house any time I choose."

"No, you will not. Not while we're involved with all this."

"Involved? It's over tomorrow, and the hell with the damn pictures! What are we going to find? What are we going to prove? All I want is Adam. I'd rather just drop the whole damned thing here and now."

"But you won't Miss Keller. Because I won't. I'm in on this too. And I don't like being threatened and manipulated. So we won't forget about the pictures. And—" with his arms crossed over his tuxedoed chest, he began to move slowly toward her, stopping an inch away "—you won't walk out of this house. I have no intention of aiding and abetting murder or suicide. I'm not going to spend the rest of my life wondering if I might have been able to do something the night I found you splattered all over the road! Don't act like a child, Bryn, or I'll treat you like one."

There seemed to be no dignified way out of the situation. She would be a fool to fight him; she could feel his strength when he wasn't even touching her. All she could do was salvage her pride with as calm a demeanor as possible.

"All right, Lee. You've been helping with…with Adam. I need you tomorrow, and you are in on the pictures. We'll get Adam—" Please make that be true! she silently prayed. But she had to believe it, and so she kept talking to Lee. She was so tautly wound inside that she was ready to fight. "We'll keep playing with the pictures. But it will all end there. I do realize that I should be ready to jump, beg, and roll over when the great star speaks, but I've already been that route once. It's not for me. Now, I'm going to bed. Alone."

He had watched her silently through the entire speech; when she finished he was still watching her. Rigidly.

The only signs of the intensity of his anger were his narrowed eyes and the pulse furiously ticking a vein in his corded neck. Bryn smiled bitterly and turned, heading for the stairway.

She walked quickly, purposefully. She could feel his eyes piercing through her back, as if they were rays of heat and her flesh was naked.

She started up the steps.

And then she felt his grip; this time she hadn't heard him move, she hadn't sensed his silent pounce. And she was so startled that she cried out in alarm.

It was just like the scene they had practiced so often for the video. She turned, falling into his embrace. She was staring into his eyes, feeling the force and power of his arms around her.

"I mean it, Lee!" she snapped out, struggling uselessly against him. "I don't want to sleep with you!"

"Shut up. You'll wake Marie and the kids. I don't intend to let you crawl back behind a celibate touch-me-not wall because you can't deal with an argument!"

They were moving smoothly up the stairway; his long strides carried them quickly along the hallway balcony. "Lee! We were not having an argument! You were making caustic, insulting remarks and not giving me a chance to defend myself. Defend myself! What am I saying! This whole thing is a joke! I don't owe you any explanations or excuses. I was a fool to have—"

Her words were cut off by the force of his mouth as his lips ground hard upon hers. Yet even in his anger there was persuasion; she couldn't twist from him as he held her, only accept and parry the heated strokes of his tongue. No matter how deep her hurt, indignity or anger, she couldn't still the tempest of excitement that swelled within her. Desire began to course through her like the wild, undeniable wash of a waterfall.

The kiss ended as she found herself tossed unceremoniously onto the bed. Shaken, Bryn tried to gather her wits and dignity about her.

"I don't think you've listened to me," she said harshly, struggling to sit with a contemptuous decorum. He still wasn't listening to her. The tux jacket fell to the floor. With precise movements, he removed his cuff links. His shirttails were wrenched from his pants, and then the moonlight was gleaming upon his naked shoulders. The click of his buckle and the rasp of his zipper seemed ridiculously loud in the quiet of the night. And all the while she saw his golden eyes upon her.

"What do you think you're doing?" Bryn demanded.

He raised a polite, mocking brow. "Undressing."

"For what?" she snapped icily.

"To sleep with the woman I'm sleeping with, of course." His shoes were tossed toward the closet with a thud, and he stepped out of his trousers and briefs. She should have been accustomed to his body by now, but she wasn't. Not quite. Each time she saw him naked again she felt her breath catch with a little thrill. She found new fascination in the bronzed breadth of his shoulders, with the gleaming ripple of his muscles, the steel hard flatness of his belly.

She even forgot his stinging words as he started walking toward her, eyeing her with the moonlight giving his golden gaze a satyr-like glitter. He picked up her foot, his touch absurdly gentle considering his heated tension as he cast away her shoe.

"Lee..."

Her second shoe was tossed aside. Sensation rippled through her as his fingers grazed the length of her panty hose to her thighs, to the elastic that wound about her waist, and skimmed them away; then his touch was upon her bare flesh.

Bryn realized that she had lain there, compliant and aching, seduced by the desire he could so easily awaken within her. She was not going to be a victim of her own traitorous needs. With a small cry of anger, she spurted from the bed, only to come crashing hard against the power of his chest and find herself swept to the bed again, a prisoner of tangled limbs and sinewed strength. His fingers wound into her hair and he began to kiss her again, his lips teasing, haunting, solicitous upon hers, then hard with need and passion....

Gentle again... and then demanding. Rough, but never hurtful, a maelstrom that roiled within her womb, making her want him, his touch...

His hands roamed with bold possession over her body, searing through the gown that covered her, covering her breasts, rousing their peaks to a betraying hardness. His palm came to her thigh, sliding beneath the fabric to taunt her nakedness and move against her with a bold and blunt intimacy.

His head rose from hers and he still spoke with anger, but she clung to the words. "You little fool! Don't you know how much I care about you, how much I've come to need you? And yes, when a man loves a woman, he gets angry. Crazy. Savage. When he sees her in the arms of another man. No, I don't own you. But you're still mine. Mine to be with in the moonlight... like this... together... intimate...."

They were shattering words. Heated, whispered words that spun in her mind like crystal. He loved her; he had said that he loved her....

He had said he loved her. But had he? Wasn't it a word that men whispered easily in the heat of the moment?

She cried out as he shifted suddenly, abruptly, easing the skirt of her gown up, wedging his body between her legs. The force of his entry was a shock, but a gratifying, dizzying shock, causing her body to shiver in liquid afterquakes. Unwittingly she dug her fingernails into his back, whimpering softly as the unleashed storm of pain, anger and untamed desire swept into and around them with the merciless vigor of a cyclone. Bryn had no thought of anything but the driving need, the sweetness that coiled and coiled within her, the wonder of feeling him move inside of her, easing the need, stroking it to frenzy....

Her release sent wave after wave of shivering aftershocks shooting through her, releasing her body slowly from the wild, tempestuous beauty of the storm. She heard him groan her name, felt him strain above her, shudder violently, and leave within her the warm liquid fire of his own release. As she clung to him, she began to wonder what was truth, the anger or the love? And she burst into tears.

He moved like silent lightning, shifting from her, taking her into his arms. And his words were no longer angry; they were anxious and filled her heart with pain and remorse. "Oh, God, Bryn, I never meant to hurt you; I would never want to hurt you. Oh, my God, I am so, so sorry. Please don't be afraid of me. I couldn't bear it if you were afraid of me...."

It took her a moment to absorb his words, to understand that he was ripping himself apart; his pain was that of a dagger twisting in his gut. She disentangled herself from his arms long enough to meet his eyes, and she shook her head in confusion. "You didn't hurt me, Lee. And I'm not afraid of you."

He was silent for a moment that seemed to slip into eternity. And then his hand moved to touch her face; it trembled as he grazed her tears away.

"Then why are you crying?" he asked her, his whisper hoarse.

"Because..." Bryn faltered. She wanted to tell him the truth; she wanted to demand to know if he really loved her. But she couldn't. Not even with him, could she be that trusting yet. And love...well, she had learned once that it could mean many things. Before she could give him her trust, she would have to believe that it meant forever and forever—and that the man could extend his love for a lifetime to three little boys who weren't his.

But she had to say something, because the anxious concern he was showing her was a baring of his own soul; she didn't understand it, but she had never seen him so upset.

"Lee, I swear to you that I'm not afraid of you—and you've never, never hurt me. I think it's just the night. I've been so worried, and frightened. And tonight was horrible, and then you started on me..."

Lee groaned. "Oh, God, Bryn, I am sorry. I don't know what got into me. Can you forgive me?"

"Yes, of course, Lee. But, please...can't you tell me why you're so...upset?"

He sighed, grazing his palm over her cheek, then lying back on a pillow to stare up at the ceiling. "Sometime, Bryn. Not now." A tremor gripped him suddenly and he spoke softly, almost hesitantly. "Bryn...you don't find me...brutal?"

Bryn smiled and laid her head against his chest, puzzled at his words, but determined to ease him. "Torrid, tempestuous, passionate, intense, strong and forceful. A whirlwind, yes. But brutal, never. You are fire and wind and gentle breezes, and I love them all."

He was silent, stroking her hair as he pulled her close and rested his chin upon her head. Bryn waited a moment, knowing that for once, it was he who leaned on her for the strength. Then she spoke softly to him.

"Please tell me about your wife, Lee."

"She died," he said tonelessly.

"I know that, Lee. But please, please let me try to understand what hurts you so badly."

"I will, Bryn, I promise. Soon."

She had to let it go at that; she couldn't give him everything yet; maybe it was the same with him. His fears seemed to be as deep as hers.

Suddenly he lifted her above him; his fingers locked about her nape and he pulled her down to touch his lips against hers with reverence. He rolled her to her side and smiled as he faced her, tugging at the rumpled gown that was still tangled around her. "Could we dispense with this?" he asked. "I need to sleep—holding you, not material."

Bryn silently pulled the gown over her head and tossed it from the bed. She settled down beside him.

There were a million things that could have been said but they didn't say any of them. They lay there, and in time, Bryn drifted off to sleep.

She awakened later—she didn't know how much later—to find she was alone. Startled, she half rose and looked around.

Then she saw him by the doors to the balcony, silently staring out into the night. The moon caught his profile and it was strong and proud...but his features, caught by shadow, were haunted.

"Lee!" she cried softly.

He came back to her, slipping beside her in the bed, and holding her close. "I woke you. I'm sorry."

"Lee, it doesn't matter. I just wish I could help. You've given me everything—"

"No," he corrected. "You've given me everything." His arms closed around her, and then he was above her, staring down into her eyes.

I'm shaking, Lee thought. *I've come to know more each day just how much I need her, and I almost ruined it all....*

"I loved you like a savage once tonight," he told her. "Let me love you tenderly, softly...."

He did love her tenderly, caressing her, loving her with appreciative eyes as his hands touched her. She was stunning, clad only in the moonlight. His fingers grazed her breasts, adoring them. His lips found their rough crests, taunting them to wonderful peaks. He suckled and nipped at each, laved them with his tongue, sheltered the luscious ripeness of the full mounds in the firm massage of his hands.

And again he looked at the length of her. The rose and creamy beauty of her breasts as they rose and fell with her quickened breathing. The curve of her slender midriff and waist. Sleek. She was sleek and long...her hips were a beautiful curve all over again. She was a dancer, he reminded himself. And she brought him with her, to dance in the clouds.

He started to touch her again, all that his eyes had cherished and devoured. His hands swept over her with hot promise; his lips tasted and caressed her flesh; his tongue traced brands of fire across her belly, down the shadow of her belly. He turned her over gently, feathering kisses down her spine, to the small of her back.

And he turned her to face him again and loved her with the greatest intimacy, losing himself to reckless passion as she writhed with a dancer's fluid grace beneath his tender touch, whispering his name, crying out his name, entangling her fingers in his hair and begging that he come to her....

He did, only to find that she could be as passionate, as demanding as he.

She rose over him in the moonlight, a sculpture in proud and naked beauty as she stared down at him with moistened lips, her wealth of copper hair curling about the swollen beauty of her breasts.

She smiled at him, her lips curling whimsically.

"Now let me love you—" she told him, leaning low to grace his chest with her nipples and sending waves of erotic heat rippling through him all over again "—like a savage...."

He smiled, enveloping her with his arms. "My love, do with me what you will...."

Much later he reminded her that they needed to sleep, that tomorrow was the day when they would get Adam back.

They needed to be rested—and alert.

Bryn smiled to herself, grateful for the abandon of the night. He hadn't given her much time to worry.

He had given her something—though she just wasn't sure yet what. But whatever did happen, he had been with her now, through the greatest trial of her life.

She was very, very grateful for Lee Condor.

Chapter 11

Bryn awoke elated; she should have been tired, but she wasn't tired at all. It was Sunday, *and she was going to get Adam back*.

It occurred to her that it was absurd to relish the thought of talking to a kidnapper but once she heard his voice again, she would be so grateful that she would readily crawl on her knees, if he asked her to.

The kidnapper had played her perfectly—right from the beginning. The tension had almost destroyed her—would have, if it hadn't been for Lee.

She tried not to believe that it could all have been a lie; that the kidnapper could still hold onto Adam. She didn't dare entertain such thoughts—she would crack.

Marie, who had proved to be a lovely woman in her mid-fifties, big bosomed with a deep warm smile and no nonsense manner, was glad to stay with the two older boys for a few hours again that morning when Bryn and Lee left. Brian and Keith would probably sleep until at least nine, and knowing that the morning would be tense with waiting, Bryn was glad that they could arrive after that part was over. She had tried to conceal the truth from them, but as children do, they had sensed that something was wrong. Marie would drop them off at the town house about eleven—in time to greet their brother and herself, Bryn prayed.

Bryn believed that Marie, too, knew that something was very wrong, but she didn't ask questions and showed herself willing to help in any way that she could.

When she had first met Marie, Bryn had been a little bit embarrassed by the relationship she was obviously sharing with Lee, but she had been gratified to see that the older woman seemed to like her on first sight. And Marie apparently adored her employer, so it seemed that the two of them together could do no wrong.

Bryn was up and dressed by 7:00 A.M. on Sunday morning—ready to leave before Lee was out of the shower. But early as it was, Marie had coffee ready downstairs. She tried to get Bryn to eat but Bryn knew she couldn't swallow a mouthful of food. When Lee did appear downstairs, Bryn barely allowed him to sip a cup of coffee, she was so anxious to get to the town house.

Lee didn't try to talk to her on the way over. They were both extremely tense.

Bryn almost burst through the front door; she remembered though— that even though it was her home, Andrew and Barbara were probably together. And they deserved a certain respect for their privacy, especially since they were staying there, courting danger, to keep an eye on things for her so that she and the boys could be safe at Lee's.

Impatiently, she rang the bell. It was only eight. The call wasn't due for an hour. Lee gazed at her, and she flushed.

"Bryn—you're going to work yourself into knots before anything happens," he warned her.

Her throat tightened. "I can't help it, Lee. You don't know what it's been like."

"I have a pretty good idea," he said dryly. "And I still think we should have called the police at the very beginning."

"No! Something might have happened to Adam!"

"And you also might have had him back four days ago," Lee said flatly.

"He's fine, I'm telling you, he's fine!" Bryn said irritably. Her voice was rising, getting hysterical.

The door swung open while she was still in mid-yell. Barbara, clad in a housecoat, looked from one to the other, backing up so that they could enter. Lee's hard features and Bryn's flushed ones warned her that the tension was already mounting. "I've got coffee on," she murmured, glancing at her wristwatch. "This is going to be a long hour. Very long," she muttered.

Bryn was already inside, pacing. "Lee, when he calls this time, I'll do the talking. You have a habit of irritating him."

"Forgive me for not wanting to get both you and Adam killed," Lee retorted, his jaw hardening still further. Barbara could feel the sparks flying and she quickly grasped Bryn's arm. "Come on, honey, let's go into the kitchen and get the coffee."

It was a long hour. Andrew appeared downstairs, and Bryn heard him talking quietly to Lee. She ran out and faced both of them.

"Please, please! Don't do anything to mess this up! There won't be any trouble. I'll give the prints back; Adam will be home. Don't the two of you do anything! Promise me that! Swear it—"

"Bryn," Barbara warned.

Then Andrew and Barbara who were nervous themselves, were left with the task of keeping Bryn and Lee apart. Personally, Barbara agreed with Lee that Bryn was wrong. The police should have been called. But then she couldn't blame Bryn for being terrified for her little nephew.

And it was said, Barabara decided. She sincerely believed that Lee and Bryn were just right for each other, that the love was there that should have helped them—had helped them—now, as in the days that had passed.

But both of them, it seemed, were afraid of the depths of that emotion, and so now, with torment and tension mounting, they were at the snapping point.

At exactly nine o'clock the phone rang. Bryn cried out and raced for it, leaving no time for a second ring.

"Ah, good, Miss Keller. You're there. All ready?"

"Yes, yes! I've got your negatives and the proofs and I haven't touched a thing. Please, when can I have Adam?"

A husky chuckle answered her. "Put Condor on."

"No!" Bryn protested. "Please, you're dealing with me; I want Adam now. Oh, please—"

"Put him on."

The command was unnecessary. Lee had grabbed the phone from her. "We want the child. Now. Or we *will* do something with these pictures," Lee snapped.

"You'll have him. As soon as I send the kid, you call that lobby and tell Miss Keller. She drops the stuff and leaves. Don't you dare let there be anyone suspicious around, you hear? I don't think you're that stupid, but I just wanted to talk to you again, Condor, to remind you I don't want any tricks."

"No tricks," Lee agreed, glancing at Bryn. "But so help me God, if anything goes wrong . . ."

"Not on my end. Tell her to go."

Lee hung up the phone.

"Well?" Bryn demanded, gripping his arm, unconsciously digging her nails into it like talons.

"You can go now," he said unhappily.

"Oh, thank God, thank God," she murmured. Then she caught his eyes with her own. "No tricks, Lee, really. You have to be here."

"No tricks," he told her grimly. "I'll be right here." He glanced over his shoulder at Andrew. "Call Information for me, will you? Verify that number of that pay phone in the hotel's lobby."

Andrew nodded, gave Bryn an encouraging grin, and stepped over to the phone. Lee turned back to Bryn. "Have the valet park your car. And as soon as you've dropped those pictures, you walk out the front door, give the valet your ticket and get into your car as soon as he drives it up. I mean it, Bryn. Don't take any chances. Don't be anyplace where there isn't a group of people around, okay?"

She nodded numbly. It was going to work out, it was going to work out, *it had to work out*!

Andrew hung up the phone and handed Lee a piece of scrap paper.

Lee accepted the paper, glancing at it, then stuffing it into the pocket of his knit shirt. He nodded to Andrew. Bryn thought that the two men exchanged a strange glance, but she was too distracted to really know or care.

"I'm going," Bryn murmured.

"Aren't you forgetting something?" he asked.

"What?"

"The pictures," he said quietly, handing her the packet that he had set on the counter. She paled. She hadn't even remembered to bring them from his house; he had been the one to do so.

"Thanks," she said swallowing nervously.

"Bryn, I mean it. Calm down or you'll get into an accident before you get there." His soft tone negated the tension between them and the anger that had sparked. It gave her a sense of security, of his caring, of his strength.

"I'll be calm," she promised.

He touched her lips with a light kiss. It was warm and giving and reassuring. Again, it was as if he filtered his own strength into her with his touch, with his subtle male scent. More than ever she wanted to cry, but she also felt as if now she could go on with her mission competently. "See you soon," she murmured and stepped out the door.

It didn't seem to take twenty minutes to reach the lush new Mountain View Resort Hotel; it seemed to take twenty years. And as she fumed at the traffic, Bryn worried herself into a state of nausea as one refrain kept going through her mind. What if something went wrong? What would happen to Adam if something went wrong? What if—what would happen to Adam—if something went wrong?

Her teeth were chattering as she drove up to the impressive portico of the Mountain View. A cordial valet stepped up to open her door, and she tripped climbing out of the van. He steadied her; she thanked him in a confusion of monosyllables, and started to leave him before taking her ticket. He called her back, and she could see in his eyes that he thought she was a crazy tourist as she thanked him again for the ticket.

There must have been half a dozen conventions going on in the hotel. People were everywhere. Bryn hurried to the large red couch that was set attractively before the forty-foot glass windows that looked out on a panaroma of greenery and fountains. She saw the phone booth; it was an elegant, paneled nook in the wall, not ten feet from the red couch. She stared back toward the reception desk at the large clock on the wall. She had ten minutes to wait.

Bryn took a seat at the end of the couch. She could see the phone booth, and by slightly twisting her head, she could keep an eye on the clock.

Tiny beads of perspiration were breaking out all over her body. Nervously she fumbled around in her purse for a tissue and dabbed at her forehead, then tried to dry her palms. She gazed at the clock again. Only two minutes had passed.

Her eyes began to follow people through the grandiose lobby. Businessmen, their attaché cases in their hands, walked to the elevators, alone and in groups. In a group of chairs near the couch, a threesome of affluent matrons sat discussing their husbands' golf games. A lone man in a dark trench coat paced behind the chairs. Bryn studied him. He had the stiffest black hair she had ever seen, and an absurdly curled mustache.

She heard footsteps behind her and almost jumped in a panic. They passed her by. She turned, ostensibly to stare at the clock, but in truth to see who was behind her. Another man, in a nondescript, very average dark suit. But the man wasn't average. He was taller even than Lee, about six foot six or seven. Bryn felt her limbs begin to stiffen in fear. He turned, walking the length of the couch once more.

She bit her lip and gazed at the clock. Six minutes to go. She heard the creak of a door and snapped her head back toward the phone booth. One of the affluent matrons had sat down in the elegantly paneled little booth and was making a call.

No! Oh, please, no! she thought desperately. She gazed about the lobby wildly. Businessmen were still milling about, the matrons were still chattering, the tall man in the suit and the trench-coated man with the strange dark hair were still pacing.

Her nails cut into her palms, creating deep crescents. An insane scream started to rise in her throat as she looked into the little phone booth and saw the woman still talking. Bryn stood, clutching her purse and the package of film. She started toward the phone booth and leaned against it, pointedly staring at the woman inside. It was very rude, but

... She managed to fluster the woman who said something, then clicked down the receiver. She rose and slammed the door open. "There are other phones in the hotel!" she snapped to Bryn.

Bryn couldn't seem to swallow so she could murmur out an answer. She glanced at the clock as she slid into the booth. Three minutes to go.

The extremely tall man started walking toward the phone booth. Was he one of the kidnappers, she wondered wildly. Or was he just a businessman about to demand that she use the phone or leave it free for others? She smiled at him and picked up the receiver. As soon as he turned around to start pacing again, she turned her back to the window of the paneled booth, using it as a shield for the hand she placed over the hang-up switch in place of the receiver. Pretend to talk! She warned herself. Lee...pretend it's Lee. "What the hell was the matter with you this morning? Keeping your music in a linen closet is ridiculous to begin with. And to jump down my throat over a set of lyrics when you're a musician is absolutely crazy. You're giving and good, but only to a point. There's a part of you that is dark and frightening and I'm half crazy that you'll leave me, half crazy to see you go...."

She bit her lip, turning to stare at the clock again. It was two minutes past the limit. Three minutes past ten. Oh, dear God, Adam! Where are you? God, if you just give him back to me, I promise I'll be the best parent in the world....

Four minutes past. The tall man in the business suit was coming toward the phone booth again.

"Lee, you rotten son of a bitch! You had no right to snap at me that way, and a simple 'I'm sorry' just isn't good enough. Lee, I want to know you. I want to know what happened in your past. I want to know what your favorite flavor of ice cream is; I want to watch you shave and have you yell at me for stealing your razor for my legs. I want to know what kind of movies you like, and I'd love to see into your past and understand how you can sometimes be so gracious, and sometimes so encased in rock that I don't know you at all and I become frightened. Frightened, but always attracted. I want Adam to be with you, Lee. I want to see Adam. I want to—"

The phone began to ring. Bryn briefly noted that the tall businessman was looking at her as if she were crazy. She remembered that she already had the receiver in one hand; all that she had to do to answer the phone was to lift her other hand....

She almost shrieked, "Hello!"

It *was* Lee. Now, she was really and truly talking to Lee. Well, she was listening to him.

"Bryn, Adam is here. Drop the pictures. Calmly. Get away from the phone. Drop the pictures on the couch—and get out. Do you hear me? Don't look back; don't do anything. Just get out."

"Adam is there? Oh, Lee, let me talk to him—"

"Bryn! Drop the pictures and come home!"

The phone clicked on her. She could barely stand, her knees were trembling so hard. She managed to stand and walk out of the booth. She walked by the couch, dropping the packet of pictures. And she continued on, straight for the revolving doors that led to the portico.

She gave the valet her ticket and extravagantly overtipped him. The van rolled beneath the portico and as the man held her door open, she crawled in. Her hands were damp against the wheel, but she gripped it firmly.

By happenstance she gazed into her rearview mirror. The man with the strange dark hair and the trench coat was staring after her. She started to shiver as if the temperature had suddenly dipped well below zero, but she forced herself to look forward and keep her eyes on the road.

Home, home, home. She was going home, and Adam was going to be there. Time seemed to crawl.

The roads were ridiculously busy. Bryn glanced in her rearview mirror to try and change lanes to make an exit off the highway. She swore softly in exasperation. There was some kind of a dark sedan right on her tail. She put her blinker on. The sedan backed off. She eased over a lane, but left her blinker on. Her exit road was coming up.

Adam. I'm going to see Adam. She thought about his chubby little cheeks and his wide green eyes. She was going to hug and kiss him so hard that he'd be ready to leave home again.

Bryn started to exit. Suddenly she felt a heaving jolt wrench through her; she heard the shattering of glass and the screech of metal against metal.

The last thing she consciously realized was that someone had side-swiped her, riding up her tail.

Her head cracked hard against the steering wheel. The van started to spin. Or was it only her mind that was spinning? She never knew. Her world dimmed and then faded entirely into darkness.

Adam's return to the household had resultled in pure chaos. The little boy entered into a new kind of danger, that of being smothered to death by the love of his brothers, Barbara—and himself, Lee admitted.

He had run in crying for his Aunt Bryn; Lee had done his best to assure Adam that Bryn would be right back. Brian and Keith started demanding to know everything that had happened. Lee tried to calm the older boys down and speak quietly to Adam.

"Do you know where you were, Adam?"

"In a house."

"What kind of a house?" Lee asked.

"I don't know. A house."

"Who took care of you, Adam?"

The little boy looked perplexed for a minute, but then he answered. "Mary took care of me. She tried to be nice, but she was always fighting with the man."

"What man, Adam?"

"The man who wore the black mask."

"Okay, Adam. Do you remember what Mary looked like?"

"She was a girl."

"An old girl? A young girl? Did she have dark hair or light hair? Was she thin, or was she fat?"

"She was skinny," Adam sniffed. He thought a minute. "And her hair was dark. I don't want to answer any more questions. I want to see Aunt Bryn!"

Lee sighed. He wanted to see Bryn, too. He wanted her to call the police. The minute she walked in, he was going to insist.

"Okay, Adam," Lee hugged him, tousled his hair, and released him. "Want some ice cream or something!"

"We have chocolate chip!" Keith exclaimed.

Barbara, who had refused to set Adam down for the first five minutes of his return, was still standing nearby. "Come on, Adam, let's get you some ice cream." She glanced at Lee with a worried frown, indicating the kitchen clock.

Bryn should have been back by now. Lee wandered back to the front porch. He glanced at his wristwatch. He had called her at the Mountain View over thirty minutes ago. But there was no sign of the van.

What the hell was taking so long?

The phone began to ring, and he hurried back into the house, diving for the receiver before Barbara could get it. He stared at her as he said a quick, "Hello?"

"Your girlfriend has had a little accident, Condor. Don't go getting excited—it was only a *little* accident. But I figured you might be getting ideas about calling the police now. Don't. She can't watch those kids all the time, and you can't watch her all the time. You hear me, Condor?"

Accident… Accident…what was the son of a bitch talking about? Lee wondered. His temper flared and snapped. "So help me God, if she's been hurt, I'll find you. Scalp you, skin you alive, and tear you apart—"

"I'd hang up, red skin. Someone may be trying to call you."

The phone went dead in Lee's hand. Panic rose in Barbara's voice as she confronted him.

"What's happened? Lee? *What's happened?*"

He shook his head at her vehemently, with his features forming into a warning scowl as he indicated the children who, as yet, were still chattering away madly over their ice cream. Adam had become a cherished celebrity to his older brothers and, thankfully, he was taking it all in stride.

Barbara lowered her voice. "What is it, Lee?"

"I don't know. That joker just told me that there had been an accident—"

"An accident! Oh, my God!"

"Stop it, Barbara! Stop it. You're shrieking. And you've got to stay calm! I'm going to go on out and trace Bryn's route. I'll call you the second that—"

He broke off, and they both froze as the phone began to ring again. Then Lee almost ripped the receiver from its cradle.

"Yes?"

"Mr. Lee Condor?"

"Yes?" the voice was not that of the whisperer. It was a male voice, calm and polite.

"Please, don't panic. I'm Sergeant McCloskey with the Nevada Highway Patrol. Mr. Andrew McCabe said I could reach you here. There's been an accident...."

The world was very fuzzy when she opened her eyes. Bryn had to keep blinking to try and clear them.

She became aware of movement. There were arms about her, and she was being carried.

She took a good look at one of the arms. It was covered in light beige fabric. The man was wearing a trench coat. Dread slipped into her heart even before she raised her eyes to the man's face.

It was him! The man with the strange dark hair and mustache who had been pacing the lobby at the Mountain View....

She started to scream.

He gazed down at her startled, and then began to talk. "Bryn! Hush! It's just me—Andrew! I had to get you out of the van—you were hit near the gas tank. Hush! It's me. Pull the hair; it will come right off. See?"

She shut up, reflexively and incredulously doing as she had been told. No wonder the dark hair had looked so ridiculous. It was a wig. She started to smile. Lee had made Andrew dress up in costume to be near her. She reached for the mustache. It ripped away with more resistance than she had expected.

"Ouch!" Andrew gasped, falling to the embankment with her, his eyes reproachful. "I didn't tell you to rip the bloody mustache off!"

She laughed, but the sound was distant and far away. As distant as the sound of sirens. The world was fading in and out once more, and her eyelids were too heavy to hold open.

She knew she was in a hospital the second time she opened her eyes. She saw the neat sterility of her sheets, the white purity of the wall. She felt the soft, fresh embrace of a comfortable bed.

Adam! Adam was all right. He was home with Lee. It hurt a little bit to move her eyes, but she did so. She was definitely in a hospital. There was a small yellow chest beside the bed, a TV suspended on the far wall and a rolling tray parked near the bed. And there was a chair at her side. A young woman was sitting in it, a blonde who had her head dipped low over a magazine.

Bryn frowned. The woman wasn't a nurse; she was dressed in a light mauve sweater and an attractive plaid skirt. As Bryn stared at her dazedly, the woman looked up and offered her a warm smile. She was very pretty with that smile, Bryn thought vaguely. She seemed full of vibrance and natural warmth.

"How wonderful to see you with us again!" the woman exclaimed, jumping to her feet. "I've got to run out and get the doctor—"

"Wait!" Bryn pleaded, discovering belatedly that when she shouted, her head began to pound. The woman paused, and Bryn said quickly, "Who are you?"

The woman laughed. "Oh, Bryn! I'm so sorry. I'm Gayle Spencer."

"Gayle Spencer?" Bryn repeated.

"Lee asked me to sit with you."

Great. Her head was breaking, she must look like death warmed over and Lee had sent a lovely blonde to watch her.

As if reading her thoughts, the blonde smiled. "I'm Lee's sister." Bryn's eyes must have widened with amazement, and the pretty girl continued with a grimace, as if she were accustomed to a startled reaction. "No, neither of us was adopted! Lee looks like my dad, and I resemble mother. And I'm married; that's why our names are different."

Bryn laughed. Gayle Spencer had spoken with such a nice sense of humor. Then she found that laughing hurt, and she sobered. "Where's Lee?" she asked softly.

Gayle grimaced again. "Flirting with a nurse, but for a good cause. They keep telling him that your nephews can't come in, and Lee is determined that you'll get to see Adam!"

"Adam!" Bryn cried out, forgetting about her head. "I have to see him!"

"Oh, don't worry. Lee usually gets his way! Now let me get that doctor, before I get myself fired!"

Bryn closed her eyes again when Gayle smiled reassuringly, then ducked outside the room. What had happened, she asked herself. She could remember the horrible jolt and the crunching sound, and then Andrew...Andrew with that ridiculous wig....

She'd had an accident with the van, but apparently it wasn't that bad. Her head hurt because she had cracked it against the steering wheel. She'd had an accident....

Because a dark sedan had purposely run into her....

"Ah, Miss Keller!" A doctor walked into the room. He was a gray-haired man with warm blue eyes that instantly inspired trust. He walked with the quick efficiency that belonged to a doctor, too, Bryn thought with a slight smile.

"Good, good," he said, reaching for her hand and patting it feeling for her pulse. "Let me just take a look deep into your eyes now...."

She flinched reflexively as he sent the ray from a pencil-thin flashlight beaming first into her right eye, and then into her left. "Good!" he said again, switching off the light. "I'm Doctor Kelten," he informed her, sliding a chilly stethoscope against her chest and smiling once more, satisfied with the results. "How do you feel?"

"Not terrible," Bryn told him. "It only hurts when I laugh or look around too quickly."

"That's to be expected. You're a lucky young lady! You've got a bit of a concussion, but a very minor one. We want to keep you overnight for observation, but we'll let you go home tomorrow. How's that sound?"

"I could probably go home now—"

"But it wouldn't be wise." He tucked the sheets back around her and began to make a tsking sound of irritation. "These hit and run things! How anyone could cause an accident and then drive off— Well, it's just beyond me! The police are going to want to talk to you, but I've fended them off for the day. You just lie quietly, young lady and tomorrow, everything will look a whole lot better!"

"Thank you," Bryn murmured, lowering her lashes. Hit and run? No, it hadn't been a regular hit and run. And she knew how Lee had felt all along; she couldn't believe he hadn't decided that enough was enough and told the police the entire story from the beginning.

"I'll see you again in a couple of hours," Dr. Kelten said, walking briskly toward the door.

"Wait!" Bryn begged, calling him back. She kept her lashes halfway over her eyes. "I understand there's a problem with my nephews coming in. Doctor, they've been through a lot. It's important that they get to see that I'm all right, especially the little one...."

Dr. Kelten interrupted her with a friendly laugh. "You can see the little boys, Miss Keller. Mr. Condor has managed to get my entire staff eating out of his hands. But only for a few minutes. If you want me to release you tomorrow, you have to toe the line!"

Bryn smiled. "Only for a few minutes!" she promised.

The doctor left the room. Bryn made a grab for the wheeled tray, searching for a flip-up mirror in the slender drawer beneath it. She found it and anxiously scanned her features.

She was very pale, but otherwise she looked remarkably well for a woman with a concussion. Her forehead was bruised, but she could brush tendrils of her hair over it with her fingers....

There was a tap at her door, and then it opened slowly. Lee was there. Tall, commanding, his eyes a golden shimmer of anxiety. He smiled at her slowly, ruefully.

But he never had a chance to say anything. Adam was pushing past him. Adam, with his blond curls, cherubic cheeks, and tear-filled green eyes.

"Aunt Bwyn!"

She didn't feel a bit of pain as she sat up and caught him to her, sweeping his little form into her arms.

"Adam, oh, Adam! Precious! I've missed you so! I love you; oh, Adam, I love you—"

"Are you going to get well, Aunt Bwyn? Are you? Do you promise?" He crushed himself to her. She hugged him ferociously.

"Yes, Adam, yes! I'm going to get well. I promise. Your silly aunt just let another car get too close, that's all. Oh, Adam!"

She started to cry, just clutching him, unable to let him go. Then she opened her eyes and looked over his shoulder, and saw Lee standing there. Then she knew that he had understood that the greatest medication she could receive was this time with Adam....

"Thank you," she whispered to him.

She might have whispered, "I love you."

Because she did. She had never known how completely until that moment.

Chapter 12

"**I** was a hit on purpose, wasn't I?" Bryn asked Lee. He was standing at the window, staring out, though at what she wasn't sure. All that could be seen was part of the roof and a lot of power lines. And it was dusk, so not even that dubious view was a good one.

It was the first chance they had had to be alone. Brian and Keith had followed Adam in to assure themselves that she was all right. At last a pristine nurse had arrived to sternly say that the boys had to leave. They had set up a minor howl, but Lee had promised them that they could play with the drums and the piano, and in a matter of moments Barbara and Gayle had been able to take them away. Lee had promised Bryn that Andrew would stay at his house that night along with Barbara, and that Gayle and her husband, Phil, would also be there. Andrew had spent the afternoon combing the place with an agent from a security company, and all doors and windows were now wired with traps that blared loudly and instantly set off an alarm at the police department. Lee, it seemed, intended to stay with her at the hospital through the night, and neither hell nor high water would move him.

"Lee?" Bryn persisted quietly when he didn't move.

He moved away from the wall where he had been leaning and came to sit at the side of the bed, idly taking her hand in his.

"Yes," he told her, his eyes following his fingers as he traced the pale blue lines of her veins. His eyes met hers. "Our whisperer called right before the Highway Patrol did. It was a warning so we wouldn't call the police now that Adam is back."

Bryn laughed bitterly. "He doesn't want the police involved, but the police do become involved in a hit and run accident!"

Lee shrugged, and Bryn was surprised to realize that he seemed uncertain. He always knew exactly what he wanted, and how he wanted to go about getting it. "I admit, Bryn, that I wanted to convince you to call the police the minute you walked back in the door. But now...now I don't think it would be such a great idea."

"You think that we should just forget the whole thing?" She wasn't sure if she was hopeful or furious.

"No," Lee said, his eyes meeting hers. "Don't you see, Bryn? No matter what, you'd find yourself living in fear for years and years to come. This person has to be caught and stopped."

"You just said you didn't think we should tell the police!"

"At the moment. Because we don't know what we're up against. And I don't think the police will know, either. We have to find out what's in the pictures."

"Oh," Bryn murmured, a chill rippling along her spine. But he was right. Adam hadn't been able to tell them anything.

"I'll start as soon as I get out of here," she said, keeping her eyes downcast so that he wouldn't know what the words had cost her.

"Good. And I think I know where you should start."

"The Sweet Dreams motel?"

"Um-hmm."

"I really can't believe that Hammerfield could...could—"

Lee interrupted her with a sigh. "Bryn, there are a lot of things in life that aren't easy to believe. A lot of ugliness we'd rather not see. I don't want to condemn the man without a trial, but he's our most likely suspect."

Bryn grimaced. She didn't feel much like arguing. She smiled at him, determined to change the subject since she couldn't do a thing from her hospital bed. "I didn't know that you had a sister."

"Two of them, actually. Sally is a few years older than I am; she's the earth mother of the brood. She moved back to the Black Hills right after she got out of law school, and she spends half her life defending the underdog, half of it raising a passel of kids."

Bryn lughed. It was easy now. Adam was back. "How many are a passel?"

"Five."

"That is a passel." Bryn hesitated for a moment, wondering why she was getting strange feelings about the pretty blonde she had met earlier. "Does your sister Gayle live here in Tahoe?"

"No," Lee replied a little uneasily, and Bryn was sure that she was right; Gayle was there for a reason—a reason that she might not like.

"Gayle lives in New York," Lee said. He bit his lower lip with an idle shrug, then gripped Bryn's hand warmly in his as he met her eyes again with a serious intent. "Bryn, I called Gayle last week, the morning after you broke into my place. I asked her if she and Phil could come out here, then go for a little vacation up to my grandfather's place."

Bryn frowned her confusion. "I don't understand...."

"Bryn, I want you to let me talk, and I want you to listen to what I'm saying. Having to protect someone else is like having an Achilles' heel. I didn't want to talk to you about this until tomorrow, but ... Bryn, I asked Gayle and Phil to come here because I wanted you to meet them and feel comfortable with them. And I want you to let them take the boys up to my grandfather's place in the Hills."

"What!" Bryn cried out.

"Would you hush!" Lee demanded, smiling crookedly. "I had to fight all the red tape in the hospital to get to stay here; if you scream like that a second time, they'll come up here and kick me out for sure."

Bryn lowered her voice. She was unaware that she clutched his arm and spoke beseechingly. "Lee, I can't send the kids away! They've only just become secure with me. Adam won't go! He'll think he's being taken away again!"

"No, he won't, Bryn. Not if you convince him it's all right."

"But, Lee, I can't let him go. Not now."

"Bryn, I know that the thought is painful to you. But I've thought this over until it's given me headaches. No one gets near my grandfather's land undetected. And I have a lot of friends nearby. Blackfoot and half-breeds like myself who are deeply into their heritage. I'm telling you, nothing could move against those kids in the Hills. And it would be great for them." He shrugged, trying to take a humorous approach to the situation. "Who knows? Maybe Grandfather can convince Adam that throwing food is poor etiquette."

"Lee!"

"Come on, Bryn! I'm serious. You're a great parent, but you're a girl. Playing Indian will be great for the boys. They can fish, ride, swim and have a wonderful time. And we can search through those pictures without having the terrible worry about what might be happening to them. We act normal—finish our video during the day and comb the pictures at night. And I promise you that as soon as we finish the video, whether we've discovered anything or not, we'll head on up to South Dakota ourselves and meet them there."

Bryn stared at him, both fear and a thrilling curiosity taking hold of her. He kept using the words "we" and "our." He wanted her with him. For more than a night, more than a brief affair...

"Brief" could be defined in many ways, she warned herself sagely. And he wanted her to let the children go away....

She bit her lip, lowering her lashes. He placed a finger beneath her chin, lifting it. There was tenderness gleaming in his golden eyes when he spoke softly to her. "Bryn, I'm not trying to send the boys away because they might be in the way. I like kids, even ones who throw food. I'm thinking of their safety."

She could feel her lip quivering. "I believe you," she said softly.

He leaned over and kissed her forehead. "Good," he whispered huskily. "You don't have to decide right now. Tomorrow, when you get to know Gayle a little better, you can make up your mind."

Bryn nodded, feeling pain enshroud her heart. But Lee was probably right. If the boys stayed now, she wouldn't ever want to open the front door; she would be afraid to take them to school.

Lee drew away from her suddenly, idly picking up the little gizmo that called the nurse and controlled the TV. He flicked the channels, then stopped at a scene of a dark and spooky castle rising above jagged cliffs.

"Ah, great! One of those old Vincent Price horror spoofs. Do you like these?"

"Yes...fine," Bryn murmured politely. He wanted the serious conversation to drop. Bryn wasn't sure that she did. She didn't feel too bad. Her "minor concussion" wasn't even causing her a headache now. She wanted to grab his arm and pull him back, and tell him that she was scared and angry...and confused. About the pictures. About him. She wanted to demand to know why he had gotten so furious over the piece of music she had picked up, and she wanted him to talk to her. She wanted to know why he could blaze hotter than a raging fire, then turn around with a gentle wisdom and empathy that was rare in any man....

What happened to your wife? she wanted to shout. Why was it that he never mentioned her name, never referred to his years of marriage? It would seem natural for him to talk about it sometimes....

She thought again about the song she had found. Beautiful lyrics, haunting lyrics that he had never sung.

Lyrics...that had something to do with his wife?

Lyrics that Bryn had discovered and thereby made Lee furious.

She closed her eyes for a minute, wondering about the song, about his wife and about Lee. Had he loved his wife so deeply that he wouldn't ever give his heart to anyone else? Perhaps he had decided to keep moving. He was very independent, affluent and famous. Why would he ever want to be tied down?

She had to be ready to let go if—or when—the time came. Events had swept her along, and now she was with him, in love with him. She couldn't let go now; she had to take the moments that were offered her, and the man. But she had to be ready. She had to accept the fact that the day would come when he would leave and move on. No man wanted to be saddled with an instant family, no matter how tolerant he was.

He had said he loved her. Was that love real? And did it matter? Love wasn't always enough.

Lee sank into the hospital chair at her side, warmly taking her hand in his.

Bryn accepted his hand. She said nothing, but turned her eyes to the screen and tried to pay attention to Vincent Price.

In a way it was nice. Sitting there quietly alone together. And she was a fan of Vincent Price....

The night passed swiftly. Right before she felt her eyes flickering closed, she spoke at last. "Lee?"

"Yes?"

"I wish I knew how to thank you and the group. When I saw Andrew in that ridiculous costume...well, it was just so nice. Of both of you to...watch over me so carefully."

"Go to sleep, Bryn," he said lightly.

In the morning Barbara stopped by with clothes. She seemed anxious, but pleased to see that Bryn looked so well.

"How did things go?" Lee asked her.

Barbara rolled her eyes. "Andrew and I are a disaster at discipline. Lee's house will never be the same, Bryn!"

Bryn bit her lip, wondering how badly the boys had destroyed the place. But Barbara only laughed. "It probably needed a little livening up!"

Dr. Kelten came in and ushered Barbara and Lee out. He examined her, then smiled. "You look fine to me. You probably could have gone home yesterday, but it doesn't pay to take chances with head injuries."

"I guess not," Bryn murmured.

"Well, anyway, the police are here to speak with you. I'll give you a minute to get dressed, then I'll send them in and tell the nurse to prepare your release papers."

Bryn thanked the doctor, then showered and dressed quickly. Was "omitting" as bad as lying in the eyes of the law? She sighed as she waited nervously for the police. She certainly wasn't going to be lying if she said that she hadn't seen a thing....

Lee came in with the young officer who questioned her. She answered truthfully when she said that she hadn't seen a thing at the time of the crash; she had only felt the thud when the car had bashed into hers. The officer thanked her for her cooperation, and she guiltily assured him that she didn't mind the questioning in the least.

Barbara had already gone on back to Lee's house, so Bryn and Lee drove alone. He glanced her way as he wheeled his car from the hospital's parking lot. "You sure you feel okay?"

"I promise you, I feel great," she told him truthfully.

Lee nodded. He didn't say much else as they continued on to the house.

As soon as they pulled into the driveway the new front door flew open. The kids came running out to engulf her in hugs, and she hugged them all back fervently.

"You should hear me on the drums, Aunt Bryn!" Brian told her. Adam, who had wedged his way into her arms and now had a death grip about her neck, told her, "Key-tar!"

Lee laughed, plucking Adam away from Bryn despite his howl of protest. "Let your aunt get into the house and sit down, Adam. Then you can crawl all over her." He grimaced at Bryn. "Maybe we have something profitable going here. How do you like the 'Keller Brothers Band'?"

Bryn chuckled softly. "It has a ring to it."

Gayle was waiting for them at the door. Bryn's smile to Lee's sister was a little shy, but Gayle was both effusive and down to earth. "Bryn! How are you feeling? Are you sure you're all right? Maybe you should have stayed another day."

"No, I'm fine, thanks, Gayle. And I'd have gone crazy in bed for another day." She found that Lee was looking at her with a sardonic smile tugging at his lips, and she flushed, casting him a murderous glare in return. He laughed and slipped his free arm around her shoulders.

"Did Andrew and Barbara go on over to the Fulton place?"

"Yes, they're going to film some individual footage of the band. Andrew said it had to be done sometime, and it would keep things rolling."

"Good," Lee murmured. "Let's get in," he told Bryn.

The first thing Bryn noticed when she entered the house was that every window in the place had new glass. And shot through the glass were a myriad of hair-fine lines. The windows were pretty; they might have been there for their beauty. But Bryn shivered. She knew that the new windows were there for only one purpose: security.

She put that thought behind her because the kids were tugging at her hands and Gayle was saying that she had to meet Phil.

Gayle's husband was a tall redheaded man with sparkling blue eyes. Bryn felt the warmth of his handshake and the sincerity in his voice when he told her how happy he was to meet her. He and Lee were about the same age, and Bryn could quickly see that Lee shared the same camaraderie with his brother-in-law that he did with the band. She experienced a twinge of envy and nostalgia. God, how she missed her brother at times.

The kids insisted that she come up to the studio and hear them play the instruments. She instantly started to protest their enthusiastic treatment of the group's equipment, but Lee silenced her with a wave of his hand. She listened to a cacophony of drums, keyboard and guitar, and then insisted that the noise had to die down for a while.

Gayle laughed and said that the pizza man was due any second; hearing that a pizza was on the way, the boys happily raced down the stairs to watch for it at the window. Gayle and Phil followed them, and Lee and Bryn were left alone.

"I think after lunch—if you're up to it—we should get over to your town house and start on the pictures."

Bryn hesitated a moment, then shook her head. She looked at him, smiling hesitantly. "If the boys are leaving with your sister and her husband in the morning, I'd like to spend the day with them. One day won't make that much difference, will it?"

Lee stared back at her for a long time, smiling slowly. "No, one day won't make that much difference." He slipped his arm around her waist and led her out of the studio. "You do like pizza, don't you?"

She wrinkled her nose. "With absolutely everything but anchovies."

"No anchovies, huh? I'll learn to live without them."

Bryn laughed, then quickly sobered. "Lee, I'm just afraid of how the boys are going to take this."

"They'll take it fine! Don't worry. All little boys like Indians."

"I'm not so sure," Bryn said dubiously. "These days, little boys like *Star Wars* toys. And Gremlins. And Pac-Man. And—"

"And quit worrying, Bryn. Things will work out; I promise you. Come on now, let's have a pleasant afternoon!"

The afternoon did pass pleasantly, so pleasantly that Bryn didn't want it to end. At five-thirty Andrew and Barbara arrived, with Mick and Perry in tow. Mick wound up at the piano, playing fifties tunes. Somehow two of the guitars made it downstairs, and Bryn wasn't sure if she was surprised or not when she watched Lee accept one from Andrew, who then slid onto the piano bench beside Mick.

"Don't tell me you play that, too?" Bryn asked him.

He shrugged, and Bryn sat back in the modular sofa with Adam ensconced in her lap. He *could* play it. She watched the agility of his fingers with amazement as they seemed to move instinctively over the strings.

Mick made a quick change to Beatles tunes, and when he teased Brian, Brian told him with great indignity that, yes, of course he knew who the Beatles were. He proved it by singing every word of "Yellow Submarine."

Dinner was a light makeshift meal of sandwiches, but Gayle tossed a huge salad and put out a platter piled high with fresh fruit, so Bryn's health-conscious-for-the-children's-sake mind was pleased. The more she saw of Gayle and Phil, the more she liked them, and the more reassured she felt. It was just going to be difficult to tell the boys.

After they had all eaten, Bryn accompanied the boys upstairs. Gayle and Barbara had handled everything well; in the strange house they had put all three in one room, bringing in a cot to slide next to the double bed. The children's pajamas were all under their pillows, and their toothbrushes were neatly lined up in the bathroom. Bryn started to help them change, then decided it was time to talk.

"How would you guys like to really play Indians?" she asked enthusiastically.

Too much had happened recently. Three pairs of suspicious eyes turned her way. "What do you mean?" Brian asked, his voice quavering.

Bryn smiled, although the tightness of her face told her how plastic it must look. "Gayle is Lee's sister, you know. She and her husband are going to go up and stay with Lee's grandfather. And he's a real Indian."

"Isn't Lee a real Indian?" Keith asked.

Bad terminology on her part, Bryn decided. Kids learned too fast in the schools these days, she thought ruefully. "Of course he's real. Or half real. Oh, never mind! You're purposely not understanding me! Lee's grandfather lives on a hill by a stream, and he lives just as they did a hundred years ago!" They were still staring at her blankly. "He lives in a teepee," she tried. "A real teepee."

Adam's lip started quivering. Great big tears splashed to his cheeks.

But it was Brian who spoke again. "You're trying to send us away, aren't you?"

"No!" Bryn protested. "I just wanted to let you have a little vacation, that's all. Adam!"

Balling his little hands into fists, Adam ran past her and into the hall. Bryn took off after him, only to pause in the doorway when she saw that Lee was coming—with the squalling Adam raised high in his arms.

"What's all this about?" he queried. Adam kept squalling. Brian faced Lee defiantly. "Us going away!"

Bryn stared at Lee reproachfully. Things would work out fine, huh? her eyes asked him.

"Are you going to marry my aunt? Is that why you're trying to get rid of us?"

"What?" Lee demanded sharply. But then he laughed, setting Adam down on the cot beside him and reaching out a hand to Brian. "Come here, Brian," he said quietly. "We need to talk."

Bryn, wishing she could sink into the floor, watched as Brian stared at Lee's hand for a long while. But then he took it and walked over to stand before Lee.

"Brian, you know that some strange things have been happening lately, don't you?"

"Yes, sir," Brian murmured.

"I swear to you, Brian, I just want you to be safe. Can you understand that?"

Brian shuffled his feet and stared down at them. Keith suddenly walked over to the pair and asserted himself, placing his hand on Lee's shoulder. "I understand," he said with remarkable maturity.

Brian grudgingly looked up. "How long?" he asked miserably.

"Not long at all!" Lee said, tousling his hair. "Your aunt and I will be up to meet you in . . . say . . . two weeks, tops."

"Does your grandfather really live in a teepee?" Brian asked, a note of excitement in his voice.

"Sure does. He can show you all kinds of neat things. How to build a sweat lodge. Carve figures. I'll bet he'll even make you a jacket out of skins if you ask him."

"Wow," Keith murmured.

Lee glanced at Bryn triumphantly. She could see the taunt in his eyes and knew exactly what he was thinking: "*Star Wars*, huh?"

But just as she started to assume that things were going well, Adam started howling again. Bryn scooped him into her arms. "Adam! You'll just be away for two weeks without me, Adam. I swear it, Adam . . . I promise . . ."

I can't do this, Bryn thought. I can't make him go away.

But could she take a risk with him—or with Brian or Keith—again? He had been taken from her once, now she had him back. But would she get him back a second time?

"Adam!" Bryn soothed. She walked over to the bed with him, set him down and lay beside him. Lee followed her, sitting on Adam's other side. The tears continued to slide down the little boy's cheeks, and Bryn thought her heart would surely break.

"Adam! Don't you know how much I love you? I would never, never in a thousand years let you stay away long. I promise, Adam, I'll be there for you, all of my life!"

His tears subsided to soft sobs; she wiped them from his cheeks. He drew a long, shaky breath as she smoothed back his hair.

"I'll always love you, Adam," she repeated softly. "I'll always be there for you."

As usual, when he was upset, his *r* slurred. "Pwomise?"

"I promise, Adam!"

"Pwomise?" he repeated, and Bryn realized that he was staring at Lee.

Lee solemnly returned his stare. "I promise, Adam."

Keith decided to cut in on the action. He came plunging onto the bed, right in front of Adam.

"We're going to stay with *real* Indians, Adam!" Keith turned to Lee. "Can we paint our faces and wear feathers?"

Lee grimaced, then shrugged. "Why not? But you'd better get some sleep, because you'll have to take a plane out early in the morning."

"A jet?" Keith asked.

"Umm."

"My father was a pilot," Keith said proudly.

"Was he now? That's wonderful. One day you're going to have to tell me all about him. But for now...well...Indians do rise at dawn, you know."

Lee stood up, allowing Keith to crawl into the double bed. Brian rose and padded over to the cot. Lee walked to the door and placed his finger over the light switch, then paused with a frown as he realized Bryn was still lying next to Adam.

"I...I'm going to stay in here with them for a while," she said. She was, in a way, lying. She was going to stay there all night. She knew it, and Lee knew it.

Don't hate me! Bryn pleaded. Please don't hate me because I need to be with them tonight instead of you.

She couldn't tell what he was thinking. His golden gaze was unfathomable. "Good night," he told her softly.

He switched the light off, but Bryn noticed that, just as at home, the bathroom light had been left on.

She hugged Adam closer to her, then stretched her arm out to touch Keith's shoulder.

Sometime during the night, Brian had left the cot and climbed in beside her. She dimly remembered waking and hugging him, too. It was crowded in the bed, but it was crowded with love.

Bryn didn't go to the airport with the boys; Lee thought it would be better if she weren't seen driving away and then returning. Lee and the group owned a private Lear, and their pilot would do the flying.

It still hurt to see them go, but Bryn kept an enthusiastic smile plastered on her lips as she kissed and hugged them all goodbye. Gayle hugged her in the entryway, swearing that she would look after her charges with the diligence of a mother hen.

"And you do me a favor too, will you?" Gayle whispered, lightly inclining her head to where Lee and Phil were exchanging a few last words.

"A favor?" Bryn inquired, whispering as Gayle had. "I'd love to, but what could I possibly do for you?"

"Look after my brother. Oh, Bryn! You're the first woman he's cared for—I mean *really* cared for—since Victoria. And all that was such a tragedy! I know that he can be as hard as rock and as cold as ice, but bear with him, huh?"

"Of course," Bryn murmured automatically. What are you talking about, she wanted to shout. But Phil was giving her a friendly hug next, and saying he would see her soon. She only had time for one more quick kiss for each boy, and then they were on their way out. Bryn thought that Adam might shatter her cheerful composure by bursting into last-minute tears, but it seemed that Phil, as well as Gayle, knew something about kids. He carried Adam and talked to him. "Did Lee tell you he had another sister, too? She lives near where we'll be staying, and she has five kids. And they have a stack of toys like nothing you've ever seen...."

Bryn waved until Phil's rented car was long gone. She closed the door and turned around to find Lee staring at her very strangely. As soon as he caught her eyes on him, though, the enigmatic assessment was masked with a smile.

"You okay?" he asked.

Bryn nodded. "So what next, Sherlock?"

He chuckled softly. What next, he thought with bemusement. I'd like to scream like a bloody conquerer, whip you into my arms and race up the steps to the bedroom. I don't think I'm really a savage of any kind; it's just that once man hath tasted the fruit...

She was still walking a fine line between courage and tears. It wasn't the right time to play Clark Gable in his stairway scene.

"Next," he said, "is that we join Barbara and Andrew and the rest over at the Fulton place. We work just like normal. You won't have to do anything but watch and supervise—everyone knew you were in an accident—but I think we should both be there. Then we'll have dinner and head for your house. What do you say, Dr. Watson?"

"I'm sure I could work, Lee."

"No way. You're too valuable to risk."

"You're the boss," Byrn said lightly.

"Hmmm. Why don't I believe it when you say that?" Lee chuckled.

Bryn smiled. As they walked out the door, she came up with another thought. "Lee, I'm going to need all sorts of things. Chemicals, paper. Almost everything I had was destroyed. But I'm afraid if I run into a camera store and start buying everything in sight, someone could get suspicious."

"Good thinking, Watson," Lee teased, "Give me a list and your door key. Mick or Perry can pick up the things and take them to the town house in grocery bags with bread sticking out of the top."

"Sherlock," Bryn replied in kind, "you're half genius."

"Umm, and what's the other half?"

Bryn stared into his eyes and answered, "I'm really not sure yet."

Rehearsal went smoothly. Bryn was touched by the concern of her fellow dancers, and of Tony Asp and Gary Wright. She remembered how much she had dreaded the work she had needed so badly. Taken aside from everything, this was one of the nicest jobs she had ever had.

The rehearsal broke early for the day. Bryn and Barbara and the group went to a Mexican restaurant for dinner, where they kept the conversation so casual that Bryn began to wish again that she could just forget everything. Surely, if she made no false moves, she couldn't be in any more danger....

When she and Lee were alone in his car and heading back to her town house, she broached the subject again. "Don't you think it might still be best just to drop everything?"

"Do you really think that, Bryn?"

She thought about the things that happened to her. Her darkroom destroyed. Adam kidnapped. The crash that had sent her to the hospital for the night. She still felt fear, but also a ripple of that fire-hot fury. She had been pushed against a wall, and when you reached that wall, there was no place to go. Except forward again, fighting back.

"No," she said quietly.

He cast her a crooked grin. "Do you want to hear an old Indian saying?"

"Sure, why not?" She smiled back.

"When the cougar stalks by night, the hunted must become the hunter."

Bryn grimaced. "Nice saying."

"Oh, we're full of nice sayings. When you get to meet my father you'll probably hear them all."

Mick and Perry had already been at the town house. Bryn almost laughed when she saw the neat line of grocery bags set along her counter, a long loaf of French bread protruding from each. But beneath the bread she found everything that she had put on her list.

"Well," she said briskly, "I guess I'd better get started."

"Can I help?"

"Can you hang paper?"

"Sure."

"Then you can help!"

Time meant nothing as they worked. The darkroom was strung with so many lines that they had to duck every time they moved. But by 1:00 A.M. Bryn had finished with the basics. They had enlarged one hundred eighty five-by-sevens to eight-by-elevens that had to be weeded through.

"These are still going to be too small to get much out of," Bryn said wearily as she grasped her stack and bypassed the file cabinet to reenter the house. "But at least we can dispense with the impossible shots before enlarging the rest."

Lee grunted his agreement, following close behind. Bryn started to sink down to her sofa, but he stopped her with a soft chuckle. "Don't get too comfortable. We're not staying here."

"We could—"

"No, because I just had an elaborate security system installed at my house."

"Yes," Bryn murmured. "I guess that makes sense."

They locked up her place and drove to his house. Bryn remembered yawning and resting her head against his shoulder. The next thing she knew, she felt movement . . . and warmth.

Lee was carrying her up his stairway. She opened her eyes and smiled at him with heavy-lidded eyes.

"Did I ever tell you I'm crazy about red-skinned tom-tom players?"

He chuckled softly, huskily. "No. But I'm glad you are."

She was still half asleep when he laid her on his bed, but she didn't stay that way long. She discovered that he had a very sensual talent for convincing her that she wasn't tired at all. . . .

Chapter 13

Bryn was lingering in a pleasant stage of comfort between wakefulness and sleep when the phone began to ring. Immediately she stiffened; a week had passed since the night of Hammarfield's dinner, a quiet week in which there had been a lot of work and a lot of learning to live together. Nothing in the least frightening had happened in all that time, yet still the sound of a ringing phone sent instant shivers racing along her spine.

The sheets rustled, and she knew Lee was rolling over to answer the phone. He glanced her way and saw her anxious features, then smiled reassuringly after his quick "Hello?" Covering the mouthpiece with his hand, he said, "It's Gayle."

"Oh!" Bryn exclaimed anxiously.

"Nothing's wrong, she's just checking in."

Bryn waited while Lee exchanged a few words with his sister, promising that they'd be there by the end of the next week.

"One more day and the video will be finished up. At least at this end. Then the editor will take over." Lee laughed at something Gayle said. "I don't like to sound immodest, but, yeah, I think it's great." His eyes fell with wicked amusement on Bryn. "I had a stunning 'Lorena.'"

Bryn smiled, and he handed the phone to her. "She's got three little urchins tugging at her. They want to talk to you."

They did talk to her, all three of them, grabbing the phone from one another. They were full of enthusiasm. Brian—she thought it was Brian—told her all about his new bow and arrows. Keith was all excited about sleeping in the teepee. "It's made out of animal skins! Real animal skins, Aunt Bryn." She didn't have the slightest idea of what Adam was saying. When he got excited his speech still got garbled into a language that only another four-year-old could possibly understand.

She sent them all kisses over the phone, warned them to be good and promised that she'd be there in no time. Then Gayle was back on the phone with her.

"I just wanted to set your mind at ease," Gayle said cheerfully. "They really are having a great time."

"They sound like it. I admit I was worried about the psychological effect all this might have on them."

Gayle laughed, a pleasant, husky sound that reminded Bryn of Lee. "Don't worry, they're absolutely normal. At least Phil says so. And he should know."

"He should?"

"Umm. He's a child psychologist. Didn't I ever tell you that?"

"No, and I never thought to ask," Bryn murmured sheepishly. "What do you do?" she added with sudden curiosity.

"What else? I'm a violinist with the Philharmonic."

"What else?" Bryn mused with a laugh in return.

"Anyway, we're so anxious for you two to get here! Mom and Dad are coming in next weekend, and they can't wait to meet you!"

"That's wonderful," Bryn murmured a little nervously.

"Well, let me go now and deal with these little Indians. Nothing new, is there?"

"No," Bryn said regretfully. "Nothing new, but nothing bad has happened, either."

"Well, we'll see you soon."

Bryn handed the receiver back to Lee and he hung up the phone, then pulled her into his arms. "Are you going to spend the day studying that new stack of blowups?"

Bryn nodded, fitting herself comfortably against him. "I glanced at them last night, and I still don't think that you can see anything clearly. Every time I blow them up the result becomes granier. I don't know, Lee. We may never be able to see anything. There *is* a couple coming out of the motel ... but ..."

She felt Lee shrug. "Keep at it, okay? That Hammarfield is sleazy."

"Lee, that's a value judgment!" Bryn cautioned.

"It's not personal. Politicians tend to be a little sleazy. It's the name of the game. The public wants its servants perfect, but no one's perfect. So keep looking. I know that things have been quiet, but there's always a calm before the storm, you know."

"Is that why you're being so calm?" she teased.

"Hmmm...maybe..." he began, but they both started as the doorbell began to chime. Lee sat up, gazing at the bedside clock. "Eleven," he groaned. "That's someone from the band."

He had mentioned last night that they were having a practice.

Bryn jumped out of bed, padding across the room to quickly grab underwear, jeans and a T-shirt from a drawer. She glanced back with a frown at Lee, who was still lying lazily in the bed and watching her with amusement. "What are you doing?" she demanded with exasperation.

He chuckled. "Enjoying the view. There's nothing like watching a nude dancer fumble her way into her clothing."

"Very amusing," Bryn retorted, throwing a pair of briefs at him. "You're the stickler for time! Get dressed. I'll get the door." She paused before leaving him. "I thought you said the sound was already mixed. What's the session for?"

"Christmas carols. We've been asked to do an album, and our business manager wants it released by October."

"Rock Christmas carols?"

"Hey, that's been my lifelong ambition! I can be the Bing Crosby of rock 'n' roll."

Bryn shrugged with a smile and left him, pelting quickly down the stairs. Checking through the peephole, she saw that Mick and Perry, as well as Barbara and Andrew, were standing there, chatting as they waited. Bryn twisted the key that turned off the security system, then unbolted the door.

"See! I told you!" Barbara chuckled to the others as they stepped inside. "They've been in bed all morning."

"Hmmm," Bryn murmured dryly. "And what have you been doing?"

"Nothing illegal, immoral or terribly exciting—but at least healthy," Andrew said with a feigned sigh. "We've been golfing."

"Golfing!" Bryn exclaimed, staring at Barbara. As long as she'd known Barbara, she'd never heard about her friend golfing.

Barbara grimaced. "It was all right. Except I landed in one of those sand traps and they made me take another point for it!"

Mick shook his head at her terminology, then reminded her, "That's the way the game is played, Barbara."

"Well, I still think you should just have let me pick the ball up and then swing at it."

"We did!"

"Yeah, with an increase to my score!"

"You were expecting to come in under par?" Andrew teased.

Barbara glanced at Bryn with another grimace. "My score was one hundred and twenty. But that's all right. I wasn't exactly playing with Mike Winfeld, anyway. These guys all were in the nineties."

"We're musicians, not golfers!" Andrew defended himself.

"Where's Lee?" Perry asked.

"He's coming," Bryn murmured.

"One of us should get some coffee on," Mick advised.

Bryn laughed. "I'm going right now!"

Barbara followed her into the kitchen. "Guess what! I'm coming up to the Black Hills with you!"

"You are?" Bryn exclaimed with pleasure. "But what about your show and your business?"

"I quit the show and I hired an assistant. I'm taking a gamble, Bryn. On this really being it."

Bryn hugged her friend. "I hope so, Barb! Wouldn't that be wonderful!"

Barbara hugged her back, then disentangled herself. "I've got to run and start getting things straightened out with the new assistant. I just wanted to tell you what was going on with Andrew. Wish me luck, Bryn. As much luck as you've had with Lee!"

"I do wish you luck! All the luck in the world!"

Barbara waved and started through the swinging doors, then paused. "Oh, by the way! I wasn't golfing with Mike Winfeld today, but I did see him. And he asked about you."

"That was nice," Bryn said.

"Umm," Barbara agreed, then added, "Gee, I wonder what he's still doing here? He should be chasing the tournaments! Oh, well, gotta go!"

Bryn finished the coffee and brought it out to the living room on a tray, only to discover that everyone had already gone up to the studio. She carried the coffee upstairs, looked through the glass window and saw them all sitting around. She couldn't hear a word they were saying, but she smiled because she knew the conversation was animated. Perry and Mick were both waving their hands around wildly.

She called out for someone to open the door, then realized they wouldn't hear her anyway. With a sigh she set the tray down and opened the door herself.

"Coffee, guys!"

A chorus of "Thanks" came her way. Lee walked over and gave her a quick kiss on the forehead. "Interrupt us if you need anything," he told her.

Bryn laughed. "Don't worry, I can entertain myself. I have the pictures, and I want to work out a bit." The den, she had discovered during the week, had a stereo and a good wooden floor perfect for dance workouts. "I'll be fine," she assured Lee. Then she waved to the other guys and closed the door behind her as she left them.

Bryn went down to the kitchen and made herself a cup of coffee, then took it to Lee's desk, where she pulled her latest batch of blowups from his top drawer. One by one she turned them over; then she flipped through them as an animator might to create a motion picture effect. There it was, a man and a woman leaving a motel room. The man hugging the woman...opening the door of a dark sedan...ushering her into it. She had captured the action.

But what did it prove, she asked herself bleakly. You couldn't see the man's features clearly. She could try another blowup, but by that time the film would be so grainy it would still be impossible to see anything.

She sighed and put the blowups back in the drawer. When Lee finished with the practice they could go back to the town house and take another stab at it.

Bryn yawned and stretched and walked back upstairs. Lee was pounding away at the drums; everyone was working. She smiled; it seemed so strange to be able to see him but not hear him.

She changed into a leotard, tights and leg warmers, and went down to the den. Setting a Bach piece on the stereo, she allowed her mind to wander as her body moved automatically to the music.

Hammarfield... If he were guilty of kidnapping a little boy and terrorizing her, he had to be stopped. He was campaigning for the senate. For public office...

Sand traps.

She frowned, tripping in midspin as the words popped unbidden into her mind.

Sand traps? What was she thinking about?

Then cold chills enveloped her, and her teeth started to chatter. Something that Barbara had said had been tugging at her subconscious all the while. She didn't know anything about golf, but what was it that Barbara had said? They should just have let her take her ball out of the sand without adding to her score.

Golf, golf, golf... In the game of golf you were trying for the lowest score possible.

Mike Winfeld won the tournament. But on the day that she had been taking the pictures, she had shot an extra roll because someone had been alone at the sand trap.

Alone... No! Not really alone. Because in the next shots there had been a dozen heads rising from behind the dune. People had been following the golfers like a giant wave. There had been only a matter of seconds when the man had been alone—perhaps twenty feet ahead of the others—and only alone for those seconds because of the slope of the dune. Seconds she had captured because of the speed of her film? Seconds...seconds were relative. It only took a matter of seconds for a quick and clever man to...what?

Bryn rushed out of the den and back to Lee's desk. She pulled out the original set of pictures that she had done and found the roll with the golfer. She could vaguely see the man in the sand, but to know anything for sure she would have to blow up those shots and do what she had that morning with others: flip through the thirty-six exposures and create a motion-picture effect.

Bryn raced back upstairs, past the glass windows to the studio door. Then she paused. The group was all wearing headsets, harmonizing by a microphone. She bit her lip. She might well be crazy; it would probably make more sense for her to do the pictures, then interrupt Lee.

Full of purpose, she changed back into her jeans and scribbled out a note telling Lee that she was developing new pictures "on a hunch." She taped it to the door and left.

She had driven halfway to her town house before she realized she had forgotten to turn the security system back on.

Bryn thought about going back, then decided that the whisperer wasn't going to attack four healthy males. And she was so anxious to see if she was right....

Bryn took her negatives straight into the darkroom. As the minutes passed, she became more and more excited. From dripping blank paper, the pictures began to emerge.

She could barely wait for the enlargements to dry. She forced herself to wait for the pictures to fully develop; then she carried them back into the house.

Chills rippled through her, but there was excitement as well. She could see it all clearly. Disjointed, jerky as she flipped through the shots, but the story was obvious.

There he was... Winfeld. Looking at the sand with dismay. Looking back to see if he could be seen. The wave of people was close, but he must have reached a conclusion with split-second determination.

The film had caught it all. A rustle of his foot hid his ball beneath the sand. From his pocket he dropped another.

Bryn must have been clicking off a roll of film one shot after the other. At 1000 ASA, she had it all. His hand in his pocket; the ball, falling; falling... and on the green.

A game! she thought furiously. It has all been over...

A game. Adam had been kidnapped, and she had been struck and terrorized because of a foolish game where grown men chased a little white ball around a green....

A game for which Mike Winfeld had earned a prize of two hundred fifty thousand dollars.

She had to show the pictures to Lee. Now she could interrupt the band without a thought....

Bryn was so engrossed with her thoughts that she didn't notice the black sedan on the corner.

She was, in fact, turning down the isolated road that led to Lee's house before she realized that she had been followed.

And then it was too late.

Panic surged within her as she at last saw the car in her rearview mirror. She had to reach the driveway first. Had to get through the front door. Had to slam it...

Perspiration beaded on her body, and her fingers began to slip on the steering wheel. Bryn raced over the gravel driveway, jerking to a stop before the front door.

The sedan screeched to a stop behind her.

She flew wildly from the van, throwing herself toward the front door. She got it open; she got inside; she turned to slam it shut and couldn't, because he was there already, throwing his athlete's weight against it....

Bryn screamed. Mike Winfeld—handsome, young, suntanned Mike Winfeld—was reaching for her, his lips menacingly compressed, his eyes hard and cold. "You can't escape me..." he began, but she could. With a cry tearing from her throat she raced for the stairs. He was behind her every step of the way. She heard his footsteps in rhythm with her heart.

She reached the glass-encased studio; she saw Lee. He was sitting at his drums. He was laughing, smiling at something Andrew was saying.

"Lee!" She screamed out his name just as his handsomely muscled arms brought the sticks crashing down on the drums. He just kept smiling. He couldn't hear her, and he was still looking at Andrew....

Bryn started to run past the glass toward the door. She was jerked to a painful stop as Mike Winfeld's hands tangled in her hair. He was spinning her around, dragging her down to the floor.

Bryn grasped madly at the glass, banging against it. But Winfeld was tackling her around the legs. She started falling, her fingers clawing furiously, desperately, at the glass.

"Lee! Lee! *Leeeeee—help me! Help me! No!*"

Lee just kept smiling; she could see the muscles bunching in his arms as the drum sticks flew and twirled out their beat at his command.

"Lee!"

Her nails made a screeching sound against the glass, horrible to her ears. Unheard inside. *"No!"* she screamed again.

And then she was on the floor, shielded from the band's view by the paneling. She kept screaming and fighting, but to little avail. Another man was coming toward them as she and Winfeld grappled. Bryn recognized him. The nondescript stranger who had tried to buy the pictures that first day.

"Took you long enough!" Winfeld panted as he held Bryn down while the second man stuffed a gag into her mouth and looped rope around her wrists and flailing legs. "Don't stand up, idiot! Condor might glance this way! Drag her past the glass...."

Bryn kept trying to scream through the gag as they dragged her to the stairway. Then she found herself thrown over Mike Winfeld's shoulder and carried from the house.

Mike Winfeld paused to rip her note to Lee off the front door. Outside, he told the second man to take her van and follow him in it.

Bryn was stuffed into the passenger seat of the sedan. She kept telling herself that she couldn't pass out with the terror. The fact that Winfeld decided to talk conversationally didn't help any.

"We're going to the old Fulton place," He told her. "You're going to have an accident while doing a little private rehearsal. You're so dedicated, you know, and loyal to Condor. And when you're discovered at the foot of the stairs, well, even dancers can be clumsy at times. I want you to know that this really hurts me, Bryn. You're so beautiful...but...well, you see it isn't just the money for the tournament. It's my career. If it was known that I had cheated..." He sighed deeply. "Over the next couple of years, it could mean millions and millions."

Bryn worked furiously at the rope tying her wrists. Too soon she could see the Fulton place looming before them.

Lee glanced at his watch, surprised to discover that they had worked so long without even thinking of a break.

"Hey, big chief," Mick called out teasingly, "are we calling it quits for the day?"

"Yeah," Lee said, stretching. "I was thinking about spending the afternoon in the hot tub with a freezing cold beer—"

He broke off suddenly, and Andrew frowned at him. "What's wrong?"

"I don't know," Lee said, puzzled. He shook his head. "I just had the weirdest feeling."

"Indian intuition?" Andrew teased lightly, but he was frowning, too. Lee strode across the room, throwing the door open. "Bryn?"

There was no reply. He hurried down the balcony hallway, staring down to the first floor as he called her name. *"Bryn!"*

Andrew, Mick and Perry chased after him. His weird feeling had communicated itself to them all.

"I'll take the upstairs," Andrew muttered.

"Outside," Mick mumbled.

Lee and Perry tore apart the ground floor; Bryn wasn't there.

Mick ran back in from outside. "Her van's gone, Lee. But I think there might just be something wrong. The gravel out here is all ripped up."

Lee stared at Mick for a moment, then barged through the swinging doors to the kitchen phone. By the time the others had followed him, he was listening to someone and scribbling information on a piece of paper. He hung up the phone with a curt "Thanks," then swung back around. "Andrew, go to Bryn's, will you? There's no answer there, but...Mick, Perry, hang around here, okay?"

"Sure," Mick said, "but where are you going?"

"To see Dirk Hammarfield."

He strode into the living room, grabbing his keys off the cocktail table. He turned and noticed his hunting collection. With an absent shrug he grabbed a bow and a quiver of arrows.

Mrs. Hammarfield opened the door with caution. "Oh, Mr. Condor! I'm so sorry, he's just too busy to see anyone without an appointment—"

Lee breezed past her. He could see a library door ajar, and he swiftly crossed through the plush living room, pushed it open, then closed it sharply behind him.

Hammarfield was behind his desk. He paled when he saw Lee walk in. Lee didn't pause. He strode with lethally quiet steps to the desk and leaned over it, grasping Hammarfield's lapels.

"Where is she?"

"I don't know what you're talking about..." Hammarfield began, but Lee gave him a shake and he moistened his lips to speak again. "Condor, I swear I don't know where—"

"You're in Bryn's pictures. You know it, I know it. Where is she?"

Hammarfield's facial color turned to a shade more sickly than gray. "All right, Condor. Yes, I'm in her pictures. But I swear to you, I've never done anything other than ask about them. I was afraid she might have gotten me into them, but I didn't do anything. I swear I haven't done anything but—"

The phone on Hammarfield's desk started to shrill. Lee barely heard it. Hammarfield stared at him nervously. "Answer it," Lee said.

Hammarfield did. A strange expression filtered over his features. He handed the receiver to Lee.

Lee grasped it and brought it to his ear.

"Lee? Lee?"

"Yes?"

"It's Andrew. Listen. Tony Asp just called here. He wanted to know why we didn't tell him about working today. I said we weren't. Then he told me that he'd seen Bryn's car parked on the roadside near the old Fulton place—"

Lee dropped the phone on Hammarfield's desk. "Call the police," he told Hammarfield hoarsely. "Tell them to get out to the old Fulton place as quickly as possible."

Bryn had managed to work her hands free. She waited until Mike Winfeld had stepped out of the driver's seat to spit out the gag and tear at the bonds on her legs. Luckily the knots hadn't been tied well. And she had been given the strength and energy of the instinct for survival.

When he opened her door she was ready. She kicked out at him with a forceful fury that sent him staggering backward. In that split second she jumped out of the car and ran.

The length of the old dirt driveway stretched before her. But she was a good runner. Her legs were strong from dancing, and it was for her life that she ran. Her lungs burned, and her breath came in increasingly painful gasps, but she kept running.

Winfeld was behind her, but she was gaining distance on him with every passing second. If she could just make the road...

Winfeld shouted something; she couldn't make out the words. But then she realized that he was shouting to the other man, his accomplice, the "fan" who had wanted to purchase the photos.

He was standing at the end of the driveway. He had parked her van in a clump of trees and was now coming for her. She was trapped between the two of them.

Bryn veered off the driveway, into the grass and overgrown foliage. Nettles and vines grasped at her, slowing her down. She kept running, but the distance was beginning to tell on her. She could barely breathe; pain was shooting through her legs, knifing at her belly.

She ran into a grove of old oaks. Where the hell was she? Where was the road? If she could just get to the road...

She stopped for a minute. There was silence all around her. And then she heard it. The sound of a car on the nearby highway. It was to her left.

She started to run again, then gasped and came crashing down to the ground as Mike Winfeld stepped suddenly from the shelter of an oak and tackled her to the ground. He wasn't messing around with her this time. He knotted his hand into a fist and sent it crashing against her face. She didn't feel any pain; the world instantly dimmed, then faded away completely.

The door to the Fulton place was partly open. Twilight was falling, and it looked like the perfect haunted mansion.

Lee jerked his car to a halt before the graceful Georgian columns. His bow and the quiver of arrows were beside him; he grabbed them instinctively, fitting the quiver over his shoulder as he began to race to the front door. He threw it fully open.

It took his eyes a minute to grow accustomed to the darkness within. And then he saw Winfeld, halfway up the long curving stairway with Bryn tossed over his shoulder like a sack of potatoes.

Winfeld saw him. "Get him!" he shouted.

Lee cursed softly. He hadn't seen the other man in the darkened foyer. The man who jumped him with a switchblade.

He was able to bring his arm crashing up against the other man's arm, the one with the knife. The switchblade went flying across the room to be lost in shadows. Lee struggled only briefly with his opponent; the man was no contender in a real fight. Lee gave him a right hook that sent him sprawling to the floor.

But when he looked up again, Winfeld had reached the upper landing with Bryn. He was moving precariously toward the railing. Lee could never reach her in time....

He looked quickly to the floor for his fallen bow, grabbed an arrow from the quiver at his back and strung it. "Winfeld!" he shouted.

Mike Winfeld paused, looking down at him. "Drop it, Condor. Or I'll throw her over."

Lee held as still as granite. "That's what you're planning on doing anyway, isn't it? Set her down, Winfeld. It only takes a second for an arrow to fly. If there's one scratch on her, I'll not only scalp you, I'll skin you alive."

Winfeld paused uncertainly. Lee realized that he wanted to kill the man, that he wanted to rip him apart piece by piece. His feelings were purely barbaric, purely savage.

Were they normal, he wondered vaguely. Because they were also tempered by something civilized. He wasn't God, and he wasn't a jury.

He moved swiftly while Winfeld was still pausing in his uncertainty. The arrow flew from his bow like a streak of silver. It pierced Winfeld's jacket and embedded itself into the paneling of the wall, pinning Winfeld there. Although his flesh hadn't even been scratched, Winfeld screamed and clawed at the arrow, dropping Bryn.

Dazed, she rolled across the floor. "Get up, Bryn!" Lee shouted to her. She looked around herself and saw Lee below her, then saw Mike Winfeld pinned to the wall, but tugging furiously at the arrow. She started to race for the stairs, but although Winfeld was pinned, his arms were long. And before she could pass him, he had reached into his pocket and with a sharp click produced the lethal blade of a switchblade.

Lee started to reach for another arrow, then paused. Bryn had raced back to the railing. In the distance he could hear the shrill sirens of police cars.

"Jump!" he commanded Bryn.

Bryn looked at the distance down to Lee. Her hatred of heights swam in her brain. She looked back. The paneling was beginning to splinter. Winfeld was almost free. It was probable that he would still be willing to kill her, if only for vengeance, now that the sirens were shrilling so loudly....

She looked back down to Lee. Sharp golden eyes blazed into hers; she gazed at the beloved contours of his bronzed face, and she saw his arms waiting.

Lee didn't speak again; he stared at her, his plea and demand in his eyes. Jump, Bryn, please jump; don't make me have to kill this man to save your life when you can come to me, and the law can make all the final judgments.

Strong arms, Bryn thought. Powerful arms. Ready to catch her any time that she fell. She had trusted him with her love and her life already.

Bryn swung a leg over the railing and jumped.

He buckled with the force of her weight, but he didn't fall. He wrapped his arms around her tightly and walked out into the beauty of the twilight just as the police cars screeched to a halt before the Georgian columns.

The night, of course, couldn't end there.

Within an hour Winfeld and his accomplice were behind bars, as was the woman who had cared for Adam.

Bryn hoped that the law went lightly on the woman; she was Winfeld's girlfriend, and she had been so terrified of him that she had been willing to do anything. She confessed as soon as the news of Winfeld's arrest had been released, and she begged only to speak to Bryn and offer a tearful apology.

Bryn, Lee, Barbara, Andrew and the rest of the group spent hours with the police, trying to explain it all.

The police were indignant that they hadn't been called in from the beginning, but they dealt with Bryn gently. She mused that they were probably accustomed to dealing with parents who wouldn't risk a child's life at any cost. She also assumed that having the whole lot of them trying to explain things had made the sergeant in charge so crazy that he was willing to let matters rest until it came close to trial time—and then a patient DA could take over.

It was late—very late—when they all congregated back at Lee's house, exhausted but completely satisfied.

It was over.

Bryn looked around at all the faces that had become so special to her. Barbara, a friend through everything. Mick, Perry and Andrew. Lee...

They ordered pizza and sat around, talking because they were all so wired with the release of tension. Then Bryn found herself making a little speech to thank them all, and the talking dwindled. Mick and Perry said their good-nights. Andrew and Barbara decided to go to the town house. Barbara kissed Bryn's cheek; so did Andrew. "We always stick together, love," he told her in a whisper for the two of them alone. "But then...you'll see more as time goes by."

Then Bryn and Lee were alone. She yawned and said that she was going up to bed. Lee kept picking up the paper plates, soda and beer cans. "I'll be along," he told her, and she knew that he was stalling.

She didn't say anything; she went on up to the room they shared, showered quickly and slipped naked between the sheets, wondering dully if it would mean anything. His attitude had suddenly seemed so...remote. Was it over? Had he helped her, then decided that his responsibilities were at an end?

No, she thought, but tears sprang to her eyes. He loved her; he did love her. He had said it time and time again.

In the dark. Whispered words of passion in the night...

She heard his footsteps and lay still, closing her eyes. He didn't turn on the light. She heard him shed his clothing, but when he lay down beside her, he didn't touch her. She rolled against him, and he did slip an arm around her. "Try to sleep, Bryn," he told her softly. "It was a long, long day for you."

She didn't answer him. She stared out into the darkness with tears stinging her eyes again. Time passed; it seemed that aeons of time passed. But she knew that he lay as she did, awake, staring blankly into the darkness of night.

At last he must have decided that she was asleep, because he rose and walked to the French doors. Through the shadows of the night she saw him there, and in a flicker of moonlight she saw his face, taut and gaunt.

She hesitated only briefly, then crawled from the bed and went to him. He seemed startled; he had been deep in a world all his own, she knew.

But he put an arm around her, pulling her to him as he leaned against the door, kissing the top of her head as he held her there. "I'm sorry," he told her. "I seem to keep you awake when I can't sleep."

His body was warm; the moonlight and the balmy night air seemed to caress them both. Still his touch upon her was a distracted one.

"I couldn't sleep, either," Bryn said, and when he remained silent, she turned in his arms, staring beseechingly into his eyes. "Lee...why don't you . , want me...tonight?"

"What?" The query was a startled one. And then he smiled slightly, touching her cheek, and she knew she had his attention at last.

"Bryn, I always want you," he told her. "I was thinking of you. Don't you know you have a massive bruise on your jaw, and scratches and scrapes all over?"

Bryn touched her jaw. It was the spot where Winfeld had struck her, but it wasn't causing her any real discomfort.

"Lee, it's—it's just a bruise, and I don't even notice it. Really. I...I need you to hold me tonight, Lee. Dear God, I'm not that fragile, really...."

He wrapped his arms tightly around her, bending to bury his face against her hair. She felt all his tension. What had she said, she wondered, and then she heard his groan, and the blunt statement that explained it all.

"She killed herself, Bryn. Victoria killed herself."

It all came out. Words poured from him. Jerky words, starting with the time when the prowler had come in and he had defended himself. Victoria's reaction. How much he had loved Victoria, and how, no matter what, she had turned from him—afraid. How she had come to think of him as a savage. How fragile she had been, so fragile that he could not touch her, or reach her. His confusion. His loss. Victoria's affairs—and that terror of him that he could never understand.

Bryn had been so afraid herself—of love. Of giving everything. Yet if ever a heart had been set before a woman, bared and bleeding, this was it. And she could not deny it. She held him tightly, her words pouring out in reassurance, and then in love.

"Oh, my God, Lee, you have to see that there was nothing else you could have done. It wasn't you, Lee. She was...self-destructive. Didn't the doctors tell you that?"

"Yes, that's what they said," he told her tonelessly.

"Oh, Lee, you've got to believe them!" she cried. "Please...I need you, Lee. I need you now, please...."

He gripped her chin in his hand, looking searchingly into her eyes. "Enough to marry me, Bryn, after hearing all that?"

"Lee, don't you see? *It wasn't you!* I love you enough to do anything, Lee," she cried, yet afraid again herself. "But I'm—I'm a package deal, Lee. I come with three little boys—"

"Do you doubt so much that I can love them too?"

"No, I don't doubt you. I just know that it can be—"

"Hard," Lee agreed. "Yes, I'm sure that being an instant parent can be hard. We'll argue sometimes; we'll have problems sometimes. But if we start out right...equal partners...we should make it. If I'm going to be their parent, I'm going to yell at them sometimes. You'll have to respect my judgment—and why are you laughing?"

"Because I love you so much! Because I can't believe that you really want to *marry* me. That you're willing to tackle it all. Oh, Lee, do you mean it? Marriage...forever and forever...?"

"And forever," he promised her huskily. "If you can really bear with me, Bryn, Bryn, I do love you so very much."

"It's magic," she said tenderly and with awe, smoothing away the taut lines of strain and concern on his face. "I can barely believe it."

He ducked slightly, sweeping her into his arms, holding her fiercely, protectively...but tenderly. She felt his love and his passion in the strength of his hold.

"Maybe words aren't enough," he told her huskily. "Actions can speak so clearly. If you'll allow me, I'll try to make a believer out of you...."

Bryn smiled. "I have an open mind. Please...show me."

Never had he made love to her so tenderly. And when they were replete and exhausted, they talked. Openly. About a future that would be real and secure—and beautiful.

Tempestuous, too, Bryn reminded herself. There would be gentle rivers ahead of them, but also raging seas. A man of his passions and vitality was seldom calm. And the past would continue to haunt him. Only time would teach him to be secure in her love. She was more than willing to give him the time—and the love.

Mrs. Lee Condor, she thought, right before falling asleep. It had a nice ring to it.

Five days later they were on their way to the Black Hills.

"We need this vacation," Lee told her as they boarded his private Lear. "A time together with no fear."

She nuzzled against him as they took seats in the richly upholstered chairs.

"I'm not afraid anymore," she assured him. "Not when I'm with you."

"Then I'll always be with you," he said softly.

She kissed him, then drew away with a crooked smile. They stared out at the mountains as the Lear cleared the runway and climbed into a crystal blue sky.

"Want to be married in the Black Hills?" Lee asked her.

She leaned against him and idly caught his hand, admiring the darkly tanned long fingers, the powerful width of his palm.

"Yes. I'd like that very much. And I think the kids would love it, too. And, oh, Lee, I know I've said this a hundred times now, but are you sure? Really sure? Three children..."

He laughed. "I told you. I like little children. I'd like to have a few of my own."

"When?" Bryn asked with a laugh.

He pondered the thought for a minute. "Umm...how old are you?"

"Twenty-seven."

"Let's make you a mother before your thirtieth birthday." He was teasing her, but then he grew serious. "I think we should wait a year and then go for it. I want to give the boys time to know me. Time to feel secure with both of us. How about it?''

Bryn smiled slowly, closing her eyes as she sighed contentedly and burrowed comfortably against his chest.

''I love you so very much...'' she whispered.

His arms tightened around her. And her whisper became an echo that wrapped around them both with warmth and tender beauty.

Epilogue

He was as one with the night.

His tread upon the damp earth was as silent as the soft breeze that cooled the night, and as he moved carefully through the pine carpeted forest, he was no more than shadow.

A distant heritage had given him these gifts, and that same distant heritage had taught him to move with the grace of the wild deer, to hunt with the acute and cunning stalk of the panther, and to stand firm in his determination with the tenacity of the golden eagle.

And it was that distant heritage that he thought of now in his secretive stalk of this dark evening. Because things had never really changed. Years ago his ancestors had trodden the same path. For all the same reasons.

He paused before he reached the stream; he could see her. She was a lithe silhouette against the moon.

Her arms were lifted to the heavens, and then she reached out to him, and he smiled, because she knew that he was there. She did not have to hear or see him; she knew his heart and his soul, and she had known that he would come.

He walked toward her slowly, appreciating the silken glow of naked flesh, and the beauty of her feminine curves. They had made love at all different times of the day and night, but this time, when the moon cast seductive beams down upon them, would always be special.

He stopped a foot away from her. The cool breeze drifted over them both in a sweet promise of sensation.

Wide, thick-lashed, cat-green eyes stared into his. He would never tire of studying her face. High, delicate cheekbones. Copper brows. Straight, aquiline nose. Well-defined mouth with a lower lip that hinted at an innate sensuality. All framed by wild and lustrous copper hair that caught the glow of silver beams and tumbled over her shoulders and breasts like a silken fantasy.

She was his wife. She had given him tenderness and love, and she had given him back his own soul. She had seen through the man to the dark corners of the heart; she had touched upon his weaknesses, and from that healing touch he had learned new strength.

He touched a lock of copper hair, felt the beat of her heart as his palms caressed her breasts. He drew her into his arms, and together they sank to the welcoming bed of earth by the shore of the stream.

Theirs was a ritual as fresh as the coming of spring, and as old as the ancient hills that surrounded them.

It was midnight, and there was moonlight.

And it was a time for...

Night moves.

* * * * *

LADY OF THE NIGHT

Emilie Richards

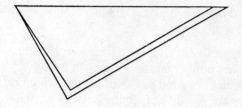

EMILIE RICHARDS

believes that opposites attract, and her marriage is vivid proof. "When we met," the author says, "the *only* thing my husband and I could agree on was that we were very much in love. Fortunately, we haven't changed our minds about that in all the years we've been together."

The couple live in Ohio with their four children. Emilie has put her master's degree in family development to good use—raising her own brood, working for Head Start, counseling in a mental-health clinic and serving in VISTA.

Though her first book was written in snatches with an infant on her lap, Emilie now writes five hours a day and "rejoices in the opportunity to create, to grow and to have such a good time."

Chapter 1

In the beginning there was nothing. An absence of form and sound. An absence of pain and fear. She created the void, and the void was good.

Then there was the voice.

The voice was life. It was life calling back life. And the voice would not be silenced.

The voice moved through the shattered wreckage that had once been a soul, slowly weaving it back together. I will not be denied, it insisted. Once again, you will exist.

Then, as always, the voice was extinguished.

The young woman opened her eyes and there was light. It beat against her eyeballs with an intensity that sent shivers of pain dancing through her body. Pain. Pain was familiar and to be avoided.

Protecting herself instinctively, she sought the darkness. But this time there was no escape.

When she reopened her eyes, they were wide in helpless terror. Words formed to summon back the void, but words spun it farther away. *Please. Please. Not again.* Each word brought her closer to reality. Each word burned away another layer of the mist that cloaked her vision.

Finally, there was sight. On a stark white backdrop lay a hand. The fingers were long and graceful, with nails cut to the quick. As she watched, the hand moved convulsively, forming a fist, then relaxed.

Over and over it practiced until, as if now ready for the long journey, it moved toward her hair.

Suspended in midair the searching fingers stilled. It's not too late, the woman called into the darkness. But the blessed darkness was gone. She was irrevocably alive.

Her hand found her head. Trembling fingers fluttered through the impossibly short strands that layered it. Slowly, inch by inch, she covered her scalp, coming to rest on a thin scar that zigzagged from her forehead to the middle of her skull. Her body twitching in terror, she dropped her hand and focused her eyes on her lap.

The training of a lifetime stilled her quaking limbs. She had gained a tenuous control when at last her eyelids fluttered up once more. Careful not to touch herself again, the young woman began a slow examination of her surroundings.

The white backdrop was a sheet; the firm support behind her, a bed. The light was from a small window to the side. It was covered with heavy mesh, more than a screen, less than bars. There would be no escape through it.

Her visual range disclosed white walls, a steel door with a small window covered with the same mesh. There was nothing else to distract her. The images were pieces of a puzzle, an old-fashioned cardboard jigsaw with no picture on the box to use as a model.

Then, finally, there was sound. A low keening came from the side of the room the woman had not yet examined. As she turned her head by terrified inches, the source of the noise was revealed.

An old woman sat on a bed like her own, rocking back and forth, her eyes blank, her body rigid. The old woman's arms tensed as they spasmodically gripped her body in a fierce, unloving hug. Back and forth she rocked, her rhythm as certain as anything in the universe.

The young woman snapped her head to the front and squeezed her eyes shut as the familiar terror overwhelmed her. But there was no longer a void to which she could retreat. The sound of her own screams destroyed the darkness forever.

Joshua Martane quietly closed the door to room 815 behind him as he stepped out into the dimly lit corridor. Closing the door quietly was one of those habitual responses that made no sense upon examination. The two women on the other side of the door would not have cared if he had slammed it loudly enough to be heard in the emergency room on the ground floor. Both of them were so out of touch with reality that the sound would have been completely ignored, if indeed it even registered.

Old Mrs. Tryon would not have stopped rocking. Years of therapy, medication and finally electric shock treatments had failed to make her take notice of the world surrounding her. A loving but resigned daughter had recently admitted Mrs. Tryon to this the psychiatric ward of New Orleans City Hospital as the first step toward permanent hospitalization in the state institution in Mandeville. There she would probably rock away her days, locked forever from the world that she hadn't acknowledged in almost a decade.

And then there was the patient in the other bed. Joshua leaned against the wall beside the door and thought about the young woman lying inert in the room behind him. Jane Doe. The "Doe" part fit. She was delicately boned and sleek. Her hair, cropped brutally short, was the soft, misty brown of a yearling. If she moved, he knew it would be as gracefully as a deer running through the woods. But she didn't move. She lay quietly in her bed, sometimes opening huge blue eyes to stare straight ahead. The eyes were like a doe's, too. A doe who had not survived her encounter with the hunter.

Jane Doe affected Joshua in a way that no other patient ever had. In all the years of his training, in his experience with hundreds of patients, no one had touched him like the young woman lying in room 815. It wasn't the huge eyes or the almost transparent skin stretched tightly over a delicate bone structure that was much too prominent. It was who she was and who she wasn't. It was the mystery that surrounded her, the secrets that would never be unlocked. It was the waste of potential.

Perhaps if she were to awaken from her long slumber, she would sit up in the bed and destroy his fantasies forever. Certainly if she was what the police insisted she was, the aristocratic features were inappropriate. If she was truly what everyone assumed, then she was a woman who had already given up on herself long before she was found bleeding and abandoned in a vacant lot.

"What planet are you on?"

Joshua lifted his eyes to those of the big black woman standing in front of him, hands on her hips and a smile twisting her full, painted lips. "Betty, I didn't hear you coming," he said, pulling himself back to the present.

"You looked a million miles away."

"It's been a very long day."

"Come get some coffee."

Obediently—because everyone obeyed Betty—Joshua followed the waddling woman down the hall. Betty St. Clair ran the eighth floor of N.O.C.H. with an iron hand she didn't bother to encase in a velvet glove. She knew everything, everyone and every nook and cranny of the extensive ward. Nothing escaped her notice, including one Joshua Martane and his interest in the young woman in room 815.

"When are you going to start dressin' like a psychologist's supposed to?"

"When I start acting like a psychologist's supposed to." He watched her face light up in a huge grin that revealed sparkling uneven teeth.

It was a familiar exchange. Joshua was a tall, broad-shouldered man who wore his faded blue jeans, long-sleeved white shirt and carelessly knotted tie with the flair of a gentleman dressed in formal attire. Betty was one of the few women who encountered him who was not impressed. Her methods of trying to get him to adhere to her standards were always well meant and completely lacking in subtlety.

"Just once I'd like to see you in a dark suit and a tie that matched what you were wearin'," she drawled. "Then we could tell at a glance that you were on the staff."

"You'll just have to tell by the good work I do."

"Been doin' any good work in room 815 today?"

Joshua lifted one shoulder in half a shrug. The pervasive disappointment he felt at not seeing any changes in Jane Doe settled back over him.

Betty nodded in sympathy then turned, squeezing past the nurse's desk to the medicine room where a pot of hot coffee was always in residence. Joshua followed her, nodding to the two psychiatric aides and another R.N. who were leaning against the long counters, sipping cups of the dark, rich New Orleans brew.

"A party and I wasn't invited?" Betty asked with a toss of her black curls.

"Trish and Malcolm are out on the floor," the blond nurse explained in a voice that conveyed her boredom. "Most of the patients are in occupational therapy."

"Thank you, Sarah. I know where the patients are," Betty said.

It was a familiar battle, and Joshua leaned back to watch. Sarah, aloof and elegant, disliked her job and disliked Betty's authority even more. Betty wouldn't give an inch. To Joshua they were symbolic of the two kinds of people who worked on the unit. Betty was strong but compassionate. Sarah was strong-willed and judgmental. Luckily the staff had more Bettys than Sarahs.

Before the discussion could intensify one of the aides turned to Joshua.

"How was your girlfriend?"

All eyes focused on Joshua, and he attempted a smile. "Quiet."

"He likes 'em quiet," Betty confided to everyone. "He likes to do the talkin' himself."

"I get my chance in room 815," Joshua agreed, purposely keeping the lingering sadness from his voice. The hospital staff, trained to pick up on every nuance of a conversation, did not need any more fuel for their teasing. His special interest in the young woman in room 815 was already a favorite topic of gossip.

"I was working the emergency room when that girl was brought in," Sarah said. Sarah rarely teased. Early in her assignment to the eighth floor, she had realized that Joshua would not support her rebellion against Betty. Sarah had worked hard since that day to pay him back. "You were filling in for the chaplain that night, weren't you, Joshua?"

He nodded, unsmiling now.

Joshua was an ordained minister who had found that his call to serve God and man had led him out of the path of the parish ministry and into psychology. Now he only reluctantly donned his clerical collar if he was needed to fill in during a crisis. Working with patients, helping them to make strides toward health, was his greatest skill. It was the long-term interactions, the giving of himself over and over again that made his job worthwhile. The night the young woman had been brought to the hospital in a police ambulance, bleeding and unconscious, had been the beginning of just that kind of involvement.

"You should have seen our Joshua that night," Sarah recalled smugly. "He was a young lion. He was everywhere, in everybody's way, trying to make sure that girl got only the best of care." She paused, minutely adjusting the belt on her crisp white pant suit. "I had to shave the girl's head. You'd have thought Joshua was going to cry."

Joshua's eyes didn't flicker, nor did his expression change. His rugged features remained under strict control. It was a skill he had developed to perfection in his youth.

The others took up the discussion, turning it away from Sarah's venom back to good-natured teasing. Joshua sipped his coffee and remembered.

Jane Doe had been brought in five months before. It had been late at night. Joshua had survived that particular evening on black coffee and the knowledge that he probably would never be asked to substitute for the hospital chaplain again. The hospital had finally agreed to hire another minister to assist the beleaguered young man who now held the job.

There had been two dead-on-arrivals already that night. One had been a fatal stabbing in a barroom brawl, another, a car accident. He had comforted relatives, repeated prayers, held hands. He had jounced a colicky baby on his knee and wiped away a little girl's tears as she was prepared to go to radiology for a broken arm.

When the police ambulance came to a halt at the emergency room door once again, its siren still screaming, he had steeled himself for another crisis and waited quietly by the door as the well-trained emergency team did their job. The young woman who had been carried past him on a stretcher was too pale and still to be alive, but the team had refused to give up on her.

It was in the young woman's favor that she had been brought to this particular hospital. Used to just such emergencies, the staff was prepared. The faint flicker of life had been nurtured. Joshua had watched as a cheap, flashy red negligee was pulled from her body and life-saving machinery was attached instead. Her waist-length hair, matted with mud and blood, had been cut, and her head shaved to prepare her for the surgery that had to be performed to close a gaping head wound. Her face had been scrubbed of its gaudy makeup. The impersonal touch of the nurses had angered him, and he had protested. They had laughed and continued to treat their patient with rough precision. And they had saved her life.

Later he had retreated to the coffee shop with the police sergeant who had followed the ambulance. The man was a lifelong friend. Joshua Martane and Sam Long had grown up on the same block in the Irish Channel section of New Orleans. Together they had fought their way from poverty and petty juvenile crime to a different life. Native sons, both were determined, in different ways, to improve the city that was their home.

"What do you know about the girl?" Joshua had asked Sam.

Golden-haired Sam, with male model looks and a deadly aim that had found a target more than once, shook his head, signaling the sleepy coffee shop waitress for a refill. "Another prostitute murder. Only this time he didn't quite finish the job. If the girl survives, we may be able to nail the bastard."

"Tell me what you know."

"Why?" Sam was curious. Although he and Joshua stayed in touch, it was rare for his friend to ask him about a case.

"I may have to deal with her. I'd like to know what to expect."

"Your kind doesn't 'deal' with her kind," Sam said bluntly. "She's a lost cause."

"Tell me."

"We found her facedown in the mud in the vacant lot behind Hootie Barn's Tavern off Basin Street. One of his 'patrons' tipped us off."

"How long had she been there?"

"Not too long, or she'd be dead. Have you been outside lately?" Joshua shook his head.

"It's cold out there, and she wasn't wearing much. Between the blood loss and the exposure I'll be surprised if she makes it."

"What makes you think she's a prostitute?"

Sam laughed, his perfectly formed lip curling back to reveal strong white teeth. "Hootie Barn's neighborhood isn't for ladies. I don't think the girl was doing social work. You saw how she was dressed, how she was made up. All the details fit with the rest of the prostitute murders we've seen. Only this time the man got careless."

"Go on."

"Well, usually, he beats them good. And then he strangles them with a scarf he leaves around their necks as his personal calling card. He did everything exactly the same this time, but he forgot to make sure she wasn't breathing when he was done."

"Don't you think that was a pretty big error?"

"I'm sure he'll think so when he reads the story in tomorrow's paper. Of course, she may be dead by then."

"No."

"You know something I don't?"

"She's going to make it."

Sam had searched his friend's face. As always he wondered how someone who looked so much like a fallen angel could ever have chosen a more unlikely profession. Joshua was obviously tired, his wavy hair in disarray around his haggard features. Only his slate-gray eyes were still snapping with life. Sam revealed his cynicism. "You got a direct pipeline to the Almighty, Josh? Did they give you one when you graduated from your fancy seminary?"

"She's going to live."

"After what she's been through, that may not be a blessing."

She had lived. Although sometimes Joshua wondered if Sam had been right. What sort of celestial joke was it that the beautiful young woman had hovered near death for three months, finally to come out of her coma unable to respond to the world around her?

At first the doctors thought that she had suffered serious brain damage from the head wound she'd sustained. Now the opinion was that the shock of her near encounter with death and the traumatic circumstances leading up to it had thrown her mind into a place it would never find its way back from. Five months from the day of the tragedy, she was catatonic. Alive and completely unaware, she was one of the living dead.

"Martane here just won't give up, will you?" Betty was addressing her question to Joshua, giving him an elbow in the ribs. "If sheer willpower could cure anyone, he'd have that girl walkin' and talkin' in no time."

"I thought I saw a flicker of response today," Joshua said, finishing the last of his coffee. "When I was talking to her, her head turned slightly as if to follow the sound, and her eyes seemed less dull."

"And old Mrs. Tryon walked on water," Sarah scoffed. "We have a miracle worker among us."

Joshua allowed his eyes to drift to the coolly elegant Sarah. She stood defiantly, but her arms were clasped across her breasts in an instinctive effort to protect herself. Joshua's scathing tongue was a well-documented fact. It was just one more way that he had never fitted the stereotype of the kind, forbearing pastor. This time, however, he let Sarah's sarcasm pass.

"Did you know," Betty asked seriously, "that Dr. Bashir has started the procedure to send Jane Doe to Mandeville along with Mrs. Tryon?"

Joshua hadn't known, but it came as no surprise. The young woman had shown no real signs of progress. Medically she had improved enough not to need any special attention. She could not be allowed to continue to take up a bed needed for other patients. At Mandeville she would receive custodial care. She would be kept alive.

"It's been coming," he said, running his long fingers through his springy dark hair. "I'm surprised Bashir hasn't done it before—"

A piercing scream interrupted the rest of his sentence. It was followed by another and then another. Joshua slammed his coffee cup on the counter, turning to run out of the room, around the desk and down the hall in the direction of the screams. Patients were gathering in the corridor, some talking excitedly, some crying like lost children. A small group trailed out of the door of the cafeteria where voluntary occupational therapy was held. One old man clutched a green-and-red pot holder with the reverence of a child snuggling a favorite blanket.

Trailing behind Joshua, the rest of the staff stopped to organize the milling patients, leaving Joshua and Sarah to confront the source of the screams. Six paces ahead of the blond nurse, Joshua stopped at the door of room 815. The terrified sounds were coming from behind it.

"Let me handle this," Joshua told Sarah quickly. "If we both go in, it will scare her even more." He pushed the door open and strode to the screaming young woman's bedside.

The change in Jane Doe was so vast that for a moment Joshua could only stare. She was sitting up, although when he had left her she had been supine. Her hands were covering her face. As he watched, her screams quieted to whimpered pleas of "No, no," that seemed to be wrenched from the deepest part of her being.

"Procedure for dealing with a patient coming out of a catatonic state." Joshua searched his memory for just such a topic in the hundreds of journals and textbooks that he had studied. Nothing he could remember began to address the present situation. Throwing the part of him that was a careful, objective psychologist out the window, he assumed the role of comforter.

"You're all right," he said quietly. "You're in a safe place. You're all right." Since Jane Doe never had any visitors, there was no chair by her bedside. Joshua pulled one from the side of Mrs. Tryon's bed and sat on its edge. "You're all right," he reassured the young woman.

Flinging her hands from her face, the young woman turned her head and stared as if she recognized him. Joshua was flooded with feeling. He couldn't begin to count the hours that he had sat by her bed, talking to her, asking her to begin the return to life. Now she had. Successes were few. He had not expected one from his work with Jane Doe.

Her hand lay stiffly on the bed, and Joshua reached for it. Immediately he knew he was making a mistake. He could frighten her back into herself by moving too fast. Her return must be gradual and nonthreatening. But the young woman did not pull away. Her hand felt fragile and surprisingly cool. He clasped it firmly but without force, letting her know that she could pull away at any time.

"You're going to be all right," he repeated. "You're safe here. Nothing is going to hurt you."

She was trembling. The delicately boned hand was alive in his. Her whole body was reacting to the ordeal. But she seemed to be trying to relax, to gain control. The whimpering was less frequent, interspersed with short periods of silence. As he soothed her, Joshua studied the terrified blue eyes. No longer blank, they were sparkling with tears that caught in the heavy fringe of charcoal lashes surrounding them.

"You're going to be all right," he said again as he smiled at her.

The door opened with a bang, and Sarah stalked into the room. "This'll calm her down," she stated. "Fifty milligrams of Thorazine. It should put her out for a while."

"Get out," Joshua said calmly, not taking his eyes off Jane Doe.

"It's a standing order Dr. Bashir left on her chart. Move out of the way."

"Sarah, get out of this room right now." Joshua's voice rang with calm authority, but the tension between the psychologist and the nurse was affecting the young woman in the bed between them. She began to whimper again. Snatching her hand from Joshua's, she thrashed helplessly in her bed.

With a sigh, Joshua stood and strode to the side of the irate nurse. "If you don't get out of here right now," he said with perfect control, "I'll toss you out on your aristocratic little behind. Savvy?"

Joshua was a six-foot-three tower of authority. Sarah turned and stomped out, muttering threats and slamming the door behind her. Joshua ran his fingers through his hair before he moved once again to the bedside chair.

"They're trying to help," he said to reassure the thrashing young woman. "But I think you need something else, don't you? I know you're frightened, but you can get through this without a shot. I know you can."

She stopped her restless movements, calming at the sound of Joshua's voice. He saw her take a deep breath and let it out slowly. With fascination he watched her do it again. It was a healthy response to fear, a search for control that was encouraging. She whimpered twice, taking deep breaths in between until finally, she was silent. Her eyes were focused on her hands, but slowly, inch by inch, she raised them to his.

Joshua fought down the urge to reach for her hand again. Instead he put all the comfort he wanted to give her in his eyes and in his voice. "Are you feeling better now?"

She nodded. Joshua drew in a harsh breath. He had not expected an answer. "You look as though you are," he said carefully.

"Where am I?"

Her voice was sweet, filled with long-suppressed music. Joshua wanted to dance or sing to its notes.

He tried not to show his excitement. "You're in the New Orleans City Hospital."

"New Orleans?" She lowered her eyes to her hands again, twisting her fingers relentlessly in her lap as she tried to absorb his meaning. Joshua watched as a single tear trailed a path to her chin to fall unnoticed on the sheet below. "I don't understand."

"I'm sure you must feel very confused."

"Who am I?" She lifted her eyes to his as though she might find the answer to her most crucial question in them. "Who am I?" she repeated. "Please tell me."

He had not considered the possibility that she would remember nothing. Joshua would have given the young woman anything he could, but her identity was something he could not help her with. She was Jane Doe, brutalized prostitute. Beyond that, no one knew anything.

The police had made a detailed investigation into the facts surrounding the attempted murder. They had circulated pictures, talked to everyone who might know, searched for information among their informants. When the trail had ended with no clues, they had stopped trying. Had she been something other than what they knew her to be, they might have continued trying to learn her identity. But in the scheme of things, what was the identity of one comatose hooker worth?

"Can you remember anything at all?" Joshua asked.

Her eyes were the deep velvety blue of a forest wildflower. They were also clouded with fear, and she shook her head. "Who am I?" she repeated with a trace of desperation.

"I'm sorry. I don't know."

She drew in her breath in a low wail, tears rushing down her cheeks to fall on the sheet tucked over her breasts. "Oh, my God," she moaned.

Joshua sat on the bed. Instinctively he reached for her and pillowed her head against his shoulder. Across the room, Mrs. Tryon was rocking back and forth, unaware of the drama unfolding beside her. Joshua took up the old woman's motion, soothing the shattered patient crying helplessly against his shoulder.

The door opened suddenly, and a short, olive-skinned man marched in. "What's going on in here?" he demanded, his voice a heavily accented intrusion in the quiet room.

The young woman stiffened, throwing her hands to her face as Joshua rose to stand beside her. Dr. Bashir moved to the bedside, grabbing her chin with a fat, soft hand. "So there's been a change." He jerked her head up, pushing her hands away in irritation. "Do you know where you are?"

Wide-eyed, she tried to shake her head.

"Still can't talk," the psychiatrist noted.

"She can talk," Joshua said between clenched teeth. "Give her a chance."

"Do you know where you are?" the psychiatrist repeated.

The young woman began to shake her head, which was now free from Dr. Bashir's grasp. She stopped and then nodded slowly. "Yes, I'm in the New Orleans City Hospital."

"Good." He lifted her wrist as if to feel her pulse. "Tell me your name."

"I...I don't know." She began to cry again.

"She's disoriented," Dr. Bashir pronounced. "Confused, probably hallucinating. I've ordered Thorazine for her. Don't interfere again, Martane, or I'll have you thrown off this ward forever."

"If you load her full of tranquilizers she'll never remember anything."

"Are you questioning my authority?" The two men moved to stand beside the door.

"Yes."

"How dare you!"

"If you don't rescind that order, I'll take you to the hospital ethics committee, Bashir."

"And what will they say about your involvement with one of the patients? You were sitting on her bed, hugging her."

"I was comforting her. Touch is an important part of healing. I'm sure you learned that in medical school, Bashir."

"Don't interfere where you know nothing, Martane," the psychiatrist said with disdain. "On paper you may be a member of the therapy team, but in my book you're an untalented do..." His English slang failed him.

"Do-gooder?"

"Yes."

"Bashir, I'm warning you. If you do anything to this patient that sets her back, I won't close my eyes. I won't be satisfied until I have you before the committee."

Both knew it was an empty threat. Psychiatrists willing to work in hospitals like N.O.C.H. were few and far between. Unless he murdered a patient, Dr. Bashir was assured of a job until he retired. But even though the psychiatrist would not be fired, Joshua could make his job more difficult for him. And there was nothing that Dr. Bashir liked less than having his life made difficult.

"I'm warning you," the psychiatrist said, opening the door to storm out into the hallway, "either you stop interfering with my patients or I'll have you working on the housekeeping staff."

Joshua stood quietly by the door, waiting for Sarah to reenter with her medication and her orders. No one came. Satisfied that the psychiatrist had backed down, at least temporarily, Joshua returned to the young woman's bedside.

If possible, she was whiter than before, her dark lashes the only relief against the paleness of her skin. As if she sensed his return, she opened her eyes and tried to smile. "Thank you," she whispered.

Joshua was sorry that she had been subjected to his exchange with her psychiatrist. It couldn't possibly have increased her feeling of security. "Dr. Bashir is a good doctor," he said carefully. "He's just a bit overzealous. We keep each other in line." Joshua sensed that she knew he was lying, and he tried to smile reassuringly.

"You were trying to help me. I appreciate it."

The words and the careful, cultured speech were at odds with what he knew about her. Joshua studied the sculpted, feminine lines of her face. The young woman's speech fitted them exactly. She sounded like a finishing school graduate, not a prostitute. There was a graceful tinge of the South in her words, but they lacked the abrasive twang of New Orleans. The mystery was compounded.

"You're here to be helped. I'm doing my job."

"Tell me how I came to be . . . here." She gestured to the four walls. Joshua watched her glance fall on Mrs. Tryon and move quickly away.

"The police found you." Joshua turned the chair, straddling it. "You were badly injured and they brought you here to recover."

"Injured?" She raised her hand to her hair, touching the long thin scar. "My head?"

"You sustained a serious blow to the head. You were very ill from it."

"My hair is so short."

He smiled at the completely feminine response. "Not as short as the new styles dictate." She frowned and he smiled again. "I'd say it was about two or three inches all over. It's beginning to curl."

"It feels ugly."

"It suits you." Standing he walked to the door. "I'll be right back."

In the hallway he waved down Betty who had just helped a patient back to his room. "Do you have a mirror?" he called to her. In a minute he was holding a plastic compact.

"Bashir is out for your blood," Betty said casually as she watched him open the door. "You've done it this time."

Joshua shrugged, taking the compact as he strolled back into room 815. "Here, see for yourself," he told the young woman.

She stared for a long time, her fingers combing through her hair once as if to test its reality. "That's not me," she said finally, her voice choked with tears.

Joshua cursed his intuition. He had thought that the sight of her face in the mirror would help jog her memory. He had not meant to cause her pain.

"What's different?" he prodded.

"I don't know. But that's not me."

"Your hair was very long," he explained. "Down to here." He gestured to her waist. "They had to shave your head when they brought you in."

A sob echoed in her throat.

"Your nose was broken," he explained, wishing that he didn't have to. "It's possible that it looks a little different now that it's healed."

"It's crooked," she wailed.

"No, it's not. Well, maybe a tiny bit. It adds character to your face."

Her huge blue eyes went dark with disapproval. "You're just trying to make me feel better."

He almost laughed at her righteous anger. "Exactly," he agreed.

Surprisingly, she giggled, then followed it with a hiccup and a small sob.

"You are really very lovely," he said gently. "And that's the truth. But you've lost a lot of weight since you were admitted. With everything combined, it's no wonder you don't recognize yourself."

"It's too much for me to understand," she said plaintively. "I don't understand any of it."

The strain showed in her face. Carefully Joshua covered her hands with one of his own. "You've had a number of shocks in the past half hour. Don't try to figure it all out. Just rest." Even as he said the words, her eyelids drifted shut. It was all too much for her to cope with. Joshua watched the tiny lines of tension dissolve as she began to slip into the blessed oblivion of normal sleep. Her voice, when it came, was very far away.

"Will you be here when I wake up?"

He was entranced with the obvious trust in her voice. His feelings were irrational, but he had to admit he wanted to be there for her. He wanted to watch her awaken, to help cushion her shock at the unfamiliar hospital surroundings. He wanted to hear her musical voice with its hint of gracious living and sultry summer nights. He wanted to hold her hand and anchor her firmly in the world she had chosen to be part of once again.

But he could not stay. She should not become dependent on him. There were others who could play a part in her recovery. "I'll be here tomorrow morning. If you wake up before then, I'll have one of my favorite nurses take care of you."

"Will she hurt me?" Her head inclined toward Mrs. Tryon's bed.

"She may get noisy occasionally, but she's absolutely incapable of hurting anyone or anything."

"Good." With a small sigh the young woman drifted off to sleep.

Joshua sat beside the bed, watching her even breathing. When it deepened and slowed, he got up quietly and went out into the hallway.

The change from day to evening staff was taking place. Joshua saw Sarah and two of the aides waiting to be let through the locked door by the nurses' station, one of the two exits from the ward. Betty was still at the desk, sharing information with the woman who would take her place on the next shift. When she looked up and saw Joshua coming toward her, she frowned and shook her head slightly, as if in warning.

The sight of the tall man coming out of the medicine room was all the explanation Joshua needed. He had hoped that Dr. Nelson, the chief of psychiatry, would wait until the next day to confront him. Obviously, that was not going to be the case.

"Martane? I want to see you in the staff lounge. Immediately."

With a nod, Joshua followed Dr. Nelson down the hall. As usual, there was no one in the tiny lounge when they entered. Since the room was at the end of the hall, it was seldom used. The nursing staff preferred to have their coffee in the medicine room, where they could escape for brief minutes to gossip.

Joshua seated himself in a chair next to the chief psychiatrist's and waited.

"I suppose you've figured that Dr. Bashir has spoken to me about your interference." Dr. Nelson was a distinguished-looking man whose voice was always calm and well modulated. He managed to convey all the emotion he needed with the lifting of an eyebrow, the tightening of a muscle in his jaw, the flash of a brown eye. Joshua clearly understood the anger that was present behind the carefully chosen words.

"I expected him to speak to you. I was hoping it would be tomorrow."

"Why?"

"Because—" Joshua looked at his watch "—as of this minute, I've been here for twelve hours straight."

"Then we'll make this short and to the point. You have no right to try and countermand any doctor's order."

"I know that." Joshua could barely keep his irritation from echoing in his voice.

"And do you also know that I could have you barred from this floor?"

"Yes."

"Then why did you tangle with Bashir?"

"Because his order was harmful to the health of the patient. I've worked extensively with her. To Bashir she's a name on a chart—no, not even that. She's a pseudonym on a chart, a body in a bed that he sees probably twice a week for a minute at a time."

"You know what his caseload's like."

"Yes. And I know what he's like, too."

"Meaning?"

"Meaning that his answer to everything is a shot of Thorazine. The patient made incredible progress today." Joshua's voice softened and pride shone through. "She's made no response in five months, Jim. Today she talked to me; she asked questions. For someone who has been totally unaware of her surroundings, she behaved completely appropriately. Bashir didn't even look at that."

Dr. Nelson was quiet, assessing Joshua's words. Both of them knew what was at stake. Joshua understood that Jim Nelson had to protect the doctors on his staff, but he also knew that the chief psychiatrist was a fair man. He had not hired Dr. Bashir; he probably didn't approve of many of his decisions. An excellent psychiatrist himself, Jim was caught exactly in the middle. It was not a good place to be.

"You're very involved with this patient, aren't you?"

Joshua nodded. "I'll admit I am. But I'm not too involved to know what's good for her."

"Tell me what you've been doing for her."

"Talking."

"Elaborate, please."

"I've been sitting and talking to her. When she was still downstairs in a coma, I'd sit by her bedside every chance I got and talk about anything that I could think of. If she was listening, she knows everything there is to know about me."

"And when she was transferred up here?"

"More of the same, but I've been spending longer hours with her."

"Do you understand why?"

"That's a psychiatrist's question if ever I heard one," Joshua answered with a frown. "I did it because I care what happens to her."

Jim Nelson was only twenty years older than Joshua's thirty-three, but for a moment he seemed much older. "I guess," he admitted, "that it's been a long time since I let myself care that much about what happens to one of my patients."

Joshua sympathized. "I can understand that."

"That's a psychologist's answer," Jim said, a tiny smile touching his lips.

"Look, Jim, you and I both know that I'm not up here just to perform tests and write up reports. I'm here as a therapist. I'm trained for it, I'm good at it, and as such, I will not sit by and watch Bashir destroy a patient."

"How did you make it through school, Martane?" The psychiatrist leaned back in his chair, forcing it onto its hind legs. "With that chip on your shoulder, how did you convince any examining board you could humble yourself enough to do anybody any good?"

"I managed it with great difficulty."

"And when you were in the ministry?"

"That was even more difficult."

"It's going to be difficult here, too, if you don't temper your opinions a little."

"My judgment in this case is completely sound." Joshua leaned forward slightly. "And we both know it."

There was a long silence. Joshua knew that the chief of psychiatry was carefully weighing all the factors. Calmly he waited.

Jim Nelson was nothing if not fair. "I'll tell Bashir that he is not to prescribe anything more than mild sedatives for the girl," he said. "Her treatment plan will have to be cleared with me."

Joshua let out a slow breath. "I owe you one."

"Several." Jim Nelson examined the younger man. "I like you. But your disrespect for authority worries me. The first time I think you're letting it control you and interfere with your judgment, I'll have you off this floor."

Joshua nodded.

Dr. Nelson stood and extended his hand. "Go home and get some sleep."

They parted company at the nurses' desk. Joshua explained to the new staff about the changes in the patient in room 815. Taking aside a dark-haired young nurse, he asked her to keep a close eye on Jane Doe.

He added some notes to several charts, made a phone call to a patient's anxious wife and prepared to leave. But there was one thing he felt compelled to do before he asked to have the front exit door unlocked.

The young woman in 815 was still sleeping soundly when he checked on her one last time. Her hands were tucked under her head and she lay loosely curled on her side like a child who has never experienced anything except love and acceptance. There were no hints of a darker past, nothing to indicate the life she had led except the intriguing lines of her slender body under the thin white sheet.

"I don't know who you are, and I don't know why it matters so much to me," Joshua said softly. "But whatever your secrets are, I'm going to make sure that you have help unlocking them."

In her sleep, Jane Doe smiled slightly.

Chapter 2

There were so many things the young woman didn't understand. The window was just one small piece of the puzzle, but it confused her as much as anything else she was trying to grapple with. The window was designed to keep patients from trying to jump out of it. What kind of hospital worried about such things? And then there was the woman in the next bed. She didn't seem old enough to be senile, and yet she lived in a different world, a world of her own imagination.

Curled up in a near-fetal position, the young woman in room 815 watched the early-morning sunlight fight its way through the closely knit mesh of the escape-proof window. She tried to quell the panic that threatened to overwhelm her thoughts. The night had been endless. Nurses had come in several times, waking her from her restless slumber. They hadn't expected a response from her, and she hadn't bothered to let them know she was awake. Instead she had watched them busy themselves with small tasks around the room.

They hadn't taken her pulse or her temperature. That had surprised her because, without knowing how she knew, she was sure that nurses in hospitals were supposed to check such things. Why was this place so different?

Why was she here? She tried to fight back the most frightening question of all, but it had hovered at the edge of her consciousness all night long. Who was she? What series of circumstances had brought her to this place and wiped away all traces of her past life?

Panic churned through her body, sending pulsating messages to every cell. She knew that if she gave in to it, it would make it impossible to find any answers at all. But the panic seemed to be larger than she was. Encompassing, annihilating.

In desperation she turned to the wall and pictured the face of the dark-haired man who had come to her rescue the night before. It was a strong face. Not good-looking in a classical sense, but wonderfully male. His eyes dominated sharp, almost harsh features, giving his face warmth that it would have lacked otherwise. She couldn't remember the color of his eyes; it was the life that was reflected in them that had impressed her. He had been completely comforting, sensing and understanding her distress. But there had been another facet of his personality that had shone through his steady gaze. He wasn't a man who liked to be crossed. He would fight for whatever he believed in.

Vaguely she remembered words of anger that had left quiet echoes in the room after he had gone. There had been another man with a strange accent that the first man had argued with. Involuntarily she shivered. She felt sorry for anyone whom the dark-haired man disliked. At the same time, she wasn't afraid that he would be angry with her. He had been gentle in all their interactions. He had held her with the tenderness of a lover. She held on to that memory as the room steadily brightened with day's arrival.

A rustle at the doorway pulled her out of her reverie. Instantly she tensed, waiting for pain to be inflicted. Tears sprang to her eyes, and she moaned involuntarily. Desperately she tried to retreat inside herself but that escape was gone. The dark-haired man had taken it from her, and he had told her she was safe.

She knew he was wrong. She could feel her persecutor approach, could feel the terror well in her throat, feel the unseen menace threaten her very existence. With the small store of courage left inside her she turned in the bed to try one more time to fight for her life. But there was no persecutor standing beside her. There was only a nurse with a tray.

The wave of terror subsided slowly, leaving nothing in its wake except a tormenting absence of memory and a body that was trembling with relief. For the moment she was safe. She was alive.

The nurse was watching with careful detachment. "I've brought you breakfast. I'm going to set it here and feed Mrs. Tryon first. I'll be back to feed you when I'm finished." The words were said in the same tone of voice a mother uses while talking to a child not old enough to answer. They sparked a small flame of rebellion in the young woman lying in the bed, and they burned away the last of her lingering terror. The night before she had allowed the nurses to feed her dinner, too exhausted and confused to respond any other way. This morning would be different.

"Thank you," she said with effort. "But I'll feed myself. Can you help me find the bathroom first?"

The nurse gasped, the tray in her hands rattling with her surprise. To her professional credit, she didn't drop it. Instead she set it carefully on the window ledge and walked to the young woman's bedside. "With the greatest of pleasure," she said with a big smile.

The young woman tried to smile in return. She understood very little of what was happening around her. She understood nothing about her fears. But one thing was perfectly clear. She had to regain her strength. She had to regain her memory. Because only with the return of both could she face her persecutor and defeat him. With a deep breath she sat up and swung her legs over the side of the bed.

Joshua slept the sleep of the dead. It had been well past midnight before he unlocked the door of his Esplanade Avenue apartment and found his way to bed. After leaving the hospital he had not wanted to face the solitude of his home, a solitude he usually appreciated. He had wanted a woman's company.

Antoinette Deveraux, a psychologist friend from his graduate school days, had not seen his last-minute invitation as an insult. They had dined at a Korean restaurant near her home in the Mid-City section of New Orleans, and they had talked until neither of them could keep their eyes open. Rather he had talked, and Antoinette had listened.

Antoinette, a declared feminist, could still play the gracious Creole belle when she felt it was called for. Completely sure of her own power and independence, she did not mind exercising the nurturing part of her personality to help a friend. She had sometimes asked the same of Joshua when she'd needed support.

He had not consciously called her to talk about Jane Doe. He thought he had just wanted someone whole, someone who could laugh and flirt and demonstrate the zest for life that was always conspicuously absent on the eighth floor of City Hospital. He had wanted the smell and sight and sounds of a beautiful woman. A woman who would make no demands on him.

Antoinette understood his needs. She had admitted to Joshua once that she was half in love with him; she also had no expectations that their relationship would ever be more than a close friendship. They had met at the wrong time in their lives. The first tentative steps into intimacy had shown what was really important to each of them: their careers, their independence, their need to guard some part of themselves that lovers cannot guard. Now she was available for long talks, for quiet support, and for an occasional, warm, what-might-have-been embrace.

"You've never talked this way about any of your other patients," Antoinette had observed after Joshua told her about the young woman in 815. She sat back in her chair for an after-dinner cigarette and waited for him to explain himself.

Joshua had watched the way the overhead light picked up the blue gleam in Antoinette's long black hair. She smoked as she did everything, with quiet, natural grace. Her hands, long fingered and slender, wove tapestries of smoke and smoldering flame. It was not the only time he had regretted that she was only a friend.

He brought his thoughts back to Jane Doe. "She's captured my imagination, I guess. She's so incredibly vulnerable. It's a miracle that she's alive and aware at all."

"But all your patients are vulnerable, Joshua. That's why they're in the hospital. Why is she so different?"

He hadn't been able to answer. Jane Doe was different. She inspired feelings in him that no one else ever had. He had shrugged.

"Joshua, you need a woman in your life."

He had shrugged again, wondering if Antoinette was seeing something that he could not see himself. "I thought we agreed that I don't want to invest as much of myself as a relationship takes."

"That was months ago. Now it seems you're ready to try."

"I'm not so ready that I'd consider getting involved with one of my patients."

"Then perhaps you should take yourself off that case. I think you're already involved."

Joshua had gone to bed with Antoinette's words still tugging at his consciousness. It was past ten when he awoke. It was his day off, but there was no time to lie quietly in bed and contemplate plans for the day. He had promised Jane Doe that he would be at the hospital to see her that morning. He had no intention of breaking that promise. It was possible that Antoinette was correct. He might be too intrigued with the soulful-eyed prostitute to be as objective and insightful as a therapist had to be, but one thing was certain. Abandoning her now would be cruel. It might hinder her recovery.

At eleven o'clock, freshly showered and shaved, he rang the buzzer that would assure his admittance to the eighth floor. Betty was waiting for him. "It's the miracle man," she said in greeting. "I thought you had a day off."

"I do. But I wanted to see a patient."

"Let me guess," she said smugly.

"How's she doing?"

"Go see for yourself. Just don't go gettin' her too excited. She's still got a long ways to go."

He nodded. "I'd like to take her to the sunroof."

Betty frowned. "She's real weak in the knees. You'll have to take a wheelchair."

"Fine."

"Then I don't see why not."

It was symbolic of the changes in room 815 that Joshua felt compelled to knock in warning before he entered. Mrs. Tryon was rocking monotonously on one bed, but the other bed was empty. Standing at the window was the painfully thin figure of Jane Doe.

"Hello." Joshua announced his presence as casually as he could.

She turned, surprised by his voice. A pink blush tinted her skin and her fingers grasped self-consciously at the back closing of her hospital nightgown. She was obviously embarrassed by her skimpy attire.

Although she had lost too much weight as a result of the trauma her body had undergone, she was still gracefully shaped and her delicate bone structure was clearly emphasized. She held her head proudly, its lovely contours starkly visible beneath the short curling hair that covered it to fall softly against the back of her neck. The muted brown wisps had been fluffed around her face and parted to cover the scar that would fade into oblivion with time and a longer hairstyle.

"I'm not dressed," she said softly.

He could tell her that he had seen all there was to see of her the night they had stripped the skimpy nylon negligee from her bruised body, but instead he smiled slightly and averted his eyes. "I'll get the nurse to bring you another gown. You can put it on over that one with the closing in the front like a robe."

Out in the hall he flagged down Betty to make his request.

"I'm surprised she's worried about her modesty," Betty said with a shrug. "Considerin' what she used to do for a livin'."

But she had been worried, and Joshua found it endearing. He waited a few minutes after one of the aides arrived with the second gown before he reentered the room. She was sitting on the side of the bed, a sheet drawn over her lap. "I'm glad you came back," she said, as if in apology.

Joshua turned the chair and straddled it, examining her face. She was trying to smile, although the haunted expression in her eyes was making the effort almost useless. "How do you feel this morning?" he asked.

"Confused."

"That's understandable." He waited.

"Weak."

"Also understandable."

"No one will tell me anything."

Joshua frowned. He knew that the nurses were afraid they might throw her back into her state of oblivion. But the apprehension she must be feeling because no one would give her any information might set her back even more quickly. "I'll answer your questions as best I can."

She seemed to relax visibly. He watched her long lashes flutter down as she looked at her hands in her lap. "Tell me about this place."

"Better yet, I'll show it to you." Joshua went out into the hall and discovered that the wheelchair was waiting. Pushing the door open with his back, he brought the chair beside her bed. "We'll go for a ride."

She hesitated, her hand unconsciously smoothing the sheet over her legs. He could almost see the struggle she was undergoing. Her bed was a safe place, the wheelchair an unknown. "Are you going to stay with me?"

He nodded.

With a small sigh, she stood, transferring her body to the chair. Joshua pulled a blanket off the bed and tucked it around her. She was so slight that there was substantial space between her thin frame and the sides of the chair. "We're going to have to fatten you up," he said, sensing that she was uncomfortable with his casual touch.

"Food tastes funny."

"Then you're obviously getting well. Hospital food is supposed to taste funny."

There were patients milling around in the hallway, and Joshua stopped and spoke to them as he pushed the chair toward the exit. Once there he waited for Betty to unlock the door.

"Do you have Dr. Bashir's permission to take this patient off the ward?" Sarah came to stand beside the wheelchair, her gaze lingering distastefully on the young woman sitting in it.

"I have Betty's permission, which is all I need."

"I'm going to make a note of this in her chart."

"Thank you. It will save me the trouble."

Sarah's cheeks were stained with red as she turned to march back to the desk. In a minute Betty was at the door with the key, and they were through the door and standing beside the elevator.

Joshua observed that the young woman's hands gripped the arms of the wheelchair. Her knuckles were white with the effort. Casually he squatted beside her so that they were on the same level. "If this is too frightening right now, I can take you back to your room."

For one moment she considered his offer. She was torn between her desire to begin the return to life and her terror that by doing so she would be forced to face the unknown menace lurking behind the locked door of her conscious mind. "Everything is too frightening," she said softly. "But I don't think I've ever been a coward." She sat a little straighter. "I want to see where I am."

"I'm just going to show you part of the hospital. I'll tell you about the rest of it."

In the elevator, he pushed the button to take them up one floor to the sunroof. "New Orleans City Hospital is a five-hundred-bed general hospital. It's well-known for its fine emergency room, its ongoing work in public health, its cardiac and intensive care unit and its psychiatric ward," he recited.

She stiffened at his last words.

On the ninth floor, Joshua turned the chair toward the sunroof, nodding in greeting to other members of the hospital staff. It was a warm day. April in New Orleans was flexible, sometimes hot, sometimes cool. Today the sun shone down with spirit. Joshua pushed open the glass doors leading to the flagstone terrace and pulled the wheelchair through. Choosing a spot where the shadow of the building would provide his patient with shade, he steered the wheelchair to a halt.

Her eyes were tightly shut as if the introduction to the outdoors was too much stimulation to handle, but with satisfaction, Joshua watched her make the supreme effort to open them. She took a deep breath to chase away the stale air of the hospital room, and for long minutes, both of them were quiet.

Finally he left her side to pull a chair into the shade next to her. By the time he rejoined her, her cheeks were streaked with tears. "Do you know why you're crying?" he asked gently.

"It's the sunshine."

He waited.

"I'd almost forgotten."

He understood. She was reacquainting herself with the simple things. They would be groundwork for the more difficult things that must follow.

"I'll try to bring you up here someday when it's raining. The drops of water scamper across the flagstone and pool in the cracks. The whole terrace sparkles."

She ignored his attempt to make small talk. "Why were the exit doors locked?"

"To keep patients from wandering out of them."

"Why aren't patients allowed to wander?"

"Because they could hurt themselves."

Joshua knew what her questions were leading up to. He wanted her understanding to expand in small stages. The truth would be less traumatic that way.

"Why don't the nurses take temperatures? Why does the old lady rock all day? Why am I in a psychiatric ward?" By the third question her voice was an unsteady plea.

Joshua reached into his pocket for the clean handkerchief he always carried. "Because you've been out of touch with reality."

Her head was in her hands, and he saw the sobs shaking her thin shoulders. There was such defeat written in the posture of her slumping body. He wanted to take her pain and share it, but he knew that no one could. After he placed the handkerchief in her lap, his hand reached to stroke the short strands of hair. His fingers were surprised by their silky feel.

"How long?" she asked finally, her voice still choked with tears.

"You were admitted in November. It's April now." She lifted her head, and he could almost see the mental arithmetic.

"Five whole months!"

"You were in a coma until after Mardi Gras. Then gradually you improved."

"I don't remember!"

"No. I know you don't."

"It's all black. And the time before that. All the time. Everything is black."

He didn't want her to dwell on the horror of a lifetime that had suddenly ceased to exist. "You're beginning to establish memories now. Tell me what you remember about yesterday."

She was trying hard not to give in to her fear, and she grabbed on to the excuse for conversation. "I remember opening my eyes. The light hurt them, and I was afraid. Everything was strange. I wanted to go back to sleep, but I couldn't. The harder I tried the more awake I became."

"That's very good," Joshua reassured her, reluctantly removing his hand from her hair. "Go on."

"Then I recognized my hands. I lifted them and found the scar on my head and I was terrified." She took a deep breath. "I think it was much later that I began to notice other things in the room. Finally I saw the old woman. And I began to scream."

"You must have been very frightened."

She gave a ladylike snort at the understatement. "You were there for the rest of it."

"I came charging into the room to see what was happening."

"And you were familiar. I felt safe when I recognized you."

He was taken aback by her words. "Recognized me?"

"Your voice." She was quiet so long that Joshua was beginning to think that she was drifting back into eternal silence. Finally she turned her head to look at him. Her eyes were luminous with the aftermath of tears. "Your voice was familiar. In the darkness I would hear it calling me. I hated it at first."

Joshua fought for his objectivity, but he could feel it slipping away. He no longer felt like a therapist asking the correct questions. He felt like a man struggling with something much more elemental. "And later?"

"Later, I didn't hate it."

Joshua knew that patients in comas or in catatonic states were thought to hear and understand voices around them. Having it confirmed so matter-of-factly by the young woman he had spent countless hours monologuing to was humbling. "Do you remember what you felt?"

"Safe."

"I'm glad." He watched the huge blue eyes search his face.

"Were you in my room earlier yesterday? Before I screamed?"

He nodded.

Her face was grave as she tried to find the right words to express her feelings. "I remember feeling as though I had been deserted. That's when I opened my eyes and the light hurt them."

They had come full circle. It was inconceivable that they could be sitting on the sunroof talking rationally about her recovery from a mental paralysis that had seemed incurable the day before. But Joshua knew that psychiatry, like every phase of medicine, had its miracles.

"Your mind had to take that time to heal itself," Joshua explained carefully. "And it's going to take longer for you to begin to put everything that's happened in its proper place. With more time, you'll begin to remember the past."

She shuddered involuntarily. "I'm not sure I want to remember." Her fingers sought the scar on her head.

"When you're stronger you'll want to remember."

"Will you tell me everything that you know?"

Joshua tried to quell the rush of sympathy he felt. He wanted to answer her questions, but he knew that all the facts were too brutal to confront her with so soon. "I told you yesterday what we know about you."

"You said that the police found me."

"That's right."

"Where?"

He tried to soften the truth. "In a lot behind a restaurant." Hootie Barn's Tavern was hardly a restaurant, but the small exaggeration seemed appropriate.

"I didn't have any identification?"

"No." Nothing but a scarf left by a madman.

"Do you know what I was wearing?"

"A nightgown."

"Only a nightgown?"

Joshua wasn't sure, but her primary reaction to that piece of information seemed to be embarrassment. What a contradiction she was. "Your X rays indicate that you're about twenty-five. Before the trauma to your head you were in good health, although there were some signs of previous bruises and dehydration."

The young woman shook her head as if to rid herself of the picture he was painting. "There must have been something else."

"I wish I could be more help," he said. It wasn't a lie. He truly wished he could. He wanted to pull her into his arms and comfort her.

The silky feel of her hair still lingered on his fingertips, and he wanted to touch her again. But the strength of his own response was a warning.

Jane Doe was not the first patient he had let himself care about. But she was the first who had captured this much of his heart. His own strong physical reaction to her was like a red flag. Antoinette was right. Therapists should not get involved with their patients. But repeating that intelligent piece of advice didn't seem to help. Beyond his role as her therapist was a personal reaction that had started the night she had been brought into the hospital.

From the beginning he had been fascinated by her, emotionally moved by her life-and-death struggle. He was a former minister, but his interest had nothing to do with wanting to set her on the right path. And it was more than the completely normal reaction of a man to a woman who has made her living pleasing others. The closest he could come to putting a name to his feelings was to say that he felt a bonding with the young woman whose name he didn't even know. Sitting beside her bed when she was comatose he had felt a commitment to her that was as strong as any feeling he had ever had. And in spite of it, or because of it, he should begin to back away. Soon he would be no good to her at all.

One major complication was on the horizon, however. The young woman trusted him. He had called her back from the darkness, and with him she felt safe. It would take time for her to develop that feeling for someone else. And she didn't have time. She was scheduled to go to the state hospital in a matter of days. Joshua was effectively blocked from doing what he knew he must. He could not take himself off this case, no matter what it cost either of them.

"Did the police try to find out who I was?" There was a slight frown crinkling her forehead. "Didn't anyone report me as missing?"

Joshua forced himself to sound as reassuring as possible. "The police tried, but no leads turned up. So far, no one who knows you has come forward. Of course that doesn't mean that they won't." He didn't add that some of New Orleans's most notorious pimps had been called in to try to identify her. More than one had volunteered to take her off the hospital's hands when she recovered.

She folded her hands in her lap and stared at them, rearranging her fingers until she felt calmer. "Why don't you tell me about yourself? Are you a psychiatrist?"

He smiled at the prejudice apparent in her pronunciation of the last word. "No. I'm a psychologist, a therapist."

"I don't know your name."

"Joshua. Joshua Martane."

"Dr. Martane?"

"Joshua."

She managed a small smile. "Now I'm supposed to tell you who I am. Only I can't."

"You were admitted as Jane Doe."

She wrinkled her nose in distaste.

"There's nothing sacred about it. Why don't you think of something you like better?"

She ignored his suggestion. "Do you see many cases like mine?"

"No."

"That's going to make it difficult to help me, isn't it?" Years of not knowing her identity stretched in front of her.

"There are some problems that we see every day and we still haven't found a way to cure them. Familiarity is not a guarantee of success. Personally I think your prognosis is good."

She raised her eyes slowly to his. "Because you want it to be?"

He was surprised at her skill in asking questions. Her thought processes were completely rational, her expression, or "affect" as psychiatrists referred to it, was completely appropriate at all times. The human mind was a mystery. Researchers probed, developed hypotheses, formulated theories, and still the mysteries could outwit the sharpest intellect.

"Why are you looking at me like that?" she asked.

"You astound me," Joshua said truthfully. "You're recovering right before my eyes."

"And for a long time you hadn't expected me to recover at all."

Now she was even interpreting facial expressions. Correctly. He smiled. "I never gave up hope."

"Thank you for that."

Their roles were disintegrating. She was no longer patient; he was no longer therapist. They were two people who believed in each other. They were two people who had shared in a miracle. Once again Joshua realized how perilous was the line he walked.

"I'm going to take you back now." He stood and moved behind the wheelchair.

"Joshua?"

He wondered how his name could sound so sweet. "Yes?"

"I'll never forget what you've done for me."

"You've done it yourself."

"Not by myself."

He watched as she wearily leaned her head against the back of the wheelchair. By the time they were at the elevator, she was fast asleep.

"She was still sleeping when I moved her back to her bed." Joshua was telling Betty about his conversation with Jane Doe. For a moment he let himself remember the fragile, feminine feel of her body as he had lifted her in his arms to tuck her back between the sheets. She had slept right through it, too exhausted to do more than sigh in gratitude.

"I've only seen this kind of recovery one other time," Betty mused. Betty, who never attempted to impress anyone, was probably the most astute and well-educated psychiatric nurse whom Joshua had ever run across. When she made an observation, everyone listened. "It was a child, a little boy abused by his parents. The courts finally had him put in the hospital 'cause his teacher at school began to complain about his bizarre behavior."

"What happened?" Joshua leaned back against the nurses' desk, mentally filing away the case history that was unfolding.

"Well, he was talkin' to doorknobs, hoppin' on one foot twice, then the other once. Just like a Bourbon Street tap dancer, only nobody was throwin' coins at him." Betty fluffed her hair. "His folks got scared 'cause the social worker started to uncover some of the stuff that was goin' on at home."

"What stuff?"

"Bad stuff. Beatin's, lockin' him in closets. Finally, his folks left town." Betty smiled, remembering. "I had to be the one to tell him that they'd gone. He just looked at me. It was the first time he'd ever looked me in the eye. Then he said, just as clear as anythin', 'Are you sure?'"

Joshua shook his head, bemoaning lost innocence.

"I told him yeah, I was sure. Then he smiled and asked me what we were havin' for lunch. He never talked to another doorknob or danced again. Last time I heard, he had finished high school and was sellin' cars on the West Bank, makin' a fortune."

"And, of course, everyone said they had known all along that he was really going to be fine," Joshua concluded.

"Goes without sayin'. But I don't think this girl's too different. She's been waitin' until she felt it was safe to get well. Takes a strong person to have that much control."

"I'm not sure she thinks that it's safe, even now."

"She might be right." Betty laughed softly at Joshua's raised eyebrow. "We get so used to discountin' what the patients up here say. After all, they're crazy folks. But this girl just might have a point. Someone tried to kill her once."

"He won't try again. As long as she's not out walking the streets, she's safe from that maniac."

Betty shrugged. "I don't know about that. But I do know that it pays to listen carefully. Even when the words aren't bein' said out loud."

Jane Doe smiled wanly at the middle-aged woman who was introduced as the daughter of Mrs. Tryon. There was no way that the surprised woman could hide her amazement that her mother's roommate had made such a startling recovery. As she fussed around, preparing her mother to get in a wheelchair for a ride around the ward, she continuously sneaked glances at the opposite bed.

"Could my mother get better like that—" The daughter's words were directed at a nurse who was helping her maneuver Mrs. Tryon's wheelchair through the doorway, and as it closed, shutting off the rest of the question, tears gathered in Jane Doe's eyes. It was inconceivable to her that only the day before she had resembled Mrs. Tryon. "Perhaps it would have been better if I'd never improved," she whispered to herself. "The miracle happened to the wrong patient. The one who didn't deserve it."

She had been sitting up most of the day except for the nap she had taken before lunch. Tired, and completely discouraged, she lay back on the bed and shut her eyes. She wanted to shut off the voices in her head, too, but they faithfully replayed the conversation she had engaged in with her psychiatrist several hours before. It was too bad that her memory of the rest of her life wasn't as crystal clear.

There were no tears to cry. She lay perfectly still, willing her mind to retreat from the truth Dr. Bashir had bestowed on her like a gag gift at a birthday party. Only the truth wasn't funny at all. It was sordid and frightening.

The door opened and closed softly, and as always, she tensed, afraid to open her eyes. Her persecutor might be waiting for her. She had no other name for the mist-enshrouded man who tormented her, instilling fear in every cell of her body. Helplessly she waited for pain to be inflicted, and when it wasn't, she forced her eyes open to search for it. Joshua was standing beside the bed, and relief flooded through her body, washing away the fleeting memory.

"I thought you were asleep."

Dr. Bashir's words returned to haunt her. They were almost as horrible as her vision of the persecutor. Tears welled in her eyes again, and she closed them tightly. "Go away."

She heard the sound of the chair being pulled beside her bed, and she turned in the opposite direction, willing Joshua to leave her alone. "Go away," she repeated.

"Not until you tell me what's wrong."

"Don't waste your time."

There was no answering scrape of the chair. Self-consciously, she threaded her fingers together, hoping that she could outwait him.

"I have all night," he said finally. "I'm here to visit—I'm not on duty."

"You're wasting your time."

"I don't think so."

His perseverance angered her. She pulled herself up to a sitting position and slowly rotated to face him. "Trying to save a soul, Reverend Martane?"

Joshua heard the anger in her voice. "Are you upset because some-one told you I used to be a minister?"

She ignored the soft-spoken question. "Are you here to hear my confession? Sorry, I can't remember any of the glorious details."

Joshua searched her face, trying to figure out what was causing the suffering he saw. "What's upset you?"

"The truth!"

Joshua waited.

"The truth you didn't bother to tell me."

"And what truth is that?"

She couldn't make herself say the words. They stuck in her throat, burning away her speech. Lowering her head, she gazed through misty eyes at her fingers.

"You've been talking to someone."

She didn't move; only the tears slipping down her cheeks signaled that she had heard him.

"A nurse?"

She shook her head slightly.

"A doctor?"

She didn't move, but the deep breath she took told Joshua he was on the right track. "So Dr. Bashir has been here to see you."

"Why didn't you tell me I was a ... prostitute?" Her voice cracked with the effort it had taken to say the last word. "Why didn't you tell me that someone tried to murder me? God, I wish he'd succeeded!"

For a moment, Joshua wanted to shake her. His anger at Bashir for telling her the truth when she was not yet ready to hear it knew no bounds. But he was angry at her, too. She was giving up. "Your life is precious," he said finally.

"At least I understand your interest in me now." Self-disillusion-ment and bitterness dripped from every word. "If anyone on the ward needed your Christian attention, it was me, wasn't it?"

"I'm here because you need help, and for no other reason."

"And of course, if you just happen to make a good woman out of me in the meantime, you won't be disappointed, will you?"

That she could be this angry and challenge him so openly was a good sign. But the human part of Joshua Martane, the part that was emo-tionally invested in this young woman, was hurt by her words. Still, when he answered, it was as a therapist. "What you do with your life is up to you. I'm here to help you put the pieces back together, but how you put them together is your decision."

She had been sure that her words would drive him away. She obvi-ously did not deserve to have Joshua Martane in her life. His forbear-ance completely dissolved her weak defenses. "I'm sorry," she said with a sob. "I'm so sorry." She hid her head in her hands, wiping her tears on the sheet.

Joshua itched to comfort her. Instead he forced himself to watch as she sobbed out her pain. "You have nothing to apologize for."

"Evidently I do," she said, struggling to stifle her misery. "Evidently I have a lot to be sorry about."

It was apparent to Joshua that Dr. Bashir's talk with her had not unlocked any new mysteries. She was still wandering in the dark, trying to fit the pieces of information they gave her into one intelligent whole. She had no memory of her past life. It was as if she had been born again, but she felt no forgiveness for her past mistakes. Indeed, they were mistakes she didn't even remember.

Finally she was calmer. "I don't want to talk about this anymore."

"Fine. We don't have to." He cast around for a safer subject. "I'm having trouble with something, and I need your help."

She lifted wet eyes to his. "What?" she asked suspiciously.

"I don't want to call you the patient in room 815 anymore. And you've already let me know that Jane Doe has no appeal for you. I want you to come up with a new name for yourself." He didn't add that beginning to establish a new identity could be helpful if her memory didn't return before she had to leave the hospital.

"I don't care. Call me what you want."

Joshua continued to prod. "Is there a story that you remember, a character you'd like to name yourself after?"

"How about Mary Magdalene?" All the bitterness she felt about the revelation of her background resounded through the suggestion. "It's such a good analogy. The prostitute saved by the man of God."

"You're no longer a prostitute, and I'm no longer a man of God. I'm just Joshua and you're a woman who needs a name." Joshua tilted his head, placing his fingers beneath her chin to lift her gaze to his. "But I like the name. Mary Magdalene led a useful, important life. I'm going to call you Maggie."

She refused to look at him, closing her eyes against the warmth and compassion in his. But his words rang in her head. Maggie...Maggie. She felt herself moving into darkness, anchored only by Joshua's touch.

Maggie, darling. Don't run down those stairs. There was a man's voice calling to her through the black fog. Unlike the persecutor, he was not mist enshrouded, only very far away. *Maggie, darling...* He was gone.

She had no idea how long she had been silent. When she opened her eyes, Joshua was still watching her, his fingers resting beneath her chin. Her eyes locked with his. Behind the compassion was a subtle flicker of something more primal. Joshua was not oblivious to her. She understood instinctively that she was not a patient like every other patient to him. That thought and the tiny sliver of memory lifted her feeling of anonymity. She was, after everything, still a person worthy of his concern.

"Maggie will be fine," she whispered. "Just fine."

Joshua noticed the change, the slight lifting of the cloud of depression enclosing her. He dropped his hand. "Maggie what?"

She shrugged.

"Maggie sounds Irish. How about Kelly?"

She shrugged again. "With a name like that, I'll have to dance jigs and eat corned beef and cabbage."

"If you can dance a real jig, we might be on the trail of something."

"Sure. If I'm Irish American, I might be one of millions instead of billions."

She was trying to joke, and Joshua smiled his encouragement. "We'll find out who you are, Maggie. In the meantime you're to work on getting well, not on regretting a past you don't even remember."

"With that attitude, I can understand why you left the church."

Her perception was amazing. Maggie was a woman with keen intelligence and sensitivity. More than ever Joshua found himself drawn to her. "Now my job is simply to help you get well. While I'm doing it, let's both throw away our stereotypes, shall we?"

She lowered her eyes and drew a deep breath. "Thank you, Joshua. I've been feeling so...soiled."

He wanted nothing more than to gather her in his arms and give her the physical reassurance she needed. But he knew that touching her that intimately was no longer safe. Instead he stood, squeezing her shoulder for a moment, before he turned to leave. "Sleep well tonight."

"Thank you." She watched him disappear through the door, and she struggled to convince herself that her courage and strength were not disappearing with him.

Chapter 3

Maggie was sitting on her bed reading a February issue of *Newsweek*. It didn't matter to her that the magazine was completely out-of-date. She hadn't been aware of the world situation in February. She hadn't been aware of anything.

It was one of the tricks of the amnesia that gripped her that she could remember general facts like the name of the president and the capitals of forty-three of the fifty states. Arguments about the economy and the environment seemed familiar. Titles of television shows came easily, and sometimes she found that she could sing along with songs on the tinny radio that played incessantly in the patients' cafeteria. Unless the songs were new, that is. Then they were totally foreign to her.

She had just washed her hair, and the soft wisps were curling around her face. She had changed into a clean hospital gown, using another one as a robe. The rough cotton chafed her thighs, and she wished for a real nightgown or casual street clothes like those the other patients had. But there was nobody to bring her anything from home. It was possible that there wasn't even a home. Trying to shake off that melancholy thought, she forced herself to concentrate on the article about nuclear disarmament.

"Maggie?"

The familiar voice sent a warm rush of sensation through her nervous system. "Joshua. Come in."

He came to her bedside, noticing with satisfaction that they were alone. It was always easier to talk without Mrs. Tryon rocking in the

Lady of the Night

next bed. He pulled the straight-backed chair beside Maggie's bed. "You look cheerful."

"I'm working on it." She smiled and her face glowed with the first steps toward health. Joshua examined her closely. In the week since she had begun to make her recovery, Maggie had gained some weight, beginning to fill out the sharp contours of her body. Color was returning to her face, tinting the white of her skin with a pale rose. Her hair seemed to grow almost daily, and she had learned to cleverly conceal her scar. Looking at her this evening, it was more and more difficult to discern signs of the trauma she had undergone.

"Where's your roommate?"

"Her daughter has her out on the floor in a wheelchair. I've never seen such devotion in my life." Maggie stopped when she realized what she'd just said. Her lips turned up in a small smile. "I wonder if that's true? How do I know what I've seen? Sometimes I forget for a moment that I've lost my memory."

"Somewhere inside you it's all still there. You haven't lost your memory, just your memories. They'll come back."

"Joshua, why do you suppose I don't remember?" She began to twist the sheet. "You say it'll all come back to me, but suppose it's something physical that isn't going to change?"

Joshua leaned forward and covered her hands with his. "Suppose you tell me why you don't remember."

"What do you mean?" Maggie liked the feel of his hand on hers, and for a moment she allowed herself to imagine that it was something other than a comforting gesture.

"What happens when you remember anything at all?"

"I haven't remembered anything. Nothing except a man's voice calling 'Maggie, darling.' But I told you about that already." She searched Joshua's face for a clue to his meaning.

"You have another memory that keeps trying to make itself known."

Maggie shook her head. "No, nothing..." She stopped and Joshua could feel her hands become fists.

"Maggie," he prompted.

"My nightmare." She watched Joshua nod solemnly. "But that's not a memory, it's just a terrible dream."

"Your nightmare is one way that your memories are trying to get in touch with you. When you can begin to face it, you may begin to remember pieces of your past." Joshua squeezed her hands and then withdrew his. "I want you to tell me about it."

"No!"

The seconds ticked by as Joshua waited. "Tell me," he said finally. "Are you afraid you'll remember the night you were brought here, or are you afraid of the life you led before that night?"

The challenge in his tone coaxed Maggie's response as silence never would have done. She lifted her head and stared straight into Joshua's eyes. "It's easy to sit beside my bed and be judgmental, isn't it?"

"I'm not judging you."

"Aren't you? You're assuming that my guilt about being a prostitute is what's keeping me from remembering my past."

"What do you think about that theory?"

"When I try to look into the past, I feel terrified, not guilty." She lifted her chin another notch. She wanted to hurt him. "Maybe I liked what I did."

He tried not to smile at her display of pique. "Tell me about the nightmares."

Maggie saw the softening of his features. She sighed. It was difficult to stay angry with Joshua, even when he pushed her further than she wanted to go.

She tried to put the dream into words. "It's always the same one, over and over again. I'm lying in bed in a small dark room. A man comes toward me. I can't see his face because there's always mist surrounding him. But I'm terrified that he's going to hurt me. I try to get away, but I can't. He bends over and whispers to me."

"What does he say?"

Maggie ignored Joshua's question. "Then just as he reaches for me, I wake up."

"What does he say?"

She tried to control the humiliation in her voice. If she refused to tell him, then Joshua would know how much it hurt her. "He calls me what you and everyone else assume I am."

Joshua could almost see Maggie withdrawing from him. "I'm sorry, I don't like to see you in pain," he said honestly. "I know you didn't want to tell me that."

Maggie tried to shrug it off. "It's just one more piece of evidence, isn't it? Even the man in my nightmare thinks I'm a whore."

"It's what *you* think that's important."

"What I think is that nothing makes sense. I go over and over it in my mind, but it doesn't help."

"It will come. In the meantime, you're getting stronger."

"And the nightmares are coming less often."

Joshua put his hand on her shoulder, his fingers brushing the soft skin of her neck. "I'm glad for that." For a moment their eyes locked, and both felt the communication that neither would dare put into words.

A noise at the door signaled the return of Mrs. Tryon and her daughter. Joshua stood. "I'll see you tomorrow, Maggie. I hope you sleep well tonight."

As always, Maggie felt a wrench as Joshua disappeared through the doorway. As he'd said, she was getting stronger. She no longer needed his support to make her feel like a whole person. That part of their relationship had ended. Instead, in its place had appeared a whole new set of yearnings that were impossible, and painful, and very, very real.

And there wasn't a hope in the world that her feelings would ever be reciprocated.

The new hospital orderly wasn't orderly at all. In fact he was the most disorderly staff person that Ida Collins, the head nurse on the sixth floor, had ever seen. And he was lazy. And insolent. She shook her head and bit back the curse that had almost escaped. She had been complaining for a week that the sixth floor was shorthanded on the night shift. A near epidemic of spring fever had cut her staff by a third. Personnel had finally heard her pleas and sent her a new man to train. If she fired him, personnel would never take her seriously again.

"After you've washed your hands," she said, addressing the man with distaste, "you can begin giving the patients fresh ice water." She almost hated to send him to any of the patients' rooms, clean hands or not. There was something disagreeable about the man that soap and water could never wash away. She hoped it wasn't catching.

"They're not going to be drinking ice water at 2:00 A.M. I've got a break coming." Under the man's heavy growth of reddish whiskers, his mouth curled up in a snarl.

"Fine. You can take care of the water when you come back. But don't forget your break's only fifteen minutes."

Fifteen minutes would just about do it. Wiping his hands on his white uniform, the man sauntered down the hall to the stairway. Inside the stairwell, he listened for footsteps. There were none. As quietly as he could, he began to climb. One flight, two...

This was where his plan had broken down the night before. He had reached the eighth floor, taken the stolen key out of his pocket and begun to insert it when the door on the floor above had slammed. He had realized that he wouldn't be alone long enough to unlock the door and disappear through it before he was discovered.

He had pocketed the key and begun the climb to the top floor as if he were going there for his break. Then he had heard the voices. He passed a couple on the next landing. Listening as he climbed, he knew that the two young interns were having a private assignation on the stairs. He had cursed his bad luck and given up for the night.

Tonight would be different. It was later. He was calmer. Tonight he would succeed. He had already done the hard part. Stealing the key had taken real brains. In contrast, killing the girl would be easy.

He took the hard-won key from his pocket, slipped it into the lock and turned it slowly. He had already peeked through the wire-woven glass window to determine that the hallway was empty. The patients were all sleeping soundly, doped up and unaware. The staff? Well, they were probably snoozing at the nurses' station. Everybody knew that the staff on the psychiatric floor took their rest whenever they could get it.

If anyone saw and questioned him, he could tell them that he had gotten confused, that the stairwell door had been ajar and he had thought he was on his own floor. After all, the locks were to keep patients in, not to keep staff members out.

His white, rubber-soled shoes creaked softly as he crept down the hallway. Finding out the girl's room number had been surprisingly difficult. He'd had no idea what name they'd brought her in under. But he had managed to figure it out. Just as he was going to manage to sneak in her room and hold a pillow over her face.

For a moment he stopped as he imagined her slender body twisting with the effort to dislodge him. The thought excited him. He only wished he hadn't waited so long to do it. He should have killed her when he'd had the chance to take care of it at his leisure. But he'd had dreams then, dreams he'd thought she'd make come true for him.

The man stopped in front of room 815. There was still no one in the hallway. He opened the door and slipped inside. His dreams were gone. Soon the girl would be, too.

Maggie lay awake listening to the small sounds around her. She could hear Mrs. Tryon's harsh breathing and the gentle swish of the cars on the streets below. In the hallway she could hear the soft squish of hospital rubber-soled shoes. One of the nurses must be making rounds.

It was a comforting thought. She was used to the hospital routine, and Joshua had convinced her that there was nothing here to fear. There was always someone nearby. Now if she was awakened by her nightmare, it took her less time to adjust to her surroundings and less time to get back to sleep. Tonight would be such a night, especially after finally describing the dream to Joshua. The images had come again, their impact no less frightening, but already she was calmer. She knew where she was. The dream had only been a dream. No one could harm her here.

Maggie heard the footsteps stop at her door. She fought back the lingering effects of the nightmare. This was not the faceless persecutor. This was only a nurse checking on her patients. Still, it was only when the door opened and closed softly that Maggie forced her eyes open. She resisted the urge to call out in order to hear the reassuring answer of a female voice. She had to learn to grapple with her fears by herself and defeat them.

The room was dark, and Maggie's eyes adjusted slowly. She could make out a white blur beside the door as if the nurse couldn't see well, either, and was waiting for her eyes to adjust to the darkness. Slowly the nurse began to move toward her bed. Maggie could feel her pupils widen, feel the beginnings of real panic. The white blur was too tall, too angular to be a woman. It was a man, faceless in the dark of the room. Suddenly she was immersed in her own nightmare. She wasn't awake. She couldn't be. She tried to fight her way to consciousness, but there was nowhere to go. The white blur was by her side, tugging on her pillow. Maggie opened her mouth to scream and a hand was clapped over it.

"Well, you're awake. Didn't they give you a sleeping pill?" The man's voice grated with a hoarse, familiar sound. Maggie struggled, using her small reserves of strength, but she was no match for the man from her nightmare. "Go ahead, keep trying to get away. I like to feel you moving against me."

Maggie could feel her terror overwhelming her. Bile rose in her throat and she could feel herself choking. "I hate to make this so quick," he said in false apology, "but I can't stay too long."

She had no fingernails to scratch with; she could only hit him as he covered her face and his own hand with the pillow. She could feel the weight of his body on top of it as he pulled his hand off her mouth. There was no more sound. She bucked and kicked and tried desperately to push the pillow off her face. Her despair was total. She was going to die. Just as the blackness began to envelop her, she thought of Joshua.

"Why in the hell didn't somebody call me?"

"Nobody called you because you're not related to the girl. You're not even her psychiatrist." Betty watched Joshua pace the floor of the staff lounge. Each time he smashed his fist into his hand, she winced in sympathy.

"I'm the only person in the world she trusts, dammit. I could have calmed her down. She doesn't belong in that cell."

"From what I hear it was a madhouse up here last night." Betty lifted her shoulders as Joshua stopped to glare at her. "Sorry about that. Anyhow, they were so busy trying to stop all that screamin' that I'm sure it never occurred to anyone to get in touch with you. They finally put Maggie in 809 so she wouldn't hurt herself."

"And Mrs. Tryon?"

"She's her old self this mornin'. Which isn't necessarily good."

Joshua ran his fingers through his hair. "What could have brought it on?"

"Maggie won't say anything now. Near as anyone can figure out, she had another bad dream or hallucination and started to scream. Mrs. Tryon woke up and started screamin', too. Or Mrs. Tryon screamed first. We just don't know."

"Something must have triggered it."

"It's just possible that Maggie's a lot sicker than any of us thought." Betty put her hand on Joshua's shoulder. "Are you gonna try to talk to her?"

"Of course I am."

"Then there's somethin' else you should know."

Joshua understood that he hadn't heard all the bad news. "What else is there?"

"Dr. Bashir is going to go through with his plan to send Maggie to the state hospital in Mandeville. He's arranged a commitment hearing for day after tomorrow."

"On what grounds?"

"That she's a danger to herself. She has no memory of her previous life, and she's incapable of caring for herself until her memory returns. After last night, he shouldn't have too much trouble convincing a judge." Betty's face radiated her concern. She understood just how much of himself Joshua had invested in this patient.

"Jim Nelson won't go along with this."

"Dr. Nelson's out of town for the next week. Dr. Timmes is takin' his place. He won't go against Dr. Bashir."

"Who's Maggie's lawyer?"

"Crofton from the public defender's office."

Joshua knew that having a lawyer speak on Maggie's behalf was proper legal procedure. He also knew, in this case, with no family or friends protecting her rights and a public defender who was probably only nominally acquainted with the details of her case history, Maggie's chances of escaping commitment were not the best.

"She's going to feel like we're coming at her from all sides. All the breakthroughs she's made aren't going to be worth a thing," he said, slamming his fist in his hand again.

"If you give up, too, then there won't be anybody fightin' for that girl."

Joshua nodded, but his expression was becoming one of resignation. "I'll need you to unlock the door to 809."

Betty was sympathetic. "If she stays calm for twenty-four hours, Bashir will probably have her moved back into 815."

"Just in time for her commitment hearing."

Maggie counted the dots in the acoustical tile on the ceiling. She wondered why the ceiling wasn't padded, too. Everything else certainly was—the floors, the walls. This is where crazy people ended up. But then, she was probably lucky. At least they hadn't put her in a straitjacket. She suspected that was next on their agenda if she got upset again. The next time someone tried to murder her, she'd have to remember to be calmer about it.

Everyone had given up on her. Even Joshua hadn't come to see her. Maybe they thought that if she huddled there on the padded floor by herself, she'd see the error of her ways. Maybe they'd learned their techniques from some Far Eastern prisoner of war camp. It was brainwashing in reverse. They weren't trying to make her talk; they wanted her to shut up. Well, it had worked.

She was still counting dots when she heard a key turn in the lock and the door swing open. Her persecutor only came in the dark. She wasn't afraid.

"Maggie?"

She started at the sound of Joshua's voice. She had a sense of sudden shame. He shouldn't be seeing her this way. She was dehumanized, an empty shell. There was nothing left inside her.

She pulled together whatever shreds of pride were left. "I'd offer you a chair if there was a chair to offer." The tranquilizers they'd pumped into her the night before were wearing off. Her voice was distinct. She was glad for that one piece of herself that still seemed to be intact.

"Maggie, I didn't know about last night. I came as soon as I heard."

She had screamed his name over and over and over again. How could he not have known? "It's all right, Joshua. You have other obligations."

She felt rather than saw him kneel beside her. Her eyes were still turned to the ceiling. "Maggie, what happened?"

"I'm sure it's in my chart."

"I want to hear it from you."

"Do you know that there are over 368 dots in each tile in this ceiling?" She looked at him for the first time. The sympathy in his eyes was almost her undoing. She steeled herself to ignore it and turned away. "Every time I count that high, I lose track of where I am. If they really wanted patients to get well in here, they'd put in tile with symmetrically arranged dots. These wavy patterns would push anybody over the edge."

"Are we going to play games?" Joshua sat back and crossed his legs, campfire-style.

"Why not? It might while away the time until somebody tries to murder me again."

Joshua felt cold chills run through his body. He didn't know whether to hug her or slap her for her flippancy. He could do neither. "Tell me what happened," he said evenly.

"You'd find it a fascinating study in true insanity. You'd probably even want to take notes." Maggie carefully avoided his eyes.

"You're very angry."

"That's insightful."

"I can't help if I don't know what happened."

She gave a bitter laugh. "Do you want the unexpurgated version? The one nobody will believe? Last night I was sure someone was trying to kill me. It was the man out of my nightmare. He came into my room wearing a white uniform and tried to smother me with a pillow. Just as I was passing out, Mrs. Tryon began to yell. I guess it scared him away. When I could breathe again, I began to scream, too. Then they shot me full of something and when I came to, I was in my own, wonderfully plush private room."

Joshua was shaken to the core. Patients often thought that someone was trying to kill them. But Maggie had never shown any signs of paranoia before. She had always been able to distinguish her nightmares from reality. "You said that last night you were sure. What about right now?"

Maggie could feel her self-control crumpling. She knew what Joshua must think of her story. After all, he was trained to probe beneath the surface. He would never believe that she was telling the truth.

"What's the right answer, Joshua?" she asked in a voice devoid of emotion. "The wrong answer got me thrown in here last night. Just tell me what I'm supposed to say? That I know it was only a nightmare and I'm sorry? That I was just trying to get attention? That I was confused but I've been straightened out since then?" She lowered her head to her hands. "I've got to get out of this place. Just tell me the right thing to say to make it happen."

Joshua ached to comfort her, to pull her into his lap and hold her until some of his strength was infused into her body. But her misery was inside him, too. He could do nothing but continue to question her. "The right thing to tell me is the truth."

She shook her head. "The truth won't set me free."

"You believe what you described really happened?"

Maggie refused to answer.

"Do you have any idea why someone would try to murder you again, Maggie?"

She sat a little straighter and lifted her head from her hands. "The man who left me for dead in a vacant lot may not be thrilled to know I'm alive. Is it too crazy to think that he may have come back to finish the job?"

"I've thought of that."

Maggie felt a jolt of hope. Joshua wasn't trying to talk her out of her story.

He went on. "But the doors on and off the ward are always kept locked. All the permanent staff on this floor have keys to the stairs in case of fire, but it would be very difficult for someone else to get hold of one. And I gather that nobody saw a stranger around during the commotion last night."

"Nobody looked." Maggie lifted her chin. "After all, it was only me trying to tell them what had happened. No one was listening."

"I'm listening."

"Are you? Or are your ears tuned to psychologist frequency?" Her hopes had died with the doubt in his voice.

"My ears are tuned to Maggie frequency, only Maggie is so busy putting up defenses that she's not communicating as well as usual."

"What do you expect?" Maggie hit the padded floor with the palm of her hand, and she knew her voice was too loud. "Everyone here thinks I'm crazy! No one has taken a thing I've said seriously. It's much easier to assume I was hallucinating than to ponder the possibility that I just might be telling the truth." With great effort she lowered her voice. Joshua's expression was intense; she couldn't tell if he understood her distress. "Look," she began again, "all I care about now is getting out of here."

"If you stay calm, you should be back in your old room by nightfall." Joshua watched Maggie turn paler at his words.

"I don't want to go back to my old room. He'll know where to find me again. I'd rather stay here. At least it takes two keys to get to me when I'm in this room."

Joshua ached with sympathy, but he kept his voice level. "You just said that all you cared about was getting out of here."

"Out of the hospital. Out of this town. I want to sign myself out, Joshua. Can you arrange it?" She turned and faced him. The palms of her hands were held out as if in a plea. "It's all I'll ever ask of you." Her voice broke and tears turned her eyes a misty gray. "Please help me."

Joshua had been able to remain in strict control under the force of her anger, but her tears were his undoing. He reached for her in a moment of weakness and brought her to rest against him. She felt impossibly fragile as she trembled in his arms. He stroked her hair and cursed whatever had brought her to such a state. He cursed the total lack of his own objectivity and the not-so-subtle response of his body to the feel of hers against him. Her soft breasts grazed the back of his arm, and he couldn't seem to ignore it. He could smell the sweet, clean fragrance of her skin. No, he had never felt this way about a patient before.

He tried to keep his feelings out of his voice. "Maggie, I want to help you. But it's not as easy as you think it is." She was silent, and he tightened his arm around her. "When you were very ill, the hospital placed you in the intensive care unit. You stayed there for a long, long time. Later, when you were finally out of danger, they moved you up here."

"Why are you telling me what I already know?" Maggie tried to pull away, but Joshua wouldn't allow it.

"In order to bring you here, your doctor had to sign what they call a Physician's Emergency Certificate. Since you weren't able to agree on your own, that's how it had to be done from a legal standpoint."

"And?"

"Because of the nature of your case, you've been on this floor much longer than the usual stay. But when it became apparent that this hospital wouldn't be able to do anything else for you, procedures to transfer you to another hospital in Mandeville, Louisiana, began."

"I'm not going to another hospital. I just want to sign myself out!"

"I'm afraid you can't. Legally, you're under the control of the state. The wheels were set in motion before you began to improve. Now a hearing's been set up to determine whether you should go to the other hospital or not. It's scheduled for day after tomorrow." Joshua could feel the rigidity of her body as she absorbed his words.

"If it's a hearing, then that means they'll want to hear my side of it. Won't they?"

"Yes."

Maggie's mind was whirling with this new piece of information. "If I go to another hospital, will I have to stay more than a week?" Joshua's silence was answer enough. "A month? Two?"

"The commitment will probably be for a year with reviews of your case every three months."

"No!" Maggie's voice was a wail. "That's a prison sentence."

"Maggie, you're going to have to stay calm. When they ask you questions at the hearing, you have to answer as completely as you can."

She wrenched herself out of his arms and turned to face him. "I have no answers. I remember nothing about my past. I can't even tell them my name. And what if they ask about last night? God, what if they ask about last night?"

"That's the first thing they're going to ask you about."

"I don't have a chance."

"Maggie, it's going to be all right."

She heard the doubt in his voice again, and she trembled harder. "Don't try to lie. You don't do it very well."

He lifted her chin in the palm of his hand to force her gaze level with his. "Whatever happens you're going to get through this. Even if you go to the state hospital, you'll be out in three months."

"What's the hospital like?"

He tried not to remember. No matter how well run such an institution was, it was not the right place for Maggie. He could think of no hopeful way to answer her question. His silence was all the response she needed. Joshua watched her begin to retreat. He could almost see her draw into herself. "It's not the best place in the world," he said, grasping for anything to stop her reversal, "but you'll be taken care of. There'll be people there who will help you."

"And somewhere nearby there's a man who will track me there and kill me." She shook her head, moving back against the wall. "Please, leave me alone," she said quietly. His presence had become too painful to bear. She couldn't adjust to the new bleakness of her future with Joshua sitting companionably at her side. She couldn't risk letting him touch her again. He had entered her life only to disappear without warning. She must face her punishment alone.

"It's not a foregone conclusion that you'll be sent to Mandeville. I'm sure the judge will be impressed with how remarkable your recovery has been."

Twisting her head slowly from side to side, she stared in front of her. Joshua could see her will her eyes to become vacant, her expression to become rigid. She was fighting the truth by trying to block her feelings. And he couldn't blame her. Under the circumstances, it was an understandable response. She was no different from anyone, anywhere, who has just been found guilty of a crime they didn't commit.

"You can't give up," he said, his hands coming to rest on her shoulders. "You have to try."

"I'll try," she said, her voice a monotone. "I'll go in there and I'll tell them I don't know who I am, where I'm from or what my life has been. I'll tell them I've been told that I used to be a prostitute, and that someone tried to murder me because of it, but I don't remember.

"I'll tell them if they just let me go, I'll go back out on the streets and try to get an honest job. Of course, I don't know if I have any skills, any skills besides prostitution, that is, but that doesn't matter. I'll give my word of honor that I'll start a brand-new life, free from any illegal activities."

She paused, finally raising her eyes to Joshua's. "I'm sure they'll believe me. Especially after my exemplary behavior last night. Aren't you?"

As usual, she had seen the truth much too clearly. Joshua willed himself to try to infuse her with hope. "You have a chance."

"Please go away. I appreciate your trying to help, but I need to be alone."

He wanted to stay, to take her in his arms again and let his hands and presence comfort her. Instead he rose from the floor. "I'll be back this evening."

Maggie's eyes were shut and her nod was barely perceptible. When the door closed behind him she didn't even flinch.

There was only one person who could halt the process that was destined to end in Maggie's move to the state hospital. Joshua knew that he should be the last person to confront Dr. Bashir and request that Maggie's case be withdrawn from the hearing. He also knew that there was no one else to make the request. Wearing stern self-control like a bulletproof vest, he found the physician in the staff cafeteria on the fourth floor.

Ignoring the food line, Joshua strode right to the two-person booth in the corner. "Dr. Bashir? May I join you?"

Dislike flickered across the psychiatrist's features, but he closed the newspaper he was reading to make room for Joshua.

"I want to talk to you about the commitment hearing."

Dr. Bashir chewed with calm precision. "Then talk."

"I want you to withdraw Maggie's case from consideration. Surely it's just an error that she's still being considered for placement in the state hospital."

"It's no error. That's where she belongs, and I intend to see that the transfer is made."

"Why do you want her transferred when she's made such remarkable progress here?"

"Do you call last night progress?"

Joshua ignored him. "I know her term of involuntary commitment is ending, but I'm sure she'd volunteer to stay until we can make suitable arrangements in the community."

Dr. Bashir stopped chewing, washed his last bite down with a swallow of iced tea and turned slightly to examine Joshua. "It is very apparent, Martane, that you are too involved with Jane Doe to see anything clearly. You've questioned my authority repeatedly, and you've blocked my attempts to use drugs to help her regain her memory. It is clear to me that in this atmosphere, the girl will not improve. She will become more and more dependent on you and less capable of accepting the reality of her position. I want her out of your sphere of influence. Especially after last night."

Joshua's eyes glittered with barely controlled anger, but his voice was calm. "So you admit you're sending a patient to the state hospital because you dislike me."

"I dislike you, yes. You are lacking in objectivity. You are too emotional to be of any use to anyone on the eighth floor. But since my opinion is not shared by my superiors, I can do nothing about my convictions. Nothing except get one patient off your caseload. And that I will do."

"Using a patient to carry out a personal vendetta is unprofessional, Bashir. Who's being emotional here?"

Dr. Bashir shrugged. "Your words, not mine. My concern is for the patient alone. It is the patient I am trying to protect."

"You do know that when Dr. Nelson comes back from his conference, I'll discuss this with him."

"I am sure you will. In the meantime, the patient in question will already have been transferred." The little man stood, leaving his tray for some hapless cafeteria employee to dispose of. "Since the hearing is open to staff, I'm sure I'll see you there. Until then, Martane."

Joshua watched the psychiatrist strut out of the cafeteria. He had not expected help from Bashir, but neither had he expected the overt hostility that he had encountered. The psychiatrist was in deadly earnest about Maggie's commitment. He would view it as a personal triumph; he was willing to go to almost any lengths to be sure that it was carried out.

Joshua's alternatives were few. Although he planned to talk to Dr. Timmes, the acting chief psychiatrist, he suspected that the conversation would only be a formality. The man had neither the authority nor the knowledge of the case to put himself on the line. He would sympathize; then he would tell Joshua to back off.

And backing off was one of his alternatives. Joshua could admit defeat. There were times when submitting gracefully to the inevitable was the better part of valor. He could humble himself, admit that he was not going to be able to change the future and help Maggie prepare for her transfer. He wasn't infallible; he could not predict what effects the state hospital would have on her.

Joshua shut his eyes and leaned his head against the back of the plastic booth. He was lying to himself. He could predict what would happen just as surely as he could predict that the sun was going to rise the next morning. Maggie would be terrorized in the new environment. She would retreat; they would medicate her; she would retreat even further. His Maggie, alone and afraid, crying out for help that might never come.

And what if her story about the man from her nightmare was true? It was farfetched, Joshua could barely admit the possibility, but there was still a slim chance that someone had gotten a key and attempted to murder her again.

Desperately he searched for an answer. He could go to the hearing and make a case against commitment. If he was calm and completely rational, the judge would listen carefully, but Joshua knew that his word weighed against that of a psychiatrist would not have much importance. If he was passionate in his insistence that Maggie be allowed to stay at N.O.C.H., he would surely lose Maggie and possibly his own job.

The only other alternative was to get her out of the hospital before the hearing took place.

He wasn't sure where that idea had come from. It was so ridiculous, so impossible that he discarded it immediately. And immediately it came back, begging to be reexamined. If he could remove Maggie from the hospital, the hearing would have to be postponed. Joshua knew that if Dr. Nelson was in town, the hearing would never have been scheduled. If he could spirit her away until the chief psychiatrist came back, Joshua knew that Dr. Nelson would agree to release her, especially if Joshua had arranged suitable accommodations and out-patient follow-up.

He also knew that he would surely lose his job. No matter what the provocation, no matter what the motivation behind his act, removing a patient from the hospital would be immediate grounds for dismissal.

He opened his eyes, smiling automatically at one of the pretty young nurses who was always trying to catch his attention. Through his concern and caring for one patient, he was being forced to face the issue that had haunted him throughout his adult life. He could be objective and predictable, working to change the world by careful inches, or he could be the rebellious reformer, the man who goes where he isn't wanted, demanding changes where changes aren't desired.

He was neither. He was simply Joshua Martane, ordained minister and psychologist, a man who didn't want to see one woman's life destroyed. What power was forcing him to make a choice between his own needs and the needs of one fragile female patient who had begun to mean too much to him?

He could no longer deny the feelings he was developing for her. Joshua Martane was completely entranced with the amnesiac prostitute with the huge blue eyes and the soul that cried out to his own.

Was he entranced enough to sacrifice his job for her? He made a difference in the lives of the patients he worked with. Cut off from this opportunity, what would he be worth to anyone?

There were no easy answers. He only knew that the time was limited to wrestle with the questions and to listen to the still, small voice inside him that would give the only answer he could live with. He stood to find his way to the exit.

By nightfall Maggie was back in room 815, but there was no hope of sleep. She tried to comfort herself with the prediction that the man from her nightmare would not be stupid enough to try to kill her two nights in a row.

It was little comfort.

The man from her nightmare had shown a desperate recklessness by coming on the eighth floor and trying to murder her with dozens of people nearby. That same desperate recklessness might push him to try again. Tonight.

Maggie knew that she was not going to be able to hold out indefinitely against her exhaustion, but she was determined to try until the early-morning hours when the activity level on the ward would begin to pick up and nurses in the hallway would make it more difficult for a stranger to hide.

Awake and alert she was able to suppress the panic she had experienced the night before. This time, if the man came into her room, she would find a way to keep him in there until her screams could bring a staff member to investigate. If she could do that and survive the encounter, her sanity would be vindicated. Perhaps she would even be released from the hospital.

That hope wasn't bright enough to illuminate a shoebox, but she held on to it as the night wore on and the noises in the hallway diminished. She felt more and more vulnerable as the ward settled in for the night. Mrs. Tryon, who had probably saved her life the night before, was sleeping restlessly, but her presence gave Maggie little sense of comfort. The old woman often moaned or screeched in her sleep. There would be little possibility that her timing would ever be so perfect again as to scare away an attacker. No, Maggie was completely alone. Even Joshua hadn't believed her story.

Joshua. She was only a patient to him, a patient who believed that a sinister nightmare was reality. She was just another one of the many people on the ward who couldn't tell fact from fiction. His doubt had even caused Maggie to question her own recollections of the night before. There had been moments during the day when she had asked herself if perhaps everyone else was right.

But finally, irrevocably, she had put her doubts behind her. She was still physically weakened from her long illness, she was emotionally vulnerable and confused about her past, but she knew that she was able to distinguish the real and the imaginary. The man from her nightmare had been real.

Reality. She gave a short, humorless laugh that sounded strangely loud in the quiet room. She was going to have to face the reality of her feelings for Joshua Martane. He had abandoned her, shown her clearly what a distance there was between them. She had become too dependent on his approval and on his warmth. Foolishly she had let herself believe that she was important to him as a person, not only as a patient. Now she could see clearly the fallacy of that belief.

There had been too much time to think and to daydream during the past week. She had made too much of Joshua's comforting embraces, his concern for her well-being, the intensity of his gaze.

A noise in the hallway brought her sharply back to her present situation. Someone was coming down the hall. Maggie could hear the footsteps slow outside her room. With her eyes wide open and perfectly adjusted to the darkness she lay quietly in bed and waited.

The door swung open with its characteristic squeak. For a moment, a man's figure was silhouetted in the sudden light from the doorway. Then the door shut behind him. The man came slowly toward her bed, his hand outstretched. Terror-stricken but still in control, Maggie waited. If she screamed now, she would scare him away. She had to wait until he was close enough to grab.

He came closer, walking slowly as if he were feeling his way across the floor. There was something different about the man tonight, she thought, frantically trying to figure out what it was. As he neared her bedside she realized that this man wasn't wearing white. He was dressed in street clothes.

"Maggie? Are you awake? It's Joshua."

She felt faint with relief. As she took a deep breath she realized that her lungs were starving for oxygen. She took another breath and another as she sat up, hugging her knees with her arms to keep her body from flying into a million pieces. "Is this some new form of shock therapy?" she finally asked, her voice low and shaking. "How dare you sneak into my room after what happened last night!" Anger replaced relief. "Did you want to prove that I'd scream at any provocation?"

Joshua had known that it was the worst possible way to approach her. He had also known that it was the only way. He had no time now to soothe her. "Be quiet, Maggie, and listen to me."

"I'm available tomorrow between nine and ten o'clock for polite conversation. Now get out of my room!"

"If you don't keep your voice down I'm going to have to put my hand over your mouth."

Maggie opened her mouth to defy him and saw the quick, upward motion of his arm. She was silenced instantly.

"Maggie, don't make me do this. Promise me you'll just whisper your abuse and I'll take my hand away."

She struggled for a moment and then when she realized that Joshua was not going to let her go without a promise, she reluctantly nodded. When she was free again, she whispered with fury, "There's a nice padded room down the hall for crazy people, Joshua!"

"We don't have time for clever conversation. I've decided to try to help you get out of here." In the near darkness he could still see that her eyes were wide, blue pools of unbelief.

"Why would you do that?" Her anger, challenged by this new information, disintegrated. All her defenses went with it. "You don't even believe someone tried to murder me. Why would you want to help me escape?"

Joshua took the time to shoot her a warm smile. "Because I care what happens to you. You don't need to go to the state hospital, and I'm betting heavily on the fact that the chief of psychiatry here, Dr. Nelson, will agree. Unfortunately he's out of town and can't be reached, so he'll be no help before the hearing. I want to get you out of here until he comes back. Then we can have you discharged officially."

"You're going to get into deep trouble over this, aren't you?"

As frightened as she was about her own future, Joshua could see that her first concern was for him. That fact was enough to banish his lingering doubts about helping her. "Desperate circumstances cry out for desperate measures."

"I can't let you take the chance." Big tears welled up in her eyes, and she extended a hand to cover one of his. "Joshua, your willingness to do this will help me find the strength I need to face the hearing."

As always, just her casual touch infused him with warmth. He tried not think about how much of his decision had been based on his attraction to her. "You're not going to face anything. In five minutes you and I are going to walk out of this hospital together."

Maggie examined the stern expression on Joshua's face. It was a face that she knew by heart. At night as she closed her eyes, Joshua would come sharply into focus. She had used it as a talisman to help ward off her nightmares. Maggie knew all Joshua's expressions. She knew the one that he used when he tried to distance himself from her in order to be objective about her problems. Tonight his face was calm, but his eyes shone with a warmth and concern that tore through her own deep depression like a searchlight in the fog.

"I can't let you."

"You don't have a choice."

She was torn between her acute need to leave the hospital for her own safety, and her need to protect him from the consequences of his act. Her hesitation was the only answer Joshua needed. It was evidence that she would cooperate.

"Maggie, if we don't get out of here in a few minutes, we won't have a chance to make this work." He realized that if he gave her any more time to think, she might refuse to come. Standing, he gestured for her to stand, too.

She was wearing only her hospital gown, and she clutched it together behind her. "I think I have another one to use as a robe on the chair over there."

"You're not going to need it." Joshua started for the door.

"I can't go outside like this!"

"Trust me. You won't have to." He turned and saw the rigidity of her stance. With two steps he was back at her side. He laid his hands gently on her shoulders and pulled her close for a quick hug. Briefly he wondered how anyone so small and so delicate could stir such powerful feelings inside him. "I have everything taken care of. Just do what I tell you to, and you'll be safe. Can you do that?"

She nodded against his chest. "You're not going to leave me, are you?"

"I'll be with you the whole time. Ready?"

Maggie straightened her shoulders and stepped away from him. She knew very little about Joshua Martane, who he was or what he felt for her. But she was certain of one thing. He wouldn't harm her. And at that moment he was the only person in the world that she could say that about.

"Lead the way," she said quietly.

Chapter 4

The lights in the hallway had been turned down for the night. At the moment, all was quiet, but there was never a guarantee that the silence would last. Joshua measured the possibilities of success as he surveyed the long stretch to the stairwell door.

"I want you to walk in front of me," he whispered to Maggie. "Stay to the side of the hallway where it's a little darker. Walk as quietly as you can. I'll be right behind you. When we get to the exit door, step aside and I'll unlock it. If we're stopped, let me do the talking."

Letting Joshua do the talking would be easy, Maggie decided. Her own heart had lodged firmly in her throat, cutting off the possibilities of speech. At his nod, she stepped in front of him, took one last look down the hallway herself and began her escape.

She was barefoot. The only shoes she owned were paper slippers that the hospital had issued her, and they always flapped loudly when she walked. Barefoot she could walk undetected, but it made her feel strangely vulnerable. She was escaping from the hospital with no shoes and a gown that was only held together by two flimsy bows. Even now, with her future dependent on the success or failure of this attempt, she was still acutely conscious of the picture she must be presenting to Joshua behind her.

There was a sharp pressure at her waist, and Maggie felt herself being shoved toward a partially opened door. She stumbled and barely kept herself from crying out. When Joshua didn't follow her inside, she flattened herself against the wall beside the door and took stock of her surroundings. There were two beds in the room, only one of which was occupied. The old man in it was sleeping soundly. With her back still firmly against the wall, Maggie slid farther from the door and waited.

"Joshua, did you find what you were looking for?"

Maggie recognized the voice of one of the night nurses. It sounded as if she were coming down the hallway.

"No, but I remember now that I left it in the staff lounge. I was just on my way to look there."

"Do you need any help?" The nurse's voice was closer, as if she had come to join Joshua.

"I don't think so. Things are pretty quiet tonight, aren't they?" Maggie could almost see the casual smile that would accompany Joshua's words.

"After last night, we deserve the quiet." The nurse gave a wry laugh. "I'm going to go check on the patients in 815 right now. I don't want a repeat of all that screaming."

Maggie shut her eyes in defeat. The escape was a failure. "I already checked." Joshua's voice was slightly sheepish. "I'll have to confess, that's part of the reason I came back tonight. I was worried about Maggie. Both she and Mrs. Tryon are sleeping soundly. You don't have to worry."

"Well, good. I won't bother, then. I sure don't want to take a chance of waking either of them up. Why don't you come have some coffee after you're done?"

"Thanks. I might, or I might just let myself out and go up to the roof for a while. It's a beautiful night." Joshua's voice became fainter, as though he were walking away.

Maggie shut her eyes and waited, praying that the old man wouldn't wake up and find her standing there. It seemed like an eternity, although she knew it was only a minute or two before the door creaked open and Joshua came in and motioned for her.

This time they made it to the end of the hall and through the exit door without being detected. Standing under the bright lights of the stairwell, Maggie knew that she was visibly shaking. Taking her hand in his, Joshua led her down to the next landing. "Put these on quickly." He leaned over and pulled a small shopping bag out of the corner.

Inside Maggie found a belted raincoat, a pair of white nurses' shoes and a triangular paisley scarf. "Where did this come from?"

"Lost and found."

"You have this so well planned!" She couldn't help it. Her voice was a whispered wail.

"Remind me to tell you about my adolescence." Joshua flashed her a quick grin that quickly turned into a frown when he realized that she hadn't moved. "Get going, Maggie."

She clasped the raincoat around her, slipped on the shoes and tied the scarf under her chin. Everything except the scarf was sizes too large. Maggie knew that she looked like a refugee, not a nurse who was on her way home.

Joshua talked softly as she dressed. "We're going to walk down the eight flights. The hospital staff rarely uses the stairs except for trips to adjacent floors. The next floor down is surgery, so we probably won't meet anyone until we get a flight or two beyond that." He examined Maggie and then smiled slightly. "I almost forgot." He pulled a pair of lightly tinted glasses out of his pants pocket. "Your eyes are unforgettable. This should help."

Maggie was surprised by the husky warmth in his voice. Instinctively she knew that it hadn't been put there to comfort her. She slipped on the glasses, which instantly slid to the tip of her nose. She pushed them up and tilted her head to keep them on. Her vision was slightly blurred.

Joshua linked his arm through hers, beginning to help her down the long flight of stairs. "If we meet anybody, smile and keep going," he said softly.

"My face is frozen."

"Freeze it in a smile, then, for Pete's sake. Don't look so forlorn. Somebody's going to get suspicious."

"What a perfect time to think of that," she muttered, as she concentrated on navigating the steps without losing her shoes.

Twice they passed other staff members, who, as Joshua had predicted, were traveling between adjacent floors. Once Joshua smiled and called a young nurse by name, the other time they just hurried on their way.

Maggie's knees were shaking from the unaccustomed exercise and the challenge of the escape. Finally they paused for a moment at the first floor exit. "The hospital has a parking garage," Joshua told her. "My car is there. We're going to go through this door, turn right and walk through the front waiting room. Then we're going to turn left, walk down a long corridor and out into the garage. Once there, we'll take an elevator to the third floor. My car is a dark blue Dodge Colt. If we get separated, wait for me there."

Separated? She shut her eyes. "I can't..."

"Yes, you can. Now I want you to link your arm through mine and look like you're enjoying my company."

"I should be good at that," she tried to joke, "I've been told I used to do it for a living." Maggie could feel herself descending into panic. She wasn't sure if she could move at all. She knew that Joshua could feel her trembling.

"Stop it, Maggie. Take a deep breath and get ready." Before she could respond, Joshua pulled the door open and pushed her through it.

The man rubbed his hand over his reddish whiskers and waited for the couple to continue their descent down the stairs. Another romantic meeting on the stairwell. He muttered a string of curses, which did nothing to alleviate his anger. He had been forced to wait for long minutes while the man in blue jeans and the young nurse took their time strolling down the stairs and past the sixth floor. Now he didn't have any time to waste.

He had never been lucky. He had been born unlucky. It wasn't fair. No matter how hard he tried, something always went wrong. The night before he'd thought his luck was changing. Another minute and the girl would have been dead. And then the old lady had begun to yell. It had ruined his chance.

Well, maybe not quite. Listening to the commotion as he hid in the bathroom next door to 815, he had discovered that no one had believed the girl's story. Tonight he would do everything the same way, but this time he'd be luckier. Tonight he knew exactly where to go and which bed to find her in. Tonight he'd finish what he'd started.

The couple on the stairs might have slowed him down, but they hadn't stopped him. He was ready now. His luck was about to change.

Maggie and Joshua made it through the waiting room without incident. They were halfway through the wide corridor when a man's voice came toward them. "Joshua? What are you doing here this time of night?"

Bearing down on them from the opposite end of the hall was the stern masculine figure of Sergeant Sam Long. Joshua bent toward Maggie and brushed a casual kiss across her cheek, his mouth lingering against her ear. "Turn your head when you pass this man. He's seen you before. Continue down the corridor and into the garage. Take the elevator to the third floor. Blue Dodge Colt parked somewhere in the middle. Now, Maggie."

She couldn't move. Joshua lifted his hand to her shoulder and gave it a painful squeeze. "Now, Maggie!"

Like a sleepwalker she turned and started down the hallway. Maggie didn't see Sam's curious glance as, intently, she followed Joshua's orders. Expecting to be stopped at any moment, she moved toward her destination, repeating the directions until they were burned into her brain.

Joshua waited for Sam. Out of the corner of his eye he noted with satisfaction that Maggie had reached the door and gone through it into the garage. "What are you doing here?"

"We just brought another girl in. Only this one was DOA. Damn." Sam's usually dispassionate expression was clouded with anger. "We came this close to catching the murderer. This close." He held his thumb and forefinger a scant inch apart.

Joshua felt as though someone had punched him in the stomach. "Are you on his trail or was it a fluke?"

"Oh, we're hot on his tail. We know his blood type, his hair color and general build, the kind of places he hangs out, his preferences in women. We know everything except his name and phone number. And I'll have that before he kills again." Sam stopped and examined Joshua. "You didn't say why you were here so late."

"I was meeting somebody."

"The girl you were with?"

"That's right."

A tiny smile softened Sam's features. "It's about time, don't you think? Hurricane Daphne's been married and divorced again already, and you've just been quietly licking your wounds."

"Spoken like a confirmed bachelor," Joshua responded, surprised to find that Sam's casual mention of his ex-wife left him with no feeling except surprise at the reminder. "You should try getting close to a woman yourself."

"The only person I want to get close to right now is the bastard who's committing these murders. I'm going to interview Jane Doe this week, amnesia or not." Sam raised his hand at Joshua's protest. "Yeah, I know what you think—you think I'll traumatize the little darling. Frankly, Josh, I don't care. I want whatever information I can get, trauma or not. There are lives at stake."

Joshua shrugged. He was in no position to argue about the patient who was sitting outside in the parking garage waiting for Joshua to help her escape. "We'll see," he said. "God knows, I want you to catch this guy, too."

"I'm going to catch him." With a nod, Sam was gone.

On the third floor of the poorly lighted garage, Joshua walked swiftly to his car, searching for the paisley scarf. He found Maggie perched sadly on the rear bumper of the blue Dodge. "The worst is over now," he said softly, sitting beside her for a moment with his arm around her shoulder. "We'll be out of here in a minute."

"Joshua, this is crazy."

"No, it's not. It's exactly the right thing to do, Maggie. Trust me, won't you?"

She nodded slowly. "But I'm worried about you."

"I can handle whatever happens."

He pulled her up, and with his arm still stretched behind her for comfort, he guided her to the passenger side of the car. "Here you go," he said after he'd unlocked the door and helped her in.

They drove out through the employees' exit, reaching the street with no incident. Once they were in the familiar New Orleans traffic, Joshua allowed himself a sigh of relief. "Well, we made it."

Maggie stripped the scarf off her head and ruffled her short curls. She was mesmerized by the sight and sounds of the traffic outside her window. She was out of the hospital. For the moment she was safe. She wondered if she would be able to sleep. "What happens now?"

"Now I take you somewhere for the night."

"Where?"

"I had planned to take you home."

"Home?"

"My home." He caught her incredulous look and smiled in response. "You'd be safe there."

"But wouldn't your family mind?"

"I have no family. I live alone, unless you count the world's nosiest landlady. After thinking about it, though, I realized that if the hospital notifies the police, my house will be the first place they'll look."

"Oh, no."

"Afraid so."

"Why have you involved yourself this way, Joshua?"

"Because you're worth it," he said simply. "I chose to help you; I was completely aware of the consequences."

"I wasn't. I didn't think it through."

"You didn't have time. But to answer your question, I'm taking you to stay with a friend of mine. The section of town isn't the best, but Skeeter can be trusted."

"Skeeter?"

"Skeeter and I grew up together. He's an artist...among other things."

"But we'll be involving him."

"He'll love it. I'm afraid it'll be one of the lesser crimes he's been involved in."

"Are you going to leave me alone?" Maggie knew that her voice reflected the utter and complete failure of her courage. Whatever surge of adrenaline had gotten her this far had finally worn off. She was out of the hospital, but essentially she was on her own. And she wasn't strong enough for that yet.

Joshua wanted to stop the car and soothe her fears. He understood her dilemma. "No," he promised softly. "I'm going to stay with you until this thing is settled and we can find you a decent place to live and a decent job."

"Why?"

The answer was too strange and too painful. He wasn't sure that he wanted to acknowledge it, even to himself. "Because I care what happens to you," he said instead. It was a watered-down version of the truth.

"Thank you, Joshua."

"You're welcome, Maggie."

Both of them were suddenly aware that the journey away from the hospital was also a journey into a new relationship. No longer patient and therapist, they were man and woman thrown together by circumstances beyond their control. Where they would go from here was as much a mystery as what had brought them together in the first place.

Skeeter's neighborhood was not the best. In fact, it was one of the worst. New Orleans, like other big cities throughout the United States, had tried to cure the problems of its urban poor by housing them in huge projects that stretched for miles, creating a veritable wasteland of squalor and crime. Skeeter did not live in one of the projects, but his neighborhood bordered on one of the most infamous.

It was one of the more ironic aspects of New Orleans life that when the housing projects had been sprinkled through the city, they often had been set down in the midst of an otherwise upper-class neighborhood. Mansions sat only blocks away from the rows of dilapidated brick buildings. Symbolically, Skeeter's house sat somewhere between the two worlds, just as Skeeter himself did.

Joshua parked his car in front of the fading salmon wood-frame house and behind the light blue van that was Skeeter's pride and joy. "Watch your step on the front porch," he cautioned Maggie as he came around the car to help her out. He had already scanned the street, checking carefully for any signs of suspicious movement. There were residents sitting, shirts unbuttoned, on nearby front stoops to catch the breeze, but tonight there was nothing out of the ordinary. Joshua knew that this was not always the case.

Together they skirted the gaping hole on the porch left by a missing board. Skeeter refused to repair the obstacle. He claimed that it discouraged intruders. At night he turned off his front light and dared any trespasser to survive an encounter with his porch. It was cheaper than a burglar alarm, more efficient than a watchdog. It was typical Skeeter.

Joshua knocked, waited and knocked again. Finally he opened the wheezing screen door and banged directly on the wooden one behind it. "Skeeter, it's Josh."

"Maybe he's not home." Maggie was so tired that she could hardly stand up, and her voice reflected her exhaustion. Joshua pulled her to stand in the crook of his arm, banging harder on the door.

"Most likely he's asleep," he explained.

The door opened suddenly, just as Joshua raised his fist to pound on it again.

"Persistent, aren't you?" A wiry man of average height stood in the doorway, scratching his bare chest with one hand as he tried unsuccessfully to cover a yawn with his other. The man was dark-skinned with straight black hair that fell to his shoulders in a shining pageboy and had a handlebar mustache that spread out almost wide enough to touch his earlobes.

"Aren't you going to ask us in?"

Skeeter stood back, making a sweeping gesture with his hand.

His arm still around Maggie, Joshua tugged her into the house. Once inside, he steered her to a newspaper-covered sofa and pushed her gently on to it, deftly piling the papers on the floor as he did.

"I'd have cleaned up if I'd known that the Right Reverend and his lady friend were coming for a social call." Skeeter grinned at Joshua, punching him lightly on the arm. "What's the occasion, Josh?"

"I need your help."

Skeeter's eyes narrowed, turning from his friend to examine the young woman on his sofa. Maggie had shut her eyes, the weariness of two nights of missed sleep claiming her totally. It was apparent to both men that she would be asleep in a minute. Skeeter lowered his voice. "What's wrong?"

"Maggie's been a patient at City. I smuggled her out of the hospital tonight."

Skeeter whistled softly. "Didn't you take a vow of obedience or something? I thought you gave up your life of crime years ago."

"Maggie was about to be committed to the state hospital. It was senseless and cruel. She's as sane as you or me. Saner than you, in fact."

Skeeter smiled, the corners of his mouth obscured by the drooping mustache. "And you rescued her."

Joshua nodded. "Can she stay here for a few days? I think I can have her officially released when the chief of psychiatry comes back into town. Until then, she needs to stay out of the way."

"No place could be more out of the way. No one with any intelligence at all will come looking for her here," Skeeter agreed. "Sure, she can stay." His eyes traveled over Maggie's sleeping figure. "I might even enjoy her company."

"I come with the deal," Joshua said firmly. "The hospital will know how she escaped and with whom. I have to stay out of the way, too. And Maggie is off limits, Skeeter. Understand?"

"That's too bad. I can understand how you got involved. She's something."

Joshua silently agreed. The tired lines around Maggie's eyes had not yet disappeared with the onset of sleep. Her short curls were still rum-

pled from their encounter with the paisley scarf, and they framed her
face like a smoky cloud. Her long, curling eyelashes touched the ivory
skin of her cheek. She looked enticingly female and totally defeated.
"Where can I put her?" Joshua asked Skeeter. "Do you have an extra room or shall I try to make her comfortable here?"

"I have an extra room. You can both sleep in there." He laughed at
Joshua's lifted eyebrow. "Don't go thinking I'm suggesting any un-
toward behavior. It's got a couple of single beds in it."

"Fine. I appreciate it, Skeeter."

"I may even have clean sheets."

"Remarkable."

Together the two men entered the bedroom, by unspoken agreement pushing the two single beds against separate walls. Skeeter found
the sheets, and in a few minutes the room was ready to be occupied.
"I'm going to get Maggie settled," Joshua told Skeeter. "Go back to
sleep, if you want."

Skeeter squinted at an alarm clock sitting on one of the two For-
mica-covered dressers. "Nah, I've got to get going. I'm sketching
portraits at one of the courtyard bars down on Bourbon Street tonight. I was just catching a few hours' sleep before I had to be there."

"Are you still doing portraits at Jackson Square?"

"About three days a week." Jackson Square was a park located in
the section of old New Orleans known as the French Quarter or the
Vieux Carré. One of its attractions was the artists who clustered on the
sidewalk doing charcoal or pastel portraits for tourists willing to pay
their prices. Skeeter was one of the best, capturing entire personalities
with a few strokes of his pencil. It was the only time that he allowed his
remarkable insight into human nature to show.

"I won't ask what else you're doing."

"Good." Skeeter clapped Joshua on the back. "It's better that you
keep your nose out of my affairs. That way, what you don't know can
only hurt me."

"Just don't bring the law down on your head while I'm here. That's
all I need."

"My sins are so petty that no one is particularly interested. I hav-
en't kidnapped anybody recently—unlike you, my old boyhood pal."

Joshua just smiled a tired smile and went to get Maggie. She was
sound asleep, her hand thrown across her eyes to block the light. He
didn't have the heart to waken her. Instead he slipped his arms under
her inert body and lifted her off the sofa. She hardly weighed more
than a child, but she didn't feel like a child in his arms. She felt like a
woman, the softness of her breasts brushing his chest, the smooth skin
at the back of her thighs sliding against his wrists.

In the bedroom he unbuttoned the khaki raincoat, slipped it over her
arms and out from under her still-sleeping body. He removed the heavy

shoes. The skimpy hospital gown left little to his imagination. Quickly he tucked a sheet and blanket over her, turned off the light and closed the door behind him.

Skeeter had dressed in a pair of disreputable jeans and a blue T-shirt advertising a popular Bourbon Street strip show. His hair was neatly pulled back into a low ponytail revealing one gold hoop earring. "There's probably something to eat in the refrigerator," he told Joshua. "I'll be back tomorrow morning sometime."

Joshua nodded. "Thanks, Skeeter."

"Think nothing of it. You have no idea what this does for my ego."

This time Joshua laughed. Everyone needed a friend like Skeeter to make them take themselves less seriously. One dose of Skeeter was all the humbling anyone could stand. Joshua locked the door after Skeeter's van pulled away from the house and rummaged in the refrigerator for a cold can of beer. Half a can later he made his phone call to the hospital.

The head nurse on the eighth floor was irate, as she had every right to be. Joshua explained the circumstances behind Maggie's removal and assured her that he would emphasize to Dr. Nelson that no one else on staff had been aware of his actions.

"You're going to be fired," she warned him.

"I know."

There was a long silence, and finally, "If you bring her back right away, I can cover for you."

Joshua was grateful that the nurse was concerned about him. "Thank you, but I did what had to be done. I haven't changed my mind. Just pass the word that I'll be in to talk to Dr. Nelson when he returns." With that, he hung up.

"Here's to you, Bashir," he said, toasting the empty room with his remaining beer. But there was no pleasure in knowing that he had bested the psychiatrist. Unlike Dr. Bashir, Joshua did not see the situation with Maggie as a personal vendetta. He would gladly have let the oily little physician win if it would have helped Maggie. Now that the drastic step of removal from the hospital had been taken, Joshua was beginning to understand that he would do almost anything to help her. There was very little of his own ego involved in this conflict. What he had done, he had done for her.

For a long time he sat on the sofa, his beer forgotten, and stared at the cracked plaster wall on the other side of the room.

"No. No...please!"

Joshua sprang from the sofa and covered the distance to the bedroom door in a dead run. Snapping the hall light on, he threw the door open and covered the distance to Maggie's side in three rapid steps. She was tossing back and forth, moaning in the throes of a nightmare.

"Maggie!"

She sat upright, her hands thrust in front of her. "Go away! Please don't hurt me!"

"It's Joshua, Maggie. It's Joshua." He leaned toward her, talking softly to reassure her.

But Maggie was responding to some inner vision. She shrank back against the pillow and covered her face with her hands. "Not again. Please!"

Joshua was afraid to touch her. He understood that she might interpret it as a new and more horrifying threat. "Maggie, wake up. Wake up, sweetheart. It's Joshua. You're safe."

Her moans softened. Carefully Joshua sat on the edge of her bed. "I'm right here, Maggie. Nothing is going to hurt you. You're safe."

"I don't...please...don't..." Her voice trailed off into a sobbing hiccup.

"Maggie, it's Joshua. Take your hands down and look at me."

Behind her hands she shook her head.

"It's really me," he reassured her. "I'm right here, sweetheart. You're all right."

Carefully he reached for her hands, talking to her quietly as he did. "I'm going to cover your hands with mine, and then, very slowly you're going to let me pull them back to your lap. Ready?"

She was immobilized.

He covered her hands with his own and gently pulled them from her face. "Open your eyes, Maggie. Now, sweetheart."

Finally she obeyed; her eyes, even in the dim light, were terror-filled, tempered only by an impossible courage. Joshua knew that she had expected someone else.

"Who did you think you were going to see?" he asked her softly.

"My persecutor."

He nodded. "Tell me about it."

The vision was fading as it always did with the light. "It was the same dream I always have. Only this time he had a pillow in his hands."

"What else?"

She shook her head, searching Joshua's face for clues. Was she truly insane? Were the visions hallucinations as Dr. Bashir had informed her in his clipped, cold voice? Was this dream no different from the one of the night before that she had thought was real?

"Maggie, you've been through enough to give anyone nightmares." Joshua could sense her insecurity, and he tried to reassure her.

"Maybe...maybe they're not nightmares at all. Maybe I really am crazy." She covered her face with her hands, this time to blot out the horrible vision of her own insanity.

Joshua understood. Sliding closer to her, he took her in his arms, not allowing her to pull away. "You're not crazy, sweetheart. You've been through a very bad time. You suffered a severe head injury; you're frightened and very unsure of yourself."

She was trying to control herself, and the effort showed in her voice. "I'm awake now. I'm all right." She said the words to convince herself as much as to convince Joshua, but as soon as she said them, she knew that they were true. "I know that I was only dreaming." The terror of the dream was evaporating. Last night's terror would never completely die; she knew the difference. "Last night was real. I couldn't wake up because I wasn't asleep."

Joshua was silent. There was nothing that he could say about her conviction that someone had actually tried to murder her again. He just continued to hold her.

Maggie was silent for long moments, too. Then finally she said, "I wish you believed me, but I'm grateful that you're not pretending to, just to make me feel better."

"What I believe is that whatever happened last night seemed very, very real to you. Real enough to make you defy everybody else's opinion."

She let his voice soothe her pain. Tentatively she put her own arms around his waist and rested her head against his chest. Joshua had held her before, but she had never held him. She was suddenly very aware of him as a man. Joshua was large, strong and in the peak of physical condition. Her arms contacted hard muscles and firm skin under his shirt. He felt marvelous, a rock to hold on to in a world too chaotic to cope with, an anchor.

His fingers were stroking her hair, playing gently with the short curling strands. Neither of them could speak. Neither of them could break the dangerous contact. They just sat on the bed, holding each other, both trying not to think about how impossible their relationship was.

"You're so good to me," she said finally, trying to find the strength to draw away.

"I'm not going to let anything hurt you." Inch by reluctant inch, he loosened his hold on her. "We're going to find out why you're so frightened, Maggie, and we'll deal with it together."

She wanted to believe him; she wanted to believe that Joshua would be there for her, with her, when she needed him. But it wasn't fair to him. Already, she might have cost him his job. "I'm getting stronger," she said. "I'm going to stand on my own two feet."

"I know. But even on two feet, you'll need a friend."

Maggie understood, with perfect clarity, that Joshua would never be just a friend. In her own heart, he was already much, much more. "I feel as though I've always known you," she said. "I'm sure it's just what you've done for me. Dr. Bashir says it's trans..."

"Transference." It was a term used for the strong feelings that a patient develops for his or her therapist. Dealing with those feelings could be a breakthrough in a patient's entire way of relating to important people in his life. In this case it was much too simple an explanation.

"Maggie," Joshua said carefully, "don't try to categorize what has happened, what is happening." He pulled away and smiled at her, wiping a lone tear from her cheek with his thumb. "We've never had a typical therapist-patient relationship. Dr. Bashir filled that need for you."

Maggie wrinkled her slightly crooked nose. "Dr. Bashir talked, and I nodded my head. Is that supposed to be typical?"

Joshua laughed, bending to kiss her on the forehead before he stood. "Not really. Can you go back to sleep now?"

"Where are you going to sleep?"

He pointed to the other side of the room. "Skeeter doesn't have luxurious accommodations. I can sleep there or out in the living room if it bothers you to have me in here."

"Please stay here." The words came too quickly. She tried to modify them. "I mean, I want you to be comfortable."

"And you'd like to have someone close by if you get frightened."

Not someone. Joshua. "Yes."

"There's no reason to be ashamed of that. I'll be right here." He stepped out into the hall and flicked off the light, coming back in the bedroom to his own bed. Sitting on the edge, he began to undress. Moonlight filtered in through half-drawn shades, and Maggie turned on her side away from him to give him privacy.

"Joshua?"

"What?"

"Why do you care so much about what happens to me?"

I'm paid well to care what happens to my patients? You need me more than anyone ever has? I'm falling in love with you?

"Because you're Maggie," he said quietly.

"Maybe I'm not," she murmured sleepily. "Maybe I'm not who anyone thinks I am. Maybe I'm not *what* anyone thinks I am."

Joshua lay down with his hands behind his head and thought of a recent conversation with Sam Long. The two friends had sat together over drinks at a French Quarter bar near Joshua's apartment. "I don't think Maggie was ever a prostitute," Joshua had said after telling Sam about her return to consciousness and her subsequent amnesia.

"Any hooker on Bourbon Street could proposition you and you'd find something good to say about her. Not everyone is a little lost lamb, Josh."

"You don't know her."

The blond police officer had inclined his head toward two expensively dressed women in the corner. "See those two young ladies over there?"

Joshua turned slightly to examine the women in question. Both were fashionable, wearing modest designer clothing and subtle makeup. Joshua smiled and turned back to Sam. "What's your point?"

"One of those young ladies...isn't. The sweet young thing on the left is a man. He's been down at the station twice for soliciting. His partner there is a female. She goes under a variety of names. Last time I picked her up it was for forging one of them on somebody else's check."

"So?"

"The papers are full of stories about people like them. An airport terrorist shoots six people; a man kidnaps an heiress in Florida and gets her killed in the getaway chase; three illegal aliens are arrested for smuggling enough heroin into the country to addict the population of New York City."

"I don't have time to read the papers."

"You should."

"Why? I'm not stupid, Sam. I was raised on the streets, too. Remember?"

"Then think again. This Maggie was picked up, half dead, in a vacant lot. God only knows what she'd been through, but one thing was for sure. The man who tried to kill her was sure she was a prostitute. She was dressed like one and that area of town is crawling with hookers. If she was somebody's sweet little girl, she'd have been identified right away."

"But nobody recognized her. Not even the pimps you paraded through her room."

"You gonna trust a pack of pimps? Besides, she could have been a loner, a new girl in town. Who knows?"

"You don't know her."

"I don't want to. I know her type." Sam's voice was heavy with cynicism. "She can look at you with those big brown or green or blue eyes and take you for all you're worth. Don't give her an inch."

Now, Joshua had given her much more than an inch. He had given Maggie his support and his help in escaping from the hospital. And he was on the verge of giving her more, much more.

Once before there had been a woman who had taken what he had to give. There had never been any question about Daphne's identity. That time Joshua had known from the beginning what he was getting himself into, and he had entered that relationship with his eyes wide open. That love, that marriage, hadn't lasted. From it he had learned to be careful, to give his attention, his friendship, but never his heart. Evidently the lesson hadn't quite taken.

"Joshua?"

"Yes, Maggie."

"I'm glad you're here."

"So am I."

"Good night." Her voice was beguilingly husky and filled with sincerity.

Joshua wanted to believe, more than anything, that he was not in the presence of a first-rate con artist.

At first, Joshua slept fitfully, expecting a recurrence of Maggie's nightmare. When hours passed and she still slept quietly, he let himself drift into a deeper sleep. When the light of late morning woke him he was surprised at how renewed and rested he felt. Turning toward Maggie's bed, he discovered that she was no longer there. He could hear the sounds of voices from the other room, and he rose and dressed to go in search of her.

Maggie and Skeeter were sitting companionably at Skeeter's kitchen table. She was wearing the khaki coat, buttoned as a bathrobe, her feet bare on the scarred linoleum floor. Skeeter, dressed as he had been the night before, was listening in fascination as Maggie told him what she knew of her own story.

"Do I smell coffee?"

Maggie's face brightened. "Joshua, sit down. I'll get it for you."

He allowed her the small pleasure. She was obviously delighted to be able to do something for him. "Thank you," he said, cradling the hot cup in his hands. "Did you sleep well?"

"Very." She didn't add that for the first time since she had once again become aware of her surroundings, she had felt safe enough to allow herself the luxury of deep sleep. She had awakened feeling refreshed. She had awakened knowing that Joshua was sleeping in the next bed.

She had opened her eyes to find him facing her, his dark hair brushing his forehead. In sleep he looked younger, less formidable. He looked as if he might have needs and dreams of his own. He was less the caregiver, more the man. She had been stirred by this new image, and she had wondered how it would feel to be held by this different Joshua Martane, not as a therapist holds a patient or even as a friend holds a friend. But as a man holds a woman.

"Maggie was just telling me about herself." Skeeter was eating a bowl of sugar-coated children's cereal. Maggie turned from Joshua and watched with fascinated awe as Skeeter shoveled spoon after spoon under his mustache. "Did you ever think about getting Sam on her case?" he asked Joshua.

"He is."

"Who's Sam?" Maggie sipped her coffee, the first decent cup she had tasted since waking up in the hospital.

"Sam's the man I stopped to talk to in the corridor last night," Joshua answered. "He was one of the policemen who brought you to the emergency room."

Maggie made a face and set her cup on the table.

Skeeter shot her a sympathetic smile. "Hasn't Joshua ever told you about his boyhood?"

Maggie shook her head.

Skeeter finished the last bite of his cereal, holding the box out to Joshua, who shook his head in distaste. Shrugging, Skeeter turned to Maggie. "Joshua, Sam and I were the three musketeers. All for one and one for all. Sam became a policeman, you've seen how Joshua turned out, and then there was me."

"Let's not elaborate on how you turned out," Joshua said, only half joking.

"Joshua and Sam are still trying to reform me," Skeeter explained to Maggie.

"I think you're very nice," she said.

"So does my parole officer. Anyway, when we were growing up we were three of a kind. Joshua, the model citizen you see before you, was actually just a young punk. And Sam? Well, Sam had been in more fights, dodged more arrests and made more contacts in the New Orleans underworld than any sixteen-year-old boy in the city."

"And now he's a policeman?"

"A damn good one. The best. I hope I never have to tangle with him."

Maggie turned to Joshua. "What made the change in you and in Sam?"

Joshua glossed over his own rebirth. "I got involved in a church. Sam's parents finally scraped together enough money to send him down to the bayous to live with an uncle. The uncle was as strong-willed as he was. Sam came back completely changed."

"I wonder why he came back at all."

"Sam says he loves the country, but he belongs in the city, on the right side of the law. In his own way, I think he's trying to do for others what his uncle did for him."

"Nobody reformed you, Skeeter?" Maggie turned back to their host.

"Jail reformed me. At least a little. I keep my nose clean...cleaner, anyway."

"I like your paintings." Maggie gestured to a series of small watercolors of New Orleans life fastened in crooked disarray to the wall above their table.

"How did you know they were mine?"

She tried to think of an answer. Finally she lifted her shoulders in defeat. "They look like you. Dark, tough outlines, with dreamy, abstract interiors. It's unusual using watercolors for such stark subjects, too." Most of the paintings were scenes of life in a New Orleans housing project. One was an old man, his head in his hands, sitting on a front porch. "You're very good, but they say a lot about you, don't they?"

Skeeter and Joshua just stared at her. Finally Skeeter turned to his friend. "I can see why you smuggled her out of that place."

"Yes."

Maggie smiled tentatively, trying to decide exactly what the two men meant. Joshua patted her hand. "You need to eat," he told her firmly.

"There's plenty of food in the refrigerator. I shopped on my way home." Skeeter got up and opened the refrigerator door, gesturing inside. "Help yourselves. I'm going to bed."

"Skeeter?"

He turned at the door and smiled at the young woman who had instantly seen into his soul.

"I hate to ask, but I was wondering if you had any clothes I might be able to borrow? I'll wash them if they need it, but . . ."

"I'll get you some things to choose from. You're so tiny I'm afraid everything's going to hang, but at least they'll be better than that coat."

"It's probably perfectly safe to take you shopping over on the West Bank, across the river somewhere," Joshua said in apology after Skeeter had left the room. "We could go this morning."

"I'd rather not take the chance. Not until I know they can't snatch me off the street and toss me into the state hospital."

Skeeter came back with an armful of jeans and T-shirts. "There's a pair of pants here with an elastic waist that might not be too bad if you roll up the cuffs and a couple of shirts that have shrunk since I bought them."

Maggie felt as though she were being given a wardrobe of designer originals. "Thank you. It'll be so good to get out of this hospital gown. Excuse me." Carrying the stack of clothes, she left for the bedroom.

"Now why didn't I realize that she'd be tired of those awful hospital clothes? I could have brought her something different to wear last week," Joshua muttered to Skeeter.

"Maybe you've been trying not to see her as anything other than one of your patients." Skeeter examined his friend. "You've been fighting a losing battle, though, haven't you?" Whistling, he left to catch up on his sleep, leaving Joshua to contemplate his coffee cup.

Chapter 5

"I think we can safely say that I wasn't an artist." Maggie squinted at the watercolor in front of her. Pools of color ran in unattractive rivulets toward the middle of her paper, destroying her depiction of the magnolia tree in Skeeter's backyard.

"At least we can say that watercolor wasn't your medium." Skeeter leaned over her shoulder and examined her painting. "No, I think your first statement was correct." He ruffled Maggie's curls. "Is that supposed to be a tree or a telephone pole with algae growing on it?"

"Maybe I play the piano." Maggie crumpled her painting and tossed it into a nearby trash can.

"I have a harmonica. You wanna try it?"

"Does it have a keyboard?" She laughed at the look of dismay on Skeeter's face. "I remember what a harmonica is, Skeeter. I was just kidding. But I think I've delved into my past enough tonight." She stood and stretched. "What I'd really like to do is go for a walk."

"We don't 'go for walks' in this neighborhood. Jogging's okay if you can do a four-minute mile and outrun the muggers."

"Is the backyard safe?" She looked at the tiny plot of land surrounded on all sides by a six-foot wooden fence.

"I keep my pet mosquitoes out there."

"I think I'll go get acquainted with them." She gave him a friendly pat on the shoulder. "Thanks for entertaining me tonight."

"My pleasure."

Outside, the night was warm and humid, and Skeeter's magnolia was perfuming the air with its sweet, lemony fragrance. Maggie sat on a wooden bench beneath the tree and listened to the sounds of a distant bird mix with rock music from a neighbor's radio. She shut her eyes and tried to clear her mind. She had discovered that the harder she tried to remember details of her life, the more confused she became. When she just let her mind drift, not pushing it where it didn't want to go, she felt as if she were moving closer to her past. Sometimes she felt as if she were only inches away from remembering.

The heavy air felt right somehow. Even the occasional mosquito that buzzed near her ear seemed right. But there was something missing. The air was too still; the bird singing in the distance was too melodic.

"Maggie?"

"I didn't know you were back." Maggie opened her eyes and patted the wooden bench in invitation to Joshua, who was standing beside her. He had gone out earlier to pick up a few things at a nearby drugstore. Despite telling herself that she should get used to being without him, Maggie had missed him.

"What were you doing?"

She hesitated. "Experiencing the night," she said finally.

Joshua understood her answer and her hesitation. "Was it familiar?"

"Yes and no." She moved a little so that Joshua would have more room. The bench was small, and he brushed against her as he sat. There didn't seem to be any place for Maggie to put her arms. Had it been Skeeter, they would have entwined them companionably and Maggie would have teased him about trying to push her off her seat. That kind of easy playfulness was impossible with Joshua. Her breath caught in her throat, and each of her movements felt curiously strained. Nothing felt natural. Nothing flowed.

"Do you want to talk about it?"

Her thoughts had gone so far afield that she didn't know what he was asking. "About what?"

"About the night. About what's familiar and what isn't."

She didn't want to talk about her memories or lack of them. She wanted to sit there under the New Orleans misty night sky and feel Joshua's arms around her. She wanted to mold her body to his and feel his lips moving over hers. She wanted to know what it was like to have his hands explore the curves of her body. She did not want therapy; she wanted the therapist. Restlessly she stood and moved to lean against the tree. "Talking won't help."

Joshua felt her withdrawal. "Is anything the matter?"

"I just don't feel like explorations into my psyche tonight."

"Is that what we were doing?"

"Do you know how often you answer me by asking a question?" she snapped.

Joshua grinned, and Maggie was struck by how appealing he was when he relaxed. "It's a professional hazard. I'm sorry."

"You like making me angry, don't you?" She forced a smile to prove that he hadn't succeeded.

"It's another professional hazard."

"When do you let down your guard? Does the real Joshua Martane ever come out to play?"

"The real Joshua Martane kidnapped you from the hospital two nights ago." He watched her eyes get larger and more luminous.

"I'm sorry. I didn't mean..."

"Yes, you did. It's okay. Does it help to know that I'm in the same boat you are? That I'm trying to feel my way, too?"

His question was a mine field waiting for her to tread carelessly and explode the tensions just under the surface. Instead she leaned against the tree and watched him in the moonlight. In the two days since she had been out of the hospital they had spent very little time alone together. The demands of her physical recovery had taken precedence.

She had slept for long periods of time, dreamless hours that were hastening the healing process of body and mind. When she was awake, Skeeter was there for casual conversation and laughter. Outside the parameters of hospital life, her relationship with Joshua seemed strained and unpredictable. Maggie suspected that the desire to avoid this kind of intimacy had been mutual.

"What am I going to do about you, Maggie?"

She pretended to misunderstand. "Hopefully before long you won't have to do anything. I'll be on my own."

Joshua considered her answer and was surprised at the hollow feeling it gave him. There hadn't been time before helping her leave the hospital to think about all the ramifications of his act. But since then he'd had the time. More time than he needed or wanted. Time to watch her cheeks tint with more color, time to watch the blue-gray shadows underneath her eyes begin to disappear, time to watch the easy affection she had developed for Skeeter. There'd even been enough time to face the fact that if she disappeared from his life, she'd be taking a part of him with her.

"Besides," she added, "don't you think you've done enough?"

No, he hadn't done enough. His body reminded him every time he looked at her that he hadn't done enough. His head reminded him that such yearnings were dangerous. "You're not ready to face the world alone yet," he said, with no trace of the inner conflict that raged through him.

"Is that all?" She tried to keep her voice light. "Just because I don't have a place to live or a job or any money you jump to the conclusion that I'm not ready to be on my own."

"You must feel frightened."

She wondered if the other things she felt were as obvious. "Sometimes. But I've proved I'm a survivor."

Skeeter opened the back door and stuck his head out. "*Citizen Kane*'s on Channel 12. The first person to tell me who Rosebud was gets to make the popcorn."

"His sled," Maggie and Joshua said together.

Joshua stood and held out his hand to Maggie. It was a casual gesture but one he had never made before. "Now tell me where you were the last time you saw this movie."

She shut her eyes and put her fingertips to her forehead as if she were in deepest thought. "I'm sure. Yes, I'm absolutely sure of it." She opened her eyes and smiled. "I was sitting in front of a television set."

"Well, you may not remember who you are," Joshua said, grasping Maggie's hand and pulling her toward him, "but if we ever play Trivial Pursuit, I want you on my team."

"Add totally sentimental to your list," Skeeter said two hours later as he flicked off the television set. On the way back to the sofa he reached for a tissue and gave it to Maggie, who was wiping away the last of her tears. "Blow hard and get it over with." She complied with a watery smile.

"What list is this?" Joshua watched the easy camaraderie that flowed between the two of them. He felt an odd stab of pain.

"A list of everything we know about Maggie. Everyone's been so busy telling her what they think they know or trying to get her to remember for herself that no one's bothered to try and total up what we're sure of." Skeeter watched Joshua with a tiny smile. Skeeter could tell his friend a few things that he had observed about him, too, but the time wasn't right for that.

"Such as?" Joshua heard the note of arrogance in his own voice. It surprised him. It had obviously surprised Maggie, too, because she was frowning at him.

Skeeter's smile broadened. "Well, tonight's a good example." He began to twirl his mustache. "Tonight's an absolute treasure trove of information."

"You're enjoying this, aren't you?" Maggie asked, poking Skeeter with her elbow. "Get on with it. I'm dying to find out what we know."

"For one thing, we know you've never popped corn before. Exhibit A." Skeeter held up the bowl filled with hard kernels and blackened remnants of the corn that had popped.

"Actually I don't think I've cooked much at all," she admitted. "Your kitchen feels like the land of Oz." They all thought back to the spaghetti that Maggie had insisted on preparing for supper. Simultaneously all three heads nodded.

"What else?" she asked.

"You're used to mosquitoes."

Maggie nodded.

"And you didn't shriek and run out of the room when that chameleon came inside to pay a call earlier."

"He was cute. And familiar."

"You're well educated. Look at your taste in movies and your speech patterns." Skeeter turned to Maggie and bowed in mock salute. "A regular Princess Di."

"If I was well educated, why was I out walking the streets?"

"Maybe you weren't."

"What good does this do?" Joshua asked. Suddenly the room seemed too small for all of them. He stood and quietly began to pace. "It's not going to tell us the essential facts."

"It could be very helpful," Skeeter began.

"No, Skeeter. I'll handle this." Maggie stood, too. She could no longer ignore the irritation in Joshua's voice. There were a few things he needed to understand. "Maybe it's not important to you, Joshua, but I want to know everything I can about myself. You have no idea what it's like being me. I'm a blank. A nothing." She waved aside his protests. "For all practical purposes I don't even exist, and yet somebody, somewhere, has tried twice to kill me. I'm willing to grasp at straws even if you think putting my life back together piece by piece is just an exercise in futility." She stopped and took a deep breath. "I'm going to bed. Good night."

Joshua stood very still and watched her walk from the room.

"You don't like it when somebody else tries to help her, do you?" Skeeter watched his friend trying to regain the perspective he had lost weeks before. He knew that Joshua was already defeated. He also knew that Joshua hadn't yet admitted it.

"I don't want her more confused." Joshua faced Skeeter. "I don't want her indulging in a lot of denial of reality."

"Denial of reality. I like that phrase." Skeeter looked at his watch. "It's time for me to go." He stood. "Denial. That's a word to meditate on, Dr. Martane." At the doorway he raised his hand in a goodbye wave. "I'll see you tomorrow."

Joshua bit back the angry words that threatened to spew out. When the door closed behind Skeeter, he began to pace the floor again.

Maggie lay awake and listened to the angry sound of Joshua's footsteps. Their relationship had become so complex that she could no longer fathom where it was going. One moment Joshua was warm and

considerate, the next he was irritated. She knew that the possibility of
losing his job was eating away at him. But there was more to his irri-
tability than that. It had to do with her. Joshua seemed to be as confused about their relationship as she was.

Obviously he felt something more for her than compassion or even
friendship. She had no name for the feeling, however. She wasn't
foolish enough to hope for love. Joshua would not love easily, although when he did it would be with no reserves. But if he gave his love
it would be to a woman he trusted, not to a woman with a shaded,
mysterious past.

She wasn't even sure she loved him. She couldn't be sure that what
she felt wasn't just a mixture of gratitude and physical attraction. But
she knew she wanted him. Some traitorous part of her that refused to
respond to her common sense longed for him with a primitive intensity that threatened to make her its prisoner.

The footsteps stopped and then started again, coming down the hall
to the bedroom door. The door creaked and Joshua was in the doorway.

"Are you awake?" he asked softly.

"Yes. Turn on the light if you need it."

He left the room in darkness and moved to sit on his bed. He began
to take off his shoes. "I'm sorry," he said. He didn't elaborate; he
knew Maggie understood his apology.

"All right."

"I just don't want you to get your hopes up. Finding out who you
are might take a long time." He began to take off his shirt. Maggie refused to turn on her side, and she watched him in the dim moonlight
through the open curtain.

"What you don't want is for me to begin hoping that I'm something I'm not." She delivered the words with no expression.

Joshua stood and pulled the sheet back. He began to slide off his
jeans. "I just want you to be realistic."

Maggie's breath caught in her throat. Joshua was so gloriously male,
so perfectly constructed. She had an acute longing to stand up and go
to him, to fit her body to his and explore the differences between them.
Perhaps it would clear the air between them in a way that talking never
would. And then again, perhaps it would prove to him that she was
exactly what he thought she was. She armed herself against her own
painful desire and concentrated on responding to his words.

"Realistic? What you really mean is that I have to face the fact that
I was a prostitute. That I walked the streets and slept with any man who
wanted me as long as he had the cash." This time her tone challenged
him.

"You can't discount the possibility."

"Don't play games. You don't think it's a possibility. You're convinced it's true. And no matter what you say to the contrary, it affects your opinion of me. I'm surprised you can even bear to sleep in the same room I'm sleeping in."

"Add overly dramatic to your list." Joshua slid between the sheets and folded his arms under his head. "I've told you before, it's what you become, not where you come from, that's important."

"And you want to be the one to play Professor Henry Higgins to my Eliza Doolittle." Maggie turned on her side away from Joshua.

"I don't want to transform you, Maggie."

"What do you want, then?"

It was fairly simple, really. He wanted to get out of his bed and crawl into hers. He wanted to pull her into his arms and absorb every particle of her into his being. He wanted to hold her until she melted into him, never to be separated again. He wanted to keep her safe, keep her happy, keep her with him always. It was fairly simple and fatally complicated.

"I don't know. But I don't want to hurt you."

Maggie shut her eyes. "Haven't you figured out by now that both of us are going to get hurt no matter what we do?"

Joshua continued to stare at the ceiling. He had no answer. The sound of Maggie's slow, even breathing filled the room long before Joshua was finally able to shut his own eyes.

The next evening Skeeter stood in the kitchen doorway with his arms folded and watched Maggie on her hands and knees scrubbing the black-and-white tile. "The floor doesn't have to be clean enough to eat off it. Did they invent the mop while you were in the hospital, babe?"

Maggie stopped and wiped the perspiration off her forehead with the hem of her T-shirt. "Doing it this way is better for everybody. Your floor gets cleaner, my arms get stronger...."

"And I get to watch your cute little rump swish back and forth."

"A dubious pleasure." Maggie sat back on her feet.

"Well, the house is shining. I'd call it quits for tonight." Skeeter extended a hand to help her up. "If you felt you had to pay me back for my hospitality, you were wrong."

"I'll always be grateful." Maggie stood and squeezed Skeeter's hand as a prelude to dropping it.

"Well, as long as you're feeling grateful, anyway, I've got something for you." Skeeter left the room and came back with a bag. "As cute as you look in my obscene T-shirts, it can't be too much fun sleeping in one. I got this for you."

Maggie opened the bag to find a pale pink cotton nightgown. It was full-length, not provocative at all, but to Maggie it looked like femininity personified. She wrapped her arms around Skeeter's neck and kissed him on the cheek. "You're such a nice person," she said. "Thank you, Skeeter."

"There's some underwear in there, too, and a blouse and a pair of jogging shorts that looked like they'd fit you."

"I'm very lucky."

Skeeter thought that nothing could have been further from the truth, but he didn't want to remind her. After an experience that didn't bear thinking about, the fact that Maggie could characterize herself as lucky was a complete testimony to her resilience and basic optimism. Standing in the kitchen watching her hold the nightgown up against her slender body, Skeeter wished, not for the first time, that he had discovered her before Joshua had.

"A fashion show?" Joshua was leaning against the doorframe watching them.

Maggie turned and flashed him a pixie grin. "Skeeter bought me some clothes."

Skeeter watched the expression on Joshua's face. It didn't change. Joshua was determined not to show Maggie what his feelings were. It was only because of her acute sensitivity that she was ever able to discern any of his emotions. With a sigh, Skeeter squeezed Maggie's arm. "Enjoy them, babe." With a nod to Joshua, he was on his way to work.

"Skeeter's very special, isn't he?" Maggie smiled at Joshua, wondering why he looked so stern.

"Maggie, Skeeter is off limits."

She wasn't sure she had heard him correctly. "Pardon me?"

Pardon me? It was the finishing school graduate again. Joshua shut his eyes. He couldn't deal with the cold feeling in his stomach. It had formed like an icy knot when he had seen Maggie hugging Skeeter, then holding the nightgown up against her lovely body for him to admire. No, that wasn't true. It had been building for three days. Every time Maggie looked at Skeeter or touched him or teased him. Every time she was in the same room with him. Joshua shook his head and opened his eyes. "I said, Skeeter is off limits."

She still didn't understand. "How can he be off limits? He lives right here...eats his..." Suddenly she understood. Her eyes widened, becoming vulnerable, bruised reflections of the inner woman. "I see." She couldn't move, she couldn't break their eye contact. She continued to stare helplessly at the man who had dared to think such a thing about her. The man she trusted completely.

Joshua saw the pain he had inflicted. He wanted to call back his words, but they were between them now. Stark, cold syllables destroying the affection and warmth that had been there before them.

"I'm sorry," he said, moving toward her.

She stepped back, her hand unconsciously clutching the nightgown in front of her. She took another step back, finding she was against the sink. "I'm going to bed."

"Maggie."

"Good night." She sidestepped, moving slowly around him and through the doorway. Safely in the bathroom she closed the door firmly behind her and turned on the shower. It was only later, when she was in bed defiantly dressed in the pink nightgown, that she gave way to bitter, angry tears.

Joshua sat in the living room, gazing out the window at a street lamp. He had never been more ashamed of himself. He was too good a psychologist to pretend that he didn't understand the feelings that had prompted his stinging insult. He had been jealous. Totally, blindly jealous. But more than that, he had been reacting to his fears that Maggie was not what she seemed. No matter what else he felt for her, unqualified trust was not one of his feelings. Too many things just didn't add up.

But tonight he had been unfair. Skeeter could be trusted completely. The scene in the kitchen had been innocent. Joshua had let himself react with a deep emotion that was a revelation. He had not felt this burning jealousy since he had discovered, at age twenty-seven, that his wife was being consistently unfaithful to him. Even then he had not experienced the gut-wrenching betrayal that had caused him to lash out at the fragile young woman who was trying to sleep in the other room.

God, the look in her eyes when she had finally understood his meaning. No one, no one could pretend to be that hurt. Her pain had been genuine. Completely genuine. And he had been its cause.

It seemed too late to make amends. She hadn't even wanted to hear his apology. With a few words, Joshua had destroyed her trust. She had been blooming with a delicate beauty, unfolding with the attention she received. Now she would withdraw to protect herself again. Joshua stood and began to pace the floor.

"Joshua?"

Joshua stopped and turned to face Maggie. She was standing in the doorway.

"Joshua, I didn't deserve your insult." She stepped out of the hallway, into the soft light of the living room. Covered from shoulder to toe in pale pink cotton, she was a feminine vision. The light just outlined the slight curves of her body, and she looked stricken and miserable. But she held herself with an innate pride that even his words had not erased. He shut his eyes in despair.

"No. You didn't. You didn't do anything. It was my problem, not yours."

"I wanted to hear your apology. We both need that much." She raised the back of her hand to her cheek then to her eye to rub it. "It wasn't fair not to give you a chance to explain."

"I'm sorry. Very, very sorry." He moved toward her, and she stood quietly as he approached. "You've given me no reason to say anything like that."

"You have all the reason in the world." Maggie's voice was calm, resigned. "We both know why you said what you did. You don't know what I'm capable of, do you? It's understandable that you wouldn't trust me."

Joshua stood in front of her, a scant inch from pulling her into his arms. To see his face, she would have to tip her head. She didn't bother. "I was jealous," he said, knowing that the truth was the only thing that might ease the pain he had caused.

She laughed. It emerged as a broken sound, a whimper encased in splintering glass. "How can you say that?"

He put his arms around her, stepping closer to hold her against his chest. "It's the truth. I was jealous."

The implications were too many for her to deal with. Her objectivity had been used up when she forced herself to face him again. "I don't understand. But could you just hold me for a few minutes, anyway?"

He tightened his arms around her and let one hand begin a slow journey over her back. At first she held herself stiffly against him, absorbing his warmth, his smell, the curious spell of his hand. Inch by inch she could feel her body respond to his, each muscle group relaxing, finding its counterpart in his body.

She slid her hands around Joshua's hips, coming to rest on her lower back. The smooth denim fabric of his jeans tantalized her fingers, and she longed for the feel of his skin. Slowly her fingers feathered up and then under his shirt to contact the heat of his body. The small intimacy hadn't gone unnoticed. He pulled her yet closer, and she could feel his lips against her hair. The moment went on until finally Joshua lifted her carefully, cradling her against his chest.

In their bedroom, he ignored the light, setting her down on her bed like the fragile object he believed her to be. Then, still fully clothed, he lay down beside her, pulling her to rest in his arms again. His chin brushed her hair, his arms held her close. "Go to sleep, sweetheart," he whispered.

Maggie shut her eyes and let her exhaustion take hold. She had no strength to examine what had happened between them. She had no strength to defend herself against this new twist in their relationship. She could only accept what was happening and trust that it wouldn't destroy either of them. Carefully she let herself snuggle closer. Joshua's arms surrounding her were stronger, better than her impossible fantasies. She let her hurt drain away as sleep overcame her. There was nothing that she couldn't forgive Joshua Martane. Nor was there anything she wouldn't give him if he asked. Her body, her heart, her soul were his for the taking.

She was completely unaware that if she had turned to him and told him her thoughts, nothing could have stopped him from giving her the same.

Maggie awoke the next morning alone. Sometime during the night she had felt Joshua slip across the room to his own bed, and although she had fallen back asleep soon afterward she had not slept as soundly. Now she turned over to find that his bed was empty.

She passed Skeeter in the hallway as she went in search of Joshua. "You're up early," she teased.

Skeeter looked at his watch. "You're up late. I'm just on my way out. Will you be all right here by yourself for a while?"

"Where's Joshua?"

"He called the hospital this morning and they asked him to come in at ten o'clock for a staff meeting."

Maggie knew a moment of utter desolation. "I bet I know what they want to talk about."

"It'll be all right. You've never seen Joshua go to bat for anyone before. He never loses."

"I wish I were as sure as you are."

"Trust me, babe."

By twelve noon, Maggie had worn a path pacing back and forth on Skeeter's living room rug as she waited for Joshua to return from the hospital. She was a solid mass of nervous energy, quickly using up her returning strength as she restlessly hiked the length of the room and back again.

When the navy blue Dodge Colt finally pulled up in front of Skeeter's house, Maggie forced herself to sit on the sofa and wait for the news that she was certain she didn't want to hear.

The day after her escape from the hospital, Maggie and Joshua had talked about his eventual meeting with Dr. Nelson. He had asked her if she would allow Dr. Nelson to make the decision about her future as well as Joshua's. "I trust Jim Nelson," Joshua had reassured her. "I know he won't send you to Mandeville, but he may want you back at City for a while. Will you be willing to go if he does?"

Stark white corridors, patients with dull eyes and insurmountable problems, screams in the night, mesh-covered windows. And a man who no one else believed was trying to kill her. Maggie had shut her eyes, fighting the fear of being imprisoned in the hospital again. "I don't know," she had answered truthfully. "I hope it won't come to that."

"We'll see."

Now Joshua had been to his meeting, and he was back.

"Maggie?" Joshua came in the front door and stood watching her. It was a warm afternoon. She was dressed in white jogging shorts and a sky-blue pullover that Skeeter had bought for her. Except for the stark pallor of her face, she was the picture of young American womanhood.

She forced herself to smile. "I've been waiting for you."

"So I see." Joshua crossed the room and sat carefully beside her. At that moment she looked so fragile that he was afraid she would crumble if he touched her. "Everything is fine, Maggie. It went much better than I had hoped."

"Tell me."

"You've been discharged from the hospital. You're free to begin a new life."

She blinked, waiting for the rest of it. "And you?"

He was surprised that she had glossed over her own good news. "I wasn't fired. I was suspended for three months. At the end of that time I'll probably be completely reinstated."

She couldn't understand the acceptance in Joshua's voice. "Three months? I never should have let you help me."

Joshua didn't know what to say. He just stared at her, watching the remorse build in her blue eyes. "Maggie," he said finally, too sharply, "don't prove me wrong and act like a crazy person now, for God's sake. They could have fired me, should have, in fact. But they didn't because they knew I had justifiable cause for my actions, and they respected me for it."

His anger stopped her retreat as his sympathy never would have. Unconsciously Maggie straightened her shoulders. "Damn you, Joshua," she said with spirit. "I am not a crazy person. And if I want to feel bad about what this has done to you, then I will. And if you don't like it, that's just too bad because I'm not under your care anymore."

Joshua smiled, the stern lines of his face softening with pleasure. "You're developing a temper to go with your name."

"You just wait until my strength comes back!"

"I'm trembling in my shoes." He put his arm around her shoulder and pulled her to rest against him. "Maggie, it's going to be all right now. I can use the time off. I've been working around the clock without any substantial free time for years. Only a few people know what I did. The hospital staff is going to be told that I'm on extended leave, and that's exactly how I'm going to look at it."

She heard the genuine timbre of his voice, and she began to relax a little, letting her own good news take precedence. "And I'm free."

"You're on your own, sweetheart. Dr. Nelson agreed that you didn't need to be hospitalized any longer."

The meeting had gone better than Joshua had dared hope. He had received a rap on the knuckles when he had deserved to lose his job. Every staff member who had been involved in Maggie's case had been present to give their side of the story. In the end Jim Nelson had listened and used his own good judgment. Joshua had been suspended because no matter how pure his motivation was, he had still gone against hospital policy. In addition, however, Dr. Bashir had been reprimanded for allowing his personal feelings to interfere with the handling of a case.

Perhaps the best news of all had been that Maggie was now free. The authorities had never been notified of her removal from the hospital; the commitment hearing had been canceled with no plan to reschedule. And because Joshua assured Dr. Nelson that Maggie was doing well away from the hospital, the staff, with the exception of Dr. Bashir, agreed that there would be no point in readmitting her. Joshua was to arrange suitable therapy for her until she regained her memory.

Afterward Betty had walked Joshua to the door. "What do you plan to do about Maggie?" she had asked.

With all its ramifications, it was the most important question anyone could ask him. Joshua chose to ignore the more complicated dimensions. Instead he had answered simply, "I'm going to find her a place to live and help her build a life for herself."

"And your relationship to her?" Betty had never been fooled by Joshua's professionalism with the young woman whose life was such a mystery.

"My relationship with her is fraught with difficulties," Joshua had admitted. "Bashir is right about one thing. I've lost all my objectivity. She'll need a new therapist. It's one case I can't handle."

"You do realize with the kind of background she has, she's probably a master at twistin' people around her little finger."

"I know."

Betty had smiled wryly, realizing that her warning was coming much too late. "Just step carefully."

Now with Maggie sitting beside him and their futures unshadowed for the first time, Joshua wondered if "stepping carefully" was even in the realm of possibility.

Maggie had been quietly trying to put the news in perspective. The impact of her newly won freedom was just beginning to settle over her. She was on her own, but she had no place to go, no money and no strength to look for a job. Freedom was wonderful, but the problems that came with it were not.

Her first problem was immediate. Turning slightly to see Joshua's face, she asked, "Will Skeeter mind if I stay here until tomorrow morning? Then I can start looking for another place to stay."

Joshua tried to think how he could best approach Maggie with his plan for her life. He had had three days to consider all the possibilities. He had a solution that he thought would be best, but he was no longer in a position of insisting that she do things his way. "Maggie, I know you want to stand on your own two feet, and you will soon, I promise. But right now, you're not strong enough to work."

"I'm going to look for a job in a store."

"You wouldn't make it through a day," he said gently. "Standing up for hours would wear you out immediately. You're still recovering from your injuries and all those weeks in bed. Will you let me tell you what I think you should do?"

"I could go back to my old job. I doubt if I'd need to stand up too often." She had tried to joke, but her bitterness emerged instead.

"Are you going to listen to me?"

She let her head fall against the arm that encircled her and nodded slightly.

"I have a two-bedroom apartment. I want you to move in with me. You'll have all the privacy you need, but I'll be there to help if you need me."

"I'm already much too deeply in your debt."

He ignored her. "Then when it's safe, and you're strong enough, you can find a job."

"Safe?"

Without thinking about what he was doing, Joshua pulled her closer, wanting to shelter her. "The man who tried to murder you is still at large. The police won't want you to make yourself available as a target again." He could feel her shudder. "Maggie, I'll protect you. Sam assures me that the police are closing in on this guy. Hopefully it'll only be a matter of weeks before they find him. By then you'll be strong enough to hold down a job. In the meantime you'll have to stay indoors when I'm not with you. New Orleans is a big city, but if you ran into this maniac and he recognized you . . ."

"Oh, I don't think there's any question that he'd recognize me." Maggie realized that Joshua's concerns came from the initial attempt on her life. "He even recognized me in a dark hospital room."

Joshua was silent.

"I know," she said with resignation. "You still think I was living through a nightmare."

"I don't think we can take any chances one way or the other," he said carefully. "As extra protection I'm going to ask Sam to issue a statement to the newspaper that you've been sent to a convalescent hospital somewhere in northern Louisiana."

"The newspaper?"

"There was a lot of press coverage back in November. Anything this guy does is news. Reporters still call the hospital from time to time asking about you."

She tried to think of a way to release Joshua from the obligation to her that he so obviously felt. "Doesn't the state have programs to take care of people like me? Why are you stuck with it?"

"Because I want to be." He turned, pulling her with him as he did so that they were face-to-face. Carefully he brushed the soft curls off her forehead. "We've come this far. Do you think I want to be cheated out of the chance to see you make a full recovery?"

"Is that it, or are you afraid that if you let me out of your sight, I'll start walking the streets again?" The question had been between them for a long time. It took all Maggie's effort to ask it with Joshua's fingers caressing her face.

He saw the pain, heard the slight catch in her voice. He wanted to reassure her, but if they were going to be almost constantly in each other's company, there was no room for lies between them. "I wouldn't be honest if I said that didn't worry me."

"Well, it's good to know where I stand." She tried to pull away.

"I don't know where you stand, Maggie. How can you? I only know I care about you, I worry about you, and I want, more than anything, to make sure you're going to be all right before you face the world by yourself again."

Maggie shut her eyes as Joshua bent his head. His mouth on hers was a surprise. She had expected another brotherly kiss on the forehead. Instead, what had probably been planned as a kiss of consoling affection rapidly developed into something else. She caught her breath as his lips brushed hers, tasting, sampling their texture. Afraid to move, afraid to respond because she knew he would pull away, Maggie lay in Joshua's arms and let him kiss her. It was a gentle kiss, but there was promise in it.

When his tongue began to stroke her lower lip, inviting her to open for him, she tentatively put her arms around his neck, expecting at any moment to have him pull away. Instead the kiss deepened, catching fire, and suddenly there was no room for control, for fear. She let herself respond with all the passion that she had repressed. Joshua was kissing Maggie. For one blessed moment the confused roles that separated them had been discarded.

Willingly, she opened her mouth, receiving his tongue, shivering as he pulled her harder against him. Her fingers threaded through the curls at the nape of his neck, and she sighed in pleasure at the feelings flooding her body. He broke the kiss to begin another, and his hands began to travel the delicate curves of her torso. Her own excitement mounted with each new intimacy. She accepted it all, knowing that there was nothing she would ever deny Joshua. She was already his, no ceremony, no ritual of consummation could make it more official. She belonged to Joshua Martane, and somehow she knew that she had never belonged to anyone that way before.

"Maggie." Joshua pulled away carefully. Her arms were still around his neck, and he could feel her fingers massaging the sudden tension there. "I'm sorry," he said roughly. "I didn't plan for that to happen."

"Why didn't you?"

She looked so vulnerable. Under the circumstances, how could she look as if she had just been kissed for the first time and was still struggling in the throes of discovery? He shook his head. Words were impossible.

Maggie saw Joshua's defenses drop neatly into place. "I see," she said, carefully removing her hands to pull away. "The therapist doesn't kiss the patient. The minister doesn't kiss a lady of the night. Joshua doesn't kiss Maggie." She stood, her legs threatening to withdraw their support. She tilted her head back and confronted him with the sorrow in her eyes.

"I'll be ready to go when you are, Joshua. And I'll do what you ask. But just as soon as I'm able, I'm stepping out of your life. Eve's going to disappear and take the apple with her. Then you won't have to worry about temptation at all." Head erect, body swaying gracefully, she left the room.

Chapter 6

Joshua's apartment was one of four carved out of an old mansion on Esplanade Avenue near the French Quarter. Joshua had five rooms and a bath. The ceilings were twelve feet high, the woodwork ornate walnut, the floors a polished masterpiece of craftsmanship, the furniture antique. Because the neighborhood was transient and the house itself in a state of semidisrepair, Joshua paid an affordable rent.

That afternoon Maggie walked through the apartment and admired everything she saw. Compared with a sterile hospital room, it was paradise.

The spare bedroom was open and airy with two windows looking out on the avenue. Both windows had wrought-iron balconies that could be reached by stepping over the low windowsills. "Up until the turn of this century," Joshua told Maggie, coming to stand with her on one of the balconies, "Esplanade was considered the 'Promenade Publique.' The Creole dandies promenaded here every afternoon and flirted with the chaperoned Creole beauties. I imagine many a young girl stood on this balcony and fluttered her eyelashes at the men parading below."

Maggie watched the traffic zipping past and tried to imagine a quieter, gentler time. "It's a beautiful street. I feel like I'm on a movie set."

"Wait until Mardi Gras." Joshua stopped. Mardi Gras was almost a year away. He couldn't assume that Maggie would even be in the city then.

"When is that?"

"Right before Lent. February or March."

She refrained from reminding him that she would not be living with him then. Instead she turned and stepped over the sill into the room that was to be hers. Joshua followed her and began to move a pile of books off the dresser.

"I've been using this room for storage," he apologized. "It'll only take a few minutes to clear it out."

"Don't bother." Maggie put her hand on Joshua's arm. "Leave it the way it is. I'm not going to be staying long."

"You can't predict that. In the meantime I want you to be comfortable."

Maggie thought that "comfortable" was a peculiar word choice. She was sure she had never been more uncomfortable in her life. "I'm not going to stay at all if you insist on putting yourself out for me."

Joshua had been careful not to touch her since the kiss that had rocked his foundations earlier in the afternoon. Now he settled his hands firmly on her shoulders. He wanted to shake her for her obstinacy. He wanted to ask her for her forgiveness. He wanted to kiss her again.

"Look, I know you're confused and angry. I'm confused, too. But there's one thing I'm not confused about. I want you here. I'm very, very sure of that. The kiss didn't change that; your bullheaded obstinacy doesn't change that. Can we please call a truce?"

"I don't like being an obligation to anyone. I may not know much about myself, but I do know that." Maggie met his eyes defiantly.

"I want you here, but I'm not going to beg you to stay. It's your decision."

Some of the fight went out of her. The situation was full of complications, but even if she'd had another place to go, Maggie knew that she'd still choose to stay with Joshua. "I want to earn my keep."

"What are you proposing?"

"I'll keep house and cook while I'm here."

Joshua squeezed her shoulders and then dropped his hands. "It's a deal."

"Were you expecting another kind of offer?"

For once Joshua let his guard drop. His anger at her question was plainly visible on his face. He took a step closer. "Stop it, Maggie."

It had been a childish, spiteful question coming out of the painful knowledge that Joshua didn't trust her. She wished that she could call it back. "This isn't going to be easy, is it?" she asked softly. "I'm sorry."

"Let's not punish each other." Joshua raised his hand to her hair and brushed the soft tendrils off her face. For a moment they stared into each other's eyes, and then each took a step backward.

"We'll go grocery shopping tomorrow," Joshua said finally. "Let me take you out to dinner tonight."

Maggie nodded, resigned to her temporary dependency.

"Right now I'm going to take you shopping for some clothes."

This time she shut her eyes, and her shoulders slumped in defeat. "I hate this."

"You can pay me back later if you feel you have to. But I like doing things for you."

"You've already done too much. Now I feel like I'm your personal charity."

"I know you do. I wish you could understand that I'm doing it just because I want to."

"Someday you'll have to explain that to me."

Shopping at a department store, Joshua had to insist that Maggie at least buy the bare essentials of a wardrobe. As fast as he pulled extra items off the racks, she put them back. It became a test of wills, and as they made their way back to their apartment, it was difficult to say who had won.

Joshua's therapist's eye kept track of Maggie's reactions to the crowds around her, to the rigors of shopping and the trip through the busy city. She had weathered the storm admirably, paying scant attention to the entire experience. When the time came to reenter the world by herself, it looked as though it wouldn't be too frightening.

"How did it feel to be back out in the world?"

Maggie considered his question. She hadn't even thought about the fact that shopping was something she hadn't done in a long time. "It felt perfectly normal." She looked out her window at the passing scenery. "Driving on the interstate seems perfectly normal."

"Do any of your surroundings seem familiar?"

She squinted, as if seeing everything from a slightly skewed vantage point would help. "Yes and no."

"Tell me about the yes."

"Well, it doesn't seem strange. The landscape is comforting, somehow." She gestured to the rows of one-story homes they were passing. "I think I've seen lots of places like those."

"That's pretty typical of most cities."

"I guess so." She brightened a little. "The water seems familiar, too." They were passing over a winding bayou.

"That's good. What do you think about when you see the water?"

Maggie considered his question. She shut her eyes and tried to form a mental picture. "Lots of it. Blue and sparkling. And waves." She frowned after another minute and opened her eyes. "That's it."

"That was a good start."

"How am I going to make it all come back?"

Joshua decided that her question was as good a lead-in as he was going to get. He had been charged by the hospital staff with the responsibility of seeing that Maggie stayed in therapy until her memory returned. "You need someone to talk to, someone who can help you reassemble the pieces of your life."

"What about you?"

"I've become one of those pieces."

Maggie nodded. "In other words I need somebody I can talk to without any constraints."

"I have a friend, a woman, Antoinette Deveraux, who does therapy privately. She's agreed to see you if you're willing."

"Do you think it'll help?"

"It can't hurt."

Maggie turned and watched the passing scenery again. "I'll do anything I can to find out who I am. I'll be glad to see her."

"So you're Maggie." Antoinette Deveraux examined the young woman who was sitting in a comfortable armchair in front of her desk.

"Probably not." Maggie looked around the small office, admiring the tasteful, unobtrusive furnishings.

"I've never heard two words used more effectively." Antoinette sat back and watched her new client. She could understand immediately why Joshua had risked so much and been so captivated by the beautiful young woman sitting in front of her desk.

Maggie turned her attention back to Antoinette. She had expected someone older and more maternal. She had not expected such a stunning combination of grace and intelligence. Maggie wondered about Antoinette's connection to Joshua. The two psychologists would suit each other. There were no mysteries, no shaded pasts to overcome. "Have you ever had a case like mine?" she asked.

"No."

Maggie smiled. "Are you in the mood for a challenge, then?"

"Always." Antoinette smiled, too.

"Do you think you can help?" Maggie tried not to make the question sound too important, but as soon as she heard her own voice, she knew that she had failed.

"Do you want me to help?"

"Of course." Maggie thought about her answer. Antoinette seemed to understand that she wasn't finished, and she waited quietly. "I don't know," Maggie amended, after a long pause.

Antoinette nodded. "Let's talk about why you may not want to remember your past."

"That's not very difficult. I may not like what I discover."

"I can guarantee that you won't like all of it."

"I'm not talking about childhood pranks or failing college algebra."

"You're talking about prostitution."

Maggie lifted her shoulders. "I don't know what I'm talking about. I only know that my past terrifies me."

"Then part of what we're going to do together is try to help you peel off the layers, one at a time, until you feel strong enough to face all of it."

"But I don't have that much time." Maggie lifted her chin and Antoinette could see the determination in her delicate features. "I have to know so that I can get on with my life."

"You can't push a river. Things happen at their own good speed."

"Can't you hypnotize me and make me remember?"

Antoinette considered Maggie's question. "Hypnosis might help you later. Right now it's not appropriate."

"I'll tell you what's not appropriate. It's not appropriate for me to live off Joshua while I sit around and wait for my memory to return. And it's not appropriate to stay in a city where a man has tried twice to kill me." Maggie managed to keep her voice calm although she felt like ranting and raving.

"It's all right to be angry in here, Maggie. You don't have to work so hard to hide it."

Antoinette's gentle statement completely dissolved Maggie's suppressed resentment. She took a deep breath and let it out slowly. "I'm going to like working with you," she said, looking Antoinette straight in the eye. "But I'm not going to be nearly as patient as you want me to be."

"I just want you to go at your own pace. I promise I can keep up."

Maggie nodded. "Then let me tell you everything I think I know about myself."

Antoinette settled back and waited.

The intimacy that had always characterized Maggie and Joshua's relationship seemed to disappear with the increased intimacy of their living situation. It was as if the dangerous attraction continually kindling under the surface of their interactions had forced them both into a guarded politeness.

Maggie was grateful for everything that Joshua did for her. She kept the apartment clean and taught herself to cook with a determination that even she found humorous. She made a habit of staying out of his way, retreating to her room when she thought he needed privacy. She rarely initiated conversations or asked anything of him.

Joshua was thrust into the position of having to guess what she might need. He gave her books to read, bought her a radio to listen to in her room, offered to accompany her anywhere that she might want to go.

But there the relationship came to an abrupt halt. Although he made attempts to find out what she was feeling, Maggie remained remote. On the surface everything was as it was supposed to be. Underneath, he had no idea what was happening to her.

A week passed and then two. Physically Maggie was blooming. They took evening walks into the French Quarter and each night, the walks grew longer and longer. She was gaining weight and sleeping less during the day. Although the nightmare still came with some frequency, its impact was less shattering. For the first time since she had awakened from her long slumber, Maggie felt that she was really getting well.

What she wasn't getting was any closer to solving the riddle of her past. She didn't talk to Joshua about her sessions with Antoinette, but she was becoming more and more aware that it would be a long time before she knew who she had been. Antoinette was helping her probe the depths of her memory, but the small bits of information they uncovered only tantalized her. Antoinette said that they were helping Maggie get ready to remember; when the time came, Maggie would be better able to face it. But Maggie found that as she improved physically she was becoming increasingly impatient.

Almost three weeks after Maggie's escape from the hospital, Joshua came home one afternoon after a visit to the police station to talk about Maggie's case. Lounging at his desk amid clattering typewriters and ringing telephones, Sam had given Joshua more assurance that the prostitute murderer was about to be apprehended. "No thanks to your Maggie," Sam had added.

A week before, Sam had finally been granted his chance to interview Maggie. He had come to Joshua's apartment and asked cryptic, loaded questions that Maggie had not been able to begin to answer. She had stood up well under Sam's probing, but she had added nothing to his information. The night of her near-death remained a mystery.

Sam was obviously not convinced that she was telling the truth about her amnesia. Now, ready to close in on the murderer, he warned Joshua again about not taking Maggie at face value. "I've seen a thousand just like her," he told Joshua. "When this guy is off the streets, send her back."

Joshua had swallowed his anger and shaken his head at his friend. "You just take care of finding this maniac; I'll take care of my own life."

Regardless of Sam's attitude, Joshua felt that he was bringing good news home with him. Soon Maggie would be as safe as anyone else was in New Orleans. But there was another aspect of the killer's apprehension that was just as important. With luck the man would be able to give the police details about Maggie that would help them trace her identity.

At home Maggie was not in the living room or kitchen. Calling out to reassure her, Joshua went to his room first. He changed his clothes and crossed the hall to tap on Maggie's door. There was no answer.

Since she sometimes spent time at their landlady's first-floor apartment, Joshua fixed lunch and waited. When Maggie didn't come back after an hour, he finally went to Mrs. LeGrand's to check on her.

Mrs. LeGrand insisted that he come in. She was an older woman, lap-dog friendly, who gauged the success of her days by how much gossiping she got to do. Joshua was fond of his landlady, but he avoided her as much as possible. Only Maggie seemed to have the patience to listen for hours on end to her stories.

"Ain't seen her all afternoon," Mrs. LeGrand said with a shake of her head. "Last time I saw her she was heading down Esplanade."

"When was that?"

"Early sometime. I was getting the mail."

Joshua excused himself in the middle of one of Mrs. LeGrand's longer sentences and sprinted to his car. Searching for Maggie along the city streets was like looking for the proverbial needle in a haystack. To complicate matters, an afternoon thunderstorm pelted Joshua's windshield with silver blankets of rain, further obscuring his vision. He drove for an hour, covering a two-mile radius from the apartment. Finally he turned his car around, realizing the hopelessness of the situation.

Trying to be calm, Joshua told himself that the chance Maggie would come to harm was very remote. The possibility of running into the man who had tried to murder her was a small one. Although that still worried him, other things worried him more. Maggie could wander into a rough neighborhood, thereby inviting new violence. Perhaps her memories had returned and she was looking for old acquaintances, or perhaps she was not as stable as Joshua had thought and was having a relapse. He knew that it wasn't uncommon for a patient to have periods of confusion after an injury to the brain. The more he thought, the more Joshua became convinced that Maggie was in serious danger.

Joshua considered calling Sam, but there was nothing that the police could do. Maggie was not in protective custody. There was no way that anyone could enforce her imprisonment on Esplanade Avenue. She had every right to leave the apartment.

He parked his car and climbed the steps. Inside he knocked on Maggie's bedroom door once again. There was still no answer. Standing in the living room, Joshua knew that he was helpless. When the rain stopped he would go back out and search for her. Until then he could only change out of his wet clothes and wait.

* * *

Even the long evening walks with Joshua had not prepared Maggie for the miles she had to cover to get to Hootie Barn's Tavern. She had looked up the address in the telephone book and once outside the apartment she had asked directions several times. Now she stood in front of the flamboyantly painted bar, watching men come and go as she tried to make her memory respond to the sight.

"I was here. I was found here," she whispered as if the words, spoken out loud, would trigger a reaction. "I was lying in that lot over there."

With acute distaste she picked her way around the building, stepping over broken glass, around old tires and other assorted debris. The vacant lot was no more inspiring than any other piece of wasted urban space would have been. There were no answering echoes in her head, no charges of excitement.

Her memories were imprisoned just as surely as she had been imprisoned in the hospital and now in the Esplanade apartment. She had nothing. No past, no future, and the present? Well, the present was especially painful.

She had been trying for weeks to adjust to the reality that Joshua would never be a part of her life. And why should he be? He had already given more than she had a right to expect. Wanting his love, his unqualified acceptance and trust was asking for the moon and the stars, too. She had no right to expect so much. Not when she had so little to give in return.

Knowing this, she had distanced herself from him, maintaining a friendly facade that did nothing to soothe the ache inside her. Until today. This morning something inside her had snapped. The enforced patience caused by her lack of strength and her lingering uncertainty about the future were finally all used up.

She had to know who she was. Somewhere in her past there might be someone who cared about her, someone who could forgive and accept her. A parent, a brother or sister, a former lover. Someone, somewhere who could explain to her why she had become a prostitute. Someone, somewhere, who could love her.

She could feel the plodding progession of her days. The loneliness of being a perpetual stranger was closing in on her. When she had awakened that morning she had realized for the first time that she didn't care who she had been. Whatever her past, she was ready to face it. What she couldn't face was the waiting.

Maggie felt tiny raindrops begin to sting the exposed skin of her arms and neck. On the sidewalk in front of Hootie Barn's Tavern, men called to her, offering invitations that she hardly heard. When several of them started toward her, she turned and began to follow a path around the other side of the building back to the front sidewalk. It was only then that she began to notice how unsavory her surroundings were.

She had been so busy examining every house, every street she had walked along, that she had not computed just how rough the section of town was. She had been searching for her identity. Along the way she had forgotten about her safety. Luckily the men who had come after her abandoned their halfhearted chase, owing, she was sure, to the increasing tempo of the rain.

The day had been warm, but the rain was cool against her skin. As Maggie hurried away from Basin Street, she cursed her lingering weakness. She was exhausted and discouraged. She was also lost.

As the rain increased, so did her confusion. She had not paid enough attention to the directions that had gotten her to the tavern. She began to wander along side streets, losing her way further. There was no one to ask since everyone with any sense was inside in what had now become a typical New Orleans thunderstorm. The small businesses she passed were not the kinds of places to stop and wait out the rain. Instinctively she knew that she was better off in the storm than she would be inside.

Maggie made a right and then a left, becoming more and more bewildered by the tangle of streets. She ended up in what looked like a poor residential section, its houses bleak and unpainted with sagging front porches and yards that were nothing more than clumps of overgrown tropical foliage. Under the dubious shelter of a massive live oak tree, she stopped and waited for a few minutes, hoping that the rain would let up before she was forced to move on.

The neighborhood might be poor and run-down, but at least its inhabitants were inside, safe and warm. For a moment she was tempted to cross the street, knock on the nearest door and ask for shelter. She could call Joshua and ask him to pick her up. Then she could be home and dry in a matter of minutes.

On closer examination, however, she decided to move on. She didn't like the looks of the house. Compared to its neighbors, it was more dilapidated, more unkempt, with garbage strewn over the yard and the rusting hulk of an old automobile in the driveway. No, she didn't want to go inside. She shuddered and began to walk swiftly down the sidewalk. Suddenly she felt as though she couldn't put enough distance between herself and the house. Between herself and the street of houses similar to the one she had examined.

She tried to convince herself that the near panic she felt was a normal response, an instinct built in to protect herself in a strange city. No one with any sense depended on strangers in an urban setting such as New Orleans. But searching her limited memory, she had to admit to herself that this surge of fear was different from anything she had felt since leaving the hospital. There was no time to explore her feelings further. She was becoming increasingly lost.

At the end of the street she made a turn and then another. The rain made it difficult to see. Drops caught in her eyelashes, nearly blinding her. The sky was getting progressively darker, illuminated only occasionally by the flashes of lightning.

Joshua had explained to Maggie about the rows and rows of brick buildings that housed so many of New Orleans' poorest citizens. When she came around the corner and found herself in front of one of the housing projects, she turned and tried to retrace her steps, hopelessly mired in the maze of streets.

At the point of total exhaustion she leaned against a sign on a street corner, too tired to take another step. Through the haze of rain and fatigue she looked up to see a white bus decorated with purple, green and gold stripes splashing its way toward her. She could just make out the sign proclaiming Esplanade Avenue.

Maggie stepped off the curb, and the bus pulled to a stop. She was a nickel short, but the driver waved her to the back without a word. She collapsed on a seat and ignored the curious stares of the other riders.

On the front porch of the Esplanade mansion, after a ten-minute bus ride, she tried to wring as much water as she could out of the loose blouse she was wearing with her only pair of jeans. Satisfied that she had done the best she could, she opened the front door and climbed the stairs.

"Maggie, where in the hell have you been?" The door to Joshua's apartment flew open, and he stomped out into the hallway in his bare feet.

Maggie shivered at the anger in his eyes and the cool indoor air against her wet skin. Snapping herself out of a near trance, she finally turned, ignoring his question, and pushed past him to get through the door. He followed close behind.

"Just a minute, you're going to answer my question." Joshua was standing in her doorway towering over her like a furious prison warden.

Too miserable to respond, she turned again and found her way to her bedroom where she pulled the shorts and blouse that Skeeter had given her out of her dresser. She was much too cold to wear shorts, but the only pair of jeans she owned were clinging to her shivering body. Switching on the bathroom light, she closed the door and locked it, starting the hot water in the big, claw-footed tub. She soaked for long minutes, adding more hot water as the temperature cooled until she was finally warm all over. Only then did she pull herself out, dress in the shorts and blouse and come out of the bathroom to face Joshua.

"It's too cool to wear shorts."

She ignored him, going back into her room to pull a folded blanket off the bed to wrap herself in as she flopped down on top of the bed covers. "Go away," she mumbled, closing her eyes.

Joshua could see the absolute, unremitting fatigue that had etched thin lines around her eyes. For once, it did not touch him. "If you're tired," he said, his voice as cold as Maggie's body had been, "it's your own damn fault. What were you doing out there? I told you not to go out without me. Not ever."

"I went to Hootie Barn's Tavern. It's one of my favorite hangouts, remember?" With great effort she opened her eyes. "That's what you expected to hear, wasn't it, Joshua? Well, it's true."

Her eyes had drifted shut again when she felt Joshua's hands gripping her shoulders. She went limper under the insistent pressure.

"Maggie, you could have been killed. For God's sake, open your eyes."

Something in his voice surprised her enough to make her look at him.

"Maggie, sweetheart, why did you go back there? Did you realize how dangerous it was?"

"I went back to find myself," she murmured, her eyes beginning to close again.

"And did you?"

"No. I wasn't there. I was never there."

She was drained. Joshua watched as sleep claimed her.

He couldn't make himself leave. He pulled a straight-backed chair beside the bed and sat restlessly on the edge. Maggie slept on, completely unaware of the man at her bedside.

Chapter 7

The apartment was dark with evening's approach when Maggie opened her eyes. As always, waking from a deep sleep confused her, flooding her body with helpless dread. Staring at the wall beside her bed, she talked sense to herself with the courage of a little girl whistling in the dark to scare away the monster in her closet. There was nothing to be afraid of in this apartment. No, she didn't remember anything about her life previous to the hospital, but yes, all her memories from that time on were crystal clear.

"Maggie?"

Joshua startled her. She had forgotten that he had been in the room when she'd fallen asleep. Turning toward his voice, she propped herself on one elbow. "Hello."

He had been standing by the window, and he crossed the room to stand beside her bed. "I wasn't sure that you were awake."

"I didn't know you were still here."

"I was worried about you."

"You're going to need someone else to worry about from now on."

"And why is that?"

"Because I'm going to be just fine." Maggie sat up, hugging her knees, her chin resting on the blanket covering them. "For the first time, I know I'm going to be fine."

Joshua had not expected this response. He had watched her for hours as she'd slept the exhausted sleep of the weary pilgrim, and he had wondered how he was going to tell her his thoughts when she awoke. Now she was sitting up, her eyes bright and unclouded, her cheeks once again tinted with color. It was another rebirth.

Maggie smiled and gestured for him to sit beside her. "Don't look so serious. I feel good."

"Why?" Instantly he hated his question, but Maggie didn't seem annoyed by it. She extended her hand and pulled him down on the edge of the bed.

"Because I'm recovering."

"Are you remembering anything?"

She shook her head. "Just tiny flashes. Enough to whet my appetite, nothing more. But I think eventually it will come back to me. And when it does, I can face it. I proved that to myself today."

He had been so angry at her for leaving the apartment that he hadn't paused to consider the fact that her experience might prove valuable. His brows drew together in the semblance of a frown as he thought about her words.

"Do you know that you're wearing your therapist's face right now?" Maggie swung her legs over the bed and turned slightly to face him. "When you're trying to puzzle something out, trying to figure out just how you should respond, you get that frown on your face. It's fascinating to watch, but I'd rather you just told me what you thought."

"I was trying to figure out how today could have been helpful."

"I faced a piece of my past, and I survived. Surviving is a talent I seem to have, and I'm proud of myself for it. I'm tired of feeling guilty about my life. Whatever I did, whatever I was, I did it because I had to do it. I'm not going to spend any more of God's precious time feeling ashamed of something I don't even remember."

This time Joshua smiled. "Good for you."

"I also realized today that I can't push the river." She smiled a little. "That's Antoinette's phrase, not mine. But it's true. I can't force myself to remember anything. I tried today and I failed. I'm going to have to settle for just getting on with my life."

"I wish it could be easier."

She nodded. "And finally, I'm tired of taking. It's weighing me down. With or without your permission, I'm going to look for a job."

"Just a minute..."

"Nope. It's my decision." She moved closer, placing one delicate hand on his knee in a gesture of intimacy. "We can't go on like this anymore. You have a life, too, but you spend all your time taking care of me. Don't you think I see what that's done to you? I know there must be places you want to go, women you want to be with. It's time for you to forget me." She successfully kept the pain from her voice. She was doing the right thing, but every word was a tiny wound inside her.

"As if I could." Joshua covered her hand with his. "Do you think you're just a millstone around my neck that I can't wait to be rid of?"

Maggie tried to smile. "No. I think I'm a patient that you got in over your head with, and you don't know how to back off gracefully. I'm telling you not to worry."

He couldn't believe that she was asking him to leave her alone. Joshua tried to examine the emptiness that her words evoked. His therapist's eye was tightly shut against his inner self. He was bewildered and angry. "What do you plan to do to make money?"

"Not what you're thinking," she said with a toss of her head.

"Stop that!" Joshua gripped her shoulders. "How dare you try to read my mind! The fact that you may have been a prostitute is way down on my list of things to think about as far as you're concerned. I'm tired of being punished because I once expressed doubts to you."

Maggie was shocked into total silence at Joshua's outburst. Eyes wide, she stared at him, her teeth sunk deeply into her lower lip.

He ignored her response. "I'm worried about your health and safety, not your morality. I care too much about you to let you jeopardize either. I care way too much."

"Do you?" she asked softly.

Joshua groaned, and his hands moved to her waist to bring her onto his lap. He settled her sideways, tipping her back to expose her face to the touch of his mouth. His lips were hungry, crushing hers with no thoughts of gentleness or caution. Joshua, who had given and given, was finally taking what he wanted. Maggie, who had taken and taken, was being allowed, finally, to give. "I care," he said between devouring onslaughts of kisses, one hand tangled in her hair. "I care more than is good for either of us."

She had no reply. Her emotions were being steadily assaulted; her body had completely succumbed to his touch. When his hands traveled beneath the blue knit blouse to discover that she wasn't wearing a bra, she trembled with him at the revelation. Holding her breath, she waited as he explored her softness. She was immobilized with longing, each feather-light touch an explosion inside her. The pleasure was unfamiliar, as so many things in her life were.

Alive with feeling, she arched her spine to bring herself in closer contact with him, her eyes tightly shut. There was a purring low in her throat, a sound of pure, unadulterated ecstasy.

"Maggie, you're so beautiful," Joshua said, his voice low and shaken. "I want you too much."

"Don't you know I'm yours?" she asked, opening her eyes to meet his. "Haven't you always known that?" With trembling fingers she began to unbutton his shirt. "You can't possibly want me too much."

But he did. He wanted her too much to be as careful, to be as gentle as her healing body deserved. He wanted her too much to do what was right for her. And the worst thing of all was that there was a rational part of him that still knew it. With Maggie curled up in his lap and the soft knit of her blouse caressing his naked chest, the pure sensual pleasure of the experience was laced with a thread of despair. He couldn't take her. Not like this. Not with so much still between them.

"We can't."

"I don't want to hear this." Maggie began to place nuzzling kisses along his neck. Joshua's hands were playing games with her spine, feathering out to caress the delicate skin along the sides of her breasts. She knew he was aroused, that stopping now was going to be as difficult as starting had been. She determined to make it even more difficult.

His voice was a groan. "Maggie, no more."

She ignored him, drunk with the knowledge that she could cause the torment apparent in his words. She had thought that he saw her only as an obligation. Now she realized just how wrong she had been. She was something much more to him, something much more special. And there was nothing that she wanted more in life than to be special to Joshua. If she could, she would gladly trade the return of her memories for one night of his love.

Maggie ran her fingertips over every inch of his chest, exploring the breadth of his shoulders, the hardness of his muscles. She rubbed her face over the sprinkling of hair, inhaling the good, clean smell of him. It was impossible to get enough of Joshua; five senses were too few. She wanted to possess him, to blend, to merge, not only in a sexual way but in a spiritual one, as well. Frustrated by the inadequacy of the human body to express what she was feeling, Maggie sighed and began to run her lips and tongue over him.

Joshua was possessed with a sweet fire that threatened to consume every cell in his body. He knew he should stop her, but his willpower was gone. There was an exuberance, a delightful lack of calculation in her touch and her kisses. She was totally engrossed in what she was doing, exploring him as though he were an uncharted island. She was a reverent seeker of new knowledge. They were both lost in her discoveries.

He had stopped his own explorations. He knew where they were leading. Her skin was so velvet soft, so completely touchable. She was lovelier to stroke than he had ever imagined, a delicate perfection that he had not believed possible. But Joshua knew he saw her through the eyes of his infatuation. Whatever imperfections there were, he was blind to them. The gift of rational insight, of logical analysis, completely disappeared in her presence. He was bewitched. For a few minutes he allowed himself the pleasure-pain of succumbing to her spell.

Maggie trailed soft, nipping kisses up Joshua's neck once more, exploring the tight skin with her tongue. She continued to his chin, feeling the slight rasp of whiskers against the smoothness of her lips. She found his mouth and pressed hers against it lightly, again and again, testing new angles, new amounts of pressure. And then, she was no longer in control; it had been taken from her by his response.

His mouth closed over hers, holding her a willing prisoner as his tongue sought the companionship of hers. She could feel the kiss all over her body as if she had become a finely tuned instrument completely sensitive to all pressures, all quivering, resounding vibrations. She knew a desire so acute that she could not think, could not breathe. At that moment she would have done anything to make Joshua hers.

"We can't."

She wondered how a rejection could be so firm and yet so poignantly gentle. Joshua had pulled his mouth from hers and turned his head. Maggie could see the regret engraved in deep lines on his face. She was struggling to catch her breath, watching him struggle to regain the control he was so rarely without. Both were shaking with their need for each other.

She wanted to protest, to let the passion just waiting to explode beneath the surface explode in anger instead. She could not. She could no longer retreat behind anger. She loved Joshua too much to punish him.

It took all her strength to accept his withdrawal. Finally she laid her head on his chest, and Joshua wrapped his arms around her back to shelter her there. Both of them were breathing audibly, and he was sure she could hear the walloping beat of his heart. "Maggie," he whispered finally, "you're still too fragile."

"No. You only think I am."

He had no answer.

"And you still don't know who I am."

He knew she was right, although not strictly in the sense she meant it. Sitting beside her bed waiting for her to awaken, Joshua had realized that no matter what they found to be true about Maggie's past, he wanted to accept it and move beyond it with her. But there was no way to put an end to a chapter of her life that they couldn't even read.

Then a new thought had crystallized. If the police were wrong and she had never been a prostitute, she still had a past. And that past might include a husband or a lover.

The thought was as shattering as the possibility of her prostitution. Somewhere there might be a man who had a prior claim on her love. Somewhere there might be a man whom she would want when she regained her memory. He was in the untenable position of not knowing which scenario of her past he wanted to be the real one.

An involuntary shudder went through his long frame at the thought of Maggie loving another man. Not loving him casually with her body, but with all of her, with the sweet intensity that flowed out of every word she spoke, out of every graceful movement she made. For the second time since she had come into his life he was shaken with jealousy. "We're going to have to find out. For both our sakes."

"What if you find out that the police were right, that my past reads like a criminal's record? Will you be able to touch me then?" With the palms of her hands firmly against his chest, she pushed away. Sick disappointment at his rejection surged through every cell.

It was time to speak his thoughts out loud, time to let her think about this new possibility. "Neither of us can know what we'll feel. Have you ever considered that there may be a man in your past that you'll want to go back to when your memory returns?"

He tried to pull her back, but she slipped off his lap to sit on the bed beside him. She shrugged off his suggestion with a lack of concern that confounded him. "Why do you assume that whatever I discover will wipe away the time we've spent together? Will you suddenly be less important to me?"

"That's entirely possible."

"I'd like to know who she was, Joshua."

He ran his fingers through the dark waves that had fallen over his brow. "What are you asking?"

"Who was the woman who's made you so desperately careful?"

"My past has nothing to do with this."

"I'm beginning to think that your past has more to do with this than mine does."

He refused to acknowledge the possibility that she was right. "Behind that locked door of your memory there may be someone waiting for you," he repeated.

With a sudden clarity Maggie understood that Joshua had his own locked doors, doors that he didn't even realize the significance of. Her doors might open with a single clue. Joshua's might never open to let another woman into his heart.

"And if no one is waiting for me, what excuse will you use then?"

Joshua was silent as though he were considering her question, but his answer destroyed her hope that he'd heard her. "It's understandable that you're impatient to have this resolved, Maggie. I'm impatient, too."

Maggie stood and straightened her clothes. Her hands were still trembling in frustration, but she struggled to lighten her voice. They had gone as far as they could go. She could not force Joshua to look at himself any more than he could force her memory to return. "I'd like to be alone now," she said, her body a statue sculpted of pride and regret.

Joshua knew that if he continued to stay, his good intentions would
be worth nothing. "I'll make dinner."

Maggie had no appetite but she nodded her head. She would not let
Joshua see how he had hurt her. "Thank you."

After a silent meal Joshua and Maggie stood in the living room
watching each other. Neither wanted the evening to end despite the
strain between them. Both knew that it should.

"Thank you for dinner," Maggie said, turning to go into her room.

"Would you like an Irish coffee before you go to bed?"

"Do you think that's a good idea?" She faced him, leaning against
the wall. Joshua's own concerns were written across his features.
Maggie wanted nothing more than to be with him, but the decision had
to be his. From this point on, she realized, the decisions would all have
to be his.

He didn't pretend to misunderstand. "I'm not sure what a good idea
is anymore." He held out his hand. "Come on."

Maggie set out the cups and saucers and then wandered restlessly
through the apartment as Joshua brewed the coffee. The dining room
was on the side of the old house that fronted Esplanade Avenue, and
there were tall windows with a view of a section of the French Quarter. Maggie stood at one, watching the traffic on the street below.
Nighttime was as busy as day on Esplanade.

Everywhere she looked she saw weathered brick, shuttered windows and iron-lace balconies. There were huge live oak trees lining the
street, and every one of the gracious old homes blended into a sympathetic portrait of New Orleans. "I was never here," she whispered.
"Never." She shut her eyes and she was rewarded with an image of
sparkling blue water. There was a boat, a cabin cruiser at a dock and
in the background there was white stucco shining in bright sunlight.

"What is it?"

"Water," she said, opening her eyes to Joshua's face. "Lots of water and a big boat. And a stucco house. A white stucco house."

"Anything else?"

She shook her head as the image faded. Wrenching sadness gripped
her; she tried desperately to hold on to the vision. It was gone, and her
eyes filled with tears. "Nothing else," she said with a catch in her voice.
"But I was happy there."

"Be glad, sweetheart." Joshua pulled her against him, intending to
comfort her. "Be glad you were happy."

Maggie pressed her body against his and slipped her arms around his
neck. "I don't want to go back. I just want to know."

"You may want to go back," he cautioned. "Don't destroy your
options."

"I want you, Joshua. The only thing that can make me leave you is if you don't want me."

Abruptly he released her. "Let's have that drink."

They sat in silence sipping the whiskey-laced coffee. Tension permeated the room to fight a battle with the whiskey-induced languor. The atmosphere was as ambivalent as their feelings.

"I meant what I said about getting a job." Maggie saw the disapproval on Joshua's face, but she ignored it. "I'm going to begin looking for something tomorrow."

"What kind of job are you planning to look for?"

"I haven't gotten that far yet. Since I don't know anything about my training or education, I'll just have to take whatever I can get."

"Without a social security card, that could be a problem. Without a birth certificate, getting a social security card could be a problem."

"Without knowing where or when I was born, getting a birth certificate could be a problem." Maggie neatly completed his train of thought. "There must be a way around all of that."

"What would you like to do if we can find a way?"

She lowered her eyes to her cup. She had not missed his implied offer of help. "I'd like to work with children somehow, but I know that's impossible. Who would trust me with a child, considering...everything."

Joshua heard the sadness and the longing in her voice. "You like children?"

She nodded. "Yes. I'm sure I do. Sometimes I can remember what it feels like to hold a squirming little body up against me, feel a pair of strong little arms around my neck...."

"Do you think you have a child somewhere?"

Maggie was startled by the question, and she raised her eyes to his. The thought had never occurred to her. She played with it like a cat worrying a mouse, but finally she shook her head. "No. I don't think so. I only feel good when I picture holding a child. If I had my own child and I was separated from him, surely I'd feel devastated with loss." She didn't miss the expression of approval in Joshua's gray eyes. "You must like children, too."

"Very much."

"Why haven't you married and had children of your own?" After all they had shared, the question seemed permissible.

He broke her gaze. "I was married once. My wife didn't want children."

Maggie couldn't imagine any woman not wanting Joshua's child. She wanted to hold him and reassure him that not all women were like that, that she would joyfully have his child. Instead she let the warmth of her voice communicate her understanding. "But you did, didn't you?"

He nodded. "I wanted children and a real family life. She wanted something very different."

Maggie guessed that telling her that small piece of his history was Joshua's own way of letting her know what she was up against. Somewhere deep inside him he understood the connection between his failed marriage and his distrust of her. She waited, but instead of more disclosures, he changed the subject.

"How would you like to work in a day-care center?"

The idea was immensely appealing. "Where?"

"At the hospital. The wages will be low and the work demanding, but your employers would be understanding. We could classify it as therapy and probably not even have to set up a social security account for you."

"Tell me about the center." Maggie could feel her excitement building.

"It's very small, an experiment really. The children are offspring of hospital employees. If we had the money we'd have three times as many children as we do, but right now it's housed in an old wing of the hospital that's waiting to be remodeled."

"Would they want me, Joshua? With my history?"

"It's very hard to find good people to work there because the wages are so low. They'll be delighted, I'm sure. It means you'll have to face the hospital every day."

"I can do that as long as they don't lock me up again."

"Will you give me a few days to check it out?"

"Will you promise not to delay on purpose?"

Joshua smiled. "You're too insightful."

"Promise."

"All right."

"Josh?" A man's voice was accompanied by a loud rap on the door. "Josh, it's Sam."

Joshua set his cup down and got immediately to his feet. As close as he was to Sam Long, Sam rarely just dropped by. "I'm coming."

Sam stood in the doorway. His eyes swept the cozy intimacy of the scene, and his pupils narrowed. "Your landlady let me in downstairs." He nodded coolly to Maggie.

Joshua motioned to the sofa. "Come in and sit down."

"I don't have time. I need to take Maggie down to the station for a little while."

"What for?"

Maggie stood and held up her hand to silence Joshua. "Why do you need me?" she asked Sam.

"Because we have the maniac who tried to kill you behind bars right now. By tomorrow his picture will be spread over every newspaper in the state. I want you to identify him before that happens."

Joshua watched Maggie go pale. In a moment he was at her side, pulling her to rest against him. "It's all right, sweetheart," he reassured her.

She turned in Joshua's arms and faced Sam. She did not miss the expression of revulsion on his face at Joshua's display of affection. "Has he given you any details about the night he tried to murder me?"

Sam shook his head. "He insists he's innocent of everything. But we have enough evidence to prove beyond a shadow of a doubt that he's not."

"Then why do you need to drag Maggie through all this?" Joshua asked sharply.

"Don't speak for me. I want to do it," Maggie intervened.

Sam ignored her, speaking to Joshua. "We need her because it will be one more bar for this guy's jail cell. I can connect him directly to three of the seven murders. If Maggie can identify him, that's one more count against him."

"I don't want her traumatized...."

"Stop it!" Maggie listened to the blessed silence for a moment and then pulled herself out of Joshua's arms. "I'll be glad to go to the police station and try to identify him. Just let me change my clothes."

The two men watched her retreat down the hall.

"She doesn't remember her own name. How can you expect her to recognize the man who tried to murder her?" Joshua faced Sam.

"It's amazing what people can do when it serves their purpose."

"What's that supposed to mean? Have you taken up psychology now?"

"I understand the psychology of certain types of people, the types I put behind bars with regularity. I could give lectures on people like the maniac we picked up tonight. Do you know how we finally got him? We set up one of our policewomen as a lure. He went into the trap like a fly into a spiderweb."

"You don't understand Maggie."

"And you do?" Sam shook his head and for a moment compassion flickered over his strictly controlled features. "You didn't understand Daphne, either."

"If you try to bully Maggie tonight, I'm going to forget we're friends. I'm warning you." Joshua's face settled into hard, unforgiving lines.

"It's gone that far?"

"It's gone that far."

Maggie came back into the room and saw the tension between the two men. She knew immediately that she was its cause. "I'm ready," she said, coming to stand before them. She searched Joshua's face, wanting to tell him that she was sorry, that she had taken too much from him already, that she didn't want to separate him from his friends.

Joshua shook his head as if he understood her unspoken apology and wanted no part of it. "I'm going with you," he said quietly. "We'll do this together."

Maggie turned to Sam, but his face was expressionless. "Let's go," he said. She had no choice but to follow him out the door.

Hours later the heavy police station door closed firmly behind them. The night had turned cooler, and Joshua slipped his jacket off and placed it around Maggie's shoulders. But he knew that nothing could begin to take away the chill she must be feeling.

She didn't even seem to notice the jacket. "I really thought I'd recognize him. When they turned on the light and all those faces stared back at me, I was sure I'd know one of them."

"It doesn't matter. They've got an airtight case." His words were reassuring, but Joshua felt much of the disappointment that he knew Maggie was feeling. He had watched her face as she'd scanned the lineup. Her concentration had been total. She had willed her brain to react, to unlock the floodgate of memories. Instead she had been faced with another failure.

"The man in my nightmare is taller, different somehow."

"Sleep distorts the truth."

"I wanted to remember."

"You're safe now," he reminded her. "Even though you're disappointed that your memory didn't return, you're safe now. The man's been caught. If he does confess, he may be able to give us some details about you that can help us. In the meantime you can build a life without fear."

Maggie turned to face him. Joshua was right. Another door had been closed to her past, but her future was wide open. "Will you call about that job tomorrow?"

"I will. Now it's time for you to go home and get some sleep." With his arm around her, Joshua guided Maggie down the steps and past rows of blue-and-white police cars. "Tomorrow will be here soon enough."

"Not soon enough," she answered softly. "It can't come soon enough to suit me."

Chapter 8

"Gray squirrel, gray squirrel, swish your bushy tail." Maggie and twelve four-year-olds were on their hands and knees in the center of the frayed area rug that covered one section of the largest day-care center classroom. Every one of the four-year-olds was trying valiantly to swish an imaginary bushy tail as well as Maggie was swishing hers. The worn seat of her jeans was arched high, and her nose twitched in rhythm with her bottom. The nose was more the imitation of a rabbit than a squirrel, but the children thought it was perfect and more than one little set of nostrils was trying to twitch, too.

"Maggie, you're silly!" One little girl, a pale blond vision in a pristine party dress, hung back from the others as if she believed that the activity was beneath her.

"You're right," Maggie agreed, sitting now with the other children flopping on the carpet around her. "Sometimes it's fun to be silly." She held out her arms and the little girl came into them, sitting carefully on Maggie's lap and smoothing her dress down over her legs. "Does anyone else have a song they want to sing?"

"It's too hot to sing!" A little boy with chocolate skin and a shining Afro fanned himself with his hand. "It's too hot to do anything!"

Mid-June in New Orleans was summer fully launched. The air-conditioning system that had originally cooled the hospital wing where the day-care center was located had long since given up the ghost. Since the wing was to be renovated someday, no money was available for repairing it. Instead all the windows were thrown open and fans set high on aluminum frames were placed around the room. Since Maggie had begun working at the center four weeks before, she had noticed this classroom growing hotter and hotter each day. By August it would be unbearable. Designed for air-conditioning, the windows were not plentiful enough or the fans adequate enough to effectively cool the room.

"Tomorrow morning we're going on a field trip to the French Quarter," Maggie promised them. "We'll walk along the river and it will be cool there. Then we'll buy milk and beignets and sit in the shade and eat them."

At the promise of the little French doughnuts liberally sprinkled with powdered sugar, the children quieted. Maggie was glad that she was going to be able to get them away from the depressing atmosphere of the day-care center. In addition to the inadequate cooling system, the rooms were gloomy, too small and lacking in much of the furniture and equipment that Maggie thought they needed. But the staff was dedicated to doing the best they could, and the children were well taken care of, even if the environment wasn't as stimulating as Maggie thought it should be.

"Maggie?"

Maggie smiled at the white-haired woman who was in charge of the center. Millie Taffin had run a nursery school in her own home near the hospital for twenty-five years. Ready to retire, she had been asked by the hospital administration to administer their new day-care program. Millie had signed on for a year. In December she would turn the reins over to someone else, if indeed the center still existed by then. So far, attempts to find new funding had not been successful.

"Maggie, Helen isn't feeling well. I don't want her handling the babies if she's under the weather. All we need is an epidemic in this heat. Will you spend the rest of the day in there? Monica can handle the fours with my help."

Maggie gave the blond child in her lap a quick hug and a push as she stood. Monica, a slender, attractive woman who assisted anywhere she was needed, came in and immediately got the children involved in a new activity.

"I hope you don't mind," Millie said, wiping the perspiration off her forehead, "but the last time Monica took the babies, she was ready to quit her job by the end of the day."

"I'm glad for the chance," Maggie reassured her. "I rarely get to spend enough time with them."

"We'll see how you feel by the end of the day."

There were six babies to one worker. Maggie and the rest of the staff wanted to reduce the ratio to four-to-one, but at the moment, because of finances, that was impossible. Helen, the woman who usually handled the babies, was a small Hercules with the stamina of three normal women. Maggie, even with her steadily developing strength, was exhausted by midafternoon.

"Are they supposed to cry that much?" Maggie looked up to find Joshua standing in the doorway, surveying the bedlam of wailing children.

She had just finished diapering every child, and now she was in the process of feeding two babies simultaneously, a bottle in each tiny mouth as she sat on a blanket on the floor between them. Although she knew that Joshua had an appointment with Dr. Nelson that day, she had not really expected to see him. The sight of the tall, powerful body in the doorway gave her a new jolt of energy. "It's triage," she informed him. "All I can do is take care of the ones who need me most. It's a terrible shame."

Joshua strolled across the room and scooped up a crying infant from one crib, humming tunelessly in its tiny ear until it quieted. For a moment, the room was peaceful. One baby was sound asleep and two others in playpens stopped fretting as the infant in Joshua's arms quieted.

"Thanks, miracle man," Maggie joked. "You're always there when I need you." She examined him as he swayed back and forth comforting the baby who was finally falling asleep. He was dressed in new blue slacks and a short-sleeved dress shirt in a soft shade of blue that complemented his coloring. She had trimmed his hair the week before on one of the infrequent evenings they spent together, and the shorter waves emphasized his strong jaw and slashing brows. As always, she found him totally appealing. She was sure that would never be any different.

What was different was their relationship. There had been no more tempting nights in each other's arms. With the advent of Maggie's job, they had seen less of each other. Despite his protests, she had convinced Mrs. LeGrand to let her move into a one-room apartment across the hall from Joshua's. The room, which for years had only been used for storage, was cramped and time-scarred with a jumble of furniture that wasn't good enough for the other apartments. Still, it represented a step toward independence for Maggie, who could manage the modest rent on her own.

When she arrived home in the evening, she was usually exhausted. Since all she had was a hot plate, she still ate with Joshua who watched her struggle to stay awake with each mouthful. But more often than not, the rest of the evening included only a few minutes of quiet conversation before she went back to her own apartment so that she could sleep.

On weekends, they usually spent part of Saturday together. They did laundry, visited local places of interest and spent time relaxing in City Park, the largest city park in the United States. Saturday evening they often ate out, talking casually and enjoying each other's friendship. There was an unspoken pact between them to let things develop slowly. Their relationship had begun in a whirlwind, and now they were catching up, developing a solid base. Maggie had no idea where any of it was leading. She hoped Joshua was learning to trust her.

Maggie lived completely in the present. She didn't think about her past, although tantalizing bits of memory still appeared from time to time in her sessions with Antoinette. She didn't think about her future, either. She lived day to day, grateful for what she had, refusing to regret what she didn't. Her life was busy, and if it sometimes seemed incomplete without Joshua's arms around her, that was just the way it was.

Today, watching him rock the baby in his arms, so completely masculine and yet so nurturing, she tried to banish the ache inside her that demanded more from their relationship. "You do that like an accomplished father," she told him.

He bent over the crib, tenderly laying the baby down and covering its tiny legs with a receiving blanket. After retrieving a teething ring for one of the toddlers who had thrown it out of the playpen, he came to sit beside Maggie, gathering one of the babies on the floor in his arms to feed it as she took the other. "I've always thought that role would suit me." For a moment his features were softened by a poignant wistfulness. Before Maggie could comment, he continued. "Millie told me you're saving her life in here today."

"I love it. I just wish there were more people to help. None of these little sweeties should have to cry for anything."

"Spoiling them, are you?"

"Not at all. An infant needs total support. When they have a need, it should be met immediately. That way they grow up trusting the world to give them what they have to have, and they learn to be patient because they know they'll get what they want eventually."

Joshua watched her cuddle the baby she held, rubbing its back gently. She was rewarded with a loud burp. "Your knowledge of child development is astounding."

"I do know a lot," she agreed. "I think I must have had training somewhere along the line."

She settled the baby back in her arms and continued to feed it. She was the picture of maternal devotion, a madonna in blue jeans and a new mauve blouse that she had bought for herself out of her meager salary. Days at a nearby playground with the children had warmed her pale complexion to a golden beige, sprinkling light freckles across her slightly crooked nose. Her hair was longer, still tousled and curly, but softer and more feminine than before. Joshua found her lovelier every day.

Maggie looked up to find him watching her intently. She gave him a slow smile. "Do I have finger paint on my nose?"

"Freckles."

"The sun always does that. My father always said…" She stopped, stunned at the revelation. "Joshua! My father always said I looked like a dalmatian puppy after a summer in the sun!" Her face was wreathed in a grin that threatened to rival the Grand Canyon; her eyes were suspiciously moist. "I can almost hear him say it."

Joshua shared her joy. More and more often, glimmers of memory broke through the barrier walls that she had built against them. Soon she would remember everything. "Your father was special to you," he said. "That's not the first memory connected with him."

She shook her head. "No, it's not. If I could just remember his face."

"Or his name." There was irony in Joshua's voice.

"I never remember anything that helps, do I?" Maggie stood, careful not to wake the baby who had finished its bottle and gone promptly to sleep. She tucked it into one of the cribs and came back to sit beside Joshua, a toddler in her arms.

"It all helps, sweetheart."

She was thrilled at the endearment. "But it doesn't help Sam trace anything, does it?"

"He's still working." Joshua didn't add that although Sam still checked the missing persons reports that came in, the police were no longer actively involved in the case. Now that Maggie's attacker had been caught, they had done their job.

She decided to change the subject. "We're taking the fours to the French Market tomorrow. Would you like to come and help?"

"Tomorrow's my first day back at work."

"A whole month early?" Maggie's huge grin reappeared. "Why?"

"They're shorthanded. And Dr. Bashir resigned."

"That's good news." Maggie had run into the little psychiatrist twice since she had come back to the hospital to work. It had been two times too many.

"It's good news for this hospital, although I'm sorry to say he's going on to become chief psychiatrist at a small private facility out west somewhere. But with Bashir gone, Dr. Nelson has agreed to reinstate me."

Maggie leaned over and gave Joshua a congratulatory kiss. "You must know how glad this makes me."

"Why don't you prove it by staying awake long enough to have dinner with me tomorrow night?"

She liked the sound of his invitation. "Maybe I could take a quick nap first as insurance."

"We'll plan on leaving about seven, if that's all right." He smoothed her curls back from her forehead, and then he stood. "I'll be sure they serve seafood." Maggie had shown an insatiable appetite for New Orleans style fried seafood. She could never seem to get enough.

"Perfect."

Joshua put the baby he had been feeding back in its crib, adjusting a mobile for it to contemplate. Maggie had helped her four-year-olds construct the mobiles for the babies' room out of colorful plastic spoons, aluminum foil and bright bits of felt. Millie had confided to Joshua that without Maggie's ingenuity the center would be a bleak place indeed. When she retired the following December, Millie intended to try to have Maggie hired in her place. Unless Maggie's memory returned and her mysterious past was cleared up, however, there was no hope that Millie would succeed.

Maggie was lifting the other toddler out of the playpen now that there were no babies on the floor to run over. "Thank you, Joshua. I'll see you tomorrow night."

He watched as she became completely engrossed in the antics of the two toddlers. She handled the children with an expertise that was not accidental. He had mentioned this new twist to Sam who had shrugged his shoulders. "She could have worked in a day-care center someplace else before she turned to prostitution. Maybe she's just from a large family. There's no way for me to check it out; it's too slim a lead."

More and more, Joshua was convinced that Maggie had never walked the streets, and he told Sam so. "You're not rational about this girl, Josh," Sam said in his tough police sergeant voice. "I've seen the way you look at her. You're going to wake up one morning and see things the way they really are, and it's going to be damned hard on you when you do."

Sam had been right. Joshua had awakened one morning, and with a sunburst of insight he had seen the way things were. He was in love with Maggie. It was not infatuation or protectiveness or sexual attraction, although all those things were present. And it was a love that he had never felt for Daphne or any other person in his life. He no longer accepted Sam's opinion about Maggie's past, but Sam had been right about one thing. Joshua's feelings for Maggie were damned hard to cope with. Nothing had really changed—only his feelings. Maggie was still an unknown quantity, and Joshua was fast reaching that dangerous point where he no longer cared.

"This is perfect. Thank you for bringing me here."

Joshua and Maggie were seated at a small table overlooking Lake Ponchartrain. The sun had just set, and the horizon was still tinged with gold and rose. An occasional gull flew overhead, and in the water right below them a trio of ducks was swimming in lazy circles.

"I couldn't find white stucco and cabin cruisers. You'll have to settle for the water and an occasional sailboat, although its too late for that, I guess."

Maggie reached across the table and squeezed Joshua's hand. "Whether I remember anything or not, it's still good to be here with you."

He covered her hand with his own, refusing to release it as they ordered huge seafood platters. "Tell me about your trip to the French Market," he said when their waitress had gone.

Maggie told him, trying to capture the excitement of the children in her words, but the whole time she was aware of his hand covering hers. Joshua had done no more than give her brief hugs or chaste kisses since the night, a month before, when they had almost made love. Now the prolonged contact was igniting a slow-burning desire throughout her body. "Each one of the children got to pick a vegetable to take back for lunch," she finished. "We ended up with one stalk of asparagus, an avocado, cauliflower, tomatoes, peppers and one wily little character got sugarcane. It was some lunch."

She listened to Joshua chuckle, and she wondered if she should tell him the most significant thing that had happened on the trip. Walking through the Quarter, guiding the children who were clinging to a long jump rope held on the other end by Monica, Maggie had looked up to find a man staring at her. He had been coming out of one of the bars along Decatur Street, near the French Market, and as they came closer, he had stepped back into the shadows as if afraid that he might be seen. As they passed, Maggie had looked in his direction, curious why he would be so interested.

His cap had been pulled down, shading his eyes with the brim. The rest of his face had been covered by a bushy red beard. Lounging in the doorway, he was no more sinister than any man who has spent too many hours in a bar. But for Maggie, seeing him had been terrifying. A cold chill had racked her body and her hands had begun to shake. It had taken every ounce of self-control she possessed to continue down the street. Each step had been torture.

Once past, she had turned in slow motion, as if in a nightmare, to get one more look at his face. He had disappeared.

It had taken almost an hour for her heart to begin beating normally and for her hands and legs to stop trembling. She had attended to the children, tried to share in their laughter, but inside she had continued to quake. Only the practice of the past months had allowed her to finally regain her composure.

Almost as frightening as seeing the stranger had been her own reaction. Maggie had finally convinced herself that her strength, both emotional and physical, was back to normal. Her abnormal reaction to the stranger seemed to belie that conviction. Apparently her recov-

ery was not as complete as it had seemed. She still hovered in a twilight world where the slightest stimulation could set off inappropriate
reactions within her.

Now she debated whether to tell Joshua of her experience. She recalled his reaction when she had tried to convince him that the night
before he'd removed her from the hospital someone had tried to murder her. What would he think about her sanity now? He was holding
her hand, talking in a husky, intimate voice that was threatening to take
her insides apart and rearrange them. If she didn't ruin it with reports
of her own neurotic behavior, the evening seemed to show great
promise.

"You're deep in thought."

Maggie smiled, certain she was making the right decision. "I was just
trying to remember if there was anything else interesting to tell you
about. There wasn't."

"What shall we talk about, then?"

"You never talk about yourself. Will you tell me about growing up
here?"

Joshua looked up to refuse and saw the intent expression on her face.
Maggie was not asking him to make casual conversation. She was inviting him to share some of himself with her just as she had shared so
much with him. He never talked about his past; indeed, he rarely
thought about it. But tonight, he owed some of it to Maggie.

"Skeeter told you about my childhood. I literally spent most of it on
the streets, running with a gang, skipping school. I was in trouble all
the time."

"What about your family?"

"I was an only child, and my father died when I was small. My
mother fell apart after that. Between working and drinking after work,
she didn't have much time to raise a son. Especially one like me. Then
when I was a teenager, I got involved in a local church."

Maggie shook her head. "I'm getting the *Reader's Digest* con-
densed version of this, aren't I? From the streets to a church is a long
journey."

For the first time since he had started his story, Joshua smiled. "You
have no problems going after what you want, do you?"

She wasn't sure he was right, but she shook her head anyway. "Add
it to my list."

"The Irish Channel, where I was raised, and the Garden District, an
exclusive section of the city, stand side by side. When I was growing up,
there might as well have been a continent between them. Reverend
Hank Carroll of the Garden District Community Church didn't like the
invisible boundaries. His congregation was wealthy and they had built
a magnificent church with a beautiful gym that stood empty most of
the time. Hank decided to change that.

"He organized a basketball team of the teenagers who roamed the streets around the church. It was in the middle of a heat wave and the church was air-conditioned. Hank passed the word around that there was an endless supply of soft drinks and popcorn for anyone who wanted to join the team. It was mid-August before I succumbed to the lure. Skeeter was already on the team, and Sam never did set foot inside the church, but I finally made an appearance."

"What kind of basketball player were you?" Maggie was entranced by the faraway look in Joshua's eyes. She knew he was a man who didn't often turn his gaze to his roots.

"I was their star center. Hank was a real taskmaster. He was small, but incredibly tough. We all tried to wreak havoc, but nobody gave the Reverend Hank Carroll trouble for long. He liked me. He saw potential and determined to shape me in a new image. I was convinced to play on the church's own team, and before I knew it I was sitting in a pew every Sunday. The next year I was given a scholarship to the private school run by the church, and he tutored me so that I could keep up. When I graduated he helped me get a scholarship to college. Somehow there was always money when I needed it."

Maggie knew something about Joshua's pride. "How did you feel about all that?"

"Different. I was the kid whose mother didn't show up for graduation because she couldn't afford a dress that was good enough."

"Why did you put up with it, then?"

"By that time I had a goal. It was very simple. I wanted to be Hank Carroll."

Maggie absorbed his words as the waitress returned and set plates heaped with fried shrimp, soft-shell crab and oysters on their table. With a small sound of pleasure she took a bite of the succulent crab. "And that's why you went into the ministry."

"And that's why I got out of it."

She shook her head. "I don't understand."

"I discovered that putting on a clerical collar didn't change who I was. I was Joshua Martane. I hated writing sermons; I hated board meetings and church politics. I hated living my life under a microscope. I continued to struggle until one day I realized that there were different ways to serve. When I looked at the things I did really well, I realized that I could do much more good as a counselor or a psychologist than I could ever do as a minister."

"Was it hard to tell Reverend Carroll?" Maggie asked softly.

Her quiet concern made him drop all his defenses for a moment. "It was probably the most difficult thing I've ever done. But when I was all finished explaining, Hank looked me dead straight in the eyes and said, 'You've turned into just the kind of man I knew you would, son.'" Joshua was quiet for a moment. "I've never told anyone that. Hank died last year. I still miss him."

Maggie ached for the man across from her who gave so much and took so little. "He was right to be proud of you."

"And there you have the story of my life."

"You didn't tell me how you met your wife."

Joshua smiled and bit into an oyster. Without even discussing it, he and Maggie had traded their oysters and shrimp as he talked. Neither had even thought about the intimacy the act had shown. "You don't suppose you've had training in counseling, do you? You ask questions like a professional. A very tenacious professional." She just smiled, and he continued. "My wife was a member of Hank's church. Her father was one of my benefactors. Daphne saw me as a challenge. I was different from the kids she knew."

"She had good taste."

Joshua ignored her comment, determined to finish as soon as possible. "When I finished seminary I came back to the area to serve a small church out in Metairie. My mother was very ill and I wanted to be near her. She died a month later. I was feeling very lonely, and one day I went to Daphne's house to pay my respects to her father. Two months later I was standing in the Garden District Community Church with Hank in front of me and Daphne at my side."

Maggie waited quietly for him to continue. "It wasn't long before I realized that I could never give Daphne what she wanted. I had been a challenge, but once we were married, she wanted to go on to greener pastures. I tried. I thought if we had a child she might settle down, but Daphne didn't want my child. And if she had given birth to a baby, there would have been no guarantee it would have been mine."

Maggie couldn't imagine anyone being given a chance to love Joshua and rejecting him so totally. She couldn't find the right words to comfort him.

Joshua continued, his voice carefully expressionless. "Actually, her father had warned me. He told me that his daughter would never be happy married to me. He loved her but he knew what she was like. When we finally divorced, he remained my friend. I still see him occasionally. Daphne's been married twice since. The last time she married a millionaire, and I'm betting that the money will make up to her for whatever else is missing in their marriage."

"I can't blame you for being bitter."

"I don't think I'm bitter. It's been a long time."

Maggie ate her last shrimp and thought about his words. He had been badly hurt, and as much as he denied it, the scars were obvious to her. It would take a very special woman to make him forget the pain he had suffered at the hands of the spoiled Daphne. "You have so much to give," she said after she was finished. "It's time you gave it to someone who could give it back to you."

"Do you have someone in mind?" Joshua reached across the table and took her hands, wiping them clean with a slow sensuous rotation of his napkin.

Maggie watched in fascination as the napkin moved over the palms of her hands and between her fingers. She couldn't tear her eyes from what he was doing. "Why didn't we meet under different circumstances?" she asked softly.

"Do you want me to say something comforting and theological? Or probing and psychological?"

She shook her head.

"Then truthfully, I don't know. Maybe we both needed a lesson on looking underneath the surface."

Dropping the napkin, he laced his fingers through hers and lifted them to his mouth. Maggie shut her eyes as he kissed each one. Even after he released her hands, she sat with her eyes closed, inhaling the tangy aroma of seafood and savoring the feeling of Joshua's lips on her fingertips. When she finally opened her eyes it was to the warmth in Joshua's.

Outside the night was dark as they walked with arms around each other along the lakefront, watching the waves crash against the steps leading into the water. "I love this city," Maggie said. "But everything I see seems new."

"Well, you don't have a New Orleans accent. And when I suggested that you order the crawfish bisque tonight you turned that crooked little nose of yours up higher than I would have believed it could go."

"What sensible person eats crawfish?"

"Everyone in Louisiana eats crawfish."

"Then I'm not from Louisiana."

"Do you want to know what I think?" Joshua watched as Maggie tipped her head to look at him, her short curls brushing his shoulder. "I think you're from the South, but not the deep South. Your drawl isn't pronounced enough."

"Would it help if we knew that?"

"It might. It would be easier for Sam to investigate if we knew just a little more."

They stopped under a massive gnarled oak that blocked the light of the full moon. Joshua's arm tightened around her, and he pulled her around to face him. Maggie knew that if she tipped her head to his again that Joshua would kiss her. But she had decided a month before that she would never offer herself to him. It had to be Joshua's choice. He had to trust her enough to believe that she was a person who would only give him good things.

"Look at me." Joshua rested his fingertips under her chin and tilted her head. Their noses were almost touching. "Nothing's changed. We still don't know who you are or how your past will affect you once you remember it. And yet everything in my life is different. Before I met you, I thought I had everything I needed. In the months I've known you, I've discovered just how wrong I was." He bent the tiny distance to take her mouth with his and Maggie responded with all the pent-up passion that a month without his caresses could engender.

They stood together for long minutes, exploring each other like lovers who have been long separated. "I haven't stopped wanting you," Joshua said in a low buzz against her ear.

"I'm very, very glad," she answered. Her arms tightened around his waist.

Joshua's laugh was husky and plaintive. "I've been trying for a month now to pretend it isn't true."

"You work so hard at denying yourself what you want. I won't hurt you. I want to give, not take."

"I'm only used to women who take." His mouth closed over hers, and his hands ran restlessly over her body as if, long denied, he was trying to make up for a lifetime of famine.

Maggie pulled away slightly and held her fingers out. The thumb and forefinger were almost touching. "Last month we were this close to being ready for each other, but you drew away from me. How close are we now?"

"You tell me," he said, watching her face.

She closed the gap until thumb and forefinger were no longer separated. "This close."

Joshua's gray eyes ignited with a smoky desire. "I want to be even closer."

The drive back to the apartment was silent as was the walk up the stairs. At Joshua's door he held her against him as he turned the key in the lock. He remembered the night a month before when he had almost taken her, almost given into the inevitable. He had stopped himself then, convinced that they would only hurt each other. Now he no longer cared. Nothing could hurt more than the constant disavowal of their feelings.

Fighting the part of himself that didn't want to give her a chance to refuse, fighting the part of himself that reverberated with the knowledge that under the circumstances they couldn't be sure that they weren't going to do each other irreparable damage, he found her ear with his lips. "Are you sure?"

"Completely."

The commitment was made. Without another word he pushed the door open. He found disaster.

The apartment had been ravaged. Drawers were flung open, some dumped upside down on the floor, some hanging only by a wedged corner in the bureau. Lamps, furniture and bookcases had been overturned; Joshua's desk had been searched, his papers scattered throughout the room. "Maggie, get back," he ordered quietly.

Maggie pulled at Joshua's arm, her eyes wide with fear. "Don't go in, Joshua. Come downstairs with me to call the police. Someone might still be there."

"You go," he said, giving her a slight push. "I'm going to see if anyone's here."

"No," she commanded in a hoarse whisper. "Please!" But Joshua had already gone inside.

Turning, she raced down the stairs to Mrs. LeGrand's apartment, knocking wildly on the door. Inside, she made the call to the police, told Mrs. LeGrand to watch for them and ran back upstairs. "Joshua?" Her heart was pounding in terror. "Joshua?"

"It's all right." Joshua came out of his bedroom. "Whoever left us this little surprise wanted to remain anonymous. He's gone."

"Thank God." She followed Joshua back into his bedroom, which was the scene of more devastation. "You shouldn't touch anything," she warned.

Joshua nodded. "I'm not, but it probably wouldn't matter. Even if they try to get fingerprints, it won't help. Do you know how many robberies the police have to investigate in a day?"

"Let's wait at my place. It won't do any good to stay here if you can't touch anything." Maggie slipped an arm through his. "Please?"

Joshua caught the faint pleading in her voice. The brush with the senseless crime had upset her more than she was letting on. It couldn't help but remind her of her own near death. "That's a good idea. Let's make some coffee."

Gratefully Maggie let Joshua guide her out the door. Her gratitude only lasted a minute. In the hallway, they both realized immediately that Joshua's apartment had not been the only one that had been broken into. "My door's been jimmied, too," she said, trying to keep panic out of her voice.

"Go downstairs and wait. Don't come back up until you hear me call or until the police come." Joshua's voice was stern.

"Please don't go in," she pleaded.

"Yeah, don't be heroic, Reverend." Sam Long's voice drifted up the stairs at the same time that they heard the door into the downstairs hallway creak shut. Maggie peered over the railing and watched as Mrs. LeGrand closed the door behind the two men. Sam and another man came up the stairs. Mrs. LeGrand remained at the bottom, her faded blue eyes big with excitement.

"This isn't your kind of case, is it?" Joshua greeted Sam.

"No, the regular team will be here in a few minutes. I just happened to hear the call and recognize the address. I was in the neighborhood." Sam drew his gun. "Now get out of my way, and get the girl downstairs."

Joshua firmly gripped Maggie's arm and led her down the steps. At the bottom, he handed her over to their landlady. "Both of you go inside. I'll come get you when everything's clear."

Maggie suffered Mrs. LeGrand's chatter until she thought she would scream from frustration. A knock on the door saved her from disgracing herself. "You can come up now." Sam stood in the doorway, his eyes impenetrable.

"Was the man gone?"

"Yeah."

There was much more she wanted to ask, but Sam's obvious dislike made her table her questions for later when she was alone with Joshua. She followed him out into the hallway.

"Any chance this could have been done by one of your friends?"

The question took Maggie by surprise. She hadn't expected Sam to say anything at all. "What friends?"

"The ones you claim to have forgotten."

Desolation settled over her. Although she had only rarely talked with Sam, she had known that he didn't trust her. But she had never suspected that his distrust was so deeply rooted. Even though she understood that Sam was a friend of Joshua's and protective of him, the scorn in his tone cut through her confidence like a razor.

"I know," she said carefully, "that you're afraid I'm trying to use Joshua. I can understand that. But have you ever thought how unfair it is to keep yourself on this case when you've already judged and found me unworthy of further consideration?" Successfully she kept her voice calm. She started up the stairs.

"Lady, as far as the police are concerned, your case is closed. Any investigating I do is on my own and strictly because I don't want Josh hurt. I'll find out your secrets, and when I do, he's going to be the first to know them."

"Good," she said fiercely. "That's what I want, too. We both have his best interests at heart."

Sam's answer was a snort.

Maggie was unprepared for the sight of her apartment. It had been totally and thoroughly ransacked. The few possessions she had managed to provide herself with were broken and scattered on the floor. Children's drawings that she had brought home from school were torn from the wall; sheets and towels had been ripped to shreds with a sharp object.

"Why?" She stood in the middle of the room, looking at the destruction around her. "I don't have anything anyone would want."

Joshua came up to stand behind her, putting his arms around her waist. "They didn't know that. Maybe they got mad when they discovered there was nothing to steal."

More policemen arrived, and in the flurry, Maggie didn't have time to consider his words. It was only after everyone departed, leaving her alone with Joshua, that she had time to think at all. Mechanically she wandered the room, straightening what could be straightened, throwing away everything that was beyond repair. "I just don't understand," she said, as if their conversation had never been interrupted.

"It was random violence, Maggie. It's impossible for anyone to understand." Joshua was setting furniture back in its place.

"But they didn't steal anything. Not from either apartment."

That had been the strangest thing of all. After fingerprints were lifted, Joshua had checked to find out what was missing. Nothing was. "The police think that the burglar started in your apartment, didn't find anything, came to my apartment and was in the process of collecting things to take when something scared him away."

"They're just guessing." There was little else that Maggie could do to repair the damage that had been done. The little apartment would show the effects of the night's work for a long time. "I think that's all we can do for now. Let's start on yours."

Joshua came over and put his arm around her shoulder. "We can tackle it tomorrow. You need your sleep."

The evening had shown such promise. Now the senseless acts of a stranger had spoiled that promise for both of them. Without discussing it, their decision was mutual. Intimacy would have to wait for a more appropriate time. "Where will you sleep?" she asked. "Your place is such a mess."

"I'll straighten a path to the bed. Will you be all right here? You can use the bolt at the top until we get your lock fixed. And Mrs. Le-Grand has a locksmith putting a good lock on the front door right now. No one can get back in tonight."

Maggie nodded. "I'll be fine. I'm too tired to worry."

"Then I'll see you tomorrow." Joshua pulled her close for a kiss. "Try to get some sleep."

"I will." She watched Joshua disappear, and she followed him to shut and bolt the door. What should have been a landmark night in her life had turned into a dismal failure. Telling herself that there would be other, better nights, Maggie turned off the lights and went to bed.

The man wasn't surprised to see the cops come. He had done a real number on both apartments. He smiled a little, but his smile was hidden in the midst of the red beard that was now so thick and unruly that it obscured his mouth completely. He downed his beer and continued to watch from the window of the bar on the corner of Bourbon and

Esplanade. How convenient that the girl was living so close to one of his favorite watering holes. But then New Orleans was good about that. There were bars everywhere. You never had to stay dry for long in New Orleans.

It was the only thing about the miserable city that he liked. He hated everything else about it; the miserable climate, the shabby little neighborhood he lived in, his job at the hospital. Just the day before he'd been ready to pack up and leave, forget the girl and what she knew about him. She was a vegetable, wasn't she? What could she tell the police? They had spirited her off to some convalescent hospital because she was no good to anyone, and besides, they'd caught the man they thought was responsible for her near murder.

He had almost convinced himself he could exit this hellhole. Of course there was still the nagging fear that she might regain her memory and tell her story. If she did, the law would move heaven and earth to find him. There was no place safe enough to hide, not considering who the girl was. But he'd almost taken the chance.

The man gave a low, squealing laugh. That had been yesterday. Today was a different story entirely. He felt good. Damn, he felt good. Here he'd almost given up hope of finding her again and now she was only scant yards away. And she'd been working at the hospital for a month. She hadn't been convalescing somewhere; she'd been working, right under his nose. He cackled at the irony, missing the disgusted glances of the men sitting at the bar behind him.

There she'd been today, towing a bunch of little kids through the Quarter. She'd looked right at him. She hadn't screamed, she hadn't gone for help. He'd watched her help the children into the van with New Orleans City Hospital emblazoned on the side, and he'd realized why she was there and where she was going. He hadn't even had to follow her. It had been easy after that to find out her new name and where she was living.

"Maggie Kelly." He tried the name out loud and then he cackled again. That was a good one. What would her father think of that? His precious daughter calling herself Maggie Kelly. There'd been nothing in her apartment to indicate that she had any idea who she was. No letters, no mementos. He was still safe. Soon he'd be safer. Soon he'd finish what he'd started.

He cackled again and downed the rest of his beer. "Bring me another," he called over his shoulder to no one in particular. He had a long wait ahead of him, but he was sure this time that it would pay off. And in the meantime he was going to enjoy every second of it.

Chapter 9

The dream started, as it always did, with Maggie lying on a hard cot in a tiny room. There were fingers of light coming from one small window above her head. She was confined, although she didn't know how. She only knew that unrestricted movement was impossible. Her eyes were focused on a door. Slowly, as she watched, the door was cracked and the figure of a man appeared in the doorway. He was dressed in black, and he had a cap pulled over his head to shade his eyes.

The diffuse light behind him made his body stand out in sharp relief, like a figure appearing from the fog. He was moving toward her. The closer he got, the more terrified Maggie became. "Don't hurt me," she pleaded. His response was a laugh and then his mouth opened to scourge her with hideous, degrading names.

Always before, she had awakened at this point. The dream had occurred so many times that Maggie had learned to pull herself from its clutches, to tell herself, even in her dreaming state, that what was happening was not real. Tonight, her will had no impact. The figure of the man continued to advance. He loomed over her bedside, peering down at her. Like a patron at a horror movie who knows she shouldn't look, Maggie found herself unable to resist the terror of staring into the man's face.

His eyes were brown, bloodshot and set too close together. The nose was bulbous and veined. The chin was covered with a sprinkling of red hair, as though he hadn't shaved for several days. As she watched him in fascinated horror, he came closer and closer.

With a small cry, Maggie woke up and sat upright, her hands clasping the one top sheet that hadn't been destroyed by whoever had vandalized her apartment. She was trembling all over. A total, unremitting fear gripped her body until she wasn't sure that she would ever be able to loosen its clutches. Fully awake, she scanned the room, now lit with the light of early morning. She was alone. The man had existed only in her imagination.

But as she tried to convince herself of that, she knew that it wasn't true. The man did exist. The man in her dream was the same man she had seen on Decatur Street. Except for the beard, which was now full and bushy, he looked exactly the same. She had taken his face and embellished her dream with it. No longer was he the persecutor enshrouded by mist. Now he had an identity. And Maggie didn't know if she had created the identity for him or if there was some bizarre truth to her nightmare.

She only knew that sleeping any more that morning was going to be impossible.

When the terror of the dream had diminished to a manageable level, Maggie got up and showered, drying herself on the remains of a tattered bath towel. She dressed and found yogurt and orange juice in the refrigerator for breakfast. It was 6:30 A.M. and her body demanded an outlet for the vestiges of fear that still haunted her. Staying cooped up in the apartment seemed like an exercise in masochism. She needed activity. For lack of anything better to do so early in the morning, she decided to go to the all-night Laundromat to wash her clothes.

One of the ironies of the vandalism was that Maggie had been saving her laundry for a week, and a small mountain of dirty clothes had been piled in a basket at the very back of her closet. Although the intruder had dumped the few clothes in her dresser drawers on the floor and destroyed some of them, the dirty clothes in the laundry basket had been saved. At least she had something left to wear.

Knowing that Joshua would be worried if he found her gone, Maggie wrote him a note and slipped it under his door before she headed down Esplanade to the Laundromat where they often went together. She hoped that he would join her if he woke up in time.

As she had suspected, her timing was perfect. The late-night laundry crowd was home asleep, and the after-breakfast crowd had not yet straggled in. Congratulating herself on her farsightedness, Maggie made casual conversation with the old woman who gave out change and kept the floors clean.

"I can't figure why anyone would come here at night," the old woman said. "Been robbed more times than I can count. I stopped working that shift. Got tired of forking over money to hoodlums."

Maggie listened sympathetically. The old woman obviously found her job boring. What else was there to do besides chat with customers? "So this shift is safer?" she asked politely.

"Yeah. Nobody's ever bothered us this time of day. And now we've got a sign out front telling 'em we don't keep more than twenty dollars on the premises."

"That's good." Maggie busied herself measuring soap powder into the washer she was using. With her back to the door, she bent over to begin piling her clothes into the machine. "I'll have to remember that this is the perfect time to come. Safe and no crowds." The door opened and she felt a rush of air fan her legs.

"Get to the back of the room." A man's whiny voice sounded right behind her. Curiously Maggie turned, wondering why the voice was muffled. Standing in the doorway, a rubber gorilla mask pulled over his entire head, was a tall man dressed in jeans and a plain white T-shirt. More alarming than the mask was the gun that was pointed directly at Maggie's chest. "Now!" he commanded.

Maggie couldn't move. She leaned against the washing machine and stared at the gorilla mask. A dreamlike lassitude invaded her limbs, and although she was acutely conscious of everything unfolding around her, she could not make her body behave normally.

"It ain't Mardi Gras," the old woman said boldly. "Get out of here."

"Old woman," the voice behind the mask intoned, "shut up or you won't be making change tomorrow." He waved the gun in front of Maggie. "Do I have to show you I mean business, honey?"

Somehow she moved. The next thing she knew she was standing at the back of the room with rows of washing machines in front of her. The man with the gorilla mask was leaning on one of them. "That's better. Now give me your money."

Maggie hadn't even brought a purse with her, only some loose change for the washer and dryer. "All I have is change," she said, fishing in her pocket.

"That's too bad, honey. Too, too bad for you."

The old woman broke in. "Here, you can have all that I've got. About twenty dollars in quarters and dimes. It's in that little room in a locked drawer." She pointed and Maggie noticed that her hand was steady. The burglary was too commonplace to frighten her.

"We'll all go get it." With the gun the masked man motioned for Maggie and the old woman to walk in front of him. In a moment the woman was unlocking the drawer. "Here," she said. "You're lucky I had just emptied the machines."

"Yeah. Real lucky." The man pocketed the change. "Now ladies, lie down on the floor. If you do what I say, you won't get hurt."

Maggie's knees wouldn't bend. She stared helplessly at the gorilla-man. "Do you need some help, honey? I could kick them out from under you."

The voice, even muffled by the mask and an obvious attempt to disguise it, was nibbling at Maggie's memory. It was horrifyingly familiar. She wondered if she would wake up in a moment and find herself safely in bed.

"Do what he says, darlin'. He's got what he came for. Just get down on the floor and you won't get hurt." The old woman was already down on the floor, resigned to the indignity of her position.

Maggie's knees buckled and she felt herself float to the ground. The old woman pulled her the rest of the way. "Just stay calm," she said, "he'll be gone in a minute."

Maggie shut her eyes. The floor beneath her felt hard and real. Without a doubt she was not dreaming this. The man with the terrifyingly familiar voice was still standing above her. The room was quiet, and then there was a click that sounded like an explosion. Maggie knew that it was the sound of a gun being cocked.

Strangely she wasn't afraid anymore. She was just terribly sad. Her life was going to end on the dirty floor of a Laundromat. She would never know what it felt like to be held in Joshua's arms as he made love to her. She would never solve the riddle of her past. She would die, alone and unmourned, except, perhaps, by Joshua. And Joshua would soon forget.

When the shot sounded, she waited for an explosion of pain. There was nothing. She opened her eyes and discovered the reason. The gorilla-man's arm had been caught by a strong hand and the gun had been knocked to the floor, probably discharging on contact. Joshua stood behind the man and the two were locked in a fierce embrace.

Joshua's presence did nothing to shake Maggie from her dreamlike state. When she analyzed her actions later, she understood her trance for what it was: her body and mind's way of protecting her from understanding the danger she was in. Now, still buoyed by her sense of unreality, she scooted slowly across the floor and picked up the gun. It slithered through her hands: plastic and metal, a terrible, lethal weapon that told her of its conquests as she sat quietly and stared at it.

Above her, the two men tumbled to the ground, rolling over and over, out into the main part of the Laundromat. The old woman jumped up and ran to the pay phone. "He's got all my change," she wailed. Rising slowly, Maggie pointed the gun in front of her and followed the men.

Joshua was larger and stronger than the man with the mask. But the other man was fighting for his freedom, and it gave him a wildness that made them more equally matched. Maggie watched in awe as Joshua matched the other man's tactics with street-fighting wisdom of his own. His movements were instinctive; Maggie could see shadows of his past.

"Stop it or I'll shoot." The words came straight off the television screen. Maggie wondered what program she had lifted them from. Her voice reflected her own suspended emotions. It was calm, almost detached.

The two men ignored her. Joshua was sitting on top of the smaller man, his strong hands, so often used for healing and soothing, locked on the other man's shoulders, bouncing them against the black-and-white tile.

With a tremendous effort, the masked man turned to his side, spilling Joshua onto the floor. Joshua twisted and grabbed the leering gorilla mask, pulling it off in one motion as he attempted to tangle his fingers in the man's hair. The man leaped up, grabbing one of the portable metal laundry carts in the aisle, and rammed it at Joshua. In the split second of impact, he turned to run from the Laundromat. But not before Maggie got a good look at the red beard, the close-set, bloodshot eyes and the bulbous nose.

It was the man from her nightmare. Calmly, with educated precision, she cocked the gun and aimed it at the fleeing man. Assuming a marksman's stance, feet spread apart, both hands steadying the weapon, she followed his moving back. The trigger against her finger felt familiar; she caressed it lightly and waited for the sound of an explosion. There was nothing. She tried again. And again.

"For God's sake, Maggie, put that gun down."

In surprise she heard Joshua's voice. She blinked, and the room began to swirl around her. Carefully she lowered herself to the ground. The gun clattered at her feet. She could hardly believe it. She had taken careful, calculating aim at a defenseless man, and she had pulled the trigger. She had wanted to kill him.

Maggie lifted her head and watched Joshua advance toward her. He seemed to be miles away, and it felt like hours before he got to her side. She noticed a tiny cut on the side of his face, and a raw, red area that soon would be black-and-blue. His shirt was pulled out of his jeans and filthy from rolling around on the floor. He had never looked better to her.

"You saved my life." It was a statement of fact. Because she was still cushioned from the reality of the situation, her voice conveyed the message in the same tone she would have used to tell one of her four-year-olds, "It's time for a story."

Joshua knelt beside her and extended his arms. The feel of his body against hers was unreal. She could think of nothing to say.

"I got the cops. I finally remembered we've got a new emergency number you can call without money." The old woman came out of the back room. "You two all right?"

Joshua nodded his head. Maggie just shut her eyes and leaned against him.

It was only a few minutes before the police arrived. Maggie and the old woman told their stories; Joshua told his.

"Did any of you get a good look at the man?" one of the policemen asked.

"I did." Maggie's voice was barely audible. "I can give you a complete description."

"Are you sure?" Joshua was watching her, a puzzled expression on his face. "The mask was only off for a second or two before he turned and ran out the door."

"I've seen him before." Maggie couldn't meet Joshua's eyes. Instead she turned to the policeman. "This is a long story, but someone tried to murder me about seven months ago. I haven't been able to remember anything about it. Yesterday I saw a man in the French Quarter and I recognized him, although I didn't know from where. Just seeing him terrified me. It was the same man who tried to kill me today."

The policemen looked at each other in a silent message of disbelief. "Lady, this was a robbery, not an attempted murder."

"No." She wished they were right. It would be easier. "That's where you're wrong. He didn't want the money. He broke into my apartment last night and this morning he followed me here to kill me. He was cocking his gun to shoot me when Joshua grabbed him. That's why the gun discharged when it fell."

"Why would he want to kill you?"

"I don't know. I wish I did."

"That's why you tried to shoot him." Joshua's voice was emotionless.

"Tried to shoot him?"

Maggie winced at the interest in the policeman's voice. "I tried to shoot him when he fled. Evidently the gun had no more bullets in it."

The policeman shook his head. "I checked. It was loaded all right. It jammed. I guess if it hadn't, we'd have ourselves a mangled suspect right now."

"A dead suspect." Joshua's voice was cold. "Her aim was perfect."

"Where'd you learn to handle a gun, lady?"

"I don't know."

The two policemen exchanged glances. "I think you'd better come down to the station," one of them said finally. "We'll need a full report and description."

"Sergeant Long can fill you in on the whole story," Joshua interjected. "I'll bring her down to the station in a little while for details."

Maggie listened to Joshua negotiate with the two men. Finally they left, and Joshua turned to her. "Come on. I'm taking you home."

"I'll do your laundry and send it to you," the old woman said. "Just leave me your address."

"I couldn't let you do that—"

"Yes, you could," Joshua interrupted Maggie, pulling out a card and scribbling an address on it to give to the old woman. "Thank you. We appreciate it."

"Considering you saved our lives, it seems like little enough." The old woman raised her hand in farewell and headed into the back room.

"You did save our lives," Maggie said, meeting Joshua's gaze for the first time since she had told her story to the policemen. The expression in his eyes wilted what strength she had left. Anger blazed in them, turning their gray depths to silver ice.

"Come on." With a hand gripping her elbow, Joshua pulled her along behind him. "I'm sure that guy is clear across town by now, but stay close to me and don't stray."

Maggie put one foot in front of the other, plodding slightly behind Joshua until they reached his car. "You drove," she said inanely.

"Damn good thing I did or you'd be lying in a morgue right now."

"I guess you're mad."

"Nothing like it. I'm furious."

The drive back to the house was silent. Maggie opened the door to her apartment with unsteady hands. "I'd like to change my clothes before you grill me," she said.

"I'll wait."

She went into the bathroom, showered quickly and changed into the dress she had been wearing the night before. She came out of the bathroom brushing her mop of curls. "Go ahead," she said, flopping on the side of her bed. "Let's get this over with."

"Let's see if you can get the questions right without my help." Maggie could see the muscle jump in Joshua's jaw. His mouth was a grim, straight line, and not one feature showed any compassion for her.

"You want to know why I didn't tell you about the man in the Quarter."

Joshua nodded.

"And you want to know why, after seeing the man and feeling afraid of him, I was stupid enough to go out by myself so early in the morning."

Joshua nodded again.

Maggie set the hairbrush down and folded her hands neatly in her lap. "I didn't think you'd believe me."

"Try again."

She lifted her eyes to his. "Just like you don't believe me now. No matter what else there is between us, you don't trust me, Joshua. I'm still the little streetwalker, scooped up out of a vacant lot, with no memory and nothing to recommend her. I knew that you'd think I was lying intentionally, or hallucinating, or—"

"Cut it out, Maggie!" Joshua jumped out of his chair and ran his fingers through his hair. His face showed weariness for the first time, and his hand massaged the back of his neck.

"You're never going to trust me."

Her words seemed to overcome the last barrier to his self-control. He jerked her off the bed, eyes blazing down at her. "You let your pride get the better of you and it almost killed you, you little fool."

"I let my love get the better of me." She refused to plead for mercy. "I wanted your love or what I could have of it. I thought if I told you, it would pull us farther apart."

Joshua held her a few inches from him. She saw the conflicts her words created.

"I'm very sorry," she said in a whisper. "I know now I was being foolish by trying to ignore my reactions to that man. I'll never forgive myself for endangering you."

"Endangering me?" His tone was incredulous. "You were almost killed and you're worried about endangering me?" He laughed a soft, bitter laugh. "Maggie, what am I going to do with you?"

"I'll get out of your life. I'll leave New Orleans. Surely that will keep us both safe if I do."

Joshua's hands released her shoulders and slowly followed the soft skin of her neck to her face. He framed it gently, his thumbs caressing her cheekbones. "You don't understand, do you? I can't let you go. It may destroy us both, but it can't be changed."

As her eyes filled with tears, he dropped his hands, turned and walked to the door. "Rest for a few minutes while I'm gone, and be sure to bolt the door behind me. I'll be back to take you down to the police station after I change my clothes."

She stared at his retreating back. It was a long time before she could walk across the room to throw the bolt.

The same boards were missing from the porch floor; the screen door still creaked like the tin woodsman before Dorothy oiled his joints. Skeeter's house looked exactly the same as it had two months before. With a sense of déjà vu, Maggie stood beside Joshua as he knocked insistently on the front door. The one difference was that they were standing in bright daylight.

"Another visit?" Skeeter stood in the doorway, covering his yawn with a fist. With the other hand he gestured for them to come inside.

The trip to the police station had been frustrating in the extreme. Sam had listened to Maggie's story with a lifted eyebrow. "So you thought you recognized the man," he said. "I thought you had am-

nesia." The interview had gone quickly from bad to worse. There was
no doubt in either Maggie or Joshua's mind as they finally left the police station that nothing she had said had made any impression on the
police, especially Sam. They still regarded the scene at the Laundromat as a robbery, not an attempted murder. Even the experience of
looking through books of mug shots had proved to be worthless.

"You can't go back home," Joshua said as he slid behind the wheel
of his car. "Obviously this guy knows where you live."

Maggie had dropped her head into her hands, aware that the tentative security she had found, both in her job and her apartment, was
now shattered. She could not go home; she could not go back to work.
Any man who would track her to a public Laundromat and try to kill
her was perfectly capable of attacking her in a room filled with small
children. "I should leave town," she said, defeat in her voice.

"Sam may not believe you, but he's too good a cop not to follow up
on this. If anyone can find this guy, it's Sam. We'll spend the night at
Skeeter's."

Now they were back almost where they had started. Inside, Joshua
told Skeeter about the events of the past twenty-four hours. Skeeter was
suitably impressed. He sat next to Maggie on the sofa and draped his
arm around her shoulders. "And you have no idea, do you, what this
is all about."

It wasn't a question. It was a sympathetic statement. After Joshua's anger and Sam's disbelief, it was very welcome. "No. I wish I did."

"Do you think you could describe this guy for me? I could draw him
and circulate his picture. I probably have as many contacts as friend
Sam does."

Joshua was standing at the window, his back rigid. At Skeeter's
words, he turned. "That's a good idea. I got a brief look at him, too,
so I can help." He had not touched Maggie since their trip to the station. His own emotions were in such turmoil that he didn't trust himself. He was angry, suspicious, hurt and above all, confused. And now,
watching the sympathetic by-play on the sofa, he was also fighting
jealousy. His voice betrayed none of his feelings.

"I'll get my charcoals. If the picture turns out well, we'll photo-
copy it and I'll pass it around."

After Skeeter left, Maggie leaned her head back on the sofa and
closed her eyes. But even with her eyes shut, the image of Joshua's rigid
stance persisted. "I wonder if either of us will live long enough to laugh
at this someday." The words had an ominous ring; she had not meant
to refer to the third attempt at murder, only to the inherent melo-
drama of their situation.

"If I live to be a thousand, I won't be laughing."

"Can't you talk to me, Joshua?" Her eyes were still shut. "Tell me how you feel. I'd rather know the worst than keep trying to second-guess you."

"There are no words comprehensive enough."

"I see."

Skeeter came back, sketch pad in hand. "Where do you want to do this? I can set up anywhere."

"Right here will be fine." Joshua came over to sit next to Maggie so that they could both comment on Skeeter's efforts.

Forty-five minutes later, Skeeter held a portrait of Maggie's assailant in his hands. It was so frighteningly real that Maggie, after giving her approval, refused to look at it anymore.

"I'll take it out and have a hundred copies made to start with," Skeeter said. "I'll spend the afternoon passing them around."

"Sam ought to have a copy."

Skeeter nodded. "I'll take him one." He teased Maggie. "You know what a sacrifice this is working on the right side of the law, don't you?"

She tried to smile in appreciation. "Thank you."

With Skeeter gone, Maggie was left alone with Joshua. She had made an attempt to understand his feelings; he had rejected her. She was too emotionally weary to try again. "I'm sure I'll be fine here," she said, standing to stare out the window that Joshua had vacated. "Why don't you go home?"

"I wouldn't leave you alone."

"You already have."

There was no answer from the sofa.

Maggie wandered through the house looking for something to occupy her. She had gone from living day to day to needing to live minute to minute. Skeeter's backyard fence was surrounded by a long-neglected border of perennials. She found a trowel and a small stool and spent the rest of the morning and part of the afternoon weeding.

Joshua watched the small figure perched on the edge of the footstool, digging weeds out of Skeeter's garden with the energy of an evangelist saving souls. She was still wearing a dress, and the fabric of the skirt billowed over the surrounding ground. The image was that of a young society matron preparing the soil for a prize rose garden. As he watched, Maggie lifted her arm to wipe the perspiration off her brow. Joshua knew that her determination to stay away from him was the only thing that kept her outside in the summer sun.

He wanted to go to her, to take her in his arms and whisper apologies for his suspicions. But no apologies could wipe away the distrust he still felt. Just the night before he had been ready to make love to her. Now he no longer trusted her. She had not told him about the man in the Quarter. She had, with professional skill, picked up a gun and aimed it at a defenseless man, and she had pulled the trigger. Over and over again. This was not the sweet, sensitive woman he had come to love. This was a stranger. A stranger with a mysterious past that hinted at crime and violence and a web of lies.

He was a psychologist, trained to objectivity and careful analysis, and yet he loved this woman with a passion that was unequaled by anything in his life. He loved her beyond his suspicions about her. And that was the part he could not change or accept.

"She's something, isn't she?"

Joshua had been so lost in thought that he hadn't even heard Skeeter unlock the door. Now his friend stood by his side. "She's something," Joshua agreed bitterly. "I just wish I knew what."

"You wear your halo well, Josh."

"What's that supposed to mean?"

"Only that you're about to sprout wings and leave the real world. When did you become so holy?"

"I've never claimed to be anything other than a man."

"Funny. I was beginning to wonder if you put your manhood in a sacred trust."

Joshua turned to sweep Skeeter with a cold stare. "What makes you think you have a right to criticize my life?"

"Are you beyond reproach?" Skeeter jammed his hands in his pockets, and for a moment, Joshua was transported back to the streets of the Irish Channel to stand on a street corner with Skeeter on one side, Sam on the other. The teenage Skeeter had stood just the way the adult Skeeter was standing. Joshua didn't love him any less today than he had two decades before. His anger faded.

"No. I'm not beyond reproach. Tell me what you see, Skeeter. I've lost the gift of insight."

"I see a man in love with a woman. I see a woman in love with a man. I see him keeping himself at arm's length because he's afraid to trust again, to give his love without doubts." He stopped as if he were loath to continue. "And I see his chance for happiness slipping away because the woman needs him now, not tomorrow. She needs him while the doubts exist, not when they've been cleared away."

Joshua couldn't think of an answer.

"I came home to change. I'm going to work at the Square for the rest of the day and at a bar tonight. I won't be home until early tomorrow morning. I'll see you then." Skeeter turned to leave.

"Skeeter?" Joshua faced his friend. "I am only a man."

"I'm glad to hear it. I'd hate to think that God chose the Irish Channel to launch His Second Coming." He smiled at Joshua's grimace.

* * *

When she could no longer stand the blazing sun, Maggie washed her face and hands under Skeeter's hose and went back inside. She was surprised to find Joshua in the kitchen preparing red beans. The beans, flavored with celery, onions and various spices, were a staple of the Louisiana diet. Served over rice they were a healthy and cheap alternative to meat. Joshua's version smelled delicious.

"Your clothes arrived." Maggie was startled by Joshua's voice.

"You had them sent here?"

He came to the door, still holding the wooden spoon he had used to stir his creation. His hair was rumpled where his fingers had combed it, and the small scrape on his cheek was already turning black-and-blue. "I knew you wouldn't be able to stay at the apartment."

"That was thoughtful."

"I put them in our room. Why don't you shower and change and then have some lunch. I was just about ready to drag you inside."

Maggie sensed a subtle change in Joshua's manner. The tension, previously apparent in his face and voice, was gone. He was relaxed. There was warmth in his eyes when he looked at her. She erected her defenses. "You don't have to take care of me."

"I realize that. You're a very capable woman. Still, even capable people can get sunstroke." Somehow the words caressed her. She refused to respond to their power.

"I stayed in the shade."

Joshua walked toward her, raised his hand and stroked her face with his fingertips. "You have a sunburn. It's not a bad one, but I'd count on at least twenty-five new freckles."

Maggie stepped back to avoid his touch. "I'm going to take a shower. Because I want to. Then I'm going to change. Because I want to. Then I'm going to eat lunch."

"Because you want to. See? You are a very capable woman and an intelligent one, to boot."

Maggie turned and left the room before he could see how his playful warmth was affecting her. In the shower she tried to whip up a protective barrier of righteous anger. One minute Joshua was ready to make love to her and the next he was distrustful and distant. The dichotomy was destroying her. She tried to be critical of his suspicions, but her anger failed her.

She was in love with a man who would never be casual about love or commitment. Her anger slowly dissolved and with it the protection she had tried to build around her heart. Maggie knew she was still completely vulnerable as far as Joshua was concerned. She could only watch their story unfold and hope for a happy ending.

Later, clad in shorts and a cool tank top, she found him in the kitchen, fixing her lunch. "Is grilled cheese okay?" he asked.

She nodded. "I could fix my own."

"It's my pleasure."

She sat at the table, watching Joshua's sparing movements. "Have you ever wondered why you spend so much time taking care of people?"

"Sure. Sometimes it's an easy way to relate to others. It gives me a role to play."

She was astonished at his honesty. "Is that why you insist on taking care of me?"

He leaned against the stove, arms crossed in front of him. "No, Maggie. I take care of *you* because I love you."

The turmoil of the past twenty-four hours had been nothing compared to Joshua's simple statement. "How can you say that?" She tried to choke back the emotion that was threatening to overpower her speech.

"Because it's true."

"You don't know me!"

"I know everything I need to know. It's not you I haven't trusted. It's myself." He flicked off the burner and came to kneel in front of her. "I've been looking for excuses not to care. There are no excuses. I care. I love you no matter what."

"What if I was a prostitute?"

"It doesn't matter."

"I tried to kill a man."

"You had a reason."

"No reason could be good enough!"

"Not when you're sitting here philosophically discussing it. But the man tried to kill you. Reacting as you did made perfectly good sense at the time."

"I handled the gun like a professional."

"I'll admit I wouldn't want to meet you in a dark alley." Joshua held out his arms. "I love you, Maggie. I want to make love to you. No matter what."

Her laugh was shaky. "That could turn out to be dangerous." She ignored his outstretched arms. "What if we find that I'm already married, or have a lover?"

"Then we'll have to deal with it when the time comes." He leaned forward and wrapped his arms around her.

She was disappointed. There was no assurance that Joshua would fight for her no matter what. He was still protecting her and himself. "I don't want any more therapy from you, Joshua." She felt him stiffen against her. There was nothing more cruel that she could have said to him. But she had not said it to be cruel. She had meant every terrible word.

"Therapy?" His voice was hoarse.

"I don't want you to make love to me because you think it will be good for me." She tried to break away from him.

His fingers on her shoulders pinned her against him. "Good for you?"

"I'm not a confused little girl lying in a hospital bed. I'm a woman who needs to be loved, who needs to be trusted. You're telling me that you'll forgive me anything. I don't want your forgiveness. I want you to trust me enough to believe there's nothing to forgive. And I want you to want me enough to fight for me no matter what we find." She tried to wrench free.

"What I'm telling you is that I need you. I need what only you can give me, Maggie. Sweetheart, I'm giving you control over my heart."

She stopped her struggle and sat perfectly still. The tears she had refused to cry drifted slowly down her cheeks. He had laid it out for her, simply and with genuine emotion. He was offering himself to her but there were no guarantees that when the facts were in, he wouldn't step back out of the picture.

Still, it was more than he had ever offered. Instinctively she knew that this much of Joshua was more than any other woman had ever had. She knew she could not turn away. "Every time we've gotten this far," she said, her voice quavering, "you've withdrawn from me. What will come between us this time?"

"The only thing stopping me from carrying you into that bedroom is my lack of preparation," he admitted. "I don't want you to get pregnant."

"You've used up your excuses, then. That's not a problem right now." She waited for a new defense to spring up, but instead Joshua's eyes softened, and he brushed his lips across hers.

"Then there is nothing between us, Maggie, my love."

She buried her face in Joshua's shirt, breathing in great gulps of air as he held her tightly against him.

The last time Joshua had carried her into this bedroom, she had been dressed in a pale pink nightgown, and she had slept through the whole night in his arms. Today she wore shorts and a tank top, and sleep was the furthest thing from their minds. He set her on her feet in front of the twin beds that had been pulled side by side.

"Do you know," he said, his voice a husky whisper, "that late at night, almost every night, I wake up after dreaming about making love to you. I can feel your skin beneath my fingers, as soft and silky as a cloud. And just as ephemeral. You slip away, and I wake up. Do you know how hard it's been to keep myself from coming to you?"

"Do you know," she answered, "that late at night, almost every night, I wake up after dreaming that you come into my room and tell me that you love me and want to make love to me?"

He smiled, his features softening with tenderness. "And what do you say?"

"I say yes. And then you reach for me, and I can feel the roughness of your fingertips against my skin. And very slowly, you bend to kiss me."

"Like this?" Joshua stroked his fingers against the sunburned skin of her cheeks.

Maggie shut her eyes, letting the whisper-soft caress work its magic. "Yes." His fingers moved down her neck, patiently exploring every inch. As he reached her shoulders, he bent to take her mouth with his.

"And like this?" he whispered against her lips.

"Yes." His mouth proclaimed that they had all the time in the world to savor each other. He nibbled lightly at her bottom lip, sucking it gently, until she sighed and opened her mouth to his trespass.

There were few visible signs of the fragile Maggie who had existed months before. But as Joshua kissed her, he was aware of her hesitation, her uncertainty. "Come to me. Give to me," he coaxed her. "I want all of you."

She relaxed against him, her arms entwining around his neck. His chest was hard against hers and her breasts flattened against it. She searched for aloofness and found none. Joshua's body was alive next to hers. His need for her complete and real. She felt his arousal and knew the force of his desire. She also knew the first tremblings of fear.

Joshua could feel it, too. "Maggie," he whispered, his lips nuzzling her ear. "I'm not going to hurt you. Are you afraid?"

She could not pretend otherwise. She nodded.

"Do you know why?"

She didn't answer.

Joshua had not told Maggie of his other dream. She was not the only one who dreamed of her persecutor. In his dream, the nameless, faceless man stood over her body, a demonic laugh rending the air around him. Joshua tried to reach her, tried to save her from the man's attack, but he was unable to move. As the man bent over Maggie, Joshua always awoke, sweating and fighting to free himself from his paralysis. It almost destroyed him to know that once, Maggie had lived through the dream. Only for her, it had been a reality. If she was frightened now, there was a reason for it.

"You can stop me if I frighten you."

Her fingers crept up his neck to tunnel through the short curls at his nape. "You don't frighten me."

"Does making love frighten you?"

"I don't know if I've ever made love."

Never in a lifetime, in a millenium, would he have expected that response to his question. He stroked her back through the soft knit of the tank top. "I can see why you're afraid, then."

"You're going to be disappointed."

"Did you think I was expecting a professional performance?" His gentle tone took the bite out of his words.

"What are you expecting?" She lifted her eyes to his, waiting for his answer.

"I'm not expecting a virgin. I'm not expecting a pro. I'm expecting to hold the woman I love in my arms and seal my commitment to her. And I'm expecting the experience to be imperfect, full of risks and absolutely magnificent." His fingers traveled to the hem of her top and then to the smooth skin beneath. "What do you expect?"

"I expect to feel whole."

"Tell me you love me."

"I love you." She stood on tiptoe to claim his mouth.

"If you love me, you have nothing to be afraid of."

"There is no 'if.'" With hands that were steady and sure, Maggie began to undress him. Joshua stood still under the ministrations of her fingers as she adored his body with her hands and lips. The past months of her life had taught her nothing if they had not taught her that life was short and full of too many twists and turns to count on second chances.

She savored each part of him: the wide shoulders, wide enough to try to take on the burdens of the world; the hard chest that was such a perfect opposite to her own; the slim hips and firm buttocks; the throbbing evidence of his masculinity that already sought her femininity; the tapering, muscular thighs; the perfectly proportioned legs. Revealed to her, he was better than a fantasy. There was a scar from a childhood battle; there was a scattering of tiny imperfections. He was human, a man like many others, and completely special because of it.

When it was her turn, she watched the expression on Joshua's face as he discarded each item of clothing. Proudly she stood before him, welcoming his gaze. She felt her nipples harden beneath his hands, felt a warm gush of desire when he stood close to her, exploring her body with his.

Together they lay down on the bed, their arms seeking the comfort of each other. She expected him to make love to her, to give her the wholeness she craved. Instead his hands and lips began a slow, torturous expedition seeking the places that she hadn't known existed. She was afraid to breathe, afraid that the magic would disappear if she moved.

"Maggie, show me that you like what I'm doing."

His words set her free. She moaned and tangled her hands in his hair. "Yes, I do... Oh, Joshua." This time when the palm of his hand began a rhythmic kneading of her most intimate space, she moved with him.

"Maggie," he said, her name a rough groaning sound. "That's right, sweetheart."

Joshua could feel the heat radiating from her, the moistness that told him she was becoming ready for him. He watched her as, with eyes closed, she began to respond to his caresses. For just a moment he mourned the careless giving of her body that had taught her so little about her own needs. He knew he was teaching her the most fundamental aspects of her sexuality. Inside he cried for women everywhere who have known a man but never the pleasure a man can give.

"Joshua?" Maggie's eyes were open, and her expression conveyed all the love she felt for him. "Come to me." She gave with the same enthusiasm with which she had taken. Half sitting, she ran her nails over him lightly, following their path with her tongue. She tasted and teased, nibbling the smooth skin of his neck, sucking lightly on the sensitive places on his chest. His response was instant and passionate as he pulled her beneath him.

His hands followed the contours of her legs, smoothing them. He levered himself over her. Her eyes were wide and full of trust. It was only that trust, expressed so poignantly, that gave him the control he needed to enter her slowly.

She was hot, and wet, and very tight around him. He was not her first lover, but he knew instinctively there had not been many before him. She was very new. He wanted to weep with the discovery.

She was surprised, too. Joshua could see it proclaimed across every feature. The feel of a man inside her was unfamiliar. She shuddered and lay very still. "Maggie. Sweetheart." His voice was broken. "My love." He gathered her close, his arms around her back, his chest crushing hers. He hid his face in the brown curls that caressed her neck.

"Joshua, love me." Her voice was a plea. She seemed unsure of what to do, how to convince him that she still wanted him. She turned her head to kiss his neck; her hands traced feverish patterns on his back. Hesitantly she began to move beneath him, her body responding on its own in a way that she could not have predicted. "Please, Joshua."

It was all he could do to overcome the heartsick guilt that he felt. No matter how many disclaimers he had made about Maggie's past, he had never quite shaken the suspicion that she was what Sam believed her to be. But the woman lying beneath him, moving her hips so sweetly against his, had never been a prostitute. Her movements were untutored and innocent; her responses had been previously untapped. "Maggie, I'm so sorry I ever doubted you."

"Just love me now."

Joshua lifted himself above her, his eyes devouring the flushed, damp skin of her face, his body consumed by the feel of her softness beneath him. Maggie shut her eyes, closing off everything except the feel of Joshua against her. She willed her instincts to control her movements. Each thrust of his hips sent liquid fire dancing through her body, yet she found the sensations confusing. They were building to a conclusion, but without help from her they faded, far removed from the intensity that she desired. Frustrated with her own confusion, she moved restlessly, avoiding rather than prolonging true intimacy.

"Maggie?" Joshua held back, his body rigid with his effort to control himself. He wanted to bury himself in her, to move with abandon against her, taking his own release. He knew if he did, that she would understand; she would take true pleasure from giving so much to him. But he wanted more. He wanted everything for her. The pleasure of giving and the pleasure of taking, too.

He moved his hands beneath her. "Move with me, Maggie." When he thrust into her again, he lifted her hips to meet him. His reward was a soft gasp of appreciation. With a patience that bordered on the unearthly, he taught her to make love to him. Hesitant at first to trust her own body, at last she let herself be guided to a place where there was no turning back.

Finally, there could be no more lessons. Each thrust, each meeting of hips, each small cry, took them further toward the place where Maggie had never been. She wrapped her legs around Joshua, trying desperately to merge. She trembled with the force of the effort, calling his name and pleading with him until there were no more words.

With one final cry, she gave herself completely, all her trust, all her faith in Joshua's love for her. The series of explosions that rocked her body set off an earthquake in the man she adored, and wrapped tightly in his arms, she felt herself brought down to earth again. Safe.

Chapter 10

Joshua wouldn't let Maggie go. He turned to his side, with her body still entwined with his. He held her, and he thought of all the times he had almost lost her, all of the circumstances that could have been different so that he might never have met her. He wanted her again. Immediately. He wanted to fill her, join together again for those blissful seconds when they could truly be one. So fierce was his need that he held her too tightly, afraid that now he had finally found her she would be taken from him.

Maggie hid her face in his neck. The heat of their bodies wound so closely together was smothering in the New Orleans summer afternoon. Maggie didn't care. She wanted nothing to break the spell that their lovemaking had cast over her. She felt loved and treasured and completely secure. She felt reborn.

"I don't know what to say." Joshua spoke first.

"I do." Maggie nuzzled Joshua's neck with her lips, her voice husky. "Thank you."

Her gratitude embarrassed him. "If I tell you it was my pleasure, will that be too corny?"

"It will be perfect."

"It was my pleasure."

"I noticed."

He hugged her tightly, kissing her before he let her go to move slightly away. His hand came up to trace the flush of her cheeks and the freckles appearing in sharp relief on her nose. "It seems to me that it was your pleasure, too."

"Oh, yes."

They lay together, touching each other with the natural ease of lovers who have been completely lost in each other. Words were more difficult. And yet words had to be spoken. When he could put it off no longer, Joshua began.

"It seems, sweetheart, that we named you after the wrong Mary."

"I wasn't a virgin."

"Not quite." Joshua ran his hand along the curve of her arm. "Nor were you experienced."

"Perhaps I've forgotten."

"I think not." His hand traveled lightly over her breasts, and he felt her shiver. "I think that we have to look harder for answers."

"The man who tried to murder me must have believed I was a prostitute."

"I don't think it was the same man who tried to kill the others. Sam is sure the man they've locked up is responsible for at least three of the murders. Obviously the man who tried to kill you is still on the streets."

Maggie waited for Joshua to continue. She could almost see him trying to work out an answer.

"What if someone tried to murder you and wanted to cover up the evidence?"

"Isn't that where cement blocks and deep water come in?"

Joshua shuddered lightly at the thought, pulling her a little closer. "Suppose this somebody had a twisted sense of humor. He dresses you like a prostitute and leaves you for dead in a vacant lot with a scarf, just like all the other prostitute murders."

"Only I don't die." She thought about the possibility. "Wouldn't someone have reported me missing?"

That was a mystery. Joshua knew that Sam had thoroughly searched all the missing persons reports that came into the station. "I don't understand that part," Joshua admitted.

Maggie shut her eyes and willed herself to remember something new. Anything. She had trained herself to bring up an image of the white stucco house and blue, sparkling water. Her father's voice...a boat...the sound of guns firing. This was new, but there was no answering jolt of fear. She concentrated on the sound of guns. Rapid firing. No screaming. She drifted with the sound. It came from a room that was semidark because the walls were painted gray. It looked like a barn or a bowling alley. On the wall in front of her was the figure of a man; part of it was ripped to shreds by tiny holes, gathered in a circle. Bullet holes. She opened her eyes.

"A firing range. At some time I've been to a firing range."

"That would explain the professional way you handled that weapon."

"But why?"

"Maybe you needed training for a job?"

Maggie shook her head. "I'm certain that I worked with children."

"Self-defense?"

"But why?"

"Maybe you lived in a big city, in a bad section of town."

"No, I lived on the water in a white stucco house."

Joshua smiled. She was as sure of that small piece of information as she was of anything in the world. "As an adult?"

She nodded slowly. "Because of what I was told about myself, I thought perhaps I was remembering my childhood, but now I think it was more recent." She shut her eyes again. "The house is two story, and it has a red tile roof." Her eyes flew open. "It's Spanish in design. Maybe I lived in New Mexico or Arizona."

"Probably not with all that water."

She shrugged. "When I imagine the house, I see lots of green shrubbery growing around it and a big yard that stretches to the water."

"What else?"

She shut her eyes again. "Sunshine and iron gates. Tall iron gates. Hibiscus and orange trees." Her eyes flew open. "Oranges! California."

"More likely Florida."

She sat up and clapped her hands. "Florida. I'll bet you're right, Joshua."

He sat up to join her. "The central or southern part of the state. Probably on one of the coasts."

"Florida." Maggie threw her arms around his neck.

He wanted to caution her. They still didn't know what she would find when her memory returned completely. He wanted to prepare her, to cushion her if the reality of her former life was painful. But he could do nothing. He could not dull the shining joy in her eyes with talk of keeping her feet on the ground. He could only be there to catch her if she fell. He hugged her, letting the soft breasts against his chest rekindle his desire. Ah Maggie, how much longer will you be mine?

They were so attuned that it was almost as if he had spoken the thought out loud. "Joshua, wherever I came from, whoever I am, it won't come between us. It can't." Her mouth sought his, her hands began to travel his body. "Love me again, Joshua. Let me show you what I've learned."

He pushed her back against the pillows, and this time there was no hesitation, no careful tutoring. They gave, they took, and for a long time they took pleasure in the moment with no thoughts of yesterday or tomorrow.

The sun set before Maggie and Joshua returned to the kitchen. Maggie's grilled cheese sandwich was cold rubber, but the red beans had cooked down to a creamy perfection. Joshua put rice on to steam, and Maggie made a salad. They sat across from each other at Skeeter's kitchen table as they waited for the rice. Neither of them needed to say a word.

Maggie noted the little things about Joshua that she loved: the way his dark hair grazed his forehead, the stern lines around his eyes that softened when he looked at her, the smooth, tanned cheeks that would be rough by early morning. Even now, satiated from their lovemaking, she wanted to reach across the table, take his hands and communicate wordlessly to him the startling depth of her desire.

Before she could, his hands had captured hers. "I've just had you, and yet, I want you still." He brought her fingertips to his mouth. "That's never going to change."

She wondered if that was enough, if wanting her even without trusting her enough to believe that she would stay with him was really enough. It didn't matter, though, because there was nothing she could do to change it. Joshua would have to be the one to take that final plunge. And he wasn't a man who indulged in blind faith.

"I hope you'll always want me," she said. "I know I'll always want you."

The timer went off, and reluctantly Joshua let go of Maggie's hands to turn off the stove. They dished up plates of rice, covering it with the red beans, and they added bowls of salad. When they finished, they cleaned up the kitchen, working together with the sensitivity of a couple who have been together for many years.

When they were finished, Maggie put her arms around Joshua's waist and rested her head on his chest. "How long do you think I'll have to stay here?"

"I don't know. Can you stand it for a little while?"

She shook her head. "I can't take time off from work without forfeiting my job. And the police don't believe my story. They may never catch the man who . . ."

Joshua gave her a fierce hug. "I'm going to call Sam and have a talk with him. If I don't get any assurances that they're really trying, I'm going to quit my own job and get you out of New Orleans."

"Where would we go?"

"Florida."

Joshua had already given up so much for her. Now he was volunteering to quit his job and undertake a wild-goose chase through an unfamiliar state just in case their theories were correct. Maggie couldn't let him. "No."

"Funny, I didn't think you'd be saying no to me tonight."

She laughed, but the sound was an audible tremble. "I won't allow you to sacrifice your job for me again. I'll go myself."

"I couldn't let you."

"I'd just be trying to put together the pieces of my life so that we can go on with our life together."

"You don't know what you'll find." Joshua cupped Maggie's chin in his hands and lifted her face to meet his.

"I have to find out who I am to put an end to this terror...."

"No, I mean you can't assume you'll want a life with me."

"You know I do."

"You do now, but, Maggie, you don't know what you'll want later. I don't want you feeling guilty because you're pulled between me and your past."

She stepped back and put distance between them. "Stop taking care of me. I don't need to be shielded from the real world. I know what I want. If you can't believe it, fine, but don't start trying to prepare me for leaving you. I won't have it!"

"And what will you have?" He put his hands on her shoulders and held her still. "Can you guarantee how you're going to feel? I can't."

"There are no guarantees that come with this life. There's only loving, and giving, and risking. We've come so far. Go the rest of the way with me. Can't you do that?"

"I'll go just as far as you want me to."

She heard the unspoken codicil. He would stay with her. But when the day came—as he knew it would—when she didn't want him anymore, he would leave. And in preparation for that moment he would keep a part of himself from her as protection.

She could only fill him with her love and hope that someday it would be enough. "I'll take what you can give me," she said, turning her head to kiss each of his hands. "No matter what you withhold, what you give is more than I ever expected to have."

Then, filled with dinner and with their need for each other, Joshua took Maggie by the hand and led her back to their room. And the evening passed much too quickly.

It was almost midnight when Joshua heard the key in the front door. He had been awake for some time, watching Maggie sleep beside him. She was lying on her side, her head pillowed on her hands and her face utterly composed, like a child who has never known sadness. Guilt had stirred deep within him for the depthless desire he had shown for her. No matter how many times they made love, he couldn't get enough of her, couldn't begin to touch the passion he felt. Tomorrow, she would know how inconsiderate he had been.

There had been no complaints from Maggie. She had come to him again and again, with the same need that he had shown. Now she was sleeping an exhausted sleep, pleasure shining on her face. Joshua was still filled with the emotions of the day and evening. At the sound of Skeeter's key in the front door, he got out of bed, pulled on his pants and went to see his friend. Maggie didn't even stir.

"I thought you weren't coming home until the wee small hours," he said in greeting.

"I was hoping you'd be up." Skeeter motioned for Joshua to follow him to the kitchen. "I've got a lead on Maggie's attacker."

Joshua was in the process of stretching when the news came. He stopped in midair. "No."

Skeeter cocked his head to one side, surprised by his friend's reaction.

It was too soon. Much, much too soon. No matter what he said, Joshua knew that letting Maggie go would be the hardest thing he had ever done. He had counted on more time with her than this. He had counted on building memories to last him a lifetime. He wanted to stop Skeeter, to scoop Maggie out of bed and take her far, far away before her past claimed her. There would be time later to deal with it. Now he needed her more than she needed to know who she was.

"Joshua?"

He knew it was already too late. Too soon and too late. He laughed bitterly at the irony. "Tell me," he said.

Skeeter was showing his flair for the dramatic. "Well, I kept the original sketch for myself. It was so well-done, I decided to put it on my display board." In order to captivate potential customers, all the portrait artists that worked in Jackson Square put their best work on display beside the little stands where they worked. Often the portraits were of celebrities, but just as often they were well-done pictures of ordinary people.

"So?"

"I didn't get any comments on it while I was at the Square, but later, when I moved to the Jazztown bar on Bourbon Street, I put it up again. About an hour ago, this guy came up, almost falling-down drunk, and started staring at the picture. So I asked him if he knew the man. He said, 'Sure.' Then he started to wander off."

"Go on," Joshua pulled a chair out from the table and turned it to sit on.

"Well, I followed him. He was pretty easy to keep up with, he was so out of it. I told him that the guy had asked me to do his portrait and paid me, but that I had lost his address and couldn't deliver it."

"And he believed that?"

"He was so drunk I could have told him I was the president and he would have tried to snap to attention. He told me the guy's name is

Stoney Cox, and he gave me directions to his place. Now get this. Cox lives over off of Basin Street. About six blocks from Hootie Barn's Tavern.''

"God."

Skeeter nodded at Joshua's stricken expression. "Trying to call out the troops? You're going to need them. The guy says that this Cox character is a real bad dude. Evidently he owed money to the guy I talked to, and when the guy tried to collect, Cox went after him with a knife. He said that Cox told him once that he was wanted in Florida for something real bad, but he's managed to keep his nose clean in Louisiana."

"Why didn't this guy report him to the police?"

Skeeter clucked and shook his head. "Honor among thieves, Joshua. What would you expect? The guy I talked to was no saint himself."

It was much, much too late to turn back. "We've got to call Sam."

Skeeter leaned back in his chair, his hands behind the back of his head. "Can you identify the guy if you see him?"

Joshua tried to imagine the face of the man in the picture. He had only seen him for a few seconds, but the image was permanently engraved in his brain. "Yes."

"I've already called Sam myself. There was no answer at home, and the woman I talked to at the station says he's not expected back until late tomorrow afternoon."

They could wait. They could wait, the man could disappear and they might not ever discover Maggie's identity. Joshua shook his head. He could not deprive her of her past, no matter how much he wanted to. And by not acting on the information now, they might lose track of the man. Maggie's safety would be in permanent jeopardy.

"I don't want to wait for Sam." Joshua stood and began to pace. "What if this guy hears that someone is circulating his picture and decides to leave town?"

Skeeter nodded. "I think that first thing tomorrow morning, we should go to the guy's house. My van has tinted windows. We'll take it and you can stay inside. I'll go to the guy's door on some pretense or other, and when he comes out, you can get a good look. If it's the right guy, we can keep his house under surveillance until we can notify Sam."

"I don't want you near this guy. I'll do it."

"He's seen you. I'm a stranger."

Joshua knew that Skeeter was right. "Then we'll just watch his house until we can get hold of Sam. We can wait to identify him without risking your life."

"I don't think so."

"Why not?"

"Because Sam doesn't buy any of this. I saw him earlier today when I dropped off the sketch. He thinks Maggie is leading you down the primrose path. I want to confront him with as much evidence as possible. If we tell him you're sure it's the guy from the Laundromat he'll jump to attention. If I tell him it's just a guy who looks like a sketch I made using Maggie's description, he's not going to be impressed. He'd come eventually, but I don't think there's time to waste."

"Sam's the one who isn't being objective."

"He loves you. We both do."

Joshua smiled at his friend. "It's not just me you love, is it?"

Skeeter shook his head. "I know where Maggie belongs and with whom. But maybe she's made me believe a little."

Joshua understood.

"I don't think we should tell her until right before we leave tomorrow," Skeeter said, standing to head to his room. "She won't want us to go."

Joshua stood, too. "How can I say thanks enough?"

Skeeter was quiet for a moment. "Do you remember when I was arrested six years ago?"

Joshua waited. Skeeter rarely talked about his arrest for selling drugs to a narcotics officer. He had been one of many, cleaned off the streets in a drug sweep that shook the city. Dealing in drugs had been a sometime thing for him, and he had never dealt the hard stuff. But everyone's sentence had been stiff; Skeeter had been caught in the furor and given a harsh five-year sentence.

"You stood by me then, Josh. If it hadn't been for you and Sam, I don't think I would have lived through those years in jail. You both jeopardized your jobs for me. Thanks won't ever be needed between us."

The two stepped together and embraced. They had grown up on the streets, tough kids who had learned early that showing emotion only got them into serious trouble. Tonight, they trusted each other enough not to care.

"Well, what are you two staring at?" Maggie knew by the bright sunlight flooding Skeeter's kitchen that she had slept much too late. Skeeter and Joshua were both up, dressed as though they were ready to go out for the morning. She met Joshua's gaze, and she knew her face was awash in color. The memory of the night's passionate lovemaking was between them.

"It's not every day a beautiful woman steps into my kitchen," Skeeter teased. "You look lovelier than ever this morning, Maggie." She blushed again, tearing her eyes from Joshua's to smile at Skeeter.

"Thank you." She poured herself a cup of coffee and came to the table to sit beside Joshua. He didn't miss her wince as she lowered herself into the chair. His guilt was mixed with teasing affection.

"I told you one more time would be your undoing," he told her in a low voice as Skeeter went to the refrigerator to get the milk for her cereal.

"You told me? I think I told you.... Thank you, Skeeter." This time her cheeks were on fire.

"You look a little feverish this morning," Skeeter said, reaching over to put his hand to her forehead.

"Yes, I thought she was feverish last night," Joshua agreed politely.

"Will you two leave me alone to eat my breakfast, please?" Maggie slapped Skeeter's hand away. The two men just laughed.

Maggie noticed, halfway through her cereal, that no one else was eating. "Why am I the only one having breakfast?"

"We ate earlier. We have to go out in a few minutes."

Maggie was surprised, but it didn't take her long to understand that something was different. "It has something to do with me, doesn't it?"

"Maggie, we may have a lead. Skeeter and I are going to check it out this morning." Joshua's voice was calm, as though he had just announced that he was going to the corner store for a newspaper.

"What lead?" She put down her spoon and stared at him. Suddenly the cereal tasted like wood chips.

"Somebody identified the picture. We think we know where the guy lives."

"Where?" Maggie shut her eyes and clutched the edge of the table.

"About six blocks from Hootie Barn's Tavern." Joshua got up and knelt beside Maggie's rigid body. His arms crept around her. "Don't be afraid, sweetheart. It's going to be all right."

"Don't go, Joshua. Call the police. Let them do it."

"We know what we're doing. Sam's going to be at the station this afternoon. We'll call him then."

"Please don't go!" Her voice was a plea.

"Maggie. Sweetheart. We can't live our life together this way. Even if the guy doesn't provide any clues to your identity, he has to be caught. Even if all we can have him arrested for is the Laundromat robbery."

"Joshua, he must know who I am. What if we find out something terrible?"

"We won't." Joshua understood her sudden absence of courage. Everything was coming to a head much too quickly. Much too quickly for both of them. Unfortunately it couldn't be helped. They couldn't wait until they felt ready to face her past.

"You and Skeeter could be killed!"

"We won't be." Reluctantly he loosened his hold, brushing his fingers across the warm skin under the back of her blouse as he stood. "We're going now. Lock the door behind us. We'll be back before you know it."

There was no color in her cheeks now. She was white, and her blue eyes seemed to swallow her other features. "Please?" She tried one last time to keep him from leaving.

"No." Joshua helped her out of the chair and pulled her close. "One kiss," he ordered her. "Then lock the door."

With her lips and with her body she tried to tell him of her fears, but Joshua was steeled to her pleas. He broke away finally. "We'll be back as soon as this is taken care of." In a moment, he was gone.

Maggie stood on the front porch and watched Skeeter's van drive away. When it was out of sight, she went back into the house and closed and locked the door behind her. Her mind whirled with possible actions she could take. Nothing that came to mind made any sense. If she searched for Joshua's car keys and found them, she wasn't certain that she would be able to find the men. If she did, she wasn't certain that she could be any help. She had no friends that she could call; she had no resources of any kind.

She paced the living room floor, unconsciously following the same path that she had followed the day that Joshua had gone to the hospital staff meeting. Why had Skeeter and Joshua wanted to identify the man first? How would they get him outside to do it? The man had tried three times to kill her; he was not a safe person to engage in a game of cops and robbers. Joshua and Skeeter, as tough and streetwise as they were, would be no match for him.

But Sam would be. There was nothing that Maggie wanted less than to expose herself to Sam's ridicule again. She knew what the police sergeant thought of her. He was convinced she was a hooker, the lowest of low-life trying to sucker his best friend. If Sam could protect Joshua and Skeeter, however, his opinion of her was of no importance. Finding Sam was her only hope.

She hesitated only briefly. She shut her eyes, and the strongest vision she had ever had of her persecutor overwhelmed her. The man in the picture was leering at her, reaching for her with dirty, nicotine-stained hands. In the waistband of his pants was a gun. In one hand, a long scarf.

She was trembling all over when she opened her eyes and ran to the telephone.

It took long minutes for her to convince the policewoman receptionist at the station that getting hold of Sergeant Long was a life-or-death matter. Finally the woman promised to call a couple of numbers to try to locate him. There were no promises that even if she did, Sam would return Maggie's call.

Maggie waited, pacing a six-foot path in front of the telephone until she was certain the floor would have a permanent rut. When the telephone rang she grabbed it in the middle of the first ring. "What trouble are you in now?" Sam asked with no polite introduction. Maggie went weak with relief.

At first Sam was unimpressed with her pleas. He was about to play tennis with his partner; he didn't like having his morning off disturbed. Finally, however, something about her pleading seemed to get through to him. He insisted that she calm down; he didn't like hysterical women. Maggie told him that she didn't care if he liked her or not, she just wanted him to do his job. Then she repeated, desperately, that Joshua and Skeeter were in danger.

She told him what little they had shared with her. No, she didn't have the license number of Skeeter's van. No, she couldn't describe it. Yes, she would probably recognize it if she saw it, but she wasn't going to have the chance if he didn't get his big blond body in his car to come and get her. In a second there was a humming noise on the line, and she knew that she had finally done the impossible. She had gotten Sergeant Sam Long to listen to her.

The car that pulled up in front of Skeeter's house only fifteen minutes later was unmarked, and Sam and his partner were in shorts and casual shirts. Maggie was down the sidewalk, opening the back door before Sam had a chance to move. "I don't know what side of the tavern they're on," she said as she climbed into the back seat and slammed the door. "They were purposely vague, I'm sure."

"They both use a lot of energy protecting you."

"Yes, and I know you don't approve, and I couldn't care less," she said, almost shouting. "Just forget what you think of me for a moment and get going."

For the first time she saw something like a flicker of admiration cross Sam's handsome face. "The sweet little kitten has claws."

"If that's what it takes." She settled back against the seat, peering out the window as though she could practice for the task to come. "How do you plan to find them?"

"We're going to cruise the streets around the tavern, starting on a seven-block radius and work our way in. You keep your eyes open when I tell you to."

"I don't need you to tell me." She concentrated on the scenery. Her body was tense, every muscle ready for action if necessary. She was a tightly wound spring ready to react when she had to.

"Does any of this look familiar to you?" Sam's question lacked its usual sarcasm.

Maggie tried to think. "I don't know," she said finally, her voice echoing her defeat. "Something always stops me from knowing. It's like viewing everything through a billowing curtain. I get glimpses and then I'm blocked.''

She expected him to snort, but he didn't.

Maggie felt as if she would explode. The terrible pressure of fear built inside her. At this moment, Joshua could be confronting her attacker. She was so frightened for him that all she could concentrate on was her terror. It was moving her toward a terrible gray place, a place with no light, no hope. Slowly, as if layer after layer was being peeled away, she began to see visions.

Joshua, at the mercy of a gunman. Joshua alone, trying to find her attacker. The scene was so vivid that she could see it in her mind. The man was wearing a mask...a gorilla mask. He was pointing a gun at Joshua. No! It wasn't Joshua. It was an older man. Medium height, heavyset, brown wavy hair. He was reaching out to her and she was trying to go to him. But she couldn't. The masked man held her, but his mask dissolved. It was not the man from the Laundromat. ''Oh, no.'' She put her hands over her face. ''No!''

Sam turned to watch her. ''Maggie?''

She didn't hear him. The scene was changing. Now she saw the man from the Laundromat. She was tied to a bed, and he was taunting her. *All women are whores!* he was shouting. *You're no different!* Maggie cringed against the seat. ''No!''

''Maggie, pull yourself together.''

She ignored Sam's voice. It was too late to turn back. Images ran into images. The first man dragging her across a parking lot. The older man with wavy hair lying lifeless on the ground. Darkness. Terrible cramps all over her body and unbearably stale air. Then she was in a room. The man from the Laundromat was taunting her, hitting her; she was trying to resist. Darkness.

''Sam.'' Her voice was a plea.

''What is it, Maggie?''

''Sam, my father...'' She couldn't put it together. The man on the ground was her father. He was dead. The first man was dragging her away. She was screaming. He hit her once, then again. Then darkness. And terrible cramps. Air she could barely breathe.

A woman. More taunting. *Please leave me alone.* It was her voice. *You've killed my father, no one will pay your ransom!*

Your father's not dead. But he was, she had seen him fall. *Go ahead and kill me!* Then darkness.

''Sam!''

''Go on, Maggie. You're safe here. What do you see?''

''I don't know. My father...the man killed him and dragged me away.''

''The man that Joshua and Skeeter are trying to find?''

"No. Another man. And a woman was there, too." She pulled her hands from her face, tears streaming down it. "But, Sam, the man that Joshua is trying to find was there later. I was tied to a bed. He called me a whore. He tried to rape me." She shut her eyes and squeezed them tight. "He'll kill Joshua. Find him, Sam."

"Then open your eyes, Maggie." Sam turned in his seat and held his hand out to her. "Grab my hand, honey. You're fine. You're strong. You can handle this. But we have to have your help now. We have to find Skeeter and Joshua."

Sam's hand was light-years away, but Maggie reached across the incredible distance between them and grasped it. She was shaking so hard that he could barely hang on to her. "We're getting close to the right area now. Can you help us? You have to help us."

She nodded, tears still streaming down her face. "I still don't understand."

"You will. First we have to find Joshua."

Maggie held on to Sam's hand and stared out the window. The streets were unfamiliar.

"We're on the six-block radius now," Sam's partner told him.

"Okay, Maggie. Watch closely. Do you remember anything about the van at all?"

"It was light blue, with a wide chrome running board and a smashed fender in the back. Big windows in the side. It's a panel van that's been converted."

Sam grimaced. "I thought you couldn't describe it."

"I wanted to come. I had to come."

She expected Sam to be angry, but instead he squeezed her hand and dropped it. He opened the car's glove compartment and pulled out a pistol. "When we get there," he warned, "you will not set foot out of this car."

"Sam?" Sam's partner pointed to the next block. Parked on the side of the street was a van like the one Maggie had just described.

"Does this neighborhood look familiar?"

Maggie willed herself to remember. Nothing came. There were rows and rows of small shotgun houses, houses built one room behind the other to save space on the narrow lots. The neighborhood was shabby. It made Skeeter's neighborhood look like a ritzy New Orleans suburb. "I can't remember." And then she did.

She had seen it in the rain the day she had gone to Hootie Barn's Tavern to find her memory. But she had seen it before that, too. It had been dark. There hadn't even been the luxury of lamplight to guide her steps. She was running past houses like these. Trying to run. She could hardly move her legs because they were on fire with the return of her circulation. *You little whore.* The voice behind her was slurred. The man, her persecutor, was chasing her. She ran between houses and tried to hide in a yard, but a dog snarled at her and voices threatened her from the house.

She stumbled on, hiding against shrubbery. There was no one else on the dark streets, no one to turn to. She turned a corner, then another one. There were no lights. There was no moon. She stumbled on. The man was coming closer and closer. She was freezing cold and crying, trying not to make any noise for fear that he'd find her. It began to drizzle. In the distance she could see a street that was brightly lit. She headed toward it. She was trying to run. And then, mercifully, everything went black.

"There were no lights," she said with a sob. "No lights. And I was trying to run."

"The streetlights are hidden by tree branches." Sam's partner pointed to one of the few lamps on the street. It was shaded by the limbs of a tremendous live oak. "On a starless night, this place would be pitch dark."

They pulled into a parking space about a half block behind the van, and quietly, Sam radioed their location to the police station. Then he turned down the radio to avoid having it heard. "Where in the hell are Skeeter and Josh?" he muttered. "Are they having tea with the guy?"

"No!"

"Hush, Maggie." He nodded to his partner. "Want to make a guess which house they're in?"

A movement from one of the houses on the other side of the street caught their attention before the policeman could answer. With a sinking heart, Maggie recognized it as the house she had stood in front of the day of the thunderstorm. A door opened, and Skeeter came out, laughing and talking as if he was with an old friend. Following him was the man with the red beard. Skeeter was shrugging, as if he had made a mistake.

"What in the hell?" Sam turned slightly toward Maggie. "Is that the guy?"

Maggie wanted to scream. "Yes," she choked out. "Oh, yes!"

"This is going to be very simple, then. As soon as Skeeter gets back inside the van, I'll knock on his door and we'll arrest him. You will stay put. Do you understand?"

Maggie was immobilized with fear. At the same moment that Sam had turned to her to give her his instructions, the door to Skeeter's van had been flung open. Joshua now stood on the sidewalk. The man with the red beard saw him at the same instant Maggie did. "Joshua!"

There was no time for thought, no time to calculate her actions. All Maggie knew was that Joshua was in danger. She was out in the street before she knew that she had moved. "Joshua! He'll kill you."

Joshua turned toward her. "Maggie!"

The sunlight glinted off a shining object on the front porch. There was a sound like a small explosion. Maggie was knocked to the ground. Another explosion. "He's been hit."

"Joshua!" Then there was silence. And darkness. Another void. She drifted. *Maggie, darling, don't run down the stairs. I won't, Daddy. I never do. Mommy told me not to.*

She was in a monstrous white castle and she was crying. *Why did Mommy have to die, Daddy? Maggie, darling, we don't understand. Don't call me that, Daddy. Mommy wouldn't like it.*

She drifted. She was on a patio, a man put his arm around her back. She felt suddenly sad. Why? *James, stop it. I'm not ready for marriage.*

There were guns firing. She held one in her hand and murdered a paper target. Over and over again. Then a man was grabbing her. *No! Her father was trying to save her. Daddy!* Her father was lying at her feet.

She drifted. There was no reason not to drift. Joshua was dead. She could feel his hands caress her, his lips on hers. Joshua was dead. She was destined to lose, and lose, and lose.

"Maggie?"

She stirred restlessly.

"Maggie. Sweetheart. It's Joshua."

It was funny how the mind could play tricks on you. She knew that when she opened her eyes, she would find herself alone in a hospital bed. The old woman would be rocking next to her. Surely Jane Doe was as insane as anyone could possibly be.

"Maggie. Open your eyes."

She wanted to die. But to die, she must first live again. Where she existed now was neither life nor death. It was the void between. She had faced so much—surely she could face this, too. She had to live in order to die. It was a paradox, but then life was nothing but a paradox.

"Maggie!"

Slowly she felt her eyelids flutter open. Joshua was kneeling above her. In the background she heard the sound of police sirens. She blinked, trying to bring the scene into focus.

"Oh, Maggie." Joshua scooped her up against him.

"I told you not to move her. I'm not sure if she hit her head when I knocked her down." She recognized Sam's voice.

Tentatively Maggie reached to stroke Joshua's cheek. His flesh was warm to her touch. He felt startlingly real. "Joshua, you're alive."

His laugh was shaky. "Just."

"Skeeter?"

"I'm here, Maggie."

She lifted her eyes and saw his outline above her. "Sam?"

Joshua answered. "Sam killed Stoney Cox before he could get off another shot. His first one missed me."

"Stoney Cox. Yes, that was his name." She rested against Joshua's chest. "I'm glad he's dead."

Joshua rocked her slowly. "He can't hurt you now, sweetheart. The worst is over, Maggie."

She listened to her name roll so sweetly off his tongue. It seemed like a shame to correct him. Still, he had to be told. She drifted with his rocking body, gathering her strength.

"Maggie?"

"Joshua, Maggie will do just fine, but for the record, my real name is Mary Margaret O'Hanlon."

Chapter 11

Joshua's arms tightened around Maggie's back as her words penetrated his concern for her. "Mary Margaret O'Hanlon?"

"Lately of Palm Beach... I guess not so lately." She stirred in his arms. "Daughter of the late Chester Gilbert O'Hanlon who was murdered by a man I knew as Bob Claiborne." Joshua could hear the tears in her voice.

"Hush, sweetheart. You don't have to tell it all now."

They heard Sam talking to some of the other police officers who had just arrived. Maggie lay in Joshua's arms as if unable to rouse herself sufficiently to get up. Joshua stroked her hair, wondering at her words. "Mary Margaret O'Hanlon." He tried the name on his tongue. Somehow it fitted perfectly.

"My father called me Maggie when I was a little girl. My mother hated it. She was very proper. She thought that little girls should be called by their given names. After she died, I wouldn't let Daddy call me anything except Mary Margaret." She trembled, and Joshua began to stroke her back.

"Josh? Is she all right?" Sam was standing over them.

"She's remembering." He tried to convey his concern for Maggie with his eyes so that Sam would leave them alone, but his friend knelt beside them.

"Maggie?"

"Sam." Maggie pushed away from Joshua to regard the man who had saved Joshua's life. "You shot Stoney Cox."

"Yes."

"He was an evil man."

"We're going to need a statement from you, honey."

Joshua was surprised at the endearment. Coming from Sam, it was the highest of honors.

"I can tell you everything."

"Maggie's remembered her real name," Joshua explained, "and where she's from."

Sam nodded and stood.

Her voice was stronger. "Mary Margaret O'Hanlon. From Palm Beach, Florida."

Joshua was bending to pull Maggie back into his arms when he caught the dumbfounded look on Sam's face. His friend looked as though he had just seen a man come back from the dead. Or a woman. "Damn!"

"What's wrong, Sam?" Joshua was honestly puzzled.

"Don't you read the papers, for God's sake?" Sam was once again kneeling beside Maggie. "Are you sure, honey? You're not still confused?"

She smiled a little. "As sure as I've ever been about anything. Don't you think I know my own name?"

Sam's laugh was bittersweet. "How did you end up here, Mary Margaret O'Hanlon?"

"I can't fill in all the details because I was out of touch for part of the time." Maggie sank back into Joshua's arms. "I'll tell you what I know, but can it wait a little while? I need some time to pull myself together first."

"That can be arranged." Sam stood. "Josh, get her out of here before the press arrives. They're going to have a field day when they find out who she is."

Joshua was as confused as Maggie had been all these months. He also knew that this was not the time to demand enlightenment. "I'm going to take her back to Skeeter's house for the time being."

"I'll see you both at the station about five o'clock, if she's ready by then. I've got to make some calls to substantiate her story."

Joshua helped Maggie to her feet. She was smiling at Sam's last remark. "After everything, you still don't trust me, do you?"

Sam reached out to stroke her check with one knuckle. "What do you expect? Resurrections are more Joshua's line than mine." He turned to Joshua. "Get her home and make her rest."

Maggie looked so drained that Joshua knew Sam's command would be easy to follow. He also understood that his own curiosity would have to wait to be satiated. Maggie was too tired to explain anything. She was still stunned over the events of the morning, still trying to put all the pieces together.

Skeeter had been giving his side of the story to one of the police officers. He came over to join them. "What happens now?" he asked.

"We're going to impose on you a little longer, then I think we'll be out of your house for good." Joshua helped Maggie into the van and settled her on one of the captain's chairs in the back. "Rest now, sweetheart. We can talk all you want later."

Her answer was a tired smile.

"Maggie?"

Joshua came into the bedroom they had so recently shared to awaken Maggie for her appointment at the police station. She was lying on the bed, arms beneath her head, staring at the ceiling. "I'm awake." She smiled. "For the first time in a long while, I'm fully awake."

Joshua sat carefully on the bed, not touching her. "Do you feel up to going down to the station?"

"Yes." Maggie turned her head to examine him. "I feel like talking about it."

"Do you want to tell me now?"

"No." She pulled herself to a sitting position and reached out to put her hand on his arm. "Joshua, love me before we go."

Joshua had carefully avoided any intimacy with her since her memory had returned. Even now he pulled away from her touch. He had managed to comfort her platonically before she fell asleep, but now just the feel of her slender fingers on his arm was making him ache with new need for her. "I don't think that's a good idea, Maggie."

"Look at me." When he didn't, she put her fingers on his chin and turned him to face her. "Nothing's changed between us. I still love you. Only you."

"Maggie." He covered her fingers with his hands and held them against his face for long moments. "You must be terribly confused. You've just gone through a trauma most of us couldn't begin to handle."

"Stop!" She dropped her hands to his shoulders and shook him. "I don't need protecting anymore. I need love. Your love. Can't you trust me?"

Joshua was silent.

"You can't, can you?" She tried to move.

"I trust you. But you need time and space to readjust your life."

"I don't want time. I don't want space. I want you." She dropped her hands and tried to pull away.

Joshua sighed and put his hands on her waist, effectively blocking her humiliated retreat. "Maggie. There was another man before me. What about him? Where does he fit now?"

Maggie saw Joshua's struggle to remain objective. She wanted to soothe him and tell him that there was nothing to worry about. But even more, she wanted to be perfectly honest with him. There had been too many clouds between them. He had to know the truth. Soon he would know everything else; now he must know about James. "I'm engaged to a man named James Darwin."

"I see."

She felt Joshua's hands tighten spasmodically on her waist before he released her. His face showed no emotion.

"James worked with my father. My father owned and managed real estate, and James was his assistant." She drew her knees up to her chin and wrapped her arms around them. "You'd have to understand my background for this to make any sense, Joshua. I was raised in a very cloistered environment. I went to a private school through high school. Then I went to a small women's college. I was shy, and though I dated a little, I really didn't know much about men. I got my degree in child development...."

"That makes sense."

Maggie smiled a little. "And then I taught in an expensive preschool for gifted children. I was living at home. The only social contacts I had were with men my father knew. My father was a wonderful man, but he was also very old-fashioned. I was the light of his life. In another age he would have selected a man for me and told me to marry him. In this enlightened time, he only selected the man and then manipulated us until James and I were engaged."

"It's the twentieth century. You couldn't have been too unwilling."

"I wasn't. James was...is," she amended, "a handsome, clever man. I convinced myself that he would be an ideal husband."

Joshua's face was still carefully blank. "How long were you engaged?"

"Longer than either James or my father thought we should be. I just couldn't make myself set the date."

"Why not?"

Maggie lifted a tentative hand to stroke Joshua's face. He didn't move. "I thought there should be more. James was good to me, very protective and solicitous, but there was no passion between us. I finally told him, and he seemed immensely relieved that I was only worried about such a minor thing. He set out to prove how wrong I was."

"You don't have to go on." Joshua's voice was not as controlled as his features. Maggie heard the lapse.

"I think I do. Evidently it matters to you." She continued to stroke his face. "We only made love one time, Joshua. James convinced me that I would realize what passion there could be if I'd only let him take me to bed. It backfired. Afterward I couldn't abide having him touch me."

"Did you break the engagement?"

She shook her head. "No. I thought I was the problem, not James. He didn't seem to care if I was cold to him. He still wanted to marry me. I thought I'd never find another man that patient and understanding."

"And so you're still engaged."

Maggie shrugged. "I've been away now for seven months. James could be married, for all I know. I hope he is."

"You can say that now, in the heat of the moment. But later, Maggie, how will you feel when you see him again?" Joshua tried to stand. "You're in no shape to be making decisions right now."

"I'm not making decisions. I've made my decision." Her fingers dug into his arm, pulling him back to her. "Love me, Joshua. Doesn't last night mean anything to you? Can you throw away what we have together so easily?"

He couldn't. The rational psychologist disappeared, to be replaced by the man who loved this woman more than he loved anything in the world. He opened his arms and she was in them. Each part of their bodies joined in agonized pursuit of fulfillment. His mouth captured hers as his hands undressed her, making short work of the shirt and jeans that she wore. She undressed him, glorying in the sleek, strong lines of his body. Maggie took the lead, showing Joshua with her lips and her hands what he meant to her. She possessed him in a way that no one else ever had, seeking all the places of his body that would give him pleasure.

Maggie loved Joshua with abandon. Joshua loved Maggie with desperation. When they both hovered on the brink of insanity, Maggie moved on top of him and with a slow, sure thrust of her hips, brought him inside to fill her completely. He watched in fascinated agony as, kneeling above him, she moved against his thighs. The hot sweetness pouring through his body blended with the vision of her, head thrown back and eyes closed in ecstasy as she gave him everything she had inside her.

Her breasts filled his hands, his body filled her emptiness. Each thrust, each twist was a new commitment. "Maggie," he moaned.

Triumphantly, she moved one more time, sending them both to the place where only lovers can go. She collapsed against his chest and he held her, burying his face in her hair.

"No matter what, Joshua. Tell me nothing else matters."

"I'll always love you."

"Nothing else matters."

As much as he wanted to agree, he could only kiss her and hope that she was right.

They were ten minutes late for their appointment at the police station. Skeeter had been asked to come, too, since he had taken such an active part in the search for Maggie's attacker. With Sam's permission Antoinette Deveraux was also to be there. In the car as they traveled to the station Maggie was silent, lost in her memories.

Sam ushered them into a quiet office, probably the only one in the low-slung, sprawling building. The police chief was there and two men in plain clothes who were introduced only by their last names. No reason was given for their presence. Antoinette arrived last, going to both Maggie and Joshua for a quick hug before she settled in a chair against the wall.

Sam made Maggie comfortable, asking her if she would like something to drink. She declined, obviously ill at ease.

"Maggie, are you nervous?"

Joshua had taken a chair next to Maggie's, and he put his hand over hers at Sam's words.

Maggie nodded. "Yes. This isn't going to be easy to tell." For a moment she turned to Joshua. "I couldn't bear to tell this story more than once. Do you understand?"

"Of course." He squeezed her hand, and then withdrew his own. Her story was something that he couldn't help her with. He knew instinctively that his touch was going to distract her. She had to withdraw in order to immerse herself in the memories that had been so long denied.

"Whenever you're ready, Maggie. I'm going to turn on the tape recorder now." Sam's voice was calm. They waited.

Maggie closed her eyes. "My name is Mary Margaret O'Hanlon. I'm twenty-five." She stopped and a tiny smile pulled at her mouth. "Just barely. My birthday was May fifteenth. I'm the only daughter of Chester Gilbert O'Hanlon who was killed by a man named Bob Claiborne."

Joshua saw the two men in plain clothes look at each other and pass a silent, mysterious message.

Maggie opened her eyes. "I'm not sure how much of my history you want. Shall I get right to the kidnapping?"

Sam and the two men conferred as Joshua tensed at her words. "Kidnapping?" His voice was hoarse.

"Be quiet, Josh. Let her tell it her own way. Maggie, can you give us some details about your life? Just a few." Sam smiled encouragingly at her.

Maggie shut her eyes. "I grew up in Palm Beach. We lived in an estate on the water in a Spanish-style stucco house. My mother died when I was six. I went to school at Our Lady of the Americas Academy for Girls and later to Rollins College." She smiled a little. "I had a German shepherd named Trixie who would cheerfully eat anyone she didn't know, and I had countless parakeets. They drove my father crazy. Once I taught one of them to say, 'Chester is a spoilsport,' and

I let it loose at a cocktail party my father was having. I was eleven, I think.''

"That's good, Maggie. I know this part isn't going to be fun, but we're ready to hear about the kidnapping."

She was silent for a moment, gathering her strength. Joshua wanted to help her, but he could only wait.

"From the time I was a little girl, the possibility of a kidnapping was just something I learned to live with. We had strict security at home, and the nice man who drove me to and from school always carried a gun. If you grow up in Palm Beach, you're always aware of the danger connected with your status. The police department there even has a special 'code red' signal so that if there's a kidnapping attempt, all three bridges to the mainland go up and squad cars cut the coastal road.

"As an adult, I hated the restrictions on my activities. I rebelled, refusing to let my father hire a bodyguard for me. As a concession to his fears, I agreed to learn how to shoot a pistol and I promised to carry one with me if I was out at night by myself.

"My father heard of a man, Bob Claiborne. ." She stopped for a moment and swallowed hard. "He lived in West Palm Beach and he specialized in teaching women to shoot to defend themselves. My father had him checked out. Bob Claiborne was an ex-policeman, and as far as my father knew, an upstanding member of the community. Daddy didn't check far enough."

Maggie opened her eyes. "Can I have a glass of water, please?" Joshua knew she was fighting tears.

Sam got her water from the cooler by the door and handed it to her silently.

"Thank you." She sipped as she talked. "I only went to the firing range to please my father. On the last evening of the training, I asked my father to come and watch me shoot. I thought it would relieve his fears. I had become very good with a pistol. Bob said I was his star pupil. My father said he'd come if he could.

"When I got there, no one else was practicing, which seemed strange, but I didn't give it too much thought. I waited for my father, but he didn't come, so Bob said we should get on with the lesson. I shot for a while, and Bob complimented me on everything I had learned. He seemed jumpy, but I really didn't pay much attention because I was so busy trying to do my best."

She had been staring into space, but now she turned her gaze to Sam. "I never thought I'd need to shoot a person. I liked shooting at targets, though. I felt like I was in a penny arcade."

"I understand." Sam nodded at her to continue.

"Bob told me that he had a certificate for me in the back room. I was proud of my accomplishment, and I wanted to show it to my father since he hadn't been able to come. I followed Bob into the back room to get the certificate. He told me to sign my name at the bottom, and when I bent over the desk, he hit me in the back of the head."

She drew a deep breath. "The blow only stunned me. My hair was very long and I was wearing it in a heavy knot on my neck. It cushioned the blow, I guess. I fell, and Bob grabbed my hands and tied them. I tried to fight and he hit me again, but it still didn't knock me out. I began to scream.

"Before he could gag and finish tying me, my father came charging into the room. He fought with Bob." Maggie put her head in her hands. Joshua ached to touch her.

"Bob hit my father with his gun. Then he hit him again. Daddy fell to the floor. He was so pale, and there was blood flowing hard from a gash on his face. I tried to reach him, but Bob hit me again and then I passed out."

Joshua watched as Maggie's shoulders shook with big gulping sobs. He reached to comfort her, but Sam shook his head in warning. Joshua restrained himself, willing her to finish so that he could take her in his arms and soothe her.

Finally she calmed enough to go on. "When I came to, I was in terrible pain. My body was one excruciating cramp and I couldn't move. Later I found out that I was in the trunk of a car, but at the time I didn't know where I was. For a long time I thought I had been buried alive. I could hardly breathe. I kept passing out, coming to, passing out."

"Damn!"

"Joshua, please try to control yourself." Sam's voice was stern. "Go on, Maggie."

"Once I woke up and I was in a motel room. Bob was there and a woman, too. The woman was rubbing my hands and legs to restore my circulation. I was still gagged, but they told me if I didn't try to move off the bed, they'd leave me untied for a while. I was still in terrible pain. I couldn't have moved, anyway. Later the woman took me to the bathroom, but they didn't feed me or give me anything to drink. I guess they were afraid if they took off the gag, I'd scream."

"Do you have any idea where you were? Can you remember anything about the room?" One of the men in plain clothes was addressing Maggie.

She shook her head. "They tied me up again, looser this time, and I fell asleep. I thought the worst was over, but later Bob carried me out to the car and put me in the trunk again." Tears rolled down her cheeks. "He apologized to me. Isn't that funny? He even put a pillow under my head." Her voice broke.

"I don't remember much else about the trip except that I thought I had descended into hell. Every once in a while I'd feel a rush of fresh air and I knew that they had parked somewhere and opened the trunk. Once I heard voices. The woman said, 'She's not going to make it like this,' and Bob said, 'She has to. There's no other way.'

"When I came to again, I was in a room. It was tiny and dark. There was only one window and hardly any light could filter through it. Bob and another man were standing over my bed.'' She stopped and sipped more water. "The other man was Stoney Cox. The woman came in and made me drink something. I vomited and Stoney hit me. Bob tried to stop him, but Stoney enjoyed inflicting pain. He got plenty of chances.'' The hand holding the cup trembled, and she set it down.

"Stoney told me that if I didn't cooperate, he'd kill me with his bare hands. Then they told me that they wanted me to make a tape to send to my father. I couldn't understand that. Bob had killed my father, but when I said that, Stoney hit me again. Stoney said, 'If your old man's dead, we'll send the tape to that pretty boyfriend of yours, but you're going to make the tape.' ''

"And did you?"

Maggie nodded.

Sam leaned forward in his chair. "What did it say?"

"This is Mary Margaret O'Hanlon. I'm safe and well. Please do as you're told and I will remain that way."

The two men in plain clothes nodded at each other.

"Then what happened?"

"A lot of the rest is hazy. They gave me sleeping pills, lots of them, and I slept. At first when I woke up, Bob and the woman were still there, but later they were gone and I was alone with Stoney."

"For how long?"

Maggie shrugged. "A century. I hardly saw him at the beginning. He'd come into the room in the evening, put a plate of food on the bed and take off my gag. Then he'd feed me big mouthfuls as fast as he could stuff it in, and he'd laugh if I choked. Afterward he'd pick me up and carry me to the bathroom. I wasn't allowed any privacy even then. He'd taunt me, and I'd cry."

Joshua was filled with a murderous rage that he hadn't even known he was capable of. For the first time in his life he understood the word "hate."

Maggie went on. "I was always thirsty. I hardly got anything to drink, and I was so weak from the pills and being tied that I could hardly move. One night Stoney came into the room in a rage. He started to call me names, awful names. He said that Bob and the woman who had been with him had been killed trying to get my ransom money. He was furious. He began to hit me. He called me a lying whore and a no-good slut.

"I couldn't resist, but I tried. The more I fought, the more violent he became. Finally I realized what he was going to do." Maggie stopped and turned to Joshua for support.

The expression in his eyes gave her the courage to go on. "He tried to rape me. I knew if I continued to fight him, he'd kill me. I went limp and that seemed to enrage him even more. He hit me over and over again, but he couldn't . . . he couldn't . . ."

"It's all right, Maggie." Joshua reached for her hand. Even if his interference stopped the flood of memories, he didn't care.

She grasped his hand as if it were a lifeline. "After that, he got more and more violent. He was drinking a lot. He'd come into my room and threaten me, call me names. He hated women. He'd ramble on and on. He told me there was a man who was murdering prostitutes and somebody ought to give him a medal. One night he came in with some horrible gaudy clothes and told me to put them on. He smeared makeup on my face and tied a long scarf around my neck. He told me the man who was killing the prostitutes strangled them with a scarf just like that one. He kept tightening the knot until I could hardly breathe. Then he told me he was going to get me some customers."

Maggie watched the emotions on Joshua's face. "It was just a horrible game he was playing with me, but I was frantic. When he retied me, he was so drunk that he didn't get the ropes as tight as usual.

"When he left the room I started to work the ropes loose. It seemed to take forever, but I managed. The scarf wouldn't come off, though. I could barely move once I was free. My legs felt like they were on fire, but I stumbled out of the room. I made it to the front door and down the sidewalk when I heard a car. I hid behind a tree. The car stopped in front of the house, and Stoney Cox got out. When he went inside, I started to run, but I was too weak. I kept falling down.

"The street was dark and it was drizzling rain. It was cold, too, and I kept slipping on the wet sidewalk. No one was around. Once I tried to hide in a yard but the people inside started yelling and a dog came after me. By then Stoney was looking for me. He saw me and I started to run. I'll never know where the strength came from, but I saw streetlights in front of me, and somehow I was running. I was getting close, but Stoney was gaining on me. I could hear him breathing hard behind me and I screamed. Then everything went black."

The room was silent. Maggie continued to grip Joshua's hand and look into his eyes. "And then there was Joshua."

"My God, Maggie. What you've endured." He opened his arms, and in one fierce movement she was on his lap held against his chest.

The police chief was speaking. "What do you think, gentlemen?"

"Parts of her story match what we know to be true. She resembles our photographs, but she's not a dead ringer. She's thinner, her hair's different and so's the nose. We're going to need a positive identification."

Sam stood. "Can we finish the discussion outside and give the lady a chance to catch her breath?"

The men in plain clothes ignored him. "It's time to bring in O'Hanlon himself."

Maggie had wrapped her arms around Joshua's neck, and he was murmuring soothing words to her. Only slowly did the men's conversation reach her. "O'Hanlon?"

Sam shot the men a look that commanded them both to be silent. He came over to Maggie and Joshua and squatted beside them. "Maggie. Are you ready for some good news?"

She nodded, afraid to answer out loud.

"When Mary Margaret O'Hanlon was kidnapped, her father was attacked and beaten by the kidnapper. But he wasn't killed, just knocked unconscious. Chester O'Hanlon is alive."

Maggie just stared at Sam. "Stoney Cox told me that my father was dead. He used to scream it at me. Over and over..."

"It was just another way to torment you. Chester O'Hanlon is alive."

Maggie brought her fist to her mouth, trying to swallow the tears that threatened again. "I can't believe it," she whispered.

"O'Hanlon's daughter was the one who was thought to be dead. You see, the police were notified of the kidnapping, against the kidnappers' orders. When Claiborne went to pick up the ransom, he had a woman with him. The police thought it was Mary Margaret. He had promised to drop her off somewhere after he got the ransom. The police were trailing him, but he got suspicious and started driving at a high speed. He crashed into the side rail of a bridge and went over the side. Both Claiborne and his passenger were killed."

"They must have gone after the bodies. Couldn't they tell it wasn't Mary Margaret?" Joshua couldn't believe the police would be that incompetent.

"The ransom was dropped off on one of the Keys. The bridge they were on was a huge monster. The car burst into flames when it hit the side and fell hundreds of feet before it even hit the water. It took days to recover the car. What the flames didn't get, the sharks finished." Sam saw Maggie pale. "I'm sorry."

"But my father..."

"Chester O'Hanlon is a lost and bitter man." One of the men in plain clothes came up to stand beside her. "We haven't told him about you yet. If you're not who you say you are, we want to spare him."

Maggie pushed away from Joshua and stood to face the man. "Just who are you?"

"We're with the FBI."

Maggie examined him. "You could fingerprint me."

"Mary Margaret O'Hanlon had no fingerprints on record."

"Oh, yes, she did. You'll find a complete set in my elementary school scrapbook. They were made when I was in sixth grade. I was a safety patrol and all of us were fingerprinted. I saved them. Tell Rosie to look on the top shelf of my closet, under the box with my swim team trophies in it."

"Who is Rosie?"

"Our housekeeper."

Something passed over the man's face. He reached out to grasp Maggie's hand. "Miss O'Hanlon, I think you can expect a visit from your father tonight."

The police chief intervened. "Are you sure she's..."

"I've seen the trophies myself. Never did get as far as looking through the scrapbook. Rosie was furious that I was poking around in this young woman's closet."

"Please, can I call him now?" Maggie was trembling with excitement, and Joshua put his arms around her to steady her.

"I think, for his sake, that the news should be broken to him gently, Miss O'Hanlon. I'd like to send one of our agents to prepare him."

Maggie nodded reluctantly. "Perhaps that would be best."

"Where are you going to be, Maggie?" Sam asked.

She turned. "Joshua?"

"We'll go to my place and wait."

"Yes. That's a good idea."

"Miss O'Hanlon, if you're feeling up to it, we have some pictures we'd like you to look at. We still don't know the identity of the woman who was with Bob Claiborne."

"I'll be glad to. Anything to get this over with." She followed the FBI man to the door. Skeeter, who had been sitting quietly throughout her entire explanation, stood and put his hand on her shoulder.

"You're a very special lady," he said, bending to kiss her on the cheek.

"And you're my very special friend." She hugged him quickly and then turned to Antoinette. "If it hadn't been for all your help, I might never have remembered."

"You did it, Maggie. I just supported your effort." The two women embraced. "Would you like me to come with you now?" Maggie nodded and together they followed the man out the door

The police chief and the other FBI man went into another office and Skeeter, Sam and Joshua were left alone.

"Are you all right, Joshua?" Skeeter's voice showed his concern.

Joshua nodded. "The amazing thing is that Maggie is all right. After everything."

"She's one gutsy woman." Sam looked sheepish for a moment. "I'm waiting."

"For what? My 'I told you so'? Forget it. You saved my life today. That's enough to keep you from eating crow."

"Why did you get out of that van when you saw Cox?" Sam asked, genuinely curious that his friend would do something so irrational.

"All I could think about was walking into that Laundromat to see him pointing a gun at Maggie. I didn't even know I was out of the van. I guess I was going to strangle him."

"I'm glad you chose the line of work you did. You'd make a lousy policeman."

"With impulses like that, I make a lousy psychologist."

"So you're human. Now maybe you'll understand some of your patients a little better." Sam clapped him on the back.

"And you, Sam," Skeeter said. "What made you change your mind and trust Maggie enough to follow her to Cox's place?"

"I don't know. I guess I just sensed how genuine her emotions were. She got angry at me a couple of times in the car, and then when she started remembering bits and pieces of her past, I could see how frightened she was. I knew it wasn't an act."

"I'm still having trouble absorbing all this," Joshua admitted. "There's a lot I don't understand."

"Like what?" Sam asked.

"Why did Maggie's father think she needed a bodyguard? Why was she so protected?"

"If you lived in Florida, you'd understand. O'Hanlon owns half the state."

"Maggie said he was in real estate."

"O'Hanlon *is* real estate. He has an empire. Maggie is the heiress to a fortune."

Joshua was silent, his face a brooding mask.

Skeeter understood. "Look, Josh. Just because she's rich, doesn't mean she's anything like Daphne."

"No." Joshua's voice was expressionless. "Daphne was never that rich."

"You know that's not what I meant." Skeeter turned to Sam, trying to change the subject. "I've got a question of my own. Why do you suppose Cox kept her so long after the first ransom attempt went astray?"

"I guess we'll never know, but I have a pretty good guess. Cox was a sadist. He wanted Chester O'Hanlon to think his daughter was dead. I imagine he realized that when O'Hanlon finally found out she was still alive, he'd be willing to pay any price, agree to any conditions Cox made. In the meantime, he had Maggie there to torment."

Joshua made a small sound of pain.

"Then why did he leave her for dead in a vacant lot?" Skeeter asked, his hand on Joshua's shoulder to comfort him.

Sam shrugged. "Maggie said he was drunk. We know he almost killed her that night. By the time he probably realized what he had done, he didn't have any choices. He couldn't carry her back to the house and risk getting caught. Maybe he went back to get her later and she'd already been found. Or maybe he thought she was dead and he wouldn't be able to ransom her anymore."

"And when she didn't die? The papers were full of it."

"He couldn't get to her. She was in the hospital in intensive care and then on a locked psychiatric unit. He was a persistent devil, though. We found out this afternoon that he's been working as an orderly on the late-night shift. I imagine he was trying to get to her even then."

Joshua's voice was bitter. "He did get to her. Nobody would believe it, though. We all thought she couldn't tell her nightmares from reality. Do you know how many times she told me a man had come into her room and tried to smother her? Do you know how many times I ignored her?"

"Don't be too hard on yourself. Even though you didn't believe her, you probably saved her life by getting her out of the hospital. Since then it's just been a game of cat and mouse with Cox trying to find her again to kill her."

"The bastard!" Joshua's voice broke.

"He's dead now, Josh. May he burn in hell."

Joshua could not reply.

Chapter 12

Maggie and Joshua fully expected to find his apartment in the confused state it had been left in. Instead they discovered that Mrs. Le-Grand had been in to clean and straighten it.

"It's good to be home," Maggie said tentatively. Joshua had been comforting, but they had spoken little since leaving the police station.

"Yes." Joshua was strangely affected by her words. "Home." Where was home for Mary Margaret O'Hanlon? "Can I get you something to eat? I think I have some cheese. I can make you a..."

"Joshua?" Maggie touched his arm. "I have to know something." He waited quietly for her question.

"Does anything that happened to me make a difference to you? I know that some of it was sordid." She was examining her shoe.

"Make a difference to me?"

She lifted her eyes. "I was never raped, but I know some of the other things that happened were pretty horrible. Does that make a difference to you?"

"Make a difference to me?" He swept her into his arms. "Of course it makes a difference. I realize, more than ever, how precious you are and how tenuous life can be." His lips sought her hair. "It's God's own miracle that you're alive."

They kissed, but Joshua was the first to pull away. "I'll go make those sandwiches."

Maggie put her hand back on his arm. "Then what's wrong? Tell me why you're backing away. If it's not what happened to me, what is it?"

"Not now. Let's eat, then we can talk."

Her eyes began to sparkle with anger. "No! Tell me now. I won't be coddled and led around like one of my four-year-olds. What's wrong?" She followed Joshua into the kitchen, standing firmly in front of the refrigerator.

"I don't want to discuss it now, Maggie. You have your father's arrival to look forward to. Let's not mar it with an argument."

"Now!"

"Are you used to getting what you want?"

She had been ready to give him a list of reasons why they needed to clear the air, but his question stopped her. "Pardon me?"

"Are you used to getting what you want? Has everyone always kowtowed to you? I'm not going to."

"Of course you won't. You're a stubborn, bullheaded renegade who does exactly what he pleases. I'll have to work hard to even make myself heard once we're married." She wondered at the look of pain that crossed his features. An icy chill stabbed through the region of her heart. "Or don't you want to marry me?"

"This isn't the right time to talk about marriage."

She didn't understand. "Don't you want me anymore?" she asked in a soft voice.

Joshua closed his eyes to block out the sight of Maggie's sorrow. "Only a fool wouldn't want you, sweetheart. But I'm not a big enough fool to believe that there's an automatic happily-ever-after waiting around the corner for us." He felt her hands on his shoulders.

"I love you."

It took more strength than he knew he possessed to open his eyes and answer her. "You love what I've been to you. But you may not need what I can give anymore. You may need someone who can fit effortlessly into your life, and I never will. My life has always been lived in a different place from yours, Maggie."

"I see." Maggie dropped her hands. "So it comes down to trust again, doesn't it?" She laughed a little, the sound falling flat in the still room. "Funny, isn't it. When you thought I was a prostitute, you grew to accept it. But you can't forgive me for being rich. In your eyes I've been eaten away by the disease of my father's fortune, and you don't want anything to do with me now that you know." She stepped away.

"It's not that simple."

"Oh, I think it is."

Joshua shook his head. "No one can survive what you've survived in the past months without feeling tremendous emotional stress. You've got to have a chance to consider what you want. You've got to be sure."

"You really don't understand, do you?" Maggie stepped back another pace. "You're the one who has to be sure. You've always been the one, Joshua. Right from the beginning."

"Maggie..."

She lifted her chin but her eyes were filled with tears. "You can't forgive me for being rich. Well, there are some things I can't forgive, either. I can't forgive being blamed for what I'm not. I won't put up with it again. Not ever. I'm not a selfish little rich girl like your ex-wife. I'm the Maggie you've always known. Nothing more and nothing less." She stepped around him to leave the kitchen.

"Where are you going?"

"To my apartment to pack. Don't worry, I won't leave without saying goodbye. You'll know when you're finally rid of me."

The hurt he knew she was feeling blocked the sting of her words. "Don't leave with this bitterness between us. You have to have time," he said gently.

She stopped and turned at the door. "No, you need time. I need you. And that's one thing you've never been willing to give me."

Chester O'Hanlon was a heavyset man of average height. He had Maggie's muted brown hair, and he had blue eyes that Joshua imagined had once been as bright as hers. He arrived shortly before midnight accompanied by a tall, dark man dressed impeccably in an expensive silk suit and one of the FBI men who had questioned Maggie earlier.

"Where's my daughter?"

Joshua knew immediately why Chester O'Hanlon had gotten as far in the world as he had. Power sat comfortably like a visible mantle on his shoulders. "She's across the hall. Come in. I'll tell her you're here." Joshua stepped aside and allowed the men to enter his apartment.

Joshua had checked on Maggie an hour before. She had fallen asleep, tears still wet on her cheeks. Never in his entire life had he felt so torn to pieces. No matter what he had told her, he could not bear to have her leave. He had wanted to scoop her up in his arms and forget his fears. He had wanted to tell her that he believed they could make marriage work, that he believed in the depth of her feelings for him. He wanted to tell her that her father's money didn't matter, the differences in their backgrounds didn't matter, her fiancé didn't matter.

Instead he had stood by her bedside and the words had sickened and died within him.

Now he stood by her bed again. "Maggie?"

"Joshua?" She stretched, and for a second she smiled. Then she remembered what was between them and her smile faded. "What is it?"

"Your father is here."

She stood on shaky legs, combing her fingers through her curls and straightening her dress. "Do I look all right?"

"Beautiful."

She crossed the room, and Joshua followed at a discreet distance. He watched her drift across the hallway to stand in the doorway that he had left open. "Daddy?"

Then she was being held in Chester O'Hanlon's arms and both of them were crying. Joshua felt tears run down his own cheeks.

It was later, after she had shared bits and pieces of her story with her father and listened to his version, that she thought to introduce Joshua. She stood, taking his arm as casually as she could. "Daddy, this is Joshua Martane, the man who's helped me so much. Joshua, this is my father, Chester O'Hanlon." She turned to face the man in the silk suit. "And this is James Darwin."

"I wondered if you'd noticed me at all," James said smoothly. He stood to shake Joshua's hand and then held out his arms to Maggie. "Now don't I get a hug and a kiss? I've suffered, too, you know."

Joshua sensed Maggie's confusion. With steely determination he loosened her grip on his arm. She went to James and gave him a kiss on the cheek. Joshua turned away, unable to watch. "Can I offer you something to drink, Mr. O'Hanlon?"

"Nothing. I just want to take my daughter home."

James was pulling Maggie toward the doorway. "If you don't mind," he explained boyishly, "Maggie and I would like a moment of privacy."

The FBI man got up to leave, too. "Well, it's all settled, then," he said. "I'll wait outside." He shook Joshua's hand and then disappeared through the door.

"Martane?"

"Yes, Mr. O'Hanlon." Joshua faced Maggie's father, waiting for him to speak. The signs were all there. Joshua understood that he was about to hear a lecture.

"The FBI briefed me on everything pertinent to Maggie's case. I understand that you and she have been very close."

"That's right."

"Are you in love with my daughter?"

It was the one question that was easy to answer. "Yes."

"Do you also know that she's engaged to be married?"

"I do."

"What are your intentions?"

His intentions? Could the confused knot of objectivity and hot emotions inside him be called intentions? Joshua had never been less sure of his intentions in his life.

Chester O'Hanlon narrowed his eyes. He seemed to sense Joshua's struggle. He was a man who would use almost anything to get what he wanted. "What do you have to offer her, Martane?" He didn't wait for an answer. "Mary Margaret has always had everything she's ever desired. She's not ready for a different life. She could never be happy married to you," Mr. O'Hanlon said decisively.

Joshua had heard the same words before. Years before, Daphne's father had spoken them with far more kindness and consideration. Daphne's father had been correct.

"I don't want you to think I'm ungrateful," Mr. O'Hanlon continued. "But I'll fight for what's right for my daughter and I won't let gratitude stand in the way. I want her to be happy. She's the most important thing in my life."

Joshua smiled bitterly. "Then we have something in common, don't we?"

Surprised, Chester O'Hanlon hesitated.

"Daddy." Maggie stood in the doorway alone, her eyes focused solely on Joshua.

"Are you ready to leave? I can't get you home soon enough to suit me," Chester O'Hanlon said.

Maggie watched the expression on Joshua's face. It gave nothing away. Regret tore through her. Regret that she hadn't been been able to make him love her enough, regret that he was going to watch her walk out of his life without a protest, regret that she would always love him. She regretted the last most of all.

She wanted to stay, to force him to see the truth, but she knew that staying would be the weakest path. This was Joshua's battle. She could not fight it for him. And she would not spend the rest of her life trying to make him trust her love. Caught in her pain, she didn't see Joshua shake his head. She didn't see the expression on his face that proclaimed the end of the most important struggle of his life.

"She's not going anywhere, O'Hanlon." The words were an explosion in the quiet room. Maggie watched Joshua walk slowly to the doorway and hold out his hand. "She's going to stay here and marry me as soon as we can make the arrangements."

They were the words Maggie had least expected to hear. She had gathered all the inner resources she had developed over the past months to help her get through the next terrible moments. But nothing she had learned about courage and survival and patience could help her now. Maggie shut her eyes but the tears spilled out to make sparkling diamonds on her lashes.

"Like hell she is!" Mr. O'Hanlon exploded. "Look at her. You're taking advantage of her confusion. How dare you make demands on her after what she's been through. Mary Margaret, you've got to have time at home to think about this."

"This is between your daughter and me," Joshua said quietly.

No matter how much she loved Joshua, Maggie knew that there were questions that had to be answered. Only then could she be sure. "You

know I'm emotionally overwrought right now, don't you?'' she asked
him, her eyes still tightly shut.

"I do."

"And you know that you're trying to take advantage of my feelings
just like my father says?"

"No question about it."

"And you know that my father is as rich as King Midas and I've always done exactly what I wanted?"

Joshua laughed softly.

"And you know that I can be strong-willed and difficult to live with
sometimes? Almost as difficult as you."

"Open your eyes, Maggie."

She did, and found his. "And you know that there are never any
guarantees?" she whispered.

"Yes, there are," he said. "I can guarantee that I'll always love you.
I can guarantee that from now on I'll trust your love for me. I can
guarantee that I'll spend the rest of my life trying to make you happy.
The rest will be up to fate." Joshua continued to hold his hand out to
her.

Maggie extended hers and their fingertips touched. "And will you
give me all of you, Joshua? The good and the bad? I want it all."

"All of me. Even the parts I hadn't known existed." He pulled her
tightly against him, and for a moment they forgot about Mr. O'Hanlon's presence, lost in a kiss that went on and on.

"Well, I'll be damned." Mr. O'Hanlon's voice had lost some of its
fury. "You do love him, don't you?"

"Yes."

"What about James?"

Maggie turned to face her father, still held securely in Joshua's arms.
"I told James out in the hallway that our engagement has ended. He's
in the car sulking. I think he's lamenting a lost empire."

Chester O'Hanlon frowned. "He would have been good to you."

"That's a poor substitute for love."

He tried one more time. "At least think about it overnight. I've got
a suite over on St. Charles. Come back with me and we'll talk."

"I'll be there later. Right now I need to be alone with Joshua. You
can start making a list of guests for my wedding." Maggie broke from
Joshua's grasp and went to her father. "I love you, Daddy. I couldn't
even remember who I was because I thought you'd been killed and the
memory was too terrible, but I'm not your little girl anymore. I'm a
woman, and I know what I want."

"And you want him." Mr. O'Hanlon nodded to Joshua.

"That's right."

He sighed and his fingers flexed. His struggle was visible. "It seems that I've lost you again." His voice cracked on the last word.

"Perhaps you've lost something, but you've gained something, too," Maggie said softly. "I think you'll come to understand that eventually."

Mr. O'Hanlon turned toward the door and then seemed to think better of it. He turned back to Joshua and nodded his goodbye.

Then Joshua and Maggie were alone.

He turned her to face him, drinking in the sight of her without barriers between them. He lifted his hand and brushed her curls, then he inched her face closer to his, taking his time to find her mouth. He heard her draw in a breath and he saw her eyelids close. Then there was only the taste and sensation of her lips as he brushed them repeatedly with his, finally entering them with his tongue, which seemed, suddenly, to have a life of its own. He had only wanted to seal his words, not begin an avalanche. They had to talk. He had to explain.

Still, he couldn't pull away. His intentions were the best, but Maggie's body was welded, now, to his. Her arms had crept around his back, and he could feel the sensuous movement of her hips against his thighs. He was a man who had walked the line between rationality and emotion for too long, a man who had tried to follow his head when his heart cried out for a different road. What caution still existed inside him was evaporating in the heat their bodies made together.

"Love me, Joshua."

"I do, Maggie."

"Show me." Her dress rustled against his legs, which were bare below the shorts he wore. He could feel her breasts under the sheer cotton, her nipples rigid beneath their covering. They repeatedly brushed his chest. He ached to feel her skin against his. Sensing his desire, she moved away just far enough to watch his face as she unbuttoned tiny pearl buttons and let the dress drop to the floor. In a minute she was naked.

Her body was a marvel of symmetry and softness. He wanted to lose himself in it forever. "Maggie, my love. I have to explain. Everything has to be right between us." His words were a hoarse plea. He could not take his eyes off her.

"Let no words come between us, Joshua."

He pulled her close and he felt her fingers unsnap the catch of his shorts. He tugged off his shirt, and they melted together. He lifted her and she wrapped her legs around him. His hands traveled her body. Even in his white-hot anguish to join, he wanted it to be perfect for her. It was Maggie who finally made them one. She was impatient for all of him, more than ready to share herself. At the feel of his body in hers, she shook with a release so profound that it defied all logic.

Joshua carried her to his bed, and whispering endearments, he came to her again. He watched her face as he led her to another, different place, a place gained by slow inches and subtle, loving torture. When she reached the glorious peak, he did, too. Maggie cried his name and he felt tears wet his cheeks. He gathered her against him and felt her heart beat. They rested, wrapped tightly in each other's arms.

Later he felt her stir and reluctantly he let her go. She moved only inches. "Are you awake?" she whispered.

"Just," he admitted, lifting his head to kiss her.

"Do you still want to talk?"

"No, but we should." He propped his head on his elbow and traced designs over her shoulders and around her breasts. In fascination he watched the immediate transformation that occurred. "You're so incredibly responsive," he murmured, his mouth seeking the evidence of her awakening desire.

"If you keep that up, we aren't going to have that talk." She didn't sound concerned.

With a sigh, he lifted his head. "You've forgiven me, I know. Still, I'd like you to understand what was driving me."

"You were afraid."

He sighed again, tilting his head to meet her gaze.

"I don't think that it's easy to be you, Joshua. You have such high ideals. You want to be everything to everybody. It's the minister that's still in you. It's been hard for you to admit you have needs. I think I frightened you because I understood that."

He smiled, brushing her hair back from her forehead. "Yes. But it's even simpler than that, really. I wanted you so much that when I finally had you, I was afraid I'd find out you weren't real."

She puckered her forehead. "I am terribly real. I have a real Irish temper and a crooked nose and I'm addicted to old Orson Welles movies."

"And you love me."

"With everything inside me."

"That's all that matters."

"I'm also rich."

"I can live with your money. It's not your fault you were born with a handicap." He avoided the playful poke of her fist.

"And I can live with your pride and your arrogance. But, Joshua, I don't intend to lean on you. This marriage is going to be a partnership."

"No more minister. No more psychologist. No more bodyguard. Just a man who needs his woman." He bent to find her mouth for a long, slow kiss. "And I do need you, Maggie. More than I'll ever be able to show you."

"I think you should try, anyway," she said, her hands threading through his hair.

With a humid caress, the New Orleans summer night closed softly around them, enveloping them in the dark protection that is a gift to all lovers.

Epilogue

In the beginning there was nothing. An absence of form and sound. An absence of pain and fear.

Then there was the voice.

"Joshua. Joshua, wake up." Maggie opened her eyes and rolled over, contacting his hard, unyielding body with her own. "Joshua, it's your turn to get up with her."

"I was hoping you wouldn't remember."

"I keep a mental list. This is the two hundred and tenth time she's awakened me from a sound sleep. I got up for number two hundred and nine."

"If I'd known the baby was going to inherit your Irish temper, Mary Margaret Martane, I'd have thought twice about conceiving her." Joshua pulled Maggie against him so that she fitted perfectly in the curve of his body. He shut his eyes again. "Do you suppose if we ignore her, she'll forget she wants company?"

A loud wail from the other room answered his question. Joshua buried his face in Maggie's abundant curls and then pushed himself into a sitting position.

Maggie lay with her hands propped under her head as she waited for Joshua to bring three-month-old Bridget Marie in to be nursed. Tiny fingers of light announced the arrival of dawn. As she watched, the big old room turned rosy and the lace curtains at the tall windows blew gently with a cool breeze.

"I love waking up in this house," Maggie told Joshua as he came into the room carrying his daughter, football-style, in front of him. "I love waking up with you."

"Well, you're getting plenty of chances these days." Joshua nuzzled Bridget's neck before he passed her, with noticeable reluctance, to her mother.

Maggie settled back against the walnut headboard and propped Bridget's head on one arm. In a moment, the little girl was hungrily devouring her early-morning breakfast.

"For all the years I lived in this house," Joshua said, watching them, "it never seemed so much like home."

When Joshua and Maggie had discovered that they were expecting a baby, they had decided to renovate Joshua's boyhood home in the Irish Channel, which he had held as rental property since his mother's death. The house, chopped into apartments years before, had taken extensive work but had yielded to loving care and skilled workmanship. Now it was a gracious example of what patience and attention to detail could do.

The neighborhood was filled with houses just like it, some under renovation, some waiting for the right owner to see their potential. Maggie and Joshua felt that they were at the forefront of a private urban renewal project that would help beautify the city they loved.

"I can't believe I start back to work today," Maggie said, switching Bridget to her other breast.

"I can't wait to have you there." Joshua traced a line up the side of Maggie's arm with his index finger. Then he slid closer and put his arm around her shoulder. Somehow, he never tired of watching her nurse their child.

"How many fathers get to have their wife and their child so close by? You can zip down and see us any time you get a break."

"Thanks to your father."

"Yes." Maggie handed Bridget to Joshua, and he laid the baby gently against his shoulder.

Mr. O'Hanlon, in gratitude to the hospital that had saved his daughter's life, had made a substantial donation to renovate the wing for the day-care center. Maggie, with Millie Taffin's recommendation, had been hired as its new director, and she had been privileged to oversee the changes. Now the center cared for sixty children in facilities that were second to none.

"Kiss your daughter good-night." Joshua held Bridget's tiny face under Maggie's nose.

"Do you think we ought to put her back to bed? We'll only have to wake her up in a little less than an hour to take her to the hospital with us."

"I can think of some wonderful things we can do in that time if the baby goes back to sleep." Joshua's voice held promises.

Maggie kissed Bridget and then snuggled back under the covers to wait. Joshua was back in bed in a moment. "As much as I love that little creature," he said, "I still need lots of time alone with her mother."

Maggie smiled and opened her arms to him. "Dr. Martane," she said softly, "I have this recurring dream I wanted to tell you about."

Joshua began to trail kisses down the side of her face to her neck.

"I keep dreaming I have everything that anybody could ever want. Then I wake up and I can't tell my dream from reality." She moaned as his mouth found the place that their baby had just abandoned. "What do you think?"

"I think" he said, his lips against the silken skin of her breast, "that I should spend the rest of my life making sure that you never know the difference."

"I think," she said with a deep, contented sigh, "that I'll just have to go along with that treatment plan."

*   *   *   *   *

A STRANGER'S SMILE

Kathleen Korbel

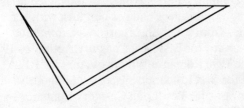

KATHLEEN KORBEL

lives in St. Louis with her husband and two children. She devotes her time to enjoying her family, writing, avoiding anyone who tries to explain the intricacies of the computer and searching for the fabled house-cleaning fairies. She's had her best luck with her writing—from which she's garnered a *Romantic Times* award for Best New Category Author of 1987, and the 1990 Romance Writers of America RITA award for Best Romantic Suspense and the 1990 and 1992 awards for Best Long Category Romance—and from her family, without whom she couldn't have managed any of the rest. She hasn't given up on those fairies, though.

Books by Kathleen Korbel

Silhouette Intimate Moments

A Stranger's Smile #163
Worth Any Risk #191
Edge of the World #222
Perchance To Dream #276
The Ice Cream Man #309
Lightning Strikes #351
A Rose for Maggie #396
Jake's Way #413

Silhouette Desire

Playing the Game #286
A Prince of a Guy #389
The Princess and the Pea #455
Hotshot #582
A Fine Madness #668
Isn't It Romantic? #703

Silhouette Books

Silhouette Summer Sizzlers 1989
"The Road to Mandalay"

Chapter 1

"Ya know, it's been a long time since I've had the chance to undress a handsome man." Anne pushed an errant strand of blond hair out of her eyes and returned to fumbling with buttons.

A masculine voice answered from behind her. "Don't you think you should wait till you get someplace warmer?"

"I will," she said, grimacing toward where Jim Thompson waited for her in the darkness. "I'm just checking him over to see whether he's worth taking home."

It was eight at night. Anne and Jim crouched together at the bottom of a steep ravine trying to assess the injuries of a man who'd been discovered there. They found themselves working in typically bad conditions. It was pitch-black and cold, the wind wet with promised snow. Bare-limbed trees set up a thrashing that drowned out the voices of the rest of the rescue party who waited above, and flashlights flickered back and forth like agitated spirits. The narrow gulley echoed with the turbulence of a gathering storm.

There was no ambulance or helicopter waiting to whisk Anne's patient away to the safety of a trauma center. He'd fallen on the wrong end of the Appalachians for that. Anne Jackson was a rural nurse; her helpers were farmers and storekeepers. Their transportation back down seven miles of negligible path to where they could reach a helicopter was horseback and travois.

Anne rubbed her hands against her pant legs to warm them up. The temperature was dropping so fast that her gloves offered little protection for numbing fingers. For a brief moment she even courted the idea of trying to finish the examination with her hands in her pockets. Then she picked up her flashlight and went back to work.

Her patient was a stranger, a tall man with darkly handsome features, probably a few years older than her. It was hard to tell much more from the brief glimpses she could manage with the flashlight. She could tell for certain that he wasn't from anywhere nearby. His outerwear was too expensive, his hiking boots spotless and too frivolous for daily use. Then there was the matter of what Anne discovered when she finally did get his jacket unbuttoned. She started to laugh. The man was wearing a custom-tailored, three-piece, pin-striped suit.

"Well, that does it," she announced with a grin as she showed Jim her discovery. "I'm going to have to take him home just so I can find out how he got here. It ought to be one hell of a story."

Jim chuckled with a shake of his head. "Who do you think he is?"

"I don't know," she said, her flashlight again sweeping the strong features and glinting against the warm-brown hair. "But I hope this isn't one of his favorite suits. I'm going to have to ruin it."

"You about ready to move him?" It was getting harder to hear Jim's voice above the wind. "I still need to have Silas and Ed send down the basket."

Anne straightened from where the injured man lay crumpled against a tree and jammed her hands back into her pockets. "Yeah, I think so. I'm going to need a little help splinting his leg first."

While Jim retrieved equipment, Anne took a moment to stretch out the kinks earned from an already long day of rounds. She felt as if there were sand in her eyes and wool in her mouth. And she was freezing. In the two years she'd lived back on the mountain she'd grown accustomed to people showing up unexpectedly at her door for help, but she'd never really gotten used to the long hours. She'd already been up since four that morning and was looking at at least another five hours before her patient was in the helicopter and she was back in bed.

Anne lifted her face to the harsh, swirling wind and took a breath of the biting air. The wild darkness made her shiver. On a night like this she could almost wish that she'd never given up the comforts of Boston.

Almost.

She took another look down at her patient with his expensive clothes and well-groomed good looks and recognized the familiar tug of antipathy. No, she decided with a scowl. On second thought, even the prospect of warm toes and a good brandy wasn't worth the thought of going back to Boston.

Ten minutes later it started to snow. They never made it to the helicopter. They never got farther than the two miles down to Anne's house, still high in the backwoods, still beyond the reach of conventional vehicles. Blinded by driving snow and wind, it had been almost more than Anne and Jim could manage to get the injured man to the horses. The rise from the gulley was steep and loose, good finger holds rare, and the footing treacherous enough to twice send Anne sliding almost to the bottom before finally reaching safe arms at the top. It took forty-five minutes to maneuver her patient that far.

By the time they deposited the man in Anne's spare bedroom, the snow was battering incessantly at the windows, and covered the ground in a thick, white blanket. A fire was stoked in the living room, and in the bright red-and-white kitchen three men huddled over cups of steaming coffee. Anne spent two hours in the bedroom before she had the chance to get hers.

She took her stethoscope from her ears for the final time to hear the clock strike midnight. The wind had eased to a dull whine, and the conversation in the kitchen had degenerated to sporadic monosyllables. The air was close with the heat of the fire and the smell of drying wool.

Anne admitted the first feeling of relief. It looked as though her patient would be all right. Even though he was still unconscious, his vital signs were finally as stable as a rock. His injuries appeared to be manageable now that his temperature had reached a safe range. And he was beginning to show signs of coming to, which meant that she might just get some sleep herself. Now all she had to do was get the rest of the rescue party out of her kitchen and on home.

Anne wondered again just who her patient was. She could almost have mistaken him for a rancher of some kind if she didn't know better. Even with the pallor and bruising from his injuries, he was deeply tanned, his angular face rugged and windburned. His hands were work roughened and strong, the fingers almost gracefully long, and there wasn't an ounce of city-bred fat to be found on his long frame. Probably six foot one or two, he was tightly muscled, with the almost hungry, lean look of a backwoods man.

But this man was not from any backwoods. From years of all-too-unhappy experience, Anne recognized all the hallmarks of social privilege. Above and beyond the beautiful suit she'd had to cut off, he showed evidence of a lot of high-priced pampering. Someone from a top salon in New York had recently had his hands in that thick chestnut hair, and a manicurist had been at those nails. The cologne he wore was exclusive, and the down outer layer that had helped save him was L. L. Bean's best.

All of which meant that the outdoor labor he performed hadn't been herding cattle or felling trees. More likely mountaineering in Switzerland or skiing the Dolomites. Anne could easily visualize him in the rigging of his sailboat as he sped up the Atlantic coast in the America's Cup race, trading dares with the other contestants. The perfect fantasy man. A brunette version of her ex-husband, Tom.

She scowled irritably, suddenly sorry that her handsome patient wasn't a farmer or miner from nearby. She had a feeling that she knew just what kind of person he'd turn out to be, and that she'd end up hating him for it—a painful reminder of what she'd escaped by running home to the mountain.

As if aware that he was being scrutinized, Anne's patient began to stir. She took hold of his restless hands and leaned toward him.

"C'mon," she coaxed gently, "talk to me, mister. I want to know who you are. Open your eyes and talk to me."

He responded, though his words were jumbled and meaningless. Only the name Charlie stood out clearly. When he began to speak in French, she answered until she realized that she was responding to a very smooth proposition.

"Not tonight," she said, smiling wryly, wondering just what memory she'd tapped. "I have the feeling you're going to have a headache."

When he did come to, he did it with a start. His eyes snapped open and he bolted upright.

"Take it easy," Anne said soothingly, pushing him back down. She stopped suddenly, the rest of her words lost within the unexpected jolt of contact. She was stunned, thrown off center by the clear lake-blue of his eyes. Bottomless, sunlit blue. When those eyes opened, features that had been handsome became mesmerizing, magnetic. There was power there, a vitality that compelled. This was a man people watched and listened to and followed. A shudder of recognition rocked through her for a man she'd never met.

Anne realized that she was staring, unable to control the surge of lightning his touch suddenly sent through her. She caught herself just short of bolting from the room.

"You're fine," she said, struggling to keep her voice level and professional even as the ground fell away. "You had a little accident."

He stared at her, his eyes unfocused and frightened. Anne found herself wanting to touch his face, to gently guide him back to lucidity. She didn't.

"It's okay," she said, smiling, trying to keep his attention focused. "My name's Anne. Can you tell me yours?"

"I..." It seemed to surprise him that he didn't have the strength to express himself. His eyes wandered again. "What...happened?"

"You fell, but you're okay. How do you feel?"

"I hurt...everywhere."

"I know. You were pretty banged up. You're okay, though." It was a good idea to keep repeating pertinent facts. People who had suffered concussions tended to have short, disjointed memories. Besides, Anne couldn't seem to think of anything else to say. "Can you tell me your name?"

"Was anyone else...?" He moved to ease some discomfort and discovered an even greater one. His face tightened with the surprise of it.

"No one else was hurt. You were alone." She was losing him again, his eyes blurring with confusion and pain. Again she fought the urge to reach out to him. She had never in her life reacted like this to a man—not even Tom—and it unnerved her.

His eyes drifted closed again, and Anne straightened, still shaken by her reaction. Now that his eyes were shut he seemed no more than another good-looking man, slightly worse for wear, who had the misfortune of reminding Anne of the people she'd once courted as her right.

She stood abruptly. The thought of her life in Boston hadn't really bothered her in a long time. The last thing she needed on this dark, snowy night was to find herself rehashing a painful past. Yet that seemed to be what she was about to do. Anne took one last look at her sleeping patient, her eyes unconsciously accusing, and turned to leave.

She met Jim heading in from the kitchen.

"He okay?" At five foot ten, he stood a few inches taller than Anne, his rust ponytail haloed in the hall light.

Anne took a minute to hang her stethoscope on the door before answering. "As far as I can tell. He's stitched and splinted and warm as toast. It would sure be nice to have some diagnostic equipment up here to make sure, though."

He grinned. "It'll make a difference when the clinic's open."

"I know," she said on a sigh, automatically checking the cracked face of her watch. "But we couldn't have even gotten him that far tonight. There has to be a better way."

"We'll get you a heliport for Christmas."

Anne finally grinned back and linked arms with her friend. "Don't make promises you have no intentions of keeping. C'mon, let's see if you guys can get home."

"Don't hold your breath. Silas is planning to camp out on your couch until we find out just who your mystery guest is."

She scowled playfully. "One of these days it's going to dawn on him that I'm not ten years old anymore."

Jim guided her back down the short hallway with a laugh. "Like I said, don't hold your breath."

When Anne walked into the kitchen the other two men stood to greet her. Wearily waving them back down, she disengaged herself from Jim and headed for the stove.

"There isn't any more we can do tonight," she said simply. "Better get on home while you can."

There wasn't an immediate answer to her offer. She filled a mug and brought it back to the big oak table. The oldest of the men who sat there scrutinized her as she eased herself into the chair across from him. She was already beginning to stiffen from the evening's exertions, but it wouldn't do at all to let him know. Taking a good sip of the hot brew, she fought the urge to confront the challenge in those watery blue eyes and be done with it. That was not the way to handle Silas, though. He defused more easily with patience and control.

"He should be okay," she said evenly, eyes back to her coffee. "I'll just keep an eye on him for a while to be sure."

"He sure was lucky Ef found him," Silas offered laconically, his own gaze retrieved. "One night like tonight woulda killed him for sure."

"He's just lucky that the fall didn't do it first. Six inches one way or the other and we wouldn't have needed to bother going after him until spring."

"I imagine his family'd be up here before that," Silas said, his eyes still as carefully averted as Anne's. "He sure ain't from around here."

Anne couldn't help but laugh. "I'll drink to that. Nobody around here's dumb enough to walk off a mountain."

"Not in a suit, anyway." Jim said with a grin. That elicited a round of chuckles and bemused head shaking.

"I don't suppose you found a name in those fancy duds?" Anne asked.

Silas laughed with a short, wry bark. "Not likely, seein' as how it was Ef that found him first."

"Yeah, I did notice that he disappeared awfully fast," she said and nodded with a rueful grin, thinking more of how the mug in her hands felt almost unbearably hot. She'd taken a good part of the slides up and down the ravine on her now-tender palms. Without thinking, she blew on the chafed skin to ease the stinging.

Jim reached out and pulled her hand over for inspection. "That looks awful," he scolded. "You'd better see to taking care of yourself."

"It doesn't really bother me." She shrugged, smiling at his concern even as she railed at his bad timing. She might never get Silas home now. "All in a day's work."

Silas frowned down at her in his patriarchal way. "Not a lady's work to go traipsin' down a mountain like that in the middle of the night."

"I told you, Silas," she chided, unable to prevent a playful grin from crinkling her gray eyes. "I'm not a lady. I'm a nurse."

He scowled, the deep creases on his weather-beaten face growing with disapproval. Anne had a good deal of trouble refraining from another grin. Silas had considered her as one of his own children since her mother had died years ago. He'd been with her on that day. He'd always been there when Anne had needed him, his gentle strength a fulcrum against which the rest of the world could balance. And he always treated her as if she were still the small girl who used to beg him for piggyback rides and make thrones from his huge, handcrafted chairs.

With what little energy she had left, Anne lurched to her feet, coffee still in hand, and turned to the silent third of the trio. John Edward had watched the preceding exchange with quiet amusement. He looked up at Anne with carefully passive eyes.

"John," she said, "I'll just go in and see if your things are dry for the trip back. Would you like to bring the horses out?"

"Sure thing, Annie."

When he stood, so did Jim and Silas. Silas took up a position next to Anne, still none too pleased.

"You can't take care of that man by yourself," he protested, as much from moral as practical considerations. Anne confronted the tall, scarecrowlike old man who all but dwarfed her.

"I can take care of him and ten others like him," she said gently. "The real work's been done. All I have to do now is baby-sit. You don't need brains or brawn for that so I'm the perfect candidate." She hurried on with the clincher before Silas had the chanced to protest. "Silas, I don't want Sarah to worry about you. You know her. This very minute she's standing by the front door watching the snow, and she won't move till you get home."

Jim and John had already edged toward the front door. Anne followed without again challenging Silas eye-to-eye and helped pick drying coats and hats from the quilt rack in front of the couch. Silas kept his silence as a matter of principle, but he began to dress along with the others.

John had just shut the door behind him when Jim poked into his jacket for gloves and came up with a surprised look on his face.

"Oh, Annie, I almost forgot. I have something for you."

Anne looked over to see him pulling a long envelope from his pocket.

"This came for you this afternoon, and when John stopped by for me, I figured I'd bring it along. Special delivery letter."

He waited for Anne to take the envelope, but she hesitated, having already seen the return address. For the second time in an hour, Anne felt her foundation slipping away, this time for an entirely different reason. Anger knifed through her stomach and brought bile to her throat.

The corner of the envelope bore the ostentatious logo of a distinguished Boston law firm. The best legal minds in Massachusetts, especially if you had corporate piracy in mind. Anne should have known. It was the law firm that Tom and her brother Brad had always used.

She'd told them to leave her alone. That she'd come home to Cedar Ridge to get as far away from him as she could, to save what was left of her sanity. She'd never wanted to hear from Tom or Brad again. It seemed that they couldn't leave well enough alone.

She accepted the letter from Jim and immediately folded it into her pocket. Silas, standing next to her, watched in growing astonishment. He'd never had a special delivery letter in his life, and considered them second only to divine revelation in importance. He simply could not understand her cavalier disregard for this one.

"Annie," he objected as tactfully as he knew how. "It must be important if they went to all the trouble of sendin' it special delivery."

She smiled, trying to keep her tone light. "Silas, it's from Brad. He sends birthday cards special delivery. But just in case it is bad news, I'm not about to read it until I've had a good night's sleep. Maybe I'll open it tomorrow after I've had my coffee." Maybe never.

Anne knew that Jim would understand. Silas did not. Wide-eyed and silent, he glared at her even after Jim had passed him his big coat. Anne was saved from another lecture by John's timely reappearance. Silas merely shrugged, as if he'd once again given up on comprehending her, and followed John back out into the night. Anne watched his angular frame bend into the white wind and wished again that she could tell the old man how much she loved him.

Jim paused beside Anne before stepping out the door. "Are you all right?" he asked quietly, motioning vaguely in the direction of the envelope.

She grinned ruefully. "Sure. It just galls me that I can still react like that to them after all this time."

His brown eyes softened with empathy. "Cassie'd say you have every right. Put that thing away until the morning and get some sleep. You won't be much good to you or your patient if you don't. The Thompson kitchens will take care of dinner tomorrow."

"Thanks, Jim." She smiled at her friend. "Give those babies a kiss for me."

He shook his head slowly, admiration in his eyes. "You know something? You're quite a lady."

"Go on and get out of here," she ordered with mock severity as she pushed him toward the door. "You keep talking like that, and I'm going to ask for a raise."

Anne stood at the window for a few long moments watching the men disappear into the darkness. Then, turning away, she pulled the crumpled envelope from her pocket and deliberately dropped it into the trash.

It took Anne another hour before she had time to relax and dry her hair in front of the great crackling fire in the living room. The lights were out in the cabin, with only the molten glow of the fire washing over the rough wooden walls. Anne eased herself down to sit cross-legged on the giant hooked rug in front of the couch, her old hairbrush in hand, another cup of coffee beside her. She'd finally taken the time to peel off her soggy clothes and slip into the comfortable warmth of her flannel nightgown and robe. The salve she'd spread on her hands was beginning to ease the tenderness even as her other joints set up a chorus of protest.

She knew that she should have been in the extra bedroom waiting for her patient to wake up. Somehow she couldn't bring herself to do it just yet. Before she walked headfirst into a new problem, she needed the time to sit and unwind from the demands the day had already put on her.

She hoped that she could relax without slipping into a coma. When she'd climbed up earlier to the loft where she slept to change clothes, her big old four-poster had almost beckoned to her. If she chanced going up there again, that old bed might just reach out and catch her.

Anne smiled wryly and leaned a little to the side, catching the braid of her hair in one hand and slowly unknotting it. When her hair fell free, cascading over her shoulders, she took the brush to it and shivered at the heady sensation. The straw-gold curtain shimmered richly in the firelight, lush and full. It had always been Anne's outstanding feature, a treasure that had transformed her patrician features into a singular beauty. Tom had always loved to touch it, running his hands through it as if it were a magical gold. He had encouraged her to wear it up, sleekly styled so that it complimented the cool gray of her eyes and classic lines of her face.

She had to admit that she'd always turned heads when she'd walked into a room of the social and political elite. She was the essence of sophistication, one of the ten best-dressed boss's daughters on the Eastern Seaboard. Now when she had finally gained the self-esteem to match the picture she'd once presented, it seemed that she was much better suited to braids: easy to take care of and practical. The way her life had become.

Anne sighed and straightened, her hair swinging behind her to brush at the small of her back. The coffee was the last of the pot Silas had brewed, and it tasted bitter and hot, helping to wake her from the comfort of warm clothes and a fireplace. Maybe enough for her to stay awake through a book. She hated it when she found herself rehashing the follies of her life, and she resented emotions that had never been properly put in their place at the conclusion of relationships. The well-groomed stranger in her bedroom and a special delivery letter were quite successfully dredging up regrets that she thought she'd given up long ago.

For some reason, she thought of Jim and how he reflected the changes in her own life. Once she would have considered him an anachronism, the kind of man one heard about in *National Geographic* or *Mother Earth News*. Who could imagine, after all, an ad exec from Chicago who pulled in seventy-five to a hundred thousand a year giving it all up for a life like the Waltons'? But Jim Thompson had done just that.

Tom would have savagely dissected Jim's manhood with the precision of a surgeon. Sipping at his vodka martini, he would have wondered how any man could survive the ignominy of running away from the real world to hide in, of all places, the Appalachians. His laughter would have been cruel and unforgiving.

Even her father would have been bitterly disappointed if she'd brought Jim home from college instead of Tom. Tom had had what her father had called an inborn knack for big business. Anne, in a rare moment of insight during her first year of marriage, had correctly labeled it the jugular instinct, an instinct that Jim simply didn't have.

Her reflections were interrupted by the first sounds of a man struggling for consciousness. As quickly as her aching limbs would let her, she got to her feet and headed for the bedroom.

Only a small night-light was on by the bed. Within its soft pool of light she saw her patient moving a bit, as if caught in a bad dream. His brow, swathed in a bandage, puckered momentarily before his whole face took on a frown. He looked as if he were trying to remember something. His hands lifted aimlessly from the bed, seeking the air and then dropping again. The pain even touched his subconscious, and he made little moans as he moved.

Anne reclaimed her seat and resumed trying to talk her stranger back to consciousness, this time with more caution and not a small amount of trepidation. It didn't take him as long this time. Within a minute or two, his eyes opened and focused on her.

Anne decided that it was definitely too late for her to still be up. Her reaction was even stronger this time. She had to restrain herself from looking away from him, afraid all of a sudden that with just his eyes he would pierce the innermost corners of her soul. Again she felt herself go rigid in response to the heat he stirred in her.

The minute his eyes locked into hers she felt that jolt, as if the chair wouldn't hold her. His eyes were clear now, not so fogged with confusion. Anne saw in them the winter sky above the pines. Alive, kinetic.

Her smile was unconsciously stiff. "How are you feeling?"

He let his gaze wander over the shadowy room for a minute and then return to rest on Anne's face. "Pretty bad. What happened?"

"You must have been hiking in the park and gotten lost. We found you just beyond it, in a ravine." She didn't think to mention the suit.

"The park?"

She nodded. "Great Smoky Mountain National Park. Do you remember being there?"

It took him a moment to answer. "I...I guess so. Is this...a... hospital?"

"Oh, Lord, no." She grinned, genuinely amused. "I'm a rural nurse. You're at my house on the backside of Bennett's Mountain. We couldn't get you any farther than this. It's snowing outside."

"Snowing." He rolled the sound of the word around as if considering a new phenomenon. "I wouldn't have...gone back...in the snow."

Anne was enough of a mind to appreciate the distinction he made. He would go in his best suit, but not if it were snowing. Real city logic.

"I'm sure you wouldn't have," she said, nodding. "It didn't start until after you fell. Can we notify anyone?"

He nodded slowly to himself as if his actions had been justified. When he winced with the discomfort of the action, Anne found herself leaning toward him, almost sensing his pain.

"What's your...name?"

"Anne," she said quietly, suddenly wanting to hold him, to rock him to an easy sleep, and just as suddenly realizing how ridiculous the idea was. "What's yours?"

His face softened into a smile, but the light was fading in his eyes. Anne bent closer as if to follow the flight of his attention.

"You're..."

"A nurse," she repeated.

"Beautiful." She could hardly hear his voice, but he managed a more wry smile before letting his eyes close. "I feel so...tired."

"Best thing for you," she agreed, realizing with a start that she'd again taken hold of his hand. "Can you tell me your name first?"

She was too late. Surprised, she watched him as he slept. He looked like a tousled little boy, making her want to reach over and brush the dark hair back from where it tumbled over his forehead. It occurred to her then that his voice matched his eyes, clear and quiet.

She sat where she was for a moment, willing the fire to die in her, listening to the silence around her as she marveled at the spark that attracted her to a stranger. Spark! Hell, it was more like bonfire. She spent all of her time wishing for the Jims of the world and still became caught in the allure of another Tom.

Maybe she'd be wrong. Maybe when he woke up in the morning he would still be as quiet and genuine as he was tonight. She found that she wanted that very much.

No matter what, she thought as she looked down at him, the mysterious electricity once again dimmed, she was going to get him back out of her house as fast as she could and get on with her life. Blue eyes or not, she was a big enough girl to be able to keep her professional distance. And that would be that.

Chapter 2

"So, you weren't a dream after all."

Anne's eyes shot open. For a moment, she couldn't remember where she was. The sight of her patient brought her abruptly back to reality. She'd ended up crawling into an overstuffed chair in the corner of the guest room sometime the night before, and had evidently not made it back to her own bed. Every muscle in her let her know what a smart idea that had been.

Wondering what time it was, she took a minute to rub at the sleep in her eyes before attempting to launch herself from the soft cushions. She was not looking forward to testing her morning-after muscles. Pain was not her favorite wake-up call.

When she finally did lurch up, there was no choice but to quickly admit to a temporary setback. She mouthed a surprised little "Ooh," and sank right back down. Her patient watched every move in silence.

Anne couldn't help but notice that his eyes were even more uncannily bright in the daylight. Only a surrounding ring of darker blue seemed to delineate the iris at all. This morning they were more alert, more in control. And even more mesmerizing.

"I'll be up in a minute," she said grinning sheepishly, her eyes only briefly meeting his as she tried to quell the sudden staccato of her heart. It was too early for this. "I'm a little stiff this morning from a bit of surprise mountain climbing last night. How are you feeling?"

"Like I tried to share a small seat with a truck," he said, his voice very quiet as if its proper use would cause discomfort. He was smiling, though. "I started to feel better the minute I woke up and saw you.... You were here last night?"

"You remember?" Foolishly, Anne felt dread, waiting for his pleasant demeanor to change, waiting to be disillusioned.

He shook his head slightly. "Your face, not much more."

She nodded to herself as she once again tried to launch herself from the chair. Every joint protested vigorously, and her knees were tender from where they'd made contact with every rock on the slope, but everything was in working order. She made it over to stand by the bed without too much difficulty.

"You were found last night at the bottom of a nearby ravine."

"And you sat up all night with me?" He snapped off a perfect, flashing smile that sent Anne's stomach plummeting. She recognized the look with sick fatalism. Barracuda teeth, she called it. Tom had a similar look. She saw the control grow on the stranger's face, the facade take shape before her eyes, and she knew without a doubt that her instincts had been right. She was going to hate this man, regardless of his magnetism.

She had wanted so much for him to be different.

"I wasn't sure how badly you were hurt," she answered, realizing with some regret that her voice had automatically taken on the smooth, icy tones she'd cultivated on the cocktail party circuit. Suddenly Boston wasn't nearly as far away as she would have liked.

"How badly am I hurt?"

"Well, I know for sure that you broke your leg, you have a dandy cut on your forehead and you're scraped up just about everyplace else." As she talked Anne took out her medical equipment and began to check the injuries she'd listed. It occurred to her that he must have had a similar conversation sometime in the past. The night before she'd discovered a number of scars that wrapped around his left side. Fine lines now from very good plastic surgery, they represented a once-severe injury. "Where else do you hurt?"

"Besides everywhere?"

"Besides everywhere."

"My back, down low. And my chest, right about here." He motioned to an area of bad abrasions.

She nodded, gently palpating the point midway across the right side of his chest. "You probably cracked a couple of ribs when you landed. You wound up wedged against a tree. I'd imagine that your backache's from a muscle strain, judging by where you say it hurts."

"Aren't you going to feel it to make sure?"

Again she froze. Why couldn't he keep that suggestive gleam out of his eyes, or come up with a half-human response? Just the tone of his voice was so much like Tom's that Anne found herself bracing for the hurt and humiliation that had to follow. It was all she could do to remain still.

"No," she told him, straightening, "I'm going to make breakfast. Do you feel like some soup and toast, or would you rather just rest awhile?"

"I'd rather get to know you better."

Her smile was rigid. "That wasn't one of the choices."

He wasn't in the least fazed. "In that case, I'll rest up so that I can have the strength later—when it is."

She ignored that. "As soon as we can get you down the mountain we'll transport you to a hospital. Right now it's a little difficult to travel. We had our first snowfall of the season while we were picking you off the mountain, and I'm afraid it was a beaut. Until we can get you to civilization, is there anyone who should be notified?"

His expression remained nonchalant, but Anne could see that he was tiring. "Oh, I'm sure there is, but don't bother. I don't think I'm going to feel like putting up with them for a few days."

"You're on the wrong side of the mountain for visitors," she said. "Phone lines are down from the snow, and nobody can get up here unless it's on horseback."

He looked astounded, eyeing the room about him as if expecting to see kerosene lamps and chamber pots.

"The peace and quiet can be deafening," she said, turning for the door. A parting thought kept her there for a moment. "If you need anything, yell. My name's Anne. I'm afraid that since we didn't find any identification on you, I don't know yours."

"My wallet? My briefcase?"

"If you had them when you fell, you didn't by the time we got to you."

"What do you mean?" he demanded, his voice imperious and condescending. "I have some important papers in that briefcase. Somebody'd damn well better find it."

"Actually," she retorted dryly, "I have it. And I'm splitting the credit cards in your wallet with my cohorts. We're going on a shopping spree in town tomorrow."

He wasn't amused. A cold disdain lit his eyes. "I doubt that any of the hicks in that two-horse town would know what to do with a credit card if they had one."

That did it. If only he could have kept his mouth shut, Anne would have gladly drowned in the tides of his eyes. She could have at least dreamed that there were still, in fact, some decent people in the society she'd left behind. This guy was making her more and more glad that she'd gotten out when she did.

"And may I say for all the hicks who had the questionable sense to pull you up a ravine in a snowstorm," she said, trying very hard to keep her voice even, "you're welcome."

For a moment he glared at her as if at a not-too-bright salesperson. Then, with a suddenness that left Anne confused, he sighed, and the emotion drained from his face as if the effort were too great. "I'm sorry, Anne. I seem to have forgotten my manners. Jonathan Bradshaw Harris. And I think I'll get a nap now and try to eat something later."

Anne walked out quickly to prevent staring openmouthed at him. He wouldn't have noticed. His eyes were closed by the time she reached the hallway.

Anne had been mistaken. Her patient wasn't going anywhere. There was a good foot and a half of snow on the ground. She saw it the minute she stepped into the kitchen and looked out the windows. The wind had eased during the night so that the snow wasn't blowing hard, but it still fell heavily and steadily, making visibility limited. The hills looked like vague watercolors painted in shades of gray, the firs by the barn spearing black and sudden into the light morning sky. If the snow kept up, they wouldn't be able to get Mr. Harris down the mountain for days, and after Anne's initial conversation with him, that prospect didn't appeal to her at all.

Dressing quickly in an old flannel shirt and jeans and shoving a heavy knit cap on her head, she threw on her jacket and headed out to tend the animals.

Her big bay gelding, Andy, greeted her by stamping impatiently against the side of his stall. He wasn't a fan of the cold weather, especially when she had to saddle him up on frigid winter mornings to make rounds. He never balked from her touch, but let her know nonetheless exactly how he felt. Anne smiled at his call and protest, knowing that he would be far friendlier when he realized that this day was to be spent lounging in the protection of the barn.

Pulling on the heavy door, she shut out the white morning and enveloped herself in the warmer, damp smells of hay and animals and leather. Her father had often said that she should have been born in his grandmother's time when the farm had been a working one. She had always loved taking care of the animals, and had spent some of her most contented moments grooming the horses or milking the cow.

Today, though, her private demons wouldn't leave her alone long enough to enjoy the peace the physical work usually afforded. The chores she did were by now so rote that she ended up with even more time to think and remember.

Maybe if she'd only gotten the letter from Brad, or just had the unexpected visit by a handsome stranger in wolf's clothing she could handle everything with more composure. But one arriving right on top of the other had proven too much. Suddenly the old pain gnawed at her like fresh fire.

For the past two years, Anne had done everything in her power to wipe out the events that had driven her back to the mountains. She'd severed her ties with the city and reestablished relationships made during the years her family had used the cabin as a summer home away from the pressures of her father's position. Leaving the power and wealth behind her, she'd resurrected the simple customs of the generations of Jacksons who had lived on the land before her. She had carefully structured her life to include only the present and those selected memories that could no longer hurt her.

She'd become so involved with life on the mountain that if it weren't for the few keepsakes she'd brought with her from Boston, she could have almost thought that there had never been a life there at all. The wealth and the crowded existence of the socially elite might not have ever existed. She could have almost thought that there had never been a business.

She frowned, hating even the sound of the word that had so shaped her life.

Business.

Jackson Corporations Limited had not been just a business, but a living thing. Her father had created it with equal parts dream, ambition and obsession. JCL had in turn bestowed her family with more status than even status-hungry Boston had demanded and given power beyond even educated imaginations. It had transformed old family names into a dynasty, a dynasty that should by rights be handed over to the oldest child. Or, in the case of Peter Jackson, who held fast to the belief that women had no place in the crucibles of power, to the oldest son.

What had been unfortunate was the fact that the oldest son, the only son, was an unworthy heir. Bradley Jackson had been blessed with none of the natural leadership, organization and charisma that had served his father so well. A weak, resentful child, he had never earned his father's respect or trust. After waiting longer than Brad had thought reasonable for the authority he equated with his birthright, and which his father, for fear of his business refused to give, he resorted to the natural talents he did have. He schemed with a willing brother-in-law to rob his father of the very empire he had created.

In the end Brad and Tom won. Peter Jackson died, a man broken in spirit, and Anne, caught between father and husband, lost everything in a fight she wanted no part of. She had come home to bury her father and stayed, too distraught by what had been done to ever consider going back.

Anne stopped a minute, the memories beginning to suffocate her. Her eyes rose, drawn to a small yellow glint in the barn's soft gloom. It was still there, above her head on a nail she'd driven into the stall post, the small plain gold band she'd hung up two years ago, the symbol of why she'd vowed never to leave the mountain again.

Unbidden, the picture of Tom taunted her. Handsome, electric, intelligent, overachiever Tom McCarthy had thrown her away in his lust for the power he saw in her father. She looked at the ring and knew that it had been Jonathan Harris, with his electric blue eyes and power-modulated voice, who had blown this particular ill wind back into her life. He was so much like Tom that it was like being forced to face her ex-husband again here where she'd finally left him and where she still sought to exorcise the memory of that last meeting.

It had been November, a clear bright day when the mountain had been brilliant with autumn. Anne had brought her father home to the cabin when the fight for control of the company had become too vicious. He'd looked sickly and so suddenly old. She'd thought that maybe the isolation would help.

Then Tom had appeared, tall and blond, well-groomed and controlled. She'd known why he'd come and instinctively tried to hide from it. She remembered it now coldly, as if it were part of a bad movie she'd seen instead of the final dissolution of a marriage she'd so long cherished.

He came up behind her, his sleek cap of blond hair glowing like a halo in the afternoon light. It was then that he finally admitted to her what he and Brad were doing, as if she hadn't already known. They were about to take final control of the company away from the man who'd given his life to it.

He reached down to touch her hair as it hung freely down her back.

"Anne, come home." His tone was smooth, well modulated, prepared. She heard no pain or grief to make the words sound honest.

She steeled herself against this. For as much as she hated him, she still, even after what he'd become, loved him desperately.

"What for, Tom?" she asked, her eyes away on the peaceful hills. "What is there to come home to?"

"Come home to me, Anne." It didn't seem to occur to him to mention love or need. "I'll take care of you."

Was that why she'd married him? Had she needed someone to take care of her?

"Like you took care of my father? He trusted you, Tom. He couldn't have given you more opportunity in that company if you'd been his real son."

"Don't be stupid, Anne. I'm giving you another chance. All that old man ever gave you was the money to mingle with the right crowd."

She'd turned on him then, the anger rising. "He is my father. And he's never in his life deliberately hurt me. You, on the other hand, seem to have made a career of it. I think you'd better go."

He'd allowed an eyebrow to arch, as he gave one parting shot. "Your father and I are the same person," he said with some satisfaction. "If we weren't, you'd never have married me. You're dependent on men like us, my love."

He had turned back to the road before she finally said it, sealing their future. "You'll hear from my lawyer on Monday."

It had been the last time she'd cried.

Anne was collecting the eggs when she heard the muffled sounds of hoofbeats. More than one horse was approaching the cabin. She picked up her basket and walked over to give a much more amiable Andy a parting pat on the nose before opening the door.

The snow hadn't stopped while she had been inside. She had to lean heavily on the door to get it open, and the tracks she'd made two hours earlier were almost obliterated. She was beginning to despair of ever getting Jonathan Harris down the mountain.

"Annie, there you are."

Silas strode quickly over from the porch, followed closely by Jim.

Anne grinned at the look on Silas's face. "What are you doing back up here so soon?" she asked. Silas took the basket and pail from her just as he always did.

"Sheriff's busy," Jim offered with a slow grin, "and since we were coming up this way anyway, we told him we'd check up on your patient for him."

"I'm not harboring a notorious criminal, am I?" she asked mischievously in Silas's direction.

"Don't know." The old man shrugged, opening the door for her. "Never did come up with any identification."

"His name's Jonathan Something-or-other Harris," she said obligingly as she pulled off her jacket and gloves to hang before the fire. The men followed her lead, stamping the snow from their boots on the throw rug by the door.

"He awake?" Silas asked.

"He was. Coffee, anyone?" She didn't wait for an answer but headed out to the kitchen and the coffeepot. She wanted some even if they didn't.

"Can we talk to him?"

"Sure, if he's awake," she said with a nod. "He doesn't have much stamina right now, but you can find him in the guest room if you want to grill him."

"Silas," Anne asked quietly a moment later, "is there any way we can get him down the mountain?"

"Is he hurt bad?" he said frowning.

"Not really," she admitted, pulling out some coffee cake she'd baked a few days earlier. "I'm afraid there's a personality conflict. He's beginning to remind me of Tom, and I don't want to end up pitching him back over a cliff in a couple of days."

Silas nodded, suppressing a half grin. "Can he go on horseback?"

"No."

"Then we can't. Snow's already too deep for a wagon, and the radio's callin' for another foot or so before it stops."

"Another foot?" she immediately protested, turning on him. He was pouring coffee into mugs for her and shaking his head in disbelief.

"Annie," he admonished, "you've got the fanciest stereo in the county up here. Why don't you at least listen to the weather once in a while? You wouldn't keep gettin' surprised like that."

It was no use trying to explain her little quirk to Silas. She'd tried once and ended up sounding paranoid even to herself. But at first even hearing the sound of a professional radio announcer had brought her too close to the city. After a while she had truly begun to prefer the comfort of silence over the repetitious babble of a radio—even the best one in the county.

"We won't even be able to get him down on horseback for much longer," he continued, evidently not expecting an answer. "That's why we came now, so we could get a name and notify kin."

Anne almost made the mistake of letting Silas know how his news affected her. She nearly screamed. But he was looking at her closely, his eyes suspiciously noncommittal, and Anne realized that he was only inches from staying for the next few days. That would have been even worse than just having Mr. Harris on her hands. She smiled without a word and handed him a cup of coffee.

After Silas went off to join the one-man posse in the bedroom Anne realized that she needed a dish towel. The extras were in the hall closet across from the guest room where Silas and Jim were interrogating her patient. She stood alone in the kitchen for a minute listening to the sounds of conversation that came from the down the hall, the compulsion pulling at her. Like an itch, she thought absently, that needs to be scratched.

It didn't take her more than a minute to give in to temptation.

By the time she reached the hallway she knew Silas had heard Mr. Harris's opinion on the notification of relatives. He was asking if there were any reason Mr. Harris didn't want his family called. To someone like Silas that was as unthinkable as it was suspicious. Anne had to repress a grin. Jim would appreciate her reaction, but neither Silas nor Jonathan Harris would.

The impulse died when Jonathan answered Silas's question. Suddenly Anne felt as if she'd missed something.

It wasn't so much what he said, which was something about avoiding company hassles, but how he said it that baffled her. Smiling ruefully, he spoke with the same quiet respect most of the people in the area expressed when talking to the old man. No condescension, none of the smug patronization Tom or Brad had always shown for someone from the mountains.

Anne was impressed. If nothing else, he was certainly a crafty animal. She imagined that whatever it was he did, that he did it very well. And if he wanted something in that rarefied atmosphere in which he. traveled, he usually got it.

At that moment Jonathan caught her staring at him. Without missing a beat he flashed a knowing grin at her that knocked into her like a kick. Those damn white, perfect teeth. Why didn't they seem to bother anybody else as much as they did her?

When her first reaction died, something else dawned on Anne. Jonathan was giving her a message. In his eyes she saw the admission that he was a different person than the men he faced. His initial reaction to being caught up here outside his universe would never do, and he proposed to change his attitude when he dealt with these people. She also had the very unsettling feeling that he considered her as much an outsider as him, which made her fair game.

She felt totally confused. Jonathan Harris seemed to be going out of his way to keep her off balance. He caught her this time with her mouth open.

"Don't worry about me," he was saying to Jim and Silas even as his eyes held Anne's. "I'll behave. My nurse trusts me even less than you do. She won't let me get away with anything."

Silas and Jim turned to see her standing across from the doorway. Anne allowed herself a slow, controlled smile just for Mr. Harris.

"He's right, Silas. I'll probably end up bringing in the shotgun from the barn. Just in case Mr. Harris tries to steal the chickens."

Jim couldn't quite control the corners of his mouth. Anne decided that if he thought it was so funny, he could stay up here instead of her.

She'd much rather run a general store than tap-dance with Mr. Harris for a week. Come to think of it, she thought as she swung the towel over her shoulder, maybe she should let Silas stay up here. Then she could just ride off and not have to worry about Jonathan at all.

By the time Jim and Silas finished the interrogation Anne had the table set and fresh bread out. Silas appeared in the kitchen doorway, a suspicious frown clouding his features. Anne knew that it had everything to do with the fact that Jonathan was playing the mysterious stranger. Knowing Silas, she was sure that he would ride straight down to the station to have the sheriff run Jonathan's name for wants and warrants. She couldn't help the grin this time as she invited him to sit for another cup of coffee.

"We'll try and have somebody up here every day to check on you, Annie," Jim offered as he sat. "And I'm sure I can get the boys at the phone company busy on your lines."

Anne sat across from him. "If you're worried about my virtue, Jim, don't. Even the best mashers I've known would have trouble making time on a broken leg. I can move a lot faster than he can."

Silas didn't take to her levity. "It won't hurt any to accept the help, Annie." He frowned his admonition. "You don't know who that man is. For all we know, that fancy name of his ain't even real."

"That just shows he has a classy imagination." She grinned. "If he's a burglar, he must be a good one. That was a five-hundred-dollar suit we cut off him. As for his true identity, get ahold of Ef Tate. I'll bet he's sporting a brand new Gucci wallet that has all of Mr. Harris's ID."

"We tried him already," Jim said grinning dryly as he finished his coffee in a gulp. "He's the soul of innocence. I'm afraid Mr. Harris isn't going to see his wallet again."

"Another cup?" Anne asked automatically.

"No, thanks, Annie," he apologized. "I think we'd better get going."

She smiled, knowing that Silas had undoubtedly been pressing to at least get as far as the nearest working phone to check out Mr. Jonathan Harris. In the perverse humor she was in, she hoped something would show up, just to see not only Silas's reaction, but Jonathan's.

Taking his cue from Jim, Silas quickly finished his coffee and followed him to his feet, the old chairs scraping noisily on the red tile floor.

Jim turned to Anne as they walked into the living room. "I could probably arrange for someone to stay up here with you if you want."

Anne shook her head. "Only if they can cook and clean windows."

"Annie," Silas admonished.

Anne waved aside the objection and stood by the front door as the men donned their coats. "I promise I'll be fine," she assured them with a gentle smile. "Unless he's a great healer or a lot more determined than he looks, Mr. Harris won't be out of bed for at least a few days. He'll be no trouble or inconvenience. Besides, if the snow doesn't stop, I don't want to have to end up feeding all kinds of people. Two's more than enough."

Anne's word sparked a reaction from Jim. "I forgot. That dinner I promised is out on the mare."

"Let me get my coat," Anne offered, reaching for her down jacket. "No sense you having to traipse in and out when I have to go out and see you off anyway."

A few minutes later, Jim handed her five large plastic containers that all but filled her arms.

"Jim," she accused, surveying them. "This isn't dinner. It's a week's rations for Fort Benning."

He answered after he'd mounted the large dappled mare he used for deliveries to the homes on the mountain. "You know Cassie. Product of an Italian mother. She just wanted to make sure you'd be okay if we didn't get up here for a few days."

"I think this should probably take me through Labor Day," she said, smiling. "Thanks."

"Is there anything else you need?" Silas persisted.

Anne shook her head. "If you can figure out a way for it to stop snowing so that I can be free of Mr. Harris's stellar company, all my troubles will be solved, and I promise I'll be a happy woman again."

She waited as long as it took for her riders to disappear into the snowy fog before turning to go back inside. Out of habit, she checked the indoor-outdoor thermometer by the door as she stamped her boots. Fourteen wet, blowing degrees. She certainly hoped Mr. Harris realized how lucky he was not to be lying out under a couple of feet of snow tonight.

There wasn't any sound from his room as she passed, so she assumed he was asleep again. She wasn't surprised. Besides the fact that his injuries had sapped his strength, he was probably bored to death already. She wondered if he had ever eaten from a vegetarian menu, as he would if he had an appetite tonight. Cassie was one of the best vegetarian cooks Anne knew. Opening the refrigerator door with three fingers, Anne piled the containers inside, unaware that the anticipatory grin on her features was almost malicious in its glee. If he were indeed like Tom, he'd choke. Anne couldn't wait for dinner.

Once the food was put away, Anne made a beeline back through the living room to work on the fire, her mind consumed with the truth of the words she'd said to Silas. If only she could get her unwelcome houseguest back to wherever he came from, she could get back to the soothing peace of her routine. Then her life would be what she'd waited two years for it to become.

As Anne bent to gather more wood from the stack by the door, she bumped into the trash can. It briefly occurred to her that it was getting full and needed to be emptied. Especially with that fancy envelope from Boston in it.

Then she turned to stoke the fire, all thoughts of her past once again deliberately shoved aside.

Chapter 3

By six o'clock the next evening the snow had topped thirty inches and still fell steadily. Anne sat in a wing-back chair by the front window looking morosely outside. She'd finally turned on the radio as Silas had suggested, only to hear that the state was under hazardous weather warnings. Most secondary roads had been closed, especially at higher elevations. The airport was shut down and every piece of snow-removal equipment had been on the major highways since early morning. And more snow was to come.

That explained why no one had ventured up to see her that day. She was glad they hadn't, really. There was probably more than enough for them to do everywhere else. The meteorologist came on the air again to give an updated report that sounded depressingly like all the others. His voice frazzled and apologetic, he assured the public that weather of this severity in this area was a freak of nature. More like one of the plagues of Egypt, Anne amended for him, able to picture him repeatedly loosening his tie and running his hands through his hair as the snow continued to pile up without his permission.

She could have told him why the state was suffering the first October blizzard in memory. It had everything to do with the fact that she had Mr. Harris as her surprise houseguest. She was snowed in with him because, with the exception of Tom or Brad, Jonathan Harris was the last person on earth with whom she wanted to be stuck in an isolated cabin.

It's Murphy's Law, she thought. When she'd worked in the emergency room, it had moved from the eleventh to her first commandment, neatly displacing all the others. If anything could possibly go wrong it would, and at the worst possible moment. Here she sat, once again living proof of that axiom.

It wasn't that Jonathan didn't need her help. He most certainly did. The concussion he'd suffered would have had him on breathing support for at least the first twelve hours. He'd slept away the vast majority of the day, not able to keep any kind of solid food down until lunch. He wouldn't be going anywhere for a while on that leg, and she'd have to guess that at least three of his ribs were broken. All that added to low back strain and exposure made him a pretty sorry sight.

It was just that she felt he had the personality of a snake. Peppering his speech with cute little clichés culled from the *Cruising Corporate Head's Guide to New York*, Jonathan seemed to believe that given enough time, any woman would melt for his hundred-watt smile and religiously unoriginal turn of phrase. And that soon that same woman would ask for no more than to serve his every whim. Anne expected to see the venom appear when it finally got through to him that she would want no part of it. Just like it had happened some three years ago with Tom.

What truly galled Anne was the fact that beneath all that gloss and party-game atmosphere, she sensed another person entirely, someone she could like and respect. Maybe it was just a newfound optimism, but she thought she might have seen a little of his true self the first night when his eyes had been so very vulnerable. She wanted to think that the word games were just a protection, maybe a habit.

Face it, she thought dourly as she watched the snow steadily pile up outside her bay window, you don't want to think that you could be attracted to that kind of personality again. You don't want Tom to have been right about needing that kind of man.

There was no question that she found Jonathan handsome. She'd caught herself peeking in at him much more than was necessary and had to admit that even with the ravages of his fall, he still stood right up there in the unforgettable-looks category. But she'd known and worked with a host of handsome men before. On more than one occasion she'd found herself in stressful and emotionally charged situations with them and had handled it with levelheaded common sense every time. It bothered her very much that she was in danger of losing that precious objectivity with the one man she most needed it for.

So engrossed was she by the increasingly depressing cant of her thoughts that it took her a moment to hear her patient's voice. When she did, she scowled, wishing that she could tape his mouth shut. She imagined that he considered himself original by calling her Florence

Nightingale. Heaving a sigh of capitulation, she uncurled her feet from beneath her and got up to answer the call.

"Ah," he said, smiling as she walked through the door, "if it isn't the light of my dark days."

"How are you feeling?" she asked, pulling the chair over again and sitting down. She took note of the fact that only a small amount of blood had seeped through the bandage on his head, and that the inevitable bruising had begun under his eyes. She also noticed for the first time how small crow's feet creased the corners of his eyes when he smiled, somewhat easing the ruggedness of his features.

"Better now that you're here." He grinned, showing her all his teeth and ruining that impression of familiarity. "Hold my hand and I'll feel like dancing."

She ignored him, pulling the cover back from his feet to check his injured leg for color and pulse. It, too, was swollen and bruised, but the circulation was unimpaired.

"Does your leg hurt?" She examined the wrappings, but they hadn't slipped or kinked and didn't really need the check.

"Only when I laugh."

"Does your foot feel tingly and cold at all?"

"No more than the rest of me."

Anne replaced the covers and straightened up, wondering how she could get around rewrapping his head.

"Aren't you going to check my chest?" he demanded, reaching for the sheet.

Her smile was a bit chilly. "Not unless you stop breathing and turn blue. Do you feel like eating some dinner?"

"What's on the menu?"

"Lentil and cheese casserole, cucumber salad, nut bread and peaches."

"Of course." He nodded with mock severity. "It all fits. The communal period, right?"

"Pardon?"

He motioned vaguely with one hand to signify her environment. "The communal period. Vegetarianism, *Foxfire Manuals* and homesteading. Are you preparing for the end of the world?"

"No. Just dinner." She got to her feet.

"I'll eat on one condition," he decided, reaching for her hand. She deftly avoided it with a move she'd perfected at Mass General. He pulled what was meant to be a handsome frown of disappointment. "You come in and share dinner with me."

"I prefer to eat alone," she replied evenly. "Besides, I have to tend the animals, so I won't be eating for a while anyway."

"You can't mean that you'd prefer to spend your time with the cows rather than me."

She offered a dry smile. "I can."

His eyes narrowed as if he were gauging her, his smile almost sly. The look of a man who was sure he had the upper hand. "What if I told you that I could take you away from all this if you wanted?"

"I'd say take yourself away. I like it here."

His smiled widened. Anne could see the challenge in his eyes. What she did not see was warmth. "I could give you everything you ever wanted."

Anne actually had to close her eyes when she heard that, the sense of déjà vu too painful. "I'll give you everything you'll ever want, Anne. Everything," Tom had promised. In the end, he had taken it instead.

She took a slow breath to quell the urge to scream and opened her eyes again. "This may come as an unpleasant surprise to you, Mr. Harris," she said quietly, "but I had everything I wanted before you fell down my cliff. And after you're gone, I'll have it again."

This time when Jonathan smiled, Anne could actually see the challenge die and be replaced by what she could have sworn was sincerity. She found herself staring.

"Please," he said, his voice sounding earnest. "I really hate to eat alone. And I'd like to have the chance to know more about my benefactor. If I ease up a little, will you stay?"

Anne had the irrational impulse to applaud the performance she was witnessing. Somehow, she couldn't. She gave him another chance to surprise her.

"It'll take me an hour or so before I can get to dinner."

"That's okay," he said, the veneer already solidly back in place. "It'll be worth the wait."

When Anne did get back with dinner, she found that he'd fallen asleep again, his face peaceful and quiet. That angered her anew. It annoyed her that the mind inhabiting that handsome, rugged face could spoil the image by constantly bartering on the sincerity and honesty suggested there. She hadn't seen a chin so square and strong since Gary Cooper; the cheeks were solid as granite ledges, as if etched by wind and water. Even his nose perfectly suited his face, straight enough to have been drawn. It was just that none of his features fit the personality. It was like watching a movie with the sound track out of sync.

He stopped her as her hand touched the door, about to leave him to his sleep.

"You're not going to back out of our dinner date at the last minute, are you?"

Anne turned to see his eyes open and gently mocking. Their light seared her enough to make her answer abrupt. "I thought you were asleep."

"As good an excuse as any," he said with a shrug. "But I don't let beautiful women shirk their commitments, especially to me. Is that the vegetarian delight I smell? It awakens gustatory anticipation."

Anne got out a small folding table as she thought how, even on his back, Jonathan Harris remained able to command control of a situation. It also occurred to her how typical it was of his kind—not the ability to do it, the need. There had never been any problems in her own marriage until she realized that she no longer wanted to delegate every decision in her life to Tom.

She set everything out on the table and then reached into the closet for more pillows to prop up Mr. Harris for dinner. He was reaching over very carefully to nibble at the salad while he waited, allowing that he was, indeed, hungry. Again Anne wondered how hungry he'd be after tasting something as alien as cheese and lentil casserole.

She walked around to the head of the bed to help him get to a sitting position to eat.

"No thanks," he told her agreeably. "I'm going to sit in that old chair you slept in."

She balked a minute. "I'm not really sure you're ready for it."

"Nevertheless," he said with a smile, "that's where I'm going to eat. With your help or not."

"Were you this stubborn the other time you were hurt?"

Jonathan stared at her, the humor dying in his eyes. Anne wasn't quite sure what she saw there instead, but it made her uneasy.

Finally, he offered a short nod. "Yes. Now, how 'bout a hand?"

Anne acquiesced with a shrug. After getting the chair situated next to the bed, she bent to pull him up into sitting position.

"This will be uncomfortable," she warned, still not sure it was a good idea, "so I'll take it slowly. Let me know if you need to stop."

"I know the routine," he snapped a little sharply. "Let's get going."

Anne moved as quickly and efficiently as possible until he was sitting on the side of the bed. Even as easy as the movement had been, she saw Jonathan's jaw clench with pain and perspiration break out on his forehead.

"C'mon," he gasped, seeing her hesitate. "The chair."

She stooped again to get him to his feet. Her arms around his chest, she felt the iron-hard tension of his muscles and the power of the arms that encircled her for support. Jonathan had been successfully seated in the chair a good few minutes before Anne could get her pulse to slow down.

Then she caught the tension in his suddenly pale face, and remembered that he'd neither asked for nor received anything for pain since he'd arrived. There was no question but that he was in pain.

"Are you okay?" she asked quickly, her fingers trapping the bounding pulse at his wrist. "Maybe you should lie back down."

"Don't you move me an inch," he chided with a grin that was a shade tighter than he'd wanted. "I can see four of you, and they all have the most beautiful frown of concern. I'm flattered."

"Do you need anything for the pain? I don't have much, but . . ."

"What pain?" He was quickly regaining control. "That's hunger you see. All I need is some of that lentil and cheese casserole you promised."

"Are you sure?" She couldn't understand him. There was no reason for him to play John Wayne. That wasn't the way his kind of man handled a situation like this. They were more apt to become demanding and loud. Yet she could see, only because she was used to looking for it, that he was still fighting against the pain and dizziness the exertion had brought on. He controlled it with a fierce concentration that amazed her. He wouldn't accept her help.

Guided by instincts her profession had long ago taught her, Anne turned for the door, leaving him the privacy he seemed to need.

"Coffee or tea for dinner?" she asked, not bothering to look around.

"Coffee's fine."

She took a little extra time in the kitchen, hoping it would be enough. Harris had spent the whole afternoon running true to form, when suddenly he had thrown her a complete curve. There it was again, that anomaly, the small bit of information that didn't fit. Realizing that if she weren't careful she could easily grow to respect Jonathan Harris, Anne found herself hoping yet again that he wasn't only what he would appear to be.

The high, shrill whistle of her grandmother's teakettle broke Anne's reverie. She reached for it, turning off the flame. Steam had filmed the window over the stove, disguising the faint white of the snow. The roof creaked a little beneath the ponderous weight, and Anne could hear the low, sad moan of the wind as it probed the windows and doors. The sounds of the cabin in the snowstorm gave her comfort, the feel of a familiar place crowded with happy memories. The house on Beacon Hill had never evoked that kind of feeling and never would. Anne assembled the things for the tray and thought yet again how thankful she was that she had this little cabin to wear around her like a warm cloak to protect her from the madness of life. She also wondered if Jonathan Harris had a place like this where he was safe.

Jonathan's attitude during dinner angered and unsettled her even more. When she first reentered the room, he was totally at ease and in control, as if the moment of weakness had never happened. Everything was a target for his caustic tongue, from the snow to her choice of attire. She did notice, however, that he made short order of the food before him. Anne only wished that her own appetite could hold up to his sense of humor.

"You're not from around here," he said suddenly as he refilled his plate from the table. Anne couldn't help but stare at him. Her Boston accent had certainly softened since she'd been in the mountains, but no fool could have possibly missed it.

"Your powers of observation, Mr. Harris—"

"Jonathan," he interrupted with a stern wave of the fork.

She ignored him. "—are overwhelming."

"Thank you." He smiled with satisfaction. "Why did you leave Boston?"

"I became tired of living there."

An eyebrow rose. Anne recognized the reaction. How could anyone give up all that, et cetera, et cetera. Maybe that was why he so delighted in baiting her. Perhaps he felt the same disdain—the sense of smug superiority that bred condescension and intolerance—that Tom had when he'd discovered that Anne wasn't returning from the mountain to the real world. Anne decided not to enlighten Mr. Harris further on the subject. He chose not to take the hint.

"Beacon Hill?"

Her startled reaction gave her away.

"I thought so," he said, nodding and returning to his food. "Most people don't have the money to run away from home in such style. What happened? Was your grandfather a robber baron, and you couldn't stand the shame of it anymore?"

"No," she answered pointedly, her eyes flashing at his attitude of smug superiority, "I got tired of swimming in the same waters as the barracudas."

Anne stood to leave, unable to remain for any more and not even bothering to take her half-finished dinner with her. She didn't even get to the door before he called out.

"Anne, I'm sorry. Don't leave." That strange note of sincerity had once again found its way into his voice. Anne stopped with her hand on the door, trying her best to understand why she hadn't already walked out, or better yet, heaved the casserole into his lap.

"I promised to behave." He spoke up again. "I guess I haven't."

She didn't answer, struggling with her indecision and angered by it.

"Anne," he said quietly, "I was out of line. Don't go."

A Stranger's Smile

She faced him then, even more irritated and confused by the contradictions in his words and actions, and wondered what capitulation would cost her. The strength of his eyes ate at her resistance.

"This isn't New York," she said with very careful control. "If you insist on playing New York word games, no one will talk to you. Especially me."

The bravado in his smile dimmed a little. "Ah, but you're such a worthy opponent."

"Worthy perhaps, but not interested. Unless some kind of truce is called, I'll be more inhospitable than a cold north wind to a bare backside. Your choice, Mr. Harris."

"You'll sit back down?"

After a small hesitation, she nodded.

"Good. I'll try to stay on neutral subjects." He motioned her to her chair and resumed his dinner. "I already have a question."

Anne looked up warily as she sat down. He immediately grinned at her reticence.

"It's only about your reading material," he defended himself, hand raised.

"You want to read something?"

He nodded, still grinning, his face disarmingly boyish. "I'm sure I will. You don't offer much up here in the way of diversion."

"You're right," she countered evenly, going back to her dinner. "The ballet left last week, our museum collection's out on loan and baseball season doesn't start for another five months."

"Touché." He bowed stiffly, his eyes almost as clear as the first time Anne had seen them. "That wasn't my point, though. Right now, I'm more interested in a far more existential question having to do with the choice of reading material available at this library. It's really...unique."

He motioned to the floor-to-ceiling bookcases that lined the wall opposite his bed and held her collection of paperbacks, old nursing manuals, magazines and a variety of keepsakes she'd never had the heart to remove from what had for years been her room. Anne's eyes were immediately drawn to the top shelf where her old dolls sat in a tumbled and comfortable row. The largest of them were her Raggedy Ann and Andy dolls her mother had made the year before she had died. They were perched on either end and watched the room with timeless eyes and sewn mouths.

"I don't throw anything away," Anne said. "It all ends up here at one time or another. The good books are in the living room."

"Then I'll have to get in there soon if this is any indication." His eyes roved among the hundreds of titles. "I must say that I'm astounded by it."

Again she followed his gaze. "Why?"

"Oh," he began, his hand up for elaboration, "the disparity. The contradictions." He pointed. "The *Foxfire Manuals*, and *Mother Earth News*, those fit. *Nursing, Guide to Medicinal Plants*, even Kahlil Gibran. Those all go with the vegetarian stew and braids. Very communal." His hand moved again, discovering more. "The classics... I imagine there are more in the living room...."

She nodded automatically.

"Those are marginal; a bit frivolous. But *Time*, *Wall Street Journal*, William F. Buckley? No self-respecting homesteader would be caught dead with those. And *Tax Shelters*? Richard Nixon's autobiography? Unheard of. Simply unheard of. Are you an imposter, *madame*?"

His tone was so easy and light, without a trace of condescension, that Anne knew he meant no offense. She found herself grinning.

"You're a victim of preconceived ideas," she accused, pointing her fork at him. "Where does it say that a modern homesteader isn't allowed to read *Time*? Just because one is isolated doesn't mean she wants to be caught unprepared." She was reminded of Silas's admonition on that very subject and couldn't help but grin again. "And who says I'm not allowed to read anything I want? I happen to belong to three book clubs and subscribe to magazines that also make the community circuit."

He shook his head with a mischievous grin. "You should be putting money into the crops and time on the chores. Sunup to sundown."

"I'm a nurse," she countered, "not Grandma Walton. I raise enough to feed myself and do enough chores to keep from tripping over hungry animals."

"What about the *Tax Shelters*?" He demanded. "The last time I heard, nursing didn't exactly rank among the most lucrative professions."

"It doesn't even rank that low," she assured him. "The book was my father's. That, Nixon and the subscription to the *Wall Street Journal*. He also had the finest paperback collection of murder mysteries in seven states."

She didn't realize that as she scanned the titles, she lost her smile.

"Past tense?"

She nodded. "He died about two years ago. You can tell what a pack rat I am if I can't even throw out a book on tax shelters." The truth was that she hadn't managed to work up the nerve to go through any of her father's things. Silas had carried most of them up to the attic for her but the books had been left here.

"You brought them here from Boston?"

She turned back to him, trying to lose the past's hold on her. "No. We used to come here during the summer. It was the only way father could escape the business. I took the house over and worked it again after he died."

She didn't notice that at her words Jonathan's eyes snapped open. "Well, that explains the Nancy Drew mysteries, I guess." He was watching her, as if expecting to find something in her face. After a moment he let his eyes wander over the room and then settle back on Anne, the color fading oddly as he squinted in examination.

Anne had gone back to her dinner. She nodded with a smile. "I kept every one. I figured that I'd give them to my little girl to read someday."

"If you'll pardon my asking, how did you come to spend summers here? It's a little off the beaten track, you know."

"My father was born here." Anne looked up and found a sudden frost in his eyes. It confused her. "This house has been in my family for about seven generations. My grandfather was the first to leave it during the Depression. When you're up and about, you'll see the quilts that are hung on the living-room wall. The oldest belonged to my great-great-great-great-great grandmother Sarah from before the War of 1812."

"The house looks pretty sturdy for being so old." Jonathan met Anne's eyes and spoke with quiet interest, but it was as if the life in his voice were dying. Anne could hardly manage an answer.

"The, uh, living-room walls are all that's left of the original stucture, and those have been refinished. The second story, kitchen and bedrooms are all new. And, of course, there's the modern plumbing. This homesteader does admit to enjoying her conveniences now and then."

"I can well imagine." His smile sprang on her like a trap. She saw his eyes sweep the room hungrily before landing with wolfish glee on her startled face. "Especially since you were the baby girl of one of the scions of Boston industry." He wagged his finger at her in an almost accusatory manner. "I've finally placed you," he announced triumphantly, the last of his easy-going manner disappearing in a chilling flash. "Pete Jackson's daughter, heiress to two separate fortunes, toast of Boston social society, patroness of the arts, marital catch of the decade . . . you were caught, weren't you? And you made quite a name for yourself by making a career of sorts well below your allotted station in life. Not exactly what daddy would have wanted you to do, was it?"

Anne didn't even bother to wait for him to finish before getting to her feet. Barely able to keep her silence, she began to gather together the dishes, the line of her jaw rigid with the struggle for control. It was all she could do to keep from hurling something at him. Not for the questions, which she had expected sooner or later, but for the attitude. With deadly, unerring aim, he had used his voice and eyes like lethal knives to humiliate her. She had spent the last two years recovering from that kind of pain, and she trembled with the familiar feel of it.

Jonathan didn't seem the least distressed by her reaction, evidently still too pleased with his coup to care.

"Not willing to answer the charges?" he finally asked.

She stopped briefly and turned on him, her eyes like steel. "Are you always this predatory, or do I just bring out the best in you?"

"An opportunity I simply couldn't pass up." His teeth gleamed almost maliciously now. "I thought you'd at least fill me in on how you arrived at this most interesting crossroads in life. It is, after all, a long way from Debutante of the Year."

"It's where I choose to be. That's the only information you're entitled to."

He shrugged nonchalantly. "I'm a bit disappointed. I at least expected some of that world famous breeding to peek through. A well-placed sneer, a haughty stamp of the foot."

"I'm sure it would make you feel right at home. These days, though, I find that I prefer a much more direct method of communication." She paused a moment, her eyes delivering the full promise of her next words. "A twelve-gauge shotgun, for instance."

And then she walked from the room.

The dishes were washed with great vigor and staccato rhythm that evening. Color flaring high in her cheeks, Anne seethed over the conversation she'd been roped into. She was furious with Harris for lulling her into a false sense of security only to spring his verbal trap with all the cheap theatrics found in a bad movie.

What was worse, she couldn't understand how she'd let him get away with it. She knew better. It was, after all, a carbon copy of the trick Tom had perfected on her with such destructive precision, especially toward the end. When she'd tried to fight his takeover of the business, he had taken to dissecting her in public with brutal delight. The feeling, she realized, was as painful and infuriating as it had always been. Mr. Harris was successfully resurrecting an ambivalence that Anne hadn't had to deal with in a long time, and she hated him for it.

She knew she should go and get Jonathan back into bed, but the thought of having to be that close to him kept her in the kitchen even as it unaccountably attacked her pulse rate again. Damn, it just wasn't fair.

By the time she did get in, however, he was so worn out that it was all he could do to carry out his part of the maneuver. Anne covered him up and wiped the perspiration from his drawn face, her mind consumed all the while with the picture of Tom as he'd told her what kind of man she needed.

"I'm going to head upstairs now, Mr. Harris," she finally said, putting her equipment back on the closet shelf. He hadn't made any comments when she'd changed the dressing around his head. "If you need anything for pain you'd better let me know now."

"I don't get a little bell to ring?"

She didn't realize how deathly tired her own voice sounded when she answered. "Not unless you brought along your own butler to answer it. I'm going to bed now."

"I'll let you go on one condition." This time he didn't even make an attempt at her hand. "You might as well call me Jonathan."

"It doesn't make any difference to me," she said with a shrug, not bothering to face him.

"Then Jonathan it is." She wondered if he'd meant that to sound hearty. He sounded almost as disinterested as she. "I mean, it's only fair since I don't know which last name to call you by if you insist on remaining formal."

She faced him then, stonelike. "I told you already that you were right. My name is Jackson."

"No. I mean your name now."

"Jackson," she repeated and left.

Chapter 4

Wednesday was traditionally Anne's baking day. Whenever she wasn't out on rounds, she spent the better part of the day baking loaves of grain, sourdough and vegetable breads, coffee cakes for breakfast and any number of muffins and rolls. Many of the proceeds were passed out among her needier neighbors, but Anne was glad that she worked hard enough to keep off the calories from what she kept and ate each week. It was a weakness she'd given in to early and often, deciding that honey and cinnamon were certainly a healthier addiction than tobacco or alcohol.

She finished tending the animals early, trudging heavily through snow that still fell and flew in fits and starts. Then, after retrieving last night's teacup from the little Hepplewhite table by the couch and patting distractedly at the cushions, she gathered breakfast together for her patient.

When Anne knocked on the bedroom door, she was invited in with a monosyllable. She thought it just as well. She wanted to get through this and on to her baking. If Jonathan were uncommunicative, she wouldn't have to waste valuable time and energy on his games.

"I thought you might like to get around a little today," she suggested without making eye contact. She kept her mind on the day ahead as she set out the food. If only she could make it through this quickly. Damn Jonathan Harris. He'd cost her sleep and peace of mind, and still the sight of morning sunlight striking the hard planes of his face threatened to steal her breath.

"You won't walk me out the front door and shut it behind me?" he asked without emotion.

"Not unless you sorely tempt me." She busied herself moving the easy chair over to the window where he could see outside. "The only thing you have to remember when you get up is to not put any weight on your injured leg. You can put your arm around my shoulder to steady yourself until you can use crutches."

"And when will that be?"

Anne positioned herself by the bed. "When your broken ribs let you." She helped him pull himself up to a sitting position and swing his feet over the side again. She worked in silence, wanting to avoid watching his face. She didn't want to see the struggle that he waged to move this far, the stoic concentration reflected in the steel-tight muscles of his jaw. It would only make her want to reach out to him again. After last night, she knew how impossible that would be.

She gave him a few moments to gather his strength before going on.

"The game plan's the same as yesterday. Put your arm around my shoulder, and when I straighten, get to your feet."

She bent at the knees, the correct physiological position, and prepared to help him stand. Jonathan slid his arm around her neck as before. Then he stopped. Anne was forced to finally make eye contact, discovering a controlled half smile that held no humor.

"Quite the professional," he taunted quietly. "I have to admit that I miss the beatific smile you bestowed on me the first night I was here. I'm afraid you've changed."

The look Anne gave him in response left him in no doubt as to whose fault she considered that to be. "Haven't we all?" was all she said.

She should have looked away again. Better yet, she should have straightened back up and walked away. Her chance for escape passed even as she glared at Jonathan, the challenge in both of them inexplicably dying.

With the devastating speed and shock of lightning, Anne suddenly found herself trapped, unable to move, unable to defend herself from the pain of contact. It was as if for that brief moment she and Jonathan were fused, united. Only his touch and the contact of their eyes held them, but it was enough to set Anne to trembling.

There was a physical reaction, she couldn't deny that. Her skin suddenly felt as if it had bumped against dry ice: burning and freezing, curling her toes and crawling along her scalp like a premonition. Her knees lost their rigidity, and she had to lock them straight to keep them from buckling altogether. Her lungs couldn't hold enough oxygen, and her heart found an entirely new rhythm. It was without a doubt a physical reaction, but if it had only been that she could have handled it, no matter how powerful.

What threatened to overwhelm her was what she found in Jonathan's eyes. Without warning, and for only the barest of moments, the veneer disintegrated over those fathomless pools of blue, and Anne became certain that she would fall in and become lost.

Like currents that shifted at different depths of the sea, Jonathan's eyes bared emotions that both bewildered and compelled Anne. She saw a vulnerability, a feeling of open space and invitation there. Beyond that, pain existed someplace she wasn't allowed to pry, a bare wound that still festered. She could see memories that she wouldn't be allowed to touch and the vacillation of a man who wasn't as completely in control as this one pretended.

But what left her more shaken than even those places in him she suddenly wanted to explore was the discovery of a deepest, primal place that stunned her. She briefly caught a flash of anger—almost hatred—that was directed exclusively at her. This was not the cool disdain of a man who simply thought her beneath his consideration, but an active, seething cauldron of hot animosity.

Just as quickly as it appeared, it was gone. Before Anne had the chance to react to the revelation in those potent eyes, the veneer was back up, the smooth patina of civilization concealing the anger. Once again Jonathan watched her with the cold, hard eyes of tolerant amusement.

Anne took a breath, struggling to regain her own composure. The last thing she could afford to do with this man was to lose control. If she did, he'd leave her in pieces scattered in the snow.

"Straighten when I do," she said very quietly, her face a careful mask.

Jonathan challenged her with a smile of smug superiority. "Are you really that cool?"

Anne faced him deliberately as she fought for the upper hand. "I really am."

Anne wasn't sure whether Jonathan's body shook from exertion or the perilously close confrontation. She knew that she was trembling too, and that made her angry. The weight of his rock-hard body against her as she helped him to his feet sent a jolt through her that threatened her heart rate again. She didn't have to look up to feel the electricity of his eyes on her. Her skin tingled with the power of it.

Of all the times for her to react like this to a man. It made her want to do rash things like confront his anger and hostility to defuse the glare he leveled at her. If he'd been anyone else in the world, she would have wanted very much to make love to him.

But he wasn't anyone else. The facade was too familiar, and she'd seen the inconsistencies that lay beneath. There was too much lightning in him, too much frost. After all the time Anne had spent constructing her fragile peace of mind, she didn't need this man to come along and shatter it with his volatile eyes and callused hands.

She'd intended to let Jonathan try walking out to the front room. She ended up only being able to make it twice around the bedroom before steering Jonathan toward the easy chair.

If she hadn't been so caught up in her own confusion as she lowered him into it, he would never have surprised her. He had both arms around her neck to ease his descent. Anne bent her knees to let him down and then leaned forward to scoot him comfortably back into the chair. At that moment, he pulled her over.

Badly off balance, she fell against him, her reaction a startled cry. He moved more quickly than she'd given him credit for, lacing his fingers into her hair and pulling her face to his for a kiss. She couldn't avoid the deliciously salty taste of his lips.

Anne's first instinct was to succumb, to match the bruising power of his mouth with her own. The heat that had been building in her exploded like a nova with the contact of his lips. His taunting caress lit fires she'd thought were dead long ago. She felt his breath catch in surprise and knew that he was as aroused as she. Their meeting could have been cataclysmic, but if there was one thing Anne prided herself on, it was control.

Jerking upright, she glared coldly at the triumph in Jonathan's eyes. "Don't expect outrage or hysterics," she suggested with frozen restraint, the taste of humiliation beginning to rise again with the look in his eyes. It was all she could do to keep from wiping at her mouth. "I don't play those games."

"You want me," he accused with great satisfaction.

Her eyes never wavered, never surrendered. "About as much as I want the flu. Listen, I don't know what it is about me that sets you off, but I won't stand for it."

"What sets me off," he countered with cold displeasure, "are spoiled little rich girls who think they're the light of the world because they packed away the designer dresses for a season. Lady, you're a phony."

"And you," she snapped back, "are a conceited, self-centered bastard who'd better enjoy his privacy. Because if you keep this up, that's what you're going to get."

Without another word she turned on her heel and walked out.

The pattern of baking day had become a comfortable ritual since Anne's first return to her mountain home. Today, she observed the custom as if it were a rite of cleansing. Concentrating on the immediate tasks at hand, Anne worked very hard to block out the escalating friction in her very small cabin.

First organizing her ingredients across the long butcher-block counter, she pulled the sourdough starter from the icebox and set the oven. Once that was done, she donned her official baking apron, an old blue gingham that had been in the house as long as she could remember. The apron was a formality, really. By the end of the day her face, hair and hands would be liberally dusted with flour, and there would be white smudges on either side of the seat of her pants where she would unconsciously wipe her hands. She pinned her braids around her head to keep them out of the way and set to work.

Anne mixed the yeast breads first and let them rise while she mixed and baked the vegetable breads. As the yeast breads cooked, she would begin to mix the rolls and coffee cakes. It didn't occur to her that the noise of her movements was a little louder today, or that when she kneaded the dough for her breads it looked as if she were punishing it. She did notice that it only took about half an hour for her to begin to feel better. The cathartic effect of baking day had been documented well enough two years earlier.

Anne had just pulled her first two loaves of bread from the oven and set them on the counter to cool when she heard a knock at the front door. She looked up, startled from her preoccupation, and found herself staring across the cabin to the door as if it would offer explanation. Then she remembered that Jim had promised to stop by. Maybe he'd also found out something about the not-so-mysterious Jonathan Harris.

"Coming!" she yelled as the knock sounded again. Shedding bread and oven mitts, she headed in for the living room.

"You sure have a lot of company," Jonathan offered as Anne walked by the hallway.

"That's because they don't trust you," she couldn't help but retort. His answering chuckle unaccountably surprised her.

When Anne opened the front door, she was taken completely by surprise. It wasn't Jim who stood before her, but Jim's wife Cassie, donned in fur-lined parka and snowshoes. Almost as tall as Anne, she was in her mid-twenties and looked for all the world like the proverbial Indian princess. Her skin was a beautiful olive color, her eyes as black as her hair. And every one of her ancestors hailed from central Europe.

"Cassie, are you crazy?" Anne demanded.

"Just frozen." Her friend grinned. "Let me in before my nose falls off."

Anne made way for Cassie to enter and closed the door behind her, all the while shaking her head.

"It's five miles to your place," she protested again. "You shouldn't have walked up here."

Cassie grinned, shedding parka and boots. "I'd rather be here than housebound with three kids. The silence was soul saving; the cold I wasn't as fond of. If I'd wanted that, I would have stayed in Chicago. Got any tea?"

"Sure I do. C'mon in."

Anne brewed up some tea and sliced into the warm zucchini bread. Then popping two more loaves into the oven, she sat down to join Cassie.

Cassie accepted her tea and sat in one of the cane-back chairs Silas had made for Anne's father. "From what Jim says about your patient, I thought you might need a chaperone." Cassie had never been known for beating around the bush.

Anne's answering scowl was more thunderous than she realized. "More like a referee."

Cassie's eyebrows lifted. "Sure didn't take him long to get on your bad side. What did he do? Make some passes?"

Anne shrugged uncomfortably. "Any number of them. All indiscriminate and well rehearsed." Until the last one. She felt the heat rise again in her cheeks.

"I see you were impressed."

"I lived with a man like that for three years, which was plenty long enough to learn the style intimately."

Cassie nodded. "What I want to know is if we're going to find that poor man down a cliff again."

Anne had to laugh, her indignation easing a little under Cassie's easy humor. "No," she admitted as she pulled the kettle off the stove and poured the steaming water into earthenware mugs. "My parents raised me to be a Christian. The worst I'd do is hang him by his feet from the loft. I'd only do that if he really provoked me."

"It got close, huh?"

Anne looked up to see the empathy in those dancing eyes. Cassie took a long sip from her mug and set it back down. "Well, I'm gonna have to go in and properly chastise him before I leave. Besides, I want to see if he's really as handsome as I hear."

"More so," Anne had to admit, her eyes on the honey she was dolloping into her tea. "But please don't say that to him. I'm the one who'd suffer."

Anne was grateful that Cassie had come. She had the knack to defuse Anne's housebound anger and restore her perspective. As always, Anne asked about Cassie's three children. She enjoyed that topic of conversation much more, having always used Cassie's brood as a substitute for the children she'd never have now she was divorced. Cassie was the kind of person who made everyone want to be a mother. Anne fed on her glow when she recounted in graphic detail the antics and tribulations of motherhood.

Anne hadn't realized how long they had been talking. When the timer went off she jumped, surprised by it. She hadn't prepared anything to follow the loaves that were in now. She hopped up, grabbing the oven mitts. Cassie followed her to her feet and started rummaging through drawers.

"What are you looking for?" Anne asked over her shoulder, the air from the wall oven hot on her cheek.

"Apron. I want to help. I haven't been able to bake bread in ages."

Anne pulled out the last loaf and shoved the door closed. "There's probably an extra one in the hall closet."

Cassie was already on her way out. "That makes sense. . . ."

Anne busied herself with the next batch of bread and didn't discover for a good few minutes just how long Cassie was taking to return. She looked over in the direction of the hall and heard voices. Cassie was in checking out Jonathan Harris for herself. Anne grinned as she leaned back and forth, kneading the bread dough with a bit less enthusiasm. Cassie was fearless and forthright, cursed with an insatiable curiosity and blessed with the courage to salve it. There were more than a few times that Anne envied her that.

Cassie didn't reappear for a good twenty minutes or so. When Anne saw her, she had a privately amused look on her face.

"Is he really so much like your ex?" she asked, dropping Anne's apron over her head and tying it in the back.

"Every inch of him, down to the cute green alligator he probably has on his pajamas back in New York."

"He doesn't wear any."

"Cassie!"

"It happened to come up in the conversation," Cassie defended herself without bothering to look over as she started measuring out flour into a bowl. Anne decided not to ask just how it had come up. "And he's not really from New York. He was born in Wyoming. But you're right. He is awfully handsome."

"He is that," Anne conceded as she worked her own bowl. "It's too bad he has to open his mouth and spoil it."

"He sure seems fascinated by you," Cassie countered casually.

"That's because there's nothing else up here to keep him occupied," Anne retorted dryly, her quiet answer contrasting with the color that flared along the ridges of her cheeks again. It made her angry that she was flattered by what Cassie had said. After what had happened that morning, she should have no room for that kind of reaction. It was just that he was a handsome man, and small vanities like that were hard to leave behind.

Cassie nodded, as if to herself. "Could be, could be."

Anne looked over to the secret smile in Cassie's eyes and straightened from her work. "What's that supposed to mean?"

Cassie shrugged. "Oh, nothing. You know me, always reading more into something than really exists."

"Out with it."

The smile broadened. Cassie still didn't bother to look up. "Oh, I don't know. He strikes me as…all bark. Kind of like the fourth-grade boy who hits the girl he likes the most."

"You've been on this mountain too long."

Cassie grinned and went on mixing. The two of them worked in a companionable silence for a time, both enjoying the quiet comfort of the Jackson kitchen. The timer buzzed, and Anne moved to the oven to pull out the latest batch of bread. She hummed tunelessly under her breath as she brushed stray hair from her forehead with the back of her arm and left another smudge of white there.

When they finally broke for lunch, Cassie insisted that they set up the table in the guest room and visit with Jonathan. Anne knew that it would be easier to survive a meal with Cassie present, but still couldn't manage to get in there soon enough to help her set up. Cassie didn't seem to mind in the least.

When Anne finally brought in the food, Jonathan was smiling and politely polished, commenting generally on the wonderful aromas that filled the house and the decaying state of the weather. He was nothing if not the perfect gentleman, which made Anne furious. She knew that he was pulling out all of his best manners for Cassie, and she couldn't understand why. Maybe the problem wasn't just Jonathan after all, but Jonathan and herself.

Anne answered when she had to with studied politeness as she helped ready for lunch, but she never quite faced Jonathan. It didn't seem to matter since Cassie was happy handling the majority of the conversation anyway.

By the time he was ready to eat, Jonathan had been sitting up in the chair for quite a while. Anne could see that he was beginning to wear thin, but it seemed that he refused to let it get in his way.

"This keeps getting better and better," he announced. "If I would have known there was so much to see outside New York, I would have left a long time ago."

Anne ignored him. She was sure that Cassie would have laughed at her reaction had Jonathan not been in the room. "Quiche?" she asked instead.

His answering smile, as he held out his plate to be served, reminded Anne of the wolf as he spotted Red Riding Hood's grandmother. If only it had happened five years ago, Anne would have found it all amusing and tolerated the leering with good-natured amusement. The wounds were still too new, though, and Jonathan seemed too much like Tom to let them heal. He'd managed to break right through the armor of isolation she'd so carefully built and instinctively attacked her most vulnerable spots.

Anne realized suddenly that Cassie and Jonathan had been talking, and that she'd been staring directly at Jonathan with undisguised anger. He couldn't have missed it, and yet he was blithely conversing with Cassie as if Anne weren't even in the room. She quickly lowered her eyes to her plate, embarrassed by her own bad manners. She'd have to try to be more civil.

"Where do you live in New York?" Cassie was saying, ignoring Anne's sudden lapse in courtesy.

"Upper Sixties, near Central Park," Jonathan answered.

Cassie nodded. "Nice. We have some friends there. Do you work nearby?"

Anne looked up in time to see a delighted, knowing smile light Jonathan's eyes as he waved his fork in Cassie's direction. "I really work in Philadelphia. I commute."

Cassie grinned right back. "We'll find out sooner or later."

"Well then, let it be a surprise. I love surprises."

"Will it be?"

"A surprise?" He shrugged. "I guess not really unless you're back in New York. But allow me my little game anyway." He took a drink of coffee and smiled ruefully. "The truth of the matter is that I don't want to be bothered with any of it right now. I'd like to consider this as my vacation in the mountains. When people know who you are, they expect certain things from you. This way there's no pressure."

Cassie persisted, quite undaunted. "Won't somebody miss you?"

"I imagine so."

"But you don't want to notify them."

"I don't think so." He went back to eating, the same irreverent smile still playing across his face. Cassie laughed and went back to her own meal. Anne stared at them both and stopped eating hers.

"You're giving up awfully fast, Cassie."

Cassie took the accusation with aplomb. "It's all in the timing, Annie."

"Yes, but you don't have to stay here with him. He could be the vicious criminal Silas thinks he is. I'm not sure I'd want to talk to him then." She caught herself wanting to grin. "Maybe we shouldn't even call him Jonathan."

"You could find something to talk about," Cassie responded as if Jonathan weren't there. "We've already discussed his sleeping attire and Wyoming. Neither of those has anything to do with his criminal career."

"You don't know that."

"She wants to know if my name's real," Jonathan said. "Tell your spies that, yes, my name is real. I don't have the energy to invent a name like that. I use all my energy just being vicious."

"I've never met a criminal with a middle name of Bradshaw," Cassie obliged as she picked lurking anchovies from her salad. "Most of them are something like Bubba or Billy."

"Bradshaw is my grandmother's maiden name." He reached over to steal the anchovies Cassie was piling at the side of her plate. "That's Emily Baldwin Bradshaw. Baldwin was her mother's maiden name...should I go on?"

"I don't think so." Anne shook her head. "That wouldn't leave us anything to talk about tomorrow."

Jonathan looked up from the fish he was popping into his mouth. "We could talk about you."

Even though Anne saw that his eyes were gentle in their teasing, she stiffened. "No, we won't."

Cassie stopped in the middle of dishing up seconds. "Her grandmother's name was Ellen Josephine McLaughlin. She was born over on the next ridge."

Anne shot Cassie a warning glance, afraid that the conversation would get around to Boston after all, and that Jonathan would attack like he had before. She had begun to relax for the first time since Jonathan had woken up, and she didn't want to jeopardize it.

Cassie chose to ignore her. "Anne was born here in the cabin, but she was raised in Boston. Somewhere near the bay."

"Boston's one of my favorite cities," Jonathan offered.

"I hate it," Anne retorted evenly, returning to her food.

His eyebrows raised. Cassie grinned, enjoying the sparks.

"Well, you've been to New York, haven't you?" he coaxed.

"I hate New York."

Cassie laughed over at Jonathan. "And you call this a vacation?"

"Don't worry," he retorted, "I'll get to her. I can be very persuasive."

Anne looked up, trying to keep her voice light. His eyes carried no further than this conversation, but she couldn't help but think of the aggression in them earlier. "Well, she isn't very impressed," she said. "She's spent better meals in the barn."

Cassie saluted with a fork. "Touché."

"I'm an injured man," Jonathan defended himself. "I should at least be recognized for making the effort."

Cassie turned for Anne's reaction. Anne shrugged easily, permitting a smile she didn't feel. "I guess I feel pretty generous today. I'll give you points for remaining an enigma in the face of Cassie's persistence."

He grinned brightly. "I'll take that as a compliment."

"Was that so difficult?" Cassie asked as she helped dry dishes after lunch.

"Was what so difficult?"

"Talking to Jonathan."

Anne flashed her a sour look. "It's so important?"

"I'm not the one stuck in the same cabin with him," Cassie shrugged. "I can go home."

"And I can put him out into the snow. No jury in their right mind would convict me."

"Ease up, Annie. You were being entirely sociable in there after the first few minutes. Why the sudden change of attitude?"

Anne thought of his kiss and the unwanted fire it had ignited. And then she thought of Jonathan's eyes when he'd done it. She finished putting away the cups before answering. "Because I'll lay odds that the minute you walk out of here, he reverts to form."

"I think you're making all this up to protect your sense of self-righteous indignation."

"And I think he's putting on a show for you. The charming, witty, much-maligned rich boy from New York. I get the picture."

Cassie shrugged her resignation. "Okay, be that way. I was just trying to help. Since you won't accept it, I might as well go on home."

Anne took a look at the clock and nodded in agreement. It would be about dark by the time Cassie got home. Anne had to admit that she would sorely miss the enjoyment of her unpredictable company.

"Well, at least take some bread with you," she offered, reaching to pull some out.

"Caramel rolls, maybe," Cassie said, nodding. She hung her towel over the white pig's head that protruded from the wall by the sink and turned to Anne. "But there's something else I want more."

Anne looked over to see that Cassie had something important she wanted to say. "Well, spit it out."

Cassie grinned broadly. "The whole darn mountain wants to know what's in that letter."

Anne found herself staring suspiciously at Cassie. "What letter?"

Now it was Cassie's turn to stare. "Come on, Annie. The special delivery letter. Except for Mr. Harris, it's the most interesting thing to happen up here in months."

"Your sense of priority is beginning to atrophy," Anne said dryly. "In Boston the snow would have at least made honorable mention."

Cassie was not to be put off. "The letter, Annie."

Anne tried to shrug offhandedly as she walked Cassie over to her coat. "It was nothing. A bit of business about my mother's trust."

Cassie might have been satisfied with the explanation if she hadn't pulled her coat off the hall tree and sent the whole thing crashing onto its side.

"Oh, I'm sorry..."

Anne bent with her to pick up the various articles of clothes now scattered over the floor. "Don't worry about it, Cass. Next time I'm over for lunch, I'll dump out your silver drawer."

"Annie..."

Anne turned to see Cassie stand up beside the waste basket, un-opened legal envelope in hand. "I knew I should have dumped that thing out," she muttered to herself.

"You didn't even open it."

Anne shrugged with forced nonchalance. "I make it a point not to correspond with people I don't like."

Cassie walked over and took Anne's hand, placing the envelope firmly in her grasp. "You can't ignore it, honey. It might be important. Just read it through once. While I'm in saying goodbye to Jonathan." She smiled with friendly warning. "Or, I'll read it myself." She waited until Anne had ripped open the envelope before heading for the guest room.

When Cassie returned to a few minutes later, it was to find Anne standing before the fireplace, letter in hand, her eyes staring and empty. Cassie's heart lurched. Something terrible had happened.

Chapter 5

"Annie? Annie, what's the matter?"

Anne couldn't bring herself to answer. She could only stare at and past Cassie as if she weren't there, shaking her head slowly. Cassie led her to the sofa and sat her down.

"I have to get to Boston," Anne finally managed to say, turning to her friend. "I have to go now before he closes."

"Closes what? Honey, what's in that letter?"

Anne took a breath to steady herself against the panic that threatened to choke her. "Cassie, he lost it. He's lost Cedar Ridge."

"What do you mean he lost it? Who lost it?"

"Brad. He put up the deed to Cedar Ridge to finance a futures deal...and he...he lost it." Her hands were at her mouth as if to stifle the enormous, overwhelming fear. It was too much to comprehend.

All she had asked was to be left alone. She hadn't wanted their money or their power or their madness. All she had wanted for the first time in her life was some peace. She had asked them for no more than the only home she had ever known and enough of her mother's estate to survive. No more. Now they'd taken even that from her.

"Anne, how could he do that?"

Again Anne shook her head, still trying to understand what her husband and brother had done to her. "Oh God, Cassie, I have to get up there and save it. I have to get to Boston."

"Annie, you can't. Nobody's going anywhere in this weather. I'm not even sure I can get a telegram out yet."

Anne stood, giving motion to the anger that was beginning to curl in her stomach, an anger that threatened to drown even the fear. She walked to the window, watching the snow as it drifted lazily across the yard. The sky was heavy with it, the wind picking up a little. The storm wasn't over, and she was trapped by it, impotent to stop her brother from selling her home out from under her to a resort developer. The snow, so benign and soft and white, whose quiet beauty she'd always loved, was stifling her and she wanted to scream. She wanted her hands, literally or figuratively, around her brother's neck. Better yet, Tom's. After all this time, she knew well enough who had orchestrated this deal.

"He can't really do it, can he?" Cassie asked. "It belongs to you both."

"It belongs to him. My father left me very little. Father was of the school that felt that money matters were better left to the men. That way Brad and Tom could take care of me." Anne turned from the window to find that Cassie had followed her over, anxiety creasing her forehead.

"You could contest it," her friend offered. "Maybe buy it outright. You have your mother's inheritance."

Anne shook her head, crowded again by the real fear that she would lose her cabin, her home. "That money is sunk in the clinic. I don't have enough to buy Cedar Ridge back." She found herself staring into the colors of the fire. The wood smoke lent a warmth to the air, a familiar comfort. The fireplace had been built by her father with stones from the mountain.

When Anne spoke again her voice was so quiet that Cassie could hardly hear it. "Cassie, what am I going to do?"

It was dark by the time Cassie finally left to go home. She tried to stay longer, insisting that Anne needed her there, but Anne was adamant. She didn't want Jim and the kids worrying about Cassie trying to get home, especially when more snow was threatening. Even though Cassie could see right through her and Anne knew it, she gave it one of the game-trooper routines as she saddled up Andy for Cassie's ride home.

"I'll be back up in the morning," Cassie promised.

"No you won't," Anne retorted evenly. "You have babies to take care of. Just set Andy loose tomorrow. He'll come home."

"Annie, you can't face this alone."

Anne's answering smile was genuine. "I won't, Cass. You can help most by keeping an eye out for the first flight to Boston. And by sending a telegram as soon as you can, telling them that I'm on my way."

"Do you want me to get ahold of your lawyer?"

For a moment, Anne blanked. "I don't have a lawyer."

Cassie stared at her. "You're kidding."

"No. I found out too late that the family friend I used for my divorce was a better friend of Tom's."

"You must know somebody."

"I'll find someone."

Cassie threw up her hands in frustration and turned to mount Andy. After knowing Anne for as long as she had, she knew better than to pursue the matter. Anne would, indeed, find someone. Cassie just hoped that whoever he was would be smart enough to save Anne's home. Cassie had a bad feeling about the whole thing.

Anne didn't go back inside for quite a while after Cassie had gone. The hard work she was able to do in the barn helped keep the terror at bay. Every time she paused, the words of her brother's terse letter returned to taunt her until she thought that the only thing left that would save her sanity would be for her to take a long hike into the woods for a good scream.

She had no idea how she would ever get any sleep until she made it to Boston. She wasn't even sure that she could stand to spend any time in the house. There were too many memories there for it to be comfortable tonight.

Surely it was a mistake or Brad's idea of a bad joke. She'd wake up tomorrow to find Jim at the door with another letter that said to disregard the previous one. Even Brad couldn't be cruel enough to pull her feet out from under her like that. Even Brad couldn't sell the land where he and seven other generations of Jacksons before him were born. It wasn't just home; it was a legacy.

Anne stopped a moment and leaned on the pitchfork she'd been using. Brad certainly would be stupid enough to let Tom do it all. And once done, Brad wouldn't give it a second thought. He had never been comfortable on the mountain, claiming that there were the spirits of too many ancestors wandering the place who probably didn't like him any more than his father did. He would never even know that the cabin was gone. Anne stared blankly ahead and fought back tears for the first time in two years.

"Have you been avoiding me again?" Jonathan demanded from his room as she walked past. She gritted her teeth, not at all sure she would be able to remain civil. She could tell that he had already discarded the gentlemanly demeanor he'd proffered to Cassie, and she was really afraid that his nasty personality would drive her beyond control this time.

"Do you need something?" she asked, going on through to the kitchen.

"A bit of beautiful company would be nice."

Anne reached the kitchen with its aroma of baking bread and suddenly wished that Cassie hadn't gone home. It was going to be difficult to even be in this room tonight where the memory of Anne's mother still lived in the warm aromas and frayed comfort of the furniture. The teakettle her grandmother had used sat on the stove, and the old kitchen witch that had hung in the sink window for as long as Anne could remember still kept the room safe. Even the old Depression dishes and glassware and the red gingham curtains that matched the tablecloth, familiar sights that had comforted her when she was first alone, now tore unbearably at her. How could she get through the night surrounded by what she would lose? How could she sleep with the memories whirling madly in her mind?

For the first time since she'd moved to the mountains Anne seriously considered getting drunk. She still had her father's old stock of liquor, so supply was no problem. Jonathan wouldn't care. Except for his leg, he was doing pretty well. Maybe if she were drunk, she could stand the additional strain of his company.

"Annie, you're ignoring me again."

She stalked to the door of his room. "The name," she said slowly, suddenly losing her temper, "is Anne. A-N-N-E. Now, what is it that you need?"

He feigned a hurt look. "What happened to noblesse oblige? We were doing so well when Cassie was here. I thought you were beginning to like me. She did."

"Cassie's a generous person."

"And I'm a tough one. You'll find that I don't intimidate easily." His smile was hard.

"More's the pity."

With her words the look in his eyes melted into the more familiar smugness. "I'll find a way, Anne Jackson. You're attracted to me. I consider your coolness a challenge. And I love challenges."

She refrained from comment. "Do you want dinner?"

"I want you." Again it seemed that his eyes didn't agree.

"That wasn't a choice."

His smile broadened. "It will be."

He ate alone. Finding that she needed most of her energy to cope with the news she'd received, Anne served dinner and cleaned up in near silence.

For Jonathan's part, even the momentary lapses he'd allowed into a gentler personality disappeared. He spent all his time true to form, goading and challenging, as if pushing Anne to react to his outrageous behavior. At any other time Anne wouldn't have given him the satisfaction. Tonight, it didn't seem to make any difference.

At nine, she found herself standing in the living room with nothing left to do to keep her occupied. The animals were bedded down, the house was sparkling clean for a change, enough baking had been done to last a month and Jonathan was quietly reading in his room. Anne sat alone with nothing to do but think about the letter.

She remained rooted in one spot searching desperately for something to do to keep her busy. It had to be involved enough that she'd have to pay attention to what she was doing. The needlepoint that sat on the sofa wasn't enough, and any of the books that lined the walls on either side of the fireplace were too much. She walked back into the kitchen and brewed some coffee, although she wasn't thirsty, and pulled out some cookies she didn't feel like eating.

"I was heating up some coffee and thought you might like some." She stood in the doorway of Jonathan's room with tray in hand. He looked up from his book, even more startled than Anne by her actions.

"What's this?" he asked. "A second chance?"

"Just coffee," she replied evenly.

"Will you sit with me?"

"For a moment." She heard herself say it and still couldn't believe it. His eyes were like aquamarines tonight, like faceted gems that flashed surface sarcasm and hid the deeper levels. She almost thought that if she moved a little she could find something else there. Well, at least sparring with him would keep her mind from Brad's idiocy.

"What shall we talk about," he asked, "your grandparents or mine?"

"Yours."

She set down the tray and stood to evaluate the condition of her patient. He'd been sitting up since morning and now looked stretched. "Would you like to get back to bed first?"

"I do that and I may not get around to the coffee."

She sat across from him in the straight-backed chair. "How are you feeling?"

He smiled, his eyes inexplicably softening. She didn't know why he seemed to be making an effort to be nice, but she was grateful. "Pretty good. When do I get to scale the living room?"

"In a couple of days if you're still feeling like it. By tomorrow I imagine you can be up and around your room more."

"Child's play."

She had to laugh. "Only with a pair of sound legs and a full set of working ribs."

"I've made it with less."

She raised an eyebrow, believing him. "In that case, let's take a turn around the block now."

He met her gaze with a challenge of his own. "All right. I've been wanting to see what the living room looks like anyway."

Anne blinked. "You're serious."

His answer was given with a wry grin. "Best way I know of getting back on my feet is getting back on my feet."

The procedure for helping Jonathan to his feet was the same; the walk was not really that far. And the spark between them just as potent when they got close. Anne felt the tension ignite in her like a stifling pressure, threatening her breath and attacking her pulse.

Jonathan stood unsteadily and leaned against her, his chest heaving. Anne closed her eyes for a moment against the urge to hold him. To find those places she could share and cherish. For these fleeting moments of contact, she felt as if she had tapped a primal energy source, and that at the core of that energy lay the secret to Jonathan Harris. For those brief seconds, Anne found herself wishing that that core was made up of the blue of his eyes rather than the venom of his words.

"How long ago did you have that injury?" she asked as they made their way toward the door, Jonathan's arm tightly around her shoulders. Her arm circled his waist, and her hand spanned the scars.

"A long time ago."

"Fall off another cliff?" She couldn't believe how well he was doing. The lines of his face were etched with a fierce concentration that awed her. He never took his eyes from the far wall of the living room.

"Something like that."

"Why do you push yourself so hard?" The question came out before Anne realized: but she had to know. What drove him? What fires fueled that will?

For a moment he took his gaze from his objective and turned to her. Anne could almost see the flames deep in that blue, and a flash of vulnerability that tore at her.

"Twice in my life I was helpless to keep people I cared for safe from being hurt," he said turning back to the wall. "The second time it happened, I vowed never to be helpless again." They walked farther, his posture rigid. "Never."

They had made it back to the room before Anne spoke again.

"I think you can use the crutches tomorrow."

He nodded. "You didn't ask any questions about what I told you."

Anne gently swung him into bed, bending to support his injured leg as he brought it up. He looked so strained, so very tired for the effort he'd made.

"You aren't ready to tell me about it yet," she answered, sinking wearily into the chair.

Jonathan looked over in surprise. Anne knew she'd read him right when she saw the confusion. The vulnerability made a brief return to his eyes.

"Will you tell me what had you so upset earlier when your friend Cassie was here?"

Anne avoided his direct gaze, her hand picking at the lint on her jeans. "Oh, I, uh...find myself helpless to save something I care about."

When she finally lifted her eyes to him, they were rueful, the pain carefully hidden. It didn't seem to matter. Anne had the feeling that Jonathan found it anyway.

"Can I help?"

She shrugged uncomfortably, wondering where the enmity had gone. In the time it had taken to help Jonathan walk through the rooms of her house, they seemed to have gained an unexpected bond. The bond of unspoken understanding and respect.

"I don't know. I'm waiting for the phone to come back up, and for Cassie to get a telegram out."

His eyes were the gentlest she'd seen them. "Do you want to tell me about it?"

She shook her head, confused tears threatening. "No. Not now. I think both of us need a good night's sleep."

For a moment Jonathan's eyes melted, the blue a sweet, warm light in response to her pain. Then, before Anne could react to the change, a wall went up, a brittle, cynical edge that forced her away again. Once more Jonathan hid away where it was safe. He rolled over on his back and addressed the ceiling.

"Would you like another kiss?"

Anne stared, not as surprised as she should have been. It occurred to her how lonely his battles must be for him. "One per patient is my limit."

He turned to her with a slick smile. "Does that mean we're progressing to bigger and better things?"

Anne stood up suddenly and glared down at him. "I'm progressing to bed. Upstairs. Alone." She couldn't account for the unexpectedly shrill pitch of her voice. "If I hear one more ridiculous proposition out of you, you'll progress outside. In the snow. Alone!"

By the time she got up to the loft, she was wondering what had so abruptly set her off like that. She hadn't really been that taken aback by Jonathan's sudden mood swing. He'd done it before, and chances were, he'd do it again, even if he had begun to trust her with a glimpse behind his facade.

Anne looked back down toward where the guest room door was, as if to better divine an answer to a question that bothered her more than she wanted to admit. Without warning she was struck by the image of Jonathan's eyes as he'd talked about helplessness. The moment when they'd been so vulnerable, when Anne had wanted to reach out and ease the struggle there. Her mouth opened silently, her chest rising a little faster.

She had been so close to him at that moment, so close to whatever the real Jonathan Harris was, that it had frightened her. She didn't want to be close to him or any man; but especially to him. And yet she had begun to succumb to that translucent fire of his eyes, the electricity of his touch. When he'd turned on her again, betraying the moment of fragile contact with barbs tipped in malice, she had protected herself by biting at him like a shrew.

The same way he seemed to respond to her.

Anne stood where she was for a while longer, unable to go on. Something Cassie had said nagged at her about the little boy who hit the girl he liked the most. Oh Lord, she thought with sick dread, what if Cassie were right? What if Jonathan were as drawn to her as she was to him and reacted with the same defense mechanism? Anne thought of the abrupt personality changes, the jibes and directed attacks, and felt worse. It made more sense than she liked.

Please God, she prayed, not now. I can't handle this. I can't even handle the fact that I'm becoming more and more drawn to this man. His quiet strength and hidden pain, the brief flashes of empathy that give so much promise all compel me. A matched set of ambivalences is more than any person can handle in a small cabin in the snow. How can I be expected to deal with it now when my life is on the line? Thanks all the same, but if you have a new love interest in mind for me, it'll have to be some other time or place. Or person. I can't afford this one.

Yet even as she consciously turned away from the thought of Jonathan, Anne couldn't avoid the fact that her heart still hammered oddly in her chest, or that she could feel his powerful arms around her as vividly as if he were actually there with her.

She knew it was futile, but she went about getting ready for bed, brushing her long hair, slipping into a long flannel nightgown and climbing in under her big down comforter before turning off the small light by her bed. Downstairs, the fire in the fireplace was slowly dying, its soft red light licking up the chimney opposite the loft. The house was quiet, the wind gently brushing through the pines outside. Somewhere an owl called, a low, mournful sound of night. It was chilly enough that the comforter felt like the embrace of familiar arms. A wonderful night to fall asleep. Only Anne couldn't.

She lay still in the pleasant warmth of her bed, trying her best to relax, and knowing that she wouldn't. She stared at the flickering shadow patterns on the ceiling without relief, the demons chasing her in the dark of midnight. First Jonathan's, and then the ones her brother and husband had unleashed.

As the night passed with agonizing slowness, the loss of her home drove everything else before it with a vengeance. Fears and ideas and plans raced madly in her head, each a desperate attempt to deal with the unbearable reality of what had happened. The irrational became plausible in the dark and the impossible possible.

It would be simple. She would confront Brad and force his hand, contest the will and buy the land back. She would walk up to Tom and laugh in his face when he told her it was all only a ploy to win her back. She'd laugh at both of them when they told her she'd never get the land back again. She could be in control. She'd worked two long years to repair the damage done to her self-esteem, and except for one incredibly handsome stranger with piercing eyes and Tom's mannerisms, she'd managed to maintain a respectable amount of independence.

All she had to do to save her home was get far enough away from Jonathan to escape his turbulent magnetism. She needed to travel to Boston where she could find some breathing room and hire a reputable, firebrand lawyer who wasn't already in her husband's pocket.

For hours she tossed and turned, her brain feverish with plans of confrontation, her body exhausted from the strain of the past three days. If only she had someone to talk to, someone she could call up and burden with the dread that refused to ease. If only there were a friend in Boston who could recommend the proper channels to take to save Cedar Ridge.

Again, she thought of the fact that she had left no friends in Boston. She'd left no friends anywhere in her former life. The relationships she'd formed when in nurses' training had died of neglect when she'd become taken up with the world her marriage to Tom had created, the world she'd been born to and groomed for her entire life.

The people she'd known in her hospital days had been the most similar to the ones she knew here on the mountain. They were a rare and good group of friends she would always regret having lost. The people she'd known during her marriage had never really been more than acquaintances, a supporting chorus to the choreography of her life as daughter to the chairman of the board. These people were only faces that filled out the background, no one she considered worth the effort of friendship. To a person, they had considered an important discussion one that debated how to best maximize the social season. She couldn't remember any one person who stood out. They had all been the same. And they were all useless.

She had no one left now to turn to for the help she needed.

For a moment, she considered asking Jonathan for help. It seemed only reasonable that after all she'd done for him he could find her someone to help her fight her way through the legal maze her ex-husband had constructed. She could go down to him and tell him how she was about to lose the only thing that meant anything to her in the world, and that he had to help her if only out of gratitude.

Then with a startling clarity she saw the look in his eyes when he'd found out who she was and what she'd done with her life. She knew how he'd react to this new twist to the story, gratitude or not.

It was with a feeling of desperation she hadn't known in two years that Anne finally fell into a tiring, fitful sleep some hours later.

By the next night Anne felt like a zombie. She'd still had to do the heavy work, and had even managed an hour-long trek into the white silence of the woods above the house, restoring some of the internal silence stolen by Jonathan's intrusion into her life.

He had been another matter altogether. Hovering precariously on crutches, Jonathan had, with her help, begun to make his way more comfortably around the rooms of the small house. In between treks, he spent his time in the chair by the window. He communicated a minimal amount, much to Anne's relief, but the time in the room with him further solidified the conclusions she had begun to form about him the night before.

Jonathan spoke little, but when he did he was again politely distant but distant, exerting the majority of his energy on recovering his mobility. He worked hard, never giving himself a break. In his silence, Anne saw the quiet, sweating determination of a man driven. Then, every once in a while, he would throw off a few biting retorts, as if making up for an oversight of some kind.

It probably would have been easier for Anne to handle just the sarcasm. That way she could have decided that her observations about a more vulnerable side to this man were nothing more than the product of wishful thinking. But she couldn't deny his courage in those moments when he tested his own will the way no city-pampered, egocentric executive would have. She knew that those times somehow connected with the brilliant smile he'd saved for Cassie. He was bitter only with Anne.

She was still worrying as she got ready for bed, her exhausted mind ricocheting from the dilemma of Jonathan to the impending confrontation with Tom.

No word had come from Cassie, and there was no letup in the snow. Anne couldn't last much longer. As hard as she tried, the terror returned, especially in the dark, when the dread grew exacerbated by the crowded night shadows. Anne knew that sleep would again be a long time coming.

When she first heard it, she thought it was her own dream. The sounds were garbled and frantic, rising and falling as if heard through a faulty speaker. Names, cries for help, more names. One name. A name she'd heard before, that teased at her memory. Anne's eyes shot open into the dark, a strange chill of prescience filling her.

Silence.

Only the soft ticking of her alarm clock broke the thickness of the early-morning hours. Even the wind had died, leaving her in a frightening void, unable to remember exactly what had awakened her.

Then, faintly she heard it again. A voice strange yet immediately recognizable, floated ghostlike from downstairs.

"Charlie... It's Charlie... He's got me...."

She held her breath, waiting, suddenly cold. The voice was haunted, belonging to a place of nightmares and pain, and she didn't want to approach it.

"Carson...get down...you've gotta... No, move back!" His voice rose to a cry, urgent and frightened. Anne tumbled out of bed. Grabbing her robe she headed for the stairs. She was afraid he'd be thrashing around and would hurt himself, the instinct of action propelling her before the plan of action had a chance to crystallize.

Anne flipped on a small light in the short hallway and stepped to the door, the light falling at an angle across the small bed. The bedclothes were snarled, and the spread was bunched tightly in Jonathan's hands. A fine sheen of perspiration reflected on his face.

"I can't get out... can't get out of his line here...." He was struggling, fighting to get free of something. Anne could see him sweating and shaking, his hands opening and closing spasmodically around the blankets. She stood motionless in the doorway, mesmerized by a stranger's dream. She knew she should go and stop it before he hurt himself, and shouldn't let him go through the terror of whatever hell awaited him in his sleep, but his strange words held her rooted to the spot. She couldn't imagine what could possibly have such a terrible grip on his subconscious. The man Jonathan Harris seemed to be would have no room for nightmares.

His next words seared straight through her.

"Eddie, I can't get to you.... I'm...I'm hit...ah, God... Corpsman..."

He was grabbing at his side, where Anne had found the scars, and writhing in the bed whimpering. "Corpsman, let him... No, I'll... I can... Eddie."

Vietnam.

Anne's hand found her gaping mouth. Oh, dear God, she thought, her stomach knotting up and unbidden tears clouding her vision as she watched Jonathan flounder in his private hell. He'd been in Nam. The Charlie he'd rambled on about wasn't a specific person as she'd assumed. It had been the Vietcong.

She couldn't take her eyes from him, couldn't move to help him. What she saw left her confused and shaken. She wanted to back out the door and escape the pain that echoed in this room. She had enough of her own to consider courting his.

He was quiet a moment, and Anne saw his hand reach out to something, as if to touch it. He made a small blind stroking motion, the way a mother might touch the face of a child.

"Eddie," he whispered. "I'm sorry, Eddie...I...I tried...."

She didn't even realize that she'd moved until she found herself beside his bed. He still writhed, the sounds in his throat rising from an anguish that cut through Anne like a hot knife. She didn't feel the tears on her cheeks as she moved to gather him into her arms.

For a few long moments all Anne could do was hold him to her, rocking him and stroking his wet, tangled hair, her murmurs meant to comfort them both. He held onto her like a lifeline, his choked sobs released with the comfort of her touch. His hands found the rich fall of her hair and wound into it. Anne eased into his touch, bringing him closer.

She never saw his eyes open, and didn't realize that he'd turned his face to hers. When she felt his lips find hers, she responded out of instinct, out of the turmoil she'd brought to this room and the anguish she'd found there. Bending to him, she met his lips with her own and became lost within him.

Anne never had the chance to question what was happening. When Jonathan pulled her down to him, she followed blindly. His embrace was desperate, his hands searching her with almost frantic need. She clung to him, absorbing the fierce possession of his mouth with her own and purging her own pain with the feel of him. Her gown was no barrier to his callused, seeking fingers. He discovered the taut nipples that strained beneath him and consumed them with chafing discovery. Anne heard a small sobbing sound and realized it was her own. Her mind was a maelstrom and her body was on fire. From the moment he'd kissed her there had been no turning away. She felt herself drowning, pulled under by the ferocious pain that had been unleashed by a nightmare and trapped there by her own need to share and salve it. She stroked the planes of his face and the rigid line of his throat, comforting, seeking, the explosion building in both of them driving her beyond reason. Jonathan bruised her mouth with his explorations and savaged her skin with his fire.

His hands trembled when he found her thighs. Anne gasped at their strength. She turned her head to the side, somehow to be free, but Jonathan found her there and brought his mouth down again on hers, harsh with his need. His lips searched her face, her eyes, her forehead, their taste reckless. She arched against him, against the fire that swept her, an agony that was hard to distinguish from the pain. Her own hands sought, roaming along muscle and sinew that stretched in unyielding lines over chest and shoulder, hips and steely thighs.

It was only when his hand forced her thighs apart that she felt any fear. He was desperate with the need for release, for union. She was afraid she'd be hurt. Instinct brought her hands up to him, to find the rock-hard surface of his chest. He was panting against her, his body slick with sweat. She wanted to beg caution and care, but couldn't manage the words. Couldn't even bear to question what fires lit those coalescent eyes. The unbearable heat built in her as his fingers found her and silenced her protest.

Their joining was cataclysmic, as if by uniting they could purge their ghosts. Anne thought she would be crushed by him, engulfed by the white hot light he ignited in her. Her arms came up, her legs circled him, pulling him even closer as he drove into her. His face was buried in her throat, his hands grinding her against him. She arched to meet him. The agony in her belly was unbearable, the sweet torment of his gasping cry, torture. They rocketed faster, their passion soaring beyond need or pain.

Jonathan lifted his head then, his eyes trapping Anne's with their wild, piercing light. She threw her head back to keep those eyes before her, but he took her mouth again, his tongue hot and searching, his breath ragged against her. He brought his hands down to trap her body against his, his pelvis sharp against her soft skin, and thrust into her with a force that made her cry out. What hunger drove her she didn't know but it matched his bruising strength. She brought her hands to his buttocks and forced him back to her again. And the explosion came, rocking them both and tearing gasps from them as they shuddered and clung desperately and spent themselves in each other.

The old clock in the living room struck three, and Anne could hear the wind outside rise a little. In this room the stillness slowly returned, and peace crept back from the dim, shadowed corners where a terrifying dream had chased it. She felt Jonathan's breathing ease, felt his hold on her relax toward sleep. Her own body refused her the release.

Her life in this house had changed tonight. Jonathan had brought out something in her that she had long hidden away. She had been compelled by more than compassion to go to him, by more than empathy for a lonely, hurt person caught in the throes of terror. She had been drawn to him because his pain had seared through her in a way that had never happened before. And she had stayed, she realized now, because her need to give to Jonathan had been greater than his need to lose himself in her. There was nothing she would not do to keep him from having to face that kind of desolation again.

The clock struck again before Anne turned from the sight of Jonathan's soft, sleeping face toward the door, her steps carrying another burden as great as her own. She had to get out of this cabin before she lost her mind. Had to get away and come back, and then maybe she could understand everything that was going on.

"Anne..."

She turned to see that he was awake, his eyes sleep-clouded and unsure. There was no guile there to confront, and Anne suddenly wished there were.

"I...was just going...." she stammered, trying to turn again. "It's pretty late."

"Anne."

His voice was strained. Anne turned again and managed to face him. But they had no more words. Their walls had gone back up, the pain of contact too great. They were already far apart, and she didn't think they'd let each other close again.

Chapter 6

It wasn't until the next afternoon, after more long hours of near-silent work with Jonathan, the tedious, mind-numbing waiting alternating with spurts of fierce work, that Anne finally heard from Cassie.

Cassie's call was the first to make it over the repaired lines. By the time the phone rang Anne was pacing around the living room.

"Annie, are you all right?"

"What did they say, Cass?"

There was a pause, a gathering of tact. "I got a telegram. And a phone call."

"A call?"

"Yeah. Hon, it doesn't sound good."

Anne stared out the front window as Cassie explained. The snow was so brilliant, so peaceful. The pine trees she'd watched grow since childhood strained under the weight of it.

The telegram had been brutally curt. If Anne wished to interfere, she would have to do so when Brad and Tom met the new owners in New York. But there was really nothing she could do. The land was sold and Anne had no say in the matter. The accompanying phone call from Tom had contained a threat, thinly veiled as a bribe: if Anne would come home, all would be well.

"Now I know why you left. Tom has all the charm of a pet cobra."

Anne looked up distractedly. "I can get to New York in time?"

A Stranger's Smile

Cassie nodded. "Tomorrow. I have it all set. But who are you going to get in New York to help?"

"I don't know. I'll find someone. I still know some people in New York." Couturiers and maître d's, she thought.

"Honey, you'd better get somebody really good. I've heard hardball players flex their muscles before, and your ex-husband made all the right noises."

Anne couldn't answer.

"Annie? Honey, are you okay? Do you want me to come up?"

"Uh, no." Anne wondered if she should tell Cassie about what had happened during the night but decided not to. She still wasn't at all sure herself about what had happened. She just knew that she could hardly bear to be near Jonathan anymore, especially when both of them were held so rigidly by their uncomfortable silence. Anne knew that whatever it was she had discovered in herself when she'd been in his arms was interfering with her ability to handle Tom's threat to her with composure and common sense. She was afraid that she was beginning to lose control.

The sound of Cassie's voice brought her abruptly back from her thoughts. "It'll be okay, Annie. You'll see."

Anne's eyes burned. The snow was too bright, the future too frightening. "I hope so, Cass. I'll see you tomorrow."

Anne hung up the phone and stood for a long few minutes without being able to move. She stared abjectly out at the scenery she had so come to cherish.

"Do you want to tell me about it now?"

Startled, she jerked around. Jonathan was standing by the hallway arch, his eyes understanding. The very sight of him, so strong and determined, brought the tears back. Anne stood silently before him, her hand on the phone, and shook her head helplessly, completely at a loss.

Before she could gather the composure to speak, he'd hobbled up to her and put his hand out. "Come on. Let's sit down here so you can tell me what's going on."

Still she balked, even as he guided her to the couch. Trust was difficult to give in her world. "You don't need this kind of headache."

"You need to talk," he retorted, easing her into the cushions and then gingerly taking a seat next to her. "And who knows? I might be able to help."

"Why should you help me?"

His smile was rueful. "After last night that's kind of a stupid question."

She gave no quarter. "It would be a stupid question if you hadn't already done several one-eighties already. How do I know you're not looking for another excuse to bare your claws?"

For a moment Jonathan looked down at his hands, as if marshalling his thoughts. When he looked back up, Anne thought she had never seen eyes so empathetic. It was as if he had looked away to allow his defenses to fall a little.

"You only have my word, I guess," he admitted, taking her hand. She felt the strength there and longed to be able to rely on it. It had been so long since she'd been able to share any of her burdens.

"But you're right," he went on. "I have been an ass. There's an explanation for it, but it's too involved. I'm sorry, Anne."

"Well," she conceded, "you do have a point." She managed a grin. "You were an ass."

He grinned back, and Anne found herself wondering how long this truce would last. It was all beginning to hurt too much.

"I'm going to lose my home," she finally said, feeling vulnerable and terrified by it. "I have two weeks to prevent it from happening."

"You'll let me help?"

It was hard to meet his eyes. She kept seeing the savage light in them the night before. "I don't know yet. What do you think you can do?"

He shrugged, wincing as his ribs rubbed uncomfortably. "I don't know. It depends on what's going on. I'm a lawyer."

Anne found herself smiling again, the light in her eyes wary. "Of course you are."

"You don't believe me."

It was her turn to shrug. "Maybe if you had some identification."

"I'm serious, Anne. I am a lawyer. I got my law degree from NYU."

"Corporate law, no doubt."

A brief twinkle touched his eyes. "This time, it might be what the doctor ordered."

She couldn't help but flash a big smile at that. "Are lawyers always so original?"

"I can only think fast on my feet when I'm on my feet. Now, are you going to take me up on my offer?"

She was weakening beneath the bright candor of his handsome eyes, and it made her furious. She knew better than to trust an attractive smile. It had taken her months to begin to trust even Cassie and Jim, months she'd spent alone in the cabin, often without venturing out for days on end. Her faith in others had been shattered because she'd once trusted a man with a handsome smile.

But she'd never seen in Tom the emotion she'd found in Jonathan's eyes. Tom had been pure predator: first, last and always. He would never have had room in his character for the compassion she'd discovered in Jonathan. He didn't have the strength, the courage or the vulnerability. Tom had never reached out to another human being in his life, unless it was to further the career and material fortunes of Tom

McCarthy. In one harrowing hour before dawn, Anne had realized that the same couldn't be said about Jonathan.

But could the aftermath of the nightmare make all the difference, when every other time she'd allowed him close he'd hurt her?

Before she knew it, she was telling him the whole story. She spoke of Tom's duplicity, her father's death and the deal she'd made with her husband and brother to set her free of their obsession with the company, and how Brad had now managed to throw away her home on a speculation.

When she looked up at the story's finish, she was surprised to see that Jonathan listened quietly, his eyes analyzing and alert. He'd assumed a professional demeanor, as if he were sitting behind a mahogany desk in a three-piece suit rather than propped stiffly on her living-room couch and clothed in Brad's old pajamas. Although his background was still a mystery, Anne was satisfied that he was a lawyer just as he'd said.

"Do you remember any agreements you might have signed?" he asked.

She had to shrug. "Divorce papers relinquishing alimony and the promise not to contest my father's will. I don't know. At that point in my life I wasn't thinking too clearly."

"That's understandable," he nodded. "Who was your lawyer?"

"Frank Wilson. Wilson, Talmadge, Pierce & Franklin of Boston."

"And you think he was in your husband's pocket?"

"I didn't have to think it. Brad finally told me so. He has the need to gloat."

Jonathan shook his head slowly, absently staring at the far wall as he contemplated what she had said. Finally his attention returned to her, his manner all business. Again, Anne had the passing feeling that she was really sitting in an office. "Could they have done anything illegal?"

"Why do you say that?"

"I don't know," he said with a shrug. "Maybe the overkill when you finally got in touch with them about this. Something's making them nervous."

Anne offered a dry smile. "You don't think my ex-husband wants me back because he can't live without me?"

Jonathan was polite enough not to answer.

Because he had no more questions, Anne knew she had to find out. The effort alone brought the fear back; an iron band tightened around her chest and closed her throat.

"Am I going to lose it?" she asked, her voice sounding very small.

Jonathan turned to her, his eyes troubled. "I don't know, Anne. You might. But you're a strong woman. Even if you do..."

Anne straightened abruptly, her eyes glittering with unshed tears. "You don't understand. This," she said, opening her arms to take in her surroundings, "is all I have. It's all I have left to remind me that I once had a family and was happy. It's the only place where there's anything left of my mother and father. I may get a new house, but I'd have no past. No memories to keep what I went through with Tom and Brad in its place." To keep what she was beginning to feel for Jonathan in its place. Her sense of stability was floundering and only the permanency of the cabin kept her upright sometimes. "This is my anchor, my sanity. Without it I would have lost my mind."

Holding her hand even more tightly, Jonathan captured her eyes with his own, offering her his strength and support, an understanding she knew to be genuine. He nodded to her and brought his other hand to her cheek.

"Then we'll have to fight like hell, won't we?"

Anne managed a small smile, fighting for some composure. "Sounds like a good game plan to me."

He gave her another nod and a smile, the winter light from the window clean and bright against him. Anne took a deep breath and surrendered her trust.

"All right then," he decided. "Let me make a call to someone I know in New York. I can give him the basics now, and you can fill in the details when you get there. He's the best you can get."

"My husband and brother don't own him?"

Jonathan's face lit with an almost piratical smile, teeth gleaming unnaturally. "That," he assured her with finality, "I can guarantee."

She finally nodded back, unaccustomed to the feeling of relief that struggled to take shape in her. "In that case, I'll get dinner while you call."

As she headed into the kitchen, she heard Jonathan dial. "Judson Fredericks, please. Tell him it's Jonathan Harris."

Jonathan finally allowed Anne to steer him to bed when she told him she wasn't staying up any longer to baby-sit him. She saw the weariness escape into his eyes as he let her cover him. He had paled a little, the lines along his mouth etched more deeply. She wanted so much to tell him to ease up on himself, to acknowledge his pain and let her help as he'd helped her. But she knew that this was a place severely guarded in him. He had to let her in first.

Anne stood next to his bed, caught between the image of the man who'd woken up in her house and the one who had offered to help save it.

"Jonathan, thank you," she said quietly. "I have to admit that until you gave me the name of your friend, I didn't know what I was going to do."

He smiled up at her, reaching over to take her hand. "Like I said, it's my way of saying I'm sorry. Besides..." His voice faded as he sought words that didn't seem familiar. "I had to thank you, too." His eyes searched hers. Something deliberate was happening and she wasn't sure she was ready yet.

"It's been a long time since someone's been that...unselfish." The struggle grew on his features, revealing the need for protection, the yearning for communication.

Anne sat gently on the edge of the bed, her hand still in his. She held his eyes just as surely. "I have nightmares, too," she said gently. "Would you like to talk about it?"

Jonathan had to look away. The ghosts were there, so close, and their pain was infecting him anew. Anne felt him stiffen and held her breath.

"You said that there were two times you were helpless to save someone else from being hurt." God, she wanted to hold him again. That dying light in his eyes couldn't possibly hurt more if it were her own. "Was that one of the times?"

For a long moment he remained very still, his eyes looking into hers. Anne waited. She heard the clock again, its rhythm the slow, steady pacing of time. The house muttered around her, and the fire popped in the living room. Her eyes were only on Jonathan as he fought his own battles of trust.

Finally, he nodded. "I was a platoon leader in Nam. Dong Ha. We were searching out VC hideouts when we ran across a whole network of tunnels." Anne felt the pressure build in her as he talked, his cadence as carefully measured as the clock's. "It was an ambush. Out of twenty men, only three of us survived. Ten were blown to hell in the middle of those tunnels." He stopped again, the images so vivid to him that even Anne imagined she could see them. The friends, the kids, the men who'd depended on him dying around him when he couldn't stop it. "We never even saw them. My best friend died right in front of me. He was supposed to be rotated out the next week."

Eddie. Anne felt the tears catch in her throat, a pain of frustration and futility welling in her. Jonathan finally looked up at her, only weariness left in his beautiful eyes, and offered a last shrug. "We never even saw 'em."

"Have you ever gone to see his family?"

"I haven't even been to the Vietnam Memorial." He found something in his hand to study. "I keep telling myself I'll go one of these days. Who knows?" he said with a shrug. "Maybe I will."

"Would it be easier if someone went with you?"

He showed his surprise. That was evidently not a question he'd often been asked. "I don't know. Mind if I think about it?"

"Not at all," she said smiling hesitantly, as surprised as he was that she'd made the offer. "I think I have to do the same."

They allowed each other tentative smiles. Things had changed a lot in a few days.

For a long moment Anne looked down at the handsome, magnetic, lonely man who had exploded into her life like a thunderclap. Unable to express herself in any other way, she bent forward and gently kissed him.

The lips she met were surprisingly tender, the feel of his cheek rough and strong. Instinctively her free hand reached for the curve of his jaw, as if it were a magnetic source of balance. Her fingers found it and tingled with the contact. Her own lips grew pliant, opening to the questioning probe of his tongue.

The brief meeting electrified her. It was as if she had found a well-spring, and the cold, clear waters that surged from it now suffused her body with a giddy effervescence that shocked her. She could hear her breath catch in a sob, deep in her throat, and her eyes closed against the delicious pain of it.

As if it were a natural progression, Jonathan reached up with his own hand and sought the warmth of her breast. Abruptly Anne straightened, his touch still searing her, her nipples stiff against the material of her shirt. Yearning leaped through her like lightning. Looking down at the message in Jonathan's eyes, she knew that she'd come perilously close to losing herself in him.

"You're a beautiful woman, Anne."

The blue of his eyes was suddenly intense, seething. For the first time in two years, Anne remembered what it was to feel beautiful in a man's eyes, to be regarded as desirable rather than capable. She caught her breath, arrested by the feeling, overwhelmingly frightened. For a long moment she could do no more than hold Jonathan's gaze, her hand still lost in his.

"I'm going to have to be able to get out of the mess I'm in before I can deal with new..." She didn't know what to call what was flaring hotly between them. She was afraid it was born of need rather than desire. All she could see was the light chilling once again in his eyes. "We have to be careful, Jonathan. Please understand."

A distance grew between them. Anne stood to a stiff kind of attention. This sudden fear was as powerful as the longing Jonathan had kindled in her. She had been betrayed by her own feelings, and now she knew that she wouldn't be able to untangle herself from this without at best involvement, at worst the kind of pain she loathed. And Anne had a feeling that it had already gone past the point of painless resolution.

She fled to her room without another word, unable to bear anything else Jonathan might admit. He never challenged her, but as the sun finally struggled up the next morning, Anne wasn't the only one who still hadn't fallen asleep.

She left in the morning without ever really talking to him. They passed social amenities as she brought in his breakfast and changed his dressings, but the air was charged and uncomfortable. It wasn't until Mary Dickey—the woman Anne had asked to take care of Jonathan in her absence—arrived with her two children that Anne finally went in to say goodbye.

When Jonathan caught sight of the preschoolers and considered their combined decibel level with a pained eye, Anne couldn't help but flash him a smug grin. He returned it with one of his own and invited the four-year-old to sit next to him. For a minute, it was as if the night before had never happened.

Anne got on the plane to New York with a sense of unease, unable to keep what had happened out of her mind. In the light of day, it almost seemed a delusion to think that Jonathan really cared for her. She'd probably read too much into the situation.

They had offered each other friendship, understanding and help. He had admitted as much when he'd thanked her for understanding what had happened after the nightmare. Unfortunately, as they became dependent on each other in the isolation of that little cabin, they could easily find themselves in a relationship neither of them wanted or could afford. Their combined emotions were fuses that ignited a pretty powerful powder keg.

Damn it, Anne thought, I'd just made it to the point of equilibrium. Maybe she wasn't ecstatically happy, but she'd been content. After all the years spent in the role of Pete Jackson's daughter and Tom McCarthy's wife she had finally forged the true cast of Anne Jackson, and she liked it. She was happy with herself. Jonathan Harris was a strong-willed, dominant personality, one who considered being in charge of his birthright. Anne wasn't at all sure that he was the kind of man who would encourage a wife to be independent.

He couldn't possibly understand what had gone into the building of Anne's self-determination. Or what it had cost. She couldn't let him tamper with it and possibly do it irreparable harm. Somehow, she'd have to hold on to her objectivity.

An awfully easy thing to decide in daylight. Especially three hundred miles away from the spell of his eyes.

Chapter 7

Anne had lied about disliking New York. She loved it. She could go there to just sit in one place for days and watch it, soaking in its kinetic energy as if recharging her batteries. Even when she'd lived in Boston, coming to New York had been like an electric shock. The amassed energy of twelve million people trapped within the high, skyscrapered canyons radiated like heat shimmering off streets in summer, charging the atmosphere like a thunderstorm. Her adrenaline shot up just by stepping onto the street.

Now, returning to the city after her isolation in the ageless mountains, Anne felt as if she'd just been thrown into a pool of cold water. She couldn't help smiling to herself as she walked along the crowded streets.

She found herself strolling down Sixth Avenue. The day was brisk, the sky, briefly seen near the break of Central Park, an almost bright blue above the smog. There had been no snow in the city and the streets were clear. Buses, cabs and limos chased along in fox and hound fashion, threatening the crazier pedestrians who stepped onto the street and challenged oncoming traffic like mad toreadors.

Dodging traffic was a game in New York. Anne refrained from trying her hand at it. It had been too long since she had competed, and she was afraid that her timing might be off. Besides, she had an armful of packages to protect.

It would be important to show a good face when she finally met up with Tom and Brad, so she'd stopped off at a few of the designer salons that were scattered along the upper Sixties. The salespeople she'd once known well had greeted her like a ghost returned from the grave. When she'd told them where she'd been the past few years, the reaction had been a universal pause and polite embarrassment for want of something to say.

Typical of these had been Madelyn, a tall, handsome woman who ruled over one of the most prestigious salons with rigid attention to suave style and judicious subservience. She had come to the door personally, hands outstretched as if greeting the proverbial prodigal child.

"Anne, my dear," she'd almost gushed. "We thought...well, of course we heard about the divorce. I'm so sorry." Feeling Anne out, she carefully cast for clues to the appropriate direction for the conversation. "We thought you'd simply gone on vacation."

Anne smiled, realizing this was like roller-skating. She'd need to work on her balance a bit more before really hitting the streets, but it was all coming back to her pretty quickly. "No," she admitted with a smile, "I've just moved."

The woman paused again, her eyes careful. "To the coast?" Those three words sounded more like, "We thought better of you." She'd probably never seen the other bank of the Hudson in her life. Anne couldn't wait to see how she'd react to the truth.

"No. I'm living in the mountains."

A nod, the same momentary confusion. "The Catskills?"

"The Appalachians." She let the woman founder only a moment, still holding both of her hands, before saving her. "My father had a retreat there. I needed the...well, the quiet. You understand."

"Of course," Madelyn nodded quickly, now on safe ground as she let Anne's hands go with a squeeze in preparation for getting down to business. "It's most understandable. And you look wonderful. The fresh air, I imagine. You positively glow, my dear."

And so Anne spent the first part of the day in New York readying herself to deal with its people again, getting her rhythm back for the games of the civilized animal. She had to worry about facing not only her brother and husband, but the lawyer Jonathan had recommended to her. After her years of experience she knew only too well how important it would be to make the correct first impression with this man, because she'd have to depend on him. There was truthfully no one else she had to turn to.

In one handshake, she would have to let the lawyer know that she was a woman to respect, not just the former arm ornament of Tom McCarthy. There could be no mistaking her intentions or commitment. And if this lawyer were anything at all like Jonathan, she would have her work cut out for her.

Now, as Anne approached the Café de la Paix on the southeast corner of the park, its striped awning rolled up, she was still smiling. It had been a good day for getting her legs back. She only wished she could have the time to sit by the window and eat a leisurely lunch, watching the human traffic pass along the park. But time was at a premium. She had an appointment to keep.

She settled for a long walk around the fountain at Fifty-Ninth where street musicians played a strange jazz piece for tuba and guitar before she turned into the Plaza Hotel. Anne always stayed there when she was in town, never quite wanting to move away from Central Park, even to the clean geometric lines of some of the newer hotels farther south. There had even been a town house Tom had kept closer to Greenwich Village when he'd found that that was the thing to do, but Anne had always returned to the old-world grandeur along the park where she could enjoy what was to her the only green in the city.

Room service supplied a light lunch while Anne painstakingly dressed and groomed herself for her appointment with Jonathan's friend, sweeping her hair once more up into the simple chignon that Tom had preferred. She wore a two-piece red wool suit with short bolero jacket whose lines fell crisp and clean over her trim figure.

She had carefully chosen her small wardrobe for its simple, classic lines, because these best suited her and her mission. Today, she wore no more ornamentation than alligator pumps and pearl stud earrings. The effect was cool and professional. Anne looked more like a high-powered executive than a rural nurse. There was no doubt in her mind as she stepped into the cab taking her to the lawyer's office that she would need every bit of control she could muster to match the picture she presented. She couldn't get out of her mind the image of Jonathan as he delivered his well-placed barbs born of this city's cannibalism. It was all she could hope that his friend had a little more class than that.

When Anne walked into the office of Judson Fredericks, she was stunned. Walking toward her with an outstretched hand and warm smile was not another Manhattan flash, but a gentleman with the air of a Southern plantation owner. Judson was a handsome, tall, ram-rod-straight, old-school lawyer who oozed confidentiality and trustworthiness. His handshake was firm and his smile brimming with the essence of cordiality. He led her into his office and sat her in a comfortable leather chair across from his desk before moving around to seat himself.

The office was decorated in dark paneling and leather, the perfect background to Judson's soft voice, distinguished head of silver hair and deceptively lazy eyes. His attitude toward her was almost openly paternal. It made her want to smile.

The first few minutes of polite observation of formal rules of office etiquette served them both to gain the other's respect. The call from Jonathan provided an easy introduction to business.

"Jonathan said he'd had an accident near your home," Judson said, frowning. "But he refused to illuminate me beyond the usual platitudes. Is he all right?"

"He's fine." Anne smiled. "He injured himself in a fall near where I live, and we were forced to keep him there due to snow and road conditions."

"There isn't any way to get him to a hospital?"

"I live in an isolated area behind the Great Smoky Mountain National Park, and it's a long, hard way to the hospital from there. Especially for a man with a broken leg and a couple of broken ribs."

He nodded, appeased. "Well, I'll certainly take your word for it. But please do tell me if there is anything he needs, and I will be more than happy to make the necessary arrangements." With this, he settled into his chair, as if to signal a change in the direction of the conversation. "In the meantime, let's look into what brings such a beautiful lady to my office. I've been able to begin gathering information on what Jonathan has told me, but I would like to hear the story again in your words."

Anne took a moment to gather her thoughts together, thinking that she already felt she couldn't have brought her problems to a better man.

She told him everything, slowly and in detail, and Judson listened attentively, not even making notes until she had finished. The window behind him suffused the room in soft gray light from the sky high above lower Manhattan. The office itself was silent but for the measured cadence of Anne's words, her manner as carefully composed as her appearance.

The silence, as comfortable as the dark overstuffed furniture, closed in again as Anne finished. Mr. Fredericks finally broke her gaze to contemplate what she'd told him, nodding quietly to himself and tapping on the mahogany desk with manicured fingers.

After a few long moments, he looked up thoughtfully. "Would you like your inheritance back?"

She wondered for a moment if he'd really heard what she'd just said. "I want my land. Nothing more."

"I ask because I'm not sure we can go only that far. You must challenge your brother's right to use that land as collateral for a personal loan. If we go so far as contesting your father's original will, you could end up with more than you bargained for."

She sighed. "All I'm saying, Mr. Fredericks, is that I don't care what they do anymore. I want none of it. I only want my home. But I will do whatever is necessary to keep it."

Again, he considered. Anne kept very still, her hands folded precisely over her bright red skirt. The rich smell of leather and thick carpeting should have soothed but somehow stifled a little.

"I'll have to do some work on it and that will take a little time," Mr. Fredericks finally said, looking back up with studious eyes. "Will you be in New York long?"

"No." She shook her head slightly. "I have to get back. I'll be back next week for the meeting with Amplex Corporation."

"Yes. Fine. And how should I contact you if I need to?"

"I'll leave you an address and a number."

He studied her a moment, considering her features and bearing, her sleek, rich hair, Gucci shoes, the well-manicured nails and faultless bearing. Then he afforded himself a warm smile of wonder. "I, of course, know of your family, Miss Jackson. And I have heard of Peter Jackson's home in the Smokies. But seeing you now, I simply cannot imagine your living there alone."

Anne returned his smile, content that she had made the impression she had sought. "Everyone has his own paradise, Mr. Fredericks. Some day you must allow me to show you mine."

His smile broadened, and again he nodded. "I think it must be a special place. I would consider the invitation a privilege. Hopefully, I'll get the chance to accept."

Anne stood to go, longing to ask about Jonathan's connection with this man, but for some reason hesitated to bring it up. She extended her hand to wish the distinguished lawyer goodbye. When he clasped it with genuine enthusiasm Anne's spirits rose. This man would indeed help her. And again she marveled at the enigma of Jonathan Harris, this man's friend.

The meeting with Judson so encouraged her that she decided to take things a step further and chance facing Tom. There would be nothing to be gained by putting it off, and she thought that he needed to be unsettled a little. It might be good to let him know that Anne wasn't the same person she was when she'd left Boston.

She was quickly surprised by a good portent. When she called to make her accommodations for the visit to Boston before heading home, she found out that both Tom and Brad were in New York on business. She could drop in on them, and without having to overcome the disadvantage of facing them on their home field. She'd have no trouble finding them: she knew exactly where they'd be.

Late in the afternoon Anne stood in her hotel room, readied for the meeting. Turning a careful circle before the mirror, she performed a final inspection. All was perfect. It was as if she'd never left. The vermilion suit highlighted the sun whiteness of her blond hair, the simple style of it offsetting her lithe legs. She had added the diamond-and-sapphire earrings her mother had left her to round out the effect.

Simple and smashing, Tom had always said. Well, he was about to get the full dose of both. Anne hoped that she was still good enough to hide the weakness in her knees and the nest of butterflies that had nested in her stomach. Standing tall and self-assured before the mirror, she smiled. She seemed smooth and cool. She could do it. She hoped.

Anne pulled on the fur jacket that would complete the picture and reached for her purse. A cab was waiting downstairs that would take her to the restaurant where Tom and Brad would be finishing their dinner. When she stepped into the taxi, the wide-eyed admiration of the cabbie was not lost on her. She wished her stomach would settle down a little.

The restaurant was small and elegant. The decor dramatically simple in chrome and burgundy. Anne had known the maître d' for years and found it embarrassingly simple to find out from him that, true to form, Tom and Brad would be dining there before flying back to Boston. She approached the desk precisely at six, knowing how well she had timed her arrival. Louis looked up from his book, his eyes widening in delight.

"Mrs. . . . ." he faltered, embarrassed.

Anne quickly saved him from discomfort. "Louis, when are you going to call me Anne?" she said, smiling.

He melted visibly. "It has been too long since we have seen you. Will you be having dinner tonight?"

"After I've taken care of some disagreeable business, Louis. Where are they?"

"The same." He shrugged. "Always the same. Would you like me to take you?"

"No, thank you, Louis," she said, smiling. "I think I'll pop in on my own."

His smile didn't quite match hers, but he nodded her on with some enthusiasm. She walked back into the darkened restaurant, knowing that she wouldn't see them until she was almost upon them. They always ate at the same table in the back, shielded by Plexiglas and muted lighting. A rush of nostalgia threatened her composure as she remembered the times she, too, had been included in the meals here.

Ever since she'd been twelve, when her father had first set up his friend Louis in a business that was now one of the top five restaurants in New York, the Jacksons dined at Chez Louis. Once a week, without fail, they'd be seated at booth fifteen.

"Tom, Brad. I see that you don't break tradition easily."

She stood by the table, praying that she could hold out, wondering what the hell she was doing here. One look at Tom had almost been her downfall. With his blond, well-groomed good looks and smoky-green eyes he couldn't possibly be more handsome or magnetic if he tried. His face was intelligent and controlled, his nose straight, his mouth sensual and his chin perfectly firm. She knew that she was still mesmerized by him and hated herself for it.

In her confusion she almost lost the satisfaction of seeing the shock on their faces. They had just finished dinner. Coffee had been poured and Tom was just about to light up a cigarillo. The match burned out in his fingers.

Abruptly, they stood. Anne smiled with cool eyes.

"What are you doing in New York?" Brad asked sharply.

She eyed him without flinching. "It's nice to see you, too, Brad dear."

It struck her again how truly unremarkable Brad was. He had the kind of face that radiated weakness. His eyes were brown and his lips thin. The only kind thing Anne could say about him was that he had grown a moustache since she'd last seen him, and that it made him seem to blend more easily into a crowd.

Anne had not always disliked Brad. In fact, at one time in their lives, they'd been rather close. That had been when her mother had been alive. Her mother had been able to bring out the best in him. When she had died, so had any spark of decency in Brad. He had become isolated and resentful, developing the facial tics that still plagued him, and blaming his lack of achievement on his father's failure to show him favor. Most of the time Brad was merely annoying, but when he felt he was about to fail he tended to strike out blindly. He hadn't really become insufferable, though, until Tom had joined the business and begun to personally groom him for usurping what Brad had always sarcastically called the "Jackson throne." From that moment, he had never again taken Anne into his confidence. Now, after five years in Tom's shadow, Brad didn't have any recognizable traces of humanity left in him.

She watched him now as he began to sweat and twitch at the sight of her and she could only feel disdain. He didn't have any class.

"Of course it's wonderful to see you," Tom said, an almost imperceptible hesitation in his voice giving away his shock. He had the class in the company. "You're as beautiful as ever, Anne. More beautiful."

"Thank you, Tom. May I join you?"

"Please."

He moved to allow her room. She ignored him and sat next to Brad, knowing that Tom was regaining his balance quickly. She didn't think it wise to push her luck too far.

"What are you doing in New York?" he repeated more conversationally.

Francis, the waiter who'd always taken care of their table, now appeared silently with Anne's coffee and Frangelica. She shot him a dazzling smile, and he bowed a bit lower than was customary. After taking a sip of liqueur, Anne turned back to her family.

"I'm here to see my lawyer," she finally answered evenly, taking note of the quick, surreptitious glance that passed between the two of them and feeling more stable for their need of it. "You?"

"Business."

She nodded absently, sipping at her coffee.

"You haven't been in the city in a while. How did you happen to find a lawyer?" Brad asked, his eye pulling oddly at the words as if he were winking at her.

"Recommendation of a friend. Don't worry, Brad, it's no one you know. And no one you own."

"Anne..." Tom reached for her hand. Anne deftly avoided it, not wanting him to feel the calluses that one manicure couldn't erase. He hesitated only a moment. "Did you get my message?"

"The one about not having any choice about what happened to my home, or the one offering new lodgings?"

"You always have a home in Boston."

"Thank you, Tom. The invitation was eloquent, but I'm going back to Cedar Ridge."

"How long will you be here?"

"I leave tonight."

He frowned handsomely, the perfect modicum of concerned disappointment. "That's too bad. I thought maybe we could spend more time together."

She smiled again, the light in her eyes dry. "See the town? I've seen it, thank you. I really have to be getting back."

"Animals need tending?" Brad's voice was quiet, his insult implicit.

Anne's answering smile, delivered over the rim of the coffee cup, was unruffled at the impotent attack. "I guess I'm a creature of habit, too, Brad. I suppose it's a matter of what one gets used to."

Tom leaned back and lit the cigarillo he'd earlier forgotten. "You know, Anne," he said, his voice soft and dark, the music that had haunted her dreams, "sitting here with you, it seems hard to believe you've been away."

It was time for her to make her exit. She knew where his line was heading and didn't particularly want to be around when it got there. She was still afraid after all this time that she wouldn't be able to walk away from it.

"But I have," she assured him, finishing the last of her coffee and gathering her purse to go. "It's been good to see you two. I'm glad I could get the chance to stop in before my flight left. I'll give Silas and Sarah your love, Brad. My best to Ellie." Ellie was the thin-blooded heiress Brad had managed to marry. Anne turned to Tom. "Anyone I can pass on salutations to for you, Tom?"

His answer was a silent smile that lit his eyes with amusement. Anne was beginning to doubt whether she'd have the nerve to sneak back into the restaurant for their delicious bouillabaisse. Tom and Brad stood with her, Tom taking her by the hands before she could escape. His movements were too smooth to avoid.

"Why don't you come back to the city?" he coaxed, his voice hypnotizing the thoughts of bouillabaisse away. "You belong here."

Anne's answer was cool, even as she wondered whether he could feel the trembling his touch had given birth to. "I'm perfectly happy where I am, thank you. It's been wonderful, but I do have to go."

Retrieving her hands from him, she turned and left. Tom and Brad stood where she'd left them, knowing why she'd come, and, she dearly hoped, more unsettled for her performance. God knew it had taken enough out of her.

Contrary to what she'd said, Anne didn't leave that night. She managed to slip back into the restaurant for some of that promised dinner and the most shameless pampering she'd enjoyed in two years, and then spent a night savoring the luxury of the hotel. Bright and early the next morning she headed home.

It was just about lunchtime when she walked into Thompson's General Store wearing the same suit she'd worn to Chez Louis. She had been coming and going from the mountain for so many years that most of her neighbors had gotten used to the disparity in her appearance. It didn't occur to her that Jim had never seen her like this until she caught the look on his face.

At first it was blank, as if a stranger had walked in. Then it slackened into an openmouthed gape. Jim and Cassie hadn't come to the mountain until Anne's last case of clothing had long since been packed up and given away. They had never seen the transition before or, for that matter, the celebrated city side of Anne Jackson.

For the first time since she'd been coming home from the city, she felt out of place and slightly uncomfortable.

Two hours later she climbed off her horse to find Jonathan comfortably seated in the front porch rocker. By the smile that lit his eyes when he saw her, it seemed that he was glad to see her. She wondered how loud the kids had been.

"Well," she offered with an appraising grin. "I suppose you're pretty proud of yourself."

"It only took me twenty minutes to get out here," he answered nonchalantly. "I was beginning to get stir-crazy."

She could well imagine that it only took him twenty minutes. There was still a fine sheen of perspiration on his forehead from the exertion, but he looked like a kid rounding third for home. His enthusiasm sharpened her pleasure at seeing him.

"A long way from mountain climbing, aren't we?" she said, laughing.

"Annie, you're back." Cassie appeared in the cabin doorway, hands on hips.

Anne faced her with an identical pose. "So, I'm away for two days and the community takes over my patient, huh?"

"We barely got started," she retorted happily. "If it had taken you a couple of more days to get home, we could have had him tending the animals by the time you got back."

Jonathan scowled. "I hardly think so."

Cassie laughed and led everybody back in, Jonathan bringing up the rear. He closed the door as Anne shrugged out of her coat and hat.

"Oh, Annie, your hair," Cass breathed. "I love it."

Anne's hand went instinctively to the tightly coiled chignon, her voice unaccountably embarrassed, her eyes straying to Jonathan's passive face. "Oh. I'd forgotten about it."

"You're going to show me what you got in New York, aren't you?" Cassie demanded, bearing down on her. "I have the feeling that you have wonderful taste when it comes to designer rags."

Before Anne could move to protest, Cassie had one hand on the suitcase and the other on Anne. Anne had the choice of going up with her to the loft to do some modeling or trying to dupe her way to the kitchen for some tea. She gave up with a heartfelt sigh and followed upstairs as Jonathan settled himself onto the couch.

Fifteen minutes later Cassie stood before her, her reaction a momentary stunned silence. "My God, I wouldn't have recognized you."

Anne hadn't realized that when she'd slipped back into the suit, she had also unconsciously slipped into the city veneer that had barely protected her from Tom.

"Oh, stop it," she objected. "You act like Eliza Doolittle just walked in."

"I feel like it," Cassie assured her with an awed shake of the head. "Do you know how...formidable you look?"

Anne stared at her, unsure how to react. Jonathan's voice interrupted.

"Don't I get a show, too?"

His reaction was even more startled than Cassie's. The minute he saw her, the teasing humor in her eyes died hard. It was as if he'd just met her for the first time, and that he didn't like what he saw.

"Not you, too," she protested, not realizing that even her posture was more suited to her clothes than her surroundings, and the sophistication of it more alien than the sight of Jonathan's three-piece suit.

"Impressive," he said, his voice barely warm.

Anne was confused. "It keeps me from being taken advantage of," she answered, trying to keep the tone of her voice light, but failing.

"Seems a bit superfluous" was all he would say, a distant look in his eyes.

"I'm changing," she decided, turning impulsively on her heel. "This outfit is definitely not the dress of the day."

Before anyone could voice protest, she slipped out of the designer suit and pulled her hair down from the sleek hairstyle into the braids that more suited the surroundings.

As she put the suit away, Anne realized that she had enjoyed donning fashionable clothes again, dusting off the old social skills and seeing how well they'd held up. It disturbed her a little.

She had come to consider that part of her life without merit, had begun to resent its waste. In the end, all she'd been given, been privilege to, had come down around her like a house of cards. It had taken a divorce and her father's death to come to grips with all the years of her life when material luxuries had been only a substitute for a father's attention and a husband's love.

Maybe, she decided, there was some truth to the adage that absence made the heart grow fonder. Or maybe she had just been able to face the old life on different terms. Her terms. For the first time in her life, she had been the one in control.

It was a true pleasure to remember the confusion she'd unleashed by pouncing unannounced on Brad and Tom. It had been only the second time she'd won any sort of victory over them, and this time she'd been in a clear enough frame of mind to enjoy it. But, looking at the clean, expensive lines of her new clothes, she wondered if maybe there wasn't more to it than that.

"Better?" she asked a few minutes later as she reappeared in work shirt and jeans.

Cassie cocked her head to one side in appraisal. "I'm not sure if better is the right word, but I think I'm more comfortable with you like this."

Jonathan was more to the point, driving home his message with the brittleness of his eyes. He spoke with as much rancor as awe. "I'd heard the legend of Peter Jackson's little girl, but I'd never had the chance to see you in action. You must have been some rich bitch, lady."

Chapter 8

Anne was more surprised than she should have been by the sudden change of attitude. Cassie was astounded—she seemed to stop breathing for a moment she was so still.

"Don't you want to know how Mr. Fredericks is?" Anne asked instead, her manner measured and even, her control spread thin over her mounting confusion. Why couldn't he just once not swing back to the attack when she least suspected it?

Jonathan's quick smile at her words was amazingly tender, considering his last words. "Judson is always the same," he said quietly. "Quite a gentleman, isn't he?"

"A refreshing change, I must admit," Anne allowed. "I'm amazed that he'd consort with the likes of you. He seems to be such an upstanding sort."

Jonathan laughed. "He doesn't. He's an old family friend. Judson was born and raised in the wilds of Wyoming, too."

"In that case, I feel better. For a while there I was wondering what the catch was."

He raised an eyebrow. "With Judson? Unthinkable."

Anne took a minute to describe the older man to Cassie, who still stood slightly openmouthed at the exchange she'd witnessed. Anne said nothing about that, just glad that Cassie had finally seen that Anne wasn't making up Jonathan's knack for lightning mood changes. Now if someone could explain them to her, she'd feel even better.

"When will I be able to get back to civilization?" Jonathan asked.

Anne raised her own eyebrow. "I thought you relished the rustic atmosphere."

"I didn't think it was much a matter of choice."

"Can you ride a horse?"

His response was in the form of a pained silence.

"Come to me when you can. Or when the snow melts."

"Why can't I go in a cart or something?" he persisted. "Surely, you at least have wagons or something like that up here."

"We do, but we can't get one up or down the mountain right now. And why are you suddenly so antsy? One foray outside does not a recovery make."

"I'm not used to being so passive."

She grinned dryly. "A real take-charge kind of guy, huh?"

"You could say that. It's been a long time since I haven't been in control." In her preoccupation with making a snappy comeback, Anne almost missed the momentary light in Jonathan's eyes that suddenly made her think of other conversations they'd had. And she stopped, suddenly unsure of what to say. The brief glimpses of vulnerability still unnerved her.

"You confuse me almost as much as he does," Cassie said as she and Anne sat in the kitchen a little while later, voices hushed with secrecy. Jonathan still sat with his book not much more than a dining-room table away.

"Me?" Anne countered with a quizzical look.

"I think I would have hit him." Cassie paused a moment in consideration. "As a matter of fact, I almost did."

Anne laughed, sipping at her coffee and wishing that she could have stolen Louis's pot. Maybe next time she was in New York. "I'm glad you saw it. Now at least you know that I haven't been making it all up to dump a load of misplaced revenge on an innocent bystander."

"But you took it so well." Cassie looked up furtively as her voice got a little too loud. Jonathan didn't react.

Anne shrugged, her attention still purposefully on the hot coffee that was warming the travel chills from her. "I'm getting used to it." A lie, but more immediately acceptable than the truth of what that little confrontation was still doing to her stomach. "He seems to defuse a bit easily if you change the subject."

Cassie shook her head in frustration. "I still can't figure why he would pick on you. He's been nothing but a gentleman with me."

Anne refrained from shooting Cassie a look of surprise. She, after all, had proposed the schoolboy theory in the first place. Anne had seen a part of Jonathan that she thought very few people had been permitted to see. And now Jonathan didn't know how to react to her anymore. Maybe he considered her to have some kind of unpalatable hold over him.

Formidable, Cassie had called her. Why would that have made such an impact on him?

"Uh, I don't know," she finally answered, careful to keep her voice as quiet as Cassie's. "Maybe I threaten him somehow. Maybe he has a wife somewhere he hates who looks like me."

"Well, I have to say that you both have the same dueling styles, that's for sure."

Anne looked over at her friend, recognizing the accuracy of her statement. Maybe she hadn't gotten as far away from the city as she'd thought.

For a few moments they sat in silence, eyes contemplative, the aroma of wood smoke and coffee comfortably filling the kitchen. Then Cassie spoke up again.

"How do your chances look for keeping the Ridge?"

"I honestly don't know," she admitted. "But it was certainly worth the trip just to throw Tom and Brad off balance. I saw them, you know."

Cassie's eyes widened appreciably. "You seem awfully calm about it."

"Sure, now that I'm far enough away. I have to admit, though, I sure confounded them with my footwork."

Cassie was still wide-eyed, studying Anne's face as she talked. "Annie, I'm really proud of you. I've never seen you this rational when you talked about those two before."

Anne smiled happily. "Maybe I'm finally getting my feet under me."

"You've done something, honey."

"Hey, I'm being ignored again! I can smell the coffee out here."

Cassie and Anne exchanged meaningful looks at the sound of Jonathan's voice.

"Ya know," Cassie said, "I think the saying for this occasion is that little boys don't grow up; their toys just get more expensive."

Jonathan ate dinner in the kitchen, but Anne begged off on the excuse that she was tired from traveling. Again, their dialogue was exceedingly polite and carefully distant, as if afraid to accidentally wander too near a weak point in their armor. Anne knew darn well that she should have walked in and demanded an explanation for his previous name-calling, but she didn't have the courage. He just might tell her. She only wanted to get herself to bed and her patient one day closer to being able to leave her to her silence and peace.

She was all too aware, as she stepped carefully around the stranger who sat in her living room, that as much as she'd breached his wall of security, he had done the same with her. He had drawn out emotions more intense than she'd allowed to surface in a long time. He had moved her. He had made her want to reach out to him, and she couldn't afford to do that. Tom had been reminder enough for any one of the risks involved, and the scene today had only served to emphasize that little lesson in life.

Yet she found herself watching him surreptitiously. There was something about the way the firelight softened his face, the way he ran his fingers through his hair as if to force it into some semblance of order as he pored through a thick volume of Flaubert. His features had lost some of their sharpness since he'd been there, until it seemed that they belonged to someone else who was comfortable in a rural setting.

Anne could imagine him on horseback now, or set in rhythmic motion as he chopped firewood, muscles straining against flannel and denim. She found herself fantasizing about Jonathan, Silas and the rest of the men in the community as they worked together in companionable humor to raise a new church or barn.

Flipping off the kitchen light, she deliberately set those mental pictures aside with the work she'd finished and walked into the living room to face the real Jonathan Harris. He looked up at her with weary question.

"Unless you're planning to spend the night out here, I'd suggest we start heading in," she suggested. "I'm ready for bed."

He simply nodded, closing the book and putting it on the table. Anne reached for the crutches, but he took them from her hands.

"Thanks, I'll get there by myself," he said a bit stiffly. "It's about time I started getting around on my own."

Anne said nothing as she watched him struggle to his feet. He was purposefully pushing her away. Anne, the nurse, was frustrated, knowing damn well that he was working himself too hard again. She could see it in the tight set of his jaw and the creases in his forehead. She was certain that Cassie had helped him earlier, probably with liberal doses of adventure and humor. Now, though, he fought in determined silence as if the whole thing were a grim battle to be faced alone.

Anne, the woman, realized that it angered her. Why was it that she got the feeling that she was such a threat to him? And why on earth did it make her feel so damn ambivalent?

She hated that feeling, always balancing on a razor's edge, wanting more and wanting less at the same time. She thought that she'd been finished with that kind of torment two years ago. After facing what her life had become the last time she'd gotten herself into a relationship with a man very much like the one she faced, she certainly didn't think she should have any trouble about handling her attraction to Jonathan. But she did, and it kept getting worse.

Not five minutes later as she followed him into his room, she discovered just how much worse.

He was trying to maneuver the corner, his progress slowing. Anne said nothing. She merely walked alongside him, watching the effort that once again brought a shine of sweat to his face and carved cruel lines on either side of his mouth. She was angry that he should put himself through this. She was also awed by the store of willpower he seemed to be able to call upon. No one she'd ever known would have put himself through this. At least not without the benefit of a generous amount of painkillers or alcohol. Jonathan had had neither since he'd arrived.

Anne found herself shaking her head, watching the broad back that strained against her brother's old pajama shirt and noting the signs that Jonathan was wearing out. Without warning, he lost his balance.

He had been trying to turn the corner to his room when he caught a crutch against the door frame, throwing him forward. He toppled quickly. Anne wasn't really as alert as she should have been, but her instincts were accurate. Her reaction saved them both from going down.

Jonathan fell to his right as he tried to catch hold of the wall, but his bad leg gave way. Without thinking, Anne clasped her arms around his waist. He gasped at the pressure against his injured ribs. Anne managed to get around and lean back against the wall, her face pressed into his chest as he fought to regain control of the crutches.

"Take your time," she told him, her voice muffled. "I'm not going anywhere." Except down, she thought as she braced her knees against his and fought to keep them both upright. Beneath the flannel shirt Jonathan's heart pounded heavily and his breathing was labored, but he stopped struggling for a minute. Taking some slow breaths, he rested his weight against her.

"We've got to stop meeting like this," he gasped above Anne's head.

Unaccountably, she giggled, adrenaline coursing through her like a heady liquor. "If Silas walked in right now," she managed, "he'd shoot you for trying to molest me."

Or maybe vice versa. She was having more trouble breathing, and it wasn't all exertion. It seemed like every nerve in her was on fire and that her heart was readying for battle. If only his muscles weren't so rock-hard, or his back so lean. Caution, or was it fear, made an attempt to break through the illogical exhilaration but failed. Her early-warning system had been thrown into shutdown.

"Wait...I...have it...." He was moving, straightening very slowly as he once again got the crutches securely under his arm. Anne straightened with him, giving him added support as he went.

"Should I pull the chair over here," she asked up to him, "or do you think you can make it the rest of the way without doing that again? I only have the energy reserves for one rescue a day."

He still leaned against her, wedging her against the door frame so that she couldn't move. "Maybe we could...just stand here for a...couple of...minutes so I can...get my breath." He caught her in his gaze, and Anne knew that she wasn't the only one having more trouble breathing than she should. A chill shot her spine like fire, another warning that she couldn't seem to heed.

"I'm not going anywhere until you do," she answered, her voice sounding breathless. She still had her arms around him and didn't seem to realize it, as if it were a natural thing. His eyes, looking down at her from the shadow-strewn hallway, glowed uncannily as if lit by a pale blue flame. The hottest fire is blue, Anne thought absently. She could feel the heat of his eyes as if it penetrated every pore. She wanted to reach up and test it, to run her fingers by that fire and challenge it, because it seemed to grow hotter even as they stood in silence.

Anne wanted to say something, to break the spell that seemed to be weaving its way around the two of them. She wanted to suddenly pull away, but knew that she wouldn't. And there in the depths of Jonathan's eyes she saw the same conflict: he was weakening just as surely as she.

They needed this; even against their wills, wanted it. Physically they needed it as if it were only to obey laws of attraction. Emotionally, neither could think of one logical reason to be attracted, one sane excuse that would explain the fact that they were so inexorably drawn to each other. Anne couldn't be certain of the reasons for Jonathan's distrust of and disdain for her. She had to assume it had something to do with the person she was, or maybe it was from his fear of dependency. She certainly knew why she loathed the idea of attraction to Jonathan, but right now that didn't seem to make any difference.

"I think I should be out getting the animals down for the night," she whispered, still unable to take her eyes from his.

He didn't move. "If you leave, I'll fall over."

Anne was having even more trouble getting her thoughts straight. "Maybe I should let you."

Jonathan didn't smile or reply. He bent to her, where her upturned face waited helplessly, and caught her between his hand and his lips. Without thinking, Anne closed her eyes against the thrill his touch unleashed in her. Her lips softened against his assault, her arms tightening instinctively around him. This is insane, she thought even as she pulled him against her to steady his balance. Nobody in her right mind would be caught in an unwieldy situation like this. She felt the hammering of his heart against hers and thought no more.

He forced her lips open gently, his own softer than Anne could have ever imagined. With the hand he maneuvered away from a crutch he explored her back, sliding it purposefully up beneath her shirt to test the softness of her skin. Anne recognized the feel of his fingers against her spine like a brand. Arching against him, she sought the heat he seemed to radiate. She met his tongue with her own and searched the depths of his mouth, the soft warmth of his lips. She'd read that women melted when aroused by the man they loved, but she'd never believed such exaggeration. But suddenly she felt as if her skin had become molten, as if she had been poured into place and that Jonathan could mold her any way he wanted if only he tried. Her knees were having trouble staying locked, even when pressed against his, and she seemed to fit his contours better than her own.

His hand found her bra and unsnapped it. She allowed his hand to progress unheeded around her side to her breast where it unleashed sparks like fireworks.

It had been a long time since she'd realized what mayhem a set of fingers could wreak when set loose against the sensitive skin of her breast. Not since Tom had she even anticipated the feel of a man's hand against the soft swelling, or ached for a slightly roughened thumb to chafe her nipples to exhilarating stiffness. Anne pressed against his hand, against the hypnotic strength of his touch. She straightened a little more so that his lips could find her neck and send her to gasping. At the same time she felt him against her, his arousal powerful.

She didn't want this moment to pass, didn't want to forfeit the headiness of his touch, the exhilaration of his nearness. But suddenly she saw the impasse and saw what she'd been ignoring. The fear she'd so far eluded suffused her with its chill until Jonathan's caresses froze her. Anne wished more than anything right then that she were the kind of person who could give in to her needs and wants without thought to repercussions. A handsome man held her in his arms, a man she was drawn to, and she wished she could let him make love to her.

She suddenly felt as if she were smothering.

"I don't know...about you," she gasped even as Jonathan's hands found another sensitive area, "but I'm beginning to lose my balance. We can't stay here indefinitely."

"Any suggestions?" he mumbled into her throat. He didn't seem to notice yet that her posture had stiffened.

"There are any number of obvious ones," she answered, her head against his heaving chest, her eyes squeezed shut against what she had to say. "But I'm afraid I can't think of one that would work right now."

He straightened at that, his eyes trapping hers mercilessly. "What's that supposed to mean?"

Anne took a deep breath to steady her racing pulse. "It means that maybe we shouldn't start something we can't finish."

"I'm not that much of a cripple," he said with a rakish grin.

She faced him with more purpose now, drawing herself up in defense of the lightning even his soft voice was unleashing in her. "But maybe I am. I'm not the type of person who can enjoy this particular recreation so erratically."

"Erratically?"

Both of them were still breathing quickly as if they'd just completed a race. Or were about to begin one.

"Maybe a better word is arbitrarily," she retorted with more force, even though the constriction in her chest threatened to suffocate her. She was too close to him to protect herself properly. She'd never been able to win with Tom, and she was suddenly very afraid that she couldn't win against this man who depended on her to even make it around the house. "It seems to me that you're the one who just finished calling me a rich bitch. That's not exactly my idea of sweet nothings."

"You were a rich bitch."

Anne was nonplussed enough to almost knock him over. "And that's all you have to say about it?"

"Anne," he said in his best conciliatory manner, the set of his shoulders softening, "we want each other. Isn't that all that matters?"

She shook her head. "No. That's not all that matters. I don't consider making love a passing sport." Her eyes flashed now and the intoxication of his touch died. "Do you?"

"No—Yes." He shook his head impatiently, easing his hold on her. "Oh, I don't know. I don't understand myself. I just know that no matter how I feel about you, you have the ability to drive me crazy. And I can't exactly take any cold showers." When his smile appeared, it was self-deprecating. "At least not without help."

His abrupt honesty threw her off again. This man who looked and spoke so much like Tom McCarthy, who showed flashes of the same bloodthirsty instincts, still had the knack of completely contradicting his image by almost grudgingly allowing his defenses to lag enough to be recognized as just that. Tom had never had defenses. He had been predatory to his toes.

Anne felt as if she were going to explode. She was literally and figuratively against the wall. Maybe if Jonathan had come along a few months later in her life she could have handled him with more aplomb. She could have dealt objectively with his confusing, compelling personality and been able to make a decision with the presence of mind she'd so desperately sought when she'd returned to the mountains.

But he hadn't waited to fall into her life, and Anne wasn't sure she wouldn't crumble beneath the pressure of his blue eyes and offhand sarcasm. She didn't yet know how to demand honesty from him. She didn't know whether to expect a commitment. She didn't know that she ever wanted one again.

"I can't, Jonathan...." Anne was beginning to have trouble breathing again. She knew what happening: she was hyperventilating. Some detached voice deep inside her commented dryly on hysterical females, but she couldn't seem to pay any attention. She knew that she had to get away, maybe out to the cool, clean air and moon-painted snow. She couldn't even bring herself to explain to Jonathan the reason she suddenly looked like a rabbit caught in the headlights of an oncoming car. She couldn't seem to pull the whirling memories and pain into a semblance of order to paint the picture necessary to make him understand. She had to escape.

"You're just going to walk away?" he asked quietly, not understanding.

"I have to." Anne felt tears threaten and was unnerved by the unfamiliar pain of them. "I have to go out and get the animals settled for the night. Can you get the rest of the way with some help?"

Her abrupt change sealed her words. Jonathan straightened, supported by the crutches so that Anne could let go.

"I told you before. I'll get there on my own."

When he turned away from her, Anne saw the frost in his eyes and realized that instead of feeling relief at the resolution of the dilemma, she felt worse.

Chapter 9

Anne and Jonathan seemed to have little to say to each other for the next few days. He was making enough physical progress to have free reign of the house. His attitude, however, had regressed. Anne knew what had caused this, but couldn't bring herself to bring it to issue with him.

She'd rejected him, had once again seemed to him in complete control of a situation that he couldn't master. She still didn't know for sure how he felt about her, but she did know now that the tensions in the little cabin had escalated sharply because of that moment of mutual weakness.

He was certainly chafing more and more at being restricted, even though it was his own injuries and not Anne imposing the restrictions. Even so, she was the one who received the weight of his impatience, his silences even more electric than his brief verbalizations. Meals were served and eaten in almost total silence. The only time Jonathan really talked to her was when she asked about his progress. He still experienced quite a lot of pain when he stretched his limits, but that wasn't something he would admit to. It seemed to make no difference that Anne couldn't help but see.

What troubled Anne was the fact that his present attitude bothered her so much. She didn't want his animosity. She wanted to tell him that she hadn't ever felt so alive as when she'd been in his arms, that she was awed by his courage and strength. More than anything, she wanted to go to him when she saw pain suddenly crease his face and invade his eyes. She wanted to hold him the way she had the night of his horrible dream, soothing away the strain, easing the frustration.

More than once she caught herself just short of reaching out to help. Each time the look in Jonathan's eyes had frozen her. Seeing that same struggle in his eyes, she wondered if he was having as much trouble sleeping as she. She wanted to have a chance to talk out the misconceptions they'd built up about each other and understand their limitations. But neither of them seemed to be able to allow the proper doors to open. Neither was able to bend and meet the other halfway. Until the day Mary Lou Sullins' baby was born.

Mary Lou's oldest girl, Emily, arrived on horseback at four in the morning to get Anne. Emily was sixteen and going to be married before the year was out, but she'd decided to wait to help her mother with the baby who would be born six months after the death of Will, Mary Lou's husband. Mary Lou was not in good health herself. She was too worn by her other seven children, Will's long illness and their crushing poverty to bear this baby easily.

It wasn't until well past midnight that Anne found herself back before her fire, a cup of coffee in her tired, aching hands. Staring into the fire, she thought of the people she helped. They were people like the Sullinses who had the babies they couldn't afford, who had more misery than should have been their share and who plodded on day after day just to survive. She thought of the baby, the joy she always felt at the new life she held, and how quickly it had been quenched when she saw the vacant look with which his mother greeted him. He deserved so much, and he would only get poverty and hunger and maybe later the chance to kill himself in a coal mine like his father or scrabble at the dirt they called a farm.

Anne turned to stare absently out the window and watched the fitful moonlight glitter on new-fallen snow like a shower of mystical sparks. She never felt the new tears that traced her cheeks.

"Hey! What's the news from the front?"

Anne lurched to her feet. Unaccountably irritated by the flippant tone of Jonathan's voice, she stalked to his room. He looked as if he'd just awakened, the night-light softening his features and sending up an unwanted aching in Anne's chest.

The sight of her stopped him short. "What's wrong?" he asked suddenly. "Is the baby all right?"

She deflated, dragged down by the bone weariness that had taken hold. "The baby's fine," she told him from where she stood in the doorway, resenting the wealth in this room, hers as much as his. "I guess that means that he has a one in three chance of making it past childhood. His father's dead, his mother's dirt-poor with eight kids and no skills. I had to send them a goat so that the baby would have milk. Other than that, he's fine.''

Jonathan's eyes seemed to melt with her words until he was left with an uncomfortable silence to fill. "Have you eaten dinner?"

"No, I'm not hungry."

Before Anne's exhausted brain could comprehend what he was doing, Jonathan swung his feet over the side of the bed and grabbed for his crutches.

"What are you doing?" she demanded.

He grinned. "Fixing you some dinner. Come on."

She watched him hobble out and still stood where she was watching the empty door.

"Get out here or I come in to get you!"

An unwanted grin tugged at her lips and she shrugged, finally following him out the door.

By the time Jonathan served up a meal of leftovers and too-strong coffee in the bright, warm kitchen, Anne had recovered some of her energy, but not much of her spirit. Mary Lou's situation gnawed at her, for it was representative of all the people she helped care for. The disparity between this world and the one she'd left only a few days ago was simply too great, too ludicrous to comprehend. And Jonathan Bradshaw Harris was the very epitome of that disparity.

They had been eating for a few minutes in companionable silence when Jonathan suddenly stopped to consider her with a very appraising eye.

"Why you?"

Anne looked up to face him. "Why me what?"

He motioned with his hands as if to take in everything around him. "Why are you the one to minister to all this? Pioneer nurse and all that."

"What would you suggest I do, start a Junior League?"

"You have to admit that it's a long way from Beacon Hill."

"Yes," she answered definitely. "It is. What's wrong with that?"

"Don't the two hats get a little heavy after a while?"

Within the span of his words Anne's listlessness disappeared, and her eyes flashed with warning. "I don't think I have any difficulty. Neither do the people I live with here. Why should you?"

His face crinkled as if he had witnessed an advertisement for a two-headed man. "The toast of Boston society setting bones and delivering babies?"

"I'm a certified midwife and an emergency room nurse practitioner. Money, after all, does come in handy for some things."

His eyes widened noticeably. "When did you accomplish all of that?"

Her eyes widened correspondingly in mock innocence. "Why, in between cocktail parties, of course."

He grinned without offense and then cocked his head to the side to consider her anew before speaking again.

"Paying the price for daddy's money?"

Anne took her time with the question. It wasn't that it surprised her particularly. She'd asked it often herself and had not always come up with a comfortable answer. She needed to make sure that she could give Jonathan the truth.

"No. I like it here. I have neighbors I can count on and something to do that's worthwhile, and that's more than I've had before. It's my home now."

"You enjoy it, don't you?"

Anne had the feeling that he wasn't referring to her work. "Enjoy what?"

"Belonging in two worlds. Famous socialite and rural nurse. It's real Walter Mitty stuff. You can indulge your expensive whims and then do penance in the mountains."

Color flared briefly high on her cheeks and she straightened, expecting to see the smug smile appear any minute. "Look around you," she snapped. "This is where I live. Do you see any designer touches? How about some calling cards from the jet set? There's not even a box from Bloomingdale's. I haven't been off this mountain two years!"

"The outrage seems sincere," he retorted evenly. "But I don't think you saw the gleam in your eyes when you slipped into those New York rags. If you won't be offended by the comparison, it reminded me of the stories of fire horses and the smell of smoke."

"Do you really think I'm going to be stupid enough to tell you that New York isn't stimulating?"

"You said you hated it."

"I lied. I can't abide smug, self-satisfied people who live their lives by a set of preconceived ideas."

"Me."

"I didn't say that. I merely admitted that I lied."

His eyes opened up a little, the sky there a little wider and warmer with honest amazement. "You really do like it here."

Anne was equally amazed. "Do you like Wyoming?"

Jonathan was fractionally taken aback. Then he shrugged, a bit too complacently. "I was born there."

"That's not what I asked." Suddenly, somehow, she was on the attack.

Again, he shrugged. "It's sometimes nice to see after I've been in New York too long."

"And you enjoy it, don't you?"

He stared, unsettled by her reversal. "Enjoy Wyoming? Sure. There's a sky in Wyoming."

"I'm talking about the double life you undoubtedly lead," she insisted relentlessly. "Maybe you're not a rural nurse, but I bet you're more the adventurer type, the sporting man. 'This executive names mountain climbing and conservation among his hobbies.' Which do you prefer?"

His smile was enigmatic. "There's no contest."

"That's no answer."

"What if I told you I prefer New York? Would you be disappointed?"

Her answering smile was just as cryptic. "I'd have a hunch that you weren't being entirely truthful."

An eyebrow went up. "Why?"

"Let's call it intuition." She leaned back in her chair a little and accused him with a small wave of the hand. "I think that you're an awful lot like me. We're able to exist comfortably in two completely different worlds, and that's hard to understand, isn't it? After living in some place like Wyoming, how do you come to grips with the other life of all the plastic, polished people you deal with? How do you rationalize living in a place where fashion is dictated by the outlandish and the rest of life is dictated by fashion? After having grown up with a moral system that taught the value of basic living, can you really define your life by who you were seen with at the Russian Tea Room or which table you get at Maxim's?"

"And if I do?"

"Then you wouldn't have said anything about Wyoming's sky, or being in New York too long. A true New Yorker would rather not bother with what's above the buildings. It's what's inside them that's attractive."

Now he caught the fire. They sat across from each other, their eyes bright with the contest. "You mean the power plays, the deals. Having lunch with half a dozen well-connected people and changing the course of history. The stock market jumping at your bidding. Politicians currying your favor because of the power you wield." He paused in friendly challenge, the adrenaline of battle warming the light on his features. "What's wrong with that?"

"You forget yourself," she answered evenly. "I may have been born here, but I was raised in Boston and nurtured in the very arms of JCL. I cut my teeth on power plays, Jonathan. It's wise to remember while you're up there lunching with the powerful that in that world the old are quickly cannibalized by the young. Don't anticipate a very long life."

"I expect to be around for a while yet. Why do you mind so much?"

Anne shrugged. "Maybe because I wonder how, after growing up in Wyoming, you could be so attracted to the kind of life I threw away." She stared hard at him, allowing an admission that she'd hardly made to herself. "The kind of life I guess I'm still attracted to. The same way you can't really abide by my decision to give up the bright lights for life in the hills. Even though you're as attracted to them both as I am. We're both social chameleons, I guess."

"Is this what comes of all that time alone to think?"

She had to grin. "Yes. Tell me about Wyoming."

Her sudden change of tack threw him off balance again. "Wyoming? What about it?"

She shrugged. "I've never been there. What's it like?"

"Have you been west at all?"

Anne thought a moment. "Does Chicago count?"

His facial reaction alone was enough to tell her. "Hardly."

"Well, then, tell me so I'll want to go. Does your family live there?"

"Chicago? No, they live in Wyoming."

She proffered a dry grimace. "Is that what you call a sense of humor?" The easing of relations was not lost on her. The constant strain of waiting for the next barb had begun to disappear with their comfortable banter. Anne looked at the handsome crow's feet that gave Jonathan's smile such character and decided that she was glad. She was very glad.

"I'm not at my best here," he was saying.

"That's good to know. I was afraid you were surly all the time."

Another raised eyebrow. This time his eyes were mischievous. "Wyoming is called big sky country, you know."

"So I've heard."

"It also has the Rockies and the Tetons. Mountains."

"Yes."

"I'm from around Jackson Hole. My family first settled there in the 1870s. Indian wars and all."

"Fascinating. Why, that's real *Roots* stuff."

"You wanted to know."

"Do you mountain climb?"

Jonathan winced. "Yes. So don't tell anyone I know how I got here."

At that she waved a finger at him. "Now that's something I would like to know. How did you get here?"

He looked deliberately confused. "You brought me."

Anne scowled. "I'm talking about how you came to do your swan dive off the Great Smokies in a five-hundred-dollar suit. That's the greatest story the locals have had since a training bomber mistook the lights on the ridge for a control tower and tried to land on Wallace Simson's front yard. And that was in 1945."

It was his turn to scowl. "I'd just finished some business with the TVA and was sort of in the neighborhood. I'd never been to the Smokies. Thought I'd take a look."

She nodded passively. "If that's just taking a look, I'd hate to see you after a climb."

His answering smile was almost brittle. "I'd had a few drinks. I'd made quite a successful deal at lunch. I'm afraid my judgment was a little off."

"Well, there's something you can certainly pass along to your friends. Don't drink and climb in the cold. It almost cost you some fingers."

"I'd only intended to look. It seems that the back of the park falls off a lot more sharply than I'd thought."

"But that's five miles off the road," she protested.

He shrugged. "In Wyoming that's no more than a couple of blocks."

"Why did you leave?"

This time he was ready for her. "I had other places to go, other things to do."

She nodded absently. "Is the rest of your family like you?"

"No, they're much more like Judson, whom I spoke with today, by the way."

Anne's head went up.

Jonathan's grin broadened. "He wanted to know if I was remaining on my very best behavior for the very lovely lady who saved my life." He tilted his head a little, taking a sip of coffee. "You seem to have made a conquest."

Anne had to smile. "Judson has very good taste."

Jonathan's expression never changed. "I know."

When Anne came in to say a final good-night before going upstairs, Jonathan motioned for her to sit a moment. She settled herself onto the edge of the bed and let him take her hand. His eyes had softened like the light before dawn.

"I think I should apologize," he started out. His fingers were tracing slow patterns against the palm of Anne's hand as he talked. She noticed how quiet the late night was, how intimate. And how warm Jonathan's touch was. "It seems that I've been behaving like a six-year-old again. I realized it when I saw the look on your face after you came back from delivering the baby." He took a breath that sounded more like a sigh. "There are some things that you're right about. New York makes a person very selfish. It's been a long time since I've known anything else."

"I don't think you're exactly a lost cause," Anne challenged with a gentle smile.

A fleeting brightness lit his eyes. "I can handle you much better when I make you mad. All this tolerance makes me nervous."

"All right," she said nonchalantly, the smile still lightening the gray of her eyes. "Have it your way. You were a jerk. Again. You were such a jerk this time that even Cassie began to lose faith in you, and Cassie would try to save the soul of Hitler."

"Better. Thank you."

"Can I ask a question?"

"Sure."

Anne considered the work-roughened texture of his hands and saw him again setting that ax into motion. "What did I do this time to warrant all the venom?"

Jonathan looked uncomfortable, as if he'd just been caught. "You surprised me. Every time I think I have a peg on you, you're not anything like what I thought." The sun neared the surface of his eyes. "I can't seem to keep up with who you really are."

"Now isn't that a coincidence? I seem to be having the same problem. Just goes to show you the worth of those preconceived ideas."

For the briefest of moments his eyes glinted oddly, as if she'd tripped over a secret of some kind. But just as quickly they softened again. An almost grudging empathy surfaced. "You know what? Your problem is that for a socialite, you care too much."

Anne saw the gentling of his smile and returned it to him. "Not at all," she disagreed evenly. "I'm only here to make the money to keep myself in designer clothes."

They sat together in silence for a few more minutes, the comfortable sounds of the house enveloping them, and then Anne stood to leave. Later as she lay in the darkness, alone in the big double bed, she finally admitted to herself how much she had missed the company of a man: the familiar warmth of him beside her as she slept, the quiet support of shared silence. She'd never realized how cold and quiet the cabin had been until it had once again been filled with companionship.

The snow continued to fall for the next three days until it became difficult to get down the mountain even on horseback. Poor Andy labored his way up and down as Anne made the few necessary trips out to settle her patients before she made her next visit to New York. On the Thursday before she left she tried to make rounds, leaving the cabin and its delicious bread-scented warmth well before dawn to haul a grievously protesting Andy out into the black cold.

The entire community knew about her plight, which didn't surprise her in the least. Everyone was pitching in to free her for the business in New York. The little Red Cross group was going to keep tabs on her patients, and the four families who lived closest to the house would take turns checking in on Jonathan.

By the time Anne once again approached the cabin it was the wee hours of Friday and she was cold and cramped. The ride back up had taken six hours beneath the brittle stars and waning moon. The scene was bewitching, a fairy tale in snow and shadows, the air clear with ringing silence. Only the occasional trill of a night bird broke in on her secluded world. Somewhere near Preacher's Seat a bobcat darted out in front of Andy, but the big bay just snorted and plodded on, anxious to be back in his barn.

It made Anne wonder as she proceeded up the sleeping mountain how she could so enjoy the pulsating racket of the New York nights where the noise and action weren't even stilled by the hush of dawn. But she did. She could easily thrive on both, living a completely schizophrenic life if given half the chance. She'd relished her time working the emergency room at Mass General, where organized chaos reigned and shouting was the only audible form of communication. But she cherished just as much her life on horseback in the primitive backwoods of the mountains. If only there were a way to combine the two painlessly.

Admitting that, Anne realized without qualification that she was really glad Jonathan Bradshaw Harris had fallen from her cliff. No matter the confusion and tension he'd created for her, his unspoken similarities had given credibility to the puzzling contrasts in her own life. The more she knew him, the more she felt their special kinship.

Much to her amazement, she found him awake when she got home. She saw his light on as she stamped her feet back into circulation on the way to the kitchen.

"Anne? Is that you?"

"In all my glory!" she called back, pulling off her gloves to put water on for tea. She was exhausted, shivering and uncomfortably aware of the pins and needles spreading through fingers and toes as the circulation made a first attempt to return after the long cold ride.

"Why are you so late?"

She couldn't help but laugh. "The last person who asked me that question in that particular tone of voice was my father," she retorted. "And if memory serves me, I was seventeen years old at the time. Want some tea?"

"Sure."

While the water was heating, Anne climbed the stairs to change into her flannel nightgown and robe, pulling heavy knee socks on to soothe her chilly feet. The rush of warmth the heavy clothes brought suddenly reminded her of the night she'd helped rescue Jonathan. It wasn't that long ago, and yet it seemed that he'd been in her house for months.

Anne absently unwound her braid as she thought of that time and how much things had since changed in her little house. She didn't see the soft glow reach her eyes or realize that she'd begun to smile. With her hair brushed out into soft waves that fell over her shoulders, she looked like a different woman than the one who had sat up with Jonathan that first night.

"Is this the woman who took New York by storm?" Jonathan demanded when Anne walked in with the tea. The lines of his face had softened, the weathered lines around his eyes crinkling comfortably with his smile. He was sitting up with another book in his lap, but his hair was sleep-tousled, and he rubbed at his eyes like a little boy.

"This is the woman who took Elder's Crossing by storm," she answered as she set the tray down.

"You look exhausted."

Sitting heavily in her chair, she offered him his mug. "You still have an admirable grasp of the obvious. I've probably ridden thirty miles, visited ten households, drunk gallons of tea and two cups of moonshine, bounced innumerable babies, argued with old ladies and been proposed to—again—by a seventy-nine-year-old widower. It has been a full day." Unconsciously, she rubbed at her frozen feet. There was a huge blister on her heel that hadn't been there yesterday. She'd need to get new boots.

"Give me your feet," Jonathan said abruptly.

She stared at him. "Pardon?"

"Give me your feet. I'll massage them for you."

She didn't move, not sure how to react.

He grinned smugly at her. "Afraid I'll try to take advantage of you? You already set down the ground rules there. Besides, feet aren't my fetish. They hurt, don't they?"

"They're killing me."

"Then don't argue. Hand 'em over. I happen to be a great masseur."

She did and was immediately glad. Having her feet off the floor was pleasure enough, but when he started to slowly work out the kinks, one foot at a time between his solid, capable hands, she thought she'd died and gone to heaven.

Jonathan kneaded the muscles slowly and carefully, almost, but not quite, hurting. Energy surged into Anne's overworked legs, making her want to stretch them. She even forgot the teacup she held in her lap. It felt so good to lean back, close her eyes and enjoy Jonathan's ministrations.

"You act like nobody's ever done this for you before," he observed.

"If they did, I can't remember when."

"Society nobility and never had a massage?" His words remained light and teasing rather than sarcastic.

She thought about it for a minute without bothering to open her eyes. "I don't think so. I can't remember ever having had time. Don't forget, I had a dual identity to support."

"In that case, you'll be happy to know that I also give world famous back rubs."

Anne opened her eyes in time to see him pat a spot next to himself on the bed.

"You should be asleep."

"I'm not the one who's been taking the light of medicine to the backwoods for the last twenty-four hours." Giving the bed another pat for encouragement, he grinned. "Go ahead and be passive for a change. You already know that I have great hands."

She studied him through half-open eyes. "You won't take advantage of me?"

He laughed, once again working on her feet. "I can't imagine anyone taking advantage of you."

"My family certainly seems to have done that," she retorted as she gave up and shifted around to the spot he'd indicated, feet now propped on her chair. Jonathan took her mass of hair in one hand and lifted it over one shoulder and out of the way. Then, gently, his fingers took hold of her neck. A delicious shiver raced down her back at his light touch.

"If you'll pardon my saying so, I can't imagine how. You hardly seem to be an easy target. Woman of steel and all." His fingers were moving slowly, working the muscles thoroughly up and down her neck, their pressure progressively more intense. Anne found herself relaxing against his hands, the pleasure of the massage as sharp as pain.

"I have not always been the confident, self-fulfilled woman you see before you." She could feel his breath on her neck and it tickled. More shivers. She wiggled her toes inside their wool socks. The pins and needles had been replaced by a kind of sweet fire that made her want to rub them against something. She could understand how a cat felt when its back was scratched. That fire was beginning to spread. "In Boston I was my father's daughter. My big act of rebellion was running off to be a nurse, but that was all right because nursing was an acceptable profession for a female. I didn't want to be a rock star or anything. And I neatly balanced the defiance by marrying Tom."

Jonathan's hands had found her spine. Subconsciously she could name the vertabrae as he passed over them. Up and down, thoracic, cervical, thoracic, lumbar, the movements slow enough to be hypnotic. She found herself stretching again as he found some particularly sore spots and began to work them out. A curious warmth radiated from his fingertips that was starting to wake Anne up again. She opened her eyes to see the hall light reflecting from the tips of her still-wiggling toes.

"Tom was your father's choice?"

"His dream. Genetically perfect for the big business. You'd love him. He's like you only blond."

It took Jonathan a moment to answer, and in that time a new tension had crept into his fingers. They moved a bit faster. "I'd be flattered if I didn't think that you just gave me your greatest insult."

Anne cocked her head at the words, wondering that Jonathan might have picked up on that. "No, I don't think so. I meant that Tom was the best at what he did."

"Sounds to me like he was a fool."

His statement surprised her. She wanted very much to turn around and find the meaning of his words in his eyes. She wasn't at all sure that she had that kind of nerve. Unaccountably she began to feel the same tension that infected Jonathan's movements, like electric wire that danced on the ground after a storm. It was more than physical proximity or the feel of strong hands searching out her weariness like potent salves. It was Jonathan.

"He's many things, but Tom is no fool," she disagreed carefully. "You remember your description of power? That's Tom. My father was the best, and Tom ground him beneath his feet."

"He threw a lot away in the bargain." Jonathan's voice was softer, surprised. Anne found herself holding her breath. He'd made a discovery, one that his touch transmitted. One that Anne already had come to know.

Her skin was beginning to ache with an addictive need for his touch. The wire jumped in her, its raw ends skittering over the deepest recesses of her belly. She knew that she should get bolt upright and get the hell out of this bedroom before she couldn't. She was too tired to resist and that was dangerous. She was much too close to falling in love, and she couldn't afford it.

"I guess that wasn't what he wanted." Her own voice was beginning to sound a little breathless.

"That's why he's a fool."

It was there in his voice. Anne turned her head to it, and his hands stopped, trapping her by the shoulders. It was in his eyes, too. The truth he hadn't been able to commit to before. For the first time Anne saw that Jonathan loved her. It was as if he'd opened a path for her to the depths of his soul, and all she could see there was a reflection of the yearning in her own eyes. She saw the imminent commitment there and was quite suddenly terrified.

She wasn't ready and might never be. Her footing wasn't solid enough on its own yet. Convulsively, she tried to jerk free, but he never moved. His grip remained strong. Anne tried to give voice, but couldn't. It was all she could do to hold his gaze.

"I'm sorry, Anne," Jonathan said very softly, his hands inexorably drawing her to him. "I lied. I'm not going to abide by the rules." His eyes were so close, his attraction smothering her. Anne dragged in a breath as if it were the most difficult thing she had ever done.

"Jonathan, please..."

He trapped the rest of her protest with his lips, gathering in her doubts with the strength and safety of his arms. Don't, she wanted to cry. Don't open that door. It holds back too much pain. I can't afford this. But there was no way out. The current arced between them, the longing to belong, the yearning for each other. It rose as sharply in her as fire and made her gasp at its fury. There was no turning back now, if there had ever been a time to turn back. Jonathan's hold on her was gentle, but Anne couldn't break free. She felt his hands hesitate, holding her at the waist, and she wanted to cry out for them to find her.

Then Jonathan pulled back, the taste of his last kiss still on Anne's lips. For a long moment he looked down at her, all of the questions he needed to ask there in his eyes. Without a word, Anne answered.

Her heart set a new record, trying to jump free of its mooring like the beating of a captive bird's wings against a cage. Her hands were like ice and she couldn't seem to breathe, but when she saw the tender invitation in Jonathan's eyes, she found herself smiling. With a deliberation that she had never known before and would certainly shock her later, she took hold of his hand and placed it against the throbbing of her heart.

"You're sure?" he asked, and she thought she'd never heard such a sweet question before.

"Not at all," she managed. And then she kissed him.

Later she would think that making love on a single bed with a man in a leg splint should have been awkward. But she couldn't remember anything at all that had been awkward. In fact, in that old brass bed that had held her childhood dreams and memories, Jonathan gave her a gift greater than any she could ever have imagined. He gave her himself. He lavished her with such an attentiveness that she would wonder how she had ever made love before.

When she stood to slip out of her nightgown, the soft durable flannel that had seen her through so many solitary winter nights, he took her hand and drew her down next to him, forbidding her the right to deny either of them any small pleasure they could share together. Jonathan unbuttoned her gown as he leaned over her, his eyes devouring hers with their bright flame. At each button he bent to kiss her throat, her chest, following the progress of the buttons with lips that tasted every part of her.

He never removed the gown but only draped it aside, as if to frame her body for him. After a last, lingering kiss that Anne shared in silent wonder, he turned to enjoy the sight of her creamy skin in the soft light. The tiniest of currents brushed across Anne with delicious warmth. She shivered, unable to stay still, yet unable to move. She could feel the heat of Jonathan's eyes wash over her as if they made contact with her. And when he bent to taste her strong body, he chose her stomach, the slightly rounded abdomen that should have held her children. The touch of his lips and the cool teasing of his tongue ignited a new ache there where he searched her hot skin with his hungry mouth, and Anne moaned with its delight.

Jonathan's hands traced the strong muscles of her thighs, the sleek calves that woolen socks hid, even as his mouth explored the ridges of her ribs. Long before his lips reached them, her breasts were taut with anticipation, the nipples waiting for his fingers to find them. He waited, though, torturing her with his deliberate patience. Sitting above her, he waited as she unbuttoned his shirt, mimicking his actions.

Anne slid her hands around his back and pulled him to her, the sensation of his skin against her like a narcotic. The hair on his chest chafed her breasts and nestled against her cheek. She could feel the taut pull of his back, the muscles there like strong rope. But again, just as she began to gather in the comfort of him, he pulled away, taking his turn.

"You're doing this on purpose," she accused, barely recognizing the anguished sound that was her voice.

"Yes, I am," he murmured back. "I want you to know what it feels like to be cherished."

He sought out her breasts then, first with his hands, which explored with maddening caution, and then with his lips. Anne could see him in the half light as he took her breast in his mouth, a gesture of giving and taking that measured a man's admission of vulnerability. When, a moment later he lifted his head to meet her eyes, she took his beautiful face in her hands and drew him down to her again. And there she held him to her, as if this would bind him to her, even as she tasted the new tears that cleansed her.

He took her with a gentle possession that made her cry out. She lay on her back beneath him, trapped by his power, bound by his commitment. Anne had never realized the breadth of her own passion until Jonathan met her mouth with his own and carefully rocked her to a shuddering peak. It was like a dark flower blooming inside, spreading its intoxicating petals so wide that it would not be bound within her. She began to move against him, wrapping herself around him as if to draw him even closer than he was. His arms encompassed her; his words united them. He vowed to make her whole again and she believed him.

Tears clouded Anne's vision, but she couldn't take her eyes from his face. He smiled at her, his eyes so close that Anne wondered that they didn't singe her. Even as the sweet pain engulfed her and she cried out Jonathan's name as if he could save her, she never lost sight of those eyes. They were the lifeline that had held and guided her. She saw them as they realized her satisfaction and kissed them as Jonathan followed her.

And when Anne and Jonathan were exhausted, their breathing ragged and worn from the gift they had shared, she took his damp, tousled head and lay it against her to rest. There he lay in sleep, nestled against the softness of her breasts, the slow rhythm of his breathing soothing.

For a long while Anne lay staring at the soft play of light against the ceiling, the chill of the late night never touching her. She knew that with the cold of daylight, though, reality would invade the sweet dream set free tonight.

Without realizing it, she gave voice to her dilemma. "What am I going to do when you leave and I'm alone again?"

There was a long silence, punctuated only by the sound of the incessant living room clock.

"What am I going to do?"

Chapter 10

Anne reached Judson Fredericks's office still in a state of anxiety over Jonathan's threat to her fragile independence. When they had awakened that morning each had dealt with the other warily, as if afraid to make too much of what had happened the night before, yet not wanting to treat it too lightly. They had ended up parting without even really talking about it. Now Anne was left with trying to distance herself enough from that crisis to deal successfully with the one Tom and Brad posed.

The office was, as ever, like an oasis of serenity hidden amid the chaos of the city. Judson stood up as she entered and smiled warmly. His sincere compliments pleased her; the dark wood and hushed lighting helped settle her. Anne held out her hand and returned his greeting.

"I've looked forward to seeing you again, Anne," he said graciously, as he guided her once more to the plush green leather chair across from his own. "I hope you don't have plans for dinner tonight. I took the liberty of making reservations in the hopes that you would dine with me."

She smiled at the almost quaint manners Judson displayed. He seemed such an anachronism in this city. He acted more like an old-style southern gentleman than a high-powered New York lawyer. "I would be delighted, Mr. Fredericks."

"Please, you must call me Judson."

Anne nodded her acquiescence and allowed the lawyer to get down to the business at hand. Judson pulled a file toward him and opened it.

"Now, I have been doing some research here," he began, picking up a pair of glasses and carefully adjusting them onto the bridge of his nose with a finger as he studied the papers before him. Perfect, Anne thought with delight. The glasses only made him look more distinguished. "You say you signed the divorce papers and those waiving rights to court approval to the executor's actions in dispensing your father's will, the executor being your brother. Am I correct?"

"I believe so. As I told you before, the time after my father's death was very trying for me. I'm afraid that I trusted my lawyer and signed whatever he told me to."

"Do you remember how many different documents you signed?"

Anne thought a moment, trying her best to pick a few pieces from within the jumbled mess of the weeks that followed her father's death. So much had been shock of betrayal and loss then, it was difficult to remember particulars.

"Four, I think. It all happened three days before I left Boston the last time. If memory serves me correctly, Mr. Martin drove me to the office himself to accommodate me."

"Four," he repeated to himself, again going over the papers in his hand. "You're certain?"

"No, I'm not certain of anything."

Judson nodded slowly in acknowledgment. "Would you have signed power of attorney over to your husband?"

This time Anne's answer was prompt. "Of course not. The last thing I would have wanted at that point was to leave him in control of my life. Besides, what would the need have been? Father left everything in Brad's and Tom's names. Father didn't consider women able enough to control their own money. I waived my chances to contest the will with the stipulation that Tom and Brad let me move back to the cabin without interference."

Judson was peering at her over his glasses in a curious way. "Did you read the will personally?"

"I had no desire to. It was read to me, and I found no surprises in it."

"By your father's lawyer."

She nodded. "By Mr. Martin."

He nodded quietly once again, contemplating the material in his hands. The lines of his face reflected only his concentration on the matter at hand, but the atmosphere in the peaceful office had somehow changed. Anne was beginning to feel a sort of electric charge and unconsciously shifted in her seat.

"There is obviously something of import in all of this," she said carefully, not feeling as self-assured as she sounded. Her hands remained frozen in her lap.

Judson looked up and smiled. "There is. I cannot, however, make any definite conclusion about it until I have a few more documents examined."

She stared, suddenly understanding. "There is a power of attorney, isn't there?"

Judson considered his answer a moment before nodding and handing over one of the papers to Anne. She examined it herself. When she again faced the lawyer, it was with eyes only a fraction as chilled as her heart. "What does this mean?"

"Did you sign it?"

"It certainly looks like it, doesn't it?" It was as if with the sight of this paper, all of the control she'd so carefully constructed shattered like thin ice. Tom was holding the strings as he had held them all along, and she felt outraged.

"Well, I'll find out for certain. If it is authentic, then your father's will ended up saying just what you thought, and I'm afraid that Tom can do anything he wants with the land."

Her head came up sharply. "Ended up?"

Why did it seem as if the clock was ticking more and more loudly in the unnatural hush? Judson removed his glasses and held them out before him for contemplation before he answered. "I have a copy of your father's will here. It does not read quite as you thought, I'm afraid."

Anne had no answer, unaware that her hands were now clasped together as if to better keep her balance, her knuckles white.

Judson continued. "Your father changed his will toward the end of his life and left the majority of his property and share of stock to you, my dear."

The silence became profound; the street below the window was filled with voiceless animation. Only the clock interrupted with its insistent heartbeat—ticking, ticking. Anne stood and walked to the window to hide her confusion. Forty floors below, an ambulance flashed through traffic, its shrillness lost outside the Plexiglas insulation. The sun lay somewhere behind the skyline, setting the windows afire in an evil blood-glow.

Anne drew a shaky breath. "The cabin?"

"It was left to you. The only direct inheritance your father left Bradley was the house in Boston."

She turned once again, facing the quietly concerned lawyer. "So I signed the power of attorney, just as Brad and Tom had been trying to get father to do before he died, and now they've had the time to legally transfer all benefits of the will to themselves."

Judson didn't have to answer. He waited silently for her to continue.

"What can I do?"

He answered matter-of-factly. "To reclaim the land you want, you must be able to prove that fraud was involved."

"Can I?"

"That remains to be seen. I have already begun to investigate the matter. We have a few avenues open to us."

"I'll have to be frank with you, Judson. I have my mother's inheritance, and most of that I have invested in a clinic to be built near where I live. I don't know how well I can afford your fee." Her smile was rueful as she reflected on the situation. "I'm afraid that's something I never had to consider before. But if I could prove fraud..."

"You will, in fact, control JCL. That was that I'm trying to tell you."

"I'm not concerned with the company." She returned to her seat so that Judson wouldn't notice the definite tremble in her knees. "I am concerned with being able to pay your bill. I have the feeling that you've already put quite a bit of work into this. Would you consider a percentage fee?"

"That would be more than generous, Anne," he allowed, "but I think I would rather simply donate my fee to that clinic of yours. At my age I have the luxury of being frivolous if I like."

Anne took his hand in thanks. It seemed to be more than enough for the older man.

"Will we be able to manage it all in so short a time?" she finally asked. "The Board of Directors' meeting is day after tomorrow, and that will be my last chance to contest the sale."

He shook his head slightly. "I have the impression that the meeting will be postponed so that we will end up with more time. But that is another matter entirely, one that I would rather take up over dinner."

Anne offered a tenuous smile. "That sounds like the best idea I've heard since we said hello."

With a return smile that showed a touch of relief, Judson stood to show Anne out. But before he did, he paused with yet another unsettling bit of advice. "Anne, there is one more matter that I feel bears mentioning."

Anne had gotten to her feet when Judson did, and now found that she felt uncomfortable before him. That he had to hesitate a moment to find the proper words to express himself unsettled her even more.

"Have you ever had cause to be...wary...of your husband?" he asked diffidently.

Anne's eyes widened ever so slightly. "Wary? Do you mean other than the fact that you'd have to drag me kicking and screaming into a partnership with him?"

Judson didn't smile at her little joke, which widened her eyes even more. She couldn't imagine a man like Judson Fredericks being forced to use clichés like this.

"It is simply a matter of a number of...well, unusual pieces of correspondence that we have received in the office since we've started to investigate your situation."

"Unusual..." Anne stiffened. "Do you mean threats?" She was furious. The idea that Tom could try to intimidate this kind man who stood before her made her want to walk right over to wherever he was and rearrange his classic features a little. She drew herself up very straight, her eyes like winter ice. "My husband tried to threaten you?"

This time she did get a smile. A quick flash of wry apology. "Only in a very civilized manner, I assure you."

Anne's own smile was brittle. "It would be the only way Tom would operate. He is powerful, Judson. And unscrupulous. If it makes you uncomfortable..."

Before she could finish the thought Judson brushed it aside with a small wave of his hand. "Not in the least, my dear. His rhetoric has only strengthened my own beliefs that this whole situation is at the least more than a little suspect. No, I was more concerned for you."

Anne didn't understand. "Me?"

Again propriety forced him to look around for his words before facing her with them. "You live alone and in an isolated area."

It had been so long since Anne had heard anyone so deliberately tap-dance around a problem that it took her a moment to understand the import of his words. She knew that her eyes once again opened, and that her mouth gaped in incredulous protest, but she couldn't manage an intelligent retort.

"Anne," he said slowly as if the whole subject caused him great pain. "If we are correct in our suspicions that your husband and brother defrauded you out of your rightful inheritance, the scope of their crime is immsense. JCL is one of the most powerful industries on the East Coast. Desperate men have been known to resort to desperate measures."

"Except for one thing," Anne said, smiling wryly. She had no intentions of even entertaining a thought like the one Judson proposed. "Tom would never believe that he could lose the legal fight since he never has before. His fatal flaw, I'm afraid, is that he believes too much in himself and too little in others."

"I would still feel less anxious about the matter if I were assured of your personal safety, my dear."

Anne saw the true concern in those warm brown eyes and wished she could have walked around the desk to give the man a hug. "I'll see to it, just for you, Judson."

For a moment he searched her eyes, only allowing the worry in his own to ease after being assured by her promise. Then he held out his hand. "In that case, Miss Jackson, I believe we have a dinner engagement."

Anne afforded herself the luxury of stopping at the Plaza to change, claiming that the suit she once again wore was strictly business attire. She arrived for dinner in an electric-blue Jack Mulqueen shirtdress that flattered her figure as well as her coloring. Her necklace and earrings were plain gold, her hair pulled up into a heavy sleek braid.

Her appearance on Judson's arm turned heads in the elegant restaurant. She smiled deferentially to him to heighten the illusion as they were seated by the magnificent two-story windows that overlooked the park. Along the walls, matching mirrors illuminated the candlelight ambiance of the lofty white room. Waiters moved silently in black, bending and nodding to the impressive clientele.

"I have to admit that this is something I miss on the mountain," Anne said as she sipped her Manhattan. "There isn't one good French restaurant in the entire town of Elder's Crossing."

Judson chuckled, his office manner relaxing to that of a Southern landowner. Anne was still having trouble placing him in Wyoming. Probably a matter of East Coast prejudices that still tended to crown everyone west of Baltimore with a Stetson.

"This can be just as wearing," he assured her. "In point of fact, I have given much consideration to moving to a small town when I retire. I rather miss it."

"Home to Wyoming?"

He nodded, the silver of his hair gleaming in the candlelight. "Very likely. I have visions of lazy summer days spent along the Snake River with a fishing pole in my hands."

"I can attest to the benefits of that sort of life," she agreed.

"Indeed you can, my dear. Your life seems to agree with you immensely." His appraising eye was gentlemanly and flattering. Anne enjoyed it all the more for the time she'd spent with the taciturn people of the hills who wouldn't consider doling out compliments so easily.

Judson claimed the privilege of ordering for them both, and they settled back to chat about his children and grandchildren, the wife he'd lost two years before and the contrasts between Wyoming and the Appalachians. They did not talk of Jonathan or of the business of the day. Anne knew that that would be served up over coffee.

She enjoyed the meal immensely, from the rack of lamb that arrived pink and succulent with a side of mint jelly to the cherries jubilee that ended the meal in grand style. Judson was the perfect host: attentive, considerate, and well versed in the sophisications of the city. Yet he had never lost the frank honesty life in his native state had instilled in him. He was able to bring Anne up-to-date on the latest in theater, opera and symphony offerings around town and offered to escort her if she were in town long enough. She thought that she would enjoy that very much.

The thought didn't escape her that this was the relationship she'd always longed for with a father who had never had the time to relax away from the demands of his empire, and who hadn't realized his mistake until it had been much too late to do anything.

It was almost eleven before coffee was poured, and Anne was served her Frangelica. Outside her window couples strolled along the street, and a hansom cab clattered into the darkness of the park. Streetlights illuminated the trees as they swayed in a fitful breeze, their limbs skeletal and gray. It made Anne appreciate even more the rich warmth of the restaurant as she sipped at the smooth liqueur.

"Dinner was lovely," she said, smiling at her host. "I'll remember this evening for the rest of the winter as I plod through the snow on my rounds."

"And I will remember it as I spend my winter attending boring meetings with lawyers and CPAs," Judson returned with genuine warmth. "Come spring, I might just visit your little town."

"I'd be delighted." Anne meant it. She'd love to see what happened when she introduced Judson to Silas. She probably wouldn't see either of them for a month as they sought out the area's finer fishing holes together.

"How long do you plan to remain in New York?"

Somehow Anne knew that this was Judson's introduction to business.

"Well, I'll stay for the meeting. I'd love to spend a few days here, but I do still have a patient to attend to."

Judson nodded. "Yes, I did want to ask after him. He sounds as if he's getting along quite well. Is it still impossible to move him?"

"For at least a little while longer. We still have some three feet of snow up there."

"That's quite unusual, isn't it?"

"I believe insurance companies refer to it as an act of God." She grinned. "My horse is about to go out on strike. He's been on rounds three times this week."

"Jonathan wouldn't be able to ride down?"

"Not yet. The nearest rest stop is seven miles down."

He thought a moment. "What about a helicopter?"

Anne shook her head. "I've thought of that, too." She didn't tell him that she had thought of it most frequently when Jonathan had still thought that cynicism was the way to her heart. "The nearest rest stop is also the nearest sizable clearing."

He nodded again as he sipped at his coffee. "I see. Well, at least I know he's in good hands. I have been in contact with his family, and they have been asking after him."

Anne waited to answer until the waiter refilled her coffee and faced away again. "Tell them that he's up and around on crutches, and if he's there much longer I'm going to send him out to milk the cows. And since you have my number, please feel free to give it to them. I have a feeling they make more phone calls than Jonathan."

"Well, he has most definitely been on the phone with me," Judson admitted. "He has insisted on being involved with every step of your case. I have employed several of his suggestions, in fact."

Anne had assumed that Jonathan had been apprised of what was going on, but for some reason she hadn't anticipated this. She'd only seen him on the phone two or three times. But if he knew about the will, he wouldn't discuss that in front of her until something was settled. He obviously had compassion. Why should that still surprise her?

"In any event, my dear," Judson continued, "you must let me know if there is anything I can do to help. Jonathan's parents are old and dear friends of mine, and you have given them an invaluable gift by helping Jonathan as you have."

"I will of course, Judson." She smiled as she decided to finally press the matter. "There is one thing you could do for me now, if you would."

"Of course."

"Well," she said, then hesitated, fingering the delicate lines of her liqueur glass. "As a matter of fact, it's about Jonathan. You've known his family for a long time." He nodded. Anne took a breath to gather enough tact together to continue. "I would ask you to be indiscreet, Judson, and tell me what you know about Jonathan."

Judson allowed himself a small frown of hesitation. "I don't understand."

She grinned wryly. "Since he's been staying with me, he has displayed some curious...oh, contradictions that make it difficult for me to understand him. There have been some incidents that make me think that he's a lot more troubled than he likes to pretend." She gave a small shrug. "I think it's important that I know all I can about him."

"He hasn't said anything himself?"

"No. Only that his family was from Wyoming and his business in New York. I do know that he was in Vietnam." Judson's eyebrow rose.

"A nightmare he had one night," she explained, seeing no need to elaborate. "He seems to prefer to play the mysterious stranger."

Judson nodded absently to himself as he studied the hands he'd placed before him on the snow-white tablecloth. "I have not been in real contact with Jonathan for some time," he admitted, looking back up with a sober expression. "My heavens, it's been since before he was in the service: maybe eleven, twelve years ago. He was, I think, a different person then."

Anne recognized the tension his words ignited in her. "How so?"

Judson considered her for a minute as if estimating the risk of further disclosure. Anne thought that he was a very worthy friend.

"Permit me a moment of explanation." At the next table a woman giggled, a shrill, silly sound that seemed to shatter the restrained atmosphere of the room. Judson never noticed. His eyes were at once on Anne and on the past. "Jonathan was born and raised near Jackson, Wyoming. I grew up with John, his father. A fine man. At one time, many years ago, I courted his mother Helen. You would enjoy Helen, I think. She is very much like you. Well, when Jonathan was old enough, he came east for college. He wanted to make a name for himself away from his father's influence, which is, of course, not terribly unusual for an oldest son. Jonathan is the oldest of three.

"Soon after college Jonathan met someone who went into a partnership with him, some type of sales venture, I believe. I never understood the details. I was in Europe on extended holiday when it happened. Evidently a loan was taken out to finance the business. When the venture went under, the partner managed to default, leaving Jonathan holding a rather large loan along with no money and no business. To make matters worse, his father had helped by putting a second mortgage on the ranch and lost it. The family had to move in with Jonathan's brother who lived nearby."

He paused to sip from a refilled cup of coffee. Anne followed suit without really paying attention to what she was doing. A quality of pain had slipped into Judson's voice that presaged the import of a nightmare.

Judson couldn't quite keep his eyes impassive as he continued. "Not long after that, Jonathan enlisted in the marines and put in a request for duty in Vietnam. His mother has always equated the action to a type of suicide note, and it is very possible that she was right. Jonathan shouldered a great amount of guilt for what he'd done to his family. He served two tours of duty and came away with a Silver Star, DSC, Purple Heart, malaria and six months in hospitals for injuries he received."

"No one could prove any wrong on the partner's part?" she asked.

"It seems that the gentleman in question had a certain amount of influence and Jonathan, at the time, had none."

"And he had no other alternatives to take?"

Judson smiled apologetically. "As I said, I was in Europe at the time. I was about the only person Jonathan could have come to for help. In point of fact, when he first called me about taking your case, I was surprised. I have always been afraid that he held my unavailability against me."

Anne shook her head numbly. It was almost impossible to conceive that this had happened to the Jonathan she knew. She understood now, though, what he had meant about being in the same position as her. She couldn't imagine having to face that kind of situation, or having to bear that kind of responsibility. No wonder he dealt so badly with the memories of Vietnam. He'd used his time as his own private purgatory for what he'd done to his parents, and had ended up failing again, at least in his eyes.

"You say you haven't kept in touch with him since then. Do you know what he's been doing?"

He nodded, sipping again at his coffee and then carefully setting the cup down on its fragile saucer. "Jonathan went to law school on the GI Bill. I attended his graduation, but when I saw him then he had changed. When I had known him before, he had been a bright, independent, enthusiastic young lad: very open and honest, and out to conquer the world. When we spoke at the graduation, I could not help but notice that he had taken an almost cynical tack. Hard. He had lost that fine enthusiasm, and was instead...well, driven. That much is easy to see in what he has accomplished since. He has founded and built a rather formidable empire in New York: Bradwell International. They deal in management turnaround. Four years ago he was able to buy back his father's ranch. Since then I expected him to relax a bit. Instead, he has devoted his time even more strenuously to advancing the position and influence of his firm."

There was much from what Judson said that Anne had to digest. Jonathan's story was not unusual in a city like New York. It was merely another tale of a young man trying to make a name for himself and failing. The values he had brought with him from Wyoming had become engulfed within the alien code of ethics he'd been confronted with, and he'd been overwhelmed.

It didn't surprise Anne, for as she'd told Jonathan, she'd cut her teeth early on that sort of thing. She'd seen better men than him fail. She'd seen her own father, who'd invented the rules, fall a lot harder. It at least helped her understand Jonathan's time in Vietnam and its repercussions. She could better appreciate his attitude and the contradictions that so baffled her. The cynicism, the slick act, the sudden glimpses of compassion. Anne represented everything that he'd once battled against in vain. This was the story behind the first time he'd been helpless to save someone he'd loved from being hurt.

And whether or not he admitted it, Jonathan was still fighting between those two sets of disparate rules. Anne was afraid that he would finally convince himself that in New York the honesty and integrity he'd brought with him from Wyoming had no place.

She could well imagine that he didn't see Judson that often, either. The older man had somehow survived with his scruples intact. That would certainly be salt in a raw wound.

Anne wished that there were some way she could make Jonathan see that he had to keep fighting. The longer he stayed with her, the more she saw the boy from Wyoming in him. It had been that side of him that had attracted her to him in the first place. She was afraid that if Jonathan went back to New York without something to reaffirm his faith in the gentler side of himself, it would finally die out, leaving him in the end no more than another Tom McCarthy. Anne was beginning to realize how important it was to her that that didn't happen.

For a moment she allowed herself to consider the memory of Jonathan as he'd slept in her arms, his face so relaxed and almost young again. But the picture brought with it pain, a sharp regret for what he'd hidden so carefully behind those brittle blue eyes. She found that she had to force it away again.

"Thank you for telling me, Judson. It does help me understand."

"Happy to do it, my dear. I only hope that spending some time with you might help him somehow."

She couldn't help but grin. "Well, if nothing else, it's helped rebroaden his horizons. Tell me something, just for curiosity's sake. Has anyone told his company where he is? He certainly hasn't."

"Oh, I imagine not. They manage quite well without him, from what I understand, because of the excellent organizational system he set up. He is often away without notice. They've become quite used to it."

"What do you mean he goes away without notice?"

"It seems that it is supposed to be his way to test the efficiency of his people. Sometimes he goes home, from what his mother has written, although more often than not, no one knows quite where he goes. My theory is that he camps alone somewhere near his home. There is much wild country where a man can be by himself with his thoughts."

"I would have thought that he wouldn't have wanted to be caught there," Anne said more to herself.

The waiter appeared silently again, the silver coffeepot in hand, but Judson held up his hand. The man nodded with a small bow of well-bred servitude and melted away.

"As I said," Judson continued, "Jonathan has not confided in me. But the tradition is one his father was fond of employing. The two of them used to camp together when Jonathan was a boy." Carefully folding his white linen napkin by halves, Judson placed it next to his empty coffee cup. "Now, my dear, I am afraid that this old man must be getting on his way. But before we go, I wanted to explain a bit more about the meeting with Amplex."

Anne nodded in silence.

"As I said before, I have reason to believe that the meeting will be postponed. It would seem that there is a request that all the board members be present and two or three of them seem to be detained. From what I have been able to ascertain, it may be a matter of weeks." Anne moved to protest, but he held up a hand with a quiet smile. "Think of it this way. The delay is to our advantage. It gives us more time to find a case against your ex-husband and brother."

"I know." Anne sighed, the evening's enjoyment dulled a little. "It's the idea that I'll have to live with this hanging over my head for so long. I never did learn to wait with grace."

So it was that when Judson saw her to the front door of the Plaza, Anne felt deflated and a bit frustrated by the lack of control she had over the whole matter. Somehow it seemed to be getting further and further away from her until she was beginning to feel like a pawn.

As she stood in the ascending elevator she slowly rolled her head to relieve the tension the idea of upcoming weeks of uncertainty had given birth to. The more she thought about it, the more she thought that the only thing that would help right now would be a long hot shower.

The idea of the hot, stinging, muscle-relaxing water got her through the walk down to her room and the ritual of undressing once she'd gotten inside. Lights dotted the black park below her room, and the music of traffic battered at her window. Anne's mind could go no further, though, than the anticipation of a twenty-minute marathon without the hot water running out just as she was getting relaxed.

Only minutes later she stood in the tub savoring the hot water like the strong hold of a lover. Steam rose in lazy clouds around her, fogging the mirror and saturating the small errant tendrils that clung to Anne's neck and forehead. The persistence of the city noise had been silenced by the waterfall of cleansing bliss, and she could almost imagine that she was home enjoying the soul-saving quiet of the mountain.

Finally giving in to temptation, Anne lifted her head to the water and let it drench her hair and flood her face. She would have preferred to stand in a mindless trance, letting the water wash away the tensions that ate at her, but images of Jonathan nudged insistently at her. His hands, the stern lines of his face that so belied his wry, offhand humor. His laugh, so sharp and crisp it sounded like limbs snapping in a dry tree.

But most of all, when she closed her eyes, his opened, and she felt herself once again mesmerized by the shifting, settling blue that had unnerved, fascinated, infuriated, and finally overcome her. Eyes that could withdraw completely into themselves to protect the kind of secret that had scarred Jonathan as permanently as the shrapnel that had opened his side, they had also reached out to her without hesitation. She had been seduced by the life-giving fire in his eyes long before she had succumbed to the magic of his hands.

She had never known any man like him before. The comparisons were certainly there to make, because he bore enough of a resemblance to them all. But he alone went beyond resemblance, not only to the men she'd known as Anne Jackson McCarthy, but the ones she'd met as Annie Jackson.

It was fascinating to her. Almost without exception, the men she had known in the city had been typical to the environment with their Hart, Schaffner & Marx mentalities and upwardly mobile outlooks. Only some of the medical personnel she had met had been unique, but she had been firmly restricted from socializing with them. On the mountain where men fashioned their lives around survival, their energies were used on farming and families and sometimes pool down at the hall in Elder's Crossing. Only Jim and a few of the other new homesteaders stood out as ever having known another way of thought.

Jonathan, though, was a real dichotomy. He straddled the two worlds like a man balancing on a knife-edge. As much as he presently loathed to admit it, he was a child of the mountain, raised on the Wyoming version. But he'd also managed to come back after his initial disaster and conquer the city.

It was no wonder to her that he had to disappear to repair his gyroscope from time to time. No matter how badly the city had burned the part of him that had been forged in Wyoming, he still considered it worthwhile to some extent or he wouldn't continue grappling with it.

How Anne would have liked to see him take what he had been taught in his own mountains and make it work in the city. Judson had proved that it would work. Anne would have tried it if things had turned out differently. If only Jonathan could match the drive the city had given him with the scruples his father had taught him, he could make a difference. A real difference. And the Jonathan whom Anne was falling in love with wouldn't have to be lost.

With a weary sigh, Anne stepped out of the tub and dried off. How she wished she were back home before her fire letting the heat from the flames dry her hair, her only problems being those of the people of Elder's Crossing. Her friends. No stranger in her life, no lawyers, no way for a special delivery letter to ever reach her from Boston. She thought that maybe when she got home she'd ask Granny Edwards to teach her to quilt. It was such a peaceful pastime.

Her robe hung on the closet door. She reached for it and caught her reflection in the mirror. For the first time in what seemed like so very long, she actually found it interesting, something she could be pleased with. She could still feel Jonathan's touch kindling life in what had become merely a tool, and remembered how it was to view herself for more than just her work capacity.

She had to admit that where she once nudged at plump, with full curves that Tom sometimes frowned upon a little, she had grown lean with the work she'd done. Her hips were small, her waist smaller, her breasts still high and firm. The times she'd stolen away to enjoy the secluded peace of the sun had left her skin with a rich glow. Ah, the benefits of the outdoor life, she could hear Jonathan say with a smug smile.

Unaccountably, the thought made her feel a bit breathless. She donned her robe and belted it, bending to sweep her hair up into a towel. Straightening, she reached out and opened the door to the other room.

"Well, Anne, I see you're also still a slave to tradition."

Anne stopped short, a cry caught in her throat. Her first thought was to run.

Tom smiled lazily at her from where he lounged on the bed.

Chapter 11

"What are you doing here?" Anne hissed.

"Why, I came to see my lovely wife," Tom answered smoothly. "By the way, Anne, you are more lovely than ever. Did I tell you that?"

He stood slowly, languorously, his words and movements making Anne uncomfortably aware of her nakedness beneath the short flannel robe. "You finally lost that weight, didn't you, pet?"

She instinctively took a step back, her composure threatened. "How did you get in?"

Tom's smile broadened with self-satisfaction. "It was painfully easy. I simply told the very pretty young lady at the desk that I was your husband and that I had managed to get to town to surprise you. She was most accommodating." He moved closer, his eyes roving her body in frank admiration. "I suppose that I must admit that there must be something to that backwoods life of yours after all," he admitted smoothly, still approaching without hesitation. Anne knew that she was breathing more quickly, his presence crowding her. "You may have calluses on your hands, pet, but your body is finally the way I always wanted it. I'm glad you came back to me."

Two bright pink spots flared high on Anne's cheeks and she stopped retreating. "You think I came back here because I couldn't live without you?" she asked with a smile that didn't touch her eyes.

"You'll always love me, Anne," he purred, his eyes boring through her. "You'll always need me."

With shattering clarity, Anne suddenly saw through him, to the very core of what drove him. And she finally admitted that his lust for power governed him even with her. She'd always thought that he had at least wanted her, if not loved her. It was more likely the truth that he'd enjoyed her, like a game. Like any game he played in his life. It was only fun as long as he had the control, the power. How it must have infuriated him when she'd walked out.

"Why did you really come here tonight, Tom?" she asked, her voice suddenly chilly. He stopped, an eyebrow arching in mock surprise. The action suddenly reminded Anne of Jonathan, and it was all she could do to keep from shivering. Jonathan wasn't like this man; he wasn't amoral. And yet, if something weren't done soon, he might be. He and Tom could be carbon copies all the way to the sneer.

"You want me to be honest?" Tom retorted, his hypnotizing eyes darkening as if he were giving serious consideration to the question. He walked closer, standing so that Anne had to look up into his eyes. A sly psychological move of dominance, but it was effective. He was so close, the faint smell of his cologne overpowering. "I came to take you back, Anne. You belong with me. You always have. I want to take care of you. To give you a real home. I was wrong before to have let you leave. I didn't realize just how much you meant to me." He laid a hand on her shoulder, gently stroking in rhythm to his words. "Anne, together we could have it all."

Anne steeled herself against the electric shock of Tom's touch, the smothering sensation Jonathan's hands had reawakened after so long.

It didn't come.

Tom caressed her arm slowly, watching his hand as it moved, something that had once set Anne off like dry kindling. But nothing happened. She watched with disbelief, waiting for something to change, for the inevitable to happen. She wanted to cry, to sing and laugh. Her knees remained rigid and her heart cold. She was finally free of Tom McCarthy.

The exhilaration was heady enough to make her smile. Tom saw the change and returned the smile he mistook for excitement, a slow seductive gaze touching the green of his eyes.

Anne's eyes hardened. "If you don't back out of this room right now, I'll start screaming rape at the top of my lungs and not stop until the entire hotel staff and the New York press corps are up here." His grip tightened on her arm, the warmth in his eyes dying. Anne looked down at his hand and then up to those cruel, hypnotic eyes she'd loved as much as she'd hated. Their power had disappeared; the glint in them was no more than selfish. "And then I'll slap an assault and battery charge on you. I'll have bruises on my arm inside an hour. Do you really want to chance it?"

For the first time since she'd known him, Tom was at a complete loss. He seemed to freeze where he was, his expression concealing any emotion he might have been battling.

"Anne, you can't be serious." His voice was strained with the effort. "I can take you back to the places you deserve to be."

Anne eyed him steadily, her feet planted a bit more solidly beneath her. The act of paralyzing him had released her. She had won; she had finally beaten his game. No matter what happened now, she had her freedom from the Anne Jackson that Boston had molded and Tom and her father had controlled as their right. She was free of them all.

"I said leave, now, Tom. Don't make me ruin your reputation."

His mouth curled into a sneer at her words. "You can't make me believe that you don't want me." Grabbing her roughly to him, he kissed her, his mouth harsh and brutal, his hands punishing. Anne stood still and waited, wanting to laugh and hit him at the same time.

He raised his head, not letting go of her, his eyes smoky with rage.

"More bruises, Tom," she said evenly. "If I were you, I'd quit while I was only a little behind."

For a moment she thought he was going to strike her. She'd never seen him so angry that he couldn't speak. The fact that she didn't flinch from him seemed to taunt him even more. He held her for a long moment, his fingers viselike, his mouth a bitter slash of scorn.

"Don't congratulate yourself too soon, pet," he hissed. "You just made a bigger mistake than you'll ever know."

And then he was gone, slamming the door hard behind him.

For a minute Anne could only stand where she was, staring after the closed door as if she'd seen an apparition. She hugged her arms tightly around her and massaged her sore shoulders with gentle fingers. She'd been right. There would be bruises: ugly, appropriate reminders of Tom's visit. She took slow, deep breaths, in through her nose, out through her mouth to ease the trembling that had set in once the fear had died.

Then slowly, inexorably a smile dawned. Rising from the corners of her mouth, it swept along the laughter lines that dimpled her cheeks to the gray eyes that sparkled with a new light of triumph. Anne had a sudden urge to call Cassie and tell her that the ghosts had been dispelled, the crutches thrown away. Mixing metaphors, she thought absurdly, not really caring. She had just stood toe-to-toe with her personal devil and overcome him. Tom McCarthy would never again intrude into her life as an unwanted obsession. She had proven to herself that she didn't need that kind of man anymore. She didn't have to fear his power or allure ever again.

Anne smiled even more broadly at the thought that he'd offered to take care of her. Once that would have been a powerful temptation.

Once, maybe, before she'd been forced to go against everything she'd been taught since childhood and had learned to take care of herself.

It had always been a foregone conclusion that she should be taken care of all her life, like an objet d'art or a helpless animal. If she'd held onto that logic, she would have remained Tom's property. She would, indeed, have given in to him tonight and gone back to the prison that had once been her home.

Knowing no other hands than Tom's, she would have succumbed to them. But as if to seal the transformation that had taken place, Jonathan had reawakened her self-awareness as a woman when he'd taken her into his arms and made love to her. He had not only made her feel wanted, but treasured in a way Tom had never thought of.

There was a special exhilaration in rediscovering something you thought you'd lost for good. Within a period of weeks, Anne had stumbled back over not only her self-esteem but the wonder of how it felt to be reflected beautifully in a man's eyes. It was too bad it was so late. She suddenly wanted to call Jonathan, too. She wanted to thank him, to tell him that no matter what, she could never be able to return in kind the precious gift he'd given her.

Anne dressed for bed and dried her hair, listening with new contentment to the discordant city pass far below her. Until tonight she hadn't really realized it, but she was a free woman, able to go wherever she wanted or do what she pleased. She could count on not only her own worth and pride, but on the fact that she was worth the love of a good man. And waiting for her like a lifeline to her strength, a symbol of her resurrection, was her home, tucked comfortably away within the mountains and her memory. It seemed that as long as she had that symbol of her past and future, she could do anything.

As long as she had it.

A brief surge of fear flared and then waned as she remembered again the victory she had just savored. The impossible did happen. She would get her home back and from there be able to make the new beginning she very much wanted.

Settling into the big, comfortable bed, Anne wondered in passing whether Tom had really meant to threaten her when he left or whether he'd just badly lost his composure. Even so, it was a relief to know that she would be escaping the city tomorrow to the safety of her cabin. Judson might have just been correct when he told her that Tom might resort to desperate measures, and Anne knew better than most what kind of influence he could manage to wield in this city.

As she fell asleep the thought occurred to her that as much as she wanted to get back to the cabin, she anticipated seeing Jonathan again even more. It didn't occur to her to feel her customary caution.

The next afternoon Judson did, indeed, tell her that the meeting had been postponed and that she would be notified of its new date in due time. Amplex Corporation sent its regrets in hopes that it hadn't inconvenienced Miss Jackson too much. Miss Jackson scowled at the statement and told Judson that she would be back home doing some real work should they feel the need to get in touch with her. And then she made the arrangements to do just that.

Jim was in the store when she pulled in. He still had some difficulty getting used to her in city attire, and was shaking his head when she walked up to him.

"Oh, stop it," she said, laughing. "In five minutes I'll be back in my jeans and you won't be impressed anymore." She walked on through to the house, where she always changed before making the trip up on Andy.

"Why are you here, Annie?" Amanda demanded in her shrill four-year-old voice. "My mommy's at your house. With David." David was her six-year-old brother who never had much of a reputation for being able to sit still for more than two minutes at a time. Anne couldn't help but grin. Jonathan would probably be having the time of his life, considering how well he seemed to get along with small children. At least she could be sure he'd be glad to see her.

For at least the first third of the journey up the mountain Anne found herself puzzled by an odd tightness in her chest, a sense of unaccustomed urgency. Her ride home had always been her favorite time to meditate. Andy preferred a slower attack on the steep path, and Anne usually enjoyed the pace he set. It gave her the time to watch the wildlife and consider the way of the world. She would think about the people she'd come to know, the grannies who held the power of folklore in these mountains and maybe the serpentine family ties that seemed to bind the hollows she crossed. The road home was Anne's chance to unwind, to catch the first shattering of ice as the creek began to thaw or watch the spiraling flight of a hawk as it dipped and soared in among the shadows of afternoon.

After flying in from a place like New York she knew that she needed the time to unwind even more than usual. Instead she found herself nudging at Andy's flanks, urging him on at a steady pace. For the first time in memory, the cabin seemed to be too far away. When she actually caught herself toying with the idea of getting a real road up to the cabin, she began to wonder what was wrong with her.

It wasn't until she topped the ridge that it actually dawned on her. She'd never hurried to the cabin before because she'd never had someone like Jonathan waiting for her. She reigned Andy in just beyond a long stand of birch and sat staring sightlessly out over the soft gray-and-white folds of winter land that stretched away from her in never-ending succession.

Jonathan. Could he make that much of a difference? Could he be the reason that her chest felt constricted by an iron band and why she had to take deep breaths to ease the alien sense of fluttering in her? Safely encased in their gloves, her hands had begun to perspire. She had never experienced this kind of delicious dread before. But then she'd never been the person she was at this minute.

She had only been gone two days, and already she felt as if a different person were approaching the cabin. When she'd left, she'd done so as a cripple, emotionally hobbled by the manipulations of the man who'd stolen her trust. She'd made love to Jonathan out of desperation, certain that she could never profit from falling in love with him. It wasn't just that she hadn't trusted Jonathan—something she could hardly consider after the example set for her by Tom—it was that she truly didn't believe that she deserved to be loved. She'd really half believed what Tom had taught her.

She returned now having taken the cure. Tom had lost his decisive power to haunt, and Anne had found hers to take charge. The scene with him the night before had illustrated that without qualification. And that, she thought, was the first step to rediscovering the conviction that she had a right to be loved.

So she was back to the question of the moment. Was Jonathan that man? Or was he nothing more than a combination of attraction, infatuation and loneliness? Was love what bound them, or was it need, something that would vanish once the snow melted and they weren't isolated and dependent on each other anymore?

Anne allowed herself a moment to consider what the cabin would be like once Jonathan left and she found at least her own answer. Once he did go, the company of memories and familiar routine would no longer be enough to fill her life. He had changed that life and had changed her.

With a wry smile she realized that she was hungry for the sight of those eyes that had once so frustrated her. The multifaceted personality delighted her where it had once only confused her. Her discovery of that specially guarded place in him had set her tumbling from the safe niche her prejudices had so carefully carved. She'd been drawn to Jonathan as if the fuel that fed him could also revitalize her. If she weren't in love with him, she decided with an odd giggle, she should at the very least tap into him as a source of natural energy.

Anne took a deep breath, filling her lungs with brisk air to try and calm the growing clamor in her. It had been so much easier when everything was hopeless and finite. She had a chance for happiness now but the uncertainty of it unnerved her. What if she were in love with Jonathan? What guarantee was there that she'd be any luckier than before? What in the end did she know about Jonathan Bradshaw Harris? She knew that he had money, a tragic past to overcome and a knack for awkward tenderness that made her want to cry. She knew that he'd made love to her with a fire and sensitivity that had brought her back to life.

Yet he had just as surely lashed out at her more than once without real explanation. It was as if every time he got too close to her, some part of him revolted, rejecting her with a venom that was frightening. She could guess all she wanted about the reasons for it, and the conclusions she had reached all seemed to be sensible. But it was possible that she was wrong; there was a deeper, darker place in him that she hadn't found. Perhaps there lay the animosity that tended to flare unexpectedly. If that were true, if there was more to Jonathan's conflicting persona than even Judson knew, Anne was afraid that she would never find it in time to save her from repeating her mistakes.

Andy turned to eye her, impatiently stamping in the wet snow. His breath rose in swift clouds that dissipated quickly. Anne patted at him absently for a moment as she gathered the courage to go on. She hated uncertainty. For the last two years she'd patterned her entire life-style to avoid it. Yet here she sat in the throes of indecision, certain that she wanted nothing less than the conflict that awaited her when she got home, and yet knowing that she had no other choice but to go on anyway. She took another careful breath, wishing she could think of a more effective way to calm down and amazed that she needed one. Then she nudged Andy in the flanks and turned him for home.

When she reached the front porch, Anne found herself hesitating with her hand on the door. She made an unconscious point of stamping the snow from her boots with just a bit more noise than usual, as if in giving the people inside some warning of her arrival she could better set the stage. A small frigid breeze found her neck and provoked a chill Anne couldn't seem to stop.

Just as she'd anticipated, she found Jonathan seated comfortably in the wing-back next to the fireplace. In the instant before he looked up to greet her, Anne struggled to control her own reaction. The sight of his bent, tousled head sent her heart skidding unnaturally and set her hands to trembling. Instead of feeling more secure for the time spent away from him, she felt as if her balance were suddenly in great peril. Getting away from him hadn't accomplished in the least what she'd hoped. The independence she'd gained the night before was in imminent danger of crumbling before the anticipation of his sharp blue gaze. Any objectivity she'd prayed for in handling this scene seemed to have been left in that quiet office in New York. Her future would rest on Jonathan's response to seeing her.

The hard lines of his face shifted oddly as he raised his face. Momentarily they softened with an almost painful pleasure, then froze with restraint. After what seemed like hours, he allowed her a genial smile of welcome.

"Well, if it isn't Miss Fifth Avenue." He dropped his book in his lap, his eyes bright with measured amiability. Probably mirrors of what he saw in her own eyes, Anne thought. She could envision them both facing each other with strained civility, waiting for a clue from the other before proceeding. She'd been steeling herself against Jonathan's acceptance or rejection, the indications he would deliver about the fate of their future. Now here he sat waiting for the same from her.

"You're going through that library pretty fast." She smiled back a bit uncomfortably. "There's no other room to work your way up to, ya know."

An eyebrow arched minimally. "Isn't there?"

"Annie, what are you doing back so soon?"

Anne started at the sound of Cassie's voice, her eyes leaving Jonathan a brittle warning of discretion before turning to greet her friend. Cassie stood in the kitchen doorway with David like a shadow behind her. Cassie missed very little and couldn't have possibly missed the static atmosphere of the room, but she refrained from allowing herself comment.

"You keep coming home early," she protested with an easy grin. "How are Jonathan and I ever going to get any time alone?"

"Take him home with you," Anne retorted more easily as she began to discard her over clothes. "I'll keep David up here with me. I'd get more cooperation and less back talk."

Cassie laughed as she walked in, drying her hands on a towel. "Jonathan, you've been insulted. If I were you I'd demand satisfaction."

"Crutches at ten paces," he said dryly.

"I'm afraid it's going to have to be something else," Anne told him. "I only have one pair." It was already easier to talk. It was always that way when Cassie was there with them to buffer what they said to each other. If only she didn't have to leave.

"Well, if you're looking for something you have plenty of, throw muffins at each other," the tall brunette offered. "You have enough in there to fight off a batallion." She stood behind Jonathan with a hand on his shoulder. Anne envied her her natural ease.

"No," she obliged. "I'd end up eating the ammunition."

"What are you doing home so early?" Cassie asked. "You told us not to expect you for another few days."

"I'll explain over some hot tea," Anne answered, hanging up her coat. "It's kind of a good-news bad-news story."

Cassie turned, almost bumping into David and preceded Anne into the kitchen.

"Don't I get to find out?" Jonathan demanded.

Anne patted him on the head in mock patronization. "Maybe when you're a little older." Then, blithely ignoring his unhappy reaction, she walked into the unusually spotless kitchen and took a seat across from Cassie. Tea was already poured and steaming from the earthenware mugs.

"David," Cassie said, her arm around the little boy's waist, "why don't you go on in and talk to Jonathan?"

"Aw, Mom," he whined, scrunching up his face, obviously afraid that he'd miss something interesting.

"Don't 'aw, Mom' me, go on," she answered evenly with a small push to the backside. David went, the look in his face leaving no doubt as to his opinion on the matter. Anne sipped at her tea to hide her smile.

"Are you sure that Jonathan wants to talk to David?" she asked under her breath.

Cassie grinned. "I think you'd be surprised. Jonathan has been teaching David to play chess all morning. David thinks that he's the neatest thing since Spiderman."

Anne's eyebrows went up. "The same Jonathan who took one look at Mary's brood and almost made it down the mountain under his own power?"

"The same. He has almost as much patience as Jim. I think that if he learns to control that nasty streak of his, he'd make someone a good father... if he hasn't already, that is."

Anne shook her head. "That's part of my New York report. I found out all about him from Judson." She went on to give Cassie a detailed accounting of her trip.

Much later, they walked into the living room together to find David carefully replacing the chess pieces in their case.

"I almost won today," he beamed up at his mother. "Jonathan says I'm good."

"Deadly," Jonathan agreed with an impressed nod. Anne walked over to help David, staying carefully away from Jonathan as if she could more easily remain objective at a distance.

The tension in the room leaped the minute she walked in. She and Jonathan didn't even have to look at each other. The unspoken emotions that had been building between them begged for release, and neither could do it in front of company. Anne wasn't even sure that she had the nerve to confront that kind of conflict once Cassie and David had gone. Again she was assailed by the urge to ask them to stay, until she had the chance to straighten out the turmoil that had erupted in the last few days.

Anne looked up from her little task to see Cassie regarding her evenly. It was as if she'd been reading Anne's thoughts and had come to her own conclusion.

"Come on, David," she said, smiling quietly. "We have to get home in time to help Daddy deliver the mail."

"Thanks for keeping me company," Jonathan said to the little boy, his voice a little tight. "When I get better we'll have to go hiking together. I bet you know the best trails around here."

"Okay." David beamed, making a great show of shaking hands like a man. Anne once again caught that flash of gentleness in Jonathan's eyes as he participated in the ritual, a quick softening at the corners of his face. She physically restrained herself from reaching out to it, as if the warmth in his expression could be soaked up through her fingertips. The tension was mounting in her chest. She could hear it reflected in her own voice as she said her goodbyes to David and accepted his overenthusiastic bear hug.

Cassie delivered her own farewells outside where she could bestow Anne with a smile that at once called up the trust of friendship and offered an almost maternal concern. Her eyes twinkled with their familiar humor.

"Are you going to be safe if I leave?" Cassie asked. Anne had told her about the messages Judson had been receiving from Tom.

Anne's smile was her thanks for her friend's empathy. "I told you. Tom's far away."

Cassie's smile broadened, her teeth gleaming against her olive skin. "Maybe I should have asked Jonathan that question instead."

"That's entirely possible," Anne conceded, trying her best to match Cassie's studied ease. For the first time since she'd made the momentous decision to leave Tom, she knew the paralysis of indecision. She was actually terrified to walk back into the cabin to face Jonathan's judgment. Smiling anyway, Anne gave Cassie an extra hug for her unstated support. She watched in silence as Cassie and David turned their horses away from her and proceeded down the path. Then with a sigh she opened the door to face Jonathan's measured gaze.

"I think," she said with enough force to surprise herself, "that you and I need to talk."

Chapter 12

Jonathan allowed one eyebrow to rise in dry caricature. "Is this going to be one of those little domestic chats I've heard so much about?"

Anne's first impulse was to slap him. She came very close, stalking up without a word to where he sat and even opening her mouth to deliver a correspondingly biting retort. But suddenly, she saw the tension on Jonathan's face was as brittle as hers. He was as shaken as she was by the sudden shift in their relationship. And just as surprised.

She realized with some astonishment that she'd begun to soften. "Would you like some tea while we talk?"

His eyebrow lifted even higher for a brief moment before returning her rueful smile. "Unless there's something more potent. I have a feeling I'm going to need strength."

"Just a keen wit," Anne retorted evenly. "And yes, I have the perfect thing. My Aunt Adelaide used to sweeten her tea with it."

Jonathan pulled a very expressive face, but kept his silence as Anne walked by to the kitchen.

A few minutes later she returned to set the tea things on the coffee table. Curling her feet beneath her, she settled onto the couch next to Jonathan's chair. Her heart was still in her throat. She noticed that her hand shook as she poured the tea and handed Jonathan his blue earthenware mug. She also noticed that his hand was a little damp as he accepted.

"I have sugar if you'd like," she offered, "but usually Aunt Adelaide's tonic is enough."

Jonathan nodded absently and took a solid drink out of the steaming mug. He swallowed convulsively and then coughed. With tears in his eyes, he turned on Anne, his breath still coming in dramatic little gasps. "What the hell was that?" He had hold of ribs that seemed to protest all the activity.

"Tonic," Anne answered evenly, sipping her own tea very carefully. The well-remembered fire of the Jackson all-purpose elixir bit at her throat with a vengeance.

"Tonic, hell," he accused, still wiping at the tears in his eyes. "That's moonshine!"

She considered the accusation quietly, finding it hard to refrain from grinning. "Oh, I guess you could call it that, too."

The next drink Jonathan took was more modest. Even so, he still found it necessary to pause after swallowing, eyes closed, breathing suspended for a moment. "Did you make this, too?"

Anne did grin then, knowing that the two of them would at least start the renegotiation of their relationship on equal footing. "No. This particular jar was payment from a lady I helped with the pleurisy."

"She should have taken this. She never would have known she was sick."

Anne savored the wood smoke flavor of the liquid in her cup. "She did. And you're right, it worked wonderfully. You see, there are some benefits to the backwoods after all."

Jonathan took another taste of his quickly disappearing tea and nodded. "I'll certainly drink to that."

"I think you are."

They then spent the next few minutes in careful consideration of the jet fuel that spiced their mugs. The fire snapped before them, and the clock marked the passing of the silence with soft staccato.

Anne listened to the rhythm of accumulating time with growing unease. There could be no more putting off the talk they badly needed. She couldn't bear to spend another night in the house with Jonathan and not come to a resolution of some kind for the strained emotions that leaped between them. She studied the solid lines of her mug without ever seeing them as she feverishly turned over opening gambits in her mind and equally quickly discarded them. She was so afraid of what she'd find in Jonathan's eyes that she refused to look up at him at all. Suddenly she felt like a high school freshman searching in desperation for a mature introduction to a summer crush. By the time Jonathan did speak up, Anne had gotten so wrapped up in a futile attempt to ease into the answers she needed that she didn't even hear him.

"Anne."

She sat like a statue, the only betrayal of her tension a vein that stood out against her temple.

"Annie." Her head snapped up, but Jonathan's smile was solidly noncommittal. "How about a little more tea?"

It took her a few seconds to answer. "Tea or tonic?"

He grinned rakishly. "Sure. Have some yourself."

She did. Only this time she went into the kitchen and poured herself a small snifter of brandy. She spent the time there as she had on the couch, with no better luck. The longer she agonized over her next move, the more foolish and frustrated she felt.

Never in her life had she found herself at such a loss for words. It was as if in the last few weeks she'd been granted a whole new life with a new set of expectations, problems and guidelines. The difficulty was that she wasn't familiar enough with the new guidelines yet to be able to use them effectively in solving the problem. The problems weren't waiting patiently for solutions until she was ready. If only Jonathan could have waited to come into her life until she'd worn her freedom a little longer.

Returning to the living room, Anne reminded herself that if Jonathan hadn't been here already, there would never have been any freedom in the first place. Whatever else happened, she still had to thank him for that.

"Jonathan," she started to say as she walked in, "I wanted to thank you for sending me to Judson...."

The words trailed limply away when she caught sight of Jonathan. He was on the floor, propped on pillows he'd pulled from the couch. Legs stretched easily before him, he patted to the matching nest of pillows he'd built beside him between couch and fireplace.

"What are you doing?" she asked without thinking.

"Making us both comfortable," he said easily, the crinkle of his eyes warm. "Come on down and join me."

Anne cast a suspicious eye even as she moved to set the tray down on the already rearranged coffee table. "You certainly have been busy."

"Profitable use of time and resources is one of my company's hallmarks," he assured her.

Before she did join him, Anne stoked the fire and turned off the lights. Immediately the shadows crept close and danced rhythmically with the firelight over the walls. The night grew comfortable and intimate, its wind only a suggestion.

Anne pulled off shoes and socks and stretched her feet out toward the fire before she took brandy in hand and leaned back next to Jonathan's companionable warmth.

"You must be an idea man," she said. "This was a great one."

He slipped an arm around her and brought her head to his shoulder. "Well, I had a feeling we weren't going to get anything accomplished on the furniture. You looked like you were waiting to go in for oral exams up there."

"That bad?"

"Worse. I was beginning to feel completely at a loss."

"You?" She instinctively snuggled closer, the strength of his arm about her an exhilarating elixir that put the glow of the brandy to shame. She felt them both ease up, as if this were the prefect position for confessing truths: in intimate contact, but safe from the uncomfortable possibility of allowing revelations to be caught in unsuspecting eyes. Anne smiled at Jonathan's uncustomary admission. "I can't imagine you ever being at a complete loss."

His answering laugh was sharp. "Well, it's happened to me more since I've been here than ever before."

Anne took a sip of brandy and thought of how Jonathan's eyes held their own source of heat. His hand was rubbing at her shoulder, an absent gesture of easy familiarity that kindled its own energy. "Has it been so bad?"

For a moment there was only the answer of a patient fire. Then Jonathan nuzzled her hair, his own head now resting against hers. "Terrible."

Without really knowing why, Anne found herself testing their closeness.

"You don't really do that well, do you?"

He looked over. "What?"

"Being at a loss. Not being in control."

She felt him stiffen a little as he turned back to consider the fire again. "No."

Anne nodded to herself, trying her best to remain noncommittal. "You haven't told me yet about the other time you said you were helpless to keep someone you cared for from being hurt. It was before Nam, wasn't it?"

Jonathan's answer was a rigid, profound silence.

"It takes a lot to make a person so...obsessed," she said gently, careful to not push. "That's the only word I can use for how you've pushed yourself to get back on your feet." She shrugged offhandedly and offered a slight smile. "Anybody else would still be demanding breakfast in bed."

Still he didn't answer, didn't move.

She kept on, feeling even more unsettled. "What happened to you in Vietnam was terrible, but I have the feeling that it was the coup de grace. The final straw."

"Why is it so important to you?" he finally asked.

"Because it's important to you. And because it might help me to understand you better," she offered tentatively. "Your mystery-man image has its drawbacks."

When she felt him relax a little, she knew this particular moment of challenge had passed.

"You didn't ask Judson?"

"Of course I did. He told me what a beautiful woman your mother is and how he used to call on her back in Wyoming."

"That's all?"

"That took two hours. I figured that it would take another four weeks to span the next forty years." She supposed it would have been easier to admit her knowledge, but it was important to her that Jonathan volunteer the information about his past on his own. He had to want to share it with her or it would end up being nothing more than emotional blackmail to hold over him.

"It was a long time ago," he said quietly without moving, his voice pensive.

"It's not that long ago when it still bothers you so much," she insisted, then carefully backed off. "Judson worries about you."

Jonathan moved then. Anne knew he was looking down at her. "He worries, does he?"

She nodded, her eyes passive.

"Do you?"

Anne took a slow breath and turned to him, her eyes honest. "I don't want you to end up like my ex-husband. And I'm afraid something's driving you down the same road."

Jonathan considered her a moment in silence. Then, his features settling into a soft smile, he moved back next to her again, his embrace closer.

"In that case, someday soon I'll tell you all about it."

"Why not now?"

He shook his head a little. "Because this is not the time or place. Soon."

She nodded. His reply was both more and less than she'd hoped for. It was a promise of a future in carefully impressive words, but not the revelation she'd hoped for.

"Jonathan?"

"Mmm?" He was sipping at his tea, his good leg drawn up as a prop for his elbow. His fingers were lacing through her hair, their touch alive.

"You're going back to New York, aren't you?"

He stroked her hair for a little while longer. She closed her eyes against the naked hunger such a simple gesture aroused in her.

"Yes, Anne," he finally said. "I'm going back."

Her voice became progressively softer. "Where does that leave us?"

He bent to kiss her forehead, the touch of him yearning and uncertain all of a sudden. "I don't know. I don't suppose we could hope for another blizzard."

She grinned tremulously. "I could push you back off the cliff."

He kissed her again, his lips lingering on her cheek. "I don't think that would be a good idea. I couldn't stand being in a snowbound cabin with you any longer if I couldn't touch you."

"Is this going to end up being a cheap, tawdry affair?" she demanded, trying very much to sound flippant. She only succeeded in sounding frightened.

At that, Jonathan set down his mug and turned to take Anne's face in his hands. His eyes, half in shadow and half filled with firelight, sought her with an almost physical intensity. Anne finally found in them what she'd so long hoped for.

"I don't think I even want to joke about that, Anne," he said softly. Anne saw the clean, hard lines of his face and thought how they lent sincerity to his words. Her heart thudded and tears stung at her eyes. His hands held her face like a wild bird that might shy away. "Would you agree to take it one day at a time?" he asked. "I want to promise you anything you want right now, but I'm not sure I can."

She felt even more unsteady than before. "Your seven children need you?"

He made a face at her. "I know Judson better than to think he would have forgotten to clear up that small detail within five minutes of meeting someone as lovely as you. There is no wife, no children; no one in my life." A grin tugged at the corners of his mouth, softened by his admission. "At least there wasn't anyone until I woke up to find you hovering over me like something out of a Raphael painting. I fell in love with you long before I wanted to."

Anne found herself smiling back, the light brighter in her eyes, a certain determination in her voice. "Isn't that always the way? If you hadn't been so darn stubborn, we could have been enjoying ourselves all along."

His eyebrows shot up again. "Me? I've seen murderers treated with more courtesy by the jury that hung them!"

Anne had no choice but to admit the truth of his charge as she snuggled back into the comfort of his arm. He immediately encircled her with the other. "I guess I was a little prickly. I had a small problem to work out."

"So I heard. A husband who talked like me. What ever became of him?"

Anne grinned again with triumph. "Oh, I gave him his walking papers. Once and for all."

Jonathan moved against her. "You don't say. Well, I'll have to check that out for myself."

Anne looked up to see what he intended and was met by a kiss. At first slow and exploratory, Jonathan's mouth gentle on hers, it began to build of its own accord. Before Anne knew it, she was completely within Jonathan's embrace, his lips crushing hers, his tongue searching hers feverishly. His beard chafed her cheek. His breath tickled her ear. By the time he drew back over a minute later, they were both out of breath.

Jonathan's eyes gleamed with satisfaction. "You know," he said softly as he brushed Anne's hair over her shoulder, "it would certainly be a shame to waste such a good fire."

Anne couldn't refrain from a wicked grin. "What do you have in mind," she said just as suggestively, "a wienie roast?"

Jonathan didn't even blink. "Only if we get too close."

She chuckled, a low throaty sound that Jonathan enjoyed. "But you have a broken leg. Wouldn't that be awfully cumbersome?"

His hand was beginning to drift from her shoulder. Anne could have sworn he'd dipped his fingers in fire. They seared easily through her blouse as he moved to her top button.

"You didn't seem to find my leg cumbersome the other night." Bending down, he kissed the flesh he had exposed by freeing her buttons. Anne was having even more trouble breathing. His fingers had almost reached her waist. Jonathan seemed to find particular pleasure in the soft mounds of Anne's breasts where they swelled above the restraint of her bra.

"The other night I was...in a...rash..." she admitted weakly, her head far back into the pillows where Jonathan's other arm cradled her.

"A rash."

She could tell that he was grinning as he deftly slipped her shirt off and teased her nipples through the filmy material that held them. The suggestion of his touch was almost more than she could bear.

"You think you'd have to be in a rash to make love again?" Rather than remove her bra, he began to undo her belt, his lips leaving blazing trails across her throat. He was taking so long it was torture, teasing her with his touch, the promise of taking her, and then holding back.

"Oh...I think the...idea...shows promise..." she managed. She opened her eyes to see his face etched in firelight, his soft lips and laughing eyes, the small cleft in his chin. Then she reached up to draw him to her.

He waited a moment, his face very close to hers, his breathing rapid. "You let me know when you think you're in a sufficient...rash." His kiss was quick, a temptation. "Okay?"

She caught his head with her hands and pulled him to her for another kiss. A long kiss that left him with no illusions as to her intentions. "Okay."

The firelight bathed them, casting their skin in living bronze as they settled into each other's arms and the luxury of discovering each other. Jonathan slipped Anne out of her jeans, his hands painting her legs with fierce chills. Then Anne helped him out of his clothes, both of them laughing at the difficulty they had getting around his homemade splint and Anne kissing his ribs when he complained that laughing made them hurt. She allowed herself to run her hands over the thick hair on his chest and then trace the scars that stood out oddly in the soft light. This time she tasted his belly, the hard, flat plane so well developed that she could trace every muscle with her tongue.

For a long while, Jonathan refused to remove her bra and panties, as if he loved the temptations of secrets not seen. The scintillation of his fingers against the silk shocked Anne to a sharp aching. Taking her own time in exploring the exhilaration of his sinewy body, she surprised moans from him and set him to gasping when she teased him with her teeth.

She took his buttocks in her hands, so firm and tight, and pulled him against her so that she could enjoy his excitement. Then she pushed him back on the pillows and took great pains to teach him how to kiss, telling him so and laughing with him. Aroused by the soft strength of his mouth, she let her tongue slip in to taste the pleasant roughness of his, the smooth curve of his teeth, the sweet warmth of his lips. It all seemed a revelation. It was as if she'd never tasted a man before, and each new place she found set her to smiling with the delight of discovery.

"Well," he finally asked, his hands teasing her so that she almost cried out, "are you in a rash, do you think?"

She paused as if in consideration. She was on fire and freezing at once, her muscles quivering with the effort of control. "I think so."

He dropped a kiss on her nose and grinned, the spark in his eyes one of tender exhilaration. "About time."

Letting his hands slide carefully down from her throat, he undid the clasp between Anne's breasts. Her bra fell away, though the straps were still on her shoulders. Jonathan didn't bother with them. He bent to her breasts, taking first one in hand and then the other. Anne had never known such gentle attention. Tears reached her eyes as she cradled his head to her, his hair so wildly black against the milky whiteness of her skin. The core of her own arousal coiled like a tensed animal within her, her love for Jonathan an exquisite pain. Yes, she guessed she'd have to take it one day at a time. She could never have asked more in life than the delicious intensity of this moment.

As he eased toward capturing her breasts, first with his tongue, then lips and finally the sharp thrill of his teeth, Jonathan slid her panties down and away. Anne allowed his hands to part her thighs, searching upwards to find her long since accommodating.

"Doesn't...all this...hurt your...ribs?" she found herself demanding, ever the nurse.

Jonathan raised his eyes to hers, his fingers trailing new, even more unbearable fire. "Not really. I guess I must be in a rash, too." He punctuated his grin with another lingering kiss.

Unable to wait even longer, Anne took him in her hand, surprised again by the power of his arousal, and led him to her. From that moment, whatever control they had managed between them vanished. They clung to each other as if terrified of their parting and reached their peak together, shuddering and murmuring, their lips bruised from the hunger of their meeting. Again Anne cried out, wondering that she could be so overwhelmed. She felt her body become electrified, even to her toes, her scalp tingling as if she'd been hit by lightning.

Lightning had never happened quite like this to Anne before. Suddenly she wondered what she'd ever found so provocative about Tom. It occurred to her that he'd treated her exactly as she'd expected to be treated. Tom had been exciting, but had never really known how to give excitement. He had taken a woman rather than cherished her.

For a long while Anne lay silent in Jonathan's arms, her head nestled in the hollow of his shoulder, her old blue-and-white afghan helping to ward the creeping chill from both of them. She would have given anything to never have to move from this spot and not have to face the uncertainty of the future. She knew that Jonathan loved her just as she loved him, but she knew too that wouldn't answer all of their questions. He still didn't seem able to trust her with the responsibility of his troubled past and had refused to address their future. He wanted to return to the city, and she wanted to stay in the mountains. And she wasn't at all sure that either would find cause to change their minds. The impasse seemed too great to overcome, and it frightened her.

"You never did tell me what happened in New York," Jonathan said lazily.

Anne had been absently running her fingers through the hair that trailed from Jonathan's chest down to his navel, a dark line that begged exploration. She moved her head to take in his eyes, sleepy and content in the dying light, and decided that she loved them more than any other of his features. She could watch them forever.

"I told you," she answered. "I exorcised myself of the ghost of one ex-husband."

He shot her a wry look. "You didn't tell me," he corrected. "You showed me. And, may I add, with great conviction."

"And enthusiasm," she added.

"Overwhelming enthusiasm." His kiss of appreciation took a minute longer. "What else happened?"

She shot him a mischievous grin. "You mean you didn't ask Judson?"

Jonathan was all innocence. "Me?"

She nodded. "I figured you'd be on the phone ten minutes after I got out of his office."

"Well," Jonathan demurred with a wry smile, "I tried. The phone's out again."

Anne nodded with a self-satisfied smirk. "Serves you right for not telling me sooner about what Judson told you about the will."

"I did that for a reason," he protested.

She bestowed her own kiss of appreciation. "I know. It would have been torture on me to have been stuck here with only half the information. Thank you."

Jonathan's eyes sparkled darkly in the firelight. "So, what else happened? Besides the exorcism?"

Anne shrugged happily. "Nothing nearly as important as that."

Jonathan made a face at her. "You were saying something about Judson before."

"Oh," she said lightly, "that. I was thanking you for sending me to him. I don't know what I would have done otherwise."

Jonathan nodded, his eyes contemplating the glowing embers. "I'm glad he helped. I wasn't even sure he'd take a recommendation from me. I haven't seen him in a long time."

Anne held her breath, hoping for more. When it didn't come, she stifled a sigh and turned to the fire herself. "Stick around. He's coming for a visit in the spring when the new clinic opens. In fact, I may name it after him. He's donating his fees to it."

Jonathan's voice still had a faraway sound when he answered. "That's Judson all right."

"He seems to think very highly of you."

"Rank prejudice. He's my godfather."

Anne turned to him in surprise. "You never told me that."

Jonathan shrugged. "You never asked."

"I suppose you're going to tell me that you went to law school because of him."

It wasn't until she'd said it that she remembered that Jonathan had gone to law school after Nam. After he'd changed.

He looked down at her, his eyes suddenly unreadable, with a hint of the old animosity flashing through. "No" was all he said, leaving her even more troubled. "No, you can't blame that on Judson."

"Well," she said hurriedly, trying to cover her confusion. "He thinks I can get the cabin back. But then, you know that. You've been helping him, from what I hear."

He shrugged easily. "Judson doesn't have as keen an acquaintance with the devious mind as I do."

Anne couldn't help but grin. "Can't argue with you there."

"Tell me what happened," he said, scowling.

So she told him, leaving out only the now shoddy-sounding threat situation. It might have been that Judson didn't tell him about Tom's boorish behavior, or maybe Jonathan didn't make much of it, because he never questioned her about it.

At the end he nodded quietly, his eyes once again beyond her, and lapsed into silence. Anne couldn't help but wonder where he'd drifted, somewhere far beyond the walls of her small home.

Was he thinking about Judson, she wondered, or the time he'd stood impotently by as his own home was lost? Whatever it was he was remembering, it brought a hard, flat sheen to his eyes. They seemed almost emotionless, as if the memory had long ago lost its power to move him to passion, and left only pictures and sounds behind. She didn't like it, or the fact that he wouldn't share it with her. Well, she thought with new purpose, I can only keep on trying.

"Tell me about Wyoming."

He started. "What?"

"Wyoming," she persisted. "I want you to describe it for me."

"Didn't I?"

She took up a thoughtful pose. "Let's see. You mentioned the Tetons, I believe. The sky and mountain climbing. Is there any more?"

His gaze was at once amused and tender. "Maybe. But if I tell you about Wyoming, does that mean you'll tell me about where you grew up?"

She took in the room with her hand. "I grew up here."

"What was Boston, a field trip?"

She looked into his eyes a moment, realizing that the tables had been turned and not sure that she was any readier than he was for confessions. "Are your memories of Wyoming painful?"

He shook his head.

"My memories of Boston are. I don't feel like digging that all up tonight, if you don't mind."

Jonathan reached down to gently stroke the pain from her eyes. "It's a deal. Tonight's for the good memories. What are yours?"

She didn't hesitate. "My mother. And the mountain."

"Your mother, then. I've seen a bit of the mountain, but you've never talked about your mother."

Anne smiled a bit wistfully. Her mother had lived in the privacy of her memory for a long time now. "No, I guess I haven't."

They ended up talking through two more hours and another pot of tea. Jonathan spoke with reservation at first and then, warming to his topic, opened up with an expansiveness that surprised Anne. He described at length his boyhood home where mule-ear deer would mingle with the horse herds to get at the winter hay; where trout flashed in a thawing spring-fed river that rushed along behind the stone ranch house his great-grandfather had built near the south end of Jackson Hole. He described it in the different seasons with the words and recollections of a small boy's awe, his eyes alight with the pictures.

His father had taken him on pack trains high in the mountains twice a year to fish and camp. This was where his great lessons in life were learned. His father had taught him self-sufficiency, Wyoming style, and how to live off the land. Jonathan even admitted the veracity of Judson's theory that he returned often to challenge the mountain much as he had in his childhood.

Anne lay still, listening intently and encouraging him with cautious questions and observations. She never was able to push him beyond recollections of his boyhood. He never even admitted to an education beyond eighth grade. She didn't mind, though. The places he'd described to her were the ones she had wanted to find, to share with him so that he could rediscover their worth. It was at least a beginning in bringing their seemingly incompatible life-styles closer. By the time he turned to hear her part of the bargain, he looked as if ten years' weight had been lifted from his shoulders.

When Jonathan did exact the price for his admissions, Anne balked. It had been too long a time since she'd talked to anyone but Cassie about herself. It was a chance she suddenly wasn't sure she wanted to take.

Jonathan, with unusual tact and gentleness, drew the story from her. Before she knew it, she was describing her mother, the shy, blond beauty who had preferred her adopted home in the mountains to the strain of the Boston social life into which she'd been born.

Anne wasn't sure if she'd ever really forgiven her mother for dying three days after Anne's ninth birthday. Elizabeth Harrison Jackson had died in the cabin with the Millers and her children in attendance to ease her pain. Silas, so tall in Anne's young memory, had shepherded Anne and Brad in and out as he'd thought necessary, never once leaving the children in the final day of their mother's life. Anne's father had arrived too late.

One of the things Anne held in memory of her mother was the baking days in the cabin. The smell of fresh-baked bread, her gentle singsong laugh and hands as delicate as porcelain.

It took Anne a moment to realize that she'd been silent for quite a few minutes. The picture of her mother dressed for a big benefit, glittering with family diamonds and cleaning Anne's bicycle-scraped knees lingered in her mind. Suddenly she had the urge to walk up to the small graveyard above the house. She hadn't been there in so long.

"I'm sorry," she said, smiling quickly. "I got a bit lost for a moment."

"That's all right," Jonathan assured her, his voice so close that his breath swept her cheek. "I was enjoying the sight of your eyes."

"My eyes?"

He nodded. "I'd always thought that gray was such a cool color. It isn't really."

She smiled up into the endless depths of blue. "Rank prejudice."

He never answered, but bent to gather her back to him, his eyes brimming with his delight in her, his lips more gentle than his touch.

Late in the night as a brittle moon shed its light through the window and time became lost in its own rhythms, Anne and Jonathan made love quietly, their passion saved for another time. As the fire once again ebbed at their feet, they explored and thrilled in each other, offering each other the salve of friendship and tenderness. Celebrating their new intimacy, they brought their bodies together comfortably, softly, their sounds of satisfaction more like the music of night breezes.

Anne slept that night where she was, covered only by Jonathan's arm and her afghan, the cadence of his breathing beside her as soothing as the murmur of the sea. It had been too long since she'd slept peacefully in a man's arms. It seemed as if she'd never slept so contentedly before, happy to enjoy the moment as it greeted her without recriminations from the past or dread of the future. She refused to consider the fact that since she'd stepped back into the cabin her emotions had vascillated more often than a wind sock in a thunderstorm. For these few hours in the cocoon of a warm house, she felt whole and happy and wanted no more than that.

She decided to momentarily ignore the uncertainties of her future: the threat to her home and life-style, the theatrical doom predicted by a vengeful ex-husband. For the hours she lay protected in Jonathan's arms, she could avoid the doubts she still had about him and concentrate only on the delicious comfort of his embrace. Tonight, she was happier than she could remember. Anne decided to let tomorrow take care of itself.

Chapter 13

Four days later when Silas returned to help with the chores he spent a good deal of the time sniffing and snorting to himself, something that amused Anne to no end. That was Silas's way of expressing paternal concern and disapproval. He was trying to let her know that he'd been a lot happier when Jonathan had been unwanted and confined to the guest room. According to Silas's solidly suspicious mountain upbringing, now that Jonathan was able to spend his day with Anne, there was too much chance for immoral hanky-panky, if not imprudent relationships. Especially now that Anne no longer seemed to object to Jonathan's presence.

It seemed to particularly gall Silas that Jonathan could spend the majority of the lunch hour in the kitchen making Anne laugh. She could actually see the old man's contemplative eye on the crutches that were propped behind Jonathan's chair. Given half a chance, there was no doubt that the old man would walk off with them in an attempt to confine Jonathan to the sickroom where he belonged.

Anne did not think it prudent at the moment to point out to Silas that that was the last room he'd want to confine Jonathan to in an attempt to keep Anne's virtue safe. She also decided with a grin toward his disapproving frown that now was not exactly the time to tell him that her virtue hadn't been safe for a few days.

So distracted was he by the way Jonathan seemed to fit so nicely into Anne's life that it wasn't until he was almost ready to leave for the day that Silas remembered the package he'd brought for her. Bundling into his heavy jacket, he walked out to rummage in his saddlebag. Anne followed to the front porch where it seemed that the cold wasn't as biting as it had been. She watched Silas with arms wrapped around her chest.

"This come for you yesterday, Annie," he was saying as he tugged a fat manila envelope from the cracked leather pouch. "We didn't know as it'd make any difference if it waited a day before I got it up to ya. You haven't really cared much for the last letters ya got."

Anne grinned, hearing Jonathan hobble out behind her. "You're right, Silas. I haven't been too crazy about any of that mess."

Jonathan filled his lungs with air and peered up into the breathtaking blue of the sky that made his eyes look like mirroring lakes. "So, this is what it feels like to be on the outside. I'm going to have to ask the warden to let me out more."

Anne flashed him a withering look. Silas turned to see him standing by her and took a long, meaningful look at the sky himself. "Gonna thaw soon," he said, nodding a bit as if to seal his verdict. "That snow'll be off this mountain in no more than a few days."

"All of it?" Anne asked, taking in the monstrous drifts that obliterated the angles of the barn.

Instead of gauging the snow as Anne had, Silas turned his speculative eye on Jonathan. "Enough." Then he nodded again, just once, and stepped back up onto the porch to hand Anne the envelope.

It was all Anne could do to keep a straight face. She had never seen Silas this upset, at least not since Ef Tate tried to make unpopular advances toward his daughter Rose. Once again Anne recognized the kinship between Silas's family and herself. His clan had been more of a family than her own since her mother and father had died. Now, they were the only family she had.

"Will you be going by Jim's on your way home?"

He nodded in his slow way.

"I may have a reply to this. Come in for a little more tea and let me go through this really quickly. Please?"

Silas could never refuse her anything. Still grumbling, he followed her back into the cabin and once more shed his jacket. The protest did ease considerably when he saw what Anne had set out to sweeten his tea. His wife Sarah, a Bible Baptist, took no hold with drinking. Silas, who attended church with her on Christmas and Easter and the odd revival, had much more liberal views on the subject.

Anne took up the best defensive position right between Jonathan and Silas at the table and tore into the package Judson had sent her. The kitchen fell into silence without her participation in conversation. After the first few minutes the only sounds to be heard were the rustle of paper, the clock in the living room and a tentative clink of china.

From the first line she read, Anne completely lost contact with the other people in the room. Judson wasted no time in telling her that he was delivering an emotional bombshell, and he didn't go far to apologize. Anne must decide, he told her in carefully reserved language, whether she wanted him to proceed further or not, since her legal option had become an all-or-nothing proposition. He had tracked down all of the information to her case and more besides. He had also obtained the proof that she had not, in fact, signed the power of attorney paper. Because of that and the provision of her father's will, everything Tom and Brad had orchestrated from the time of her father's death had been not only unethical, but illegal. Copies of all documents were enclosed for her elucidation.

The bottom line, Judson wrote succinctly, was that if Anne wanted her house back, she'd have to accept the whole empire. Before she made that kind of decision, he suggested she read the enclosed copy of her father's will. It would, he hoped, help her better assess her position.

Anne picked up the accompanying forms, separating the will out to be read last. Judson had arranged everything chronologically from the power of attorney to the futures deal Brad had made. The documents were all in tortuous legalese, but it didn't take Anne long to recognize the pattern Judson had outlined. By the time Brad had made the mistake that brought the situation to a crisis, he and Tom had acquired complete control of the entire Jackson empire, leaving Anne no more than the family jewelry they knew she would never sell and her mother's small trust that they couldn't break anyway. As she'd told Judson, they'd contrived to create a situation she'd assumed had already existed. Frustrating yes, but no bombshell. They'd already come to these conclusions.

She looked down at the will and didn't notice how profound the silence had become in the bright kitchen, or that Jonathan and Silas watched her with identical expressions. Afraid of what the will would tell her, she picked it up as if it were alive.

It took no more than four paragraphs for Anne to be dealt the blow.

The will had been made before the last time her father had returned to the mountain, at the height of the power struggle. Anne could suddenly see again the gray of his face in those days, the stubborn refusal to disbelieve his son. She remembered his increasing dependence on her, and that he'd almost reached a point of expressing a love for her she'd sought as long as she'd remembered. He'd died still searching for the way to bridge a lifelong gap. And she had been left behind still wondering, as it always was with children of a hard man.

She wondered no more. What he had never been able to say, he'd expressed eloquently in his gift to her.

. . . to my daughter Anne, the only member left of the Jackson or Harrison families worth the honor of those names and histories, I leave all that is her inheritance, both in fortune and in heritage. I leave her the responsibility of directing both of these in the honorable, farseeing fashion she so often suggested to me. And in bequeathing my entire estate to her with the exception of the house and furnishings in Boston, which I know she wouldn't want, I have every belief that she will carry out her responsibilities in a way that will justify the pride her family has always had in her.

For long minutes Anne stared at the words, unable to focus on them, unable to move beyond them. Why hadn't he told her? Why couldn't he have, just once before he died, verbally expressed the love that echoed from these stringent pages? She could see now that it had always been there, though expressed only in a manner he could manage. Money and schools and opportunity. It was a tragic thing when the most important words a man can give his child could only be offered in his will.

Without a word to Jonathan or Silas, Anne stood and walked toward the door. She didn't see Jonathan move to follow, or Silas hold him back with a hand on his arm.

"Leave her be," he said, his eyes on her retreating figure. "She has business to attend that you got no part of."

The evening air was softer than it had been in a long time, the sunset less crisp at the edges. Beneath Anne's feet the snow folded into shadows cast in a painter's blue. Anne stumbled along, blind to the beauty around her, her eyes clouded with the tears of futility. The graveyard was only a short pathway up beyond the house, nestled in among pines and the oaks her ancestors had planted. Her parents were buried here together, their headstones as simple as the rest with only names and dates on the slim rounded stones.

Just the sight of their names brought back the pain, all of the different unresolved aches of their leaving. Her mother, so frail, fighting so hard to stay with her children, the apology in her eyes still fresh in Anne's memory. And her father.

It was because of her father that she'd avoided the graveyard so assiduously. It was a hard thing to face someone who caused anger and guilt at the same time. It was harder still when death had removed the chance to explain or be understood. Anne stood at the foot of her father's grave as if she could absorb there the feelings he'd never been able to share face to face. She wanted to understand the man who had written the words of that will.

She stood as the sun disappeared over the next ridge and pulled most of the light with it, until the first of the stars came to life in a peacock sky. She couldn't say for sure that she felt any great relief in the time she spent alone with the memories of her father. A lifetime of ambivalence didn't disappear like shadows with the flick of a light switch. But she did know that she felt different. Now, when she asked the questions she'd asked herself for so long, she found answers. Someday, she thought, they would be enough. She knew at least that the love she had so frantically tried to lavish on her father had been in its own way returned. She hadn't been the fool she'd feared.

When Anne returned to the kitchen, she found Jonathan and Silas where she'd left them. She could tell by the empathy in Jonathan's eyes and the pride in Silas's that they'd read the will. It didn't upset her in the least. She smiled at them with watery eyes and sat down to finish her tea.

"Silas, would you ask Jim to send a telegram for me?"

He nodded, more animation in his eyes than she could ever remember. "Ya goin' for it?"

Her smile widened, and she cocked her head at him in mock disbelief. "Well, what do you think?"

When he answered, his eyes were dead serious. "I think he had a right to be proud of you."

Anne couldn't think of anything to say, but as Silas left, she stood on tiptoe and delivered a hug that had him crimson.

That night Anne slept quietly in Jonathan's arms, savoring his silent understanding and companionship. In the morning she invited him outside to help her with the chores. He followed gladly, precariously balancing himself in the snow, his head on a constant swivel to take in the scenery he'd only viewed from the porch below.

"It's not the Tetons," he said as he worked his way through the door Anne held for him, "but it has its points."

"Why, thanks," Anne retorted dryly. "You've made it all worthwhile."

Due to obvious restrictions, Jonathan took over the less strenuous chores of feeding, milking and grooming. That and, when the mood struck him, kibitzing His company taught people efficiency, he said, and it was the least he could do to teach Anne some. He also said that Anne's rather ascerbic retort was not unusual for someone who refused to see that they needed professional help. Anne's reply to that was a simple but effectively threatening display of the fertilizer she was in the process of mucking out. Jonathan took the hint and kept his peace.

"When do you think I'll be going down the mountain?" he asked a little later as he sat milking the cow. Bessie swung her head lazily around at the question, munching her hay as if in calm consideration of answering herself.

Anne looked toward the animal's back from where she was cleaning some tack to see what had prompted Jonathan's question. His eyes betrayed nothing as he rocked easily back and forth with his task.

"Silas almost dragged you down yesterday," Anne told him, going back to work.

Jonathan chuckled. "Does he not like me for the same reason you didn't like me?"

"More or less."

"Him and how many others?"

She shrugged noncommitally. "Let's say that the older people in the valley feel compelled to look after me."

"Would they mind if I didn't go back down at the first chance?"

Anne smiled more to herself than to him. That kind of scandal would be consumed with relish and condemned with fervor. She could almost hear the whispers already: " . . . that fancy gigolo taking advantage of our Annie . . ." She would have to stock up for all the curious and concerned visitors.

"They would," she finally admitted, "frown on it."

"So I figured. Well then, how much longer do you think I can successfully hide out in Shangri-la?"

Anne looked up at him and saw the genuine regret that was taking shape in his eyes. For a long moment she stood very still, sharing it with him as she saw the consequence of his trip back to civilization. Unable to face new pain, she said quickly, "Oh, a week at best. That's if Silas's thaw doesn't come. But I've never known Silas to be far wrong."

They would now measure their time left in hours, hoarding it like water on a desert. The uncertainty of the future colored the present with bittersweet light. Anne rubbed slowly at the soft, fragrant leather, using the activity as an antidote for the fear.

"Tell me something." Jonathan spoke up after a long silence. Anne turned to him. His eyes, gemlike in the morning light, were laughing, the crow's feet at their corners wrinkling suggestively. "Have you ever made love in the hay?"

Anne stopped what she was doing. "What?"

"You heard me." With a brisk twist of his hand, he indicated the loft, spilling with winter hay. The warm, fragrant hay was suffused with animal scents and age-old illusions.

"Jonathan," she objected instinctively, "I've just finished chores. Cleaning chores."

He would not be deterred. "Your cheeks are glowing and you have bits of straw in your hair."

"And I smell like horse..."

"Anne," he objected gently, a hand out in invitation. "Don't you want to find out what all the notoriety is about?"

Now her eyebrow arched, the enticement of his offer already waking tremors of excitement. "Do you mean that *you've* never made love in a hayloft?"

"No. I mean that I've never made love to you in a hayloft. And right now I want to. Very much." His hand was still out to her, his face still inviting much more than even his words as he got slowly to his feet. Anne only hesitated a moment longer before she walked over and held out hers in kind.

"Tell me one thing and I'll say yes," she said grinning. "How do you plan to get up the ladder?"

By now Jonathan had a tight enough grip on Anne's hand that she knew he wasn't going to let go, no matter the answer. "Very carefully."

He did, too. Balancing on the injured leg, he hoisted himself up with the good one, using his phenomenal set of chest and shoulder muscles.

What had begun in fun ended in earnest. Anne barely had the time to spread out an old blanket over the hay before Jonathan pulled her over next to him and took hold of her with an intensity that startled them both.

"This...is what happens to you," she panted between heady kisses, "in a barn?"

His smile was rakish, his eyes alight with their peculiar fire. "This is what happens to me," he amended, holding her beneath him and burying his face in her throat, "with you."

His impatience infected her as his hands undressed her. In no more than a few minutes she lay naked in the sweet, soft hay as Jonathan got out of his own clothes. Anne couldn't wait though. With an aggressiveness she wouldn't have recognized in herself before, she pushed him to his back and finished the job.

The sight and feel of his strong body beneath her hands set her pulse rocketing. Suddenly she was damp with perspiration. She couldn't seem to hold still, moving against him as if the friction of their bodies could further feed the flame that raged in her. She reveled in the coarseness of his hair against the smooth skin of her thighs, stomach, chest. She rubbed her cheek against him and nipped at the tight skin of his belly. And when she took him in her mouth, full and throbbing with power, she heard him groan with pleasure.

Jonathan could only take so much of that before he pulled her back to him, trapping her beneath him as if afraid she'd escape somehow. His excitement fed hers until it seemed unquenchable. His lips found her neck, the back of it where the small hairs anticipated pain and pleasure, and his tongue teased her unbearably. When she moved to meet his lips with her own, seeking the delicious heat of his mouth, his hands sought out the small, special places of her body that brought her even closer to the precipice.

Anne had never remembered such abandon, such fierce primal release. It was as if between them she and Jonathan had found a uniquely kindred energy source, a passion neither of them had ever really realized. They had also learned, instinctively, how to prolong their pleasure in each other until they were both drenched and gasping, eyes uncannily alike in their intensity. Together they teased and held back, promised release and then withheld, until they could bear it no longer.

"Please," she begged for the first time in her life, her voice shrill and breathless with the intensity of him inside her. "Please...now..."

With her plea, Jonathan took her to him almost brutally, his arms all but crushing her, his mouth ferocious. Captive within what could have been a prison, Anne met her freedom head on, the brilliance at the pinnacle so overwhelming that its delight was agony. Unbelievably, when Jonathan reached the same peak moments later, Anne followed again, wide-eyed and trembling.

For a long while later they lay exhausted in each other's arms, too spent to even marvel aloud at what they had shared. Anne supposed that she dozed for a while once the delicious fire that had coarsed through her limbs finally ebbed to a pleasant glow. She lay for a long time savoring the feel of Jonathan against her, the heady aroma of him and the slightly scandalous comfort of the hayloft. When she should have been inside her house making preparations for going out on rounds, she curled into the curve of Jonathan's hip and tested the texture of his chest with lazy fingers. All the while she found herself smiling and thinking that this sort of thing could easily become a habit.

"They were right," she finally said.

"Who?" Jonathan's voice sounded sleepy and content.

"Whoever decided that haylofts were so notorious. They should be."

He chuckled, his fingers just as lazily exploring the softness of her breast. "It's something about losing your inhibitions," he suggested.

"Inhibitions, hell." Anne grinned back at him. "That's not what's usually lost in haylofts. When I'm a parent, my daughter's not going anywhere near one."

It didn't occur to her until after she'd said it that until only a few days ago, she had given up the idea of children for good. The realization would have been more exciting for her if it weren't for the fact that she just as quickly understood that she had meant parenthood with Jonathan. She knew what her chances were there. A little of the light died in her eyes.

Jonathan must have sensed her feelings. "Tell me something, farm girl," he said, neatly changing the subject. "What do you plan to do if you win the suit?"

She didn't hesitate. "Stay here. Help run the clinic like I'd planned."

He shook his head. "What about the rest of the family holdings? Do you think that if you ignore them they'll go away?"

Anne thought a minute before moving up to her elbow. Leaning over to talk to Jonathan, she let her hair fall in a curtain to his chest. Her eyes were cautious. "I'll find someone to run them."

Jonathan's eyes were patiently amused. He didn't move. "Where did you say you cut your teeth? I suppose you think you can simply have everyone send résumés to the cabin so that you can pick the person to run seven industrial divisions and all the other subsidiaries right here from the mountain."

A new wariness crept into Anne's voice. "Applying for the job in person?"

The hint of a smile brightened. "That's the Anne Jackson I know and love. No, I'm not applying. I'm trying to tell you, my lusty wench, that no matter how you try to avoid it, if you win, which I think you will, you'll have to spend some time in the big city settling your affairs. And that I will also happen to be in that big city."

There was a moment of silence before Anne replied, unable to keep the memory of Jonathan's New York bred personality from her voice. "We've passed the country test. Let's see if we can do it in a corporate boardroom?"

Jonathan reached up and kissed her firmly on the mouth. "You do have a way with a double entendre."

"Still no promises?"

It was Jonathan's turn to pause. "Do you think it would be wise?"

Anne knew what would be wise, but a hayloft was not the place for common sense. She stifled the new uncertainty his words had given rise to and smiled provocatively. Without a word, she began to slowly rock back and forth, her hardening nipples grazing against Jonathan's chest, the shower of her honey-colored hair enclosing them from the world.

Jonathan groaned in mock exasperation. "What do you think I am, Superman?"

She grinned down at him, her movements more pronounced. "I was thinking that it takes you such a lot of exertion to get up and down from the loft, we might as well make the most of our time up here."

"Much more of this kind of exertion, and I won't be able to get back down at all."

Anne's eyes lit up with an even more wicked light as she looked over to see that Jonathan wasn't nearly as nonchalant about her advances as he made himself out to be. "Another double entendre? If it is, I can't wait."

He groaned at her humor and pulled her back down to him.

Anne wasn't the least surprised when Cassie showed up the next day. When she opened the door to find her friend on the front porch, Anne hugged her warmly.

"Silas came to see you, huh?"

Cassie's grin had frozen into surprise the minute she saw Anne. "My God, Anne," she gasped. "What has happened to you?"

"What do you mean?"

"You look positively pregnant."

"I beg your pardon." As yet, neither had made the first move to go inside.

"I never thought I'd say anything so trite, but you're honest-to-God glowing!"

"Get inside, Cassie," Anne suggested dryly, moving to accommodate her. "You're getting snow-blind."

Cassie walked in, never taking her eyes from Anne as she shed her coat and hat. "Annie, I mean it. You look wonderful. No wonder Silas was so indignant."

Anne had to laugh at that. "You should have seen him."

"Oh, don't worry. I got the whole show. He snorted and stomped around the store for a good twenty minutes before he decided that he didn't need to buy anything at all. I've never seen him so upset."

"He thinks that I'm about to repeat my mistakes." They headed as usual toward the kitchen, and Anne stopped a moment to throw another log on the fire.

"Are you?"

"I doubt it. Coffee or tea?"

"Coffee. Where's Jonathan?"

"He's still asleep. He's been pushing himself pretty hard the past few days." Even before she got the words out, Anne was struck by her latest unintentional double entendre and found herself grinning like a high school girl.

Cassie didn't miss a bit of it. She allowed a half smile to touch her eyes. "Before I forget about it, I have a good reason for visiting. A telegram."

Anne reached for the envelope with a scowl. It wasn't until she saw the return address that she relaxed. "Oh good, it's only from Judson."

Anne had hardly begun to read before Cassie saw the relief in her eyes grow to puzzlement. "What's the matter now?" she demanded.

Anne looked up, quickly trying to cover the worry that must have shown through. "Oh, nothing. It seems that we've stirred up a bit of a hornet's nest."

Cassie's eyes became immediately suspicious. "How, and what nest?"

"I'm sure that Silas told you about the papers that he delivered yesterday."

"And your decision to do unto your husband what he's done to you. Yes, and I think that congratulations are in order. What nest?"

Anne used her hand to brush away the concern in Cassie's expression. "Just Brad. He overreacts. Judson says I should be careful around him." Anne saw Cassie's expression sharpen and held out a threatening finger. "Don't you dare tell anyone in town," she admonished. "I'll have 'em all up here sitting on my front doorstep with their shotguns."

"Maybe that's not such a bad idea."

"Don't be silly. This isn't the Hardy Boys. Judson said that Brad had been 'visibly upset.' That means that Brad's been a jerk. I'm sure he stormed into the office and made a few vague and silly threats, and that Tom had to pull him back off. Brad never did know how to handle a threatening situation."

Cassie didn't give up easily. She was leaning forward now. "But this is a threatened jail sentence and a loss of everything he has, Annie. Maybe you should move in with us until this is all resolved."

Anne reached out and took her friend's hand. "Cassie, I grew up with Brad. He's all bark and no bite. Believe me." But Tom wasn't, she reminded herself uneasily. How threatened would the two of them have to be to do something spiteful like a little trumped-up blackmail or sabotage at the clinic? Damn it, she was tired of having to worry about those two. It was about time she let them know in no uncertain terms that she'd had about enough of their neat little squeezes. She wasn't impotent in the face of their attacks anymore. For not the first time, she realized that she was glad that she'd thrown down the gauntlet.

"You weren't going to let me have any of the coffee cake?"

The two of them started at the sound of Jonathan's voice. Looking up, they found him lounging in the doorway, clothed in Brad's old plaid shirt and corduroy pants, crutches propped against his sides. Again Anne noticed that his frame strained the material of the clothes.

"I didn't know you were up," Anne greeted him, darting a warning glance at Cassie.

"Congratulations, Jonathan," Cassie said blithely. "You look great."

Anne decided that Cassie had meant that to be significant and ignored it.

"Thanks," he said warmly. "Getting dressed only took me forty minutes start to finish this morning." He hobbled in and gently lowered himself to the seat next to Anne. "If it were a competition, I could beat every little old lady in Miami."

"You do in my book," Cassie retorted offhandedly. "None of them looks that good in their work clothes."

Anne ignored her again. Jonathan laughed, holding his chest to support irritable ribs.

"Cassie, I'm going to miss you."

Cassie shrugged with a mischievous grin. "Don't go."

Jonathan returned her grin, but with an odd loss for words.

Chapter 14

Three days later Anne stood at the front window watching the melting snow drip steadily from the eaves. Silas's prediction had come true with particular vigor, almost as if nature itself were conspiring with him against her. Jonathan would be gone in another day.

Anne sighed and rubbed at her eyes with a hand as she tried to hold off tears that had threatened all morning. It wasn't fair. Just when they were becoming really close, when the tentative forays into commitment had begun to gel into something tangible.

Jonathan had begun to find a new ease with the softer side of himself, content in the evenings to do no more than talk in the comfort of a fire lit room or read a good book. He'd lost much of the restless impatience that had marked his early days in Anne's home. More than once she caught him in moments of amused surprise as if he found it hard to recognize himself anymore.

Anne, watching him grow, had discovered a new matching place in herself that flowered within his reach. She was beginning to tap into a reservoir of love that she'd never known existed. Her time with Jonathan only fed a hunger for him that grew instead of diminished. Anne Jackson realized that for the first time since her mother died, she could love someone selflessly and completely.

Now, however, Jonathan would return to the city and the life that had forged and still supported the part of his character she wished she'd never seen. No matter how hard she'd tried in the last few days, she

couldn't seem to move past that idea, past the picture of the man he'd
been when he'd first arrived on her doorstep. Because of that, she
couldn't seem to see her way to anything but an all-or-nothing relationship. New York or West Virginia. Choose, Jonathan.

And she knew what he would choose.

"Annie." Jonathan put a hand on her shoulder.

She jumped, not having heard him, his touch burning with new unquenchable fire.

"You're getting pretty good with those crutches," she said, not
turning away from where the sun lit her strained face. "I didn't even
hear you."

The night before they had made love in front of the fire again, but
their words had had a ring of desperation, their laughter an uncomfortable shrillness. The snow had begun to melt yesterday.

"You weren't paying attention," he said easily. She didn't answer.
He stood just behind her, a hand now on either shoulder as he looked
out above her head. "Two weeks ago I would have paid any amount
of money to see that sight."

Anne sighed wistfully. "Me, too."

Jonathan chuckled. "You mean you were about to throw the toast
of New York out in the cold?"

"Right on his ear."

It was a moment before he asked the next question. Anne faced the
silence like a penance. "When are you throwing me out?"

She took a long breath, the weight of his hands almost unbearable.
"If this thaw keeps up the way it is, Jim and Silas could be up here tomorrow."

Say you won't go, she begged silently, the knot of unshed tears
choking her. Change your mind and make a commitment to me, please.
I can't let you go and survive.

Jonathan's voice, when it came, was quiet and strained. "Come with
me, Annie."

She shook her head, struggling to keep her voice under control. "I
don't think so, Jonathan. I don't think I'd like you in New York."

"You're locked in too tightly to those preconceived notions of
yours," he argued quietly. "I might surprise you."

Still she didn't turn, but stood very still, her hands shoved deep into
her pants pockets. "I'd like to think you would. I just...well, it's hard
to get past old disillusionments. I don't know if I could compete with
the lure back there anymore. I don't know if I really want to try."

"Then what do you think we should do?"

She could only shake her head. She felt his leaving already, and a
great gap widened in her, a void where the life-giving force of his love
had laid.

With gentle pressure, he turned her around to face him. She could hardly bear to look up at the sky-blue of his eyes.

"What do you think we should do?" he repeated, never releasing her from her gaze or grip.

"I think you should probably go back as you planned. Then you can give yourself some time in the real world to balance out your time here. Maybe we'll see each other when I'm there on business. Then if you want, you can come back for a while and we can decide what to do."

He drew her even closer until the ache of desire grew indistinguishable from the sharp pain of loss. "What about you?"

"I'll be here." She looked down, control almost impossible within the range of his eyes.

His one hand moved against her cheek, his touch caressing. Barely suppressing a moan for the agony of his touch, she lifted her head away from him, her eyes closing against the tears that began to spill. He followed and kissed her, his mouth searching hers with tender yearning.

"I love you, Annie."

Anne opened her eyes and thought that the morning sun in Jonathan's eyes would blind her. His face shifted and melted beyond her tears, and she saw the pain in its lines. What he had to do was no easier for him than it was for her. She was so afraid that when he walked away from her, he would walk away from himself. If that happened, he would have to forget her or never be able to live with himself. She wanted to tell him that. She wanted to be able to bribe or coerce or beg him to stay. She could only manage a half smile.

"I love you, Jonathan. You've given me back my freedom."

"No," he said with a slow shake of his head. "You did that, Annie. I happened to be around when it happened. That's why I think you'd survive in New York."

It was becoming increasingly difficult for her to answer without giving way to pain-wracked sobs. He wouldn't change his position. No mention yet of his staying. And she couldn't change hers. There were only so many steps she could manage at one time. "I'm not that strong yet, Jonathan. Until I am, I have no business back there with you."

"You're stronger than you think, Annie."

She couldn't answer at all. She could only look up at him, the eloquence of her turmoil glinting in tear-filled eyes. Without another word, Jonathan gathered her into the strong comfort of his arms, his lips finding that hers tasted of bitter salt. In her quiet desperation, Anne threw her arms around him, clinging to him as if he could save her. The kiss deepened as Jonathan eased her lips apart. His hands were around her waist, sure and sustaining, his hard body easing gently against hers. Slowly, inexorably, as his mouth took command of hers, his embrace tightening until the two of them swayed with the power of their need.

Anne felt his hands against her skin, fingers exploring and remembering, their touch igniting her own hunger. An obsession, a sure, sudden knowledge that she had to be next to him right now, to touch him and rouse in him the same unbearable tension he had sparked in her. Right now she needed him more than anyone or anything else in her life. She needed to know that what she'd given him had not been wasted or foolish, and it seemed to her that his most beautiful statement of that had to be made without words.

Jonathan understood as if her thoughts were telepathic. With his arms tight around her, he lifted his head a little and smiled. Anne found no guile there, none of the smugness that had once ruled their relationship. She saw only tenderness, the warmth of his love like the sun in the endless sky of his eyes.

Her tears still fell without restraint, but she smiled tremulously back. "Well," she managed in a throaty, hesitant voice, "it's probably a good thing you are leaving tomorrow. I haven't been able to get a thing done for a week."

"Yes you have, farm girl," he said. "You've made me fall in love with you. And for the first time in fifteen years, you've made me wonder whether I really want to go back to New York."

Jonathan took her to her own bed, the high old four-poster with the goose down mattress that overlooked the sunlight and felt the firelight. In the bed that had been her grandmother's and hers before her, Anne lay next to Jonathan in much the same way her ancestors had, giving and receiving the same timeless gift. Jonathan's eyes smoldered as they ranged the length of her body, their gaze raising goose bumps as surely as if they'd grazed her skin. The strong light from the front window threw him into a soft kind of relief, shadows outlining the taut muscles of his chest and arms and settling into the planes of his face.

Anne thought of the chiaroscuro of the painting masters, the dramatic play of light against dark. It couldn't be any more breathtaking than the pattern of white sunlight against Jonathan's skin. Without thinking she used her fingers as imaginary paintbrushes, stroking the rich, healthy colors into the contours of his body, the rounded edges of his shoulders and arms, the hairy coarseness of his chest. Along to narrow hips and strong, muscled thighs.

Still the tears came, as if contact with him were as painful as it was essential. Jonathan kissed them as they fell, following their traces to her throat and breasts, tasting the saltiness in her hair as she lay. With gentle hands he untangled her braid and fanned her hair out beneath her like a gilt frame. His eyes were tender but his touch hungry, impatient, and it was the contrast that was compelling to Anne.

She drew him to her breasts and begged him to savor them. She felt his fingers flutter against the sensitive skin of her thigh and invited them to explore. When they found her, their touch so light as to send her gasping, she arched against him, aching for union with him.

Jonathan whispered into her hair and nuzzled her ear, his hands driving her to a new, more urgent rhythm. The nerves in Anne's skin jumped to acute life, teased by the soft, curling hair of Jonathan's chest against her taut nipples, enticed by the scratch of an hours-old beard against her cheek and tortured by cool fingers against hot flesh. Unable to remain apart any longer, Anne led him to her, begged his arms to enfold her, his legs imprison to her. He waited long enough to capture her eyes with his own. Then together they moved in a like rhythm to a world beyond the finite one they inhabited. The sun was an explosion within them; the day, for a moment, endless; the future contained within a heartbeat and the gasping cry of release.

After Jonathan had drifted into a contented sleep, Anne lay wide awake within his embrace. She couldn't sleep, couldn't relax into the mindless peace Jonathan had found. Comfortably enclosed within his arms, she was even more painfully aware of the relentless passage of time. By tomorrow night she would once again sleep alone in her big bed. She would reclaim the isolation of her world only to find that it no longer gave her comfort.

When Jonathan left, her home, the haven she'd come to treasure for its secluded severity, would become for the first time a lonely place, a place not so much safe as empty. Another voice had become ingrained into the memories of these wooden walls. Another presence had become incorporated into the essence of what Cedar Ridge was. Only this presence would not easily relegate itself to the past.

Moving quietly so that she wouldn't wake Jonathan, Anne slipped out of his grasp and got dressed. Without any conscious intent, she made her way back down to stand before the big front window to look out on the softening snow.

The sun was rising high, and it glittered metallically. Small rivulets were beginning to cut paths into the white lawn that sloped away from the house toward the road. Soon its brown would be visible, parallel lines of sodden mud that wound down the mountain toward the town. The river would rise with the melting snow, and the trees, so deformed with the weight of the heavy snow, would begin to spring back up at the sky. As she watched, a large mound tumbled off a pine to the left of the porch and thudded to earth, the tree straightening a little. It wouldn't be long.

Anne couldn't exactly decide why she always brooded at this window. It seemed that the serenity of the scene before her helped to settle her so that she could gain a better perspective on the priorities in her life. The world around her home was always the same and always would be. It was stable.

More snow fell, the sound like a body falling. Anne watched it like the approach of a flood.

She tried, one last time, to find the resolve to follow Jonathan to New York. Looking back carefully she assessed her time there, the scant days she'd spent testing the city and corporate waters. She'd done well, she knew that. The old demeanor had slipped on as easily as the new clothes. She knew that if she went back with Jonathan now, she'd probably end up enjoying the games she would resume playing. At least to a certain extent. And she truthfully thought she could live anywhere as long as she was assured of his love.

The dilemma rested not so much in her own reaction to New York but in Jonathan's. She had to know what it would do to him before she could make a commitment. The drug of that world was far more alluring than any chemical known to man, and far more lethal. It had changed Jonathan before the eyes of his friends and family and left scars more unforgettable than those he carried from Vietnam. Anne knew all about that drug. She'd seen firsthand too, what it could do to a person.

Jonathan was going back to see how he would handle the kind of power that moved the nations of the world. It had beaten and claimed him once, altering him so thoroughly that Anne knew his parents must look at him now with the eyes of frightened strangers. She had no more guarantee than they'd had, those who'd loved him so much, that he wouldn't succumb yet again. She had known him for only weeks out of his life, and no matter how much she wanted, she couldn't hope that that time would automatically protect him.

If she went with him as he'd asked, it would only be worse. There she would be, the constant reminder of what she thought he should be, nagging at him with silent, anxious eyes. If he were going to hold onto what he'd gained here he'd do it on his own. If he weren't, her being with him would do no more than make their final parting resentful and bitter.

If she were to lose him, she would much rather it be while they still loved each other. If he had to go, better she saw him turn from her with regret.

Anne was so preoccupied that for a few minutes she lost track of what was before her. She didn't see the visitor approaching until he was through the clearing. Startled, she shifted her concentration to him.

It was a man, but not one of her neighbors. They didn't dress like that. She couldn't see him very well yet, but she wondered whether it might be one of Jonathan's corporate executives come to pay a social visit. He was attired in a manner suspiciously similar to Jonathan's when he'd arrived. Maybe, she thought dryly, it was a kind of corporate uniform for the woods.

She supposed that she should go out to greet him, wondering half-heartedly why anyone would make a trek like that on foot in snow that was still a good foot deep. The man was either very determined but stupid, or just plain stupid. Someone in town would surely have lent him a horse with the directions to her cabin, if only he'd asked.

Anne was about to turn for her coat when something caught her eye. A familiar posture to the visitor's walk. He looked as if he were denying the fact that he was walking up a mountain even as he did it, as if he wouldn't be caught dead here if he didn't have to be. She wanted to laugh.

It was Brad.

No wonder he didn't have a horse. After what had been going on in the last few weeks, no one in his right mind in Elder's Crossing would go out of his way for Bradley Jackson. In fact, she was surprised that Silas wasn't giving him an official escort to make sure he didn't give her any trouble.

Brad was the last person Anne expected to see. After all, the only time he'd been to the cabin in the last five years had been to bury his father. Brad believed that if a limo or air service couldn't get you there, it wasn't worth going. Now, looking at his rather clumsy approach, Anne desperately wished she could get her hands on a camera. Pictures of this would make delicious blackmail material, if for nothing else than to remind him in his worst moments of megalomania what a fool he really was.

She waited until she heard him on the porch before throwing the door open, the grin on her face not so much welcoming as smug. She decided it might be a lot more fun than what she had been doing to gloat over Brad's discomfort instead. When he looked up from stomping his two-hundred-dollar L.L. Bean boots on the porch, he had nothing but malice in his eyes for her, his mouth twitching irritably. Her grin broadened in delight.

"Well, if it isn't the prodigal son," she greeted him. "What brings you so far from the big city?"

He straightened and smiled in return, the light in his eyes brightening oddly. "I'm glad you're here," he told her almost amiably. "It'll save me some time."

"Time for what?"

He motioned to the door. "Can I come in?"

"Why not?" Anne moved in to allow him by. "Coffee, tea? I have some semistale cake, if you like."

He stood inside looking around as if reorienting himself. "I'd almost forgotten how very...rustic this all was." He spoke as if the words had a slightly bad taste to them.

"I kept it just the way you left it," Anne assured him dryly. "I knew some day you'd come back."

He looked over at her with the same attitude of distaste with which he'd considered the cabin.

"I'll take some coffee."

Anne nodded agreeably. "Convention usually dictates that one remove coat and hat before sitting at the table."

"I'm still cold. It was a long walk."

She couldn't help but grin again. "I'll bet it was. What was the matter, all the horses already hired?"

He wasn't amused, but Anne certainly was. She wanted to go and get Jonathan. It would probably do him good to see what the other side of him could resemble. Maybe he hadn't been as bad as Brad—few people were—but he'd certainly worn that look of disdain when first considering life in the boonies. It was lucky for him that she didn't have the heart to wake him just for Brad.

Anne sat across from her brother as he sipped the steaming liquid in his cup and thought about the time she'd spent with him in this house. His memory should have been imbedded in this place like everyone else's. There should have been pictures that popped into her mind when certain things were handled, or aromas sensed. Like the way she could still see her father fishing down at the stream, his back sunburned and hair bleached blond, his pleasure in the silence brightening his stern features. Or her mother's delicate hands as she and Sarah worked over the wedding ring quilt that hung highest on the living-room wall. Sometimes, she even felt a pull of Tom's personality, filling the rooms like heady smoke.

But try as she might, she could not conjure up any kind of special feeling for Brad here. Even as he sat at the table where he'd eaten so many meals and worked so many jigsaw puzzles, he didn't conjure up any sensation that he had once belonged to this place. It was as if he were truly a stranger in his own house. What saddened Anne was that he didn't care in the least.

By the time he finished his cup of coffee, he'd lost much of his original antagonism. The side of his face had calmed to slow fluttering motions along the side of his mouth, and his lips didn't curl back so much in that perennial sneer. Anne knew that it was because he was anticipating the bombshell he obviously planned to drop. He wouldn't have gone to all the trouble of getting to the cabin for a trivial matter, and they both knew it. What pleading he might have done for leniency from his sister, he would have left up to Tom and adept lawyers.

She exchanged monosyllables with him, willing to play his cat-and-mouse game for the time being. She didn't want him to know how frustrated and worried his sudden appearance was beginning to make her, how very much she wanted to ask where Tom was while Brad made the jaunt up the Appalachian Trail.

Judson's carefully worded warning was still too fresh for her to take Brad's casual arrival lightly. He had something unpleasant up his sleeve, something like another legal paper Judson hadn't unearthed that would negate Anne's hold over her own destiny. But if she were going to get Brad's goat, she couldn't allow him to start with any kind of advantage.

"So tell me, Brad," she finally said quite civilly into her coffee cup. "Have you come up here to reacquaint yourself with historic architecture?"

"Just a leisurely stroll in the woods," he retorted.

"Of course," she said with a bright smile. "Well, it's always nice to see you. Oh, I'll tell you what. Since you're here, there are some clothes that you might like to take back with you."

"No, thank you."

Emptying his cup, he set it down before him and allowed Anne a measured gaze almost completely free of tics before a slow, sporadic smile caught at his mouth and made Anne uneasy. His look was anticipatory. He considered her leisurely, then took hold of his coffee cup with a corner of the tablecloth and slowly wiped its surface. Anne couldn't help but stare at the odd behavior. Brad's eyes turned to his work.

"Well, Anne, I'm afraid that I'm too greedy to put this off any longer, even for you. I have a tight schedule, so I don't have the time I'd like to sit and socialize about old times." His eyes sprang on her, their look of expectancy now boiling uncomfortably. Anne recognized the look. He was feeling cornered, and thought he'd found a way out. Brad simply couldn't help gloating. What worried her was that there was very little control in his eyes right now.

"Put off what?"

He smiled again, his one eye blinking absurdly. "Simple, Anne my dear. The solution to my problem. This cabin has become a millstone around my neck, and you're the one who put it there."

She couldn't help but laugh. He'd taken his juvenile attempt at revenge too far. "Brad, honey, how long have you been rehearsing that? Why you sound almost threatening. It must be a line you read in one of father's mysteries. Just what does it mean? You've called in someone new to handle the case?"

Her sarcasm didn't seem to bother him. It had always awakened a storm of facial irritation in the past. Instead, he continued to smile as if relishing some private joke. Anne was becoming hard-pressed to sit still.

"No lawyers, Anne. They seem to have come up empty-handed." He paused to let her carefully digest his words. "Just like Tom did when I sent him."

"You sent Tom?" she laughed. "Be realistic, Brad."

"I sent him."

There was a mad kind of glee in his voice now. Anne watched him, realizing that he was serious. He really thought that he had sent Tom to bribe her. Brad might have had his petty delusions in the past, but Anne had never known him to completely lose his touch with reality.

"Brad," she tried more gently, suddenly very uneasy with the picture that was forming. "What did you come here to say?"

"Say?" he echoed hollowly. "I didn't come here to say anything. That's all finished."

Within the space of his words, something else appeared in his eyes, something Anne had never seen there before. Beneath the avarice, the sarcasm and disdain, a new glow began to flicker: a manic purpose, a look of hungry malevolence.

A real madness.

Anne froze, suddenly very afraid of her brother. He watched her with eyes that seemed to see something else altogether, something she didn't recognize. With uncommon perception, she understood that he was acting out a scenario he had practiced many times. He was living a dream he had created within the walls of isolation he had built long ago.

She could see now the revenge he had plotted and savored through the long, ineffectual years when he had lived on jealousy and resentment. The revenge was to have been carried out against her father. And now, because he was out of his reach, against Anne. Whatever he was about to do, Brad had done a thousand times before in his fantasies. Now he had lost the ability to comprehend the difference.

Anne noticed again that the facial twitches had stopped. Brad was in perfect control. She suddenly realized how far the game had gone when Brad pulled a gun from his coat—a short, ugly little .22. The famous Saturday night special, whose availability was legend and whose bullet did an obscene little dance inside the human chest cavity. And this gun was pointed directly at her.

Chapter 15

"Brad, this is absurd," Anne protested without thinking. "What do you think you're doing?"

Brad smiled giddily, his mouth an almost perfect crescent, and leaned comfortably back in his chair. "Actually, I think I should be grateful to you for bringing this whole mess to a head. You can't imagine what a pleasure it will be to put a match to this white elephant." He looked around with a little giggling sound, as if savoring the thought. "Pete Jackson's place. The legacy, the symbol of history and family, everything that he preached ad nauseam but never practiced. 'The tie that binds.'" His lips curled into a sneer and his gaze returned to his sister. "But Bradley didn't belong. He wasn't the bright, the gifted, the beautiful. He was only second best, and old Pete didn't even acknowledge his existence until he made good his threat to usurp the throne. You know, Anne, you never knew what you missed. You were never in the contest for the real world, at least not as far as Pete was concerned. Women didn't have to compete for something that could be theirs. So it was safe to lavish the worldly goods on you as the royal princess. The household pet. Weren't we all surprised when ole Pete decided to get back at Brad by leaving the household pet everything."

Anne's mouth was dry. Her heart raced painfully. All she could think of doing was trying to run. Every tactic she'd ever used with gun-wielding patients suddenly disappeared and she was afraid she'd lose control. The sense of unreality was increased by the fact that a part of her still refused to believe that it was Brad who sat so nonchalantly before her with a gun in his hand.

"So what are you going to do," she challenged instinctively, still reacting as she always had to him, "shoot me because I was cute and cuddly? Or is it that I'm the only one left to blame?"

His silent, smiling shrug made her want to scream. She didn't know how to talk to him, what to do to defuse him. Looking at him now, she knew with a sinking finality that he was long past reason. He was acting out his cruel fantasy, and try as she might, she couldn't get beyond her feelings of disdain. She wanted to scream at him, to insult him for the stupid way he was handling this. She also realized that she wanted to beg for her life.

"Brad," she said, her voice barely in control. "If it means that much to you, I'll forget the lawsuit. Take the land. Do whatever you want with it."

He shook his head with a smug grin of satisfaction. "Too late. That fine lawyer of yours didn't waste any time before contacting the authorities. I've been checking on it, you know, and I figure that if Tom and I were convicted, maybe we'd serve eighteen months in minimum security. I'd come out of it with the house on Beacon Hill and a comfortable living. But Anne, with you dead, I'd inherit the estate anyway, so I'd walk away from the whole thing in under two years in an even better position than when I went in. And Tom wouldn't have his fingers all over my money anymore." He waved the gun at her, punctuating his enthusiasm.

"Now, here's the fun part. I have an alibi. At six tonight, as usual, Tom and I will be waiting for Louis to seat us at our booth. And I've been seen going into my room earlier today to work on our unfortunate financial setback that could well cost me my ancestral home. Every once in a while my voice has been throwing recorded tantrums just loud enough to be heard and noted." He was enjoying himself immensely, like a small child getting the last piece of cake. Anne was frightened. The gun was once more leveled very steadily at her chest. "You know," he went on blithely, "I can't thank you enough for showing me such a good time today. Being able to see the look on your face right now is worth all the trouble I've gone through. I've been dreaming of something like this for years." He looked around the room with malicious glee. "As for the cabin, well, let's call that a settlement of old debts."

"What an interesting turn of phrase."

The interruption jolted Anne. She whipped around to find Jonathan lounging in the doorway. Even knowing that he gave them no physical advantage, she breathed an instinctive sigh of relief. Jonathan would know what to do. He would help defuse the situation by just being there.

Then she noticed that something was wrong. Jonathan seemed to not even notice that Anne was in the room. He gazed passively at Brad, but the light in his eyes burned eerily. A new, unexplained tension suddenly exploded.

Anne instinctively turned to Brad, maybe for some kind of explanation. The sight of him only added to her confusion.

Brad had turned white. His mouth hung slack as if he'd been hit, and his expression, which had only moments earlier been smugly pleased, caught fire. The left side of his face contorted madly. An evil enmity Anne had never seen before glared in his eyes as he struggled for control.

"What are you doing here?" he hissed.

Jonathan smiled lazily. "Waiting to run into you, it would seem."

There was a moment's silence Anne somehow couldn't break. It was as if a field of physical malevolence had sparked between the two men that no one could interrupt. They were two men Anne didn't know, consumed by something she didn't understand but instinctively feared. She watched each in turn, seeing a similarity in their expressions. She wasn't sure which one to be more afraid of.

Brad got slowly to his feet, the gun still steady, still poised at Anne. His eyes never left Jonathan.

"So it was you all along," Brad finally said with some wonder. "I should have guessed."

Jonathan shrugged with that strange smile that made Anne chill. "You've been outclassed, Bradley."

Brad nodded absently, still pondering something. "You managed to hide yourself well in that dummy corporation. It was, wasn't it?"

Jonathan nodded with a small grin. "I'll take that as a compliment. I went to a lot of trouble."

Suddenly Brad turned on Anne, his malice threatening to consume her. Still too stunned to comprehend what was taking place, she flinched from him.

"And you, little princess. Your part in this was a stroke of genius, especially after the wonderful act you put on two years ago. You like your revenge served cold, too, do you?"

Anne was too overwhelmed to react. "What are you talking about?" She turned to the stranger in the doorway. "Jonathan, please tell me what's going on. How do you know Brad?"

Somehow she'd gotten to her feet, though she didn't know how. She faced the two of them as she held the back of the chair for support, her hands sweaty.

Brad came after her and she started away. He looked from her to Jonathan, amazement dawning.

"She doesn't know," he breathed, again facing Jonathan and ignoring her in her small corner. He actually smiled at the man in the doorway, shaking his head with grudging admiration. "My God, what a masterful game. Jonathan, you have my respect. It was a brilliant move." He was really beginning to enjoy himself again, that little giggling sound escaping from him. It was as if he'd just remembered that he was the one with the gun in his hand, and that his new victim was far more amusing than the old.

Anne turned on Jonathan again. "What didn't I know?"

Brad wouldn't be denied the pleasure. "Anne, my dear, you know that Amplex Corporation Board of Directors you've been waiting to hear from? I'd like to introduce you." He made a show of indicating Jonathan with a grand wave of the gun, and then giggled again.

Anne blanched, trying to understand. Reality was fast leaving her behind. When she turned to Jonathan for explanation, he merely acquiesced with a passive shrug. She felt herself go deathly cold. The last of her foundations was beginning to crumble away beneath her.

"Why?"

Again he shrugged. "A story too long to tell in the time we seem to have."

She turned on Brad as if expecting help, but he just grinned. Her helplessness seemed to delight him all the more.

"An old score to settle," Jonathan added evenly, his eyes noncommittal.

His words set off a chain-reaction in Anne. A flurry of disjointed memories clicked together into place like a slot machine: Jonathan's odd trek back into the winter mountains in a custom suit, his animosity, the bits of out-of-the-way knowledge he'd collected about the family. His interest in Peter Jackson's daughter, Brad Jackson's sister.

Anne realized that she'd stopped breathing. She faced Jonathan and tried to discover some of the affection that had filled his eyes when he'd looked at her only hours ago and found none. His eyes were as cold as treacherous ice, a fragile covering for dangerous emotions below. His emotions were directed only at Brad. She challenged him to look at her again, her eyes bright with disbelief.

"Brad? Brad was the man who swindled you?" She knew she'd struck home even before he answered.

His answer was conversational, his voice as unemotional as the surface of his eyes. "Then Judson did tell you?"

"He told me. And because of what Brad did twelve years ago, you engineered the futures deal so that he would be sure to lose his family's home, too?"

He didn't offer an answer.

She swung on Brad. "Did you do it on purpose, Brad? Did you set out to ruin him?"

"Of course I did," he sneered, his reaction classic. His eyes gleamed maliciously as he looked at Jonathan and remembered whatever had set him off twelve years ago. "He was always so perfect, so *right*. So I outclassed him, didn't I, Jonathan? I got him caught between a rock and hard place to teach him a little lesson in where the real power lies."

Jonathan didn't bother to answer Brad either. Anne found that she was shaking her head as if she could deny what was happening. She wanted to lash out and didn't know at whom. It was too much to accept. Brad probably couldn't even remember what incident had been the catalyst for sending him after Jonathan. Jonathan had spent over a decade in return to exact his own brand of revenge, and Anne was the one caught in the middle.

Anger crowded her almost as closely as the terror of Brad's eyes. She lashed out at Jonathan for deceiving her, for according her a false security and then callously stripping it away again. She attacked him because she loved him.

"Was this all your quaint idea of Biblical justice, or did you think that I had a hand in what Brad did?"

She got no reaction. Jonathan was watching Brad.

"God, this is too good to be true." Brad giggled, his face jumping erratically. "It seems that I'm about to have my cake and eat it, too."

Jonathan finally gave Anne her answer then, his eyes still rigidly veiled. "I think Brad plans to make the point moot."

Brad laughed, the sound grating. "Indeed I do. But you sure have helped make this a most unforgettable afternoon. It's just too bad that I can't tell Tom how I found Jonathan Harris playing house with my sister, and that she didn't even know that he'd come to steal her precious home." His excitement was peaking as he considered the two people he held at bay.

At that moment Jonathan moved slightly to ease his bad leg. Brad jumped, swinging the gun around at him. "Don't you move, Harris," he shrilled a bit too loudly.

"Don't worry, Bradley," Jonathan answered calmly. Tugging at his pant leg, he revealed his homemade splint. "I'm not in good enough form for heroic gestures today."

"Why, Jonathan," Brad said with new delight. "I think you're keeping something from me. What happened to you?"

"I fell."

"You don't say. That's too bad. Hope it wasn't anything serious."

"I'll recover." Jonathan smiled evenly.

That seemed to appeal to Brad's sense of humor. His laughter was strident and loud. Then, abruptly, he stopped, his attention newly diverted. "Well now, let's see. Jonathan, you do complicate matters a little. I guess I'll have to get Anne to tie you up first. You see, the robbers tied the victims and ransacked the house before they...well, you know. It was too bad that Mr. Harris had suffered his injury and was able to offer no help to his hostess." He giggled again. "Really, Jonathan, you appeal to my sense of poetic justice. But remember, I have the gun. I'll be just as happy to shoot you now as later."

He backed up to the pantry and opened the door, never turning his back on his hostages. "Anne, I assume you still keep the clothesline in the same...ah, here it is. I should thank you for being such a creature of habit." He showed the roll to Jonathan. "It's been in the same place for the last twenty-five years at least. This place always has been a shrine to the fallacy of permanency. And Anne, as the dutiful daughter, has served it quite well, I think. Something like a vestal virgin." Still watching Jonathan, Brad flipped the ball of twine at Anne. She caught it instinctively.

When it seemed that Brad was about to head off on another self-serving tangent, Jonathan interrupted with a small, rueful smile. "I hate to be a bother, but could we continue this when I'm sitting down? I'm wearing a bit thin."

Brad stared oddly at him, as if his concentration had been broken. Then he smiled. "All right. I guess the next act takes place in the living room anyway. Please proceed."

Anne walked over to the door to see that Jonathan's crutches leaned against the wall beyond him. He moved now to reach for them. Edging aside enough to let her through, he slipped them under his arms and leaned heavily over. If Anne hadn't been so close when he turned to follow her, she never would have heard him.

"Can you tie something I can get out of?"

She nodded automatically, just enough, and moved past him.

Jonathan turned to follow, walking very carefully, just as he had the first few days he'd been up. At first Anne was confused. He had been careful all along, putting as little weight on his injured leg as he could. But she knew darn well that he had no reason to be having so much trouble. He was breathing heavily as he lurched a single step at a time across to the couch. When he lowered himself very carefully to a sitting position, a small gasp escaped that sounded very real.

"You're not telling me everything, Jonathan," Brad accused with relish. "How did your accident happen?"

"I...told you...I fell."

Brad shrugged. "Be that way. All right, Anne. I'd like your best Girl Scout knots. Hands behind his back. And even though I doubt sincerely whether it would make any difference, tie his ankles together. Jonathan, you do look awful. I guess I can assume that more was injured than just your leg."

Anne piped up, beginning to get a glimmer of Jonathan's strategy. "Quite a lot more. He shouldn't be anyplace but bed." Absurdly, she thought of how she sounded like an old English movie.

"Ah." Brad nodded, his eyes wide. "Compassionate to the bitter end, Anne? This is the man who made you the fool of the century, and you still think of his welfare. Good instincts, you nurses. All right, Jonathan, after she ties you up, feel free to lie down." He shook his head with glee. "To think that you went to all that trouble just to surprise me."

"You know...me...any little...revenge...I can...get...." Jonathan still seemed to have trouble breathing, his chest heaving with exertion as he tried to speak. Anne was impressed, even though, as Brad had said, Jonathan had just finished making a fool of her. His quick thinking could still save her life. Even now he was putting on the act of a lifetime as he wiped away nonexistent perspiration from his upper lip with the back of a trembling hand. He even managed somehow to look gray. Anne decided to ask him later how he did it.

"Isn't there some kind of...code," he gasped, his eyes coldly amused, "about taking...advantage of...an...injured man?"

Brad stood by the front door, alternately watching Anne's work and the scene outside. Anne's pastoral landscape. The sun rode straight up in the cold winter sky, glittering brightly off the snow so that the glare from the window cast the house in an uncomfortable gloom. Brad blinked repeatedly as he turned his attention back on them. His expression had frozen into disinterest, his smile faded. "None whatsoever, Jonathan." Anne couldn't see his eyes well, but she thought that the tic was worse.

Jonathan did smile, a chilly and rueful sight. "Funny...I had a feeling that would be...your attitude."

Anne straightened, hoping that Jonathan could manage to get the knots free and wondering what he intended to do once he did. She thought as she watched the tableau before her how dim the big fire in the fireplace appeared in contrast to that of the sun, how its dull red glow seemed almost evil.

Brad moved close enough to give Anne's work a half-hearted check and nodded, again motioning to her with the gun. The fact that she flinched again amused him. "Now, Anne," he directed, his voice businesslike and distant, "if memory serves me once more, there's a big can of gasoline in the barn. You'll walk there ahead of me to get it."

The band that constricted her breathing tightened. She stared at him, still fighting the belief that he could really carry out his threats. She was still not able to accept the fact that Brad was doing this, enacting a well-planned murder, torturing them like a great, slimy cat with his prey. Jonathan tried to catch her eye and nod, attempting to calm her, but she couldn't even accept his assurance. She didn't, after all, really know him, either. What did he want from her after all this? What had he wanted all along? The ground was falling out from under her, and she had nothing left to grab onto. She couldn't function anymore.

"Anne!"

She started, Brad's voice cutting into her. She looked over at him, at the tic that pulled again at his eye as if he were winking at a lewd joke, at the absurdly small gun that he wielded so ungracefully, and at the inappropriate walking boots he'd bought new to make the trek up here. It was at that moment that somewhere deep within her mounting terror a black rage was born.

This was all wrong. There had to be something she could do to stop him. He was lost up here in these mountains. His arena was the inside of a corporate office. This was her home, her world. Brad couldn't walk into it from his world of climate control and lawyer-spawned courage and expect to overcome her with such a silly little gun. He was on her turf, and it should have been to her advantage.

She caught Jonathan's eye and found reassurance in his calm gaze. They'd make it. Together they would be able to outwit Brad. She'd have to fight the bitterness of Jonathan's betrayal long enough to manage it, work with him until they were free and then rip his lungs out. He'd help to save himself if nothing else, and he was as comfortable in this world as she. They just had to get Brad to stumble.

She had to keep her head. Oh, God, if only she could keep the picture of Jonathan's eyes at bay long enough. She had to forget the soft blue of a mountain stream.

"I'm going, Brad," she said evenly, trying to hide from him the deep breath she had to take to steady herself. As she walked by him, the tic pulled again, more spastically. Maybe he wasn't as controlled as he seemed. Unless Anne were even more wrong than she'd been so far, he probably hadn't even had the courage to pull the official strings of Jonathan's ruin those long years ago. How could he possibly be expected to retain the temerity it took to do something this awesome face-to-face? She didn't want to think of the real power that obsessions gave to the delusional person. She didn't think she could survive the idea that Brad was invincible.

Anne walked ahead of him into the brittle afternoon air, the clean touch of it helping to settle her a little. Brad said nothing as they traversed the way to the barn, but the gun never wavered far from the center of her back, the feel of it a very unpleasant reminder.

Stepping into the barn calmed her even more. Andy whinnied over to her and Bessie stamped in her stall. The smells were familiar and warm, the sounds muffled. Somewhere in the back, melting snow dripped steadily from the rafters. Wanting to give Jonathan as much time as possible, she stopped as if to orient herself to the dark building.

"Don't play games, Anne," Brad warned irritably. "The gas is in the old tack room. At least that's where Pete used to keep it, and I can't imagine you defiling the sacred memory by moving it."

"I had my canning equipment in there this year. I moved the gasoline." She paused as if in thought. "The question is where..."

Brad shoved the gun into the small of her back, his patience wearing. "I'd rather not shoot you here, but that's always an option, Anne. Does that help you remember?"

"Oddly enough, it does." She led the way to the back of the barn.

Only five minutes later, unable to stall any longer, Anne started back, the half-full ten-gallon can heavy in her hands. Brad had checked it when she had pulled it out, evidently convinced that she'd also kept a gas can of water handy on the off chance that anybody would come up and force her to set fire to her house. His tic was becoming worse with the passing minutes and now pulled sporadically at his mouth. He'd begun to finger the gun like worry beads, which didn't encourage Anne at all. It was still pointed straight at her back.

She opened the door to the cabin and had to once again adjust her eyes to the gloom. At first all she could see was the fire to her right, still burning steadily and making the air close. Then, she was able to make out the furniture. it wasn't until Brad stepped in behind her that she realized that Jonathan was gone. It took no more to galvanize her. Almost without hesitation she dropped to the floor, the gas can landing upright in front of her.

"What the hell are you...?"

Then Brad saw, too. His eyes shot open as he began to swing around. He never got started. A poker whistled out of the darkness and caught him on the left shoulder. He cried out and fired, the sound deafeningly close. Anne rolled away from it without giving another thought to the can by the fire. She saw Jonathan lunge from behind the door. Brad saw him and screamed, the sound a mix of fury and fear.

From where she'd taken cover Anne watched the struggle, the two men's shadows against the throbbing glow of the fire. For a moment they were one silhouette, indistinguishable. Then Jonathan moved. Getting a hand on the gun, he tried to force it away from Brad. The two of them fought for it in silence. Jonathan still had the poker in his other hand. He brought it up to strike and lost his leverage on the gun. Anne could see it, small and deadly, caught high between the two of them and glinting dully in the light. The shadows still wavered in sweating silence, the only sounds now oddly the melting snow and the crackle of the fire. She watched impotently, unable to move or even breathe for the fear. Jonathan couldn't take this much longer.

Suddenly Brad lunged hard. The two men crashed against the wall, sending the hall tree over in a clatter. Jonathan lost grip on the poker and gave a sharp cry as he hit the wall on his weak side, his bad leg buckling beneath him. He never let go of the gun. Sweat glistened on his face as he brought the other hand up and pried at Brad's grip, trying to slam the gun against the wall to loosen it. Jonathan was losing his balance. His right leg was almost useless, and Brad was trying to aim for it in an attempt to cripple him. Frantically, Anne looked around for help.

The poker lay exposed by the door. Quickly, she scuttled out from where she'd taken refuge by the chair and scooted over to get it. She could help Jonathan with it. He was rapidly wearing out. She could hear the rasping of his breath as he struggled.

She got hold of the poker as Brad shot an elbow at Jonathan and caught him at the ribs. Jonathan gasped; his hold loosened. Brad began to edge the gun down toward him. They didn't see her. Crouched behind them, Anne had just enough time to warn him.

"Jonathan!"

She made her move. Swinging with everything she had, she caught Brad flat against the kidney. He screamed and reeled around, pulling the gun with him. Anne dove away in an effort to put the couch between them. He fired seconds later. The bullet thudded into the couch inches from Anne's head. Already flattened, Anne peered out to see the astonishment in Brad's eyes.

"Damn it!" Jonathan lurched away from the wall to keep Brad from getting to Anne. He caught him against the couch. The gun rose between them again, glinting oddly like a sacrificial offering. Jonathan pushed and pushed more, bending Brad back at the waist. Anne was so close to them now that she could almost smell Brad's terror, and Jonathan's rage. She brought the poker up again, moved just beyond Brad's field of vision and stood waiting.

Jonathan's eyes were fire, their only color the terrible glow of blood and fury. He had a hand around Brad's throat and began to squeeze. Anne could hear the gurgling noises as Brad fought for air. The gun wavered between outstretched hands, slimy with sweat. Jonathan was gasping almost as loudly as Brad.

Brad kicked hard and Jonathan jerked upright, his mouth contorted in soundless agony. Anne raised the poker above her head.

Brad got ahold of the gun. He slammed it against the side of Jonathan's head. Then he swung it point-blank at Anne.

She froze.

Jonathan staggered, unbelievably still on his feet, trying to clear his head. Blood streamed down his face, glittering blackly in the light.

"Brad..." Anne saw him pulling at the trigger and couldn't move. She couldn't move. Brad's breath came in sobs. His hands shook and his face contorted cruelly, but he pulled steadily, almost casually at the trigger, ignoring Jonathan as if he didn't exist. He was enjoying the realization of his fantasies, feeding on the blank terror in Anne's eyes. A split second that filled an eternity.

"Anne!" Jonathan lunged. His football tackle caught Brad at the waist and sent him over backwards. The gun clattered hard against the chimney as Brad fell back over the couch, his body buckling oddly at the waist. He slammed to the floor, knocking into the gas can.

Anne screamed. Jonathan seized Anne at the knees and pushed her over. They hit the floor together behind the couch just as the can fell into the fireplace and exploded. The blast deafened her, knocking the wind out of her. She lay stunned and disoriented. With a rush, flames shot straight up, their brilliance consuming the chimney. Anne could only lie and watch, detached. Through the sudden roaring that filled her ears she thought she heard a long, terrified shrieking and wondered who it was. Then she saw the roaring flames, leaping along the walls and dancing patterns across the ceiling. She couldn't breathe.

"Anne, get out!"

Jonathan was pushing at her, yelling in her ear. She could only see one of his beautiful eyes. The other was caked shut. His eyebrows were gone. He was coughing and choking, his face washed in sweat and blood.

"The window! Come on!"

He jerked her up and she turned to look. The shock stunned her anew. The whole cabin was engulfed, the fire already devouring the loft and staircase and turning the furniture into kindling. She doubted they could get to the door. Even the hall tree, wedged at an angle against the wall, blazed, her down jacket melting into bright liquid. The quilts, generations of Jackson heritage, were already almost gone.

Jonathan had her by the arm, his hand a vise. She couldn't move and couldn't keep trying. There was nothing left, nothing to fight for. It was coming down around her, like another house of cards. Her beautiful bed, the one her great-grandfather had made, was burning. Lost.

"Annie, come on!" Jonathan screamed at her, his face almost hideous in the blood-red light of the flames. "We have to get out now!"

"No..." She pulled at him, trying to get free, but she was too numb, too overwhelmed to move. She wanted to curl back into a ball and give in. She couldn't do any more.

Jonathan never hesitated. Grabbing her around the waist, he pulled her back down and literally dragged her across the floor. "Keep your head down."

Thick black smoke blocked out the brilliant sunlight. It looked like a halo, a far-off streetlight in the fog. Anne kept her eyes on it as the terror woke in her. She was coughing, tears streaming down her face as she stumbled along next to Jonathan. Cinders, bits of wood and quilt fell around them. The heat was terrible. Anne could hear Jonathan's coughing, sobbing breath and wondered how he thought they could get out of this furnace alive.

Halfway across the floor, Anne had to rip through Jonathan's shirt to get a flaming piece of upholstery from his back. He never felt it. He never stopped moving, head down, his leg dragging painfully behind him, his arm tight around Anne.

Anne followed him blindly, looking up only to try to find the window again. It was getting harder to see. Harder to breathe. God, they weren't going to get out. She could hardly move. Where was the window? Had they gone the wrong way? The room couldn't be this far to get across.

Then the smoke shifted, just enough. There it was, a few feet ahead. Jonathan stopped, his back heaving with the exertion of just breathing.

"A little farther!" he screamed above the din of the fire that sought them. She nodded, sobbing now with the effort to breathe. He moved on and found the chair, still miraculously whole. Next to it was the floor lamp.

Pushing Anne's head down to the safety of the floor, he grabbed the lamp and swung it through the window. Cold air rushed in with the shattering of glass and the fire exploded over their heads. Anne felt the heat across her neck like a scald. She brought her head up, terrified.

"Jonathan?"

He was out, reaching back in for her. She climbed, the light of the sun hurting her eyes. She wondered why. Nothing was more brilliant than the orange of the fire. She took Jonathan's hand, and he pulled her through the broken glass. Good old jeans. They kept her from getting cut.

Anne tumbled out onto the snow-packed ground, landing next to Jonathan. She couldn't get a breath. It seemed enough to stop there and heave in great draughts of air, but Jonathan pulled at her again. She looked up to see that his face was black and wondered offhandedly if hers was too.

They made it to the door of the barn and fell, gasping and choking to the cold dirt floor. Anne thought her ears were still muffled. She couldn't hear anything but her own labored breathing and a dull roaring sound. She shook her head, trying to clear it. Then she heard the slow dripping of the snow back at the far side of the barn. She realized that nothing was wrong with her ears. The world outside was quiet. She looked up to see that it was a beautiful, crystal winter afternoon, the white light almost surreal. Even the brushing of the wind was silenced. There was only the dull rush of the flames as they consumed the cabin.

She looked over at Jonathan as he leaned against the other side of the doorway, his legs outstretched. His breathing was harsh and loud, and he wiped at the sweat on his face with a trembling hand. Immediately, Anne slid over to him.

"Can you breathe?" she demanded. He nodded, not very convincing. "How is your leg?"

"Fine...broke a...couple of...ribs...again, I...think."

He was clutching at his side and leaning to favor it. She tried to get his shirt up so that she could better check him, but her hands shook so badly she couldn't work very well.

Jonathan shook his head at her, not enough breath for words. She took the hint and let what was left of his shirt go. Jonathan managed a grin and carefully lifted an arm in invitation. Hesitating only a second, Anne accepted his offer and stayed within the comfort of his embrace.

"Do you...believe I never...wanted to hurt you?"

"We have plenty of time to discuss that," she said. "Concentrate on breathing right now."

"Whatever happens," he insisted, still breathing with short, painful gasps, "you won't ever...lose Cedar Ridge...I promise."

Anne looked over at the inferno that had once been her home and realized with some surprise that she forgave him. "You saved my life," she said quietly. "The rest, I think, is gravy."

"I...wanted you to...know."

Anne turned to him, to see the genuine regret in his eyes, the pain o a man who saw the woman he loved suffer, and she found a smile for him. "I know."

Farther inside the barn Andy stomped and whinnied, the smell of the smoke unsettling him. Jonathan turned at the noise.

"Do you think we...should try and get down to...town?"

Anne shook her head. "No. I have the feeling that the town will be coming to us." The roof of the cabin gave way with a long crash that demanded their attention. A wide column of thick black smoke lifted straight up into the sky. "They'd never pass up an opportunity like this to tell me how much I need a real road up here."

She watched the destruction a while longer, her mind still too stunned to sort it all out.

"Anne?"

She turned to him with a crumbling, watery grin. "All of my Nancy Drews are gone. I had the... whole collection... for... when..."

It was a long time before her sobbing subsided. And an hour later as the sun impaled itself on the western trees, twenty riders crashed into the clearing at a dead run to find Anne and Jonathan sitting together at the side of the barn door watching the last of the fire as it licked the charred ruins of the cabin.

Anne stood in the cabin doorway and watched the new spring sun warm the top leaves of the trees, the first light refreshing and clear. It had been her first night home since the fire. Since that time she had been living the life of a Gypsy, traveling to Boston to settle family and business affairs, New York to consult with Judson and then back to Elder's Crossing to oversee the clinic construction and her practice.

It had only been a week since she'd closed the door for the last time on the house in Boston. She had dreaded that especially, anticipating the pain and remorse of selling it. She had, after all, spent much of her life there. But when it was over, she'd stood in the echoing marble foyer to look around at the sterile surroundings and felt only the emptiness of the place. She had left nothing behind.

It had been while she had been on that final trip to Boston, flying out as the last of the snow had given way to crocuses on the mountains, that the cabin had been finished. A completely new modern structure, with a lot of glass, whose design had been decided the day she'd buried Brad next to the father he'd so envied and hated. It had been at that moment that she'd realized with inescapable finality that her family was gone. All her childhood memories and dreams had been put to rest beneath white headstones and black ashes. It was time now to move on to a new life, symbolized by the radically new structure on her ancient mountain.

Anne turned from the door and walked back through the house that still had a loft and a high wall for the quilts her friends had already begun to collect for her.

She'd made it into the shiny white kitchen where she was pouring herself coffee from a new pot when she heard the sound of a vehicle approaching. A smile of anticipation lit her features. Pouring a second cup, she slipped out of her thick robe to reveal a pale pink lace-

and-silk teddy. Then, picking up the cups, she walked to the front door, golden hair swinging gently down her back.

"You up already?"

"I'm a farm girl." She grinned lazily, leaning against the open door and waiting for him to turn to her.

When he did, Jonathan dropped the box he'd been lifting with a flat thud. "Good God, woman," he gasped, "you're not supposed to shock a man like that." His eyes didn't seem to mind so much. Anne couldn't get enough of the sight of him, so tall and handsome and whole. He had not dealt well with the hospital, nor it with him.

"And you're not supposed to run out on a woman the day after she's married."

"Important mail," he assured her, bending to pick the box back up. "Special delivery."

Anne scowled a little. "I was afraid you'd run back off to New York."

"Not for six more months." He stomped up onto the porch and nudged her backside. "That was the deal. And may I say," he leered, depositing a quick kiss on eager lips, "I can't wait to see what it's like to ravage the chief executive officer and chairman of the board of Jackson Corporations Limited."

"You ravaged her last night," Anne reminded him, settling onto the couch and putting the coffee cups on the glass-and-wood coffee table.

Jonathan set the box down before her and grinned. "No. Last night I ravaged the finest rural nurse in West Virginia. Open the box."

"What is it?" She studied it before going to the masking tape.

"Your wedding present."

Anne eyed him suspiciously. "The pearls were my wedding present."

"Open it."

When she reached into the packing a few minutes later, Anne drew out a book—a small book, no more than one hundred and ninety pages. Then came another. The rest were packed lovingly beneath, some new, some originals, all familiar and treasured.

Anne looked up at Jonathan, tears in her smiling eyes. "How did you...?"

Jonathan's eyes were bright and happy, the pain at their depths long since exorcised. "You once said something about collecting Nancy Drews for our daughter to read."

She put the books down and eased herself into Jonathan's arms. "Did I tell you that I love you?"

Jonathan kissed her with a gentleness that brought more tears. "Seems to me you did."

She grinned suggestively and stretched against him, the silk whispering against denim and flannel. "Did I show you?"

"Yes." He kissed her again. "But I think it would be okay if you showed me again."

She did.

* * * * *